in color

and frequency

*in color
and frequency*

Vivienne Paul

Hibiscus Tea Publishing

To DK Sr., my first music teacher and the one who shared his gift of art with me. I love you, Daddy.

And for A, J, and G.
My sweet, curious artists and emerging musicians.
You'll always inspire me.

Love, Mommy

♥ ♥

"A painting is music you can see, and music is a painting you can hear."

-Miles Davis

"In the garden of existence, there exists two beautiful roses:

Music and Love."

-Mehmet Murat Ildan

♪♫♪

prologue

"I feel like I'm competing for your time, India."

I'd been at Brandon's house for less than an hour, and this was what we had been doing. Arguing yet again about not spending enough time together.

"Brandon, there's no competition! You have my heart."

"You know what I mean, India."

"I don't. There's absolutely no one else, and you know that. So, make it plain."

Brandon sighed in frustration, and I raised my eyebrows, prompting him forward. "Your folks, man." He ran his hand down his face.

My eyebrows raised even higher. They had to be at my hairline. "What do my parents have to do with this?" I had a feeling I knew what this was about… but I refused to believe he would do that to me. So, I needed him to say it.

"Fucking everything India!" He tossed his hands up in the air.

"Okay." I returned, deadpan.

"We haven't had any time. All of our time is infringed on. They call for you in the middle of everything. I can't even make love to you. Last time I tried, I could barely finish before you were rushing out the door to get to them. Morning, afternoon. Sometimes you don't even come back. I go days without seeing you, let alone hearing your voice."

"It's not like I'm cheating Brandon. You know where I am."

"I hate this shit, India. I'm over it." He shook his head repeatedly.

"Over it? What is *it*? Me?"

"How do you expect us to have a relationship like this?" he asked, avoiding my question entirely.

"I'm here right now. I'm right here with you, Brandon."

"But are you really? You're always mentally elsewhere. And the second that phone rings, you'll be gone again."

"That's not fair."

"To whom?" he challenged.

He had me there. But I was conflicted.

And I said nothing. Just hung my head.

Brandon and I have been together for about two and a half years, and he gave me a key over a year ago. I still live at home with my parents, and Brandon wants me to move in.

He'd begged me multiple times to move in, but my parents need me. Also, Brandon lives more than a half-hour drive away. But he kept trying to convince me and eventually gave me a key. Often reminding me that the offer still stood. He would say I was welcome anytime, even if he wasn't home, like if I just needed a break. I took him up on that offer, too. Plenty. I'd come take naps more times than I can count. If I tried to nap at home, it wouldn't last long. He understood my situation. Or at least he used to. These days, it doesn't seem like he understands at all.

It remained silent for a few moments. I guess that was enough time for Brandon to calm down.

"Baby." His voice was soft. He placed his finger under my chin and gently lifted my head as his gaze met mine. "All of this shouldn't be on you."

I gave him a small smile, appreciating his thoughtfulness. Maybe he wasn't only thinking of himself. "I'm an only child. They have no one else. I can't just leave them all alone."

"Maybe you should reach out to a social worker or something. Maybe they can set your folks up with some resources."

"Brandon, to me, family means everything. Taking care of my parents is very important to me, both personally and culturally. We support each other."

"Well… to put it bluntly, maybe they should move closer to where they'd have more help. At least then you'll be free of all this." That was out of the question. If they left, I was going with them, and that was a fact. They're all I have.

I cut my eyes at Brandon and snatched out of his grasp. Shaking my head. And I said nothing.

"I'm just saying, India. you're taking care of them, but at what expense? You can't live your life if you're wasting it wiping their asses!"

"How dare you!" I snapped. "You have no idea what you're talking about." He hadn't the slightest clue.

"For your information, both of my parents have urged me to live my life, focus on my dreams, and follow my passion in art. They want me to find love and start a family. I'm the one who won't do it!" I crossed my arms, so angry with him.

"I'm sorry. I didn't mean it that way, baby. Come here." He pulled me back into his arms, wrapping me in a bear hug. Brandon continued, "I swear I didn't mean it that way. But, for your sake. For their sake. For our sake. You'll have to make some decisions." He kissed my forehead. "Honestly. You're running yourself ragged. You're so young, baby. You haven't truly been living; you've just been existing. You never have time for anything fun. You're always tired."

Brandon was right. My energy was constantly depleted, and I didn't do much except work. Thankfully, I painted for work, which gave me a bit of an outlet.

Painting was my first love. Not only did it pay the bills, but it also calmed me like nothing else. I'm a creative at my core, and thriving in my creativity is my happy place.

The extra art gigs I would have gone after were less frequent because I didn't have the bandwidth. Speaking of which, I hardly spent time with Destiney either. Destiney is my best friend, and we collaborate all the time on painting projects. But not lately. I haven't hung out with her in a while. Not even to shoot the breeze. She's my only close friend. My best friend and I felt terrible about neglecting her, too. Beyond that, we'd created some of the most beautiful collaborations when we got together. Our chemistry was unreal. Destiney is so talented, and we were unstoppable when we worked together creatively.

The last few times she reached out, inviting me to join her on a project, I had to decline. I hated having to do that. But the truth was, I couldn't commit to any projects with so many unknown variables. She understood my situation better than anyone else, but that didn't make the guilt any less.

I moved away from Brandon's arms and sat on the couch. I could see his point. I'd definitely need to make some decisions. And soon. But he left a bad taste in my mouth. He basically told me, without saying it outright, that an ultimatum was coming. Soon I'd have to choose. That, I was certain of.

I pulled out my phone and sent my father a message to let him know I'd be sleeping over and that I'd see them in the morning. I really hoped he wouldn't try to call me for anything, especially since he kept urging me to focus on my relationship. I knew my father wanted me to marry soon, so he wouldn't have to worry about me. But I was worried for the opposite reason. It was clear that marrying Brandon would pull me away from them. Brandon isn't a family man. That much was evident from his soliloquy a minute ago.

This couldn't work. It wouldn't work.

Family is everything to me, and if I felt this way, that only meant one thing: Brandon isn't the one. Ironically, telling myself that didn't ignite sadness. It brought clarity.

I closed my eyes and sat still for a few minutes, too exhausted to move. Actually, I was past exhausted. Physically and mentally. I closed my eyes for a moment to gather some energy. I wanted to go to Brandon's bedroom and lie down. I sat quietly for a few more moments, my eyes still shut. I could always sleep right here.

I felt Brandon move to sit beside me on the couch, then pull me into his side. "You good, baby?"

"Yeah." My eyes were still shut.

"I need to get in the shower. Care to join me?" Brandon was right on my heels as I got up from the couch and headed down the hallway toward his bedroom. I still hadn't given him an answer as I sat on my side of the bed. Brandon stayed in the doorway, shirtless and wearing a pair of black basketball shorts. That shit used to turn me on. How things have changed. I set my overnight bag down beside me. He approached the bed and stood right in front of me, gently pulling me to stand up. I did. He held me, and I wrapped my arms around his waist. Still said nothing.

But I loved being in his arms. Even though I was only across town, I hadn't seen him in person for about ten days. The time between visits kept getting longer. We haven't talked much lately either. Recently, our conversations mainly consisted of text messages to check in with each other.

This was no way to maintain a relationship, and I knew that. We were slowly drifting apart, and I didn't know what to do about it.

I don't even know if I had the strength for a fight.

"I've missed you." He pressed our lips together and kissed me softly yet hungrily, showing me just how much he missed me.

I kissed him back, but I knew that letting go and getting carried away might give him the idea that he could get more from me. It always led to more, and that was the last thing I wanted. I couldn't use the excuse of being on my period; that was played out now. We kept kissing, and I knew he wanted more. Asking me to join him in the shower made that clear.

Brandon reached for the button of my jeans, and I gently placed my hands over his. Brandon understood the silent gesture all too well.

"I can't keep doing this with you, India," he sneered after abruptly breaking away. His sweet tone was gone, nowhere to be found.

I sat down again.

"Doing what?" I asked, feigning ignorance. I knew exactly what he was talking about. I'd been curbing his advances for weeks now. Brandon was probably sick of me. I was sick of myself.

"I was just telling you this! I'm not trying to have parts and pieces of you. I rarely see you, and when I do, you're too exhausted for anything," he walked around to his side of the bed, scooting back toward the tufted headboard.

"You mean sex? That's all you want from me, Brandon." I sighed in frustration.

As much as I hated to admit it, he was right. This relationship was hanging by a thread. I cared about him, but he was making things difficult for me. I had so much going on at home. I thought coming to him would give me a break. I wasn't in the mood for sex, but I would have loved for him to hold me for a while. Maybe it could even help me forget everything that's gone wrong in my world. We would have gotten to sex. Eventually, I felt bad because none of this was his fault, yet he was the one being neglected. I could do better. But… it was hard to compartmentalize. I had no outlet. He was supposed to be my outlet.

Wasn't he?

"I mean, I'd like to have sex with you. You are my woman."

"It seems that's all you've wanted lately." I lay on my back.

"India. Ain't that what healthy couples do? Have sex? Lots of it?" He glared at me, practically burning a hole in the side of my face. But I said nothing. "What? You don't like sex now?!"

"You don't have to snip at me," I snapped. "Even if I wanted to have sex with you, I don't anymore." I crossed my arms. Something was definitely off with me, and this was a clear sign. I am a very sexual being. Not so much these days. So much has been happening, and all my rushing around finally caught up with me, taking its toll.

"Man, India! *What do you want from me?!*" His voice had shot up at least two octaves.

"Fine, Brandon! Fine! You want sex? Then come get it." I spat as I sat up and started unbuttoning my jeans, lifting as I slid them over my hips and off, mindlessly tossing them into a corner. "Come on!" Brandon said nothing but slowly turned to his left to look at me. I was just about to take off my underwear but froze when our eyes met. His face was blank. But his eyes. They looked dark and hollow. The realization of what I'd said hit me hard.

"Brandon... I'm so-."

He raised his hand to stop me. "Don't even worry about it." He swung his legs over the side of the bed now, with his back to me.

"Brandon. Baby, I didn't mean it like that." Sitting up on my knees, I crawled over to him. Just as I went to hug him from behind, he stood and stepped away from the bed before I could reach him. Standing at his full height, he turned completely to face me. I sat back on my heels with my head lowered, feeling terrible and unsure of what to do. I knew I had messed up. Yet, he was eerily calm. I looked up slowly just in time to see him shake his head slowly, clearly indicating disappointment.

"You thought I would want it after that," he finally jested. It wasn't a question, and I knew it. He held my gaze, and I was frozen. "I don't want anything from you offered to me like that." His voice was cold as ice. Brandon backed away and walked around the bed toward the bedroom door. On his way, he grabbed a shirt from the hamper of clean clothes sitting right beside his dresser.

"Brandon. Please. Can I talk to you? I reached out to grab his arm as he walked by me.

"Now you wanna talk? Come on now, India." He stood against the wall, giving me a deadpan expression, and I took that as a sign to go ahead with my elevator pitch.

"Brandon... I just... there's so much going on. I'm tired. I'm stressed. Ma and Dad aren't well, and it's just..." I started to get emotional, and my voice cracked. "I don't even know if I'm coming or going." Tears welled up in my eyes, but I kept them at bay. He stood by the door, watching me. I know I could have communicated better, and I realize that.

"And amidst all that, you forgot about me."

I couldn't refute his claim. I was definitely neglecting this relationship. Even if it wasn't intentional, it still remained. Brandon had been sitting idly by, accepting whatever scraps of attention I tossed his way. Our conversations were few and far between, and spending time together was even less frequent. When I saw him, I would fall asleep. We didn't talk much face-to-face beyond surface level, and I wasn't giving him any intimacy either. My man was starving for my love, attention, and connection. Meanwhile, I was starving for rest and reprieve, and he was the one suffering for it. This was unfair to him.

"You're right. I'm sorry, Brandon. This is all so overwhelming. I can't… I don't think I can keep doing this. To you. You don't deserve this."

"What are you saying to me, India?" His voice firm.

"I don't know." And I truly didn't. My head was telling me I needed to let him go, but my heart was urging me to fight for us and work things out. The truth was, I had no fight left in me. All my energy was drained by caring for my aging and ailing parents. As an only child, everything fell on my shoulders. They had no one else. If I weren't there to help, they wouldn't have anyone. It was taking a heavy toll on me, and I was starting to feel like I was losing it. I felt like I had already lost Brandon.

"You saying we're done here?" he asked me. His tone was unrecognizable, and that scared me. I looked up into his eyes. They were still dark and empty. "You're done because you can't do two things at once?"

"I don't want to be. But I don't have anything to give you right now. I'm stretched too thin…I can't maintain a healthy relationship." A single tear fell, and I didn't bother to wipe it.

"But I want you, India. I'll live if we don't see each other as much for now. It won't kill me if we can't make love as often. But you shut me out."

"Brandon. I can't maintain a relationship and my other obligations."

"So that's it? You're done? This is the real world, India. You're an adult. Walking away isn't the answer! Figuring it out is."

I looked away. Saying nothing. I wasn't sure how else to communicate this. I had to end things here for now. There was nothing else to it.

"I guess I have your answer. Fucking unbelievable!" Brandon left the room, and shortly after, I heard the front door open and close. I could have communicated better, and I knew that. But he didn't seem to get it. In my world, family is everything.

Maybe he was right. I'm not good at maintaining both.

I decided to leave as well. I didn't need to stay here. I took the key off my key ring and placed it on the side table next to the bed. I looked around the room to gather my things. Once I had everything, I headed out the door.

Unsure if I'll ever step foot in this place again.

♪♥♫♥♪

one

INDIA

Today is one of the worst days I've had in a while.

My mom's glaucoma was worsening, and she was undergoing treatment. She also had moderate hypertension, which seemed to trigger her glaucoma. Despite following her doctors' recommendations, we couldn't figure out why. Meanwhile, my dad's arthritis was flaring up badly; his hand joints, in particular, were bothering him. Both of them had been in pain, unable to do much for themselves, and needed me a lot more than usual.

Add to that, my ex-boyfriend Brandon and I were constantly fighting. We broke up some weeks ago, then got back together but things were even worse this time. All we do is argue. We argue all the time. He believed I was neglecting our relationship, and he was right, although it wasn't on purpose. I can admit we barely spent any time together.

We were on the phone arguing about something we always fought about, and we just couldn't see eye to eye.

And we wouldn't.

Square pegs don't fit into round holes.

Brandon was beyond frustrated with me, and he wanted me to choose. He was mistaken if he thought I'd pick him. His parting words for me were that I wasn't ready to be with someone living in the real world. My world is as real as they come.

But I knew we were done. For real this time. When I hung up the phone, I thought about everything. We'd broken up before. A few times. Gotten back together. Had wild make-up sex, only to repeat the cycle. I couldn't change my circumstances, nor could I expect him to accept them. The world doesn't owe us understanding.

Just as well, I knew this was the end of the line for us. Our relationship had run its course. An apology or promises to do better couldn't fix this.

We were done.

I lay back on my bed, and something interesting crossed my mind; even though Brandon and I had been together for nearly two and a half years, I wasn't feeling sad about the breakup. Not right that moment, at least. I genuinely felt a huge sense of relief. I had no idea how long that feeling would last, but it wasn't on my mind right then.

My past relationships have been complicated for many reasons, and I wondered if I was capable of anything lasting anyway.

After checking in on Ma and Daddy, I called Destiney to see if I could visit her. I needed some fresh air. I grabbed my tote and called her as I headed to my car. Visiting her was never a problem. Destiney always let me visit whenever I needed. When she answered, she said she was with Micah, but being the bestie she is, Destiney dropped everything to be there for me.

I'd do the same for her. In a heartbeat. She's been my girl for almost a decade. She's been solid and loyal.

Destiney and I met as volunteers for a community mural. We were the only two Black girls there, out of dozens, and I immediately noticed her incredible talent. She picked up that paintbrush, and I thought, okay, Sis did not come to play around.

We worked closely together on that project, and we were fast friends after that.

We still work together often. Destiney and I are part of an independent artist collective called Zaffre, and we try to book the same gigs whenever we can.

The collective is awesome. And I love the name.

Zaffre is a deep blue pigment created from cobalt oxide. It resembles shades like azure or sapphire. Zaffre has been used in glassmaking since ancient times.

Destiney and I have been part of the collective for as long as we've known each other. When we joined a decade ago, we were the youngest members and the only two Black women. But we stayed involved, and the collective helped advance both of our artistic journeys, opening many opportunities for us: creative projects, community exhibits, grants, and building strong relationships with other independent artists.

Just like our friendship, Zaffre has grown beautifully over the years, increasing in size and diversity.

Something I'm very proud of is that Destiney and I are affectionately known as "the big sisters of Zaffre." By staying involved in the collective and encouraging their growth, we've paved the way for other artists of color. We provide them a place where they belong, where they can be themselves. We've had the opportunity to mentor many, and that makes me feel good. The collective grew from a few dreamers into a vibrant, diverse network of about twenty artists from many different disciplines and backgrounds. Different cultures. Now, we have a strong community. It's truly amazing.

As I drove to her place, I smiled wide. I knew she was with Micah, and it wouldn't have mattered if she hadn't been able to get away. She was so happy and blissfully in love, and I absolutely loved Micah for Destiney. Watching them fall for each other was the sweetest thing I'd ever seen. Once she got out of her own way. That was an uphill battle, but everything worked out. I'm just glad I could talk some sense into her before she missed out.

When I got to her place, we chilled for a bit, and I filled her in on what's been happening. The terrible day I had, my parents not doing well, and my now-ex-boyfriend's parting words to me. I told her I felt like this was it. That we were done, done this time.

"Alright, Best." Destiney began. "We're going out tonight. Get your mind off of things."

I groaned. "Des. I'm not up for that. As much as I love to dance. Tonight ain't it."

"Oh, trust! You'll love this place. It's a lounge called Home-GrownSol. They have a live band. Micah's best friend, Solomon, plays the sax. That band is so dope! We can get some dinner. There's a full restaurant. The food is amazing. Have a drink too."

Once she put it that way, it didn't take much more convincing. That all sounded good to me. I love a good lounge, and Destiney was right. I needed to get out. I was starting to feel down.

HomeGrownSol was a vibe, with a grown-and-sexy atmosphere. The food was delicious too. I had no idea this place existed. I told Destiney we needed to come back, and she said she and Micah go all the time. At least once a week for dinner. Yeah, the food was bomb.

Even though Micah was with us, he hung back and relaxed at our booth. We had great seats close to the stage. At one point, Destiney and I went to the ladies' room and then to the bar. When we returned, Micah was talking to a tall, lean, ebony-skinned gentleman. Short locs pulled back. He was dressed in a black T-shirt and jeans. No idea who he was, but as we approached, I could see how handsome he was.

He was leaning against the post of our booth. Destiney got in, and I slid in beside her. Then, I observed everything about him as subtly as I could.

I instantly noticed his quiet confidence.

"You girls good, Destiney baby?" Micah asked Destiney.

"Yes. Thank you." She pecked him sweetly on the lips. "Hey, Sol! We're so excited to hear Smoke tonight!" Destiney excitedly gushed.

So, this is Sol. I've heard that name before.

When Destiney first started seeing Micah, I'd heard of his best friend Solomon. Naturally. They met as sophomores in high school, and they've been best friends ever since.

"Excited for you, too. Thanks for coming out." He was charming and smooth as silk. I noticed his eyes had found me, and they were lingering now.

"India." Micah cleared his throat. "Forgive me. This is Sol, my brother from way back. He's in the band you'll be hearing soon. Solomon, meet India. Destiney's best friend."

Solomon extended his hand to me.

"Your name. Say it one more time for me. Please." His tone was gentle. And warm.

I had a small smile when I offered, "India."

"Pleasure, India. I hear you're the mural queen."

I shook his hand and looked him in the eyes. I swear something inside me shifted. He's heard things about me?

My smile was easy, "I can do a thing or two with some paint. But *queen* might be a stretch."

"Don't sell yourself short, Artist Girl," he said, smiling back.

I blinked. *Artist Girl?* We're doing nicknames? He was laying it on thick, but I quickly recovered. It wasn't unusual to be hit on, but something about him felt different.

I tried to play it cool after he headed back to the stage. I think I succeeded. Destiney didn't ask me any questions, so I'm sure I didn't let on that Sol had my interest piqued.

We enjoyed the band; they were fantastic. I really enjoyed listening to him play the saxophone because he was incredible at it. Halfway through the set, they took a quick break, and he came over to talk with Micah again. I was deep in my conversation with Destiney, and he seemed busy with Micah. We didn't speak again.

But I knew we'd eventually cross paths again.

two

SOL

When my eyes find her for the first time, in an instant, she's all I can see.

I was at HomeGrown on a typical Thursday evening, and my bandmates and I were getting ready to entertain the intimate crowd with some great tunes. I play in a few bands, but Smoke was my favorite, and the house band at HomeGrownSol.

There are six of us in Smoke. Joe plays bass, Mike handles lead guitar, DK is our drummer, James is on keyboards, Carlton is our vocalist, and I play alto sax. We perform live at HomeGrown-Sol every Thursday and Friday night.

We tuned our instruments, warmed up, did a quick sound check, and then we were ready to groove.

About fifteen minutes before our set, I went over to talk to Micah. He'd text me saying he'd be coming through, and that was always cool.

"My favorite Part" by Mac Miller played softly over the chatter and clinking glasses. Folks were out tonight. The lounge was moderately full. And there was a chill ass vibe in here. Which is typical.

"Mich!" We slapped hands. "Good to see you, man."

"Always great to see you, bro!"

We shared a quick embrace.

Micah and I have been friends since we were fifteen. We met in high school and later played basketball on the same AAU team, and now, twenty years later, here we are. Micah is my best friend and truly feels like a brother to me. We've shared countless moments, high and low, over these past two decades.

"You here with your lady?"

"I am."

Micah was all teeth and gums, and I chuckled.

"Man! Look at you." By now, I was cackling, shaking my head, but it was all in jest.

I loved this for Micah. Honestly. Truly.

Destiney is the best thing that could have happened to him. She's good to him and for him, and they were so good together.

"Destiney brought her best friend out," Micah said, gesturing toward where they were standing. "Apparently, she's been going through it and needed a night out."

I followed Micah's line of sight and saw Destiney.

Then I saw her. It didn't take more than a second for me to spot her in the crowd. They were near the bar, and she was talking to Destiney. And she took my breath away. Instantly.

The very moment I see her, something inside me shifts.

I could barely focus on whatever the hell else Micah was saying. He was saying something, but I couldn't even tell you what.

I continued to admire the impeccably gorgeous tall glass of water, tuning out everything else. And yeah. She was tall. And modelesque. She looked to be at least 5 feet 10 inches tall in her high heels, dressed in blue jeans, a white blouse, and gold hoop earrings. To me, her physical presence is striking. As I watched her from a distance, appreciating everything I saw… everything else seemed to fade away like vapor. The sounds, the scents, the people moving around the space. None of them existed anymore.

Yeah. She's a work of art. Stunning.

I love her brown skin. It was like toasted cinnamon. Her big brown eyes were bright and warm. Her smile was rich and inviting. Her wild curly hair framed her face.

Her energy radiated across the room. I felt it as she approached the table. And somehow, I managed to avoid acting like a complete idiot while Micah introduced us.

"India. This is Sol, my brother from way back. He's in the band you'll be hearing soon. Solomon, meet India. Destiney's best friend."

I'd heard of India, and it hit me then that Micah mentioned Destiney and her best friend being a force in the indie art scene.

Micah showed me a few pictures of their projects, and they were… stellar. *Magnific.* I was beyond impressed.

Extending my hand, immediately, I asked her name again.

"Your name. Say it one more time for me. Please."

As if I hadn't just heard Micah say it. I wanted to hear the way she said it.

"India."

Beautiful.

"Pleasure, India. I hear you're the mural queen," I said.

She had a small smile that settled somewhere in my chest.

And I swear, the night shifted. It felt like I was the only one who noticed. And I didn't know what the hell had just happened.

This started out as just another Thursday. Another gig at HomeGrown, my mind on the music. But there was something about her that stills me.

When I stepped onto the stage with my saxophone, I kept my eyes on her, sneaking glimpses whenever I could. She looked so beautiful sitting there, tall and regal, listening intently to the band as the melodies drifted through the lounge. I watched the way she leaned into Destiney whenever she laughed. Something in particular had her so tickled she squeezed her eyes shut and threw her head back. And I was mesmerized.

I arrived home hours later, and I should have been exhausted. I'd played two full sets and had a drink. Usually, that would have mellowed me out. Instead, I was sitting on the edge of my bed, thinking about how she said thank you when I complimented her work.

And her work was incredible. I almost texted Micah to get some insight on exactly what her story was. I know, "going through it" is usually code for boyfriend problems.

But I thought better of it. I'd see her again. She's Destiney's best friend. Since Destiney and Micah were joined at the hip, we would definitely cross paths again. Eventually.

three

INDIA

"That mural you girls did at the Boys and Girls Club is fire!" Ella shrieked. "The colors. The shapes. Y'all are amazing!"

"Thanks! But we can't take all the credit," Destiney laughed, sipping from her glass.

"Yeah, we had help and worked with a crew of people. But thank you," I told Ella smiling.

Ella waved her hand, "No, don't even start. Both of y'all are dope on your own, too. But y'all together are *a force*! Y'all could have painted that, and it would have looked just as amazing. Maybe better."

"Don't come for the collective!" Destiney cackled.

I joined her. "Yeah. They're cool people. The collective put our names out there. Put us on. It's been such a blessing."

"That's dope too. You know I'm kidding," Ella said.

"There's plenty more where that project came from, too," Destiney said, nodding. "Indie and I might branch out and start our own Artist Collective someday."

I nodded. "Yeah, we've tossed the idea around. I think that would be cool... Just have to find the time. We'll see."

"You two are such creative visionaries. Bringing life and color to us all! I'm so proud to be your big sister! I want to be just like y'all when I grow up! Let's toast to growth and opportunities!" Ella beamed as we laughed, toasting to that.

We were at Micah's brother Malachi and his wife Ella's house for a cookout they were hosting. I'd been relaxing in the kitchen with Destiney and Ella, sipping on some rum punch Ella made for us. It was so good. It had fresh sliced lemons, limes, strawberries, pineapples, and peaches, mixed with coconut rum, pineapple juice, orange juice, and fruit punch.

I've only met Ella twice before, but I love her energy. She's so sweet and funny. She treats me like family, even though I'm only here because I'm Destiney's best friend. Ella owes me nothing, but she's always so kind whenever I see her.

We kept talking as the patio door slid open and Sol entered the kitchen.

Sol is just as handsome in the daylight. More even.

"Excuse me. Just heading to the restroom." He politely told Ella as he walked past the kitchen table.

"No worries! Go right ahead."

"Hey Destiney!"

"Hey, Sol!

I saw him before he saw me.

When he saw me, he did a double take but quickly recovered. He probably didn't know I was in here.

I didn't realize he was out there either.

It was a pleasant surprise.

"Hey India. Good to see you."

"Hey Solomon. Likewise."

He smiled wide, saying that, and I did too, even though I was feeling a little kittenish. This was my second time seeing him. That time at HomeGrown was a number of weeks ago.

I had been thinking about him the whole time.

I couldn't help but laugh a little when I realized I was feeling shy. Usually, I'm outgoing. Even when I don't feel like talking, I can find the words. Then I paused for a moment and understood why, since that wasn't typical for me. I didn't know Sol would be here, so I was pleasantly surprised. And I believe the feeling I got when he greeted me with his smooth presence made me giddy.

Sol walked down the hall. I took a generous sip of my rum punch, pretending my stomach wasn't swarmed with butterflies.

He was so damn smooth with it.

Coming in here looking the way he did, talking the way he did, sounding the way he did, and moving the way he did.

Saying my name like that.

Des and Ella kept their conversation going. When Sol went through the kitchen again, he gave me another look, and this one lasted a little longer. He smiled, and I smiled back, trying not to make it obvious. I knew the girls were watching, even though they pretended not to pay attention.

The second Sol was outside again, with the patio door securely shut behind him, Destiney cleared her throat.

"Okay Best. Let's talk about how you froze like a statue the second Sol walked in here."

"No, I didn't." I casually took another sip.

"Girl, please! You hardly breathed!" Destiney said.

"Yeah. He was checking for you, too! He almost got whiplash looking back at you," that was Ella.

We all laughed.

"You guys are exaggerating," I said, attempting to downplay it. But Destiney wasn't trying to hear that.

Destiney smirked. "You're a single woman. And he's single too, as far as I know. So what if you two were giving each other googly eyes?"

"Yeah. And he's a great guy. I've known Sol for quite a while. Next time he comes inside, maybe you can chat?" Ella said.

I nodded saying nothing. I wasn't against it, even though things were complicated for me. My heart, my emotions, my family situation. But there was something about Sol that felt like a breath of fresh air, a calming presence. His energy was so... put together.

Yeah.

It had been several weeks since I last saw him. I wouldn't mind talking to him again.

I decided I would if he came back inside before I left.

I was just about to leave when he stepped back inside. I was hanging out in the kitchen, and I happened to be alone at that moment.

Just a few minutes ago, Malachi came in and whisked Ella away. Kissing her all over. Those two didn't stop, and they disappeared a lot. Grown folks' business. I love it!

Destiney was in the living room with Gabby, Mal, and Ella's daughter. She's around twelve, I think, and is very well-mannered. She's pretty, sweet, and mature too. Well-spoken and just a lovely girl. Gorgeous and looks just like Ella. Gabby and Destiney were nerding out over books. Destiney is a huge bookworm, and Gabby is an emerging book lover herself. They started talking about black historical fiction titles and went to the living room where they continued their conversation.

I wanted to tidy up the kitchen. It was the least I could do. Ella and Malachi opened their home to us, and they were so hospitable. The food was fantastic. Ella can cook! I had a great time, but I had been here for a few hours and needed to head out.

Sol entered the kitchen expectantly, as if he had come looking for me.

"Hey India." His charming smile was right there to greet me. "Have a good time?"

And mine was back. Easy. "I sure did. You?"

"Always a good time with the fellas." he returned, light-hearted, nodding.

I perched on one of the stools in the bright, spacious kitchen. Mal and Ella's home was grandeur. This kitchen was immaculate.

Sol stood a few feet away from me. Near the entrance to the living area.

"Haven't seen you in a while. How've you been?"

His thoughtfulness made me smile again.

Actually, I don't believe I ever stopped smiling. Sol's energy was so mellow. So… centered. Collected.

And I could dig it.

I felt tranquil as hell just being in his space.

"Really well, thank you."

"Good stuff," he nodded.

I didn't tell Sol any of this, but since I last saw him, I'd been reconnecting with Brandon.

Dipping back.

I even considered trying to figure shit out.

Somehow.

But Brandon liked to remind me that I was "emotionally unavailable" and that "I continued to put everything and everyone else first."

After having sex with me.

But Brandon wasn't wrong about any of that. His delivery was just harsh. It sucked, actually.

At the same time, Brandon was being insensitive to the emotional toll things at home were taking on me.

I hated watching my mom suffer through her glaucoma eye drops. I felt so helpless. And my dad's joints were so stiff and painful that he couldn't even apply arthritis balm to his own knuckles. So, I did it for him with pride.

Brandon didn't realize that I couldn't simply compartmentalize this. I couldn't just flip a switch and become a different version of myself. Honestly, that version of me didn't truly exist. If it did, it was buried deep down somewhere. I wouldn't mind experiencing the softer parts of myself now and then, even if only for a moment. But that wasn't realistic. I had to close this chapter with Brandon once and for all.

As I hung out in the kitchen talking to Sol, my mind was filled with those thoughts.

Then I realized Sol had a playful side to him.

Bringing me back to the present, he began teasing me about my art tote.

"So, you just carry your whole world around with you?" he teased.

I cracked another grin. Wider than the last one.

"Oh. This? She's just misunderstood."

Grinning, too, he posed, "She?"

"Yeah," I laughed. "She's like a dysfunctional pet, following me everywhere. Very committed."

We laughed.

He called me 'Artist Girl,' reminding me of the nickname he used the very first time we met.

I loved that for many reasons and felt special. It was incredibly endearing when he called me that. I also gave him the nickname Music Man, which he seemed to embrace just as eagerly.

"India. You're someone I'd like to keep talking to. You've got a dope vibe. Like... quietly electric. I'd love to keep this energy going. Can I get your number?"

I gave it to him. Without hesitation. I was into his directness and confidence.

Yeah. It was sexy as hell. But I told him what the deal was right then and there.

"I like your vibe too. Your energy. But... I just got out of something after two years, so I can't promise anything. Still, I'd like to keep getting to know you."

And I did.

We vibed so well just having a conversation. The heat between us was impossible to ignore. Definitely sexual chemistry.

Neither of us mentioned it.

We didn't have to.

It didn't need to be acknowledged, but it was undeniable.

four

SOL

"So, what's up with India though?" I asked Micah.

Micah, Malachi, their cousin Raymond, and I sat on the back patio at Mal and Ella's, talking and enjoying a few beers.

Malachi is Micah's older brother, and Mal is like an older brother to me too. And such good people. He's looked out for me since we were teens, just like he looked out for Micah. Cousin Ray is cool too. Usually a riot. But still good people.

We'd been out here shooting the shit for the past few hours. Mal grilled for us. Ella cooked a few sides, and we had a great time. The sun was setting now, but it was still early.

I saw Micah raise his eyebrows. Then he asked, "What's up with India? What do you mean by that?" Surprise evident in his voice.

"What you so surprised for?" Ray said. "Shorty is bad!"

Yeah. India is incredibly beautiful. It had been several weeks since that night I met her at HomeGrown. I thought of her from time to time, too. She isn't someone easily forgotten.

I'd only seen her once, and she's even more beautiful than I remembered.

And I knew my question had Micah surprised for two reasons.

We'd been relaxing on the patio all day, and I was just now saying something.

"I didn't realize you were back out here. You swore off relationships," Micah continued.

That was the second reason.

"Fine as she is, my ass would come up off the bench too," Ray said.

We laughed.

Nodding, I said, "Yeah. I certainly didn't set out to meet someone. But India is beautiful. I mean, damn."

"Destiney is beautiful with a beautiful ass friend. The fuck are the chances of that? Malachi, you ain't bout to be known as the only one with a badass wife on your arm." Ray chimed in.

We all cackled. Malachi has been with Ella for years, and from day one, everyone was captivated by Ella's beauty.

I'd been out here with the guys and at some point, India showed up. I didn't even realize she was there. I went into the house to use the restroom and saw her sitting in the kitchen, chatting with Destiney and Ella.

I gave her a friendly smile, schooling my features and doing my damndest not to grin like an idiot during the brief moment we locked eyes over the rim of her glass.

Then I went back to the patio and rejoined the conversation the guys were having. But honestly, I spent the entire afternoon wondering if she felt what I did in that moment.

"Well, you've already been introduced to her," Micah said.

"Gone in the house, she's still in there, I think." That was Mal.

I wondered if I'd crossed her mind at all since we met a few weeks ago back at HomeGrown. Spent the whole afternoon lost in thoughts of her before I decided to put myself on Front Street by asking Micah, right in front of the guys, what the deal was with her. Surprising, even to myself. But as beautiful as she is, I wasn't sure I wanted to further complicate my already complicated dating life. I hadn't even been out here like that.

But I decided I would talk to her again, check in and see how she's doing, and go from there. I was far too curious about her not to. Past intrigued.

Before I left, I went back into the house to speak with her. I made good timing because she was about to leave herself.

She stood, pulling an oversized tote over her shoulder, and it was nearly bursting with color. I could see the edges of canvas boards poking out and the worn bristles of a few brushes sticking up like wild hair.

"So, you just carry your whole world around with you?" I teased, making conversation.

India cracked an adorable grin, "Oh. This? She's just misunderstood."

"She?" I had my own grin.

"Yeah." She laughed lightly. "She's like a dysfunctional pet, following me everywhere. Very committed" She pulled the tote higher on her shoulder.

"What's inside?"

"Oh, art supplies. And… unreasonable dreams." Her smile was easy, and my interest was piqued. A dreamer.

I moved a bit closer to her, nodding. "I see. You're an artist carrying half a studio in a tote."

She cocked her head playfully. "Yeah. Have to. Never know when I'll need to catch inspiration on paper."

I grinned, nodding again. "Oh, I get it. Music is my canvas. But I don't think I can haul my guitar and a bag this size around all day."

She shrugged. "Our art is different, but we both chase moments. Me and my colors. You with your melodies."

I nodded again. "Artist Girl."

"Is that what I am?

"Sure. I believe that's what you've always been in my head… just calling it out."

India smiled. I love her smile. And something else happened. There was a shift in her posture. She seemed to be looser now.

"I'm so glad I got to see you again," I said.

"Likewise." Her closed-mouth smile spread as she regarded me just a little longer.

I admired her too, quietly. Subtly.

Then, "If I'm Artist Girl, you're Music Man."

My chuckle was deep. "Music Man, huh?"

"You're a badass on the saxophone. You play guitar too? You're definitely Music Man."

There was a beat of silence between us. It was easy.

I was quick when I said, "India. You're someone I'd like to keep talking to. You've got a dope vibe. Like... quietly electric. I'd love to keep this energy going. Can I get your number?"

She smiled, studying me before she said, "Direct. Confident. I like that." Then there was a heavy pause. "I like your vibe too. Your energy. But… I just got out of something after two years. So, I can't promise anything. But I'd like to keep getting to know you, too."

My grin returned. I pulled out my phone and handed it over. "That's fine. All I'm hoping for."

She handed me my phone back after tapping in her number, playfully tossing out, "I don't want to regret this, Music Man."

"No way you would, Artist Girl."

I didn't waste a moment. Texting her that very evening.

Artist Girl. I forgot to ask if that tote comes with a user manual. Or is chaos the whole point?

She replied instantly.

Artist Girl: LOL! Chaos is the point, and this is a curated mess, thank you very much!

Me: Oh, I respect it. Just don't want it to swallow you whole.

I'll send a search party if needed. You in there?

Artist Girl: That depends.

Me: Blink twice if you need help.

Artist Girl: LOL!

Before turning in for the night, I sent her a voice memo. *"Seriously though… I meant every word. You have a presence, India. It was great seeing you earlier. Thank you for allowing me to remain connected with you."*

We kept texting, though.

Well into the late hours.

And for the next few weeks, we talked about all kinds of shit. Flirting back and forth, laughing a lot, and getting to know each other better.

I shared details about my students this semester, about jazz gigs, and music.

India told me about her community artwork and mural projects. She sent a picture of a sketch she was working on and challenged me to guess what it was.

We don't talk every day, but we talk quite often. Some days we text, and other days we exchange memes. Voice memos go back and forth, and she always keeps me laughing out loud. India is silly.

Some days are quieter, but our connection never ends.

It intensifies.

five

INDIA

Music Man: Hey, Artist Girl. I can't seem to get you out of my head

That Artist Girl was so cute. And I smiled from ear to ear.

He'd been on my mind too.

Glad I wasn't the only one.

Me: Hey, Music Man. Same here

Music Man: Tell me what colors you're painting on my mind tonight?

I'd just seen Sol a few hours earlier at Malachi and Ella's, and the connection we shared was off the charts.

The attraction. The chemistry.

The synergy.

It was undeniable.

I was happy to hear from him. My face lit up like a Christmas tree when I saw the notification.

I didn't need to wonder if he was thinking of me too because he told me so. With no shame.

He'd sent me a voice memo too. Making my heart squeeze. Then melt.

Yeah.

And… Sol was a flirt, and I liked that. I could flirt a little bit, too.

Me: You sound like you want to be my canvas. Watch out. I'll leave marks all over you.

Music Man: Oh trust. I'm more than ready to be marked. Each note I play is practice for the touch I want from you.

Me: Careful. Get me started and I won't stop til you're begging for a masterpiece only I can give you

Music Man: Paint me like your favorite sin, Artist Girl. I'll serenade you for hours. Now I'm curious which art form can make the other melt first.

Damn.

We went back and forth like that all night.

And the next day, then a day or two later. All the while, our connection and sexual chemistry grew stronger. For weeks.

We talked about everything under the sun and really got to know each other. Sol is interesting and layered. He shared openly and willingly about himself, answering every question I asked. And asked a lot about me, showing a genuine interest in learning everything there was to know about me.

I loved that.

We never met up. We never saw each other. But I thought about it. Plenty. I wondered if he was thinking about it too. Weeks passed, and neither of us asked to see the other.

I had my reasons, and I wondered what his were.

six

SOL

It was the first Saturday evening in January, and the crew had gathered at Micah's house to celebrate his thirty-fifth birthday.

Destiney did her thing, the house looked nice, and she'd had the party catered. Plenty of drinks. A vibe. Great energy.

I was mid-conversation, chilling with the guys, but the second I saw her, I completely forgot whatever joke Ray had just cracked.

It was impossible not to notice India when she entered a space.

She was across the yard, a bottle of water in her hand, in their covered patio area, talking to the ladies. And I took her in. All over again. Somehow, she was more lovely than the last time I saw her.

Her long black curls were soft and wild, cascading down her back. She wore gold hoop earrings and a wrap-around marigold dress that stopped me in my tracks.

She was art in motion.

Walking poetry.

The cookout back at Malachi's, when she gave me her number, calling me Music Man was almost two months ago.

Yeah. We had been in touch, texting each other. Sometimes flirty or offbeat, but we managed to learn the small details about each other. She loved midnight blue and mangoes. She hated bananas. She had an adorable quirkiness about her. She was smart, sensitive, and sassy. She loved to paint and was fiercely devoted to her family.

And now she was standing across the yard, talking to Destiney.

We were in the same space again.

And damn, she looked good.

I was really into her. I can admit that now, at least to myself.

Yeah. I had a crush. Plain and simple. My thirty-four-year-old grown ass had a crush on this Artist Girl who carried an oversized canvas tote around that defied physics.

I saw her a few weeks ago when the crew went out to a taproom. Our conversation was light, which was fine.

As Micah strolled across the yard, I followed. Without a second thought. I decided I needed to make my way over to her somehow before I lost my nerve. I wanted to talk to her.

Really talk. Converse.

She was animatedly chatting with Destiney and a few of the other ladies in attendance, and as I approached her, she looked up, her beautiful face settling into an easy smile.

Micah escorted Destiney to dance, and I knew this was my chance.

"Music Man." she greeted me kindly, and her voice had warmth. It was gentle and familiar.

"Artist Girl. Hey," I spoke at a measured tempo.

We stood close, but we didn't touch. I thought over the months of messages exchanged between us, almost connecting us like an invisible thread. As comfortable as I felt, it was also strange. But intimate in a way. Seeing her in person again.

"It was getting late. I was thinking you weren't going to show."

"Yeah. Had to make sure Mom and Dad were situated.

"Glad you made it."

"Same."

We had a pause, but it wasn't awkward. It was a moment where unspoken feelings were communicated. Energy was exchanged. We both understood everything.

I could smell her faint citrus perfume. It was light, fresh, and lovely. Totally her. And her dress was fire.

She told me I looked good, and it made my chest tighten.

"You always look good," I told her. And I meant that. "That color complements your complexion beautifully."

"Careful. You're spoiling me with all these compliments," she told me playfully.

I didn't miss a beat. "That wasn't a compliment. That was a fact."

Our eyes stayed fixed on each other.

I don't know what she was thinking, but I kept replaying all the voice memos she'd sent me. Her sweet voice and the magic in her waves of laughter. Those voice memos kept me company some nights, and I played them on repeat, saving a few of my favorites.

Our conversation resumed. She asked me how long I had been at the party. We talked about the food Destiny catered and how great the cake was.

Of course, we segued into what we shared through all those text messages.

India is so proud of her family and her heritage. It was profound and pivotal. Seeing her that way was as a reminder that I lacked that knowledge, but it made me ache even more to learn it.

"So, Artist Girl, I've been researching Port Mourant and Guyana overall. I love the culture. Indo and Afro. That's dope, by the way. That mix."

She nodded, smiling sweetly. "Thank you. It's home. I haven't lived there in forever, but I spent my formative years there."

"You said you were there for eight years?"

"Yes. From when I was seven to fifteen. Started high school when we moved back here. Big years."

I nodded, wishing I had something like that to reminisce about. I have traveled internationally. Many times. Since childhood. That's the lifestyle you have with wealthy parents. But there was no real sense of connection to any of those places. We were on holiday.

"I don't even know where I'm from. Not really. I know where I grew up, but it's not the same."

Her face softened. "You told me. You're adopted."

I nodded. "Yep. As an infant." I sighed softly. "Not knowing where my roots are. What country. Language. You talk about your heritage, and it's inspiring. It sparked something in me. Like someday I'd love to find mine."

There was a pause, but it felt natural. "Next Lifetime" by Erykah Badu started playing. This song was ethereal and made us vibe on a deeper level. At some point, India looked at me. Like, she really looked at me. Then, gently she said, "You can belong even if you don't know where you're from, Sol."

That caught me, and it hit me in a good way. Many things she said did that to me.

I sat with that and processed her words. She was right. And for now, I could roll with that. We went quiet again, but it wasn't awkward.

Deciding to lighten the mood, I teased, "That accent of yours. It's adorable."

Her brows dipped. "What accent are you speaking of?"

I nudged her playfully, grateful for the excuse to touch her. "Yours. It pops out sometimes," I told her matter-of-fact.

She shot an incredulous glare.

"Soft. Subtle, but it shows itself. It's nice. Like music."

She was smiling again and shook her head slightly. "I think it's gone. Sac swallowed most of it."

"Nah. It's there. I hear it. Especially when you say, "paintin" instead of "painting." I did my damndest to keep a straight face while I butchered the accent and raised my voice an octave trying to imitate her.

She found that so funny. And started cracking up, playfully shaking her head. After she calmed down, she said, "I don't even sound like that."

I laughed too. "You do."

"Mocking me, Music Man?" she teased playfully.

I smiled wide. "Not even a little bit, Artist Girl. I like it a lot. It makes me wanna know if there's another way I can get that accent to come out." There was a sensual undercurrent to my tone when I said that. "Makes me want to know even more."

The music around us slowed. "Fortunate" by Maxwell started playing from the speakers, and without hesitation, I stood and extended my hand to her.

She came willingly.

And we swayed, pressed closely together.

I was respectful, keeping my hands firmly at her waist. At one point, they were at the small of her back, but I didn't dare venture anywhere else.

Yeah. It was magical having India in my arms. We swayed and breathed in sync under the string of lights. She had her arms around my neck. And… all of this felt familiar. But brand new at the same time. I hadn't slow danced in years. But this slow dance with India… I felt everything.

I felt a sense of closeness and sensitivity. I sensed the tension we had been building, and silence lingered between us as I drifted into her reverie.

By now, the hour was far spent. And most of the guests had already left, and now it was just the crew.

We weren't the only ones up close and personal. I could see everyone paired up, as if the energy had shifted and we were all on some grown and sexy shit.

As if someone had cranked up the heat.

I could see that Micah already had Destiney wrapped in his arms, her cheek pressed against his chest. Malachi held his wife, Ella, close to him. Destiney's sister Daijah and her soon-to-be husband Julian were cuddled up tightly.

Yeah. I felt good right where I was and with who I was with.

Then she whispered to me, "Sol. Do you always dance this well?"

I tittered softly, murmuring back, "I think you're bringing it out of me."

And I think I knew then.

I believe I knew it at that very moment.

I knew this was more.

There was no way I would keep flirting with her through texts and shooting the breeze whenever we happened to cross paths. I was convinced. The way her body felt pressed close to mine was one thing. But the way I felt in her space. Her vibe, her energy…

I wanted her.

I wanted her to rest her head on my chest when her world was in chaos. I wanted to understand what she meant whenever she sighed, what she was thinking whenever she grew quiet. I wanted to know her inside and out.

But I wouldn't rush this. No way.

I was close to her ear, saying, "India. I'm not going to rush any of this." I took in the citrusy scent that smelled wonderful on her warm skin. "But I want you to know… I want you."

Her soft almond eyes fixed on me in nanoseconds. Filled with wonder, and I think I sensed desire. Lust, maybe?

The sexual energy between us was undeniable. Sure. But I wasn't talking about that. Not strictly that.

Her eyes stayed on mine, but she didn't speak. She didn't need to.

I walked with her to her car and asked her to text me when she got home safely. She promised she would.

I went back into the house to check if Micah needed any more help before I took off. He was laughing about something Destiney had just said, and I had no idea what it was.

I was past distracted.

My whole body was still humming from my contact with India. That dance.

India had already gotten to me.

It wasn't just in the way she looked. Although, damn, that woman was fine. It was so much deeper than that.

"Thanks again for your hospitality, man," Micah and I slapped hands.

"Oh, you know it. Thanks for spending time with us." He leaned in for a quick embrace.

"Anytime."

He followed me to the front door.

"I saw you hugged up with India."

I knew it was coming. I smiled despite myself.

"Making something shake?"

"We'll see. I like her."

Micah nodded. "She's a good girl. She's fragile, though. Been through some shit. Be gentle with her. Plus, she's Destiney's best friend." He narrowed his eyes playfully, and it was all in jest. Micah knew I wasn't a reckless slimeball out here.

"I'm already knowing."

When I slid behind the wheel of my BMW, I just sat there for a moment. I placed my hands on the steering wheel, but instead of cranking up, I sent India a text while it was still fresh on my mind.

After texting her, I started my engine and drove home.

I live in Greenhaven, and it usually took me about fifteen minutes to get home with light traffic at this time of night.

I thought about the connection I felt when I touched her. It was something I didn't expect. Something I definitely didn't plan.

I knew where this could lead. I'd been down other paths that started passionately but ended in silence.

But I got the feeling this was different. Like perhaps, this one would hold.

I said I wasn't going to rush her. I knew she hadn't been out of her last relationship for very long. I knew she was healing. Her heart was probably tender.

But. I also knew I wasn't just in this to have fun with her, play in her face. Looking for a good time.

If India would let me, I would be in it for her.

seven

INDIA

So, tonight was Micah's thirty-fifth birthday party.

I was at Micah's house most of the day. I came earlier this afternoon and spent a few hours helping Destiney, her older sister Daijah, and Ella decorate and set up everything for tonight.

We had a great time, laughing and talking. Destiney is extremely close to her sister Daijah, and we share a great friendship as well. Daijah and I have been cool since the moment I met her. She's so much fun to be around. I'm super excited for her, too. Daijah and Julian will be married in two Saturdays from today.

Destiney and Micah are getting married about a month later, near Valentine's Day, which couldn't be more perfect for them.

I went home to check on my parents, make sure they had dinner, and get them settled. Then I took a nap. After I woke up, I showered and headed back to Micah's. I was running late, so by the time I arrived, the party was in full swing.

The party wasn't packed or loud. But it was filled with familiar faces, laughter, and the people who meant most to Micah. A few guests were inside the house, but most of us were outside on the patio. It was a nice vibe out here. String lights, music, candles. I loved the playlist, too. Neo-Soul mostly. Jilly from Philly. Ms. India.Arie. Maxwell. Anthony Hamilton. Musiq. That good shit.

I was glad to be here and out of the house. I hadn't gone out in a while. Weeks, I think. Besides work, taking my parents to their appointments, or running errands.

There was an evening a while back when the whole crew got together at a place in the Delta Shores area of Elk Grove called Wine & Graze Taproom. That was cool. And the whole crew was there. Des and Micah, Mal and Ella, Daijah and Julian.

When Destiney invited me out, she told me who was coming, and when I learned that Sol would be there, I was down. Though I didn't mind being a seventh wheel, I have been before.

And the tap room was cool; I'd never been, but I loved being there. It offered pour-your-own wines, beers, cocktails, hard ciders, and even coffee. An array of appetizers. There were plenty of cozy spots to sit. Music played softly in the background. Flat screens were everywhere.

When we first arrived, everyone was coupled up, leaving Sol and me. We exchanged hellos and talked for a minute. I remember him telling me how great I looked. He looked great himself, and I told him so.

I was a little shy because we'd been texting and flirting, and now we were face-to-face. And yeah, I was awkward for some reason. But I hid it as best I could, sipping from my glass of wine and keeping it cute. Later, the men gathered around a flat-screen to watch the game, while we ladies hung out and chatted.

Here we were again.

I had only been back at the party for about ten minutes, and I sensed him before I saw him. Destiney and I had been chatting, cracking up at something, when Micah approached and took her, strolling off toward the makeshift patio dance floor. I sat near the drink table, and I heard his voice behind me.

"Artist Girl. I was hoping you'd be here," he said, grabbing a chair beside me, his eyes grazing over me with a slow, warm touch.

And his voice. It was smooth, deep, and flirtatious. He was teasing me already.

He had a wide grin, and I canvassed his look. He was wearing a fitted black button-down with the sleeves rolled up. The litany of tattoos on his forearms on display. I loved his ink. His locs were at his shoulders, freshly twisted with a clean taper.

Sol was trouble. I could tell that just by looking at him. His chair was extremely close to mine. Hardly any space between us.

My eyebrows went up, a tiny grin teasing. "Why?"

Sol leaned in closer, and I could smell his intoxicating cologne. Damn, he smelled good.

"You have a way of making the room much more interesting."

Okay.

I casually tried to laugh that off, just as "Lady" by D'Angelo came on, and the atmosphere between us had shifted.

Just that quickly, it was thick with the sexual energy we'd been dancing around. We were always flirting, sexually suggestive flirting. Albeit via text. But now that he was talking to me directly, it was potent. As hell.

I took a sip of my bottled water, and I noticed that his gaze had fallen to my lips.

"You look great, Sol," I offered, trying to shift things away from me.

"Appreciate that. Likewise, India," his voice was low. "But you always do."

Damn. Okay.

I took a few measured breaths. He hadn't even touched me yet. But the heat passing between us was like an inferno. I felt my stomach flutter. I hadn't felt that in years. Seriously. What the hell was going on?

I was so aware of him, it was crazy. I don't think I've ever been affected by a man this way before. But Sol had me unraveling. His quiet confidence and the way his tongue tapped the corner of his mouth after he smiled.

Sexy.

He made me a drink, and when he handed me my cup, his fingers brushed mine, sending sparks right through me.

We kept talking. And talking and talking. A couple of hours passed.

Before I left for the night, we danced.

Just one, to a slow jam, and he pulled me close. His large hands warmly settled low on my waist, and I placed my hands on his chest. It felt natural, and I was so comfortable. We silently swayed to the music. We didn't need to talk. Our bodies did the talking.

Then, he whispered close to my ear, "Indie. I want you to know...I want you."

I didn't answer. Couldn't find my voice. At that moment, I was stuck, but I was convinced I didn't need to speak. The way I looked at him said everything.

I wanted him too.

eight

INDIA

I texted Sol as soon as I got in. As promised. I already had a text from him by the time I got there.

Music Man: I swear the music dropped a few decibels when you left

Me: LOL! I'm home. Thank you for such a good time tonight.

Music Man: I'd say you're welcome… but you know you wrecked me, right?

I cracked up. He was beyond silly.

Me: Didn't look wrecked to me

Music Man: I'm good at holding shit together

Another text came in right after

Music Man: Still thinking about the way you moved

Me: Can't stop thinking about that either

My breath was bated as I waited for a reply

Music Man: Sleep well, Artist Girl. And... if you find yourself up painting at 2 am, send me a pic. I want to see how your mind is working.

Well.

Me: Who says I sleep? That's a bold assumption LOL. For your information, I'm reorganizing my brushes.

Music Man: Makes sense. It's almost scientific that artists are chaotic at night.

Me: Compelled to agree.

Music Man: I like your chaos, tho. I bet you could tell me what color sounds like...

Damn.

We could really go back and forth like this. Teasing each other and flirting way too much. For hours. It was almost midnight now, but knowing how we got down, we would. And we have, many times. We talk about so many things. Art and music, of course. But thoughts, ideas, and family. We also discuss the things we like to create when we're working in solitude. Those are some of my most creative moments. Turns out, it's the same for Solomon.

Another message came in.

Music Man: Also, you are stunning India. Tonight especially. I saw you in that dress. Then you smiled. One word... Dangerous.

Me: Thank you. Now stop gassing me up Music Man.

Music Man: These are facts Artist Girl. I've had a little crush since meeting you at HomeGrown. You hardly looked my way, but your energy stuck with me.

Okay. Well.

Me: I have a crush on you too. And I like the way you do your thing with me.

Music Man: Do you?

Me: I do.

And I did.

I so did.

Tonight especially. That slow dance. That conversation. The way he was talking in my ear.

And I liked the way he spoke to me. I really did.

The way Sol handled me, period. Careful. And certain.

While making me weak in the knees at the same damn time.

The way Sol did his thing with me was second to none.

Yeah.

Music Man: I love the way you do yours with me. You're easy to admire.

Me: That's sweet. I'm inspired by you.

Music Man: I'm obsessed with you.

Aww shit.

I sent a bunch of hearts and smiles. It literally captured how I felt in that very moment.

Neither of us said anything else for a while. When I started to nod off, I sent, **Getting sleepy. Talk tomorrow?**

Music Man: Always. Sleep sweet, Artist Girl.

nine

INDIA

Before I opened my eyes, the scent of turmeric and ginger drifted into my bedroom, while bright sunlight filtered through my thin drapes, casting a soft glow across my bed.

Ma was already up, and I knew Dad was sitting in his chair having tea. I might as well get the day started too.

I got out of bed, stretched, pushed my wild curls out of my face, and then padded down the hall toward the kitchen. I'd go say good morning and have some breakfast before I took a shower. I had a few commissioned pieces I'd been dragging my feet on, so today the plan was to focus on those.

"Good morning, Ma," I hugged my mother Marva with both arms as she stood at the stove, transferring food into a dish.

"Good morning, baby," she kissed my cheek, and I kissed hers.

I kissed my dad's forehead and hugged him tightly. "How's your pain today?" I asked him as I took a seat at the kitchen table.

"Not so stiff today, baby girl." my father Vijah told me. I doubted he was being completely honest about that, but I gave him grace. Dad never liked it when we made a big fuss over him. But it was hard not to, especially when his arthritis really flared up.

My dad was a carpenter and tradesman for over thirty years, working on construction projects all across Sacramento. He did residential and commercial work, building furniture, kitchen tables, and cabinets.

He was known for his precision and quiet work ethic, and arthritis developed gradually after years of hammering, sanding, and sawing.

Recently, he has limited dexterity and painful joints in his hands. But he's mostly independent on his better days.

My mom placed two fragrant plates on the table. "You sleep good?"

"Yes, Ma. How about you?"

"I did," she returned with a smile.

I tucked one of my legs under me, ready to dig into this food.

Salt fish with tomatoes and onions, fried plantains, and roti. My stomach rumbled. "Thank you, mommy," I said before taking a bite.

"You're welcome, baby girl."

I didn't make a sound as I filled my mouth with food, eating with my hands as we usually do. I could fix salt fish, but not like my mom's. It was so good.

I was distracted too. My mind was already drifting back to memories of Sol's hands on my hips. The way he held me, the way he'd whispered in my ear. He was on my mind when I woke up, and I already had a message from him to greet me with the sunrise.

Music Man: Good morning, Artist Girl

My mom joined us at the table, arranging the pills she needed to take after breakfast. Her eyes were slightly foggy from glaucoma, which was getting worse, so her doctor was trying a new medication.

"You dreaming 'bout that young man again?" Ma kept her attention on the pills she was lining up. And I nearly choked on the food in my mouth.

I blinked; my mouth was half full. "Who?"

"The one you're smiling about." She carried on with her task without missing a beat. "Your whole face was glowing just now."

My dad's hearty chuckle floated around our small kitchen. I'm glad he could find joy, even if it was at my expense. It wasn't lost on me that he was massaging the swollen joints in his left hand, which bothered him more than his right. I know his hands are stiffer this week.

"Haven't seen this side of you in a while. I'm glad he's keeping a smile on your face, baby girl," my dad said. He was right. When I was with Brandon, especially toward the end, things just… they weren't good.

But Brandon was in the distant past. Because now… right now, I was thinking about Solomon's hands on my hips and his sexy cologne. That was a damn aphrodisiac, unraveling me right there where we stood.

He said he wanted me.

And I want to be wanted. By him.

And I want him.

But I can't even say I have the bandwidth for any of that. I'm still healing. Still level-setting. But I'm steadily catching feelings.

"I was young before. And your mother isn't blind, Indie. You floated in here this morning, silly grin," she chuckled. "It's okay." Daddy joined her when her chuckle turned into full-blown laughter.

Blushing, I shook my head, neither confirming nor denying. I hadn't told them about Solomon. Mentioning him would imply this was something, and it wasn't. Even though we admitted to having crushes on each other, and the sexual tension was undeniable. Our chemistry was magnetic.

This wasn't that.

It likely never would be.

It could never be.

My mom's laughter faded as she gently rested her hand on my knee, rubbing it softly. My mother was incredibly affectionate. "He's different," she said pointedly. "Whoever he is. Smiles all in your eyes and nowhere to put it." A beautiful smile lingered from her laughter.

Ma was a knockout. The most beautiful girl in her village. According to family lore, Dad saw her in the morning and asked her father to marry her that very evening. They married just three months later and have been together ever since, through so much. It's a true testament of for better or for worse.

I look just like my mom, and it's such a trip sometimes. My complexion is a toasted cinnamon, and she's about a shade darker. We have the same full lips, the same high cheekbones, and the same warm almond eyes. My long, wild black curls are hers, too. I used to tie them down or twist them up, trying to make them smaller. Now, I wear my hair wild and free. Almost all the time.

We even smile the same, but mom's smile held much more certainty.

My father has been steadiness to her.

An anchor. So good to her.

I love the love they share.

Since my earliest memories.

I've seen my father press a kiss to my mom's cheek, especially when he thought I wasn't watching. Their love didn't have to announce itself loudly; it was there in the quiet moments. Sure.

But I'm her mini me. Even though I surpassed her height at just twelve, people always say I inherited everything from her. They're right. I notice it more as I get older. And it's not just about my looks. As I've matured, I've embraced my blackness. The blackness she gave me as a proud Afro-Guyanese woman. She holds space the way she always does, blending sweetness and gentleness with just a touch of fire. Like brown sugar in hot tea.

I bit my bottom lip. "Nothing to see here," I teased. My parents chuckled softly.

My father held a tender gaze, "That's something special, my Indie. Don't run from it."

If only it were that simple.

ten

SOL

My love life is complicated.

I've been single, officially, for six years.

I was expected to be married by now.

My parents, especially my mother, had been trying to marry me off. "To a suitable girl who would make a great wife and blah blah blah."

Somehow, I managed to ward them off, insisting that I needed to focus on completing my doctoral program. It was intense, and that was a convincing argument.

Now that I've graduated, my mother is back at it, pressuring me. And I've been feeling that pressure a lot more lately.

I was here on a lunch date. Simply out of obligation, based on what is expected of me.

I'd been sitting here at this overpriced restaurant with lousy food, across from a young lady who couldn't care less about what I was saying to her.

And I felt bad for a few reasons.

I didn't want to be here.

I wasn't interested in dating her.

Certainly, I didn't want to marry her.

I was here out of politeness and because my mother strong-armed me into promising to take her to lunch. Well, she didn't really strong-arm me, though.

I mostly felt bad because I was thinking about India. Wishing it were her sitting across from me instead.

India had been heavy on my mind these past forty-eight hours. India and the promise of something I can't even put into words.

India was incredible.

It began with a slow song.

Then, a slow dance.

And I knew the very moment she came into my arms that this wasn't going to be like anything I'd experienced before.

I realized immediately that India wasn't going to be a casual thing. Definitely not a one-night stand. None of this concerning her was about getting her into my bed.

India was different.

That much was clear off rip.

It was in the way she sighed when my hands slipped to the small of her back. When her soft hands griped my back as if she needed to anchor herself to me. It was in the way she looked at me with her deep, quiet eyes. They held depth. They held soul. They told a story. I got the impression she was letting me see something she wouldn't reveal to most people.

I'd been chilling. Getting to know her. Being cognizant of her situation and her heart healing. But I told her I was into her. I told her I liked her.

Been told her. And. I wasn't in pursuit of her initially, but now... now, I was preparing to shoot my shot. We were moving like we were beginning to become something.

I hadn't said anything. I hadn't hinted at anything. And neither had she. But the way she looked at me that night at the party when I told her I wanted her made it clear she felt the same way I did.

The night of the party was when things shifted.

Going up a notch. Or four, or five. And the tension didn't ease afterward. It stretched and hummed into the next few days. I was still feeling the residual effects of that moment we shared during that slow dance. I was still floating. I'd come so close to kissing her. I wanted her lips. I wanted her tongue. I wanted to give her mine.

And I hadn't seen her, but we were texting constantly. Very flirty, always friendly, but thoughtful. Or bold. Depending. All that. I thought about a conversation we had last night. I'd just gotten back from a gig in Rancho Cordova with a group of guys I play with now and then. The band is called Wind & Brass Funk; about seven of us. My buddy Teddy and I played sax. They had a couple of trumpets, a trombone, a flute, and a clarinet.

I've played with them for a few years now. We jam really well together. Teddy asked me last minute to come out if I wasn't busy, and I'm glad I wasn't. The guys are cool and talented. I always enjoy myself when I get to play with them.

We performed at an outdoor amphitheater in a neighborhood park. I had a wonderful time. But India was on my mind all the while. I wished she were in the audience, watching me…watching her.

The band and I took a group photo, and I sent it to her say-ing, **"Thinking about you, Artist Girl."**

Later, when I checked my phone again, she responded with smiles, music notes, and heart eyes, saying, **"Thinking of you, Music Man."**

When I got home a few hours later, she texted me asking how the show went and how my day was.

Artist Girl: How was your day Music Man?

Me: My long day. Three classes back-to-back. Half the students want to learn, and the others only want beats for their TikTok.

Artist Girl: LOL! You still love it.

Me: I do. Wbu? When you get a minute, send me some pics of the magic you made today.

Artist Girl: Sure. Painted for six hours at the rec center. Love seeing it all come to life. Destiney's on this crew with me.

She shared pictures of a mural she was working on. Lots of blues and violets.

Me: Looks amazing!!!

Artist Girl: Thank you. It's kinda everything.

Me: Dope. FR. You are literally painting the city. Ever look around and think you're exactly where you're meant to be?

Artist Girl: Hmm. Not often enough, but this feels good

Me: Side note… I'll confess that I listened to your voice memo three times. Sexy

Artist Girl: I'll confess the same. Your voice is nice. It's like you can tell me a story that will put my ass to sleep. Sexy and deep. Dangerous combo.

Me: What's dangerous is you giving a man like me that knowledge

Artist Girl: LOL! Use the info wisely, Music Man.

I sent a voice memo. *"Indie. Imagine something. We're up late, and you are painting a masterpiece. Wild and colorful. And I'm nearby with my acoustic. Playing melodies. We're just being… creating in the same space. What do you think of that?"*

**Artist Girl: Just listened. And that sounds like peace.
Also, dangerously sexy.**

Yeah. Shit like that.

I needed to see her, and I was going to remedy that.

In the meantime, I had this situation. Sitting right across from me.

We were at a stylish rooftop bistro in downtown Sacramento. A curated, expensive menu with an overly lengthy wine list.

And I was bored out of my mind.

Noelle reached across the table, her fingers lightly brushing my wrist, bringing me back to the present.

"Solomon," she tilted her head. "You're so quiet."

I lied. Forcing a smile, I said, "I'm a little tired."

Noelle didn't ask any questions. She didn't lean in, and I didn't either.

Yeah. I was supposed to be married by now, to a young woman like Noelle. And she was young. I think she'd just turned twenty-four.

Pretty.

Polished. Poised.

Confident.

Dressed impeccably. Flawless hair. Practiced grace. Always conscious of her image.

Noelle was a self-assured debutante born into privilege.

The privileged world I grew up in was full of status, tradition, appearances, and expectations. And lately, I've been feeling that pressure more than ever.

I managed to keep my parents at bay, insisting I needed to focus on finishing my doctoral program. It was intense. By the grace of God, blood, sweat, and tears, I earned the letters behind my name. Shit, and the ones in front. But now that I've graduated, my mother is back at it, pressuring me into something with Noelle.

I arrived on time, but Noelle was already here, about ten minutes early. She wore a tailored dress, heels clicking, delicate earrings, and subtle makeup. Looking perfect. On purpose.

I complimented her. She looked lovely. And we had a decent conversation.

She asked some questions. I responded in kind.

But.

Sparks hadn't flown, and none of it was impressive. Not to me, it wasn't. And this had nothing to do with India. Honest to God.

This wasn't our first "date." My mother first mentioned Noelle over a year ago. And we'd gone out to lunch then too.

And the mothers. They were dedicated to the process, acting as producers and casting directors, searching for the perfect candidates to fill a coveted role. My mother was proud and hopeful, showing me the picture of Noelle that her mother had sent. Noelle is a pretty girl, and it should've sparked something. Would have sparked something for someone following the status quo. In my parents' eyes, Noelle is the perfect match. But I knew things would fall flat when we met.

Noelle was well-bred and well-educated. She knew how to carry herself in social circles.

But she's everything safe. And nothing soulful.

I wanted something more.

Something authentic. Genuine.

We were halfway through our lunch entrees, and I was already zoning out. Noelle had been talking about her new role as a private duty nurse.

She was sure to mention "this type of work being designated only for affluent clientele."

It's a big deal, apparently. She emphasized that her private client required personalized care, and the agency is quite selective about who it hires. Earning this position would also be great experience for her nursing career.

I gave a subtle eyeroll.

I understand how this works.

Noelle didn't earn anything.

Noelle has rich ass parents with power and influence. That position was given to her, not based on merit but pure nepotism.

I can guarantee others were more qualified but didn't have parents in influential positions who just needed to make a call, and the job was theirs.

Add to that, her client was wealthy, hiring through a private agency.

That meant they would offer a generous salary.

Money Noelle didn't even need.

Then, she made sure to mention that she would be more than willing to quit the whole "nursing thing" to start a family.

I completely checked out at that point.

My mind wandered.

I was thinking about a beautiful Caribbean woman.

Her warmth. Her passion. Her sex appeal.

I stirred my tasteless risotto. And remembered to smile politely every few moments, pretending to be engaged.

But I felt nothing.

I was so done with this whole thing; I didn't even want to walk Noelle to her car. But I thought better of it.

When we reached her car, I gave her a quick hug goodbye. It was respectful and meant nothing.

And I couldn't even imagine kissing her. Not now. Not ever.

I wasn't detested or repulsed. I just wasn't into her.

There is a difference.

I headed to my parents' house with Miles Davis flowing through my speakers.

And I was still thinking about India.

Her wild hair. That oversized tote. Her free spirit.

eleven

INDIA

My love life is complicated.

Kieran, my first love, was back in Guyana. We were fourteen.

I remember his easy smile and his laugh. We were just kids. It was puppy love. Simple and pure. But back then, it felt like the whole world.

I cherished those moments for years.

I saw his glances, but he was so shy that he sent his friend to ask about me. And when we finally spoke to each other, he was even shyer.

We shared our very first kiss on the way home from school. Sweet, shy, and clumsy. Both of our hearts were pounding. I told him I was worried I wouldn't be good at it. He said he was too.

We met in the middle, and our lips brushed like a question neither of us knew how to ask or answer. When we pulled apart, our eyes were full of wonder. It wasn't explosive, but it was real. It was ours.

My heart was shattered when we left. I remember sobbing in my mom's arms.

She comforted me and then shared something profound: *"It's alright to miss him, baby girl. Sometimes love is not forever, but about the lesson it leaves behind."*

I held onto those memories of Kieran and me, always grateful for that first love, even if it ended too soon.

So, moving here at fifteen, I felt homesick and heartbroken.

And extremely guarded.

I missed Kieran. The boys sniffing around me were the last thing on my mind. An entire year went by before I even thought about getting to know anyone.

And I resisted it. My heart was closed. I was emotionally shut off, and I was simply not interested.

But Amir.

This was a guy who wouldn't give up until he had me. And eventually, he won me over.

He was consistent and sweet. His approach was unbelievably smooth and caught me completely off guard because I wasn't checking for him like that.

Not at first.

I met him during my junior year. We took an art class together, and I had been taking art classes throughout high school. That year, I was in Advanced Art Studio, which was my favorite class of the day. I had it during seventh period that semester, but I hated that time slot.

Amir wasn't like the other boys. He'd tell me things I hadn't heard before.

I knew he thought I was pretty. He had a subtle, flirtatious swag about him, and I knew he was attracted to me.

I definitely thought he was cute once I gave him the time of day.

I initially thought he was a transfer student or something. I remember asking him if he'd just started here, and he gave me an incredulous look.

"I've been here since freshman year." When my face showed my embarrassment, he laughed it off. *"You good. I noticed you when you transferred here last year,"* he told me.

My eyebrows were up on my forehead.

"You appeared out of nowhere. February twenty-third. I saw you for the first time and learned you'd just got here. A girl named India transferred here from Guyana." I listened intently as Amir kept talking, *"I didn't know what to think of all that then. But when I saw you..."* My breathing slowed, waiting to hear what he'd say next because I was almost sure he'd say some typical, predictable, teenage boy knucklehead shit.

But he completely surprised me, saying, "I loved your jeans. The patchwork. The uniqueness of your style. I loved your backpack." I'd drawn whimsical designs all over my lime green backpack with a black Sharpie. *"And then I learned you were an artist. I saw your work featured in the school newspaper. "India Rampersaud, featured artist of the week." It all made sense after that."*

I slowly exhaled. "I decided I'd have to introduce myself at some point. I was kinda shy. Honestly. I wasn't sure what I'd say after I told you my name. But I kept watching you from a distance. When we got new schedules, I saw you head in here, and I knew this was meant to be." He had my undivided attention at this point. *"So."* He stuck his hand out. *"Lovely to meet you, India Rampersaud. I'm Amir Gregson."*

That was it. I immediately had a crush on him.

Amir would say the most incredibly thoughtful things. He loved my clothes and my style.

My mom hand-sewed many of my clothes, making me unique outfits that no one else could wear. One of a kind.

Mom was a seamstress and designer, and she could make anything I asked for. That's where I got my talent.

She could draw and design anything.

Anything I came up with, and she would deliver if she could get the material.

Amir was a bright light in our Advanced Art Studio class. He could draw well, too, and we bonded over that.

Amir was amazing at cartoons. I couldn't believe what he could do with markers. He also had a side hustle. Kids would pay him to draw caricatures, like the ones people do for you on the boardwalks or at Six Flags. Amir would have people lining up to get couples' pictures drawn during lunch.

He drew me all the time. He was incredibly talented. And Amir would compliment my artwork. He loved my paintings and drawings.

So, we hung out all the time, and I started developing feelings. When I told him I liked him, he said he liked me from the beginning and was just waiting for me to catch up.

Smooth.

In the next breath, he asked me to be his, and we made it official.

And we went to homecomings and proms in junior and senior year.

We lost our virginity to each other.

My heart was fully in this, and this love was very intense. At least for me. Simply because Amir and I had a chance.

And we were together for nearly five years.

I was twenty-one when it was all over.

After we graduated, I wanted more. I wanted to get married, so I started asking questions.

"Where do you see us in five years?"

"Do you want to get married someday?"

Initially, he laughed it off, saying, *"We were still young,"* or *"Let's not ruin things by planning too far ahead."*

I suppose we were young. We were only eighteen. I agreed we could wait a little longer. So, a couple of years passed. And eventually, I asked him directly, *"Amir, do you see yourself marrying me?"*

He became eerily quiet. Then he uttered three words that shattered something inside me.

"We're not ready."

At first, I was confused. I have loved him since I was sixteen. I cried about it, and he threw it back in my face. Gaslighting me.

"This is what I mean, India. You crying when we're talking about something serious. How are you gonna handle real life? I'm not ready. And you're not either."

He declared it as if he knew my heart better than I did. Like he was doing me a favor by withholding what I wanted more than anything else.

I withdrew after that.

Convincing myself he was right.

I was overly emotional and naive.

Honestly, though, I would've married Amir in a heartbeat.

Despite how his words had cut me.

I recall him sighing heavily when I brought up marriage again. I think I asked him where this was heading. If he still wanted me.

He rolled his eyes, *"India. We talked about this already."*

No, we hadn't. Not really.

I asked, I cried, and he gaslit and deflected.

And I cried again when he rolled his eyes and pinched the bridge of his nose.

"You gonna keep falling apart like this every time I try to talk to you?"

As if my tears could alter the truth.

Like my feelings were too deep for him to comprehend, and therefore, something was wrong with me.

"India, you're always crying. How can we have a proper conversation if you're going to be so emotional?

So, what did I do?

I started apologizing.

For being too sensitive. Convinced, wanting clarity and wanting my love to be reciprocated was some kind of weakness.

Oh, and he said we lacked passion.

We weren't "freaky."

Honestly, I wasn't sure what to think of that.

But I kept giving him everything.

Everything in my power to give.

My body. My loyalty. My time. My future.

I loved him.

I would follow Amir anywhere.

But he couldn't even engage in a genuine conversation.

Something I didn't realize until later was that if someone doesn't answer your question, they're hiding something.

And if they blame you for how their words hurt you, they aren't being honest. They're cruel.

Amir decided to attend the Art Institute in San Francisco. I was proud of him and excited, but also anxious about doing things long-distance.

But he would only be about eighty miles west of Sacramento.

And he came home to visit me at least twice a month. We talked all the time. FaceTime.

He even sent for me to come see him occasionally. I'd take the Amtrak and spend a long weekend.

And he promised that when he finished his program, we would talk about marriage and our futures.

I felt good about that.

It all came to head when I found out he was sleeping with someone else the entire time.

He had a whole baby on me, and I only found out because she sent me a picture.

He was leading a double life. She knew she was the side and decided to reveal his secret because, in her words, *"She was tired of waiting for him to end things with me."*

I was blindsided.

I felt humiliated.

I was utterly devastated.

Amir didn't have much to say for himself. Just some flimsy stuff about us outgrowing each other, and he wasn't sure how to end things otherwise, or some shit like that.

And can you believe he married her?

Weeks later. What's even more unbelievable is that she actually married him, knowing what he did to me.

And Amir did more than just cheat on me. He did something incredibly unfair. Something I carried with me for years and still struggle to forgive myself for.

Something no one else knows except him and me. Something he pressured me into doing, and something I felt I had no choice about, without fearing I might lose him.

Looking back, I guess it was a blessing in disguise, given how everything turned out.

At least I managed a clean getaway.

After Amir, I shut down again.

At twenty-one years old, usually the prime of a young woman's life, I was freshly heartbroken and newly single.

Amir left me for the woman he got pregnant, then married her, posting pictures as if we never existed. As if everything we shared from sixteen to twenty-one years old meant nothing.

That crushed me, and I quietly retreated into myself. I was extremely withdrawn.

Destiney was there for me when things took a nosedive. She let me cry on her shoulder and helped me put the pieces back together. I'm beyond grateful for her.

A little while after Amir, I casually dated a few guys here and there. But I never got involved in anything serious. I think I was way too afraid.

Then I met Brandon.

And he seemed different.

I met him at the park, of all places.

One early spring afternoon, I was at McKinley Park, which is in East Sacramento and just a short drive from my house.

McKinley Park is one of the most popular parks in Sacramento. It's sprawling, covering more than seventy acres. Most Saturday afternoons, nearly every spot in the park is filled with picnics, basketball games, joggers, and walkers. Dogs on leashes. Baby showers. Birthday parties. Even weddings and photoshoots.

There are lots of benches scattered throughout the park. You'll find many couples spending time together or people, by themselves, having peaceful moments of reflection.

McKinley Park is rich with inspiration. There's a pond in the center of the park with swans, ducks, and geese.

There's a rose garden, and it's breathtaking.

I would sometimes spend my entire afternoon there, painting. I love visiting in spring. It's magnificent. The rose garden is full of hundreds of roses of various kinds blooming again. I read that there are over twelve hundred rose bushes there.

So, I had my easel set up and was painting some roses, using a mix of primary and pastel colors. I was in my zone, with one earbud in, music playing on one side. The joyful sounds of children laughing and playing at the nearby playground drifted in from the other.

"That's amazing."

The voice was smooth and easy. Commanding.

I looked to my right, and a handsome man was standing a few feet away. Casual attire: sneakers, shorts, and a tank top. He had warm brown skin, a low fade, and a goatee.

"Really. That's the most phenomenal thing I've seen in a long time." I turned completely to face him. He didn't come any closer, but he now wore a smile. I counted one dimple.

"Thank you." I smiled as well. Not my megawatt smile, but I was polite. I didn't engage. Neither did he.

He went on his way, and I returned to painting.

Exactly one week later, around the same time, I was back in my usual spot. In the rose garden, my easel was set up, brush in hand.

"Must be my lucky day."

I looked over my shoulder, and there he was again, several feet away. It was déjà vu. He was dressed down but still looked as handsome as the last time.

But he didn't linger.

"Carry on. I don't mean to disturb you." And then he was gone.

About an hour later, I heard his voice again. "It seems as if you paint like the world is watching." I turned toward his voice, and he was a little closer this time. "I like that."

His lines were incredibly smooth. His tone was steady. It was really casual, actually. And open. I wasn't quite sure how to handle that.

He glanced at his watch. "If you haven't eaten, there's a café on Broadway that I like. If you want to take a break, I'll be there until three." After rambling off the name of it, he was gone again.

I stood there with my mouth slightly open.

He didn't push or ask for my number.

Or my name.

But I can say with one hundred percent certainty that he got farther than another man would have, if they had asked for either of those things.

After all that shit with Amir, I had my emotional defenses up. I was twenty-five years old at this point and still guarded because of that trauma.

My reluctance to engage was obvious, but he gave me an option. He didn't pressure me, which meant a lot. He was respectful and clearly able to read the room, demonstrating his emotional intelligence. I appreciated that.

I didn't move immediately. Instead, I stood there, thinking about it and having an internal battle.

I could meet him in a public place, and I could always leave if the vibe was off.

After debating, I decided to meet him.

I remember seeing him as soon as I entered the café. As I moved toward the table, he looked up, grinning. That same grin from the park. Friendly and welcoming.

He stood as I approached the table. "You came."

"I did," I replied, internally asking myself why.

"Brandon." He extended his hand. "Thank you for joining me."

"India." I shook; then timidly sat in the chair he'd pulled out for me before he sat down as well.

"India." he echoed, nodding. "It suits you, beautiful."

"Thank you," I replied politely. Speaking through my nerves, I teased, "Had to see if you were actually interesting."

He chuckled. "That's fair. I can't promise you that. But I'm so glad you came anyway."

We didn't speak much at first. I just observed him, and he watched me. His eyes appeared gentle.

Then I asked if he had already ordered.

He hadn't. Said he'd been waiting for me.

Smooth.

We had an enjoyable conversation over iced lattes. Brandon was thirty-two when we met and was already an accomplished real estate agent.

As I got to know him that afternoon, it made sense. Brandon was charismatic and confident.

He sold million-dollar homes in Folsom, El Dorado Hills, and Granite Bay, the affluent foothills about forty miles east of here. A world away from my life in Oak Park.

He was very proud of the life he had worked hard to build. I understood that and appreciated it too.

I was intrigued. A few hours later, when we parted ways, I gave him my number, eagerly looking forward to his call.

That was how Brandon got me. He charmed his way in without even sweating me.

He kept things casual and let me decide when to let him into my life. He simply loved being around me and spending time together. I enjoyed it too. The thing about Brandon was that he didn't try too hard. He wasn't desperate; he flirted just enough but gave me space. And when we made things official, I thought maybe I would be safe this time.

SOL

"Solomon. How was lunch with Noelle?" My mother, Claudine, asked immediately. I'd barely settled on their fancy sofa in their sitting room. The room was elegant, decorated with high-end furniture and imported pieces, like the rest of their Curtis Park home. My childhood home. I was sitting across from them. My father had a book open but closed it, placing it aside as I sat.

"Hello to you, too, mother." I said with a hint of sarcasm.

My father, Leonard, chuckled softly. He was definitely more easygoing of the two.

"Forgive me. Hello, son." She smiled pleasantly. Then she repeated her question, waiting silently for a response.

"Fine," I returned, measured.

My mother raised an eyebrow. "Fine? Just fine?"

"She's a nice girl, but there's nothing there.

"She told me things went well."

Now my eyebrows went up. She'd called my mother. I can't even say I'm surprised.

"Solomon. Honey. It was just one lunch." Her tone was pressed and pleading. "You're not in college anymore. It's about time you started thinking practically about your future. You'll be thirty-five soon. Noelle is a lovely young woman. She's from a nice family. You know she just finished her master's in nursing."

I bit back my smirk. "She told me twice, mother." I watched my father pour himself a glass of scotch in silence. When he raised his brow at me, I waved my hand, declining the silent offer. I wasn't planning to stay much longer; I was already ready to leave, even though I'd only just arrived.

"Noelle would be a great fit, Solomon. And I suspect you know how this works by now. This isn't about feelings or sparks flying. It's about honoring your family and respecting our hard work. We've laid a path for you. We have a reputation. You're expected to build something lasting. A legacy."

I was adopted at weeks old. My parents tried for years, unsuccessfully, to conceive.

Spent tens of thousands of dollars on fertility treatments. But that was just a drop in the bucket.

My upper-class, well-educated parents come from a long line of wealthy Black people.

Old money. The kind of money that truly bought you the finer things. They carried themselves with understated elegance. Raised me with a rigid structure and grand expectations.

Being adopted at all is a blessing. But being adopted into wealth was a world of privilege.

I grew up with everything that should have made me feel safe.

A beautiful home in Curtis Park with manicured lawns, tree-lined streets, and quiet prestige. Located in an affluent, historic neighborhood near East Sacramento.

That came with isolation. Although my adoptive parents are Black like me, I never truly felt like I belonged.

None of the children in my neighborhood looked like me. The same was true for my prestigious private school. None of the children there resembled me. None of the kids on my soccer team looked like me either.

I have been studying classical music since third grade, and I have always enjoyed music. It came naturally to me, and I excelled at it. But it was another situation where I was one of the few Black kids in an elite setting.

That always left me looking for something.

I've been searching for something more for a long time.

That thing… whatever it is, I'm sure I'd recognize it when I find it.

Maybe a face like mine or a story that was mine. A family name. I've been searching for a long time. Hit a few roadblocks… and felt discouraged, so I left it alone. Returned only to face setbacks again.

But then I met India, and it ignited something in me. Something akin to a boost of confidence. To try again.

Yeah. India is already inspiring me.

"Solomon." My mother's voice was frantic, pulling me out of my thoughts.

"Mother. I'm not interested in Noelle or building anything with her." I said, surprising myself. There was a sharpness in my tone that I never used with my mother. But I needed to say this with my chest.

"She can't be that terrible. You had lunch with her."

"For you. I was doing you a solid."

"A solid?" Her tone was incredulous. I said nothing more, and my mother looked from me to my father and back again. He still hadn't said anything, and that pissed me off.

"You've finished your program, Dr. Solomon Avery. We're very proud of you, and you've had your freedom. But your father and I… Solomon. We…"

My father didn't even look at me. His attention was fixed on something outside the window, several feet across the spacious sitting room. Then my father cleared his throat and said, "We have expectations. You've indulged, now it's time to prepare for your future and the next generation."

I silently looked at my father for a few moments, feeling betrayed first of all. His silence indicated he was siding with my mother. I suppose that's not a surprise. But I hoped, deep down, that he would support me. Tell my mother to back off. Let me choose who I want without hassling me about it.

He wouldn't even meet my eyes.

It's not even about Noelle. It's about the pressure to conform to expectations from a family that adopted me but didn't truly see me.

That's evident even from my father's word choice just a moment ago.

I was stunned. "Indulged? Is that what you think this is about? You believe I'm just out here, sowing oats willy-nilly or something?"

Neither of them said a word.

"Wow." I stood from my seat on the sofa.

"Solomon! Where are you going?" My mother asked urgently.

"I need some fresh air."

I'd been standing outside on the stone patio for a while when I heard my father open and close the sliding door softly behind him. He was quiet when he stood beside me and remained silent as he looked out into their pristinely trimmed hedges along the property line, as if they held all the answers.

I reflected on my thoughts, and they felt crowded and heavy.

But there was something so inexplicably clear that I couldn't contain myself when I said, "I'm seeing someone."

I knew I had my father's attention, but he said nothing. So, I added, "I like her. I like who I am when I'm with her. I like the way she makes me feel. I like her. A lot."

My father continued to look straight ahead. "This is serious?"

"Not quite. But I'd like for it to be. I think it could be." This was the first time I admitted any of this. Even to myself. Just thinking about it had me smiling on the inside.

There was a heavy pause. The silence seemed to stretch.

Finally, "You know Solomon. Your mother..." He sighed. "She's going to need time. She wanted Noelle for you. She won't give up so easily."

I turned toward my father immediately. When I had his eyes, I said, "Respectfully, I don't need her permission. This isn't something I am asking for her approval on."

My father gave a slow nod, possibly in understanding. I wasn't certain. He didn't appear to resist what I had just revealed.

"You'll be careful." It wasn't a question, more of a reminder.

"Absolutely. I am with her.

He patted me on the shoulder and turned to head back inside.

thirteen

INDIA

I was in my art shed, working on a commissioned piece. This was my art studio space, where all the magic happened.

We call it "The Bee Shed" because my dad carved a tiny bee into the wood above the doorway. It was a little joke. He said that when I was really little, I was always buzzing around. Drawing, coloring, or painting, never sitting still.

It's a little shabby, but I wouldn't trade it for anything. My father built it just for me with his own hands, before his arthritis really set in.

I spend most of my time here. Creating, thinking, and praying sometimes.

This is where I store all my paints, brushes, canvases, and easels.

I was sitting on my stool with my bare feet on the paint-splattered floor. I had a Bluetooth speaker here as well. Midafternoon sunlight streamed in, my playlist going.

A blend of R&B and Reggae.

A brush in my hand, I streaked the oversized canvas in front of me with reds and oranges. I was trying to get in the zone, but it wasn't happening.

I knew why.

I was distracted.

I'd been thinking about Solomon.

I've always had a man chasing me. Interested in me.

But I had a hard time trusting that they wanted me for who I am and not just because I'm pretty.

Some men just wanted a pretty woman on their arm, and that's all you were. The only thing you were good for. A fucking trophy. They weren't interested in you beyond your physical presence. Not at all concerned with what you have to say, your thoughts, opinions, or feelings.

I was feeling frustrated with myself because I didn't think that was the case with Solomon at all.

I just had a gut feeling that he wasn't like that.

He was so interested in me. Absorbed, attentive, and now, I'd say invested. He wanted to learn about me, my culture, my opinions, and my family.

I also learned about him.

Yeah.

But I shared those things with him openly. Nothing on my radar detected an ulterior motive.

I shared my brief twenty-seven-year story, and he listened intently.

Sharing that my parents moved here in the early 90s as newlyweds from Berbice, Guyana, specifically Port Mourant.

My dad received employment-based immigration because he was offered a job as a tradesman. They didn't have much, aside from their love for each other and their dreams. They settled here in Sacramento, California, and eventually obtained permanent residency.

They had me a year later. I am a first-generation American by birth. When I was seven, we moved to Guyana. My grandmother was falling ill, and my parents wanted to be close enough to help care for her, as well as raise me near relatives.

I loved living there. Those years hold my fondest childhood memories. I climbed mango trees, chased cousins through my grandma's yard, running barefoot and laughing with tears in my eyes. The warm sun kissed my shoulders. Living life surrounded by lots of aunties, uncles, and cousins.

When I was fifteen, my parents decided we would move back to the U.S. They wanted me to get a high school education here and have better opportunities in the future.

I was devastated and cried like a baby. Returning to the U.S. was one of the hardest times in my life. The girls at my school were so mean. They called out everything different about me.

I can still hear their voices, teasing me about my height, how thin I am, and my body. *"No curves, no hips, no boobs."* I'd never felt so insecure. They also teased me about my accent.

But the boys liked me. And that made the girls even meaner. Maybe they liked me because I was different. I don't know. I am different. Biracial.

My father is Indo-Guyanese. I'm brown, with a darker complexion than some other Black girls, but my hair was long and fell wild and free.

Not the same natural curls they had.

I have thick, black, wild strands that refuse to be tamed.

According to them, I was acting as if I were better than them.

All I did was keep to myself. I barely spoke because I didn't want to be teased about my accent. And as proud as I was of my roots, I wanted to be like them. I thought maybe then I wouldn't feel so alone, even as a Black girl in a sea of other Black faces.

Sometimes, even now, I wonder if I am too much of everything and not enough of anything.

Too tall. Too thin. Too Guyanese. Too Indian. Too creative. Too damn pretty.

I just want to be truly seen for who I am. Not as an outsider or as a girl with an accent and an exotic vibe.

As me.

It's been tough to carry all of that, and I do a good job of hiding it. I've shared some things with my mom since we're close, but not everything.

I haven't shared any of these things with Destiney.

I'd rather harbor than harp.

But in so doing, it has caused me to second-guess myself. Hold back.

Internalize. Scrutinize.

But in the meantime, I just keep painting. I keep creating. I continue to be wild and free-spirited, even if it means doing so in solitude.

And I guess that's what had me so distracted. Sol seemed to see things deeper than my art. It's crazy how he speaks in sound the way I speak in color. We speak a different language, yet we still understand each other.

And being understood. Being seen. That's all I have ever wanted.

fourteen

SOL

Dr. Kollie: I'll be in town at the end of the month. Let's plan to get together.

I'd just walked in the door of my house when I felt my phone vibrate with a message. I put my bag down and checked it quickly, eagerly, thinking it was India.

It was Tasha. I looked at her message but didn't reply immediately. I wasn't sure if I would respond at all, and if I did, I wasn't sure what I would say. So, I stared at the message a few seconds longer. My thumb hovered over the screen.

If I were being real, Tasha was fine.

Smart. Confident.

She wore sleek rimmed glasses and had an East Coast wit that made her even cuter. She had a nice laugh and a sharp tongue, but could be soft when it mattered.

Like in bed.

We'd been doing this song and dance for a few years.

Our connection was based on mutual attraction, convenience, and intellectual synergy. Nothing emotional. Not at all. That's the truth.

Dr. Tasha Kollie.

I met her at Cal Berkeley. I was there for a Black Studies symposium, invited to speak on Black Musical Traditions. She was on a different panel, but I caught some of her presentation.

And wow. Tasha was brilliant.

She had an incredible stage presence, was very well spoken, and articulate. She was magnetic. I didn't expect to meet her, but I admired her from afar.

The symposium lasted a few days, and I met her at the end of the second day. I was giving a lecture on Music Senses and Cultural Memory when I noticed her standing in the back. She wore a black tailored blazer, a white blouse, and black slacks that followed her every curve. Red pumps. Her arms were crossed, and she seemed to be listening intently.

We made eye contact a few times, and she smiled at me. I didn't think much about it at the moment. I saw in her bio that she was part of the hosting faculty, so I figured it was all just part of the hospitality package.

She stayed behind as the hall cleared out and approached me to ask about Sonic Rebellion and Music Resistance. She politely introduced herself as a distinguished professor of Africana Studies, having recently completed her doctorate and already tenured in the department by her early thirties. Her research focuses on the globalization of Hip-Hop, especially as it relates to the African diaspora and the less-examined African diaspora sites.

I was beyond impressed. I enjoyed her confidence and conversation. We had lunch together spontaneously at a campus cafe and exchanged contact information.

I settled into my hotel room, and after a couple of hours, she texted to ask if I had dinner plans.

We met up and had dinner. We laughed, talked, and had a few drinks. When she asked if I had plans for the rest of the evening, I knew where things were headed.

I ended up at her place afterward.

We had amazing sex and kept it going. When I planned to be in the Bay Area, I'd reach out to her. Whenever she planned to come to Sacramento, she'd contact me. It was always discreet.

We'd meet for a late dinner and drinks. There were even a couple of times when we met in other cities or states.

We both traveled quite a bit. It's part of being a renowned professor in your field.

I was invited as a guest lecturer at UCLA and casually mentioned it to her. She decided to meet me there, turning it into a weekend trip.

I gave a TED Talk in West Palm Beach. It was an experience of a lifetime. Such an honor. She met me there, surprising me.

She told me she would be speaking at a conference at the University of Houston, so I booked a flight and a room and spent a couple of days with her.

We never had that talk. About what we were doing. About what this was. Where we stood.

Tasha never asked, and I didn't either. Our conversations were always surface level. We never went deep with anything. She kept that part of herself closed off, compartmentalized. I followed suit.

Yeah. The sex was incredible. But I hadn't seen her in a few months. Hadn't had sex in a few months. I wasn't intimate with anyone else.

Since we'd been sexing for a few years with no talk of an end game, it was obvious where Tasha stood. This wasn't that. I figured she wasn't concerned. She would have brought it up by now, I'm sure.

Tasha is young and pretty, and she's at a point in life where she'd want to think about settling down. If that's what she wants.

And it isn't as if I'm not concerned. But. Tasha doesn't seem to want those things. Wanting stability. To put roots down somewhere with someone. Nah. That's just not her style.

Tasha is a globe-trotter. We've talked extensively about our international travels. She has been to twice as many places as I have. She's a frequent flyer. Already diamond status. And, I'm saying this parenthetically, it's not as if she couldn't travel with her husband and a baby in tow… but I digress.

Though our conversations were mostly superficial, I got the sense that Tasha wanted to rebel against her parents' expectations.

She told me she was a first-generation Liberian and always followed her parents' guidance. She went to Berkeley at seventeen and stayed on the dean's list throughout her entire undergraduate studies.

Based on what I gathered, I believe she decided that was her stop. She decided that now was the time to live her life on her terms. Her words, not mine.

And let me just offer some perspective: men know which category they'll place a woman in from the beginning.

That's just the way it is.

Don't hate the player. Hate the game.

Not that I'm playing games, and I realize that would piss a woman off. But Tasha isn't trying to belong to anyone, at least not right now, I don't think. And I'd bet my last dollar she's sleeping with other people.

I don't think about that, but for the sake of this argument, I'm sure that's the case.

And. Honestly... I'd be extremely disingenuous if I said I wanted anything more with her.

Tasha isn't a wife. Tasha doesn't give me wifey vibes. She's way too out there and too damn scattered.

Not to be mistaken for a free spirit. They're not the same. But she never asked me what I wanted. Never leaned in or showed any interest in that.

Tasha is incredibly smart and very articulate about her discipline, and I respect that. Nothing but respect. As an academic. But she's not someone I'd bring home to my mother. She probably ain't trying to meet a man's mom anyway. So, I let the message sit there. Didn't reply. I'd figure something out later on.

Because now? I had the incomparable India Rampersaud in my head. On my mind. Catching my breath.

Her laugh. Her voice. The way she said my name.

I didn't want to pretend any longer. I didn't want to fall into reckless habits that would leave me emptier than when I started.

The party was exactly two weeks ago. I saw my parents the day before yesterday, and I was annoyed with that whole situation. Still, I was proud of myself for speaking my mind and standing firm on my position.

And I was floating through lectures, grading papers. Had my weekly gigs at HomeGrown… but… underneath all of that was an ache.

This gravitation.

For India. Only India.

I missed her, which I hadn't expected to. Not in this way. But it was hard not to. We kept texting. Late nights, early mornings, sometimes past 1 a.m. Sending messages that were flirty as hell, with sexual undercurrents.

But let me mention that she sees things deeper than my music. It's crazy how she speaks in color the same way I speak in sound. Like we speak different languages, yet we still understand each other. She'll have me rolling at her weird little paint metaphors.

I still can't believe it. She was a stranger not too long ago, yet she occupies so much space in my mind and heart. And I've missed her. Crazy. I've missed her. With a full schedule. Classes, gigs, rehearsals. I still catch myself wondering what she's doing and if she's okay. If she's had a chance to paint, I know that grounds her and keeps her sane. I know she has a lot on her plate.

I've reminded her that I have a crush on her. A real one. A couple of times. It's cute how she laughs it off, telling me she has a crush too.

Yeah. I like her a lot, for reasons beyond just physical attraction. And India is stunning.

But I want to make a move and let her know I desire something more with her. However, I don't want to push her too quickly. I want to wait for her, listen to her unspoken needs, and let her heart heal.

But I'm sexually attracted to her too. And it's intense. Especially right now.

Right. Now.

It's easy. The energy she exudes makes my whole body hum.

I just like her vibe. I love her rhythm.

And I admire her strength. Her dedication to her family and her refusal to apologize for it.

So, I'd just taken a shower. I already had dinner. I went to put my dirty clothes in the hamper, and I had a voice memo from her when I returned to my bedroom. I'd sent her one just before I got in the shower. I was responding to something silly she'd said, and I was cracking up at her.

I listened to her reply, then sent one right back. I removed the towel from my waist, applied some lotion, and started to get dressed. I was just pulling my shirt over my head when my phone lit up with another memo notification. I pressed play.

"Sol. I need you to warn me when your voice is gonna come through like that. I wasn't ready."

Then she sent a picture.

Of her thighs.

Stretched out on her bed, a soft light tracing her curves. No caption to go with it. Only the image.

I had to sit down for a second.

INDIA

I really should have gone to bed.

But I knew what I was doing.

And I knew exactly what I wanted.

And I was wide awake, especially now that I've sent Sol that picture.

And now that I was waiting for a response, my heart was pounding with anticipation.

Yeah. My ass was wide awake now. Freshly showered. Lying in my bed, in a T-shirt, panties, and nothing else.

Scrolling through our thread like it was gospel.

Sol had been a welcome distraction, and he had no clue.

But more than that, Sol wasn't asking for anything. He didn't demand anything. He was just there.

Sol was incredible. He made me feel more like myself than I have in a long time. The place I was in now, feeling a sexual gravitation toward him, almost seemed inevitable.

He was extremely supportive.

We talk about many things all the time. One night, I was feeling vulnerable and shared my dream of learning to tattoo with him.

"Artist Girl, you have talent, and I believe you'd make a damn good tattoo artist. I'll support you in every way I can."

I needed his encouragement right now. Things at home were stressful. Earlier today, my mom had to see a specialist because her eye pressure had spiked again. They wanted to see her and insisted that she come in this week. So, I took her to another office across town, the only one with an opening. It took a quarter tank of gas. When Dad checked Mom in, I noticed his subtle nod when the receptionist mentioned the $85 copay had to be paid upfront.

I stepped in, swiping my debit card before he could reach for his wallet. I knew Dad's account didn't have enough to cover that. He wouldn't be getting paid for another two weeks.

Then we had to pick up mom's prescription, which cost another $60, but she needed it today. We also needed to grab a few groceries.

I opened my banking app while we waited at the pharmacy. Not zero, but pretty damn close.

I knew we would be okay. I knew we would figure it out because we always did.

I spent some time sketching when we got home to ground myself. Once I got mom and dad settled, they both wanted to take a nap, and I couldn't blame them. I went out to my shed to draw.

Money was a fleeting thing around here. The subject of money made me feel very uncomfortable. I didn't like discussing it because it caused me extreme anxiety.

Sometimes there was a cushion. Not a big one, but enough to breathe. Enough for groceries, utilities, and a cell phone. Sometimes, there was even a comma in my checking account. Infrequent, but nice when it happened. It didn't last because there was always something. But I never dwelled on it. That was fruitless.

It was one reason I wanted to get into tattooing. I knew I could earn more money doing it. I still love painting. Doing murals and commission work. That was my passion. But I needed to bring in more money somehow.

The stack of bills on the kitchen table, past due, had me in a tailspin. But I reminded myself we'd be fine, and we had done worse with less before.

Today has been a lot.

And Sol had been a steady presence, helping me forget all my troubles when we talked at the end of the night. He kept things light. He made me laugh.

And it's the sweetest thing that he's a grown-ass man, always telling me about his crush on me. He's always saying it. And he's not the only one. I like him too. Hella. And I've told him so.

And Sol is incredibly talented in music, beyond just gifted. He's so clever. His conversation and his mind... I just love how it works, how he sees things, how he sees me. His vibe is amazing. Sexy.

He's such a flirt. No one has flirted with me as intensely as he does. One second, he's cracking me up, and the next, he's saying some freaky shit, turning me on.

He's always turning me on.

I didn't mean to send that picture, not at first. But when I listened to his voice memo, his voice… it was a little rough, maybe because it was getting late, but it hit me. Put me in the mood, and my body reacted before my brain had a chance to think.

And it wasn't just lust. Not at first. It was something about the way he listened to me. I could be open and vulnerable. I could unload my thoughts and speak freely, and my mood swings were welcomed. Some days I had a lot on my mind and I was moody. Sol always responded in kind. Listening intently and encouraging me.

Speaking life.

That gave me space to trust him. I wanted to get closer to him. I think I'm still hesitant. But right now?

Damn. Right now, I need Sol. I want him. My body is craving him.

I'd just gotten out of a messed-up situation. I was honest about that when we first started talking. Months ago. I told him I wasn't even sure I had the capacity for anything. Barely even a friendship. I thought about him. His feelings. Sol's a good guy, and I didn't want to hurt him.

Here I was, nervously waiting for a response to my picture. It was 11:04 pm.

Before the picture, we exchanged a few voice memos. He randomly asked what was on my mind this late. We laughed about something I saw on TikTok. He sent another memo, and I told him his voice was doing things to me.

Music Man: Tell me. What kinds of things?

Then I sent the photo. My bare thighs peeked out from the hem of my T-shirt.

He took a while to respond, and even though I was here and he was there, I swear I felt a shift.

Music Man: You playing with fire tonight Artist Girl

Me: These are the things you're doing to me. Come put it out.

His response wasn't momentary. And I stared at my phone, my heart pounding loudly in my ears. Then a notification.

Music Man: India. If I come to you this late, I need your transparency. Don't have me guessing. What do you want?

Me: You. Let's not pretend this hasn't been building. I want you here and your hands touching me. Your mouth. I want all of it.

I saw three dots. Then,

Music Man: Send your address.

I paused for a moment, contemplating something stronger than lust. I didn't want him to think I moved like this. I definitely didn't want to regret anything.

Me: Sol. Before I give you my address. I'm not the type to do stuff like this. I've only been with two men, and I was in long-term relationships with them. I'm kind of embarrassed that I sent that picture, and I'm asking you to come over. But I do want you. I have wanted you for a while now.

I reread it three times. I finally sent it and waited again, my stomach in knots. I was convinced either he would ghost me or something real could come of this. Seconds felt like they dragged on. Then my screen lit up.

Music Man: India. No need to be embarrassed. I knew from the beginning you aren't like that. From the start, I felt that. And I swear that if I come see you, it isn't just about

tonight or just about right now. It's because I want you. **More than your body. YOU.**

My heart rate tripled, and I felt warm all over, but not from arousal.

He sent another message.

Music Man: Tell me where I can find you. If you still want me to come. But only if you're sure, India. I respect you. Tell me what you need.

Oh my gosh. Sol knew exactly what to say.

Me: Come through, Music Man. I sent, dropping a pin.

Then I put my phone down because my heart was pounding again. I was feeling nervous, excited, anxious. All the things.

I quietly walked down the hall and checked on my parents. Their ceiling fan made a soft buzzing sound. Ma was curled up on her side, her hair wrapped in the silk scarf she wore to bed. Dad's snores were faint, but he was out. Good.

I returned to my room and closed my door behind me. Took a few deep breaths.

This wasn't us hooking up. For me, it wasn't. I had the feeling it wasn't for Sol either. But I wasn't wired like that. I didn't do casual or meaningless. Although I'm extremely sexual, I've never been the type to give my body away. I wasn't raised that way. Most of all, my parents were asleep in the next room.

Tonight, I was a woman who wanted and needed. Him.

I cracked my window and lit some incense, the real shit. My cousin sent it from back home in Port Mourant. I loved the scent. Jasmine and clove. Then I turned on my Himalayan salt lamp, casting a soft, warm glow in my bedroom. Perfect.

I stood in front of my full-length mirror, teasing out my curls. I slipped on some shorts even though he had already seen my bare thighs. I looked around my bedroom. It wasn't perfect, but it was neat. Layers of artwork covered my walls. Art supplies were scattered across my desk. My large tote sat on my chair. He loved to tease me about my tote, but I knew it was all in good fun.

My phone buzzed.

Music Man: Outside. No rush.

God. My heart rate picked up again. I took a few calming breaths and then typed back.

Me: Coming. Please remove your shoes.

I was as quiet as a mouse as I moved toward the front door. Opened it. He looked at me with an easy smile. I smiled too. Then I pressed my finger to my lips, whispering, "My parents are asleep."

He nodded, understanding everything. I let him in, carrying his shoes.

I entered my bedroom, he came in behind me, and I closed and locked the door.

When I turned around, he was already close.

"Hey, Artist Girl," he whispered as he leaned down to put his shoes by my door.

"Hey." I took a few deep breaths. Now that he was finally here, my nerves were starting to settle.

We were face to face when he asked, "Can I have a hug, India?"

I silently nodded, falling into his arms. He embraced me quickly and securely. His arms felt like home. And security. And he smelled so good. Like a fresh shower and the cool night air.

Then, he was in my ear. "Can I kiss you, beautiful?"

I nodded again, my eyelids fluttering faintly.

It started slow.

Our lips pressed together softly. His hands at my waist. I wrapped mine around his neck and got lost in the bliss.

His lips were so full and so soft. His tongue was in my mouth. Mine was deep in his. It was as if we'd done this before. But it felt so new at the same time. The tension dissipating.

My body arched into his as if it had been waiting to be connected again. Reunited once again. The months of restraint were unraveling, thread by thread. He backed me into the wall and continued to kiss me slowly. Deep. Nasty.

Damn, Sol was a great kisser.

He sucked my bottom lip and went deeper still. His hands started to move upward under my shirt. His fingertips brushed the curve of my hips.

He broke the kiss, softly murmuring against my lips.

"You tell me if I'm moving too fast or if you want me to stop."

I was breathless, whispering, "I don't want you to stop."

His nod was silent, and he pressed our lips together again. We kissed a little longer, and his hands moved up to cup my breasts. I tensed just slightly. As a reluctant member of the 'itty-bitty titty committee,' my small breasts are one of my insecurities.

Sol must have noticed. "You okay?" he softly asked against my lips.

"Yes."

"Good." He kissed my lips. "You're so sexy, India."

"Thank you."

"You're welcome. I've been dreaming of this moment with you. To be alone with you like this."

"So have I." And I really had. And he was right. This was our first time being alone. We'd just shared our first kiss. Had plans to be intimate. *Mmm.*

He was close to my ear, his large hands caressing my body all over. "I've been wanting to taste you." My breath hitched, and Sol pulled back, looking me in the eyes. "Can I do that, India?"

"Y—. Yeah. Yes." My response was quick. Almost embarrassingly so.

He let out a faint chuckle. Then his lips brushed mine. "Yeah?"

"Yes. Please."

He still had my eyes. His face darkened, as if my permission sparked something.

"Are you sure?"

I nodded. "I'm sure. I've been thinking about it too."

Still whispering, "Lie down for me, Artist Girl."

He took my hand as I led us to my queen-sized bed. I lay on my back, my hair falling like ink across my pillow. My breaths were uneven, my chest rising and falling under my shirt. He stood beside the bed, watching me as if I were a sacred painting he needed permission to touch.

He took off his shirt. "Can we take yours off, too?"

I nodded. Sitting up, I pulled my shirt up, and he gently guided it over my head. I removed my shorts too, leaving me in only my black lace panties. "Goddamn India. You are so fucking beautiful."

I had a shy smile, but I was open and ready.

Anxious and in need.

I was Sol's for the taking.

He lowered himself in front of my bed, and as he settled between my legs, I let out a breathy sound, barely audible.

He was gentle as he eased my thighs apart. Then he hooked his hands underneath them, pulling me to the edge of the bed.

"Are you sure, India?" he murmured again, looking up at me.

"Yes. Never been more sure. I need you, Sol."

It was something I said.

Or maybe it was just the way I said it. It felt like I'd given him everything.

He lifted himself, kissing my flat stomach. Down to the lace of my panties. So slow. So gentle. He went lower, leaving a trail of kisses. Then peeled my panties down my hips, and I lifted for him.

I knew I was wet. Already. And he confirmed it when he murmured, "Mmm… already slick and warm for me, India. You are glistening right now." I heard him swear under his breath. "If you only knew how hard I am in these joggers." He let out a light titter. Then, *Tu es si belle,"* he whispered. "My Belle."

Damn. He speaks French! He sounded like a native speaker. I didn't understand, but I knew it was French, and he spoke it beautifully. Surprising the fuck out of me.

I moaned softly, shifting my hips toward him. I couldn't wait any longer.

He lowered his head, then connected us. The first stroke of his tongue was gentle, deliberate. Just enough pressure to make me gasp. Oh my gosh.

"You taste like honey, Belle," he murmured softly against my lower lips.

He dragged his tongue up slowly. Circling my clit. It felt incredible. He flattened his tongue, pressing in deeper, sucking gently. Then flicking in a rhythm, teasing me and making me come undone.

I fisted the sheets, my knuckles were probably white; I was gripping them so tightly.

"Sol. Baby… oh my gosh."

He kept eating me. So good. Kept licking me. Flicking me. Sucking me. His face was buried deep in my pussy. He slid a hand around from underneath my thigh to my waist. His other hand slipped between my thighs. And then his fingers were inside of me, stroking me, alternating with his tongue. Fuck. Gentle pressure driving me crazy.

His voice was strained now, "There you go… that's it." he murmured. "Give it to me, Belle."

I lifted my hips, moaning. My body writhed, edging toward something beautiful.

"You taste so good. So... fucking sweet, baby. I could stay down here all night."

My voice breaking, even in a whisper. "Sol. Baby. Don't… stop. Please don't stop…" I was so close. I know he could feel it. The way my breath hitched, I was trying to twist away and pull him closer all at once.

Sol doubled down. His tongue and fingers stroked me deep and slow. I moaned his name. "Solomon..." came out of my mouth like I had been waiting for this moment all my life.

He didn't even pause. My thighs were trembling, and I called his name again as I emerged from euphoric oblivion.

When he lifted his head, his mouth was drenched. His lips glistened with my essence. His eyes looked satiated. He kissed his way back up my body. My inner thighs, hips, and belly. And then my mouth as I tasted myself.

He kissed my neck, then he was in my ear. "You good?"

I could hardly nod.

He had a faint chuckle. "Can I hold you a minute, Belle?" he whispered.

I nodded, then slipped into his arms, and he came into mine as if it was the most natural thing we'd ever done.

"Sol."

"Yeah?" we were still whispering.

"Do you always do that?"

"Do what?"

"Start with your mouth. Like that…" My voice was light. I felt incredibly vulnerable, but my curiosity was too strong not to ask. "You make a girl forget her damn name."

He smirked. I felt it in my neck. His mouth was pressed there, kissing me softly now and then. "Only when I mean it."

"Hmm. Nobody's ever done that for me." My voice was quieter now, barely above a whisper. I hadn't intended to share that, but it slipped out before I could stop it. In that moment, I felt more vulnerable than I ever had in my life. Honestly. Sol had pulled that out of me.

"Done what?"

"What you just did."

His tone was measured. "India. You telling me you've never had your pussy ate before?"

Suddenly, I felt defensive. I don't know why exactly, but I did. I regretted this entire line of questioning.

"Well... I've done it. For them." I shrugged. "But Brandon never... He just didn't really do that."

Sol sat up just a little. The lamp provided enough light for me to see his furrowed brows. "Never?"

"Never. No." I said that as if I wasn't sure whether I should be ashamed or annoyed. "Not one time."

Still propped up slightly, Sol looked at me as if I'd just told him water wasn't wet.

"Wait a second." He shook his head. "All that time. For more than two years, that clown never went down on you?"

"Clown?" my eyes widened.

"Yeah. He's a fucking clown. Brandon the Clown. Doing clown shit."

I buried my face in my pillow, snorting. Sol leaned over, giving me a serious look.

"Deadass, that's wild."

"I asked. Hinted. But." I shrugged my shoulders. I couldn't offer much else. And Brandon wasn't here to defend himself.

Sol slowly shook his head. "I'm genuinely offended on your behalf. A man let you love on him with your mouth and couldn't even return the favor." He leaned closer to me and said in my ear, "Nah. Not even gonna lie. That shit pisses me off."

He settled back beside me; I was in his arms again. I touched his jaw gently. "Well... for what it's worth, you made me feel wanted. Like my pleasure matters."

"It absolutely does matter," he returned without delay. "It always will. I'm going to make your body forget what selfish feels like."

I exhaled. "I think you already have."

sixteen

SOL

"Good." I moved over her slowly. "You okay?" Still whispering. I wasn't trying to get us caught, even though we were grown.

"Yeah. I just... damn, Sol."

Chuckling softly. "I know, right. You taste so good, baby," I told her in her ear.

"Thank you." Her arms were around my neck. "What did you say when you spoke French earlier?"

"*Tu es si belle.* You are so beautiful. And you are. My Belle."

"You speak French fluently?"

"Yeah. Studied French since I was nine."

"That's awesome. I love how it sounds."

"Thank you." I kissed her cheek, then her neck. "I want more, Belle. Want to be inside you... If you want that too." She looked up at me with a gentle gaze. "I'm not rushing. Or assuming. I'm asking you."

"Yes," she whispered. "I want that too."

"You have condoms?" I asked, already reaching for my joggers on the floor. I'd come prepared just in case.

"Just a couple. Top drawer." she murmured, nodding toward her nightstand.

I pressed a few kisses to her forehead before I took one out. She watched as I rolled the condom on. My body was buzzing, and I couldn't wait to connect with her.

She reached up and cupped my face.

"Are you ready, Belle?"

"Yes."

I moved over her again, slowly. Gave her more kisses from her shoulder to her collarbone, her neck, her cheeks. I kissed her as if she were both fragile and powerful. All at once. And she was. She was art. Like a beautiful porcelain doll. Delicate and fragile.

I was close to her ear. "Have you ever had a man take his time with you?" My voice was thick and low.

"No, baby."

"You're about to baby... taking my sweet time pleasing you."

I ran my hands down her thighs and spread them open again. I wasn't in a rush, but I was reverent. I kissed her all over, giving her the attention she deserved.

Then I slid inside. Slow. Deliberate. Taking my time, inching in gently. I held her as I entered her, and once I was fully inside, I held her gaze.

"You feel that, Belle?"

She nodded.

"That's mine now, baby." Damn. She felt good.

"That clown can get the fuck on somewhere. I respect you, and I see you. All of you." I started to move my hips. Slow. As if I had all night. I angled just right, dragging moans from her lips with every stroke. She clung to me, her eyes wide. "India... I'm not him." I whispered in her ear again, kissing her neck. "I would never take from you just to leave you empty. Ever."

She moaned quietly.

"You hear me, baby?"

"Yes."

I continued to stroke her slowly, taking my time to appreciate her beautiful body. Slender and smooth, she had a tiny gold hoop in her left nipple. I ducked my head, licking both of her nipples. She enjoyed that, so I did it again for her.

"I got you. All of you." I moved deeper. Our bodies were slick with sweat. And I kept stroking her. Wasn't nothing hurried about what we were doing.

She held me close and wrapped her legs around me. We were breathing in sync. Heated breath and aching passing between us. "Belle. You feel so good. *Mmm.*" I managed. "You feel like heaven, baby."

India came first. I felt her tremble around me. Soft cries dissolved into my shoulder.

I followed, whispering her name and telling her how pleased I was.

And we lay there afterward. Her head on my chest and our limbs tangled.

We didn't speak, just held each other tighter.

Yeah. This was a promise of what was to come.

This was just the beginning of what I would show India.

seventeen

SOL

So. Since that first night… a night I can't stop thinking about, I've gone to India three more times, with zero hesitation. Not one second thought.

India will text me, and then I go. It's as simple as that.

For real.

I'll be planning for lectures, literally in the middle of typing on my computer. Or just relaxing, almost ready to go to bed. And I'll see *Artist Girl* on my screen. And. My chest will do this thing it's been doing. Where it tightens up and lights up at the same damn time.

Artist Girl: You up Music Man?

And that's all she has to say. I'm already on my way to her, all the while grinning like a teenage boy who just started to smell himself, as if I ain't ever got none before or something.

But she's different. This is something different.

But I'll go to her, all the while telling myself it's no big deal.

But it is. It always is with her.

Then I get there and see her, in all her beautiful fucking glory. Her hair is wild, her eyes are sleepy but longing. She takes me in as if I am exactly what she was waiting for.

And we don't talk much at first. Not really. We just fall into each other. I lose myself in her every damn time.

Once she's let me have her, and she's had me, and then she's settled in my arms, softly breathing into my neck, I think about all the things I still haven't said. The questions I still need to ask, the answers I desperately want from her.

I want to know what we're doing. I want to know if this is just a physical thing. Just sex for her. If she ever thinks of me when I'm not in her bed. It seems like she does; we text as we normally do. But things have changed now that we've started doing this.

But I want to understand. Because… It's not just about physicality for me. It's not just sex. Not even close. And I constantly think of India when I'm not sharing space with her.

But I don't even ask. I worry that I might risk shifting this, whatever it is, even more. Shifting energy. Pressing her when she's just starting to let me in. Finally. I noticed that too, and I am so pleased with it. It makes me feel like I am doing something right. With her heart being broken and fragile, it's huge that she's letting me in. So… I keep my questions to myself and continue to show up in the meantime.

I keep caring for her without calling it anything. Thinking, maybe that's foolish of me. And irresponsible. But I'm sure I am already too far gone. I'm man enough to admit that. My feelings are involved now. Have been.

Another thought I had… which is crazy, the more I think about it… these feelings aren't love… yet. But. It's on its way there. I can admit that too. And that's wild. For me, anyway.

We're lying together right now in India's bed, and she's facing away from me. She drifted off not long ago, her back pressed to my chest. I have one of my arms tucked under her, while the other is wrapped around her waist. Her skin feels warm against mine, and her breathing is steady. She's tired. She told me she had a busy day taking her parents to appointments and running errands. She works so hard, always on the move. Painting masterpieces and leaving her mark around the city. I hate to wake her, but I'll need her to lock up behind me.

I shifted slightly and gave her a gentle kiss on the shoulder. "Indie," I started, pressing a few more kisses there.

She took her time turning toward me, giving me a lazy grin. She blinked slowly, rubbing her soft hand up and down my bicep. Her voice was quiet, "Didn't mean to fall asleep on you."

"No need to apologize, Belle," I whispered. My goodness, her eyes. They looked like open doors. I could stare into her eyes and get lost there.

I should say it now. I should… ask her. Not for a title… but maybe ask her, just… if she feels this too. What I've been feeling.

Still holding her gaze, I brushed back one of her curls. Her lips part as if she is about to speak, and I lift my eyebrows expectantly. But she says nothing. I hear a faint hum. She does that when she's comfortable and settled. Especially when she's satiated, after a pleasure-filled session like the one we just had. I feel the same way. India does that to me. It's so easy with her. So natural.

And I want to ask her right now. I want to say to her, "Belle, what are we doing? What is this to you?"

Because this isn't casual. Not to me, it isn't. But, what if this is casual to her?

I sighed softly. After a few beats, I leaned in and brushed her ear, whispering, "Indie…"

Her eyes were on mine as she murmured, "Hmm?"

Then I hesitate, having an internal battle with these loud ass thoughts in my head.

Ask her! Say it!

And. I don't ask her or say anything. Instead, I softly kiss her temple, full of feeling. I wonder if she can feel that. It's such a reverent kiss. How could she not? Finally, I say, "Uh… nothing. Please come lock up behind me, and you get some rest. We'll talk tomorrow, Belle."

"Alright." I heard a sigh. It was subtle, but I caught it.

When I got up from the bed, I reached for her hand, and she accepted, intertwining our fingers. We took a few steps toward her front door, hand in hand. We did this every time I left. And I liked it, a lot.

I drove home and hopped in the shower again once I got there, trying to wash my thoughts away and hoping I could settle down enough to get some rest.

I looked at my cell phone when I returned to my bedroom. 1:07 am.

When I took off my clothes before stepping into the shower, I could smell her all over them. Smelled just like her. Her coconut body wash, her warm, soft skin where I pressed my face into her neck. I loved inhaling her mass of curls and the sweetness of her shampoo. I loved breathing her in. Inhaling deeply as if she were my source.

And I lay there, staring up at my ceiling. It was dark in my bedroom, but my heart was pounding loudly. My mind kept racing, wondering.

How long can I keep doing this? Not asking.

And I should be asleep. I have a class in the morning, but all I want to do is go back to her.

I'm a night owl, typically anyway. And she is too, apparently. Some nights, she texts me earlier, maybe around 9:30 or 10 pm. I'll show up closer to 10:30. Some nights, she takes her time, waiting until her parents are fully asleep. If she hasn't had a chance to shower, she'll do that, and I get a text around 11 or 11:30 at night. I usually arrive just after midnight.

But it's no big thing. I'm always up late. Grading papers or watching performances online. Tiny Desk… I've seen them all. Maybe I'm playing something, practicing, or composing. Then I hear from her, and I go to her. Late doesn't bother me at all. I like it. The night, the quiet. It's sacred, like something just for us.

I kissed Indie twice at the door. She kissed me three times back and said, *"Get home safely, Music Man,"* in that sleepy voice of hers. The voice that makes my body hum.

And there's something else; something I couldn't understand, no matter how hard I tried.

Brandon never once put his mouth on her. All that time.

What kind of man has a woman like India and never gets on his knees for her?

A woman like India. Soft. Warm. Art covering her skin. She was clean. Always. And I don't just mean hygiene either.

She takes care of herself. I could feel it on her skin. India felt like she lived right. Like she drank water and ate fruit. But she cared for herself. She smelled as if she layered herself with love, from the bath to her lotion to the perfume oil she tastefully dabbed behind her ears.

Clown shit. That's what it was.

Some of these dudes are selfish. They see sex as only involving their dick. Some of these dudes fear intimacy, as if being vulnerable is a weakness or something. Some have a weird ass power dynamic and believe that if they go down, that then makes him beneath her or something.

And then there are these wackos who don't know what the hell they're doing and would rather act like it's nasty, rather than admit they never learned.

Worst of all, they refuse to even try.

None of it made sense when it related to India.

Now, make no mistake; some women don't take care of themselves. And men know it. Quick.

Poor hygiene, dry skin, sour breath, or just their vibe.

Some of them didn't make you want to. If they don't care about their body, why should he?

But India isn't like that.

And she was… I honestly don't know. The words that come to mind don't do her justice.

There is something about how she shares herself with me. She opened up for me, and there was an unspoken trust there. I'm so glad there was, as if she knew I would treat her just like the gift she is.

And she's so soft. So warm. So sweet. She gets so wet too. All the water she drinks, all the fruit she eats. She tastes clean and delicious, as if her body was made to be devoured. And. I swear… I could live between her thighs.

I lay in the dark, still wide awake, reflecting on the first night we shared. I remember how her scent clung to me. Warm, clean, and faintly floral.

And. I couldn't stop smelling my hands.

And… there was a voice memo.

"You made me feel like it mattered to you…"

I closed my eyes and sighed, "Goddamn Belle."

She opened her legs for me, like a prayer. I went to my knees without hesitation. Every time she's let me taste her since then, it's not out of lust. It's out of respect and instinct. There's no way I could have access to a woman like her and not honor her.

For India, honoring was precisely what it was.

The first night we were intimate, so much happened. It was way more than just physical. That's all I can think about now. It was crazy.

The pussy attached to India was the best I've had. Ever.

It anchored something. It connected us. At least, that's how I see it. I'm curious to know what she's thinking, and I really should ask her.

But before that... before the pinnacle, I tasted her.

Her very first time, she told me later. But I would have known if she hadn't. She gasped, as if the sensation shocked her. She moaned, as if something inside her awakened. She gripped her sheets and trembled, as if the pleasure rewrote something in her.

You can't fake a reaction like that. I knew. But I appreciated her vulnerability in sharing that with me.

She was a woman who had suffered from starvation.

Fucking clown. He only took from her for over two years.

Yup. Clown shit.

Giving is not optional when you're taking. Only a clown would leave a woman like India deprived. I never wanted to be that kind of man. I never will. I'd rather not touch a woman than give her less than she's owed.

She met me where I was and let me in. She melted beneath the touch of my tongue, with gratitude.

Fuck.

Belle didn't even know what she was worth.

Not yet.

And that broke something in me.

She was so convinced this was rare and new. And maybe it was to her, I guess. But I was about to show her something. Taking my Belle sightseeing.

I found my phone in the dark and opened her voice memo again.

"You made me feel like it mattered to you…"

Oh Belle. It does. And you do matter.

And she is so flexible. That shit is insanely sexy. Her legs open without apology. Without hesitation. I had all the space I needed. No barriers.

Her taste and scent are now imprinted in my mind. Fresh. Earthy. Sweet.

I never rush that. Ever. I want her to enjoy it. Every single moment. This is for her. After being unfairly deprived, I am setting a new standard for her.

And the way she looked at me after I'd pleased her that way, I knew I'd shown her something no one ever had.

And when I returned to my quiet home that night, I sat in the dark with her taste still on my lips and listened to her voice memo.

She spoke softly, a little shy. But her voice carried everything we hadn't yet said out loud. I listened to it four or five times that night. I lost count.

It didn't matter. I listened to it all the time. I knew it by heart, damn near.

"Hey… I realize I could have texted you. But… I didn't want to type this. I wanted you to hear me say it to you…" She cleared her throat. *"…I'm lying here… thinking about you. About what just happened. And. I just… I've never felt like that before. Felt those things before."*

She had a lazy giggle, then a soft breath. *"…I felt wanted. Like…my body wasn't just something to tolerate. Like I was art. Like it mattered to you."* She sighed. It was a little heavy. *"And… I don't think I even realized how much I'd been settling until you looked at me the way you did and touched me the way you did. Sol. It just felt like you meant it. And you saw me."* She murmured, *"And then you started speaking French… oh my gosh…"* She had a light titter. It was silly and adorable at the same damn time. *"I have no idea where this is going. If it can go anywhere… but just… thank you. I'm not trying to be weird about it. But thank you for seeing me and making me feel that I'm allowed to want more and that I can have that. Anyway… sleep good, Music Man."*

Yeah. After that, when she called for me, I didn't touch her just to please her anymore.

No. I touched her as if I were memorizing her, mapping all of her reactions, learning her spots, and establishing a language from her breath patterns and gasps. The way her legs would softly tremble when I whispered her name in her ear.

And I'm taking my time with her. I've slowed down even more than before. Every kiss I press on her soft, warm skin is deliberate, from her belly to her thighs, to her hands. She's sacred. Not just beautiful.

Yeah. I cherish these moments with her. Even when she gets excited and urges me to go faster. I want her to enjoy being appreciated. And get used to it.

It was clear in her voice memo that we had achieved something she didn't think was possible.

After that, I gave India more of the same. And I planned to keep showing her what it feels like to be pleased. Not just wanted.

I vowed to be the man to ruin her for anyone who doesn't touch her the way I can.

And as I slowly drifted off, I reminded myself, for the umpteenth time, that I needed to talk to India about us. About what we were doing and what this was becoming. Because I wanted her, and I wanted that.

All of it.

eighteen

INDIA

When I woke up this morning, I was aching. And not just between my legs. That was part of it, for sure. But the ache was in my chest, my thighs, and at the corners of my mouth, where Sol's name still lingered from the kiss he left there last night. Or should I say this morning?

First of all, it wasn't in my plans to sleep with Solomon.

Honestly, it wasn't. And I didn't even need to tell myself that. But I did anyway. I kept saying I wouldn't sleep with him, a few times. None of it made any sense. For starters, I don't usually move like that. But there was something about Solomon, and the easy way he had me feeling so damn comfortable. So comfortable, so chill, that I wasn't using any of my good sense.

I sighed lightly. I could hear birds chirping outside. I'd left my window slightly cracked, and now the sunlight was filtering through my curtains as well. It was still early, but I could hear Ma and Daddy moving around in the kitchen. They usually get up early since they go to bed early. Most of the time. I needed to take a shower before I went up to greet them. I wanted to wash away the remnants of last night.

Not that I wanted to, but I couldn't risk Ma calling me out. She did that a few days ago, the morning after the very first time Sol came here. And then came again. Twice, I think. Had me coming too.

And the very next morning, my mother noticed. But of course, she would notice. She notices everything. She kept giving me this look, and I pretended not to notice. But she wouldn't stop. It was pointed and lingering.

"Who has you waking up smiling like that, girl?"

I brushed it off and kept my neutral expression, but I was screaming on the inside. I mumbled something about a dream I had as I raised my cup of tea to my lips, but she knew. She always seems to know these things.

And she just wouldn't let it go. When I started fixing lunch for her and Daddy, she was watching me again. I was just slicing potatoes. That's all. I had a skillet on medium-low heat with a fresh onion, garlic, and ginger mix. It smelled fragrant, and I'd be tossing in some freshly diced tomatoes soon. Ma stood in the kitchen entryway, watching me, as if I was doing something suspicious. And I could feel her eyes on me.

"Are you feeling okay, baby?" she asked casually, like it was nothing. But I knew better.

I slowly stirred in the tomatoes now that the onions were translucent. I kept my eyes on the skillet on the stove.

"Yeah, Ma. Why?" Damn. I didn't need to ask her why. All I had to do was answer the question. I kept my eyes away from hers, though.

"No reason." Ma's voice was light, then quickly turned sharp and curious. "You been smiling to yourself all day."

I finally dared to look at her, but not before I could school my features, and I knew it was too late. I could tell my face had given me away. I hadn't even realized I was smiling.

"No, I'm not. Not smiling any more than usual," I bit the inside of my lip.

"Mmmhmm." Ma moved past me and opened the fridge as if she wasn't still bothered about this. It wasn't a big deal. I'm a grown woman. And I know my mom. She'd love Sol. Daddy would too. I'd have their blessing to see him. Romantically. But. This isn't that. And the less they know, the better. I haven't even uttered his name around them, and I didn't plan to either.

She stayed silent as she moved things around in the fridge, and I kept stirring.

"Indie. Baby girl, is this the coconut or the condensed one?"

Ma's glaucoma was gradually stealing her sight. Some days, she needed help. Another pair of eyes.

I shifted slightly to face her. She had both cans close to her face, squinting. "The one in your right hand is the coconut milk." I turned back toward the stove, stirring again. The fragrant aroma of the ginger and tomato was just beginning to bloom in the oil.

"Yes, I thought so. These letters are so small. You using the last of the soaked chickpeas?"

"Yes, Ma," I answered, keeping my back to her. "No meat today. Figured this would stretch and still taste good."

"Yes, baby, this will be just fine. It's a gift to know how to make do when things are tight. Don't lose that."

"Yes, Ma," I said, nodding. She stood beside me, milk in her hand, squinting. "Take this before I pour too much. I can hardly see the line anymore."

After I wiped my hands on the towel nearby, I turned down the flame.

"I think you just want me to do the messy part."

Ma laughed heartily. "I'm supervising. You can fix this better than me."

I quickly shook my head. "No way!" I tilted the can over the skillet as the thick white milk poured into the simmering tomato base. Mom was nearby, her head tilted.

"Slow. That's good…"

"Mommy! I thought you said I could handle this?" I playfully nudged her.

Her laugh was easy, "I can smell when it's about right. You don't want too much."

"I know, Ma."

I kept stirring, and Ma walked over to the table, slow and quiet. Our kitchen was small, so she was just a couple of steps away. My back was to her now.

"I remember when you used to smile like that." She said softly.

The wooden spoon in my hand paused mid-stir.
I knew she wasn't finished with this. I didn't look at her; I just resumed slowly stirring the contents in the skillet.

She wasn't even done. "Is that man from the party?"

I almost choked on the spit in my mouth. How did she know that? But I said nothing, careful not to give her any nonverbal cues.

"I don't know what you're talking about, Ma."

She laughed softly and satisfied. Meanwhile, I hated how warm it made my chest feel.

"Indie. Let that curry simmer and come sit down."

She was right. This was the part where you let it alone to allow the ingredients to marry each other under the low heat. I was just trying to buy myself some time.

I put the lid on the skillet and headed to the table, sitting in the seat closest to her. I didn't really look her in the eye, though. "I was only cooking lunch, Ma."

"Mmmhmm." She had a playful tone. Ma could be silly, and I loved her quick wit and banter. I finally looked up to see her eyes on me. A gentle smile appeared on her beautiful brown face. Her eyes were smiling too. "I don't need to know everything, baby girl. I know you're grown."

I exhaled softly, still controlling my demeanor.

"But I'm your mother. It's okay to share with me. And I can tell when a woman is smiling to herself over a man when I see it." She gave me a pointed nod. "That kind of smile… that doesn't come from painting or some mangoes from the flea market."

I burst out laughing. Couldn't help myself.

She wore a slight grin. Her gentle brown eyes held a quiet understanding. "Is he treating you right, my Indie?"

Yes!

I swallowed hard. The answer was a resounding yes. But that was the problem.

I decided to humor her. She wasn't going to let it rest. "Yeah. He's so kind, Ma. Very gentle with me. And smart."

Her smile widened, but it was still controlled. Her voice remained steady as she said, "And is that what's got you smiling, baby girl?"

I laughed again; I couldn't help it.

She nodded. Satisfied. "Mmm." She stood and kissed my cheek, gentle and knowing. She always knew. She went back to the cupboard, fishing out her favorite teacup. "I'm just sayin. And I may not say much, but I see you, baby. Glowing lately. Walking different. That man is feeding your spirit."

My eyebrows had to be at my hairline. My heart was pounding loudly in my ears. Is it that obvious?

"Don't wait too long to say what needs to be said. Daddy and I didn't get to where we are, guessing our way there."

She turned on the kettle and went about fixing herself a cup of tea as if all she'd just said didn't shift this whole kitchen.

♪♥♫♥♪

After lunch, I was in my art shed. I had my playlist going. I was in the mood for Ms. Lauryn Hill, and she'd been flowing through my speakers these past couple of hours. Getting me together.

And I was trying to concentrate. I had an appointment later on with Kingston. He owned a tattoo shop in the Triangle District of Oak Park, and I was going to head down there in a little bit and talk to him. See if he'd give me a shot at learning to tattoo.

Of course, I was thinking about Sol.

And everything Sol had been doing to me.

Fuck. I wanted him to do it again.

"I'm not trying to get you caught, Belle."

He was here super late this morning. The latest he's ever stayed. And we both dozed off.

A few times. I didn't want him to leave. And when he finally did, I honestly wanted him to take me with him. But I didn't say so out loud.

"I don't want to leave either, but… I should get going."

I gave him a sleepy smile. He'd just stroked me into oblivion after he ate me so damn good.

My eyes were closed. "I know."

"I could stay in my car. Sleep right outside. Just so I'm close to you, Belle."

"You would do that?"

"For you. In a heartbeat." He whispered, softly kissing into my neck.

There was a stretch of sleepy quiet. I was dozing off again when his warm lips were pressing onto mine.

"Tu es ma lumière," Sol murmured, just a whisper of air between us. "You are my light, Belle." He told me before I even had to ask. Another light kiss followed.

And my damn heart was thudding in my chest. I couldn't believe his words. His reverence for me.

That scared the shit out of me, too. The possibility of what it could all mean. Where it could go. How beautiful it could be. Knowing… I couldn't. We couldn't.

Make no mistake. I… want this. I want him. But I don't have any-thing to give him. So, I didn't say anything. I just nestled into the warmth of his body. Even for just a moment longer, my fingers finding his in the dark, I threaded them. And I whispered in a small voice, "Stay just a little longer. Please."

I smiled at that, but as soon as I realized what I was doing, I wiped it right off my face.

I heard my phone buzzing and on the upside-down bucket beside me. I had a few of them in here that I used as a table. They served their purpose.

Mala: Cousin! Mom and I will be there in twenty minutes

Me: I'll be ready. Drive Safe!

My cousin Maelle is a lifesaver right now.

The car had been acting funny all week. Dad had been under the hood most of the morning, trying to figure things out. I didn't really have the money for an Uber, so before I settled on taking the bus, I asked my cousin for a ride. I just had one stop to make.

Sounds like my Aunt Gloria would be coming by to hang out with Ma. I started cleaning up the shed so I could get changed and ready to head out once Maelle got here.

Back in my room, I looked over myself in my full-length mirror. This meeting with Kingston had the potential to change my life. I knew I needed to wear something with just enough allure. Not just something presentable, but something impressive. I needed this gig at the tattoo shop. I needed it bad.

I chose a flowy wrap-around dress. Deep magenta. It was fun, flirty, and perfect. Not too sexy.

Last night, I looked through my sketchbooks, and it took a while; I kept all of them.

I finally decided on two that would be perfect. They were past full; not one blank page remained, but I packed them in my tote so I could bring them along. I knew if I showed some of my best work, I'd have more of a chance at landing this gig. I wasn't new to this; I was true to this. I'd been on my own from day one. And as an independent artist, I was constantly looking for work. Selling myself. It was the nature of the beast. As part of an artists' collective, I received a decent amount of work, but I was always looking for more opportunities. Exposure. And always down to network.

I put some gold hoops on. Simple ones that catch the light but aren't too flashy. Then I decided to brush my hair back. I'd style it into a low ponytail, I could braid it, and let it fall down my back. Something neat and uncomplicated. I didn't want to draw the wrong attention to myself. Not today.

I tried to practice my elevator pitch. Going over a few things, I would say once I got there. I needed Kingston to do me this solid, and I didn't want to mess up any chances I may have.

But as hard as I tried, I couldn't focus.

I knew why.

Sol.

It didn't matter how much I wanted to pretend. I was distracted. In my head. But damn, I couldn't help myself.

Sol left me with vivid thoughts and parting words.

And I could still feel him. The weight of him. His hands mapped my body like they always belonged there.

I was thinking about the way he looked at me. It was a look, like I was his. Not just some girl he'd been texting for months. And the way he kissed me when he left this morning. I love his kisses. And his words. They were full of promise. It was almost like they were meant to hold me until our next time together.

And I already wanted to call him back tonight.

As if I'd thought him up, I saw my phone light up on my vanity. Buzzing with a notification with a message from him.

I picked up my phone and read it twice.

Music Man: Didn't want to leave you last night, Artist Girl

My stomach flipped. What the hell was he doing to me?

Me: I didn't want you to leave, either Music Man

I double-texted.

Me: Still don't if I'm honest.

Music Man: I'm ready for you as soon as you're ready for me, Belle

Damn.

Three dots.

Music Man: You sleep okay? I woke up tasting you. Again. Do you feel that too?

Yeah. Sol was reading me. And I was completely honest with him.

Me: I can't stop thinking about you, or any of the things you do to me. Was shifting in bed earlier, like it would help

Music Man: Goddamn. If you were here right now, I wouldn't let you leave the bed. I'd have you again. Slow. Face down again. Would you like that, Belle?

Me: Hell yes.

Music Man: Can I taste you again first?

Me: Please do, baby. I would love that.

Music Man: Whatever you want. Getting hard now, baby. Tell me when I can come back to you.

My breath caught. Then I groaned. I wanted Sol right now.

I sat on my bed. Clenching my thighs. Flustered, but feeling bold, open, and teasing. I was so into Sol; he brought it right out of me.

Me: You aren't playing fair, Sol. Making me miss your mouth. Now I'm squeezing my thighs.

I sent another message right after that one.

Me: Come back tonight? I'll be waiting. Can we do it slow, baby? I'll be face down, and I want you whispering in my ear the way you do. I can't wait to have you again. And yes. Start with your mouth. Please.

Music Man: Say less. Won't be rushing a damn thing, taking my time with you. Gonna whisper in your ear all night. And yeah… starting with your sweet pussy in my mouth. Wanna feel you shake, hear you try not to moan too loud.

Fuck.

Me: Can't hardly wait, baby

Sol was so… He took me to another level, satisfied me far beyond anything I could have imagined. For starters, he shared every thought with me, like a real-time play-by-play. Seriously. I knew his every thought about me, how he felt, what he saw, what he enjoyed, and what he could do for me.

And he was pretty explicit. Then, sensual and sweet as hell in the very next breath. Always respectful. That was new for me, and I was so fucking turned on by that. I could have come without him even touching me. And every other statement that left his lips was some form of a compliment. Sol was analytical. Analyzing everything and then reciting it as if he were performing spoken word poetry. So. Damn. sexy. The fact that we had to whisper everything made it all the more emotionally intense.

Yeah.

He's a musician. An artist just like I am. None of this surprised me. But experiencing him… It's been clouding my every thought. Ma was onto me, and I wouldn't be surprised if Maelle caught me slipping, too. Our first night together was unlike anything else, far beyond anything I could have imagined. And it kept getting better each time he came to see me. Fuck.

I think back on our first time.

He tasted me. The first time in my life I felt a man's lips on my lower set. All the fantasizing I'd done over the years. The toys… none of it came close. He felt so good. But the way he expressed his pleasure.

Before, during, and after, that was what made the moment intense; it was like a form of reverence. Then I told him I'd never experienced that before. He was pissed. But he handled me with such care.

My vulnerability. And I'll admit, I was a bit defensive as well.

Just after I'd come undone for him, Sol kissed his way back up my body. He had just eaten me out, taking his time, his M.O., and now he was moving his lips upward again. He lingered in a few spots, not just kissing softly but leaving words and his warm, gentle breath in his wake, just as intimate as his touch.

Sol had a unique way of handling everything. The mood was set: emotionally and physically intense. We moved slowly, kept our voices low, and touched each other softly. I wondered if he would be this quiet if we weren't in my parents' house. And let me clarify. By quiet, I mean with his volume.

Sol had *plenty* to say.

So, his mouth traced a path up the inside of my thigh. I was still coming down from my orgasm. I'd just come moments before, and I felt his warm breath dancing across my sensitive skin. His lips brushed over the crease where my thigh met my hip. He lingered there, taking a deep inhale. Then he moved to my belly, kissing there. Kissing my ribs and the underside of my left breast. He kissed my nipple, then licked it, gently taking the tiny gold hoop into his mouth and sucking on it. He told me he hadn't expected that but adored it. And by the time he was back in my ear… he had one of his large, warm hands gently resting on my belly. His other hand was moving along my side, softly. Up and back down again. His fingers had a light callus from years of guitar playing. I loved how his hands felt on me, wherever they ventured.

"Belle…" He was whispering in my ear now. "You taste like heaven." I moaned. I didn't know what else to say. Not right then, I didn't. But he wasn't concerned about it. He was very close to my ear, making it clear that what he was saying was just for me. Murmuring, "So soft. So wet for me. Sweet. Like you drink water and eat fruit… like you take care of yourself. Mmm. I've been dreaming about this." I felt his lips lightly graze the shell of

my ear before he licked me there. His fucking tongue, man. "You drive me wild, Belle…" He wrapped his arm around me even tighter, pressing his chest even closer to mine. He held onto me silently. I closed my eyes, brought my arms around him, and our breathing synchronized within moments. "Damn, Belle. The way your legs parted for me. It was like you already knew I'd take my time with you. Like you wanted me to live there." We shared a lazy chuckle. His finger traced a light path on my hip. "You're so fucking pretty down there. Soft. Smooth. Bare enough… that little patch of hair is perfect. I could see everything. Felt everything. I took one look at your beautiful pussy, and I knew I wanted to get lost."

I moaned again.

I loved that he was so pleased with me. My lady parts. No one had seen them before. Not like this. Close enough to taste them.

He kissed my neck slowly, wet and hungry, letting his words drip from his mouth. "I've seen some things in my life. But this…" He gently palmed between my thighs again, careful, as if he knew I was still sensitive there after what he'd just blessed me with. I hadn't spoken a word, but I let out another breathy moan. It was more of a sigh, I think.

Sol was still in my ear, still whispering. "You move so easy. Flexible as hell." After a few beats, "You ever train for that? Or you just good like that?" He was kissing beneath my ear again. Didn't seem he was waiting for an answer. "The way your thighs locked up around me when you came." His voice was a hush now. Very quiet. Reverent. "You damn near broke me, Belle."

I shivered. He broke something in me, too, in the best way.

And eventually, I told Sol he was the first one to do that. I told him I had never experienced that before and had never been eaten out before. Never felt what he did before. Never had anyone take their time like he did.

And my confession, vulnerability, and transparency opened the door to Sol's reaction.

First, he was in disbelief. Then… frustrated?

Yeah.

He was definitely frustrated.

On **my** behalf.

But then… there was this, I don't know. This carnal satisfaction he felt. Once he moved past his offense, he relished being the first to have me like this. To do this for me.

He set the standard that's for sure.

"*You gave it up so honestly when you came. Like you've been waiting on me. Goddamn Belle. I swear… you're in your own category.*"

And he was inside me too. It was… incredible. Every time has been an experience.

The first time, he asked me if I was ready. Brandon never asked me that.

And I remember gasping as he entered me.

He was slow, deliberate, and thick. No pain, just pressure. He stretched me, making space inside and expanding me inch by fiery inch, causing my toes to curl. I knew my eyes were fluttering closed because he asked me softly, a few times, to look at him.

I could feel myself opening around him. Of course, I was already slick and ready; he'd just eaten the entire fuck out of my pussy. But he was more than I expected. I remember him leaning in, placing his forehead to mine.

"*Is this too much, Belle?*"

"*No. Just… full.*" I said, catching my breath.

He captured my lips, sucking my bottom lip, then pushing his long ass tongue into my mouth as he groaned softly.

"*You feel so damn good. You feel like a perfect fit. As if you were made just for me.*"

I'm inclined to agree. We fit together perfectly. And I felt all of Sol. He took his time. His strokes were long and deliberate.

Yeah. He took his sweet time with me. No thrusting. He stayed right there, letting me adjust to him. Aware of what he was working with.

Reverence.

Eyes on eyes. His thumbs gently brushed the corner of my mouth. "*Talk to me, Indie,*" Sol murmured. His voice controlled and low. "*I need to know how you feel.*"

I felt all the things. I didn't even know how to respond to that. I couldn't think clearly at all. I was in pure bliss.

"*Indie… Artist Girl… I can tell you that you feel like heaven to me.*" He was long stroking me slowly, and it was so fucking amazing. "*We're taking our time. Got all night to do this. Tell me when you find the words, Belle.*" After a beat, "*No pressure. No rush… just us.*"

Why was he saying this shit to me, man? Oh my gosh.

I managed to find my voice. After a few moments, "*I feel… I feel everything, Sol.*"

He nodded, "*So I'm doing it right. Good.*"

Hell yeah, you're doing me right. And please don't stop what you're do-ing.

He continued to move. Slow. Deep strokes. And I swear each one drew a whimper from me.

And Sol was watching me. His eyes were locked on my face as if I were the most captivating thing he had ever seen. I felt extremely vulnerable, but also incredibly turned on at the same time.

I had been so insecure about my body, yet I was doing a damn good job pretending I wasn't.

Sol was a grown ass man. A man like him, a man of his caliber, could have any woman he wanted. And I didn't feel like I measured up to those women. Not physically anyway.

"Artist Girl. Look at me." Sol paused his movements. His slow, steady rhythm grinding to a halt. And shit. That got my attention.

I gave him my eyes. His already found mine. Even in the dim light, I could see his focus on me. His care. And this unspoken demand for my hon-esty. "Where'd you go just now?"

Damn. Sol was so present to have noticed that.

But of course, he did. He was so attuned to me; he felt me drift away the exact instant it happened. No one had done that before, and he cared enough about me to catch me mid-thought. Mid-doubt.

And as much as I appreciated that, I struggled internally with how much I wanted to share. This didn't seem like the right time. No doubt in my mind, it would kill the mood.

He wasn't here for that. He was here for this.

Still holding his expectant gaze, I hesitated, trying to come up with some-thing.

This was so stupid, so damn shallow.

But this was real. This was me.

I bit my lip. "Nothing," I whispered.

Sol didn't move. He just kept holding my gaze. I looked away, and after swallowing hard, I said, "I just… I know you could have anyone, Sol. Some-one thicker. Curvier. Fuller." I shrugged, still avoiding his eyes. "You're… you." The words started to spill out. "I'm… just me. No breasts. Slim hips. I'm not voluptuous or anything. Sometimes I wonder if I'm enough." I ges-tured downward at my naked body. As I shifted on the bed, embarrassment began to take over.

I was so caught up in the moment just minutes earlier, only for my insecurities to take over. *Sol must think I'm crazy.* His thumb brushed my cheek, and when he spoke again, his voice sounded different. The tone was confident and rough, but still low and steady. *Sure.*

"India."

When I said nothing, Sol reached out, cupping my face gently, and his thumb traced my cheek. He looked at me, waiting patiently for my eyes to return. And he was still inside of me. Present and anchored. *Damn.* An intentional stillness. So present. I swear our physical connection had intensified. Right then. It was more emotional now. Charged by my vulnerability and his patience.

Sol wasn't trying to get back to what we were doing. His hips hadn't moved a millimeter. It felt like an afterthought now. He stayed right there. Hard as hell, but still inside of me. And he didn't pull away. He stayed connected with me. His body, his gaze, his attention. He was giving me space to sit with my thoughts and words, while gently calling me back at the same time.

And I began to feel grounded. Realization hit me. *This wasn't sex to him.* Sol's thumb was still tracing my cheek, and I finally looked at him. Right into his eyes. And he looked deep into mine. It was intimate as hell.

"India. Please stop that. You are more than enough. I love everything about you. Everything. Your wild spirit, your slim frame, your small breasts. I love all of it."

I held his gaze as he continued. "I've seen women. Touched a few. Sure." He leaned into me, brushing my lips with his. Then moved to my ear, "But I'm inside you right now. You. Your body and your skin…" His hand slid down, his fingers softly caressing me, then he pulled me closer, anchoring me to him.

"Your legs are wrapped around me. Your heart is beating against mine. I'm exactly where I want to be, *Artist Girl.*" He left soft kisses on my forehead, then leaned in my ear again, "You're small, but you're taking me so damn well, Indie. I love every inch of you." Somehow, his voice has turned softer, yet more possessive. "The way your body fits so perfectly with mine… you're irresistible. This wasn't an accident. And I don't want you disappearing on me over some shit that don't matter."

God. Why did he say stuff like that?

Then Sol resumed, moving his hips slowly and steadily. And I felt it even more now. His care for me, his desire for me, the truth in every word he'd just spoken.

"You stay right here with me, Belle," he whispered. "Stay in this moment, right here with me."

And I did.

And each time we were together after that, I did.

And Sol always made sure I stayed out of my head, asking for my eyes every time they wandered.

"Look at me, Belle."

"I need you to see what you're doing to me."

I knew he could see what *he* was doing to *me.*

Yeah. And he kept me informed. Moment by moment. Play by play.

He had his hand wrapped around my thigh, and I was positioned just right so that each of his strokes was so deep I felt wave after wave of pleasure. He held my hand, his fingers intertwined with mine, and placed above my head.

"Damn… you're so tight around me. Taking all of me. You want all of me, baby?"

"Yes," I cried out, keeping my voice low. "Sol, please don't stop." I arched my back as he continued hitting that spot that sent me.

He kissed me. And another thrust. Then another.

"You gonna come for me again, Indie?

"I think so… yes… I think so. *Mmm.*"

"Yeah. Gonna make you come again," Sol whispered. "Real quiet, though, baby. You can do that for me, right?"

I was whimpering now. "Yeah. Sol. Please."

His chuckle was deep and low, and I felt it. "That's it. Let it go for me, Belle."

And when he came after me, I almost fell apart all over again.

It was incredibly sexy. All of it. His quiet curses. He spoke into my skin, but he barely made a sound. When he pressed his sweaty forehead to mine, he groaned my name, dropping kisses along my collarbone and shoulder. "Belle, you are something else."

And we stayed tangled up in each other just like that, catching our breath. Then we did it again. Yeah. Our first time, our first night together, was one for the books. But they've each been explosive. And we were both beside ourselves after that first night.

That much was clear. I sent him a voice memo as soon as he left, and when I woke up the next morning, he'd sent me one. And it was so... it was the kind of message that made me pause.

Especially the next morning, with that morning-after clarity.

Feeling the weight of what we'd done and where it might lead if I wasn't careful.

The message he sent was heartfelt and tender. He spoke softly, and it felt incredibly intimate. It seemed so perfect after the night we had together. As I listened to his memo, I could picture Sol sitting on the edge of his bed, freshly showered and still shirtless, with his eyes closed, wrapped in his thoughts of me. I felt the same way, and my breath caught as I listened.

"Indie. Hey... I know you're still asleep. But I just..." He had a soft chuckle, "I had to send you this. There's no way I could just let last night be last night." His pause was brief. "India. You undid me. Do you know that? And I can't stop thinking about you. The way you tasted. The way you opened up for me. How quiet you tried to be. My God, Belle. The way you bit your lip. You gave me something so real last night. It wasn't just your body either. You let me in. You let me see you. All of you. Not just your beautiful naked body or those tiny tattoos. How you get when you're turned on. And I could talk about that for days..." He softly chuckled again. "But Indie, it was so much more. You trusted me. I get the feeling that you shared parts of you that you've never let anyone else see before. And that's sacred, Belle. And that means something to me. Listen... if you ever feel shy about something you've never done, don't. That isn't a shortcoming, Belle. That's just a door no one else had the key for. And I don't mind being the first... if anything... I'm honored I can be." There was another pause. "Indie. You don't owe me anything, but I want more of you. If you let me, if you're comfortable, I'll take care of you. Alright. I'm going to shut up now." He chuckled. "Text me when you're up. And for the record, I can still taste you on my lips, my Artist Girl."

Damn.

I listened to that so many times, all the while tangled in my sheets, my heart pounding. Hell yeah, I was still aroused. More so now even. And I was torn. On the one hand, I was glad I didn't regret any of that, and so happy he hadn't ghosted me after he had me. But I was scared.

Scared that this might be too real, much too fast. Still, I slept with him. And more than that, I let him see me, taste me, and touch me. And he did. In a way no one else ever had. Days had gone by since the first time, and we'd done it three more times. My body was past satisfied. Never have I ever felt so fulfilled.

Yet still humming in that *what did we do* kind of way.

And each time I called him back, I noticed how different he looked at me, as if I were the whole damn universe. My heart is aching. He wants more. And I want that too. Not just the sex, either. It scares me how much I want him. This was supposed to be simple. Just relieving some late-night tension, not promises of more. Yet here I am, days later, all caught up in my feelings. And I'm not alone. Here he is, making my heart squeeze and triple in size, saying things like 'honor,' 'sacred,' and 'you let me in.'

I clench my thighs together right now, just thinking about the sound of his voice and how his tongue moves. Still sore in the best way. Still feeling sensitive and tender down there. His marks were left behind even in the invisible places.

There was a light tap at my door. "Indie!"

My cousin Maelle.

I need a minute, though. Just one. To breathe and figure out my life. And to process the reality and the truth. I might already be falling for this man.

"Focus India," I told myself. "You have bills. You have goals. You have responsibilities. There's no time to be sprung."

I pulled my tote over my shoulder, grabbed my phone and keys, then stepped toward my bedroom door. Ready to open it and face the task ahead.

And despite my pep talk, I knew my mind was elsewhere.

Well, not just my mind. My heart, too.

They were still caught up in Solomon.

nineteen

INDIA

I'll be right back."

"You're good, cousin. I'm chillin." Mala reclined the seat, reached behind her, and dug through her backpack. When she pulled out a notebook and some flashcards saturated with handwritten notes and highlighter everywhere, I already knew.

Typical Mala. Always preparing for some upcoming exam and always studying for something or other. That backpack of hers went everywhere she went, just like me and my tote.

She's incredible. So bright, driven, and ambitious.

"I look okay?" I pulled the mirror down in front of me and did a quick once-over. I touched up my berry wine lipstick, checked my teeth, then popped a piece of gum in my mouth.

Maelle killed the engine. "Yeah, you look amazing. Beautiful. As always."

"Thank you, My."

She nodded and turned in her seat to face me more. Her big brown eyes fixed on me, studying me like her flashcards. Then she gave me a look. The one she always gave when I tried to play it cool, even though she knew better.

"You okay?" she asked finally, all the while chewing her gum uncharacteristically slowly. Maelle was a gum popper ordinarily. And her glare zeroed in on me as if she already knew the answer.

And I shrugged silently. I glanced at the storefront, my stomach already in knots.

I took a few calming breaths.

I've been to this rodeo many times.

Needing to prove my worth. Sell myself. I didn't revel in this process.

"Yeah. A little nervous, I guess."

Mala sucked her teeth. "Indie." She shook her head, reaching over to grab my hand. Then, in a calming voice, "Girl, stop. You got this. You are talented. Dope! And you work your ass off. You are exactly what they need in there. Don't you dare go doubting yourself."

I nodded. Mala wasn't wrong.

I took pride in my work ethic and my talent. Anyone would be lucky to have me. I just needed Kingston to see that. I knew I had value to add, and I knew I needed this. We could help each other out.

I just needed to learn how to work that gun, and it would be up from here.

"Thanks for the pep talk. I love you, cousin." I opened the car door and stepped out, straightening my dress. I spritzed myself with a little body spray. Then I grabbed my tote, slinging it over my shoulder.

Mala rolled down the passenger side window as I shut the door.

"Anytime, cousin. And if they can't see any of that?" She popped her gum loudly, pausing as I leaned into the window, "That's on them! But I promise you. Somebody's gonna snatch you up!"

I laughed under my breath. That's Maelle. Always cute. Always sweet. But don't let that fool you. Mala was coming for the whole damn system.

She pointed at me, kinda playful, but her voice and expression were firm. "Fix your face before you go in there! You look too good to go in there looking like you're worried about bills and shit."

I sighed heavily. "You know I am, though."

She nodded sympathetically. "I know. But they don't need to know that. Chin up. Go handle business, Indie."

"Love you, Mala."

"Love you more. Go be great."

I stood tall, fixed my dress, and headed toward the entrance with my chin up.

All of this was meant to be.

The car acting up and not having the money to spare for an Uber. Maelle giving me a ride. I needed her badly in that moment. And she was right there. Just like she always is. Always there for me. Always my voice of reason. Sometimes I wonder who the big cousin really is. Maelle is only twenty-five, just a couple of years younger than me, but she's so mature. Wise beyond her years. Level-headed. So fucking dope, and I love her so much. My Auntie Gloria, Maelle's mom, and my mom are sisters. Maelle and

I were raised like sisters, and besides Destiney, there is not a soul on this earth I trust more than her.

I stepped into King Tattoo Parlor, immediately greeted by the scent of ink and antiseptic. It was slow. I'd say that's typical for Tuesday. Most people were probably at work. I've been here many times, and this shop gets really busy. That was a good thing, I decided. Fewer distractions.

The soft, steady beat of music filled the space. I could hear Smino's "Anita" floating through the speakers. Smooth and playful, layered with that soulful bass that made the walls vibrate just enough.

Chill rap was usual here.

The faint buzz of a machine drifted from the back of the shop. The front was empty. No clients flipping through flash art, no loud voices. And the place looked great! It always did, and I was more than proud of Kingston. He worked hard, stayed on his hustle, and made this one of the region's most successful Black-owned tattoo shops. And King was only thirty-two.

The shop was spacious and always clean, with a bold design. I loved the exposed brick walls, and there was deep charcoal paint in the corners that added richness. Gold fixtures glinted here and there, enhancing the royalty theme. Eight stations lined the walls, four on each side, separated by sleek black partitions. Each station had tattoo chairs, stools, and neatly organized trays of ink. Everything was spotless. Since it was midweek, about half the stations were empty, but I knew how crowded this place could become later in the evenings and on weekends.

I looked up when I heard someone approaching.

Fatima.

I have always loved her style. Today, she was wearing a black crop top with tight ass high-waisted jeans. Gold jewelry was tastefully arranged on her neck and wrists. Ankh necklace and a couple of stacked rings. Minimal yet bold.

And Fatima is gorgeous.

Petite and curvy. If you can picture it, she is the complete opposite of my tall, lean frame.

"India!" Her arms were already open. "Hey, gorgeous! How you been?" She was smiling at me like I was the best part of her day. I returned a warm hug, and hers lingered longer than it needed to. She smelled nice. Whatever she was wearing was fire.

Fatima is Kingston's longtime girlfriend. She took care of the piercings. He did the ink.

Yeah. She was gorgeous. Intimidatingly so. Rich brown skin, smooth and glowing. A gold hoop in her nose. Locs that she kept long for years, but now she had them cut into a cute ass bob. Loc jewelry woven in. Tattoos peeked out from her arms and collarbone. Perks of having a boyfriend who tattoos.

And I knew part of me getting this gig would mean getting her buy-in.

And. Fatima was cool and all, but honestly… it was the way she looked at me that always made me a little uncomfortable. That slow, suggestive, knowing kind of stare. The way her energy pressed in. Confident, sexy, openly flirtatious. With no apologies. It wasn't anything she said outright… it was everything else. She knew she was sexy. Sultry. And there was this sharpness beneath it. I wasn't used to women coming at me like that. Definitely not used to how much it made me think. Fatima was probably five feet even. But you knew she could handle herself. Hold her own. A firecracker, that one.

Her hand slid down my arm as she finally let me go. Her hazel eyes examined me with that same lingering curiosity. I guess it was her subtle reminder of the things she and Kingston had asked me. More than once. And yeah, I thought about it. Then I thought better of it. Then, politely declined.

Judging by how Fatima's hand slid down my arm... she might still be thinking about it.

"Hey girl!" I kept my tone light, not letting on that she made me more nervous than I already was. We caught up for a few minutes, making small talk. Fatima always managed to calm my nerves and then stir me up in other ways.

She leaned back against the desk, arms crossed. "When you gone let me do your septum?" she teased, flashing a sly grin. "That would be fire on you!"

I laughed. "Girl who knows. I'm chillin on piercings for now."

Fatima tilted her head. "Mmm. You say that now. Next thing I know, you'll be asking me to do your tongue."

Crazy because Fatima had done my nipple piercing.

That little adventure was all Destiney's idea. We came together; she got one side, I got the other. And Fatima was professional. But her eyes lingered.

I barked out a laugh, losing all of my resolve. I shook my head. "Girl, you're wild."

"So, you here for King?" Fatima asked, narrowing her eyes playfully.

"Yeah, is he here? I need to talk to him." I pressed lightly, smirking.

She nodded, "Alright then, pretty girl. Sit tight."

She disappeared down the side hallway and my eyes drifted across the shop as I waited.

There was a merch corner near the host desk, stocked with black hoodies and T-shirts featuring the King Tattoo crown logo, stacked neatly in piles. Aftercare kits were also available.

Then I drifted toward the mural again, taking in the details as if I hadn't seen this and studied it too many times to count. The mural covered the entire back wall, serving as a focal point as soon as you entered the shop. Bold, intricate, and impossible to miss. Deep golds, emeralds, and rich browns brought it alive. It was a lion's face, with strokes that seemed to shift if you stared too long. The whole piece pulsed with pride, filled with the black culture that made the entire place feel alive.

Drew truly outdid himself. Every time I looked at it, I discovered another detail. Something new, another layer to appreciate, a hidden shape tucked somewhere within the patterns.

I smiled to myself. Andrew, but everyone called him Drew. Crazy talented. An old timer. He's in his late forties now and has been creating some of the coolest murals you've ever seen. His work is everywhere, even internationally. He was invited overseas to contribute to murals in South America, the Caribbean, and Canada. Humble as hell for someone who's always in demand, using his talent to bless every space he touches.

A deep voice cut through my thoughts.

"My favorite canvas," he announced. His commanding voice echoed through the shop.

I turned back toward the hall as Fatima pranced back toward me, Kingston right behind her. His eyes landed on me, slow and deliberate, and the grin that followed was nothing but trouble. The slow grin that appeared told me he already had plans. He was dressed in his usual crisp black T-shirt and black joggers, tattoos for days, trailing down both of his arms. As Kingston strolled out, tall and broad, probably around 6'1", he made Fatima look even smaller. But somehow, beside him, she never seemed overshadowed.

"To what do I owe this pleasure?" he asked once he reached the host desk, leaning back with a grin. And just like that, the flirting began. "You finally come to your senses?"

Fatima and I both laughed. I crossed my arms, offering a smile that matched his energy. "Relax, Kingston. I'm just here to talk business."

His eyebrows shot up. "Business."

I saw Fatima glancing between us, biting back a grin.

Someone from one of the stations called out to her, so she walked over, but not before tossing me another flirty glance.

Kingston nodded his head. "Business. Cool. Come on."

I followed him back down the hallway, past the stations, and into his office.

It wasn't fancy. A little cluttered. But clean. Art prints everywhere. Sketches lined the wall. Flash sheets. A few photos of tattoos. A shelf with neatly stacked portfolios. A black leather couch sat against the furthest wall.

A little of his cologne clung to everything. Woodsy, warm. Damn near distracting me if I let it.

He sat behind his sleek, modern desk. I sat in one of the two chairs directly in front of it.

"You cheating on me, Pretty Thing?" His voice had dropped low. Kinda teasing, but there was an edge of heat there. His eyes flicked at my forearm.

"Stop it, Kingston." My voice held a teasing tone.

"I'm for real." He reached out, gently lifting my arm, turning it so he could get a better look.

Breathe was written along my inner left forearm in delicate script. Small. Just under three inches long, thin and clean. Barely there, but it meant everything to me.

Though it wasn't new at all, I've had it for more than six months now. I haven't been here and haven't seen him. His eyes flicked to my forearm again.

Knowing King, he likely noticed it immediately.

"You're my canvas," he muttered, releasing my arm gently. He sat back in his chair, spinning it slowly. Lazy. "Don't appreciate you giving it away." After a beat, "Who did that?"

"Mateo." I returned.

King's eyebrows bunched. "Puerto Rican cat?"

"Yeah." Small world. Guess the tattoo community stayed connected.

Kingston shook his head, grinning slowly, that cocky energy never far. "I would've inked you for free."

"I don't want anything free, Kingston. I would've paid you." My lips curled in the faintest smile. "Walked in and y'all were hella busy."

He was quiet for a second. His eyes, though. They were still locked on me. Sharp. Amused. And I was sure he was still undressing me in his head.

And as much as I love my permanent reminder to breathe, Mateo did a great job on it, I would have absolutely preferred Kingston do it.

But I was dealing with some shit. Something I was fighting with Brandon about. During our… oh, I don't know, tenth break-up? I needed the pain, and I needed the escape. Most of all, I needed the reminder. So, I walked in here on a random Friday evening, hoping he could squeeze me in. But the shop was so busy. Crawling with people. Kingston was my first choice. Then Drew. Both of them were booked with appointments. So, I looked up another shop and drove across town to find someone with an opening.

Something I never did when it came to my ink.

I didn't play about that. But like I said… I needed the reminder; I needed the pain. I needed the escape.

And King was dope with the gun. A steady hand, clean lines. Always flawless. That's why I kept coming back.

Kingston did one of the first tattoos I ever got, a small infinity symbol beside my left breast. I liked how he did it. Smooth ass linework. It healed beautifully. And now, almost a decade later, it still looks as vivid and pristine as the day he finished it. I had a dozen tiny tattoos scattered across my body, like hidden stories. And I came back to King for all of them.

He nodded once. "That's why you finally decided to come back to me?" he began, "You finally ready to let me mark you properly, Pretty Thing?" His voice had dipped even lower.

"Kingston." I forced a plastered smile, keeping my tone light and friendly.

I wasn't going there with him. I wasn't doing this. We weren't doing this.

"Dead ass." His smile was easy. And King had a nice smile, I'll admit.

Kingston was handsome. Bold. Rough around the edges. Deep brown skin with tattoos crawling up his broad, solid arms and around his neck, as if they belonged there; his shirts never stood a chance against his biceps. Yeah. He had ink for days, like it was part of his DNA. Dark brown eyes. He rocked a low fade for as long as I can remember. Always fresh. His low-cut beard was neatly groomed, always. And he was cocky. As hell. Past confident. King knew he was skilled, talented, and sought after.

And he'd always had Fatima. Beautiful, dangerous, and right by his side from the start. No matter the label they used or didn't use, everyone understood Fatima wasn't going anywhere. And even though their relationship was open, I never crossed that line, especially because they were open. I never planned to step across it. I always had Brandon. It was messy, but it was familiar. No. Kingston and I never happened. Never would. He flirted with me all the time. Sure. But that was just him. I wasn't for sale, and I sure as hell wasn't about to be one of his side projects. I don't care how good he looked doing his thing.

"I'm serious." He brought me from my thoughts. He was tracing over me with his eyes, mapping out his next spot. "You know you're mine."

I smiled despite myself. Then I gently shook my head. Subtly. I playfully reminded him, "Stop saying that. I'm not your anything, Kingston."

"I'll stop, soon as you stop playing. Pretty Thing." His grin stretched lazily, cocky as ever. "I'm sure we can work something out."

I snorted but maintained a neutral expression. Calm. I had to play my cards carefully. His ego was as large as Texas, but like most men, Kingston enjoyed the chase. He held my gaze just as I held his. Neither of us blinked.

I casually folded my arms. "King. I'm not playing. You know exactly what this is. You have something with Fatima. That's ya'll. And I respect that." I leaned in a little, tossing out a flirty tone, eyebrow cocked, "And I don't share." Then, steady and unbothered, I said, "Besides...I'm not for sale, Kingston."

He chuckled quietly under his breath. Nodding once as if he appreciated the reminder. "I know you're not... that's half the reason I like you." He sat up in his rolling chair, placed his hands on his desk, and interlocked his fingers. Still watching me, "Alright then. Business."

I smiled and told him what I wanted.

I'd been thinking seriously about learning the craft. How much I respected the work. I always had how this wasn't some whim.

And he listened intently. Really listened. His eyes never left mine. "I brought some sketchbooks," I added, nodding toward the chair beside me where I'd set my tote.

He nodded once and leaned back. "I've seen your work. No doubt you're talented." He tapped his fingers on his desk. "I've seen you sketch," he added. "Your hand is good. But tattooing is different, Pretty Thing. You mess up? It's on somebody for life."

"I know." I kept my voice steady, starting to feel excited, thinking maybe this meant he was considering it and might say yes. "I'm not trying to shortcut anything. I'll put in the work."

He studied me quietly for several agonizing beats. His head tilted slightly. "This is a grind. Cleaning stations. Watching sessions. Learning hygiene. All of that comes before you even touch a needle."

"That's cool," I replied immediately.

"You'll be starting at the bottom, Canvas."

"Been there," I shrugged.

His grin returned. "Oh, you really want this?"

"I do." I nodded, offering a friendly smile for good measure.

Another beat of silence. His eyes still fixed on me. "Alright. Let me think on it. You already have the art. The question is whether you got the grind."

I lifted my chin. "Watch me."

King's smile slowly stretched. "Pretty Thing… you gone be trouble."

"Oh, I've been trouble."

We both knew I wasn't there for him that way. And still… I wasn't backing down either.

Let him look. Let him wonder. It didn't cost me a thing.

And from the way King nodded, eyes shining, he seemed fine with that.

twenty

INDIA

"Okay, Smarty Pants, what are you studying for now?" I teased Mala as I slid into the passenger seat.

When I stepped out, Mala was curled up in the car, her legs tucked under her. She was flipping through her stack of flashcards. Her lips moved in quiet repetition. I peeped highlighter stains on her fingertips.

She didn't look up. "CHES. You know I'm not done yet."

I turned to toss my tote onto the backseat. Of course, she wasn't finished. Mala was driven; she always had a plan. She'd earned her Master's in Public Health and was focused on rural communities for now, but global health was always the bigger goal. She was deeply passionate about medical research, which matched her ambition and intelligence. I wasn't mad at any of it.

I admired it. I admired her. The way she pursued what mattered so deeply to her. Mala was a passionate visionary who didn't flinch at the size of her dreams. I knew she was considering PhD programs soon.

"Which one is that?"

"Certified Health Education Specialists."

"Ah." She'd said that before.

We sat in the car for a few more minutes. I checked my phone, then glanced over at Mala. Her flashcards were still spread across her lap. Her CHES study guide was open on the center console between us, with multicolored neon tabs lining the edges. She didn't look up immediately, just kept flipping a card back and forth between her fingers.

"Mala, you don't know how to chill," I told my cousin jokingly.

She finally looked at me and said, "And… you don't know how to believe in yourself sometimes. But here we are."

We shared a laugh. Couldn't argue with that.

"Touché, My."

"So. How'd it go?" she asked, her eyes flicking over me as if she was searching for signs. Good or bad. She started gathering her flashcards, closed her study guide, and slipped it back into her backpack.

"Pretty sure he's actually considering it."

Mala nodded as if she expected nothing less. "That's great! Looking forward to your good news. Besides, one of us has gotta land something today." She snorted. "I'm still trying to memorize disease prevention frameworks on my damn day off."

She zipped up her backpack and put it in the back seat. "You ever think about how different all this could have gone?" she asked suddenly. She had returned her seat to its normal position and was now facing forward. Her hand rested lazily on the keys in her ignition.

I frowned. I was loosening my braid, pulling out the hair tie, and teasing out my tresses. I needed my hair to be free. As often as possible. "What you mean, My?"

She looked over at me, wearing a thoughtful expression. "Our parents left home to give us better. Say they hadn't… You wouldn't be sitting here hoping for a shot as an apprentice. I wouldn't be sitting here worried about this CHES exam. We'd be worried about… clean water. Or clinics closing. I'd be worried about how to keep babies alive in some underfunded hospital." Her voice was soft. She was knee-deep in her purpose, and I admired that tremendously.

And I sat with her declaration. The weight of it sharp and familiar. I always count my blessings the very second I even think about complaining. And I didn't say anything. I look at my beautiful baby cousin. Took her in. The way she zeroed in on something in the distance when she gets to talking about this stuff. There is a quiet fire underneath all of that sweetness. Maelle wants to change the world. She has always been that girl. Smart as hell. Cute. But beneath it all, steel, strength, and focus.

"Global health isn't just a career goal; it's personal, too. I want to be a part of fixing that."

I smiled, gently nudging her shoulder. "You will, My."

"Damn right, I will." She held my eyes, giving me a bright, confident smile.

"We're celebrating, cousin," Mala declared.

We'd barely pulled out of the strip mall parking lot when she sharply cut the wheel.

"It's not official yet," I protested, though I was already smiling. Mala and I are two foodie cousins raised on Caribbean food, but we're adventurous and curious, always down to try something new. There are so many options near the Broadway Triangle in Oak Park.

"I said what I said." Mala grinned. "Manifesting good news in advance. Plus, I'm hungry."

We shared a laugh, and I turned on the radio as "Just Friends" by Musiq Soulchild played through the speakers.

"We aren't going far," Mala said as we cruised down Broadway. "Some Ultimate Taco Tuesday event happens every Tuesday night right up here. Saw it on TikTok."

"Mmm. Sounds good to me." I love authentic street tacos.

Mala pulled into a lot off Broadway around 6:30 pm, and I noticed a line of taco trucks lined up along the curb. The sun was beginning to dip, casting a warm honey-colored glow over South

Sac. It wasn't dark yet, but the whole block felt vibrant. The place was loud and bustling with people who clearly knew good food when they tasted it. People were already waiting in line at the trucks. The smell of grilled meats and fresh cilantro hit me the moment I opened my door.

Mala had already grabbed her purse and was walking around the hood of her car, her eyes sparkling. We were on the same type of time.

"Before you start, it's my treat. You get it next time," Mala told me.

I opened my mouth to argue, but it was no secret that my wallet was tight. One glance at my cousin and I knew arguing was pointless anyway.

"Thank you, cousin."

"I always got you."

And she did. She knew I always had her back, too. Music floated from the speakers around us. Mostly Reggaeton and Latin hits. Chatter filled the air. Orders were called out, ready for pickup. Mala and I scanned our options. It wasn't an easy decision; there were eight taco trucks, each offering something different. The "Ultimate Taco Tuesday" featured tacos with a global twist, and it didn't disappoint. An indecisive person could stand here all night trying to choose.

One truck offered Caribbean Tacos, with jerk chicken or oxtail tacos. A Korean taco truck served barbecue beef or spicy pork in tortillas, topped with kimchi slaw. Another was a Cali-Mexi-American style, which seemed to have larger portions and plenty of toppings like cheese, sour cream, and guacamole, similar to a Tex-Mex style.

One immediately caught our attention: Taco Tinga, a fusion taco truck featuring spicy chicken Tinga and mango habanero sauce. Their colorful menu made Mala and me feel adventurous.

"Crispy fish tacos with pineapple salsa?" Mala read off the chalkboard menu.

"Hell yes." I nodded, grinning as we moved closer to the window to place our order.

We both ordered a spicy chicken Tinga, a fish taco, and a grilled shrimp taco with fresh lime.

About fifteen minutes later, we were perched at a tiny table, foil-wrapped tacos in hand, salsa dripping from our fingers onto our napkins.

The lot buzzed with life. I knew it would get even busier as the early evening turned into night. I'm so glad Mala brought me here. The music was steadily floating from the speakers. The playlist included Cumbia, reggaeton, and some Afrobeats too.

And the smells were heavenly. Grilled meat and fresh cilantro. People danced near their cars, while kids chased each other. Everyone was eating well and having a good time.

I took a bite of my shrimp taco and groaned softly. "Damn, cousin. This was such a good idea. Thank you again."

Mala grinned with her mouth full. "Anytime is a good time for food." We laughed. Mala mused, "I swear, tacos hit different everywhere you go."

I nodded in agreement, "Exactly. Different flavors, all delicious in their own right."

I grabbed my chicken Tinga taco and took a big bite, closing my eyes. "Yup. Life-changing."

She laughed, nudging me playfully. "Cousin, we're some foodies, huh?"

"Born and raised." And I had no shame. I couldn't even argue. I appreciated this time with her. The food was delicious too, but my nerves were finally settling. I was relieved that I'd finally taken a step. And though it wasn't official, I felt good about King giving me a shot. It all felt right in my gut.

"To good news," Mala declared, lifting her taco and bringing me out of my thoughts.

I smiled wide, "Even if it's early," I teased, clinking my half-eaten taco to hers.

"Especially because it's early."

Another truck caught my eye across the lot. Somehow, I hadn't noticed it before. It was bright green with bold orange lettering that read, "Masala Tacos."

"Oh wow, plant-based tacos with Indian flavors."

Mala turned around to see for herself. "That is so you! Chickpea masala, tandoori, cauliflower…"

I laughed. "Yeah. They're plant-based. That is so Destiney. I should bring her here next time."

Mala smiled and nodded. She knew Destiney well. Naturally, my cousin and my best friend would.

I pulled out my phone and FaceTimed Destiney. It rang twice, and then Destiney's face appeared on the screen.

"Best!"

"Des!"

"Where are you?" she asked curiously, likely noticing my surroundings.

Mala was beside me, leaning into the frame, looking cute and smiley.

"Hey Destiney!

"Oh, hey Mala!" Destiney's smile grew wider. "What are you girls up to?"

I turned my camera around and scanned the food trucks. Mala and I were talking almost at the same time, telling her about all the tacos, and I made sure to mention the vegetarian one.

"Come with us next time!" Mala chirped from beside me once I had the camera facing me again.

"Yum! I'd love that, especially if there are tandoori tacos."

We didn't talk for too long. Destiney was with Micah. But before we hung up, I told her I'd met Kingston earlier. I mentioned I was looking into the apprenticeship weeks ago. She gave me her good vibes, and I promised I'd let her know once it was official.

We ended our FaceTime, and Mala was sipping the last of her Agua de Jamaica. I had some too, and it was perfectly sweet and refreshingly cool.

My phone vibrated.

Music Man: You went for tacos and forgot about me?

I bit back a smile as I unlocked my phone to respond. I'd sent Sol pictures when our order first arrived.

Me: These tacos are bomb, but you're winning. You've still got my undivided attention.

Music Man: Good answer. Finishing up grading…
thinking about my Artist Girl. You look good in my mind.

Damn.

I shifted in my seat, trying to play it cool, but my stomach did that slow, familiar flip. I knew I had a silly-ass grin because Mala clocked my face immediately.

Music Man: Can't wait to have you again, Belle. You're all mine as soon as I get to you.

I bit my lip. Sol knew exactly what he was doing.

Me: Can you come late?

Music Man: I can come as many times as you'll let me, baby

Music Man: Inside you. On you. All over you. Just say the word

I nearly groaned.

I sent the fire emoji, quickly followed by the water drop one.

Music Man: Oh, you like that?

Another one.

Music Man: I've been thinking bout that sexy little whimper

of yours all day. The way you sound when you can barely stay quiet… when you're coming all over my mouth. Love the sound of you coming apart for me. You can hardly keep quiet.

I shifted in my seat, pressing my thighs tightly under the table.

Shit.

I shifted in my seat. Again. My stomach doing that slow flip. I was aching too. And I was getting wet. Right here, right now.

Me: Sol

Music Man: Yes Belle

Me: You'd ruin me if you were here. By the way…you talk a lot for somebody who couldn't even pull his mouth off me last night.

Three dots appeared immediately.

Music Man: lmfao. I'll beg. Gladly. Drown me. Let me spend the whole damn night lost between those pretty thighs. All I need is your word. Just say it and I'm there.

Me: You're getting me wet right here at this table. Can't hardly sit still. Dripping for you. Right. Now.

Music Man: Goddamn. That's mine, Belle. You keep dripping for me. Soon as they're asleep, I'm coming to collect. Hard for you already, baby. Don't keep me waiting too long.

Fuck.

Three dots. Then,

Music Man: Don't bother with any panties once you get out of the shower tonight

Me: Shit baby. I can hardly wait. But how we go from tacos… to you talking nasty like this?

Me: You got my thighs pressed so tight under this damn table I can't think straight.

I sent another.

Me: You're ridiculous. And I like it way too much. lmfao. Might skip the panties if you behave

Three dots.

Music Man: I don't plan on behaving, baby. I plan on having you. Panties or not… I'm in that sweet pussy tonight.

Me: It's yours. Any way you want it, baby

Music Man: Just say the word, Belle

I was still staring at my phone, thighs pressed tightly together, trying to steady my breathing. I swear I read every word in Sol's voice. He was explicit, and the vivid imagery of his tone really excited me.

Mala cleared her throat, and I knew I was busted.

I looked up, trying to school my features. Just that quick, I forgot she was sitting there.

Mala was leaning over the table, her eyebrows raised expectantly.

"Who's got you all tight-legged and grinning like that, Miss Ma'am?"

I opened my mouth, then quickly shut it again.

"Uh-huh… start talking."

I casually locked my screen and placed it face down on the table. "Talking about what?"

Mala sucked her teeth. "Cousin! You sitting over there like you just got devoured whole. Who has you shifting in your seat?" Mala had a wide grin, her expression curious.

Me? My whole face was on fire.

"Music Man?" Her voice rang sing-song. "You might as well spill it. I already saw it."

I let out a small groan and then hid my face in my hands.

And Mala thought that was so funny. After she gathered herself, "I wasn't going to say anything, but you can't do all that grinning and not spill it, cousin!" she teased, tossing a tortilla chip in her mouth.

I lightly tittered, shaking my head. I looked around us, feigning nonchalance, but as I thought about it, I wanted to share this with Mala. I knew she was good at keeping things between us. We grew up very close and shared our deepest, darkest secrets. Nothing was repeated to anyone else. Ever. Nothing ever came back to me. And honestly, I was about to burst. Destiney didn't even know what was really going on. Not the recent stuff anyway. When things took an intense direction. Yeah. Destiney and I needed to catch up.

Plus, Sol is such a good guy. Treats me well and sexing me good. It was no problem sharing with Mala. Besides, she never cared much for Brandon. She was never a fan of his. Even when things were better between us. At the very least, she'd be happy to know I'm done messing with him. Both physically and emotionally.

She brought me from my thoughts, "And for your information, I promise I wasn't even going to say anything. Not today anyway. But we're here now. You got sex skin."

I laughed so hard, I damn near choked.

"Sex *what?*"

"You heard me. Sex skin. That afterglow, only good sex can give you. That deep stretch, soul-snatching glow. You got that."

My eyes were wide. And Mala was relentless.

"You've been floating all week. I noticed it when I stopped by the other day. Floating and grinning. I clocked that limp too."

My jaw dropped. And I froze.

"Okay. Wait. First of all..."

"Girl, please." She cut in, waving dismissively. "Tell me about Music Man."

She didn't know his name either. I'd been good about that. But I realized she'd picked up every nonverbal cue I couldn't hide.

But I could share with Mala. She was a safe space.

"Yes. He's a musician. A badass on the sax. His name's Solomon."

And that was all I had to say. The grin that spread across her face was slow, smug, and completely too satisfied.

"Damn, cousin. If you could see your face right now. He must be fine and talented." She had a somewhat dreamy look herself.

"He is. And so much more," I admitted, softer than I intended.

"Where'd you meet?"

"Destiney's man introduced us. They've been best friends since high school."

"Wow. Imagine that. Besties, with besties." Mala held my gaze for a few beats. "You caught feelings already, haven't you?"

How could I not?

I sighed softly and didn't respond immediately. I probably didn't need to answer at all. I'm sure it was written all over my face.

I absolutely did. Even before we started sleeping together, I had no problem being honest with myself. Being sexually intimate only intensified my feelings, and that wasn't the plan at all. But yes, I did have feelings. My feelings were strong too. Mala saw that. Nope. I don't think she needed me to confirm anything; she knew me just like I knew her.

And as expected, I saw her warm brown almond eyes gaze over me when I finally looked at her. Her sweet, fierce, protective spirit was always present.

"Just be careful, Indie," she said softly. "A good man is a blessing. But your heart... just be careful."

I nodded silently because there wasn't much else I could say at the moment. Not right now, anyway. I already knew. But Sol didn't seem like trouble. He felt so right. Like the start of something that could be so damn amazing.

We were still sitting at our table, about to leave when I noticed two guys across from us. Watching. That wasn't anything new. Heads turning. Not for me and not for Mala, with her cute smile and big, curious eyes. One was a little taller; I saw that when they both stood and headed toward us.

"Sorry to bother you, pretty ladies," the taller one began, smiling warmly. "But we couldn't just sit here and not say hello."

Mala was already looking at me when I turned to her. One of her brows raised.

"Appreciate it. You guys enjoy Taco Tuesday?" I asked, keeping it friendly.

"Sure did." The taller one smiled smooth and harmless. "How could we not? Good food. Good music, and now good company."

His friend chuckled softly. Co-signing.

I looked at Mala again, and she grinned but said nothing.

My polite smile never faded, but I knew this wasn't going anywhere. We wouldn't be rude, though. Never that.

"You ladies from around here?" he asked, his eyes shifting between us.

That was my cue. "We appreciate it, but we're not interested."

Determined, the shorter one still tried. "Just conversation, pretty. We don't bite."

Mala finally spoke, using just enough sweetness to shut it down, "Conversation turns into numbers. Numbers turn into situations." She shrugged, her eyes twinkling. "We're good."

My laugh was soft and sweet.

And the guys caught her drift. "Fair enough. You ladies have a good evening," the taller one said.

As they walked away, Mala turned to me, grinning. "You still got it." she teased, bumping my shoulder with hers.

"*Still?*"

She burst out laughing. "Can't take you nowhere, Indie!"

"Can't take you nowhere!" I chuckled, shaking my head. Yeah. Mala was cute. And the men liked her.

We stood, collected our things, and headed back to the car. I pulled out my phone and scrolled straight to my thread with Sol. "There's only one man I wanna see tonight."

Mala smirked, catching on immediately. "Mmmhmm. Solomon."

And I couldn't help the smile that spread across my entire face. "Yeah. I can't wait."

Mala laughed, knowing good and damn well what I meant by that.

Me: Can't wait to see you

Sent another one right after that.

Me: Already wet thinking about it

We were back in the car, Mala had already cranked up, when his reply lit up my screen.

Music Man: Keep that same energy, Belle. I'm hungry tonight.

I replied instantly.

Me: I'm ready to feed you, baby.

twenty-one

SOL

"Excuse me! Professor A!"

"Hey, Lorenzo."

"Hey. Great lecture today. "

"Great discussion," I replied, giving him a pointed nod. Lorenzo was one of the eager ones. Always sitting in the front, actively contributing to the discussion, and consistently asking questions. A passionate up-and-coming talent and a thought leader for sure.

"Just one more question. Gotta minute?" Lorenzo hovered near the edge of the desk as I put my laptop into my bag. Lorenzo's eyes were bright and full of restless curiosity. He's taken a few of my classes, and I'd noticed that hunger from the start.

We'd just finished my early evening Music Theory II class. As the last few students left, the soft buzz of chatter drifted out into the hallway behind them. I took my time packing up, not in any rush. No office hours tonight. This class meets Tuesdays and Thursdays from 4:30 to 5:40 PM. Office hours are Monday at midday or Tuesday after class, or by appointment, of course.

I faintly chuckled and nodded. "What you got for me?"

"Okay, do you ever think that theory ever… limits creativity? Like, once you know all the rules, is it harder to break them?"

I smiled, adjusting my bag over my shoulder. "Good question." Before responding, I let the question hang in the silence. I wanted him to hear his question, think about it, and truly hear the answer.

"Theory." I tilted my head slightly. "Theory's not there to limit you."

His eyebrows raised.

"Have you considered that theory exists to provide structure? Or to give language, a way to understand what lies beneath the sound? What do you think?"

Lorenzo nodded slowly, absorbing that, but I could still see a hint of doubt.

So, I added, "But, if you get so attached to the rules that you forget the music? That's what will limit you. Remember, music didn't begin with textbooks. It started with people. People who played. Experimented. Through feeling. Or circumstances."

I could see the lightbulb turn on.

"You learn the rules so you know which ones to break… on purpose."

He cracked a grin at that, and my whole day was made. That's what this was all about.

"Rebellious musician energy. I like it." He nodded, his grin growing wider now.

I chuckled. "Controlled rebellion. That's the sweet spot."

Lorenzo grabbed his notebook and tucked it under his arm. "Thanks, Professor Avery! I'll miss your classes when I leave. This is my last semester, and I'm transferring to Sac State after this."

"Congratulations! And stay in touch with me, please," I replied. "I'm not hard to find."

"That's a deal." He nodded.

"Good stuff." I said, rounding the desk to head toward the door. Lorenzo, a few steps ahead of me.

"So..." he backed into the door, holding it open for me. He also dragged the word out like he wasn't in a rush to leave. "Thursday night huh?" he posed slightly mischievously.

I raised an eyebrow. Amused. He wasn't slick.

"Yeah. Thursday night. What about it?" I already knew. My cover had been blown a long time ago.

Lorenzo shrugged, pretending he didn't know. "You know... as a musician, the music scene is small. Word gets around. Heard about a house band at HomeGrown. Pretty solid, I hear." He paused, his eyes shining. "You're really *professorly* on the saxophone, from what I've been told."

I let out a deep chuckle as I adjusted my bag over my shoulder. "Is that so?"

And he shrugged. Fake nonchalance.

I chuckled again.

"Yes. And... strictly for academic enrichment purposes, some of us may want to check it out."

I shook my head, laughing heartily throughout. "Academic enrichment? Right." I felt a buzz in my pocket, so I pulled out my phone and unlocked it. "Doors open at six. The band is up by seven. I don't tutor scales between sets. So, manage your expectations."

Lorenzo nodded, his grin widening.

And I shook my head. Laughing again.

"Appreciate you, Professor A. Have a good evening!" He headed down the hall in quick strides.

"You too, Lorenzo." Commencing my stroll in the other direction, I called out to his back, "Don't make it weird, Lorenzo. It's still my night job."

He turned and called after me, "Wouldn't even dream of it!"

I planned to go straight to the parking lot after class, but a text from my dean appeared during my brief exchange with Lorenzo. He asked to see me before I left. So, I made my way through the Performing Arts Center, the PAC, where all of my classes were held in this building. My office as well. I passed it on the way to see my dean.

And Lorenzo's question still lingered, trailing after me long after he'd disappeared down the hall. It stuck with me, heavy in the quiet, as I headed toward the dean's office. My thoughts were running further ahead than my steps. It lingered, not just about music theory but also the balance I still wrestled with. This balancing act I was performing well, but simultaneously losing myself in the process, on the inside. Whatever semblance of an identity I held. I was so good at presenting something that wasn't remotely close to what I desired to know. The void I wanted to fill. And following the rules. Always following the rules.

The halls were much quieter now. The evening classes were more mellow than the morning and daytime sessions. As I walked through the mostly empty hall, Lorenzo's question kept echoing in the silence. It stuck with me. Rules. Rebellion. How knowing too much can, in fact, confine you, if you're not careful. It all felt so familiar.

Rules. Especially these high-class, uppity rules my parents gave me. I admit I felt some resentment about that. And I rebelled. Within reason, I suppose. My way of rebelling was refusing to study anything but music. Not medicine. Not law. Not engineering. Nothing STEM-related. I initially refused to go to college at all. At one point, I was even threatened with disinheritance. That idea was intriguing. I knew I'd be fine. I work hard, holding down a nine-to-five job, earning my own money, and doing multiple side gigs. Passion projects that bring me fulfillment and happiness.

We reached a compromise, and I headed to college. I studied music, pushing myself as far as one could go. I earned a Doctorate in Ethnomusicology. I was like a damn circus act. A constant battle. Fucking rules, man. Juking and jiving. Knowing when to follow the rules and when to finally and fully break them. To truly find myself.

I glanced at my watch. I had just enough time to stop at my dean's office, get home, shower, and make it to HomeGrown with plenty of time to spare.

I couldn't wait to get out of here. Tonight, I'd be seeing India, and I was so damn excited. We'd been seeing each other for a few weeks now, a few times a week. But… sleeping together, which I rather enjoyed. And I knew she was enjoying herself too. I was making sure of it. Certain.

But at the same time, I didn't want to reduce her to just this. She deserved so much more. This was starting to get to me. I wanted to pursue her, properly. I'm a gentleman. I know how to treat a lady. And. I knew exactly how I wanted to handle India. I wanted so much with her. I wanted to take her out, show her a good time, love on her, spoil her, and show her off. I didn't care what we did; I just wanted to be with India.

And I wanted to *be* with India, too. I wanted all of her attention. Lord knows, she had all of mine. I want to be her man, to show her how it's really done. Yeah. I wanted her for myself. I realized that a long time ago. I don't know exactly when it happened, but here I was, pinning after so much more than anything physical. India was the woman I wanted to be with, and I planned to discuss this with her this weekend. No excuses.

But I wanted to share space with her, not just in her bed. And. I also wanted her in my bed. I asked her about spending time with me at my place, but she evaded the topic.

Didn't seem interested in that, or a date, or anything beyond this physical thing, late at night, at her house.

Which made me wonder what that was about. Was it a security thing? I knew I didn't scare her. I knew I made her comfortable. Maybe this would take some time. But the other thing I worried about was whether this would ever become more than this. So I knew we had to talk this weekend.

I didn't want to admit it, but it seemed she was starting to answer my unspoken questions without explicitly answering them at all. And I didn't want room for confusion on either of our parts. I wanted to tell her exactly how I felt and what I wanted. I also wanted to know the same from her.

And honestly, I wanted to meet her family. Her parents, the people who made her. It's no surprise that I do; she lights up with pride when speaking of her parents.

But India is incredible. One of the coolest people I've ever met. And I've met many. I'm a professor and a musician, traveling quite a bit for both. I also network a lot.

She's such a daddy's girl. I love that. And she and her mom are incredibly close. I would be honored to meet them. But I get the impression that it won't happen anytime soon. Especially if all she wants to really do is sleep with me.

I don't like to second-guess my choices. I value the peace and harmony that come from well-thought-out decisions. To that end, I'm not usually someone who stays silent. Usually, I would speak up about something sooner rather than later.

But, this situation we've found ourselves in... found myself in... I still haven't talked to India about it, and I had my reasons. I was waiting for the right time, and I don't believe it presented itself. I figured I would need to make time for it, and I was. This weekend, we'll finally have this talk face to face. All this time passing us by, and I was no closer to getting any clarity or answers. Meanwhile, my feelings for India are steadily growing. Rapidly.

And the more I thought about it, the more I felt a little uneasy. Deciding for the moment that I would 'let things be' probably wasn't the best choice. Making the conscious decision not to say anything seemed to have negative effects. But I'll get this sorted out. This weekend.

Now, about our conversations. I loved those. India was so down-to-earth and silly. She would crack up at herself, and it was adorable. As beautiful as India is, she has such a grounded personality. Super chill, a great listener, and really easy to talk to. We chat on the phone, and hours can just pass by. Just the other night, we were up late talking about a couple of my all-time favorite movies. Top five for sure. It turned out that one of them is also a favorite of hers. We naturally shifted into that topic after a few questions of mine led us there.

I liked India for many reasons. Shit, I was falling for her. Simple as that. One reason is that she let me ask her so many questions, always answering them truthfully. Gracefully. In transparency. I gave her that same courtesy. Of course. I wouldn't consider otherwise. But I asked her a lot about her life. Her family, her culture, their customs, and their food. I was like a student, soaking in everything she proudly shared. Some questions seemed small or silly, but not to her. She welcomed and answered them all. Having such a void and a desire to know all of these things about myself, I found comfort in that.

And she saw me. She listened intently when I shared about my life or myself, which wasn't as beautifully detailed or vividly cultured as hers, in my opinion. But she was very interested and eager to learn just as much about me.

Yeah. Belle had me falling in love with her.

"Okay, Artist Girl, describe the sounds in your home growing up? Was it loud?"

She let out a lazy chuckle. It was late, and I knew she was tired. I was getting tired too, but neither of us wanted to go.

She'd started an apprenticeship at a tattoo shop and had been working long hours, learning. I was so proud of her, and she was so excited.

*"Loud? Hmm. Yes sometimes. But... it was... **alive**. That's the best word for it. Back in Berbice, especially. Aunties, uncles, cousins, in and out. Music always playing. When we moved here, our home was still very much alive. Just a little calmer. You?"*

I shook my head, though she couldn't see me. "Nah. My folks were... polite. Super structured. Dinners were quiet. They played music, but it was classical." I paused for a beat, then chuckled. "You know... this will sound random," I said, "but Crooklyn is still one of my all-time favorite movies. I used to imagine having a family like the one in Crooklyn." I chuckled again.

*"**Crooklyn**. Really?" Suddenly, India seemed to burst with energy.*

"Yeah," I answered, chuckling again. "That movie meant everything to me. The siblings. They argued, but they loved each other. Stuck together. Then the father trying to make it as a musician. That hit too. Doing his best to create while putting food on the table. The trials of life weighed him down, but he kept going. The whole brownstone full of life and love. I always wondered how life would be if I had that. And the soundtrack? Man! A masterpiece. Spike did something special with that one."

*"**Crooklyn?** Are you serious?"*

"Dead serious. What? Never seen it?"

"You're kidding! I can quote the whole movie! It was one of the first films I saw after we moved here. That film changed me. Coming here feeling lost, angry, heartbroken, and isolated. Then seeing a Black American family

like that... chaotic, messy, but so beautiful. It just... man! All of it made me feel like maybe we could belong here, too. Just in a different way. You know?"

"Oh, I definitely do! That's what I loved too. The way they all moved around the house. Kids on top of each other, laughing, arguing. Parents right in the middle of it all. The warmth. I never had that, but I really wanted it. Bad."

There was a silence. It felt comfortable. And it was unspoken, but the silence said, "I see you." For her. And for me.

"Wow! Imagine that. We share a favorite movie."

"Yeah. Crazy. A movie we enjoyed as kids." After a beat, "You own it?"

"No. Not yet. But I watch it whenever it comes on. It's free on YouTube sometimes. You?"

*"VHS, DVD, and Blu-ray," I said casually. But it was everything. "I searched high and low for a pristine copy of Crooklyn on VHS. And found it. In the original box. **That** was in mint condition, too."*

India giggled, "Liar! You for real?"

"Dead serious. When you come by, I'll show you."

"Wow." she laughed again. "You own all three. That's wild."

"I had to, and the soundtrack. Vinyl and digital. That's how serious I am. I'm telling you, that soundtrack? Someone could write a whole thesis on it."

"You're nerding out right now, Music Man!" Her chuckle was light. "Nerdy in the best way."

I chuckled too. "But wait," I pressed, "Want to know the other movie I own in every format possible?" I gave her a beat. Then, "You won't guess."

"Uh oh. What is it?"

"A Goofy Movie."

"Aww!" She cracked up. "Seriously? I haven't seen that in forever!"

I sat up, eager to nerd out all over again. "Powerline was my idol. Like Michael Jackson, Prince, and Bobby Brown all rolled into one animated king. And that concert at the end! That song? Yeah. Tevin Campbell had no business going that hard in a Disney movie."

"Oh my gosh!" India was rolling.

And it was adorable. This was the most tickled I think I've ever seen her. And I let her get all her giggles out.

I was serious as hell.

"Okay. So you're definitely very passionate about this." She was still laughing.

"Don't act like I'm wrong," I said playfully. "You know 'Eye to Eye' still goes!"

"I'm compelled to agree." She finally got her last giggles out. "You're really something, Music Man."

"You like it," I said confidently. Without hesitation.

"Hell yeah, I do." she replied immediately.

As I walked down the hall, one of the elevators opened a few feet in front of me. The ding announcing its arrival brought me from my thoughts.

"Evening, Professor Dodd," I offered.

"Dr. Avery!" she gushed, her eyes lighting up as she clicked toward me in heels and a fitted dress. She'd spun on her heels to head in my direction. I was sure she was just headed the other way.

Professor Monica Dodd. Sociology.

Sharp dresser. Cute. She always carried a flirt in her smile whenever she saw me. Like now. I noticed the way her eyes lingered just a second too long. Good thing I had somewhere to be.

"Where are you headed? You don't have another class this evening."

Okay. She was keeping tabs. Not that it wasn't public information. Our schedules were listed in the faculty database. But still. I wasn't checking for Monica. And I wouldn't be. Ever. I didn't mess where I ate.

"Meeting with Dean Whitaker," I said simply. Nothing more. And I never stopped walking. But I took my time strolling, and since my legs are long, Monica took a few steps for each of mine.

"I see. Well, if you're free afterward, I was thinking... there's a sushi place over on Freeport. A low-key, quiet spot. We could review my notes for the symposium at UC Davis, I mentioned?

And she had. I nodded once, offering her the briefest moment of eye contact.

Her eyes lit up. "I'll be speaking on the intersection of race, class, and resilience in post-pandemic education. They've pulled together a strong panel."

She paused, tucking her long braid behind her ear, her tone softening just enough. "I could really use your insight. I'm still new to this kind of thing… maybe we could go over it together?" A gentle laugh followed. Light, flirty, almost coy. Like she was trying to play helpless. But Monica wasn't helpless. Not by a long shot.

She was sharp and passionate about her work, and she was going places. And if I could guess fast. Which is a great thing. Phenomenal, actually. Monica didn't need me to read her notes; she just wanted an excuse to interact with me beyond pleasantries. No, this wasn't her first attempt. Second. Or third.

Still, I kept it smooth. I slowed down once I reached the glass-paneled corner office. Offering a polite nod, I told her, "Congrats again on the invite. That's a great opportunity. And it sounds like a solid event. If you want to send your notes my way, I'd be happy to give them a read." I gave her a kind smile. "Thank you for the invite."

I realized right after I said that it sounded like an afterthought. Too late now.

Her smile wavered slightly, but she quickly recovered. "Oh… sure. That'd be great. Thank you."

I nodded once, "Well. Gotta run. Dean's expecting me."

"Of course," she said, stepping back, but her eyes still lingered. "Another time, then?"

Instead of an answer, I gave a half a nod that time, saying, "Take care."

I cleared my throat as I knocked on my dean's office door and stepped inside.

"Dean Whitaker," I said as soon as I crossed the threshold, stopping in front of his desk and shaking his hand firmly.

"Dr. Avery." He greeted me pleasantly. After the shake, he removed his glasses. "Have a seat. This will be quick."

I sat in one of the comfy leather chairs facing his large desk. The walls behind him were filled with degrees, academic certificates, and awards.

"I sent you a couple of postings. Well, a few actually. You said you'd think about spreading those wings." I watched him, and just that quickly, he'd put his glasses back on. They sat low on his nose as he gave me a pointed nod.

"Dean Whit," I chuckled. "You're not letting up, are you?"

He zeroed in on me. "Avery. I wouldn't be doing my job if I did. Now, would I?"

"Fair enough," I admitted.

"You're made for more than this, Dr. Solomon Avery. And I'm not giving up my job just yet." We both laughed.

"Your reputation preceded you. You hadn't even stepped on this campus, and I'd already heard about you. Your talent. Your music. The stages you've performed on. Your work with the youth."

"Thank you, Dean," I told him gingerly.

I hugely respect and admire my dean, and we've had this conversation before. A few times, matter of fact. When I first joined the department about four years ago.

At the time, I was still a few years away from finishing my doctorate, and we discussed my background and goals in detail. Dean Whit maintained his respect for me as an individual, and the feeling was mutual.

He's so accomplished yet one of the humblest men I know. Dr. Harold Whitaker. Respected. Thoughtful. Experienced. Educated. And an educator for decades, both in K-12 and higher education before moving into leadership. From the very beginning of our working relationship, he's been more than a superior. He's been like a mentor. Holding me accountable and always encouraging me to reach my full potential.

"I appreciate you sending them. I'll take a look," I said.

I knew the postings were for universities. More money and tenure tracks. But the truth was, I liked it here, especially at Sacramento City College, within the community college space.

There's nothing glamorous about it. But there's a realness. A rawness. An honesty that you'll only find in this setting. Community college is the reason I started teaching in the first place. I encounter students from all walks of life. There's no nepotism or privilege. No trust fund kids. These students, both young and mature, are working-class. Trying to make it. Some of them are the first in their family to even make it to college.

Some of them were hustling. Working two jobs, raising children, and still making it to class. Eager to learn, just trying to make it, trying to better their circumstances. I respected that. The drive. The hunger. The ambition. Immensely.

And a place like Sacramento City College is a place where I could help motivate, encourage, and give back. But. I told my Dean I'd review them, and I would. He had my word. Dean Whitaker also reminded me of his standing offer to write me letters of recommendation if I need them.

As I headed toward the parking lot, I glanced at my watch again. I chuckled, shaking my head. That really could have just been an email. But maybe my dean thought he could get through to me by talking face-to-face. Who knows? It wouldn't hurt to review those postings.

Honestly, I figured I'd take more than just a few minutes reviewing them. Maybe then I'd have something else to talk about when I saw my parents this weekend. I was expected to join my parents for dinner every Sunday afternoon. And I went. According to my mother and father, few things were acceptable excuses to miss. And I knew that I'd hear something about Noelle if I didn't manage to fill the space with something else.

Noelle. Pretty, well-bred, safe Noelle. The young lady, my mother, seemed to desperately want for me. A young woman I didn't feel a damn thing for. Lately, it's more like pestering. A busted ass record I didn't want to hear anymore. And no matter the subject, somehow, Noelle was conveniently brought into the conversation.

My father and I hadn't spoken about India since the afternoon I shared my thoughts with him several weeks ago. That was fine. He didn't mention this to my mother either. Evidently. Which was even better because I needed to be the one to do that.

Yeah. I knew I needed to impress upon my mother, very soon, that I wouldn't be pursuing anything with Noelle, and I wouldn't marry her. But I wouldn't worry about that now. In just a couple of hours, I'd see India. And the thought alone made my heart smile and my body hum.

My beautiful Artist Girl.

I was so happy she agreed to come out tonight. It wasn't a date. Her cousin Mala would be with her, which might be why she agreed. But that was okay. I'm fine with that for now. Baby steps.

I was still doing good on time. Sac City was almost close enough to my house to throw a rock at, and HomeGrown was in midtown, just a ten-minute drive from me.

I strapped my backpack on, secured my helmet, and pointed my bicycle toward home.

twenty-two

INDIA

If only I had met Solomon sooner.

I'm sure I'd be drunk in love right now. Crazy in love.

Dangerously in love. Queen B knew exactly what the hell she was talking about. Two nights ago, Sol texted me. It started out innocent.

Music Man: Can't sleep. You up, Artist Girl?

I was.

It was late, later than we usually text. These days, I'm always up late, even after a long day. I'd be completely exhausted, but my mind keeps racing, and I can't settle it no matter what. So many thoughts flood my head, thinking about so many things.

I had a few commissioned watercolor pieces that I needed to finish. I was always grateful for commissioned work. Whenever they came, I welcomed them like a fresh harvest. But I was burning the candle at both ends because I was working long hours at the shop. I needed to streamline this apprenticeship so I could get my license. I needed the money. And I was overwhelmed by my feelings for Solomon. He'd been asking to see me outside of these late-night rendezvous.

They'd slowed down just a little bit. We were still doing it… but less often. I was trying to figure all of this out because it seemed that this was more to Sol than just sex. And, I'd be lying to myself if I said this was only sex to me. It was so much more than just sex. This wasn't the plan.

Nowhere in the plans were we supposed to get caught up in all of this. Wrapped up in each other for this long. This was supposed to just be something we did sometimes, with no pressure for anything more on either side. I knew we both had crushes on each other, and maybe that was our first mistake. Sleeping together when feelings were already involved. On both sides.

Mistake number two, we never really established anything. We just flirted like it was going out of style, then started fucking. Like some horny ass teenagers.

Shit.

We already had feelings, and now they've grown stronger. I knew Sol's feelings for me had intensified. I could tell. I could feel it. And he wasn't the only one. Mine had grown too. I was starting to like him a lot. Fuck that. It wasn't *like* anymore. Things were bordering on love. And I don't even know when it happened.

Destiney and I finally talked about it, and I told her the best way I knew how.

Honestly.

I told her we had been sleeping together for the past few weeks. I explained how well he'd been catering to my body. My spirit. How good a lover he was. And I shared that my feelings were growing deeper.

Let her tell it; she could tell the second she saw me. I planned to bring it up and casually mention how things had been going. But I didn't even get that far.

"Okay, Best. Spill it. You've got that glow!" she said teasing.

We met at our favorite coffee shop, *Barista Nia's Cafe.* We've been coming here for years. It's a Black-owned business located in the heart of Historic Oak Park, surrounded by many other Black-owned establishments.

Melanin Pages, a bookstore Destiney loved visiting, was right next door. They carried an inventory exclusively made up of books written by people of color. They frequently hosted book signings.

A soul food restaurant called *Roots and Flavor* is on the other side of Nia's. They serve the best macaroni and cheese you'll find around here.

Recently, very recently, I discovered that a close second would be the mac and cheese at HomeGrownSol. But Home-Grown is in Midtown Sacramento, maybe ten minutes away without traffic.

Just as I took a bite of my orange-glazed scone, Destiney said, "Someone's been rearranging your insides. Who is it, Indie?"

My answer was instant, and although I tried to laugh it off. She wasn't wrong.

"Sol."

She gasped, "Solomon? *Really?* How long has this been going on?"

"We've been talking on the regular since the barbecue at Mal's." She nodded, sipping from her mug slowly. "But we started messing around in January."

"Messing around?" Her eyebrows shot up to her hairline. "*Oh. Okay. Wow.*" She had a satisfied smile. "Sol is a good guy. And he's handsome. I guess I won't be mad at you for not telling me." she said sarcastically. Then she took another drink, rolling her eyes dramatically.

"Oh, Des. It wasn't supposed to be anything. We'd kept things pretty low-key. But..." I sighed, then took a sip of my Cinnamon Dolce Latte: It was the perfect temperature and just the right sweetness. This was my go-to whenever we came. It was espresso, steamed milk, cinnamon dolce syrup, and whipped cream.

"But..." she looked at me expectantly, sipping her Café de Olla.

Destiney bravely tried a new drink whenever it appeared on their menu. That one was Mexican-spiced coffee with cinnamon and piloncillo sugar.

After a moment, I told her, "I think about him so much. He's all I think about. When I'm away from Sol, I miss him. And when I'm with him, I want to touch him."

"Best... sounds like some serious feelings. And for the sake of this conversation, are you sure it isn't lust talking? It can be easy to confuse the two. Especially if it's good. And by the way, you're glowing, I can surmise it's good?"

"Girl..." I lifted my mug to my lips and took a generous gulp. We laughed. I didn't even need to say it.

But Destiney had a point there. And this was a textbook example. Each time I called Sol, he came. And he made me come too. Every damn time. The way he ate me, as if he were starving for me. The way he whispered in my ear. The way he stroked into me. Fuck. He said my name like it meant the entire world.

I shook my head. Vehemently. "No way. This isn't just sex. Not the way he does it. The way he does me. Des. He's so patient. And so damn thorough. Solomon knows exactly what he's doing and takes his time doing it. It's like he's trying to memorize my every curve. Like I matter to him. I've never felt this with anyone before."

Destiney nodded her head, wearing a warm smile. My smile was bright; I knew it reached my eyes. I continued, "Everything with Sol feels different. And I trust him implicitly. I never thought… I never knew I could feel this way. Not just physically. I feel it deep in my soul."

"That's your heart yearning for him. And the heart knows what she wants," Destiney shared, her warm smile never fading. "I love this for you." She gently set her half-full mug on the table in front of her. After holding my gaze for a moment longer, she added, "I know you Best, and I know there's a but." Her tone shifted slightly, almost cautionary.

My smile faded. I could feel it.

She gently shook her head. "Best. You need to surrender to those feelings. You deserve that kind of love."

I smiled and gave her a look. "Not you, giving me romantic advice!" We burst out laughing. For a little while.

"Hey! I've learned a thing or two by now."

I swear. There's just something about those tables. They always turn. I remember giving Destiney similar advice when she and Micah were trying to figure things out. I was worried for a second. I knew Micah was a great catch and a perfect match for her. I knew he was a good guy. Between Destiney's sister Daijah and me, we knew she wouldn't forgive herself if she missed out on a love like the one they'd cultivated. Love truly looked great on her. She'd been married for only a couple of months, and they'd already faced so much. But every challenge brought them closer. Made them stronger. It was such a beautiful thing.

Truly, I was so happy for my best friend, who happened to be married to Solomon's best friend. That was the other thing. I thought about how messy things could potentially get. I knew full well neither of us was going anywhere, whether Sol and I made something more of this or not.

"I'm getting another scone. Maybe I'll try the raspberry one," Destiney offered, pulling me from my thoughts.

"Damn, I didn't even realize you'd already finished the other one," I said jokingly.

"Girl, don't judge me. You know I'm eating for two!"

I cackled. "No judging, I promise! I'm just glad you can eat again. That morning sickness was pretty bad."

"Right! I still feel a little nausea in the morning, but it's not too bad. I won't complain. My appetite is back and stronger than ever. That Café de Olla is fantastic too, but I want another scone."

"When are you out of the woods?"

"Soon. But not soon enough." She briefly had a distant look in her eyes.

"Everything will be fine, Best," I told her with the most confident tone I could muster.

Destiney and Micah experienced a miscarriage during their first pregnancy. That was tough, and my heart broke for her. But she and Micah supported each other through it. And I was so glad they were brave enough to try again. I know that takes courage.

She'd told me that the risk of miscarrying drops significantly after the first trimester. Other than Daijah and me, no one else knew she was pregnant again. Destiney said Micah hadn't told anyone, but once she passed her first trimester, they planned to share the news.

Destiney stood. "Can I get you anything, Best?" she asked with a knowing look. "Don't even start, Best. It's my treat. Now, what would you like?"

I smiled, "Thank you, Best. A blueberry muffin?"

"Yes! Warmed up?"

"Yes, please. Thank you." I'd been eyeing those fluffy muffins but decided on the scone in the end. I couldn't afford both. And I appreciated Destiney so much.

"So. Tell me what you're so afraid of," Destiney asked as she returned to our table. I had already started eating my muffin, and it was scrumptious.

She had a raspberry scone and a cup of yogurt.

I sighed. "That's such a loaded question, Best."

"We have time."

I knew she wanted to know because she cared about me, and she wanted to see me happy. She'd seen all the ugly shit I dealt with when I was with Brandon. Well, some of it. No one really knew *everything*. I look back on that relationship and wonder why the hell I stayed as long as I did. Either way, it was a lesson learned. A lesson I would never repeat.

I heaved a heavy sigh. "I mean. I... First of all, I'm never alone. I've been in one committed relationship after another. I need to know that I can stand on my own two feet. I wonder if I have a deep underlying fear of being alone or something."

I meant this sincerely, too. I wasn't making this up as I went along. This was something I had thought about. Extensively. Taking my time before entering another relationship and being by myself. That was important to me. I hadn't been single for a long time, and even when I was officially single, I still entertained someone in some capacity. Even if we weren't sleeping together.

But I needed to be alone. That had to happen. It was for the best. I needed a damn palate cleanser. A change up. I've thought about that too. Like, was I seeking something? In an attempt to boost my self-worth that I can't find on my own? The fact that I was always in a relationship and never single… was there some underlying reason for that? Yeah. I needed time by myself before entering a new relationship. And I needed to see a therapist to level set.

I shared all of this with Destiney. My best friend and I always spoke openly with each other.

"Alright, Best. That's easy." Destiney nodded. She'd torn into her cup of yogurt and sprinkled the granola on top. "We can do that." She said as she took a spoonful. "You can see my therapist.

I feel so great about her. She's so amazing. If she isn't a good fit, I have a list of some of the best black therapists in the area."

I nodded. "Alright."

"What else?" Destiney pressed. "You said this was a loaded question. And you gave me a legitimate excuse just now, but I feel like you're stalling. Trying to avoid the inevitable."

I opened my mouth to respond, but no words came out. I exhaled a frustrated breath and then chuckled lightly. My bestie could read me like a book, which was crazy. I could read her too. We'd mastered each other's idiosyncrasies. Just like best friends do.

"You know what I think of all this?" I looked up and into her eyes. My beautiful bestie had a beautiful smile. With big, brilliant brown eyes. Shit, my bestie was beautiful, period. And she'd been glowing. She kept talking, "Well, I'm so glad you asked…" I laughed, and she continued, "I believe you're falling in love with Solomon. And I think you want to be with Solomon. You're just looking for excuses not to."

Damn. She wasn't wrong. At all. No lies detected. At first, I was against it. I knew I was falling for Sol, which was crazy. But I'd also thought about, really considered, being with Sol.

When I allow myself to, that is. Yeah. Lately, I've been at war with myself. My mind has been opening up to the idea. The idea. That's all it was. But for me, that was significant. I looked just past Destiney, saying nothing for now. I was musing over her question and her declarations. Destiney let me rock. I could hear the grinding and hissing sounds from the espresso machines, the clinking of cups, and the stirring of spoons. The chatter among the patrons floated through the café, along with the music. I listened closely and heard "Mine" by Alex Isley. It was the irony for me.

"Falling in love feels like I'm handing him a loaded gun," I said finally. I didn't even think first. The words just came out of my mouth. But it wasn't anything personal. I knew Sol was a good guy. I knew he'd care for me. I knew my heart would be safe with him.

Since my first encounter with Sol, I haven't been the same.

I can admit that. Mentally and physically. My skin still tingles from the tender way he touches me. My heart still swells from the sweet way he whispers my name against my neck. Or softly in my ear. What's been happening... the feelings developing. Hell, they were deepening at this point. Yeah. This is so much more than lust. Solomon listens when I speak, wanting to understand. He hears me, but more than that, he sees me. He cares so much about me. He always has something sweet to say. He cares about my family and often asks how Ma and Daddy are doing, as if he knows them personally.

And here's the thing… they weren't doing so well, and money was tight right now. Always fucking money shit. There was always something. A prescription to pick up, bills past due. The car was nickeling and diming us, draining any "disposable income" we might have had. At this rate, I could see our car bankrupting us. I knew that was causing stress for my parents.

We'd spend money we didn't have to fix something, only for something else to go out. We couldn't get it to start, and when it finally did, I couldn't trust it would start again. I didn't want to drive anywhere because I didn't want to end up stranded. We didn't have the money to tow the car back home. So, I'd walk to the tattoo shop. Luckily, it wasn't a bad walk. About forty minutes one way. I'd take the bus home because Daddy didn't want me walking in the dark. Mala gave me rides anywhere I needed, and Destiney did too. But I savored those favors.

And. Sol had no idea about any of this. I was making it work. I never dwelled on money issues too much because it wasn't a good idea. Instead, I stayed a practical thinker, solution-focused. I'd been looking at some positions at after-school programs for art instructors. I didn't want to go back to corporate America, but a steady paycheck was what we needed right now. The challenge was fitting that into my full-time apprenticeship schedule.

The plan was to put in as many hours as I could each week so I could earn my license faster. But the apprenticeship was unpaid. To make up for that, I'd been taking on more commissioned work.

Destiny and I worked together a lot on art projects, but I hadn't been able to commit to many of them because I was so busy with all of this.

And yeah. All of this was taking a toll on me. I was much more exhausted, but I had to keep going. I had an endgame. Just had to get through this.

And it helped to hear Ma and Daddy cheer me on, encouraging me and always being proud of me. As always. Even if they didn't understand the logic behind what I was trying to do. Of course, Ma was concerned about all the work I'd been doing, and Daddy too. He's very protective of me. The late hours I'd spend in my art shed, he'd fight sleep just to come check on me.

Having Destiney here was such a blessing. It took my mind off everything. It helped me feel a little better about my feelings. She's been here for me all the time. The highs, the lows. She's always there. She keeps sending me info on paid gigs. She even covered my phone bill before. This friendship means the world to me. She means the world. I couldn't be more blessed to have met her. When we work together, we create some of the rawest, sickest art you've ever seen. I'm serious. Destiney and I have an amazing collaboration, painting murals all over the city and beyond. Murals that leave people struck. In awe.

I've seen it. We did a lot of community beautification projects, and crowds gathered to watch us work. I've heard the murmurs.

"Black girl magic! These two beauties can paint their asses off yo!"

"Got damn... they're so beautiful, you almost forget they're painting something even more beautiful."

I'm active on social media. Destiney isn't. But I'll post from a site we're working at; we might hardly appear in the clip, but you'll see us if you don't blink. And then I'll check the comments.

"Peeped India and Destiney!! Man... it's wild!! I know their work. These two can stop traffic with their faces and their brushes!"

"Dead ass! Watching them paint is almost a distraction. They're so fine. These black queens don't miss. Hands like legends."

We haven't been able to work together much lately. I've been focused on my apprenticeship, and Destiney has been busy being a new wifey and soon-to-be mommy.

But yeah. Destiny and I were almost inseparable right after we met. It was so easy. My girl is incredible! But more than that, Destiney has always been kind. So sweet, just like me. Quirky in an adorable way. And she understands me, which is rare because I'm often misunderstood and judged.

Destiney really understands me. I didn't know a soul on this earth with a heart as big as hers. She's such a gem. And she's always looking out for me, checking in on me. Late last year, she asked me to work with her on a mural she was painting inside Micah's home. I was so honored and agreed right away. We worked on it for weeks, putting in hours on different days after a full day of painting at work, and it turned out to be something so fucking amazing. I'm so proud of what we created.

When we were all done, Micah tried to pay me, and I refused, begging him not to. I wanted to do this solid for Destiney. She'd done so much for me. And I remember her softly nudging my shoulder, encouraging me.

"Best. Let him bless you. Please. You never ask for anything." She insisted the mural wouldn't have been as amazing as it turned out without me. I was incredibly humbled by that. So, I reluctantly agreed, and when I got home and opened the envelope later, I cried. Micah paid me so generously. Much more than I expected. That check set us up for a while. We caught up on our bills and still had plenty to spare. It truly changed my whole season.

I had a few small gigs coming up, and I'd make it work. There was also a consultation scheduled for a custom piece. Yeah. I would make it work. I always made it work.

"Sol isn't like that, Best," Destiney reasoned with care. Bringing me back from my thoughts. She understood. "Sol and Micah have been best friends for twenty years. I bet Micah had an idea about you two; he knows you're my best friend and how much you mean to me. If he didn't trust Sol with you, he wouldn't have let it happen."

I didn't disagree with any of that. But I said nothing.

"Best. You'll miss out on a blessing by resisting."

"I don't have anything to offer Solomon. Mom's glaucoma is getting worse. Dad's arthritis is flaring up again. They need me more now, and I have to be there. Taking care of mom and dad is what cost me Brandon."

"Sol isn't Brandon. And Brandon was in that for himself Best. That's the truth." She paused for a moment, then asked, "Have you and Sol even talked this over? I get the feeling he'd be understanding and supportive."

I shook my head, "There's quite a bit we need to talk about, actually." I revealed absently. "But I'm so damn broke I can hardly pay attention."

We sat in comfortable silence. Ella Mai's "Trip" came on.

"Okay. I know you're not *that* girl. But I'm telling you, Sol has coins, Indie. He'd change your life."

I didn't say anything. But there was a shift in my demeanor.

Initially, I was surprised. If Sol had money, he sure was quiet about it. He appeared like an average Joe, which was fine with me. Sol was reserved and so chill. Super laid back, just a low-key guy. He could be silly and charismatic, but he had an underlying calmness about him. And I liked that. A lot. But we never talked about money. Money was a topic I generally disliked discussing. In hindsight, I realized Sol didn't talk about money either. Ever. Yeah. Money was always a sensitive topic for me. And by now, I was in a place where money didn't impress me anymore.

Brandon had money and was pretty successful in real estate. He sold million-dollar homes and a few multi-million-dollar ones. But I never liked asking Brandon for anything. Brandon had everyone fooled, including me. His success in real estate afforded him the finer things, and he was flashy. I guess, considering where he came from, he had something to be proud of. Yeah, Brandon had a lot of money, but he was stingy. We dated for two and a half years, and he never gave me anything or helped me with anything.

And it wasn't like he didn't know my situation, and I became severely independent in the process. Subconsciously at first.

These days, I hardly like to bother my dad for anything. I realize that's not a good thing. Mala always points it out to me. Since she's hip to it, she checks in with me often because she knows I probably wouldn't say anything. And thank God for her. Life is meant to be lived in community.

Brandon having a bunch of money didn't mean shit. Brandon didn't really take care of me. Not really. It was weird. While I was with him physically, I benefited. We'd go places, and he'd handle everything. But I never liked to ask him for anything. And I don't mean money or anything materialistic. Brandon made it seem like doing anything for me was a chore. Not even anything big, just small things. For example, if I brought bags from the store to his apartment, he'd make such a fuss if I asked him to help carry them upstairs.

He lived out in Rocklin, about twenty-five miles east of my house. So, I would stop by, and everything would be fine, but if I couldn't stay the night, he'd get a horrible attitude with me. If I left when it was dark outside, he wouldn't even walk me out. I asked him once, and he mumbled something about it being an upscale neighborhood and nothing would happen to me. Yep. And he wouldn't even stay on the phone with me while I drove home. Wouldn't even check to see if I'd made it safely.

I cooked for Brandon at his place a lot. He loved my food, and I could make many different dishes, not just the Caribbean food I was raised on. Sometimes he asked me to cook something specific, and I'd need to go to the store. I'd ask him if he wouldn't mind coming with me since he wasn't busy, just because I wanted his company. He wouldn't.

I realized that I couldn't even call Brandon if I didn't know what to do, and with no one else to turn to. I eventually stopped asking Brandon for anything. In my mind, these were everyday things. Nothing major. Ordinary things that would show his care and dedication to making me feel secure and safe. And I didn't feel that. I wasn't. Not emotionally. And that affected how safe I felt physically with him too. If a robber approached us, I didn't even believe Brandon would protect me. I knew he wouldn't. When I needed something, I didn't call Brandon. And I didn't ask him for a damn thing. I'd call my father.

"Nothing the matter with letting a man do for you. Take care of you."

I reflected on Destiney's words. To me, it wasn't even about dependence. Though I'd become fiercely independent, it was about feeling confident enough in someone and choosing to trust them because they've proven they will show up for you. My trust in that was shattered. And I worried it was beyond salvage.

While we sat here talking, Destiney managed to polish off both scones and that yogurt. And I was so glad she was in better spirits these days. We hung out at Nia's for a couple of hours, and it was the best time seeing my bestie. I loved catching up with her. I gave her space to be a new wife, so I didn't overstep, letting her tell me when she could get together. I welcomed it each time. Destiney dropped me off at home, and I took a few minutes to relax before heading out to my shed. I had to get to the commissioned pieces.

Later that evening, I was back from the shop. I spent hours cleaning stations and then worked on station setup. Helped at the host desk. Booked a few appointments. Did some observations. I took a shower, and just as I settled into bed, I heard my phone vibrate on my nightstand. It was after eleven p.m.

Music Man: Missing you, my Artist Girl

I responded right away. I missed him too.

Me: Aww. Miss you too, my Music Man.

Sent another.

Me: You okay?

Music Man: Nah. Missing you too much. I'd love to pick you up. Take you out. Spoil you. When will you let me do that, Belle?

Damn. He's asked to take me out a few times already, and I've avoided his requests each time.

And even though this wasn't part of the unspoken agreement, I appreciate that he saw me as more than just a sexual object. But I needed to find a way to tell him this wasn't going to happen. Even after my conversation with Destiney. All of that. I just… Yeah. My thoughts were all tangled up. In work, in family. And how he made me feel.

Just two nights ago, he texted me, asking if we could get together and do something. In my mind, I was screaming Yes! I would love to! Why wouldn't I? The way Sol listens when I speak, how in tune with me he is. He knew I was exhausted before I even said a word.

But I told myself I wanted something I could do without any commitment. No pressure. No expectations. I laid on my back with my phone in my hand, quickly typing away on the screen.

Me: You have a show tomorrow, right?

Music Man: Yep. Playing at HomeGrown. Can you get away tomorrow? I'd love to see you.

I waited a minute. Thinking. I wouldn't mind hearing the band.

Me: Going to try. I'll see if Mala can come with me.

That would do for now. It wasn't a no. And it was noncommittal, which was the best way to handle this. That was the issue. I wanted to let these reservations go, and they were free to go. To fucking hell. I already knew that letting myself fall into Sol the way I know I'm capable of falling, the way I know I want to fall… I would worry about who would hold things together when it all fell apart.

twenty-three

SOL

Have a great show man. Let's get up this weekend.

I reached out to Micah earlier, asking if he might have some spare time this weekend. I chuckled to myself because I knew I was asking a lot, especially these days. Micah spends every waking moment with his new wife, Destiney, which was totally fine with me. I loved that for him. It's been beautiful. Those two were made for each other, and my boy was gone behind her a long time ago. Micah said he could swing something, and I looked forward to chilling with him. Maybe we'd play ball or something. We had a few things to catch up on.

I tucked my phone back into my pocket after responding to Micah as the familiar sounds began to fill HomeGrown, layered with the usual buzz of anticipation. Glasses clinking. Murmurs of conversation. HomeGrown was a vibe. A great place to chill any day of the week.

There was music playing now, flowing through the speakers. Music was always playing here at HomeGrown. A few neo-soul tracks had been spinning, setting the mood. The energy felt great here. No doubt, we'd have a good show. We played Thursday and Friday nights, and it was always a blast. So, naturally, we attracted a crowd. I always enjoyed playing with the guys. It never felt like work or a chore. Smoke was something I was so damn proud of.

The guys and I had taken our places on the stage, but we still had about twenty minutes until showtime. As I got things situated, I looked out into the crowd of melanin faces, searching for one in particular, but I didn't see her. She said she would be here, so I knew she'd walk in any minute. I don't think she would have been a no-show.

I glanced at my watch, then at the doors, then at my watch again. Sixteen minutes. I was hoping for a moment to chat with her before the show, but if not, we'd have a break between sets.

Sol. You good? Why you keep looking at your watch?" Joe asked me, bringing me out of my thoughts. The guys in Smoke were like brothers, but Joe, our bass player, was more like an un-cle. The oldest in the band but cool as hell. Once he got in his groove, he was smoother than silk. That man stayed in the pocket. Joe and I always set up right beside each other, closer to the left rear of the stage.

"Yeah. Just seeing how much time we got."

He gave me a look. "You sure? I saw you kept looking at the door, too." His tone dripped with sarcasm. Joe was quiet, but he picked up more than he let on. Of all the guys in Smoke, I've known Joe the longest, and he was the very first person I asked to be part of this band.

I adjusted and readjusted the strap of my sax, trying in vain to occupy myself, but it didn't matter. I was a little nervous for some reason. India had seen me play. Here. Where we first met. And I've serenaded her on FaceTime many times. But tonight, I was feeling something else.

When the corner of my lip lifted, Joe's eyebrow went up, and I knew I was caught. He gave me a beat, "You waiting for someone." It wasn't a question. I was glad he wasn't blasting me in front of the other fellas. That wasn't his style anyway.

"I am." I turned toward the door again. "A special someone," I revealed, my smile was content, but it was there.

His eyebrows were high on his bald head. *"Oh?"*

I knew my answer had caught him off guard.

I hadn't been checking for anyone, not lately. Honestly, none of the guys in Smoke acted that way. That was the whole point. Smoke was curated by yours truly.

My boy Tim and his wife Janelle own the place. Tim handles the front of the house, and Janelle manages the kitchen.

People come for the food because Janelle can cook, but they come back for both the food and the music. Tim approached me, wanting an in-house band for HomeGrown. I understood the assignment, and by the time our conversation was over, I knew exactly who I would ask to join me. Thankfully, everyone I asked agreed. I hand-selected these musicians, not just for their talent. And make no mistake; they were very talented. These cats were some of the dopest, coldest musicians.

So. Fucking. Talented. These guys could play anything.

Any style of music.

By ear. By sheet.

Rehearsed. Cold.

And that's the thing. I've been in this industry for a long time.

So many guys are talented, but you couldn't work with them. Egos and shit.

Or they were messy. Moving foul. And I knew that was something to consider.

Tim was my boy. We've known each other for a long time. And this was a place of business. There was a certain level of decorum expected. The truth was, attractive women came in here all the time. Usually in groups.

Shit, they come in packs. Like harems. Laughing loudly, wearing tight ass dresses. Their chests out. Eyes scanning the stage, their intentions clear. Vying for the seats in the front. Hoping to catch someone's eye.

A wink. An invitation.

But none of the men in Smoke moved like that.

Every one of them had an old lady. Either very married or very committed. They all had families, and a few of them had babies at home. None of us moved thirsty, unlike some of the other bands I've seen.

These men were committed. On lock. Thriving on some grown man love. You could hear it in the way they played. There was stability there. Each of them had a muse inspiring them. And they were utterly lost in the grooves of the music because their hearts were content. As the lone single man of the group, I got the impression, a long time ago, that they wanted the same for me.

I felt my phone vibrate, so I quickly pulled it out, thinking maybe India was texting me.

Spence: Showtime confirmed! You'll see me. And don't embarrass the fam, cuz.

I smirked and shook my head before tucking my phone in my pocket. Typical of Spence. Always talking slick, as if we shared the same set of expectations. As if I had purposely carved out my own path miles away from their bougie ass world. A world I never really fit into anyway. I glanced at my watch. Twelve minutes. We always started on time. I looked at the door again and decided to put that thought aside for now.

Then it all happened at once. Joe asked me something, but I didn't catch it. Just as I looked away from the door, I saw her silhouette in my peripheral vision. I quickly turned my head back toward the entrance and saw India weaving gracefully through the tables in search of a seat. When Joe let out a low whistle, he temporarily broke the spell I was under.

"There she is." he said in jest. Joe chuckled. "No wonder you were so pressed."

DK held down the drums, and his tempo was the heartbeat of Smoke. He kept time as if it were sacred. It didn't matter if we were improvising or playing a set we'd rehearsed for hours. DK was set up close enough to hear Joe. He looked at Joe, then at me, and followed my line of sight.

"Okay, Sol. I see you," DK said, his voice low. Not to alert the other guys, I guess.

I didn't even care. I saw that India found a seat, and she wasn't alone. A young lady, whom I assume is her cousin, was settling in right beside her.

"You headed over? You have time." Joe asked.

I chuckled because I was way ahead of him. I had already taken the strap off my neck.

I made my way to their table, which was a bit further back. The best seats were already taken, but she'd still be able to hear the music just fine. As I approached India, my smile grew wider. She looked up and met my eyes just as I arrived.

"India. So glad you could come out tonight," I said, reaching for her hand and kissing it. I couldn't help myself. I wanted a hug, but I'd get one later.

"I'm glad too, Sol." Her smile was warm and relaxed.

She was dressed casually, wearing a pair of dark-washed jeans and a red blouse with a black blazer. She looked fresh-faced with bright red lipstick. Her lips were heart-shaped, soft, and kissable. India rocked some of the boldest lipsticks, and I loved that. Her warm brown complexion complemented each shade she wore.

"This is my cousin Maelle. Maelle. Solomon," India gestured between us.

"Nice to meet you. Been hearing so much about you, *Music Man*." She had a sly grin as I reached over to shake her hand.

I chuckled at that. "All great things, I hope. It's nice to meet you, too, cousin."

"Oh, absolutely." She gave me a knowing nod as we shook hands, smiling the whole time.

India shook her head playfully. "Wow, My. Okay. Just bust me out, why don't you?"

Maelle continued, "Word is you're super talented. I'm so excited to hear you guys."

"I just love to play," I shrugged. "The guys and I groove well together. I'm glad you could come out. Enjoy the show. The kitchen is open if either of you would like anything. Please, be my guest. I'll take care of it."

"Thank you, Sol."

"Thank you."

They returned in unison.

I glanced at my watch again. "Well. I'll need to get back up there." I lifted India's hand to my lips again. I'd since reclaimed it. I could smell a warm scent on her freshly showered skin. Whatever it was, it smelled incredible on her. A gourmand vanilla. It was lovely and complemented her body chemistry perfectly.

Talking directly to her now, I said, "We take a break between sets. At about half an hour. Will you be here so I can talk to you again?"

She'd given me her eyes.

My goodness, me. She was so beautiful.

She had that easy smile. Her hair, wild. Just the way I love it, framing her face. Large gold hoop earrings added the perfect touch.

Shit.

India was so damn sexy.

"Yes. I'll be right here. Watching you. Come by on your break." Her tone was sultry, as if she'd forgotten all about her cousin sitting right beside her.

As if it were only the two of us.

Alone.

Talking like we did in the quiet stillness of her bedroom, late into the evening hours.

Or early in the morning.

She sounded like she wanted to give herself to me. Right now. She was looking at me as if she wanted me to have her.

I sure as hell wanted her. And he knew what time it was. He was growing stiff. Right now. I stood there, my feet planted, my mind gone, enchanted by her. How long exactly, I have no idea. I still had her hand in mine, softly caressing her fingers. India had beautiful fingers. Long and slender. Just like the rest of her. I told her once that she had the perfect fingers to play piano and offered to teach her if she ever wanted to learn.

Someone behind me cleared their throat, snapping me out of the spell I was under. A spell I would gladly surrender to anytime. Any day of the week. Deadass.

"Professor A! About that time." The familiar voice laughed.

I chuckled. "Hey Lorenzo. You made it, I see." I gave him a fist bump with my other hand. I never let India's hand go.

"Been here! When you came off stage, I figured I'd say hello. I'm just a few tables over, here with my brother," he gestured toward a nearby table.

I nodded. "I'll have to meet your brother before the night is over."

"Sure thing." He lowered his voice. "And who are these lovely ladies?"

"Right. Forgive me." I turned back toward the table. "Lorenzo. This is India. She's special to me. She's been the one keeping me sane lately. And her cousin…"

"Maelle," she interrupted me before I could finish, offering her hand to Lorenzo.

"Pleasure to meet you, May-Elle." Her hand was in his within moments.

"*MY-Elle.* It's French. And it's nice to meet you, too."

"That's stunning. It really suits you."

My eyebrows raised, and I heard a faint chuckle pass from India's lips. I chuckled as well, shaking my head.

Returning my attention, I told her, "Indie. I'll be back at break, beautiful Artist Girl." I finally released her hand.

"Have a great show. Music Man."

By the time I was back on stage, all five of the guys were in position, and all ten eyes were searching for answers.

"What?" I pretended to be clueless as I put the strap of my alto sax around my neck.

Mikey, our lead guitarist, gave me a slow clap. "Gentlemen. Gentlemen. The lover boy returns."

The others cracked up, and I shook my head, laughing too despite myself. That comment didn't surprise me. Mike was a fool like that. Very charismatic. Always making us laugh. And always wearing sunglasses indoors, just because he could get away with it. And Mike could play that guitar.

Joe didn't even look up from tuning his bass. "My boy is in deep. Ya'll see that? Kept kissing her hand too."

James chuckled from the keys. He was the quiet one. Didn't say much, and sometimes you hardly noticed he was there. But once he started playing, there was no mistaking his presence.

James was awesome on the keys. His fingers could tell a whole damn story.

Joe continued, "You tell her we play requests?" The guys laughed again.

"Absolutely! Say the word, and we'll play something real sexy for you two lovebirds," Fresh offered with playful banter. Fresh handled vocals.

We called him *Fresh Prince* or *Fresh* for two reasons. He could sing his ass off, and his real name is Carlton. So, of course, we would call him Fresh.

"Love birds?" I asked. But I was full of shit, and they knew it.

All of them had incredulous expressions, and I couldn't hide my smile either. I felt good. India was here, and I was about to play with my bandmates. My boys. When they all laughed, I glanced back out toward the audience. Yeah. I was feeling something like that. They could see it. Of course. And I knew their banter was all in jest. All the fellas were cool. The six of us had been playing together for a few years. We'd become like a unit. Like a family. Chosen family. And Smoke wasn't just the name of the band; it was the vibe we carried.

A laid-back, rich, full-bodied sound that left an impression wherever it landed. It stayed with you long after the sound ended. And we vibed so easily with each other. Leaving space for each of us to shine individually, yet we blended cohesively like a well-known recipe. The six of us shared mutual respect and a deep love for the music. A brotherhood unlike anything else.

"Y'all finished or y'all done?" I asked with a friendly smile, shaking my head.

We shared a laugh, and everything felt right. I knew more questions would come later, and I would gladly share. I looked forward to telling them about my Artist Girl because I wanted her to be mine. More than anything else at the moment.

"Alright, Smoke. Showtime. Let's get it!" Fresh turned toward the crowd, taking the mic in his hand. *"What's happenin', Home Grown! Y'all looking good! You feeling good?"*

Cheers and applause erupted throughout the building. It was time. We had already prayed backstage. We always prayed before the show. Each of us was a man of faith. That's just how we did it.

We prayed for a great show and an enjoyable time playing together.

I wiped my hands, rolled my neck, and set the sax into position. DK counted us in, and we started right on time. Fresh let the lyrics flow out of his lips effortlessly.

"Breaking My Heart" by Mint Condition.

I looked out and found her. Yeah. I kept my eyes on her all night, and I could feel her watching me right back.

The alto saxophone sounded warm and pure, with just the right bite. I played a few instruments well, but the saxophone was my absolute favorite. Every time I raised it to play, I could see her. Watching me, as if she could hear something no one else could. I liked that. And I played for the room, but I felt it for her.

Smoke was mostly a cover band, but we played original tunes from time to time as well. Tonight, during our first set, we covered some classic R&B songs by Tony! Toni! Toné!, Bilal, and Prince. A typical set for us includes about six solid songs. Usually, we have a quick interlude and brief solo moments throughout.

James delivered a smooth solo during the intro of "Anytime" by Brian McKnight, highlighting his skill on the keys. Mike played a sharp riff on the lead guitar when that song shifted into "Get You" by Daniel Caesar. The crowd always loved it when we got to showcase our talents.

As we transitioned from one song to the next, Indie was the reason my solos stretched out a little longer. During "Ascension" by Maxwell, my Artist Girl was the main reason I stayed in the lower notes. Indie had me caught between discipline and desire.

Joe called it before I had to, when we hit the halfway point, "Aight, fellas. Let's take twenty," he said, stretching his hands out.

Fresh nodded, leaning into the mic. *"We'll be right back, ya'll. Take a breather, but don't go too far. Get a drink. Tip your bartender. Order a dessert. See you in twenty!"*

There was a mellow applause. The crowd was satisfied. We gave them just enough to think about, but not enough to fill them up. Not yet. We were just getting started. The opening set was always a slow burn. But the closing set would light up the whole room. We'd raise the temperature with some Neo-Soul and Jazz influences. That was the point. We liked to send everyone home on a high note. Put them in their feelings. Make them feel warm inside. Help them start the night right once they leave here.

After I took off my neck strap, I gently set my sax down. It was still warm all over. The other guys stepped off stage, leaving Joe and me.

"Go head," I looked up to find him already grinning. Like he knew my next move. "She's still sittin' there."

We laughed.

"You must be doing something right if she ain't left yet." he offered, still chuckling and wiping his brow with a towel. "Man, I've never seen you light up like this. You're smiling right now."

I shook my head, but my smile stayed. "You sound like somebody's auntie."

Joe guffawed and took a seat on his stool. "Listen. Ain't nothing wrong with letting yourself be happy. She's beautiful. And she seems good for you. Don't think I haven't noticed you moving different." He tossed back his water bottle, drinking nearly half of it.

Now I was curious. "What do you mean?"

He gave me an incredulous glare. "You know exactly what it means. I'm not mad at it. Glad to see you letting someone in."

I shrugged. But my expression was telling, I'm sure.

"Must be serious." Joe was grinning again. "You don't bring anyone around like that. Ever."

I nodded, revealing, "I like her." I looked over at India's table and offered a smile. She caught my eyes and smiled back. "She and I have been spending a lot of time together. I haven't felt this good in a while. She's solid."

Joe nodded and sincerely told me, "Don't mess it up."

I wore a silly grin now. "Not a chance."

After I took a generous sip from my water bottle, I headed her way. I had been waiting for this break, and I'd been thinking about what to say for the past thirty minutes. And India looked up as I approached. Her kissable lips curved into that easy smile before I reached her. And I swear… her smile had gravity to it.

"You good?" I asked, leaning in just enough. The playlist was going again, and "I Wanna Know" by Joe floated from the speakers.

She nodded. "I'm great." Her eyes met mine. "You all sound amazing."

"Thank you, Belle. Just doing my job."

Her delicate fingers wrapped around a glass of white wine. She took a sip, her eyelids fluttering slowly. *Fuck.* She was gorgeous.

Low and easy, I told her, "You're welcome to another glass. Whatever you're in the mood for. Stronger. Or sweeter. I'm taking care of you."

Her smile grew slowly. "Sweeter."

That one word did something to me. "You got it, baby. I'll go handle that for you right now."

"Thank you."

"Sure thing." I furrowed my brows, looking around. "Your cousin leave?"

India giggled, gesturing toward the back of the lounge where some high-top tables were, and another set of doors leading to an outdoor patio. "She's been chatting with Lorenzo all night."

I looked over and saw them sitting close together on one of the plush velvet sofas, side by side, clearly deep in conversation as if no one else existed.

"Ah." We laughed.

"So. A glass of sweet wine. Can I get you anything else? The red velvet cake here is to die for."

India smiled. "Sounds marvelous. Maybe next time. The wine will do for now."

I nodded. Then, "We've got one more set, Artist Girl. Can you stay?"

"I wouldn't miss it."

I nodded again. Pleased. "Good." I let my eyes scan her. When I looked back at hers, she held my gaze for a moment. Locked onto mine.

India didn't look anywhere else. Maintaining eye contact, she took another sip of her wine. Then, before I could stop it, "Come by tonight. I'll take you home." Fell right from my lips.

I didn't regret what I said, and I didn't phrase it as a question. It was more of a suggestion. But really, it was a plea. A request. Low and easy. And honestly, I didn't expect her to say yes. I'd asked her before. More than once. And India would deflect. In a playful, noncommittal way.

But not this time. She didn't hesitate at all. She kept her eyes on mine as she said, "Okay."

And, for a second, a very brief second, it caught me off guard. I guess she was in a good mood. Hell, maybe she just finally felt like agreeing. I didn't know, but either way, I wasn't going to question it.

I nodded, grinning. "Sounds good." Trying my damndest to play it smooth. But something warm was brewing in my chest. "Hold on to that smile for me, Artist Girl. Let me grab that wine for you."

♪♥♫♥♪

"Hey Laney. A sweet red, please. Roscato is perfect if you have that. Thank you. And I'll have an Old Fashioned. Neat."

I'd been standing at the bar for just a few minutes when someone nudged my shoulder lightly.

"Nice set."

I turned toward the familiar voice and met the green eyes of my older cousin.

"Spencer." I gave him a fist bump. He held a tall glass of bourbon in his other hand. Just that quickly, his eyes were casually scanning the room, lingering a little too long on the women.

Typical.

"Solomon. Good to see you. You're looking great."

"We can't all be like you, but I try."

He smirked as he kept scanning the room.

"Didn't expect to see you here. Slumming among us commoners."

His chuckle was low. "I like to get away from the same faces." I saw his eyes flick toward a table not far from us, where a few attractive ladies laughed over their drinks. "Sometimes good scenery is worth the drive." Nope. I didn't miss the implication there.

I gave him a beat. "Where's your wife? Kennedi know you're down here basking in the scenery?"

160

He looked at me, smirking. That practiced, politician-in-training façade he'd worn since we were in our early twenties.

He swirled the amber contents of his glass, then sipped. "She knows where I am." He looked past me again. "She always knows where I am."

It's crazy too because he wasn't even defensive about it, just matter-of-fact, as if it were part of some contract.

Wild.

I sighed softly. "She signed up for this open secret stuff. Right."

His confident smile never faltered, but Spencer's jaw clenched. "You're about to lecture me now, cousin? I'm not one of your students." He took another sip of his bourbon. The soft hum of conversation and music filled the space around us.

I decided not to humor him. It was rhetorical anyway.

Spencer's mother and my mother are sisters, making him my first cousin. He's a year older than I am, and even though we were raised together, we couldn't be more different.

And Spencer is biracial. My uncle comes from a wealthy Italian family in New York.

Like me, Spencer had been groomed for legacy.

A private education. Double Ivy League for undergrad and Law school. Then he got into real estate, and now he was moving in political circles. Spencer fully embraces that bougie world of keeping up appearances. He is fully committed to the affluent, polished world of doing everything "acceptable."

Oh, and he's recently married to a woman who ticks all the boxes on paper. Pedigree, education, a respectable career, and very pretty. But from where I'm sitting, their marriage is dry. They hardly speak to each other. There's no spark. Just looks and status. I'd like to think Spencer wanted passion at some point. But somewhere along the way, he convinced himself it wasn't important. I couldn't disagree more. I saw Spencer's dull, passionless life a long time ago, and I vowed never to end up stuck in that situation.

Glenn Lewis' "Don't You Forget It" played just as I accepted my Old Fashioned. I offered a thank you, taking a small sip. I looked over my shoulder to where India was sitting. Her legs were crossed, and she was leaning back in her chair now, looking beautiful and relaxed. Her long, slender fingers brushed her now empty glass, waiting patiently for me to return.

I'm coming, baby.

He was mid-lift of his glass, and I could see Spencer's movements still. His eyes drifted past me and lingered there. Then, a subtle smirk curved his lips. "Speaking of scenery…" I regarded him silently. As soon as the bartender set the wine down, I nodded, carefully gathering both glasses.

"Who is that?" His tone was sharp with inquiry.

No reason to turn around; I already knew. "My business," is what I offered. I looked him in the eye, knowing there was more. There's always more with Spencer. First of all, he was smug as hell, and he tended to be nosy and dismissive.

He released a quiet, knowing laugh. "Mmm. Pretty. Real pretty." His eyes stayed fixed on her. Hungry but restrained. The way rich men master. "Wouldn't have thought you'd go for the hippie bohemian type. But damn, cousin." Spencer whistled softly. "She's worth breaking the mold for."

I narrowed my eyes. "Eyes up, Spence."

He chuckled for a while, clearly amused by the whole situation. It wasn't actually that funny. He finally looked away from her. "Relax, man. I'm married, remember?"

I glared at him. "You've been married. That shit never made a difference."

He raised his glass in a weak ass mock surrender, still smirking. He couldn't deny the truth. We shared another moment of eye contact. Hearing an offhanded comment wasn't anything new. Lately, Spencer has been really coming down on me about the Noelle situation, which wasn't a situation at all. *"You've had your fun, cousin. It's time to do what's expected."* Annoying shit like that.

"So, you're really not gonna tell me who that is? I saw you talking earlier. You two looked pretty close."

"I told you. That's my business."

"It's my business too when I'm here cheering you on as the family golden boy and you're keeping company with another woman. A woman who isn't Noelle."

"India."

"India? That's her name?" He had a sly ass smirk now. "She is… stunning. Claudia had you messed up for a long time. I figured it would take someone rare to pull you out of that... But come on, Solomon. You know where this will lead."

I carefully turned both drinks in my hand to head back. "Yup. This will lead exactly where I want it to lead."

"You know your mother won't approve."

"She doesn't have to." I locked eyes with him again. I was unbothered. Cool as a cucumber. "Appreciate you coming. Now. Excuse me."

I commenced my stroll back to her table.

Spencer was right on my heels.

"You going to introduce me? Or..." His brow was raised. His lip curled with amusement. "That's off limits too?"

I exhaled, slow and measured. Past irritated. "Why? So you can look twice as hard while you're up close?"

He laughed. "Just being polite. Pretty girl like that. Got all my little cousin's attention. This is someone I have to meet."

I gave him a look.

I knew this news would hit the press by morning. I didn't care. I was planning to talk to my mother about India during dinner on Sunday anyway.

"Come on," I offered reluctantly.

We headed toward the table. They would have to meet each other eventually. I planned to keep India around.

But I know Spencer. He wasn't slick. There's no way he would pass up the chance to meet a beautiful woman. A woman he doesn't even have a shot with. Still, Spencer prides himself on charm and connections. And his annoying ass commentary.

I believe Spencer cares about me… in his own condescending, self-appointed big brother kind of way. I'd introduce them, but with boundaries. He's family. But I know my cousin's habits.

And wandering eyes. Married or not.

Fucking weirdo.

twenty-four

INDIA

I'd had such a great time at Homegrown tonight. I'm so glad I went.

I wasn't even tripping over Mala ditching me. We'd catch up later. Yeah. But HomeGrown was a whole vibe. A whole grown folks vibe. I loved the energy there. I loved the crowd. Everyone was just chilling, looking to have a good time.

Mala and I shared a basket of potato wedges, and they had to be the best potato wedges I've ever had. They had a light peppery batter I'd never tasted before, fried to perfection with a light crunch. There was a sprinkle of freshly grated Parmesan cheese and chives on top. The insides were fluffy, and there a house sauce that paired perfectly with them. It was creamy, tangy, and had just the right kick of spices. I was really curious about its ingredients.

The band sounded fantastic! Tonight was my third time visiting, and they keep getting better each time I hear them. There are five musicians plus a lead singer, and everyone is incredibly talented. I had the chance to meet all of them before Sol and I left for the night. They are such nice guys. Sol said he's great friends with each of them.

I met Sol's cousin right before the band had to get back on stage for their closing set. And that was... *interesting.* First of all, my Spidey Senses went off immediately. I don't know why, but he gave me the ick.

My eyes landed on Sol as they both approached the table.

"Artist Girl," he greeted me with a smile as he gently placed a glass of red wine in front of me, then claimed the space right beside me. I felt his hand lightly graze the small of my back, and I was hip to his unspoken, unmistakable signal.

Sol spoke in a cool, casual tone, "This is Spencer. My cousin." He paused briefly, "He wanted to meet you."

Ah. Okay. I knew my senses were right. I was way ahead of him.

Keeping my expression friendly and my voice polite, I said, "Nice to meet you."

Spencer extended his hand. "Pleasure's mine. I've heard a lot about you."

"Oh?" I asked softly, curiosity in my voice. Glancing at Sol, I added, "Can't say the same."

Spencer didn't miss a beat, chuckling. "Well then, I suppose I'll need to make a great first impression. The first impression is the lasting impression."

Okay, he's charming. I could tell Spencer was quite sure of himself. He reminded me of Brandon, his archetype to a T. Eww.

I could smell his cockiness. And it was a foul ass odor.

He was handsome. Sure. Not that I was looking at him that way.

But men like him? Hell no. Brandon fucked that up.

And Sol stayed close. I knew he needed to get back on stage soon, but his hand was still on my lower back, making it clear. And I was okay with that.

I was not available. And I get the impression that men like Spencer got whatever women he went after.

"Thank you for the wine." I softly told Sol, taking a sip. I loved it. Nice and sweet.

And it felt good to have him so close, right here. Just like this. Yeah.

"You're so welcome, Belle," he replied, rubbing up and down my back. He kissed the top of my head, into my mass of curls. I know Sol. He probably took a deep inhale, too. He always says how much he loves the scent of my hair. The texture and the color. I have natural highlights that love to show themselves in the summertime. But Sol loves my hair. Especially because it's mine. He'd actually told me that before.

I cast a subtle glance at Spencer, and he was watching our every move without shame. I knew he was taking mental notes and probably would have a series of interrogating questions for Sol later.

When Sol introduced him to me, he was just vague enough to leave a few questions unanswered. I figured Spencer was the type who liked to know everything. He smelled like money, had that smug attitude, and a sense of entitlement to match.

I looked at his left hand and noticed the bare strip of skin on his ring finger. It was just light enough to leave an imprint that confirmed my suspicions.

I flicked my eyes up, and he was already looking at me. He sipped something amber from his glass with a flirty grin.

Wow.

I schooled my features quickly enough to remain unbothered.

"Well, it's nice to meet you. Did you forget something tonight, or...?"

Disarmed, Spencer's grin faded. His brows furrowed. He met my eyes, and I looked at his bare ring finger.

He chuckled. His recovery was smooth. He's probably a smooth ass talker too, talking his way in and out of anything.

"Ah. You're sharp. I like that."

Fucking creep.

I brought my glass back to my lips and took a sip. Then, evenly, "I bet your wife would too."

In my peripheral vision, I saw Sol take a sip of his drink. I glanced at him, and he was fighting a grin but winked at me.

Spencer chuckled again, not missing a thing. The tightness around his eyes gave him away, though. Oh well.

And then Sol murmured quietly enough for only me to hear, "My Belle ain't here for the games."

Damn right I wasn't.

Sol had to get back on stage, so after promising to return as soon as the set was over, he and Spencer walked away.

I texted Mala and asked her to come back to our table at some point. I'd be leaving with Sol, but we needed to check in with each other first. When she came over, I asked what her plans were for the night. She was coy as hell at first, but eventually said she planned to go straight home. I wasn't worried about her. Mala is a good girl, through and through. Smart. Mature. Most of all, she didn't have any reason to lie to me. She wouldn't. I knew we'd catch up later. And I knew she'd have a bunch of questions for me since I'd be going with Sol tonight.

The second set lasted about forty minutes. They finished by nine-thirty. After that, Sol and I walked Mala to her car. There was still a decent crowd even after Smoke finished on stage. Home-Grown stayed open until eleven on Thursday nights, and the kitchen remained open until ten. Music was still playing, and the bar was still open as well.

When we got to Sol's car, he put his saxophone in the trunk.

"Where's your tote?" he asked me, teasing.

"She's not here. Wasn't invited to the show." We chuckled.

"I'm almost not used to seeing you without her."

Sol didn't know it, but these days I don't always have her with me. I walk much more now without reliable transportation, and it's a lot of extra weight to carry. After Sol closed the trunk, he turned to me, his smile easy and his arms out. "Can I have my hug now, Artist Girl?"

"You may." I willingly went into his arms. It felt so good.

I heard a faint moan, and I couldn't tell if it was him or me. It didn't even matter. I'm sure we shared the same feelings.

"So, you're coming with me?" His arms wrapped around me warmly and securely as he spoke in my ear. We weren't far apart. I'm 5'9. I'd say Sol is 6'1.

"I am," I said. My arms wrapped around his neck as I pulled myself closer, pressing into him. And we stood there. Body to body.

"I'm juiced."

I let out a soft giggle. "Are you?"

"I'm juiced and squeezed."

"Wow." My giggle turned into full-blown laughter. "Me too." And I was. I had two glasses of wine, and I still felt a light buzz.

And yeah. I was feeling good for several reasons. Being in his space. Knowing we'd spend more time together. The mystery of what was to come being in his territory. I wouldn't have the home court advantage tonight.

All of that was a turn on. So damn exciting. I could kiss him right now, especially since we're alone. But we've never kissed outside of a sexual setting. Maybe we'll kiss later. I love his kisses.

Whether Sol and I became more than friends or not, he was such a dope ass person to be around. The chillest person you could possibly spend time with. And my comfort was his top priority. Once that was straight, he was all about making me happy. Mind. Body. Spirit.

"Ready to roll, Belle?" he asked, bringing me back from my thoughts.

"Yes. I'm ready."

"Alright."

He had my hand in his as we walked around his car to the passenger side. He opened the door and closed it softly once I was seated and settled.

Brandon never opened my door.

And. something else occurred to me.

I'd be here all night if I kept track of everything Sol did that Brandon didn't do.

I should stop now because it's obvious who the winner is.

Another question I had was, why the fuck won't I give Sol a chance?

twenty-five

INDIA

"Make yourself at home. I'm going to change out of this shirt, and I'll be right back."

"Alright."

Sol walked down his hallway, leaving me in the living room of his house.

We'd just walked in the door, and he offered me a seat on his ridiculously comfortable couch. It wasn't even that late, but I could knock out on this couch. His deep black velvet sectional was so plush and comfortable, broken-in just enough, yet still had some firmness and spring to it.

I looked around, unable to believe I was really here. Even though I'd never been before, the energy and vibe felt both new and familiar at the same time. Solomon's home matched his quiet, soulful energy perfectly. The rustic, charming décor reflected his taste. I'd only stepped through the front door, but even in his wood-paneled sunken seating living area, his touch and finger-prints were everywhere my eyes landed.

I'd been through Greenhaven before. It isn't too far from Oak Park. However, it's a bit off the beaten path, so I don't visit often. I've delivered commissioned artwork here once or twice. Greenhaven has a classic suburban charm and is one of Sacra-mento's most desirable neighborhoods.

Sol lived deep in Greenhaven. The sun had set long ago, and even in the evening hours, I could see that his home was tucked into a well-established neighborhood. Beautiful homes. Mostly ranch style, but I'd seen quite a few mid-century designs as we drove in. It was a world away from the tiny urban bungalow-style houses in Oak Park.

Yeah. You can see the money. Old money. These houses are likely to stay in the families for generations. Worth over six hundred thousand or more. Mature trees line each block. Evening walks around here are probably serene. Curved driveways. Brick or stucco exteriors. Some homes have been updated with new windows and fresh paint. But most still retain their original charm.

Sol's was a classic. A single-story brick mid-century with a low roofline. Two-car garage. A large front yard, a long driveway, and a deep-set porch. Neatly trimmed hedges in the front. The inside was clean. Very tidy. I loved the original hardwood floors.

There was a fireplace against the furthest wall in his living area. It was a stonework fireplace from another era, but it still worked. In the corner, there was an upright piano. Built-in bookshelves held music books, textbooks, some Black classic titles, and a few trinkets tastefully arranged on the shelves. These included souvenirs from his worldly travels, a few awards of recognition, and framed Black art.

Yeah. There was warmth in Solomon's home. Not flashy, which wasn't his style. But it felt lived in and well-loved, I could tell. No. This was no bachelor pad. Not even close. That made me curious. I wondered if he'd lived with a woman before. Here.

I didn't see a woman's touch. Not really. The colors were dark with warm hues. But this was a family home, just like the others on his tree-lined block. I get the feeling Sol can find respite here if he seeks peace and space. There was plenty of both, but not in an extravagant way. It was warm, cozy, and perfect.

"What time will you need to be home, Cinderella?" Sol asked from behind me, bringing me out of my thoughts.

"That's cute."

We laughed.

"I'm a grown woman, Solomon. Remember?"

"Don't I know it." He walked around the sectional and took a seat beside me. He sat close, and our thighs touched. "Didn't know if you needed to check on your parents or if you want to get in at a decent hour. It's already past ten."

I nodded. My smile was easy. He held my gaze as I said, "Appreciate you. They're fine. And I can chill for a while longer. I'll let you know." I'd already told them I wouldn't be home tonight, right after Sol asked me to come here, and they'd gone to bed.

He didn't realize it yet, but I planned to stay the night finally. I didn't have a bag packed… but he'd asked a few times.

So. Why not? I'm sure he had something I could sleep in.

"Alright." Sol nodded too. "Can I show you around? I'd like you to feel comfortable here."

I was still smiling. "Sure."

He took my hand, and we intertwined our fingers at the same time.

"The kitchen is straight ahead. I have an enclosed deck back there."

It was an open kitchen with a retro style and tile countertops. To me, retro kitchens feel warm and homey. The bright white tile and dark gray grout on the countertops extended to the backsplash. It looked great with his white cabinets. The counters weren't cluttered, with just a few modern appliances. There was a breakfast nook by an oversized window. I loved that. Just past the sliding glass door, there was a modest-sized backyard.

We descended the hallway from an entrance just off the kitchen. "Restroom right down here to your left. My bedroom is at the end of the hall. These are guest rooms." He gestured as we passed a few doors.

It wasn't a flashy house, but I loved everything about it.

It was so him. I felt a sense of serenity in his space. I could tell that everything in his home had a meaning and a place. Just off the main living area, we stopped at a set of double glass doors.

Somehow, I missed these the first time. He opened them to invite me in, and as we crossed the threshold, the air inside shifted. He flicked the switch, lighting up a vintage lamp in the corner. The light was softer here, like amber. The space had a faint sandalwood smell. It didn't smell bad, not at all. More vintage, almost like the scent you'd find in an antique shop or something. But I could smell hints of incense wafting on top.

Then, I took in everything around me. Sol had a music collection I couldn't believe. Shelves lined the walls, and they were packed.

Jazz. Blues. Billie Holiday, Nina Simone, Charles Mingus, Etta James. R&B and soul, both classic and modern. Aretha Franklin, Donny Hathaway, Marvin Gaye, Sade, D'Angelo, Jill Scott, Maxwell, Brandy, Jazmine Sullivan, Cleo Sol.

There were pop and crossover icons: Michael Jackson, of course; Whitney Houston; Beyoncé; Prince; Rihanna; Amy Winehouse; Janet Jackson; Adele; Bruno Mars.

Hip hop giants: Lauryn Hill, Kendrick Lamar, Nas, Missy Elliott, A Tribe Called Quest, J. Cole. I mean, so many others.

Alternative or indie artists who have had a global influence. Lianne La Havas, Sudan Archives, Corinne Bailey Rae, Fela Kuti, Esperanza Spalding, and Moses Sumney.

On vinyl. CDs. Cassette tapes.

Gospel. Both new and old. Walter Hawkins Singers, The Clark Sisters, Bebe and CeCe Winans. Commissioned. The Chicago Mass Choir, Georgia Mass Choir, Mississippi Mass Choir. Tye Tribbett. Yolanda Adams. Jonathan McReynolds.

There were crates stacked neatly against the wall with even more vinyl records. And crates of additional CDs. Cassette tapes were stacked carefully on a top shelf, handwritten labels showing their contents.

No doubt, this collection was carefully curated. It was probably something he'd grown over many years. There had to be hundreds of different pieces of music. It was incredible.

This music spanned across genres. I had never seen such an eclectic collection in one place before. It was extensive. The only other place would have been a music store. When those were a thing.

The music was neatly shelved and arranged in some way. I couldn't quite say how. It seemed Sol knew exactly where everything was. He moved toward the CDs, searching for something specific.

No. This wasn't junk like the stuff you'd see piled up in a garage, long forgotten. This was a cherished collection that Sol clearly still enjoyed listening to. There were two well-worn armchairs against the wall. Low and cushioned. A coffee table sat right in front of them. A music book sat open and undisturbed. Just as he'd left it. A few more music books sat on the shelves here, too. And a few worn spiral notebooks.

I stepped closer, taking in more of the artists. Too many to name. Some I hadn't heard of. Some were household names. Some I had completely forgotten about.

Quite a few soundtracks: The Wiz, The Preacher's Wife, The Best Man, Poetic Justice, Soul Food.

This collection was so impressive and inspiring. Music was his passion. It's one thing to be a musician, but I don't know anyone who lived and breathed music the way Sol did.

There was soulful, abstract art hanging. I noticed a ceramic incense holder on a small side table. It was one of a kind, surely handmade and painted in blues and greens.

Two black cases sat against the wall. One shaped like a violin, the other like a saxophone case. An acoustic guitar rested in a stand.

A window faced his front yard. The room was a decent size, nearly big enough to serve as both a master bedroom and an office. It was a space dedicated to all things music.

"This is where my restored stereo system lives," he said, bringing me from my thoughts.

"Teachme" by Musiq began to fill the room, with a warm, big sound. Clear as a bell.

Damn.

This entire album is fire. All of his albums have been. Did he know what the fuck he was doing? I love Musiq.

I turned to him as he came and stood beside me.

"She plays everything. Records, CDs, tapes. The radio still comes through nice and clear... Mostly." He chuckled at that.

I eyed the beauty. It reminded me of a much simpler time. We all had something like this in our homes once upon a time. The stereo system was black with a wood panel finish. A turntable. Twin cassette decks. A 5-CD changer. AM/FM radio tuner.

"Wow." I was in awe. I hadn't seen one of these in years. "Where'd you find this?"

"Yard sale. Years back. Completely by chance. I was heading home from a gig across town and took the scenic route back. I passed through a neighborhood I'd never been to before. And they had a few things for sale out front. I took one look, and I had to have it. Crazy because I'd been looking for something, but I never quite found what I was looking for. And I know they sell modernized systems. But it wasn't what I wanted."

I nodded and said, "That's amazing! Was it working when you found it?"

He cracked up, shaking his head. "Hardly. But I spent months working on her, taking my time with careful hands… restoring her, piece by piece. Replaced the belt on the turntable, cleaned the needle, swapped most of the wires, and oiled the wood…" He shrugged. "Didn't know what I was doing, but I was determined to bring her back to life." He smiled with pride. "She's just like new."

I smiled too.

And we remained silent for a few moments as Musiq serenaded us, talking about the need to learn the best way to love his woman and sincerely asking her to teach him how.

Lately, these songs… I must be crazy because I swear, they all seem to be speaking to me.

Directly. About my feelings and my dilemma. I knew Sol would teach me how to love him, and he'd happily and gracefully learn how to love me… if I teach him. Yeah. Shit is getting out of control. Maybe I should not have come here. And I don't mean in a messy way, not at all, like my feelings. It's like I can't fight them anymore. What a difference a day makes. Here in Sol's home, surrounded by the peaceful, dope energy he gives off, I found myself overwhelmed with emotions. I'm terrified because I feel like I'm losing control, but I don't even want to stop. I like him. More than I intended. I feel very strongly for him, like it's becoming more than just liking, beyond the physical connection.

Sol is such a good guy. The way he sees me, listens to me, notices when I'm off, and asks about Ma and Daddy. He makes it so easy to just be with him. And I want him. *God, I want him*. So much that it hurts. It breaks my heart because I know he wants me too, and not just physically. He wants to be with me, and I can feel it because I want that too. And I could cry. Because I can't. I can't commit to that; I'm afraid to. I don't want to let him down. He doesn't deserve to get only parts of me. I wouldn't want to be with him like this. That's what happened with Brandon. Sol deserves someone who's ready, without damage. And Brandon was still calling me, convinced he could spin the block with me. I did dip back, twice. But then Sol happened and… nope. Brandon and I are done.

And the more time I spent getting to know Sol and him getting to know me, the more I realized Brandon never saw me. He didn't care to. He wanted me to fill the role he thought I should be. Someone who was his pretty, quiet trophy. Brandon was a different kind of mess. Solomon only wanted me to be myself. If only things had been different. All this caution would have been blown in the wind a long ass time ago, and I'd be on a fucking cloud somewhere, letting my man love on me the way I've dreamed about. A love so deep it's almost indescribable. Those feelings would carry me wherever they wanted to take me, high above this place.

A black-and-white poster of Quincy Jones hung on the wall above the stereo system. Next to it, I noticed degrees hanging. One was significantly larger than the other two. When I looked closer, my jaw dropped.

"You're a doctor?"

"Yeah." He said it so casually.

Humble swag man.

"Okay… why am I just now learning this about you?"

I was shocked. We've talked about so many things. I knew he was college-educated. He taught at a community college. But he never mentioned this detail.

He shrugged. "I don't know. Guess we just haven't talked about it yet."

"I'm really intrigued. What type of doctor are you?"

"I hold a doctorate in music, specifically in Ethnomusicology."

"Wow, Sol. That's so interesting. Can you tell me more about Ethnomusicology? That's a new term for me," I pressed, smiling.

He smiled too. "Absolutely. Ethnomusicologists study the relationship between music and culture, and the ways music functions within different societies and communities around the world."

"I see. That must have taken a lot of effort. I really respect academics. I know it wasn't easy."

"Thank you, Belle. It definitely wasn't. I just finished recently. Graduated a few months ago."

"I had no idea! Congratulations!"

"Thank you."

"Any big plans now that you've achieved this? Any major career moves coming up soon?"

He had a heavy sigh, and my interest was piqued.

"I mean, not particularly. I enjoy teaching at community college. Maybe someday, but... I'd have less time to pursue my music full-time. So, a few things factor into that."

"Sure. I get it. I enjoy working as an independent artist, but it definitely has its pros and cons." I decided to leave it there. I wasn't about to ruin this mood. It was lovely.

"It definitely does."

"So. I have to ask. Of all these artists..." I lifted my arms, gesturing around us. "Who's your favorite?"

Sol thought that was so funny. "That isn't a fair question, Belle. Come on." He cracked up."

I joined him after a while. I guess he had a point.

"Thinking Bout You" by Frank Ocean floated around us as I said, "Give me your Mount Rushmore. All-time top five." I finally reasoned with him.

"That's a little better. But top five of all time? Man…" He placed his hand on his chin in thought. "Okay. Quincy Jones for sure. Just because he did so much. He composed, arranged, produced, conducted, scored. He was a talented musician in his own right, and he put so many other artists in the game. He's a legend. Rest his soul."

I nodded.

"So I have four left..." he grinned at me. "I'm going to get you back somehow, Artist Girl! Gonna ask you an impossible question just like this one."

We laughed.

"I know it's tough. My favorites can shift depending on the day or my mood."

"Right. Glad you understand the predicament you put me in!"

We laughed again.

"Well. How about I share the artists I've been listening to lately?"

"Okay, sure!"

"Alright. First, OutKast. They meant a lot to me when I was younger, especially in my teens and early twenties. I was an outcast. Different. I loved the way they expressed themselves artistically, especially Andre. They just seemed to get it, with an 'I don't give a fuck attitude.'"

I nodded. "For sure. I like them too. And I can relate to that. Feeling like an outcast." We'd talked about that at length.

"Miles Davis. He's the reason I love jazz music so much. He's incredible. When I was younger, I used to try to play the trumpet like he did," Sol laughed. "I love Queen. They were ahead of their time for sure, but so much of their music is still very much alive today. Still. And that's how you know it's good music. It transcends generations. And... I'll go with someone newer for my fifth; I like Elmiene. That cat is cold. He's young and has so much ahead of him. His future is so bright it's blinding. He's got great energy. I've watched a lot of his interviews. Mad respect for that guy."

"Oh, I like him too! I watch his Tiny Desk a lot." I gushed.

"Love Tiny Desk."

"Me too!"

"I'm grabbing a drink. Can I get you anything?" Sol asked me after a moment. The music was still playing. I knew it was coming from his CD changer because I could hear the shifting of drives. A sound I haven't heard in years.

"Is there tea?

"Yeah. Follow me."

We could hear the music just as clearly in the kitchen. He must have had some speakers placed throughout his house.

"I have a few herbal teas." He pulled a canister down from his cabinet. Removing the lid, he slid it over to me. Then he filled his kettle with fresh water.

"That's perfect. Thank you."

"Thank you for agreeing to come by," he told me, holding my eyes for a moment.

I smiled at him. "I'm glad I did."

We returned to the living area with our warm mugs in hand. I sat down on his couch. Sol set his mug on the coffee table.

"Excuse me for a quick second, Belle. Going to turn this lamp off." He padded over to the music room and quickly returned.

"I love your place, Sol. It's so cozy. And so, you," I told him once he took a seat beside me on the sectional. We sat facing each other, my leg propped under me. There wasn't much space between us, and I could touch his knee without reaching far.

"Thank you. It's home, and I feel blessed to spend so much time here. Between lesson planning and gigs, I'm often composing and arranging, which has been great. But mostly, I'm a homebody anyway."

"Yeah. Me too." I took a sip of my tea. It was black, with sugar, cinnamon, and a splash of whole milk. It was a nice cup. "I think about how nice it must be to have your own space. I've never had my own space. I've always lived with my parents. It's part of my culture since I'm not married... And I love them. And I appreciate them... but it's a bit much sometimes.

He nodded, allowing me to continue.

"I used to spend the night with Destiney sometimes, just for some privacy. But she got married, so..."

We laughed.

"Isn't it great, though? I'm juiced for my boy! So happy for them."

"Me too! I couldn't be happier for Destiney. Micah is so great for her. They belong together."

"They sure do."

I took another sip of my tea. Sol took a few generous gulps of his. And that love-and-marriage talk had me thinking. Though Sol and I talk a lot, on the phone and through text, there's still so much about him I don't know. I feel like he knows a lot more about me. I wondered why he shut off specific topics. And I wanted to get to know him better.

"You're a mystery, Music Man," I told him, taking another sip.

"A mystery? Am I?" he asked earnestly, raising his eyebrows.

"Hell yeah, you are. I mean, when it comes to your past relationships. I don't feel like I know much about you. It seems like you know everything about mine. But. You've been really private about those details."

He shrugged. "It's nothing personal, Belle. I don't like to dwell on any of that. It's in my past for a reason. I'm a forward thinker."

I nodded, absentmindedly swirling my tea. "I get that, I guess it's just… I feel like it would give me perspective, and maybe if I had that, I'd have a better understanding of you. The moments that made you who you are now."

He nodded, then finally said, "That's fair." He lightly sighed. "How about we take turns asking each other questions. Ask me anything you want to know."

"Sure."

"And we have to answer them honestly."

"Of course."

"And anyone who asks must also answer the same question."

"No problem. I'm an open book." I returned eagerly.

We both had a chuckle.

"You ready Music Man?" I asked him, teasing.

"Let's do it."

"Alright." I took a long sip of my tea, then set it down on the coffee table.

"What would you like to know?" he volleyed.

"Hmm …ooh, I know what I want to ask! Tell me about your first kiss!" I was so giddy for some reason.

Sol's brows furrowed, then raised. "Uh… " he shrugged, laughing. "It was awkward. Not much to tell."

"I mean, of course it was!" I chuckled as well. "But go ahead and tell me more. How old were you? Who was the girl?"

He nodded. "Okay. My first kiss was in seventh grade. Her name was Skylar."

"Skylar…that sounds… *suburban.*" I wondered if she was white.

I didn't have to wonder long.

Sol chuckled at that. "Definitely suburban. She was white."

My jaw dropped. My eyes wide. "White! Oh shit! *Really?*"

He shrugged.

"I didn't know you date white girls. Why am I here?" My mood shifted immediately. I don't know why. But it did. And Sol picked up on it.

"Hey, Belle, what's going on? You good?" He asked with care.

"Damn Sol. I mean…I'm everything a white girl *is not.*"

I never would have thought. I didn't get that vibe from him. They have a vibe, and that's just it. Especially those who exclusively date white.

"Got damn right." He said without missing a beat. "You absolutely are. And I *did.*"

"Did what?"

"I *did* date a couple of white girls. I haven't in several years. Literally. I love black women. I always have. There's nothing quite like a beautiful black queen. But when I was younger, the black girls didn't like me back." He shrugged again. "They never gave me a chance."

"Get out of here." I couldn't imagine why not. He answered my unspoken question.

"Dead ass. Not smooth enough, I guess." He shrugged again. "I was into different things."

"Hmm."

"I went to school mostly with white kids, and the few black girls there weren't checking for me. As much as I liked them, I was too different. The white girls liked me, and they're the girls I grew up around."

I had a subtle nod.

"Make no mistake. Artist Girl. *I love black women.* The reciprocated attention didn't start till closer to the end of high school."

Sol was matter-of-fact. I knew he was speaking honestly. And. I could relate to that to some extent.

I faced similar challenges. Hearing, *"You're not really black,"* the second I arrived back on American soil. I was constantly reminded how different I was from the other black girls. And when I replied without pause that, *"Yes, I am."* There was always a rebuff.

"We all had a glow up." I offered.

"Yeah."

We were silent for a beat.

"You good now?" Sol pressed with an ounce of sarcasm.

I shook my head, laughing. And kind of embarrassed, I guess. That shit was a touchy subject. To me it was.

"Yeah. I'm good."

"Good. Now. Tell me about *your* first kiss."

I smiled right away. "Kieran. My very first boyfriend, when I was fourteen, kissed me on the way home from school. Right under my grandmother's almond tree."

"Fourteen? You were in Berbice?"

"I was," I said. Smiling. He remembered that detail. And that was Sol's M.O., the little things I mentioned in passing… he remembers those things. It was incredibly sweet. "This was right before we moved back."

"I see. Awkward?"

"Oh, you know it!" We laughed. "But it was a perfect first kiss. I wasn't half bad."

"Oh, I'm sure."

We laughed some more.

"Tell me about your first love," I volleyed. "Since you know about mine." I'd told him about Amir. Everything.

Sol's demeanor shifted. There was a heavy sigh.

"My first love. Claudia. We knew each other our whole lives. We went to the same private school since kindergarten, and we both attended the music academy from third grade. We were friends. We both played the violin and always sat near each other. Claudia was friendly, pretty, and incredibly talented at the violin. Eventually, she became first chair. Around junior high, I realized I had a crush on her, but I didn't say anything right away. I was awkward and didn't think she'd like me back. By the time we were teenagers, I'd gained some confidence, but she already had a boyfriend. Then, in tenth grade, I found out she was single again, and I finally worked up the nerve to shoot my shot." He had a faraway smile. It was sweet.

"She was funny, smart, and nice to me. She understood me because she was a band geek just like I was."

We both laughed.

"So, I wrote her this note. It said that 'I liked her and would she be my girl or something.' I had another girl in my first period show me how to fold it up in this strange contraception thingy you girls do."

I nodded, knowing exactly what he was talking about. I remember writing letters to my friends, folding them in all sorts of unusual ways, and giving them to them during passing periods.

"So, I gave it to her when I saw her, and I begged her not to read it until I walked away. When she found me later, she told me she liked me too, and of course, she'd be my girlfriend, and she wondered what took me so long or something." He had a faint smile.

"*That's so sweet! Oh my gosh! Sol!* That's like a young adult romance novel. Like a teen romance movie!"

He had a light chuckle, but I could also sense the looming emotions.

"Yeah… things were sweet with her. Until they weren't."

"I hate to ask… what happened with you two?"

"Well. We dated for years. I was in love with her, and we dated all through school. Even after I changed high schools, we kept our relationship. She was just as in love with me too." He let out a heavy sigh. "We started talking about our futures, marriage, college, and she kept putting off the conversation. I wanted to marry her."

Damn. That sounded familiar.

"So, we maintained our relationship even when we went off to college in separate directions. As much as I missed her, none of that mattered to me. I knew we'd be reunited eventually. Then I started putting pressure on her closer to the end of undergrad. I wanted to start setting things in motion. Make concrete plans for a

future together. Get married." He was focused on something just
past me.

"Yeah."

"Well…she finally revealed that her dad would never approve
of us getting married."

My eyes grew wide. "What's wrong with you? Who wouldn't
want their daughter to marry you?"

He chuckled, but it held no mirth. "I mean…" He sighed. "He
didn't want a black son-in-law for starters."

"Was she white?"

"They were black. But her father had this sick-ass obsession
with his children marrying and reproducing with white people.
Fascinated with the idea of a biracial grandchild. Something about
elite genes." He shook his head.

My eyes had to be at my hairline. *"Are you serious?!"*

"Dead serious. He isn't the only one, either. Professional ath-
letes do it too. I'd never heard of it until she told me, so I looked
it up. There are notorious examples. Black men saying it themselves. Black men seeking out tall European women who are super
athletic to procreate with, solely to produce offspring with these
bionic, superior genetics."

My jaw dropped. Just when you think you've heard it all.
"That's wild."

"Right. I was disgusted. Her father didn't want me for his
daughter. He wanted a white son-in-law. And Claudia knew that.
All the while, she knew that. Yet she stayed with me, continuing
the relationship, knowing it had an expiration date."

"Wow."

He continued. This question clearly unearthed raw feelings
for him. But I was here to listen. "Her folks didn't like me. They
never said it, but it's so clear in hindsight. Cold smiles. Comments.
Nah. I wasn't who they wanted for their daughter."

"I'm sorry Sol."

"Thank you. That isn't even what hurt the most. Trying to
prove my worth… Speaking the part and dressing the part and ac-
complishing all I did as a musician. None of that mattered. I
would never be good enough for them to approve of us. Then she
started pulling away… and never fought for us. For *me*."

"For what it's worth, you shouldn't have to perform to be loved. Or accepted."

"Yeah. I've come to realize that. I didn't have that wherewithal at the time. I mean… I always felt different. Being adopted. I was quiet. An odd one. A classical music student, just trying to find my place. Where I belong, she seemed to understand me. And… well, you know the rest. Rich parents who are powerful and influential meant she couldn't marry me without being disinherited and cut off from all her resources. She chose all of that over me." He shrugged. "I guess she had to do what she had to do."

"Sol, I'm so sorry." I reached out, grabbing his hand.

He shrugged again.

"Wasn't meant to be."

He looked at me. "Wouldn't be sitting here with you had that worked out." He gently squeezed my hand.

I smiled wide. "Very true." I sighed. "That was heavy. I'm sorry."

"You're okay. Don't even worry about it… been focused on what's in front of me." His lids were low. "I haven't felt seen, truly seen… understood… in what seems like forever. Until *you*."

"Oh, Sol…" I began. And I was stuck for a second. That was so sweet. And it made me feel so good. Because honestly… it was the same for me. My voice smaller for some reason, I revealed., "With you, I feel this gravitation because you've seen me too."

He lifted my hand and placed it right over his heart. I covered his hand with my other hand instinctively.

"You feel that?"

I nodded, "I feel it."

"My heart's been beating for you, Belle."

"I can say the same."

We leaned into each other, sharing breath. Our foreheads touching. We remained that way for a while. Jazmine Sullivan softly crooning in the background.

"We're getting sappy, Music Man."

We laughed. Sitting back on the couch again.

"The only way I know how. I just care about you. My Artist Girl."

We sat there for another moment. Eyes on eyes.

"Close to midnight now, Cinderella."

"You're okay." I tossed back. "I don't have to be at the shop until four tomorrow. I'll be working there late since they're open later on Fridays."

Sol nodded. "I don't have any classes tomorrow. Just Home-Grown in the evening."

I nodded.

"Forgive me for being a boring host. This wasn't planned."

"You're perfect, I'm having a great time, Sol."

"Are you?"

"I am. I like the way you handle me."

"Do you?" His tone was a shade darker now.

"I do," I told him, with my lids low.

I gulped down the last of my tea. Then reached for his mug. "I can take these back."

"Nope. I got it. You're my guest."

"You're so sweet."

"Another cup?"

"No thank you."

Eyes on eyes, comfortable silence surrounded us. The music still going.

"Belle?"

"Yeah?"

"Can I kiss you? Please?"

"I'd like that."

"Would you?"

"I would. I thought you'd never ask."

He had a light chuckle. "Trying to be a gentleman."

"You're so much more than that," I told him.

I leaned toward him on the couch; he leaned in toward me, and our lips connected.

We got lost in the bliss.

Yeah, this felt so right. Sol kissed me as if he'd waited his whole life. It wasn't rushed. It wasn't careless. It was intentional. Slow. The moment his tongue met mine again… I stopped pretending. I moved closer, pulling myself in. I melted. All parts of me. Any reservations, any guards I had, began to fade away. The warm weight of his large hands gently held my face. Then he threaded his fingers in my tresses. Moans escaped us both. He shifted to my neck, kissing and sucking. I know he left marks. I lifted my chin as he kept kissing my neck. Sol told me he loved kissing my soft, long neck. I used to hate my neck. It's long and narrow, and I was teased relentlessly about it. For years. But Sol loved my neck.

Yeah. His mouth was on my collarbone now. My head was tilted back. My hands were around him, low on his waist, and I'd slipped them beneath his T-shirt, grazing his abs.

He broke away, "Getting wet for me, Indie?" then was back kissing my neck, my cheeks, our lips meeting once more. Our kisses grew deeper, our tongues slow dancing again. After a moment, I pulled back just a little, fixing my low-lidded eyes on his.

"You'll need to check." I had a sultry smirk. "You can touch me again, Music Man," I whispered.

He didn't need more than that. I leaned back on the couch slightly, throw pillows behind me, and Sol went for the button fly of my jeans.

"Yeah," he drew the word out. His arousal evident. "You are *wet*. Damn, Belle."

We resumed kissing. Sol hovered over me, his hand still in my jeans. Rubbing and stroking my slick pussy with his fingers. Getting me going. My moans gave me away.

He'd lifted the bottom of my blouse, kissing there and licking there. The rhythm of our bodies naturally coordinated. His hands intimately familiar to me. Inside me. Driving me wild.

I had my hands around him, rubbing his back. Softly. Up and down. But with need.

"Sol?"

"Yeah?" He never stopped sprinkling his kisses; his warm lips seared my skin. His wet tongue leaving a trail of pleasure.

Through a moan, I teased, "You planning to keep kissing me everywhere but where I want? Or… are you going to be good?"

Sol's breath hitched, and he laughed lightly. "Oh…Belle. I plan to be very good."

I laughed nervously, suddenly feeling… a little shy. I'd never had to ask him. But I wanted it. And I could hardly wait anymore.

I covered my face with one hand. Deciding to be transparent, I revealed, "Oh my gosh, no idea why I'm being shy. Timing is all off." My voice was kinda muffled.

Sol gently eased my hand away from my face. "Look at me, Belle." When I did, I saw that he had a soft smile. "You want it. I want it. And baby… I *love* giving it to you." He softly kissed my hand. "You can ask me for anything. No shame here, Artist Girl."

I exhaled. *Damn.* Sol was everything. I threaded my hands into his locs again.

He was still low on my body, near my waist. His hands were caressing my thighs now.

"Sol. Baby… please touch me with your mouth. I've been aching to feel you there again." He brought his eyes up; his lids were incredibly low.

I gave him mine.

Then softly he said, "I need your beautiful pussy on my face, Belle."

Surprising the hell out of me.

That was new for me. And. As turned on as I was, that made me nervous.

He saw it.

"You shy, baby?"

"Little bit," I revealed. Eyes on eyes.

"You're safe with me, Belle. Always."

"I know I am."

He nodded. "There's nothing to be shy about. I'm craving you too."

Sol sat up on the couch, and I lifted myself as he helped me pull my jeans and my thong over my hips. Once they were off, we switched places. He lay on the couch, and I was straddling him.

His hands were around my waist. We kissed again, but it felt different this time. There was a fierce devotion, at least from me. I knew I was safe with him because he had shown me that I could be a long time ago. His arms tightened around me. I think maybe the conversation we just had… opened him up even more. This was such a vulnerable moment for him. We'd never talked about his first love turned first heartbreak before.

"Bring her to me, baby."

I made my way up his body, with his arms around my hips. As soon as I settled where he wanted me, gently and immediately, he held onto me. Anchoring me. My fingers threaded into his locs again.

Then. Sol started eating. Licking. Sucking. Slurping.

Loud. As. Hell.

He liked this. His moans left no room for confusion.

I was right there with him. My cries of pleasure intermingling.

Yeah. It felt nice, and I slowly rocked my hips, his tongue following my every move. I reached forward, holding onto the arm of the couch for better leverage, then I started to relax a little more.

Fuck. It all felt incredible, it always did, but right now… Oh. My. Gosh. Sol's tongue. His lips. His sounds.

After I came, we lay on the couch. My head on his chest. I'd found his hand, and we had our fingers threaded. He'd been caressing mine, silent. Just our steady breath. Eric Benet was crooning now.

"Sol."

"Yes, Belle." His free arm was around me. Rubbing my back and my naked ass. I hadn't put my jeans or my thong back on.

"I'd love to please you, too," I revealed. "I want to take care of you tonight."

"You already please me, Belle."

My chuckle was quiet. "No, I mean..." My voice was soft, but confident.

Pulling his card and putting a spin on it, I told him, "I want your dick in my mouth."

"Do you?" He pressed, not missing a beat. But I likely took him by surprise. I'd never done this for him. Not yet. But this seemed like an opportune time.

"I do." I reached down between us and found his dick standing at full attention. I freed it from his joggers and stroked his length.

"Indie…" he groaned. No, it was a growl. Definitely a growl. "India. Artist Girl. Look at me, please," he said through bated breath.

Yeah. My head was still on his chest. But I looked up to find Sol's brows lifted.

And. The tiniest grin tugged the corner of his lips.

He kissed my cheek, and there he was again, giving me that reverent look he always had when he studied me.

"You sure?" He volleyed.

"Sol. You're so…" I sighed. "It's amazing. The way you make me feel. I've never felt this with anyone. And it makes me want to give it back to you. Freely."

He searched my eyes.

"I want to show you how good I can be to you, too."

He nodded once.

"Can I?"

"You may."

I made my way down his body and rested on my knees. I took his length into my mouth and started to suck softly, attentively, giving it my very best. I knew I was good at this. I've done it many times. But for once, it was something I genuinely wanted to do.

Something I asked to do. My hands moved tenderly and deliberately. This was about connection. I wanted him to feel how much I cared for him. Sol's hands gently held my head, not to guide me but because he needed to touch me, needing the anchor. And Sol enjoyed it; he told me so. Many times. Even if he hadn't, he expressed his enjoyment audibly. That shit was sexy. I'd never heard him like that before. We always had to watch our volume when we were at my house. When he was ready to release, he politely asked me to move aside, but I told him to go right ahead.

I wanted all of him.

Yeah.

He was lying back on the couch again, and I was on top of him, my head resting on his chest. Our breathing was in sync once more, and our fingers were threaded again.

"Belle… felt like you reached my soul." He let out a light titter. I felt his vibrations beneath me. "That was something else."

I smiled against his chest. "That's the way you make me feel, each time you touch me."

We lay there on the couch. In silence. Still being serenaded.

Eric Bellinger, "Keep Me in Mind."

Our hearts in sync, wrapped in closeness. No words needed. But the silence spoke everything that was unspoken.

And I was feeling wide open.

Wide the fuck open. Solomon could have anything from me right now.

There was definitely a synergy. He wanted more from me, too; I could feel it. The air around us was thick with intimacy. Our bodies were warm, our eyes heavy. It was getting late, but we still felt charged. He was still awake and firm between us, and I know Sol. He would say something. Ask for permission. In his emotionally present, quiet, grounded, and sensual way he always does when he wants me. Respectful. Explicit. Quiet hunger and reverence. No pressure. No rush. Just us. Because this is so much more than sex. Both for him and for me.

Solomon brushed my hair back, his soft lips grazing my temple, his voice low and deep. He pulled me close against his chest.

"Come to my room with me, Belle. I want to be one with you." He kissed my temple again, his fingers trailing along my bare thigh. "Can I? The way I've been dreaming about."

"Yes, please. I want that too." My emotions and desires were intertwined. I was completely open and turned on. We stood up from the couch. I was naked from the waist down. I took off my blazer as we walked in. My jeans and thong were on the floor somewhere. I was only wearing my blouse, no bra.

Sol grabbed my hand and led me ahead of him. Taking me to his bedroom, he pressed me against the wall as soon as we arrived. Our kisses were deep and hungry. But we didn't rush, even though we both wanted to.

His fingers traced my bare waist, my back, and my hips. He handled me the way he always does. Careful and confident. We kept kissing, deeper and hungrier, making my knees weak.

He pulled my shirt off, and I slipped his shirt off too.

He took his time licking and sucking each of my nipples, marveling at them.

"Look at you. Sexy Artist Girl. I love your body. I love your figure…everything about it."

"Thank you." After my moment of doubt those weeks ago, he constantly reassured me that he found me irresistible and sexy. And I appreciate that. I could sense that he was trying to be patient, but his breathing was faster. Mine too. He finally backed me into his bed, and it felt like both a first time and a homecoming. He climbed on top of me and kissed me. Everywhere. Every part of me. Slow. Memorizing me with his mouth. He asked me many times if I was okay, and I told him I was more than okay. And he asked if he could have me, and I told him I wondered when he would ask.

He chuckled softly and found me in the dark again after strapping on a condom. And he pressed into me, filling me up and making me feel so good. We moved together slowly as he began to stroke me. I wrapped my legs around him instinctively, and he told me how great I felt. Talking in my ear, he said he wants me and asked if it's okay. I pulled him closer, losing my damn mind. He kept that dirty talk going, those declarations.

How much he enjoyed being inside me, how pleased he was with me, how sexy he found me. I told him how good he made me feel, how special I felt. I wrapped my legs tighter, anchoring him, and we moved together breath for breath. Yeah, our bodies spoke truths we hadn't yet said out loud. We'd slept together more than a dozen times by now, but this right here was catapulted to the very top.

I knew I would never forget this moment. I'd never experienced anything like this before. And I knew it was him. No one else ever made me feel like this.

More than desired.

Loved.

Even if neither of us ever said the words. I understood that was why everything felt so much more intense. My senses were heightened. Sol felt precisely the same way I did. It was unmistakable.

And *so beautiful*.

As Sol stroked me even deeper, he said, "I don't want this night to end... want to wake up next to you. Stay the night, Belle."

My answer was simple. Instantaneous. As he stroked me into oblivion.

"I was hoping you'd ask. Yeah… I'll stay."

twenty-six

SOL

She shifted against my chest, waking me from the light sleep I had fallen into.

The sunlight filtered through the linen curtains in my bedroom. My arm was draped over her waist, and I held her tighter as she moved closer to me. Her eyes were still shut.

I'd woken up a long time ago and had been up for a while, hypnotized as I watched my sleeping beauty. I listened to her calm breathing, watching the rise and fall, basking in the stillness and quiet. I loved waking up with India in my arms. It was a feeling I couldn't put into words. Not right now anyway. I was too full. So full.

Yesterday evening, I told her I was so juiced that she agreed to spend time with me. And I was. Ecstatic. And I was beyond excited when she agreed to spend a night with me.

We were up late, which isn't anything new for us. But, in this setting, things felt a little different in the best way.

We didn't have to whisper, for one.

We could take all the time we wanted.

And we could express our pleasures freely.

I encouraged India not to hold anything back. Encouraged her to tell me everything, to reveal all the thoughts she'd been having, to tell me exactly what she needed from me. To share what she desired me to do for her. I wanted to fulfill those desires and more.

And… India took me on a ride. When she reached her peak… her sounds… they were so beautiful. So melodic. It was becoming my favorite sound. I loved it whenever I got to bring them out of her. And she gave them up so honestly. Last night I told her she looked so damn good when she let go for me. When she came apart for me. I remember kissing her lips after she came undone all over my mouth. And she shared that I made her feel so beautiful. I told her I'd continue to do that as often as she would let me. Our connection was much stronger now. It seems we've taken a step closer to maybe becoming something. Though in my head, we already were.

I shared my past relationship with her. I told India about the only woman I ever loved, a woman I once planned to spend the rest of my life with.

Claudia. That's a situation I don't like to think about, and I especially don't like to talk about it. And I don't. But I'm grateful that India was there for me in that moment. I felt better after sharing, and I was glad to have that out in the open.

Yeah. Claudia broke my heart, and after her, I didn't even consider opening myself up again. Being vulnerable again. I'd made a vow not ever to get caught off guard like that again. ... until her. Everything I'd written off... everything I'd sworn I wouldn't do... India had me going back on all of it. And I was falling in love with her. My eyes were closed now, still basking in the stillness and quiet. It was hardly seven-thirty in the morning, still early, and I knew eventually we'd have to part ways, get our prospective days going. But I hoped she wasn't in a hurry. I wanted to do more with her before I took her home.

"You woke up before me?" she asked in a sleepy voice, stretching a little.

I opened my eyes to her soft smile. "Only because I don't want to miss the moment." Her smile grew. "I don't want to miss a single moment with you, Artist Girl." I leaned in and kissed her forehead. Her wild hair fanned out in a mass of curls. "Good morning. You good?"

She nodded. "I am. More than good. Thank you." Her mouth was behind the collar of the T-shirt I'd given her to sleep in. "And good morning."

I nodded too, taking in her bright eyes. Even first thing in the morning, India was stunning. Breathtaking. She tilted her head slightly.

"Stop staring at me. I know I must have sleep in my eyes or something!" she giggled. "Gotta talk from back here. I know I've got morning breath." She kept the collar over her mouth.

We laughed.

I shook my head. "Actually, you don't. You look beautiful, Indie."

Artist Girl was the epitome of 'I woke up like this.'

Damn.

I realized something else now that we were in the natural sunlight.

"You're sun-kissed," I told her.

"Huh?"

"There's sun kisses all over you."

"What are sun kisses?"

"Freckles."

India had a few brown freckles sprinkled on her nose.

She giggled, then pulled the shirt completely over her face. "Oh my gosh!" Her voice muffled now. "I used to hate my freckles!"

"I love them!" I told her, softly pulling the shirt down.

"You've just been kissed by the sun, Belle."

She told me, "I always thought they made my face look dirty. But… sun kisses. I like that."

"I like you," I told her.

"I like you too."

We lay there, facing each other. Eyes on eyes.

"Last night..." she began. "It was different."

I slowly nodded. "You gave me all of you. Thank you for trusting me. And spending a night with me."

"You make me feel safe and comfortable. Thank you. I don't think I've ever fully given myself before. I don't think I even realized I was holding back."

I reached out, brushing curls away from her face. Then I looked at her for a moment.

"I appreciate that. And you never have to hold back with me. Ever."

"I know," India nodded with a closed-mouth smile. Then, "Do you have any extra toothbrushes?"

"Plenty."

"Okay. I need to take a shower, and I want to feed you before I leave."

I pulled her closer. "You already did. But I can eat again."

She giggled, covering her mouth. "Sol! I meant breakfast!"

I chuckled. "That's so thoughtful of you, Belle."

India took a shower, and while she did, I put her clothes in the washer. I'd given her another one of my T-shirts and a pair of joggers to wear in the meantime. Once she got out of the shower, she headed to the kitchen, and I took a shower. By the time I finished and got dressed, I opened my bedroom door, and my nostrils were instantly greeted by a delightful aroma.

A warm, rich, savory aroma filled the air. When I stepped into the kitchen, the scents grew even stronger. Familiar, yet not quite. Spices and seasonings hovered in the air. Fresh garlic, onion, and a hint of ginger. I noticed three different pans on the stove, and I could hear something sizzling softly. And then I saw her. Her damp hair was loosely tied up on top of her head, and my T-shirt hung off her bare shoulder.

She didn't notice me, busy making whatever she was working on… I kept watching her… and it was the most beautiful thing I'd ever seen. India was pressing something flat into a cast-iron skillet. She had a spatula she was turning, and her face was calm and focused. She hummed quietly under her breath. India was barefoot in my kitchen, standing at the stove in my T-shirt. The blinds were drawn, letting in the natural sunlight that made the room even brighter. Her phone was beside her on the counter, playing reggae music, and her hips were swaying. Yeah. This was definitely the most beautiful thing I'd ever seen. And this thing between us… it wasn't even official yet.

It didn't have a title. Not yet.

But I know I liked waking up next to her. In this house. And I enjoyed seeing her in the kitchen. I liked the smells. I liked the sounds. I liked the way she kept doing something she seemed so damn good at. I hadn't tasted the food yet, but if it tasted as good as it smelled… Yeah. I liked her. And I liked all of this. And I wasn't trying to let any of it go. I wanted this all the time. I want her to want this too. I stepped further into the kitchen, and India looked up.

"Hey."

And I had a huge grin. "Hey. It smells amazing in here," I shared. I wanted to step behind her, hold her, and kiss her neck, but I didn't want to get in her way. Instead, I leaned against the counter opposite her and stood there, stunned. This was real. And she was really here.

"Aww!" She initially had her back to me, then she turned her head and looked over her shoulder, grinning. "Thank you."

"You're welcome." I tucked my hands into my pockets, enjoying the view. I watched India move through the space confidently. It was natural and intimate. She knew exactly where to find what she needed.

I saw my cutting board covered with bits of green onion and a red bell pepper. Then I watched her move confidently and calmly, as if she belonged there. Like it was just an everyday thing. I wish that could be. I would love for it to be.

"You can have a seat. Foods almost ready."

"Nah. Loving this view too much," I teased. And I did. "You look good in my clothes, Belle."

She chuckled, glancing over her shoulder again. She replied, measured, "I look good in anything."

I threw my head back, tickled. Indie was quick on her feet. And silly. So silly. We stayed up late laughing into the wee hours. "You absolutely do. Can I help you with anything?"

"No thank you. Just about done..." she flipped something that looked like a tortilla in the cast-iron skillet. Focused. "Just one more roti and we can eat."

"Is that what that is?" I'd tried roti before, but never homemade. And how did she make that with the things here?

"Yup. Paratha style."

"Paratha," I repeated. She'd taught me some of the names of the traditional dishes she made. I'd also been teaching her French. Here and there. She understands at an elementary level. She shared that her cousin Mala and her uncle speak Haitian Creole. She has developed a limited understanding after years of hearing it while visiting her aunt's house.

I stepped closer, amazed. She used the palms of her hands to flatten the ball of fresh dough into an almost perfect circle. In fact, it was very close to a perfect circle. Then, I placed it in the cast-iron skillet and added a drizzle of oil.

"You made roti from scratch?" I saw the steam rise. "How did you manage to make that?"

She had a light titter. "Well… you had everything I needed. Flour. Baking powder. Salt. Oil. We would normally use a tawa…" She flipped the roti. I saw more bubbles. "But this cast-iron skillet works perfectly."

"Wow. Excited to taste this magic of yours. That's what I'm calling it," I told her.

She shook her head, her back still turned to me. Focused. "No magic. You had everything I needed. And, I love your kitchen. That big window brings in so much natural light. And I know how to make do."

"So, it appears," I said. "Artist girl, I'm going to connect your phone to the Bluetooth."

"That would be great, thank you, Music Man!"

She flipped the roti onto the pile of others. "Please sit, Sol. I'll bring your plate over in just a second."

As Bob Marley's "Jammin'" began to surround us, I sat.

And my eyes never left her.

Then she brought over two plates and gracefully placed one in front of me. And it was... It smelled heavenly, first of all.

But the sights and colors, the arrangement. I mean…

"India..." I couldn't find the words. "This looks wonderful."

She smiled. "Thank you. Let's pray. I'm hungry!"

I took her hand in mine and prayed over our meal.

Thanking the Lord for this beautiful morning and for this gorgeous woman who prepared this lovely meal.

For real. That's precisely what I said.

Anyway, my plate.

There were scrambled eggs with tomatoes, scallions, and fresh thyme. Lightly fried potatoes with garlic and peppers, and spiced ground turkey with green onions and a touch of paprika. I could tell by the color. And on the side, a roti, folded and still hot.

I looked at my plate, then up at her. She'd already torn into her roti, using it to eat her potatoes.

So I picked up my fork, not even sure what to try first. But I took a forkful of eggs and potatoes since that was closest to me. And oh my! I loved it.

The eggs were fluffy and tasted great with the potatoes. Those were delicious as well. They were gently fried and perfectly seasoned with garlic, herbs, and maybe cumin. They were so good.

Then I tried the spiced ground turkey. I realized that's what was quietly sizzling beside the roti. As soon as it hit my tongue, I closed my mouth as my palate exploded. It was seasoned with green onions, fresh garlic, fresh ginger, paprika, and something else I couldn't quite place. Something warm. It was subtle, but I tasted another layer.

"Okay," I finally said, and India looked up at me. "Belle, this turkey is the star of the plate." I swallowed. "All of it is delicious, but this is seasoned so well."

She paused mid-chew, grinning. "Thank you. Aside from the fresh herbs, I used paprika and something you had with a hand-written label." She looked over her shoulder at the stove, nodding. "Sol's curry blend."

I laughed. "That was an experiment."

"Guess it worked." She shrugged, teasing, giving me a pointed nod. "What's in it?"

"I can't remember exactly, but cumin and cardamom are the first spices that come to mind. I need to sit down and figure it out so I can replicate it."

"Good idea! It elevated that turkey to another level, according to you."

"You didn't try any?" That's when I noticed it was missing from her plate. No eggs either.

She shook her head.

"You don't eat meat?"

"I do. Just not all the time." She tore another piece of her roti with practiced fingers. She used the same hand to pick up some of her potatoes, which I noticed were a bit mashed. That was interesting. "Wasn't in the mood for meat. And I'm half Indian. We fast from meat a few times a year."

I nodded and watched her eat with her right hand. Her left hand rested casually in her lap, and I was captivated. I'm a world traveler; I know that many cultures around the world eat with their hands. Maybe I was making it a bigger deal than most would, but this was the first time we shared a meal. I guess I was just surprised, delighted, and fascinated. All at once.

Yeah. She gracefully pulled off a piece of roti; she was on her second one now and folded it around pieces of potato. Using her fingertips only, she neatly placed it into her mouth. It was clear this was something she'd been doing her entire life.

"Do you always eat with your hands?"

She looked up and replied softly, "Sometimes."

"Belle. No judgment here. I'm intrigued. I've never seen you… I love that."

She smiled, shrugging. "Well. I've never slept over and cooked you breakfast either."

"True." After a moment. "Will you show me?" I placed my fork beside my plate. "I want to learn, Artist Girl. I want to do it too."

She smiled wide. "Okay."

"Come sit on my lap."

India settled in my lap, gently lifting my left arm. Glancing over her shoulder at me, she said, "You keep this one off the table. Unless you're drinking something."

"Not complaining." I said, beginning to rub her thigh.

She had a light laugh. "So, you'll do everything with your right hand. That's a common rule in cultures that don't use utensils." She turned my palm up. "Only your fingertips. Avoid using your whole hand or getting food on your palms."

I nodded against her. My palm was still raised, and India rubbed the soft palm of her right hand against mine. Her left hand intertwined with mine. And I loved everything about this moment.

My dad says that in India, food is considered a gift. Eating it with your hands is a way to honor that gift. It's believed that the fingertips are an extension of the five elements: Earth, water, fire, air, and space. It's said that eating with your hands can awaken these elements, which enhances the taste and digestion and helps connect you to the meal and the people you share it with."

"That's beautiful."

"I think so too." She pulled my plate closer to us. "Alright. We'll go slow because there's an art to this. The key is only to take smaller, manageable bites. You don't want to drop any and make a mess. Are you ready?"

"I am."

India took my hand and placed a torn piece of roti in my fingers. She guided me as we scooped, folded, and pressed into the spiced ground turkey.

Still guiding me, she slowly and gently lifted my hand from the plate to my mouth, "There." She glanced over her shoulder, smiling proudly. "Try again, Music Man. By yourself this time."

And I did. It wasn't as smooth, but I did okay. And as I chewed, I swear the food seemed to taste better. Yeah. The flavors absolutely hit different when eating with my hand.

"It takes practice and skill, but you're doing so great."

"Thank you for showing me."

India returned to the chair beside me, pulling her plate back toward her.

"Mash your potatoes and mix them with whatever you're trying to pick up… makes it easier." I watched her as she demonstrated.

"I see." I nodded. "India..." I mumbled through another bite. My eyes closed. "Damn."

She found that amusing.

"I still don't understand how you managed to cook all of this. Roti from scratch in my kitchen. And these flavors. I'm so impressed.

"So, you like?"

"You kidding, Artist Girl?!" I shook my head, still chewing in delight. Glancing at my plate, then at her beautiful face. Her easy smile. "I'm amazed. It's delicious. Thank you."

"You're welcome." She shrugged playfully. "You did all the shopping. Your fridge is stocked pretty nicely. Your kitchen is sunny, sexy, and open. Just couldn't help myself."

Sade's "Smooth Operator" floated through the space.

"Sade? Let me find out!" I teased.

"I know good music."

"You do."

We kept eating, and I kept watching her. A few loose curls framed her beautiful face. My shirt still hung off her shoulder. She sat with her foot propped under her. I noticed she liked sitting that way.

And she looked like she belonged here with me, part of my morning in this home.

"You're dangerous, Indie."

"Dangerous?" she tilted her head, a hint of a smile playing on her lips.

"Dangerous. Feeding me like this and looking the way you do. I paused for a moment. "You trying to move in or something?"

She grinned wide. "With this big open kitchen? Don't threaten me with a good time!"

We laughed.

"I'll be remiss if I don't mention..." She gave me a pointed nod. "Your spice cabinet. You out here collecting?"

I chuckled softly. "I guess you could say that. I cook and enjoy trying new things, even if I don't always know what I'm doing. But I'm not afraid to experiment and try new recipes."

She nodded. "That's the best way to learn."

"Sure is."

"That's exactly what you've got there. Right on your plate. Black fusion with Indian and Guyanese vibes."

"And to think this is only breakfast. I can't imagine what else you might do, but I'm excited."

We shared another laugh, and I stood up to add a bit more of everything to my plate. "Can I get you anything, Belle?"

"No thank you. Roti and potatoes are a quick way to make me feel as full as a tick."

We laughed.

"I haven't heard that expression in a while."

On my way back to the table, I grabbed another bottle of water from the fridge. India was still drinking hers, but mine was almost empty.

"Artist Girl. This is crazy. Like good crazy. Can't have ordinary scrambled eggs now. You've ruined me."

She smiled again. "Thank you."

"You have an open invitation to come here anytime."

"You told me that. Last night."

"I meant that. And you can come cook anything. Anytime."

India laughed as she got up from her seat. "Thank you. I really do love your kitchen. Your home in general."

"Thank you kindly. Artist Girl. Thank you for being here."

I kept eating, noticing I was slower when using my hand. Maybe that was the point. Slowing down and savoring, being mindful of everything. Not just what I was eating, but my feelings and thoughts as well.

And I loved everything she shared this morning about her cultures, as I always do. Having India here with me, I felt a quiet, steady feeling. While I sat there enjoying the meal she prepared with so much love, care, and intention, it settled deep in my chest.

I heard the unmistakable snapping, and I knew it was the start of "Nothing Even Matters" by Lauryn Hill and D'Angelo. This was a good one. She'd told me she listened to music for hours every day, especially when she was in her art shed. Or any space where she was creating. I could relate to that. Not just a musician, but an artist.

Something incredibly dope we've done a few times was having a creative session together on FaceTime. India in her shed, and I'd be either at my piano or in my music room. And for a couple of hours, we'd both be in our zone. Making it happen. It's amazing to watch her work, too. I've only seen it on camera, but I look forward to seeing it in person.

Live. She's so talented. The mural she and Destiney did at Micah's was sick. If I could get her to come back and see me... and bring her tote. I had all kinds of plans for us. I can cultivate a creative space for her.

Something else I've been thinking about but keeping to myself is that I'd love a collaboration. I would really love that. I've considered a few different ideas, and I'd talk to her about it when the time feels right. I didn't want to get ahead of myself. But we could talk art all day, India and I. Even though we express our art through different media, we understand each other. I loved the way her mind worked creatively.

Yeah. And I was really impressed with India's playlist. So many great songs floated into the space, deepening the connection we'd already built. It fostered an atmosphere that feels even more intimate than last night.

I was already relaxed, but this was leading to a deeper sense of intimacy. A closeness. And it wasn't physical. I kissed her on the forehead this morning. I'd had my arm around her waist and rubbed her thigh when she was in my lap, the first time she'd ever been in my lap, by the way, but… that's all we've done this morning. So far. We showered separately. We haven't hugged. And it seems like more than enough. Plenty. And now… right now? I feel so close to her. So connected. Without touching her at all.

I saw India at the sink, preparing it for the dirty dishes. There were only a few, so she must have been washing along the way. I could see the clean dishes in the dish rack on my counter. She was quick, washing the remaining dishes in the sink, and before I finished my second plate, she had moved on to cleaning the stove and wiping down the counters.

I stood to put my plate in the sink to wash.

"You didn't have to do all of that. I would have gladly done the dishes since you cooked us breakfast."

"It wasn't much. Besides, my mother raised me never to leave a messy kitchen. Especially after making roti." She laughed lightly.

Then turned to wipe down the kitchen table as well.

"Well, still. Thank you."

She turned to look back at me, smiling easy. "You're welcome."

"She's taught you so much, Artist Girl. She raised a queen. Your father, too."

A queen and a catch.

"Thank you."

I nodded, regarding India as she padded toward me from the kitchen table.

I was leaning back against the kitchen counter by the sink. She stopped right in front of me, eyes locked on mine. We weren't touching, but in this moment, I could feel the connection between us. It had clearly grown stronger, somehow, for reasons I couldn't quite place. I looked at my watch, then pushed off the counter and said, "Wanna ride bikes?"

Her brows were at her hairline, and I laughed. When I asked her, I had a wide grin, and she looked at me like I had two heads. "Ride bikes? Today? Right now?"

I nodded. "Right now." Then shrugged. "Why not? It's just about nine a.m.. Still early. You have time?"

She looked down at herself, then back at me. "I can't ride a bike in these."

"We can wait until your jeans are dry, and I can lend you a hoodie."

She seemed to be considering it. Then, "You serious. Ride bikes?"

"Yeah. I live close to a trail. And I have one you can fit."

I studied her carefully. Then I asked her, gently, "Do you know how to ride a bike, Indie?"

She nodded. "I know how... It's just been years. I was probably thirteen years old the last time I rode a bicycle. Back in Guyana."

Ah. "I see. Well, as cliché as the saying is, you never forget. And we'll take our time, practicing around here before we head out. And if the trail isn't a good idea, we don't have to go. I want you comfortable and I want you safe."

"Alright. I'll call my parents and check in with them."

"Sounds good, Artist Girl."

twenty-seven

INDIA

"Still a little chilly out. Wear this over the shirt."

"You may not get this back!" I joked, slipping the charcoal gray hoodie over my head. And it was the perfect hoodie. I could tell he'd had this hoodie for years. It was soft and slightly worn, with stretched cuffs from being washed dozens of times. It was clean, but I could still faintly smell Solomon's scent on it. It re-minded me of his warm hugs. And I love Sol's bear hugs.

I'd waited in the hallway while he rummaged through a hall closet, coming out with it. My jeans had dried and I had them back on, and I was also wearing one of his T-shirts.

The hoodie and T-shirt were both swallowing me since I'm so thin, but it helped that I'm tall. I pushed the sleeves up to my forearms. Yeah. This would work just fine.

Sol chuckled, sliding the closet door shut, then turned to face me. "I like the way you look." He gestured to the small space be-tween us. "Here. Wearing my shit. You look good. All of this looks good."

I lightly chuckled, pulling my curls out from the back collar of the hoodie. I met his eyes, smiling too. "I've really enjoyed my-self."

"That's what I love to hear. That's all I want for you."

We stood there for a moment. No words, but it felt comfort-able. We had enough space between us, yet we were close.

So far, aside from the kiss he gave me on the forehead this morning and the brief moment I sat on his lap, we hadn't touched at all. We weren't being affectionate and hadn't indulged in each other again. But it didn't bother me that we hadn't. I still felt a strong emotional connection, just sharing space with him. I was truly enjoying simply being with Sol. The physical aspects... we didn't need them. Our bond was much more profound. So much more. And when we were intimate last night, it felt completely dif-ferent. I can't even explain it or find the words. But what hap-pened last night... I swear, that feeling will carry me for days.

I could live in this space. In this energy. In this vibration. And never move. I had no troubles, no worries. Nothing but the feel-ings Sol had quite literally stirred in me. Feelings that were running rampant in my mind and my heart. Rampant, but certain. I knew I liked him. I knew I was falling for him. Yeah. These feelings were intensifying. Feelings that validated any doubt I might have had once upon a time. Feelings I rather enjoyed. But these were feel-ings I didn't know what the hell to do with.

Because we couldn't be us. As much as I would love that, I can't.

And I'd made the decision that I needed to tell him before we parted ways today. This conversation was necessary and long overdue. It was also intimidating. Really damn frightening. I didn't want to hurt him. Brandon told me many times that I wasn't ready. Amir had even said the same. That I couldn't handle real life. Brandon liked to remind me of all my flaws. That I was in survival mode, and he's right. I am. And I don't believe I'm in a place where I can fully give myself to someone without somehow dropping the parts I need to keep intact. I can't do both: maintain a healthy relationship while trying to hold everything else together. I've already proven I can't. Looking back at my pathetic track record. Brandon is a fucking asshole, but I couldn't refute that. At the same time, Sol never asked me to be anything or do anything. Never made me feel bad or expect me to be perfect as if I needed to earn his affection or something.

No. I could exist, and Sol adores me just the way I am. Yet, I have thoughts, doubts, concerns, and worries. What if I can't be enough for someone again? Say I try this… and I want to so badly. But what if I try this us thing? And he walks away, too? Still, I don't think he would. Sol has been so consistent and reassuring, without even saying anything reassuring, that the fear I have has quieted down. It hasn't disappeared, but it's much quieter than it used to be. Then I think about how selfish I've been, and this persistent guilt gnaws at me. I've been thinking about it for a while.

But I never voiced it. I tried to drown it out. But I was raised with a conscience, a moral compass, and I should feel guilty. And I do feel guilty for letting things go on this long without clarifying with Sol what this was. My endgame. For disregarding his feelings and his time, even after realizing he wanted more with me, and I wanted the same, but I probably wouldn't pursue it. Yeah, I feel guilty and scared. Scared of losing him and losing this. I can't commit to a relationship with everything I have going on.

But I still want this. This… thing. It's definitely a friendship. And I still want him, but not a relationship. Not right now. Yeah, I plan to talk to him about this before we part ways today. I'll tell him that maybe we could have something, continue this physical connection, but without any pressure for anything more. No definitions. Just who we are when we're together. Enjoying each other and spending time.

And I can see him more, do things together. I don't see the harm in that, and I know that's something he's been wanting. It's been so real and sweet with him. Yeah. I can tell him that, see where his head is. God. That is so fucking selfish of me. But this is better than stringing him along, pretending there's more to come, because I can't do that.

"Let's head to the garage. The bikes are there. We'll see how rusty you are and what we can get into," Sol offered playfully, pulling me from my thoughts. He headed down the hall, and I followed.

"Hey! I might not be so bad," I tossed back.

"Let's see."

We entered his two-car garage through a side door off the kitchen. The space was filled with bright morning sunlight as he opened the garage door. It was a tidy garage, with a wall of tools and a few built-in shelves. All the things you'd typically see. His shiny silver BMW was parked next to a white early 2000s Volkswagen Jetta with a bike rack on top.

Against the furthest wall, two bikes hung on a rack. He easily pulled one down. "You can ride this one." He propped the grey bicycle on its kickstand and turned back toward the wall to pull down the other. When he faced me again, I looked up at him. I still hadn't moved or even gone near the bike.

"It'll fit you, I promise," Sol assured me. He leaned his bike against the wall and stood beside me. "You got these long, sexy-ass legs. These long arms. It's a perfect fit, Belle."

I cracked a wide grin at that. "Oh my gosh!" I chuckled, lightly shaking my head.

"Have you forgotten how to get onto a bike, Artist Girl?" he asked softly.

"No… It's just…" I sighed softly. "No. I haven't." I moved closer to the bike and climbed on. Then leaned over to kick the stand back down. I slowly rode down the driveway, not perfectly smooth, but I did it. And gradually, it all started to come back to me.

"No shame in a wobbly start," Sol called out from where he stood watching me. "You're doing so great, Indie."

I rode around in a circle a few times in the quiet street right in front of his house.

I don't know when exactly, but eventually, I found myself wearing my megawatt smile. I could feel it. And I swear, I think there were tears in my eyes, too. I honestly couldn't even remember the last time I had felt like this… this childlike thrill… this carefree feeling of riding a bicycle. Things had been so heavy, everywhere I looked, in every direction I turned. And now, my once bruised heart was somehow, in some way, in the hands of someone I never meant to give it to. And right now, I was experiencing something I hadn't felt in years.

Joy.

"Not so fast, Artist Girl! Safety first!" Sol called out to me.

I was two houses down, but he was waving me back, holding a helmet in the other hand. And I laughed loudly and freely when I almost tipped over trying to turn and head back.

"You trying to leave me or something?" he volleyed as he gently pressed the helmet onto my head. I snapped it underneath my chin.

"I wouldn't. I'm trying to see this trail."

His chuckle was easy. Sol had his legs straddling the bike, holding it up, already wearing his helmet. The garage door was closed now. "You'll love the trail. We'll get a good ride in, and there's a place where we can stop and rest. Call out if you need anything."

"Okay."

We rode through his neighborhood and onto the American River Trail. It was close to his home, just as he'd said. Sol led us at first, but we eventually pedaled side by side once we hit the trail. And the trail was more than I could have imagined. The air was clear and crisp. The sun shone brightly, but the trees lining the trail shaded us. I could hear the faint sound of the river as the wind whipped past my ears, my hair flying behind me.

After about thirty minutes, we stopped at a bench near the water. Sol offered me a water bottle, and I drank from it immediately. Guzzling a lot of the ice-cold water. I hadn't realized how thirsty you can get riding bikes!

"You ride often?" I asked after we sat quietly for a while. Occasionally, bike riders passed us. And aside from the birds chirping and the quiet stream, it was silent. Peaceful. I wish I had my tote.

"Yeah. Very often. Great way to clear out the noise. Helps me think, "He had his arms stretched behind his head."

"Yeah. I see that." I nodded. I was quiet again for a moment longer. Then, "Thank you. For inviting me."

He looked at me and said, "Thank you for joining me."

He took another drink from the water bottle, then looked at his watch. "It's not quite ten. If you have a little more in you, we can ride a bit further and stop at another place. About another mile or so."

"I'd love to." I returned without pause.

"Cool."

We followed the trail, then took a different route through a neighborhood, stopping at a small shopping plaza with just a few shops. My eyes lit up instantly when I saw a sign.

"Froyo! Can we get some? Please!"

Sol's chuckle was light. He nodded. "We can get whatever you want."

We locked the bikes onto a rack, then went inside.

"So. Artist Girl." I looked up into Sol's eyes just as I tasted my yogurt. "How are things going at the tattoo shop?"

We were sitting at a tiny table just outside the yogurt shop. Sol right across from me. The small plaza had a tranquil water fountain in the center, just a few feet from us. Trees shaded the area, with a few benches and tables.

I nodded silently, taking another spoonful. It was delicious. I'd never been here. But I wanted to come back and try their other flavors.

He laughed. "Must be good."

"So good! You'll have to bring me back here!"

"Anytime, Belle." He gave me a pointed nod, using his spoon for emphasis, "Couldn't get away from the mango? All those toppings to choose from?" He laughed at me teasing.

I'd gotten raspberry yogurt topped with fresh mango, fresh kiwi, and coconut flakes.

And Sol was right. He knew I loved mangoes and ate them all the time.

All. The. Time. I preferred fresh mangoes, but I devoured a bag of dried mangoes any chance I got.

"Don't do me!" I giggled. "You're just jealous mine is prettier than yours." Sol got vanilla yogurt with blueberries and almonds, using my own spoon for emphasis. "You could have used some color." Then I lowered my voice to a sultry tone, "Besides… eating all this fresh fruit is the reason I taste the way I do."

He thought that was so funny. "Touché, Belle. Touché." He laughed, shaking his head, and I joined in.

"Things are going well at the shop. Learning a lot. Just putting in the time," I told him once we'd settled down. "The artists there are amazing! So talented. There's a girl named Kam; she's the one I work with the most. She's been cool. Then there's Malik and Drew. All of them are just… I have much respect for that level of talent."

Sol nodded. "That's dope. That'll be you someday, Artist Girl."

I smiled at that.

"Have you been able to start tattooing?"

I shook my head. "Unfortunately, no. Not yet. But I'm itching to!" I glanced just past him at the people moving in and out of the small plaza. It was late morning now. Still quiet. Most of the people were women with young children, along with a few older couples. The plaza had a charming feel. There was a used bookstore, a coffee shop, and a cute gift shop filled with trinkets and jewelry. It's the kind of place you'd visit if you were just passing through as a tourist. "I feel like I'm ready. But I have to wait for King to think I'm ready."

"King?" His voice carried a slight inflection, and I looked up into his eyes.

I waited a moment. Eyes locked on his, I said, "Kingston is the owner." I spoke in a steady tone. Was he jealous? That's cute. He had no reason to be. None.

Sol slightly nodded. "I see."

We both kept eating our yogurt. "So what makes you so sure you're ready?"

"Well… I've been observing the other artists, and I know I can do it. I can handle cleaning the stations. I know hygiene with my eyes closed. I want to move forward. Learn to handle the gun." I sighed in frustration, looking just past Sol again. "If only…" I left the words hanging in the air, not bothering to finish, deciding instead to eat more yogurt. It didn't even matter.

"If only what?" he asked me after several moments had passed.

"It's nothing." I shook my head and kept eating. "Tell me how things have been going with finding your birth family? Any leads?" I asked, in a shallow ass chirp, attempting to shift the focus away from myself. I was done with that subject, and I didn't want to talk about it. It would only get me in my feelings. And I didn't want that. Not now, or ever. I just wanted to leave it alone and move on.

"Come on now, Indie. Please don't do that," he said, his tone firm and pressing.

I looked into his eyes and saw care, warmth, and safety. I was familiar with those feelings when it came to Sol and me. It seemed these qualities were never far away. I could tell by the way he treated me. The night I felt insecure about my body, he showed those same qualities. If I wasn't having the best day, he'd talk to me, distract me, and help me feel better, even if just for a moment.

"I'm sorry," I told him. "I didn't really mean anything by that. Can't even remember now." I shrugged. Full of shit. And I knew it.

Sol knew it too.

"Okay." He nodded. "We're lying to each other now." His entire demeanor changed. He set his spoon in his cup of yogurt, pushing it aside as if he didn't plan to take another bite. He seemed to have lost his appetite.

And I couldn't tell if that was a question or not, although we both knew I wasn't being honest.

After I set my cup and spoon on the table in front of me, I hung my head. I'd lost my appetite too.

He let me rock, but I could feel his eyes on me. I could feel his attention focused on me.

Several moments went by. Every so often, we heard the bell ring above the door as people came in and out of the yogurt shop.

"India," he said gently, his voice nearly a whisper. "You went somewhere... and I'd like to know if there's a reason you didn't want to finish your thought? Are you uncomfortable sharing with me?"

I looked up into his waiting eyes. They were gentle and reassuring. He wore a slight smile, and I could tell his focus had zeroed in on me. I had his full attention.

Shaking my head vehemently, "No. It's nothing you've done wrong. Sol. You've done everything right," I told him sincerely. He was hanging on my every word. "It's silly. And I shouldn't have lied to you. I'm sorry."

He nodded again. "Tell me what's so silly," he queried. Eyes still holding mine.

I inhaled lightly, releasing it slowly. "Well." I faintly chuckled, but it wasn't in mirth, and my eyes drifted off just past him again. "I was just thinking, if only I could afford my own tattoo gun and some skins. I'd already be practicing. Probably be pretty decent by now."

Seemingly disarmed, he nodded again. "That isn't silly."

I shrugged and offered him a small smile.

"It's a pipe dream." Slipped out before I could stop it. My eyes grew wide, but it was too late. I schooled my features, trying to play it off, and quickly added, "They have guns at the shop I could use. Just have to wait until King says I'm ready." I shrugged again. "Just anxious to start that part."

"I get it, Artist Girl. It's the same for a musician. Nothing beats your own guitar, keyboard, or drum set. That changes everything."

"Yeah." I looked away again and went back to my yogurt. It had melted just a little, even though it was a cool morning. I brought the cup to my lips when he spoke again.

"So, a gun and some skins. What else will you need? Ink? Gloves? Needles?"

My eyes widened. "Why do you ask?" I think I already knew why.

Yeah. I'm pretty sure I knew why.

"So we can take care of that for you."

"We can't handle anything right now. I don't have the money, and guns aren't cheap. Even used ones aren't cheap. Sol. Really. Don't worry about it."

"No problem. I'm willing to invest in your dream. You're talented; I see it. And you say you're ready to try, so let's do it," he said matter-of-factly. Reaching into his pocket, he pulled out his wallet. When he peeled off seven crisp Benjamins, my eyes widened again. Handing them over, he said, "Promise I get a tattoo, and you've got a deal."

I sat there with my mouth slightly open.

He chuckled after a pause. "We have a deal, Artist Girl?"

I nodded slowly.

"Okay. Can we hug on it? Shake on it? Fist bump?"

I smiled as I stood to give him a warm hug. He hugged me tightly in a bear hug like never before. Or maybe it was just me. Either way, I was so grateful.

"Solomon. Thank you," I said while still wrapped in his arms.

"You're so welcome."

We took our seats, and I was overwhelmed with a flood of thoughts.

As much as I appreciated it, it was bittersweet. I felt conflicted. I couldn't buy a bunch of tattoo equipment when we could barely keep groceries in the house. It didn't sit right in my spirit. We were so far behind. The money I'd spend on all that could go toward paying our past-due bills. It would give me some breathing room. I thought about how much better I'd feel earning that money myself, after making sure everything at home was taken care of.

"Artist Girl. You good?" Sol asked, pulling me out of my thoughts.

Deciding to be honest, I spoke transparently, "Sol. I appreciate this so much. I really do. But. I can't. Things at home… we're behind on a few bills. I couldn't buy these things and enjoy them if we're in financial distress. I've been juggling commissions, but we're barely making it work." I slid his cash back toward him. "I appreciate this. Really. But." I shrugged. "I'll get around to all of that eventually. It isn't the end of the world." I cracked up. "I don't even know why I'm telling you all this."

"Because you trust me," he said without missing a beat. "Thank you for sharing that with me. I appreciate your transparency."

I sank back into my chair, shaking my head slightly in embarrassment. "Forget everything I just said."

"Indie." His voice was low and steady. Calm. "If you need help, let me help. You don't have to carry all of that by yourself."

"Sol." I kept shaking my head. "I'm not asking for a savior. We'll figure it out. We always do. My father is a hardworking man. He worked his entire life with his bare hands and took care of Mom and me. Both of my parents are dedicated workers. They came here with nothing."

He nodded a few times. "You've become someone so precious to me, India. And when I see you drowning, my instinct is to pull you up."

I said nothing, but he continued, "I love that you're so proud of your parents and your family. I absolutely love that about you. And I see you. The way you take care of everyone else. Let me handle those bills. I'll feel better knowing you're breathing easier."

I looked into his eyes. "I appreciate that. But accepting help will make me look like a charity case. We've just fallen on some hard times, that's all. And I don't want to owe anyone anything. Not even you."

"I would never see you as charity, India. And you wouldn't owe me. No strings." His voice remained calm and steady. And his eyes, honest and sincere. "You pay me back each time you let me hear your laugh. Each time you let me into your world. Answering my questions," he said. "When you share your artwork with me. When you tell me what's on your mind, calming my spirit after a long day. That's the return. Let me do this for you."

I looked away, speaking in a quiet voice. "None of this is your problem," I said, still resisting. "Sol. I couldn't."

"India. Yes, you can. Friends look out for each other. Just this once. Let me take care of you the way you take care of everyone else."

I was torn between the pride in my chest and the tenderness of his words and thoughtfulness.

There was definitely an internal tug-of-war.

I can handle myself. I don't need handouts. But there's a relief in being caught up, being able to focus on other things, and slowly rebuilding my savings.

I hesitantly picked up the money again. Sol had since slid it back toward me, and I held it between two fingers. I bit my lip, staring at it, with Sol watching me.

I sagged my shoulders. Not in defeat, I don't think.

Maybe in acceptance. Yeah. I was accepting the help.

The help up. Not the handout.

"You know…" I began, looking into his expectant eyes. "This is different for me. And I couldn't just take your money. I'll pay you back every penny. I mean it, Sol."

Eyes on eyes, he said reassuring, "I'm not worried about that." He said it without making me feel small or like I was just some project. "And should you find yourself needing anything else, please don't hesitate to ask."

♪♥♫♥♪

"So. I've been searching again, trying to find my birth family."

"Glad you're back at it!" I said with excitement. "How's that going?"

We were back at Sol's place, sitting at his kitchen table. We'd been out for almost three hours riding bikes. On the way back, Sol challenged me to a race. There was about a quarter mile to go, and he somehow got a head start, so he won, but he cheated, and I demanded we have a rematch someday. He agreed, insisting that even if I'd had a head start, he'd still beat me. I laughed the entire ride back, and by the time we reached his house, my cheeks hurt from smiling so much. My legs felt like jelly, but it was all good because my heart was so full. In a way I hadn't felt in so long, maybe ever.

The bike ride today was exactly what I needed. And it was so easy with him. We cruised, pedaling side by side. Undeniably intimate. Just being. The stretches of trail with just the two of us. Talking. Rediscovering each other. The wind in our faces. We were both hungry when we got in, and Sol made us sandwiches. Simple, but it didn't mean boring. It was perfect. And it hit the spot! I hadn't had a turkey sandwich in ages, and Sol makes the best turkey sandwiches! Classic and flavor-filled. Wheat sandwich bread lightly toasted. Garlic aioli, mustard, provolone, leafy green romaine, roasted turkey slices, and the juiciest heirloom tomatoes ever. The tomatoes were my favorite part. They were thick-sliced and made up the bulk of the sandwich. I loved them. They were a treat! We didn't buy heirloom tomatoes. Ever. They were more expensive.

And it's no wonder. Sol and I discussed these tomatoes at length. I knew they were heirlooms, but he told me this variety was called Mortgage Lifter, his favorite among tomato types. They have a sweet, earthy aroma; they're large and smooth, with pinkish-red skin, few seeds, and a great, low-acid flavor. Not to mention, they're stunning to look at! I love that heirloom tomatoes come in a kaleidoscope of colors. I wished I had my tote; I wanted to paint some in watercolors.

Sol took a bite of his sandwich. "It's not. Keep hitting dead ends. But I don't want to give up. I want to find my people."

I was working on my second sandwich now. We were also sharing a bowl of green grapes, and I popped a few in my mouth.

"I'm sorry about the dead ends." This was something that Sol had been looking into for several years now, and I felt for him. I know how important this was to him. I wanted something to happen, and I wanted it sooner rather than later.

"Appreciate you." He shrugged, chuckling lightly, "At this point, I'm so desperate for something. Anything. I'd be grateful to find a distant cousin or a great uncle. Something."

"No kidding." I lightly tittered as well. "You'll find your family. Just keep searching. Your determination isn't in vain."

"That means a lot," he told me with a warm smile. "Thank you."

"You're welcome."

"I don't want you to leave, but I should get you back so you have some time before you head to the shop." It was close to 1 pm.

I nodded. He was right. Plus, I needed to check on Ma and Daddy. And face the music. I knew they would have questions for me.

And I was prepared to speak.

We'd cleaned up, and now we were sitting on the couch. Sol had music playing. I put my blouse back on. His T-shirt and hoodie were unscathed.

I really had such a great time, starting the moment I stepped through the door last night. I didn't want our time together to end. I told him so.

"You're welcome here. Anytime, Belle. I love having you here," he said, looking into my eyes.

We were on the couch, his arm draped behind me. I felt his fingers gently grazing the nape of my neck. My hand was threaded through his, feeling like home. We had managed to keep our hands off each other all day, and now we were being affectionate again. Maybe because we knew we'd be parting ways soon.

As he absentmindedly grazed my skin with his warm touch, I felt a heavy weight because I knew what I needed to do. I knew I should say it now. Right now. While it was quiet and we weren't naked and breathless. Distracted. No. I was still distracted.

I could faintly hear Jesse Powell's "You" just as I said, "Sol…" before I could change my mind.

"Yeah," he murmured, low and warm.

Shit.

I looked across the room, gazing at a painting of a black jazz ensemble hanging on his wall. It was beautiful. Sol had quite a few pieces by Black contemporary painters displayed in his home. Notably, a limited edition print by the incomparable Kehinde Wiley, signed and numbered. That blew me away.

"What are we doing?" I hadn't meant to ask that, but that's what came out.

His response was immediate.

"Enjoying ourselves. Learning. Growing." He brought my hand up to his lips, softly kissing it. "That's what I've been doing. Shit feels amazing. You're amazing." He gently lowered his arm from around my neck, then took my other hand and kissed it all over.

I sighed. I was still looking off, just past him, almost as if I knew I'd lose my resolve if I gave him my eyes. "Sol… I feel like I am doing way too much with you. Like things have gone too far or something. But I can't help myself. I like being with you. I love the way I feel when I'm with you."

"I feel the same way. It's the easiest thing ever being with you."

Fuck.

"Aww." I couldn't help myself as I looked into his expectant eyes. Eyes that I knew I could trust. And I've known this for a while.

"Dead ass. I love how I feel when I'm with you, too. I don't want you to hold anything back. Let it all go for me, Belle. I want to keep this going. I want to be with you, India. I'm letting you know I'd love that. I'd want nothing more, honestly." He had a warm smile. I love his smile. "That cool with you? My Artist Girl."

Yes!

My eyes were on his.

But I said nothing. I couldn't. And I knew I had a faint smile curling at the corner of my lips. Gosh, Sol had such a way with words. Even though I could feel this, and it wasn't a surprise, hearing his declarations straight from his heart just… it was so sweet. So special. It made me feel so good. I was at a fork in the road. A junction, faced with two choices. Like I had two doors to pick from. Earlier, I thought I knew what I would say. I was so sure. Or so I thought. But Sol had me second-guessing. Reconsidering. And he waited for me to answer. Patiently. Soft. Kind. Safe. Expectant eyes fixed on me.

Our fingers were still linked, all twenty, tangled in silent caresses. Sol kissed my forehead. Sweet. I loved his forehead kisses. He brought me back to the present.

"I just…" I began, my throat tight with emotion, but I pressed on, "I can't. I'm not in a place for anything serious right now. Taking care of my parents. So much going on. Sol… You've been incredible. A perfect gentleman. I have issues I need to work through."

The sparkle in his eyes faded, but he didn't say a word.

"As much as I want to, I can't right now. I'd feel horrible. My time, my energy, it's so limited. Starting something right now would be incredibly selfish of me." I felt my eyes start to well up.

Sol was such a great guy. If things weren't screwed up right now, if I'd met him sooner, I'd be with him in a second. He nodded slowly, still saying nothing. I couldn't read his expression either.

"I want to keep seeing you," I quickly added. "I love seeing you and being with you. Just these past eighteen hours. It's been incredible." I managed to smile somehow.

He finally spoke softly. "But?"

I lightly nodded. "But… I don't want to hurt you, Sol. I don't want to let you down. Overcommit to something I can't guarantee. I don't even know if I have anything to give."

He looked away from me. I could see gears turning. The silence between us stretched. It wasn't awkward, but it was heavy and loud. I knew I'd caught him off guard. I knew he was disappointed. I'd argue he was hurting. I certainly was.

He moved closer to me. Murmuring, "Belle."

We met eyes again. "Think about it for me. Will you? At least consider it." He gently squeezed my hands. "I respect you and whatever you've got to carry. I care about you. India. God, I care about you. And I like you. What I've learned so far and what's to come. I like spending time with you, and I want a chance with you, India. I won't leave you lacking for anything."

"I like you too, Sol. I really do. I'd be with you if things were better. I care about you. You're such a great person. I'll only disturb your peace."

He didn't like that. "Don't say that, Indie." He sounded frustrated with me.

I shrugged. "That's how I feel. This is no way to start a relationship."

"I want you to leave caution to the wind when it comes to us. Feel free to fall… I'll catch you."

Oh Sol. I fell a long, ass time ago.

"India," he pressed when I said nothing.

"Yeah."

"You wouldn't need to make any guarantees. You'd only need to give us a chance. Think about it for me." He didn't sound disappointed. Just honest. And hopeful.

"Maybe we should slow down."

"We can do that. Whatever you want."

"Alright," I whispered. I glanced at him, unsure of what all this even meant.

"Just don't disappear on me," he said softly.

"I wouldn't do that to you. I couldn't."

"So you'll think about it? About you and me?"

I told him, "I'll think about it."

"Can I have a hug, India?"

We stood as he held me close, wrapping his arms around me. I responded by wrapping my arms around him securely, and I leaned into him.

"Solomon."

"Yeah?"

"Want your money back?"

"No. Nothing's changed. And I stand by my word. Get what you need, Artist Girl."

He kissed my temple just as sweetly as he usually does. "We'll figure this out."

I nodded, saying nothing.

And. My chest felt lighter. I could think about us. Being us. Maybe we will. Or maybe not. I didn't know. Only time would tell.

But I could confidently say that for the first time in a long while, I knew I wasn't alone trying to figure things out. The drive home was quiet, with music playing softly, though I wasn't really listening. Not sure about Sol. And I still felt full.

From the sandwiches, the bike ride, the love we made, the time we spent, and our conversation. Somehow, it seemed like we took a step... forward? Maybe. We were definitely shifting into something more. I couldn't call it anything. We didn't have a label for it. But it was real, and I certainly couldn't unfeel it.

And Solomon. I got the sense that he felt good about that, which made me happy. There was a slight glimmer, a trace of a silver lining. It seemed he felt a little more confident about this becoming something. A lot surer than I did.

And although I told him I would consider it, honestly, I would, I wasn't quite ready yet.

twenty-eight

SOL

She beat me to it.

"I want to be with you, India."

I'd told her after pouring my heart out. After an intense eighteen hours where I felt the best I have in years. I experienced feelings so intensely intimate, so exceptionally profound, so deep, familiar, and natural. India had me grinning like a fool from the moment I saw her last night at HomeGrown. She did that to me effortlessly. Everything had been going so well. India agreed to come out and hear me play. She spontaneously decided to come back to my place. She chose to spend the night with me when I put her on the spot. She had been in my space, letting me take up hers, letting me do for her, and she did for me.

She gave herself to me. She pleased me with her mouth for the first time, asking me if I was okay with that. And she was incredible. The things her tongue could do. I was hard just thinking about it.

Yeah. She let me have her. All night she did. I held her in my arms until she fell asleep. She woke up beside me. She cooked for me. She fed me straight from her fingers, right on my lap. She let me feed her too.

I knew we needed to have this talk, in person, and that was the plan for the weekend. But she beat me to it, letting me down easily, killing me softly with her words. I'm not even mad. Just shocked and surprised, sure. But that was my fault. I was the one carrying unresolved questions around for weeks. Questions that should have been answered a long time ago. What are we? Does this mean anything to you? Where is this going?

And that's the thing. I know India shared the same feelings. I'd bet my last dollar she did. I knew that before she told me. We were both moving in tune with our feelings. She's a passionate woman with her heart on her sleeve. We spoke of our mutual crushes. Many times. Making light of it. Teasing and flirting about it. But when things began to shift, we never put words to it. But I felt it. I knew she felt mine.

When I discovered I felt the way I felt… when I realized I felt strongly for her, I should have spoken up. No way I'll ever know if it would have made a difference. I guess I would have known where she stood…sooner.

Yeah. I'd carried my feelings and my words around heavy in my chest like stones I didn't know how to put down.

Telling myself that I didn't want to disrupt things. Or push her. And that we would continue this and we'd talk about it at some point. And we'd… see.

But she beat me to it. And she confirmed what I'd dreaded hearing.

I was disappointed. And I admit my feelings were hurt. I'm man enough to admit it.

I exhaled an exasperated breath as I drove down Broadway in Friday afternoon traffic. I could have taken the freeway but chose to take the streets instead. I wasn't in any particular hurry. Just lost in my thoughts.

I'd turn off the radio once India got out of the car. When we reached her house, I offered to walk her inside or at least to the door, but she insisted she'd be fine. I wasn't sure how I felt about that. I figure she didn't want me to meet her parents, and that was fine. I guess. If that's where she was with it. Still, I didn't think it felt right just dropping her off. I waited until she was inside before driving off, but I would have liked to walk her to the door at the very least.

She'd kissed me on the cheek before leaving and said she'd text me later. I kissed her forehead and wished her a good day. Despite my feelings being in disarray, she was heavy on my mind. My chest felt warm as I reflected on the past several hours. Yeah. Everything intensified; feelings were catapulted. And we connected.

The sex… it was… well, first off, it wasn't sex. It hasn't been for a while. But last night, I can say with 100% certainty that we made love. Made magic. Honestly, it was so beautiful. More beautiful than any of the other moments we'd shared. Not that the other times weren't, but there was something more that time. I won't soon forget that experience. I don't believe I ever will, honestly. I think back to the throwback song by Az Yet, "Last Night," and it was just like that. I saw heaven when I made sweet love to her. And… man, I swear. Had it not been for the barrier between us, had we not taken precautions, I would have put a baby inside India. I'm convinced.

We were both completely open, like never before. Emotionally and physically. She let herself go with me, for the first time like that. And I had, too, after sharing my past heartbreak with her. I was willing to give my Belle what she had brought out of me that evening. We talked, we spent time. All the time we wanted. No whispers. When I came inside of her, I mean inside the condom, it came from somewhere deeper than any other place. Can't explain it really.

Yeah. India was so open. Wide open. I could feel it. And her body… it would have received what I'd given her. Shit, I'd bet she was ovulating even. There was something different. And something would have come from that. Something would have manifested. Someone. A life. We would have had proof of the night we shared that love. That time. Those feelings. Yeah. Damn.

But then she asked what we were doing. And initially, I was excited, hopeful, and relieved. We were finally going to establish ourselves and make things official. Then, as I sat there listening to her tell me all the reasons she couldn't, my heart hurt more with each word she spoke.

I watched her. She seemed conflicted. She wanted me just as much as I wanted her. She wanted us. But I listened to her. I didn't interrupt. Her voice was soft. Her words were careful. Not confident, but she tried to convince herself she was.

"I'm not really in a place for anything serious…"

I chuckled to myself as I made my way home.

I understood what she meant, but I didn't.

Because what we've been doing these past few weeks… this thing we've been slow dancing around. The talking. The texting. The voice memos. Day after day. Night after night.

The mutual feelings. The attraction.

The pull I felt toward her and from her. All of it felt like more.

When we touched. When we kissed. There was gravity.

When we talked on the phone in the wee hours, we'd both had long days but still wanted to chat. Catch up. Be that soft place to land at the end of it all.

And when she laughed at something silly, I'd say, or when she teased me about something we talked about. The way she listened to me gripe about my students who had so much potential but wouldn't try harder. I couldn't understand why that didn't mean something more.

And beneath all the words she spoke, I sensed everything she wasn't saying. Her fear. Her guilt. The idea she seemed to believe wholeheartedly was that her life is too complicated for anyone else to care for her the way she deserves.

How she's stretched so thin, carrying so much. And here I am, right here… a man with open, strong hands. Able. Willing. Wanting. And nowhere to put them.

She told me she had nothing to give. I desperately wanted to tell her that she already gave me something.

When she said that, I thought back to last night. I couldn't help myself. She shared communion with me. And art. A soul meeting another soul in the dark.

I didn't say any of that. That would have been selfish of me. So I listened to her, intently, nodding, and eventually told her we'd figure it out. After trying unsuccessfully to convince her that she didn't need to make any promises or guarantees. She didn't need to guarantee anything; she just needed to be. Just remain the woman she'd been all along. The woman who sent me with her smile alone.

And I'm disappointed. But not in her. No. I'm quite disappointed in the timing of all this. If only we'd met sooner. Life is funny. The way it lifes. Situations happen that leave things in ruins, and in response, people build fences around the very people they should want to run toward. I wanted to define us, and I'd told her so. That I want her. Not just her body, though… my goodness, I want that too. And having her, I've taken the best care of her, and I would continue to. I've been taking my sweet time with her, savoring her.

But I want her. All of her. Her art, her fire, her chaos, her laugh at 1 am. I hadn't fully expressed the depth of my desires. I kept it classy, but I wanted to tell her how I truly felt, as passionately as I did. I also longed for her to want me in return. But India made it clear. She can't.

I disagreed. But what more could I do?

I'd need to wait for her to figure it out. The trouble was, I worried she might not. And then what?

More specifically, now what?

I sighed, rubbing my hand down my face.

Now? Now, I wait. I honor her words. And mine. I'll continue to be here. Present. Unassuming. A friend. An ear. A safe space.

I'm going to be here because something about India feels like home. And a part of me hopes that maybe one day soon, when her hands aren't so full, she'll reach for mine.

I pulled into my garage when I arrived home.

The bikes were still leaning against the wall.

I smiled, picturing her joy earlier and hearing her laugh. She laughed today. It was such a carefree laugh. Her head was tilted back, the wind blowing her hair. Her eyes squinted. I wanted to keep chasing whatever had brought it out of her.

Yeah. India looked so alive out there. Free. Relaxed.

She told me it had been years since she last rode a bike. But she rode that bike as if she had been transported back in time, recalling a time before everything changed for her. Got heavier.

And damn. She was so beautiful.

In the sunlight, she was swimming in my hoodie.

I wanted to kiss her. Could have. Thought about it. A few times. Her mouth was right there. Soft kissable lips. Familiar and close enough. And I knew India would have let me if I'd asked.

But it wouldn't have been right, not after a day like today. I'm so in tune with her, and in hindsight, I could tell she had all of that on the tip of her tongue. Waiting for the right time to drop it on me. Something that bothered her.

Yeah. Looking back, she seemed tense. Distracted. I saw it on her face once we got back from the trail when we sat at the table. The couch. I saw the battle. The pull and push. Part of her wanted this, and the other part of her was scared. And I could see why. I get it.

She needed to see this for herself.

And I wouldn't rush her. Not now. Not ever.

So. I made her a sandwich. We talked about heirloom tomatoes, and she had all sorts of questions. It was the sweetest thing. Her gratitude. I promised to take her to the farmer's market. But I fed her and offered her my ear, my space, and my quiet. When I asked about riding together again, she said, "Yes. I'd love that." I swear, those four words could carry me for days. Especially now.

Before I closed the garage door behind me, I tuned up the bike she used. Then I entered the house through the kitchen. I leaned against the counter, taking a sip of water. I could still smell the faint scent of the breakfast she made for us. This was crazy. I glanced at the kitchen table. I could still see her sitting there. Her soft eyes, her hair sitting on top of her head. One leg tucked under her, looking comfortable and making me feel good.

God, she was stunning.

She caught me watching her while she was eating.

India glanced at me, making my chest ache. My body hum. My heart thump. She'd just put food in her mouth, so she didn't say anything. She chewed slowly, measured, then took another bite.

Me? I hadn't moved.

And the silence between us was warm and full. Music was floating throughout the house, filling the space.

Finally, "You going to keep looking at me like that?" Eyes on eyes, she teased playfully.

"Like what?" I flirted, playing along. I already knew. I'd never tire of looking at her.

She waited a beat or two. "Like… you're thinking of last night." The top of her lip curled.

"I am." I responded immediately.

Her smile was easy, her lids low. "Well, stop." Her tone was sultry as she pointed to my plate. "Eat."

"I could…" Her eyes never left mine. "I'd eat you up right here off this table, Belle."

She threw her head back laughing. I'd caught her off guard. This was my second time within the hour, alluding to having another taste of her. I knew how much she loved the way I ate her. Savored her. Pleased her with my mouth.

Damn. I loved it too.

Yeah, this was wild.

After Claudia happened, something broke in me. Something profound that I avoided.

And India managed to permeate that. Effortlessly. I swear, I never let myself drift anywhere close to commitment, after all these years. No promises, no feelings. Just music, travel, and occasional sex when I wanted it.

I went to my bedroom, sat at my desk, and opened my laptop, deciding to fine-tune a grant proposal I was working on. I had a few hours to spare.

I've served on the board of a Music Academy for the past two years, but I've been involved with the program since its inception nearly a decade ago. The funding would sustain and expand our music academy, offering high-quality music education to underserved youth. Youth who otherwise wouldn't have the opportunity.

It's a great program with a great cause. Our core belief is that music can significantly contribute to children's mental and social development. And we wanted to provide underserved children with the gift of music.

And music truly is a gift. We serve nearly fifty elementary schools across the greater Sacramento area, helping build confidence, fostering creativity, and providing opportunities that might otherwise be out of reach.

The proposal wasn't due for a few more weeks, but it wasn't something I took lightly. I knew this could determine whether our program sponsors would agree to continue supporting this effort. And it could garner additional donors.

But it was daunting. I don't mind writing. I write all the time. As a professor and musician. I contribute thought pieces to a quarterly music magazine.

But academic writing is a whole different beast. Ask anyone who's written a thesis.

I thought back to India's vulnerability earlier. Sharing with me her desire for her own tattoo equipment.

And the hard times they'd fallen on.

I understood her hesitation in sharing that. She's so proud. I knew that was a big deal for her. But I'm really glad she shared it with me.

I'll keep being there for her. If she needs me, I'll be right by her side. I genuinely care about her.

She was hugely mistaken if she thought for a second I'd let her stress over that alone.

Even if it didn't make sense to anyone else.

I didn't care.

I heard my phone vibrate on my desk beside me.

Micah: Ball tomorrow?

Me: Yup. Usual spot. How's 10 am?

Micah: Works for me. See you tomorrow

Me: Bet.

I'd been so eager to see Micah, catch up with him, and share everything that had been going on with India and me.

I cracked up thinking about the sudden change of events.

It is what it is.

twenty-nine

SOL

"So. How's married life?" I asked my best friend of twenty years. When Micah smiled, that was all the answer I needed.

"That good, huh?" I teased as I took a seat on a bench near the court. Micah was standing nearby and already gulping his water.

It wasn't too chilly when we arrived this morning, and the early afternoon was warming up just a bit. It felt just like an early spring morning in Elk Grove. I appreciated the light breeze. Playing ball, we broke a sweat. We were at a park near Micah's house. He lived about twenty minutes from me. We often met here to play ball.

Micah lived in Elk Grove, a rapidly growing suburb just south of Sacramento. His neighborhood was very different from mine. Modern homes are popping up everywhere you look. And it's no wonder. Elk Grove is a great place to settle down. It's multicultural and multigenerational, with friendly people, affordable living, plenty of jobs, excellent schools, and beautiful parks to enjoy. Families were outside now with their young children, climbing all over the nearby playground.

"Indeed. Never better," Micah said, nodding. He capped his water bottle, placing it beside the bench, and took a seat. "Destiney's pregnant." His smile never leaving.

"Is she?! Congrats, man!" I said as I immediately stood up, slapping hands with Micah.

I didn't expect this news, but it wasn't a surprise either. I knew Micah wanted a family and had been searching for his wife since college. I was over the moon for my boy.

"She is," Micah beamed with pride and excitement.

"I love this for you, man. You two will be great parents."

"Appreciate you." Micah looked away, focusing on something in the distance. "A little nervous, but we're hopeful." Another beat, "We lost one late last year. It was early, but it hit us pretty hard. And I hated to see Destiney go through that."

My eyebrows were at my hairline as I looked at Micah. He was still focused on something beyond me.

"Anyway... that's part of why we didn't want to share with anyone too soon this time.

"Yeah, man. I get it," I told Micah gently. "Damn… I had no idea."

Micah smiled weakly. "We kept it close. And we're so excited this time, but I'd be lying if I said I'm not scared as hell, too. Been trying to be the strong one. My wife's been leaning on me. And I want her to be able to. Grateful for you."

"Of course! You already know." I paused for a moment or two. Fortunate that Micah trusted me with this. His vulnerability, above all.

And it was mutual. I trusted Micah with my life.

I sighed deeply. It hit me hard. I really had no idea. "I'm so sorry you had to go through that. Can't even imagine. But God has a plan and a purpose." Micah nodded. "For what it's worth, I'm proud of you, man. So proud of you. For being there for her. And trying again. That takes guts."

Micah nodded again. "Thank you. Things are different this time. Every little thing will get in my head if I let it." He chuckled, "But I'm overprotective as hell this time. I know Destiney is over me already! And I have a list of questions every time she sees her doctor." We shared a laugh. "Just hoping and praying things work out this time."

I nodded. "They will. And this little one is already so blessed. You're already fighting for them. Just take it a day at a time. I got you. Anytime you need to talk. And praying with you, man."

We slapped hands again and leaned in for a quick hug.

"Appreciate you, fam."

Yeah. Micah is my brother. It's a trip when I think about how much time I've spent the past several years searching for my people.

False hopes dissolving almost instantly.

Leads that end up being dead ends. Stopping and restarting only to still get nowhere.

Maybe I was searching for something that wasn't meant for me to find. I knew I had family in Micah. The strong, vulnerable, and unspoken loyalty we'd built as teenagers had grown into open support. A support I was incredibly grateful to have in my life. A support I knew many people didn't get to experience.

And Micah's family, my chosen family, also chose me. And his parents. His mother is lovely, supportive, wishing me well, and still asking about me. And Micah's father. He treated me like a son and still does. He's an inspiration and a source of strength. Many people forget that strength isn't always loud. Its significance often lies in quiet resilience.

"So, what's been up with you, man?" Micah's question pulled me out of my thoughts. "You been making something shake with India?"

I chuckled softly. I had plans to bring Micah up to speed, although things had changed very recently. I wasn't as confident about being with India anymore. I was. But now, I'm not. I wasn't planning to give up entirely, but I didn't even know how I would approach us now. We're still friends. I told her that nothing would change. And I don't want anything to change. I don't want to lose her. I care about her.

"Sol." Mich volleyed when I didn't answer for a while.

I chuckled lightly. "Honestly. I don't want to kill this vibe. You just shared some great news with me, and I'd rather keep things up here." I gestured with my hands.

Micah's eyebrows were raised. "Kill the vibe?" his tone was tinged with concern. "What happened?"

"Nothing like that," I clarified quickly, chuckling.

"Okay. Well, whatever it is, say it with your chest."

When I remained silent, Micah said, "Bro. We been rolling since CD players and flip phones. Lay it on the table man. We can figure it out."

I nodded my head. He was right, and I appreciated his concern.

I sighed, finally sharing, "India… We were chilling at first and having fun. Messing around. But man… I've caught some serious feelings for her." Micah nodded in understanding and let me rock. "Just last night, we talked about it. She feels just like I do. But…" I sighed again. "She's not trying to lock anything down. Said she can't." I shrugged my shoulders. "She's just not ready right now."

"Hmm." Micah paused briefly, sitting up straighter. "Sounds familiar." After a moment, he added, "I mean... who else do we know that was out here saying 'she wasn't ready for all that'?"

I chuckled as I thought about it. It didn't take me long to figure it out.

"You talking 'bout your now, wife."

"Right. She's my now wife. I'm a husband. Soon to be father. About to be a diaper budget planner." Micah had a goofy grin, and we laughed. "For real though. You remember how pressed I was."

"I sure do!" I jeered playfully.

"Hey! I knew what I wanted, and I stayed solid. Showed her what life would be like with a man like me around. Minus the pressure. Just had to give her time to catch up. And eventually she saw it. She saw me."

"Yeah. I see." I bounced the basketball between my legs as we sat there. Recalling just how patient Micah was in his pursuit of Destiney. It really was a beautiful thing when it all came together for them.

But there was no guarantee that would be our story. As much as I wanted it to be. I mean... having a shot with India. Being her man. Her being my woman.

Marrying her. Eventually having children… I wasn't thinking about that. Not just yet, but it wasn't something I was opposed to.

Crazy because I was. Once upon a time.

And I wanted all of those things with Claudia. I desperately wanted those things with her. And, well, India restored my faith in love. I can't even say when it happened. I couldn't draw a line in the sand if someone offered me a million dollars. And in opening my heart to her and us, I subconsciously accepted the idea that forever with India sounded so good. It sounded like the most mesmerizing melody. Yeah. India exhibited the qualities that would make a great life partner, a great wife, a nurturing mother. Yeah. India checked all the boxes.

But she had to see that. How could I get her to recognize something right in front of her? She had to see it for herself; that was the only way it would work. The possibility that she might never see it was something I worried about.

"Mich... what if I wait around for her and she never gets there?"

"That's a legit question, man. And I gotta be honest." Micah paused. "That's always a possibility. But at least you know you showed up in good faith. On some real shit. But if you come through the way I know you can, on a white horse, doing everything you're capable of, handling her heart the way it's meant to be handled... she might surprise you."

I nodded saying nothing. I understood.

Micah cracked up. "Women have layers, man. You know that. Just stay the course. Be patient with her. I believe she'll come around."

I cracked up too. "Oh. This you being wise cause you a whole husband now?" I said in jest. It was all love. And I appreciated him. His time, his words, the fact that he cared so much for India and me.

Micah threw his head back. "Nah! This is me being right."

We laughed.

"I'm telling you, man. Patience and consistency. That's it. You want India? Let her feel that. Show her. Then fall back a little and let her miss you. You don't want to smother her too much."

I shook my head, smiling. "Okay, Love Guru."

Micah found that so funny. He shrugged, "Worked for me. She married me. Now she's growing me a son."

"How you know it's a boy?"

Micah leaned back, grinning wide. "I just know."

We burst out laughing again.

"I'm glad you told me, Sol. Seriously," Micah said once he'd calmed down. "And don't ever think you have to hold back. We're brothers."

"Thank you."

"Bet. And it was no surprise. I knew you'd eventually tell me something about you two. I remember when I introduced you. I noticed those glances. Didn't think much of it when you didn't say anything. I honestly forgot about it until that day at Mal's when you asked about her those months later." Micah had a lazy chuckle. "India is solid. Destiney speaks of her on the regular.

They've been best friends for a decade. And you have so much to offer, bro. Even if she doesn't see that yet."

I had a lazy cackle to match. "I had to fuck around and catch feelings?" It was rhetorical. Not a question Micah could answer. I couldn't even answer.

"Nothing wrong with catching feelings. It happens to the best of us. And I'll be just as honest as I am supportive…" Micah waited for me to look at him."Sometimes people just need time."

I nodded silently, understanding. That was something that kept coming up.

Time. It was as if we were on two different wavelengths. Strange, considering we had such an incredible synergy. But the concept of time seemed to be moving at different speeds for India and me.

And timing.

I was ready for a commitment with her. I was prepared to go all in and do this thing. She was convinced she wasn't ready. And she couldn't.

And if only we'd met at a different time…

But I believe we met when we were meant to.

I believe in divine timing.

And I'm hopeful, without relying on false promises. That could be tricky.

"It's frustrating wanting more than the other person does, but keep that line of communication open. Continue to be genuine with her and yourself. You aren't crazy for wanting more. I respect India. She's my wife's best friend. Love her like a sister… but listen, man: if you keep showing up for her and she doesn't end up on the same page as you at some point… you have to ask yourself some tough questions. Most importantly, don't lose yourself in it. Don't forget your worth."

I nodded. After a few moments, "How long am I supposed to wait? I don't want to end up holding on to nothing."

"Indeed. And I wouldn't expect you to wait forever," Micah sighed. "It's not easy sitting in that in-between. Believe me, I know. Especially now that your heart's involved. But… you laid it all out. If you really care about India, give her space to meet you. And if she has something real for you, she'll come around. She isn't shutting the door completely... seems like she might just need some time. And if not... you didn't hold back. You showed up, and that's what counts."

I nodded in understanding. Yeah, I could rock with this. I had nothing else to say for now, just reflecting on his words. His wise advice. The brotherly connection between Micah and me was layered with vulnerability, humor, banter, and heart. Christ-centered above all. We prayed for each other.

Later that afternoon, as I drove home from the park, I thought back over the advice Micah had generously shared. I was alone again, and that was the best time. The radio was off.

Micah offered advice like a supportive friend would, without giving false hope or toxic positivity. We're in our mid-thirties now, and even though Micah is only a few months older than me, his protective older-brother vibe was on full display this morning. But that was okay. I appreciated him. Immensely.

We were both vulnerable for two very different reasons. Our dialogue reflected our emotional maturity. We're grown men. Past posturing. With faith in God and in our relationship, all while respecting boundaries. This was a dynamic we created, having been friends for more than half our lives, and always wanting to see the other succeed and be happy in any space they inhabit.

And I knew Micah wanted to see things work with India and me. He won't push me to walk away too quickly. He wants to see me happy. He was there to lend an ear when I fell apart over Claudia.

And that's precisely who Micah is.

Solid. Loyal. A man of valor and faith.

And I knew Micah wanted to see things with India and I work. He won't push me to walk away too quickly. He wants to see me happy. He was there to lend an ear when I fell apart over Claudia.

And that's truly who Micah is.

Solid, loyal, and full of valor and faith. He's supportive, honest, and reassuring, always grounded emotionally. He's encouraging, even when he's facing his own challenges. Yeah, Micah is my brother. The closest thing I've ever had to a brother. I thank God endlessly for him.

♪♥♫♥♪

It was about 2:30 in the afternoon when I arrived at my parents' house. Dinner was promptly served at 3:00 sharp on Sundays. I rounded the front of my car, took a few deep breaths, and as I walked up their circular driveway, I noticed a black sedan. Maybe it was hired help or a chef. My mother was a decent cook, but she liked to hire a chef to do the cooking occasionally. Usually, that was only on special occasions. Just as I reached the front door, my mother was already swinging it open, as if she had been waiting for me to arrive.

"There you are, son!" she chirped excitedly.

"Hello, mother." I kissed her cheek, and we exchanged pleasantries.

After closing the front door, I proceeded to the living room where I knew I could relax until dinner. My father was probably there now, and we'd be able to talk. Maybe even watch some of the game.

I needed to calm my nerves.

I'd be informing my mother that I did not plan to continue seeing Noelle. That nothing with Noelle and me was going to happen. Regardless of how my conversation with India the other day went, I wasn't planning to pursue anything with Noelle, and it was best for both of us to move on separately. But. Even after talking with Micah, my thoughts were all over.

The thing was, Noelle was a sure thing. Not that she was even a contender, but. Anyway, India, I was still pursuing. With no guarantee it would happen. Despite her mutual attraction and shared romantic interest in me. I thought about that too. How things have shifted for me again. Before Claudia shattered my heart the way she did, I wanted a family once upon a time. And India restored that. Rekindled that. And I was open to the idea of a wife and a family again, at some point.

Yeah. I'd been lost in my own thoughts, confronting my doubts and wondering if I'm making a mistake by pursuing a love that might never give us a chance. I'm risking my heart again with no guarantee of a reward. And India has my heart now. I told her my heart had been beating for her. I'm falling in love with her. I want to. I want India. They say it's better to have loved and lost than never to have loved at all. Love is a risk. They say, no risk, no reward. They also say, the greater the risk, the greater the return. I silently exhaled in frustration. They say a bunch of shit.

And I don't know that I necessarily agree with those sentiments. Not completely. My thoughts were all over the place. But one thing I was absolutely sure about was that I wanted to pursue things with India, even without knowing where we'd end up or if we'd even be together. Either way, I was willing to take that risk. Besides, my mother had been trying desperately to get ahold of me, and I needed to shut this whole cookie operation down. Today was the day.

I know my mother wanted some answers from me. She'd been texting me, calling me, demanding I answer her calls. When I didn't, she insisted I give her a call. She even tried calling from my father's phone, as if that would make a difference. I will admit, he and I communicate much better. He's much more easygoing, levelheaded, and easier to talk to. Usually, I would have answered, but I wasn't a fool. I knew it was her calling from his phone. So, I didn't answer those either. And I knew she'd gotten the news hot off the press. Spencer went back, telling everything he saw and heard when he came out to HomeGrown those weeks ago. And I know my aunt and my mother talked about it. That was fine. I'd fill her in on the details before I left this afternoon.

And I was really looking forward to getting out of here. I'd call India as soon as I got home, and we'd be able to chat. It had only been a couple of weeks, but I missed her. Like hell I did. We'd only been texting. No voice calls, no voice memos. I needed to hear her voice in my ear.

Since that conversation, things weren't quite the same. I could see India maybe feeling unsure about how to navigate this space between us. I was feeling the same way. I told her everything was the same, and I meant it. The safe space we had created was still there for her to exist in and land softly whenever she needed to. But figuring out how to handle these feelings we had. That was the tricky part. For me. They continued to grow even after being shut down. Wild. I couldn't help myself.

Meanwhile, I planned to consider the sage advice Micah gave me, especially that feelings don't move at the same pace.

And India and I have still been texting. I never wanted to lose that. Or her. Even if she won't let me have her. I still loved hearing from her. Every time her name appeared on my screen, alerting me of a notification, I loved it. I sent her a few bike trail suggestions. We talked about riding again soon. I mentioned that when we rode out next, I had something I wanted to show her. She sent heart eyes and then star eyes, telling me she couldn't wait and that she was "so freaking excited." Her words exactly. I grinned at that. Yeah, India being so excited made me very excited. Him too, which was fine. India moves me in so many ways, and I haven't been the same since experiencing her. Yeah.

"Solomon, not so fast." My mother called after me, pulling me out of my thoughts. I had already descended their expansive corridor, heading toward the living room. I stopped and turned to face her. With graceful strides, my mother was beside me in moments. A warm, pleasant smile lit up her milk-chocolate face. Her tone wasn't pressed or frantic, surprisingly.

And my mother looked lovely this afternoon. She was always well put together, even when lounging. Her hair was pinned up, with a few long bangs framing her face. Nothing fancy, but she was dressed up a little more than she usually would be for dinner.

"I know you've been calling me mother, trying to get ahold of me," I began.

"It's alright, dear." She waved her hand dismissively. "You're here now. That's all that matters." She then turned back.

Uncharacteristically nonchalant.

Hmm. Okay.

"Right." I nodded, unsure of what else to add. This definitely caught me off guard.

"Well. I'm headed to the living room to speak with Dad. We'll chat more at dinner." I commenced my stroll, but hardly took two steps when my mother briskly grabbed my arm.

"Solomon. Honey..." She raised her hands to my collar, smoothing it out. Then she brushed invisible dust off each of my shoulders. I raised my eyebrows expectantly. "Do you mind going to the sitting room first? There's a post for you on the table. Arrived a few days ago."

"Sure." I turned the opposite way, heading toward the sitting room. Not thinking much of it. It was sporadic, but I still received mail here at my childhood home.

I guess the odd part was why my mother was so insistent that I go there first. I could have grabbed it on my way out later.

As I approached the sitting room, I thought it might be from a university. I'd submitted a few applications. My parents also believed I was holding myself back by staying at Sac City College. However, I think it's just their desire to brag about me. Teaching at a prestigious university would give them something to boast about. Still, I had been applying here and there. Most recently, I applied for each of the positions my dean shared with me, just because I said I would.

Some universities would reach out to me unsolicited, offering faculty positions sight unseen based on my credentials and my extensive online presence. I received invitations to guest lectures. Guest panelist invitations. I wondered if it was an invitation to a state dinner, gala, benefit, or fundraiser. I moved through several different circles, and many of them sent me correspondence.

Wait. Maybe it was something about my birth family. I'd been facing so many doors closing in my face. Was this finally a lead on something? I picked up my pace, excited at the possibility.

The double doors of the sitting room were closed, so I slid them open and, to my surprise, I found Noelle perched on the sofa. She immediately stood up.

"Solomon. Hello." She spoke in a measured tone. Friendly. Practiced. Polite.

This was clearly a power move by my mother. Claudine Avery, not to be outdone, she invited Noelle over without telling me and tried to force this issue. Bless her heart. Convinced this forced proximity would spark some interest… or perhaps push me into submission.

Noelle smoothed her dress after she stood completely. She was dressed to impress, with a pleasant, plastered-on smile. Me? My irritation was back, and had gone from zero to one hundred in nanoseconds.

"Excuse me for just a second," I told her in a calm tone. It was clipped too, and at this point I didn't care. Noelle probably knew she'd be surprising me. She and my mother have a pact to overpower me.

Or try to. It won't work, though. I promptly turned on my heels and headed back toward the kitchen where I knew my mother was. Yeah. I was very frustrated. But felt betrayed and sad too. She sent me to the sitting room knowing what I would find and didn't think to tell me. And although I was upset, I wouldn't completely explode. I planned to save this conversation for dinner, but it couldn't wait. That was fine.

Just as I expected, I found her in their spacious kitchen. It was bright, open, and modern. My mother stood near the kitchen island, casually chatting with the chef and housekeeper, who were busy plating our meals.

"Solomon." She greeted me calmly, smiling as if she hadn't just blindsided me. "You all can wash up. Dinner is about to be served."

"Really, mother?" I let the silence hang for a second.

So did she, giving me a look of indifference, yet a faint smile still lingered.

"You invited Noelle here without telling me? Is this some kind of ambush?"

"Oh, son. You're being dramatic." She waved dismissively. "It's only dinner. I thought you might come to your senses if you could see what's right in front of you. Besides, we'll need to get together more often since you two will be married soon."

She was calm. Smiling even. And I was furious. I took a deep breath in an attempt to stay respectful.

"Mother," I said firmly but calmly. "What's clear is that you won't trust me to make my own choices. You went behind my back, trying to control something. Like you always do. I'm a grown man. I've already told you I'm not interested in anything more with Noelle."

"Oh, Solomon. You're not thinking clearly. You're emotional. And Noelle is a woman who understands the world you're from. She…"

"Mother. No." I interrupted gently. "I've told you, I'm not interested in anything more with Noelle."

My mother beckoned for the housekeeper to start taking the plated food into the dining room. "I've told you, Solomon, honey. The woman you share your life with reflects everything your father and I have worked so hard to build. This is legacy. Our name carries weight. In rooms and in history. And while I'm sure she's… sweet in her own way…" I narrowed my eyes. "…Sweetness doesn't translate into grace, refinement, or understanding." She shrugged dismissively.

My eyes were narrow slits.

I nodded once. "You heard me. I know that's what this is about."

She spoke in a calm tone. "Your cousin mentioned her. And I had a few questions, that's all."

"Asked a few questions and immediately called in your reinforcements?"

"I tried to talk to my son about it, but he wouldn't answer my calls," she said sarcastically. I rolled my eyes, huffing in frustration.

"Oh, don't get yourself all upset. Talking with you isn't working anymore. It seems you've decided to ignore everything we've built for you, and I had to remind you of what you already have. Noelle knows how to carry the name and what we stand for."

My tone was clipped as I seethed, "Noelle knows what *you* represent. Not me." I continued, "My love life is not a business deal, and if you want to remain a part of my life at all, you have to start respecting me. Not just the version of me you want to control."

My mother had been rummaging through the fridge and turned to face me, her eyes wide.

"You think you're protecting me, but you're only trying to control me. You knew I'd be here for dinner. I was planning to talk to you about India this afternoon. But when you found out I was spending time with another woman, you went behind my back again, instead of giving me a chance to discuss it with you."

My mother had a cold smile, her voice still calm. "I already know what she's not." My mother stood straight, slowly crossing her arms. "No need for me to know her."

I followed suit, straightening my own back. "Mother. I won't let you disrespect the woman that means something to me."

She shook her head, a faint chuckle escaping her lips. "We're worlds apart. And it's not about love. It's about alignment. Alignment of our visions, values, and social fluency. We've raised you to move in circles with dignity and distinction. That girl…" She paused, forcing a polite smile. Wow. "I'm sure she's lovely, but she's not the best woman to stand beside you at a charity gala. Can she represent our family at a board dinner or a foundation fundraiser without stumbling?" She paused briefly. "Or is she more concerned about taking selfies and posting about manifesting her come-up on Instagram?" My mother cracked up. But wasn't shit funny.

My jaw clenched. I was furious. But I stayed calm because my calmness was my own form of power. My mother believed she had all the control, but she was mistaken.

"I came here this afternoon out of respect. You used that respect to manipulate me. I need you to understand something. This can't keep happening."

Her smile disappeared. Her eyes were as wide as saucers.

"Solomon. Honey." Her tone was pleading. I'd struck a nerve with her somewhere. "I'm not questioning her worth as a person… it's the fit. As your mother… I… It's my duty to protect you, son. I'll protect you with my life. Until my dying day, I'll protect you. I want what's best for you. And who's best for you." Her tone was telling. She was growing emotional. She hung her head. A sign of her uncharacteristic vulnerability. My mother was great at controlling everything.

I took several deep, calming breaths.

"Mother." I softened my tone but stayed firm. "I want to live the life I choose. This life…" I raised my arms, gesturing around me, "It isn't me. I want love. Not a business deal. Happiness isn't optional for me. You might not like the idea of the woman I'm falling for, but she knows me in ways no one else ever has. She sees the man I am inside. Beyond what I have to offer on the outside. And that's what I want in a future wife. Not some legacy partner."

My mother slowly turned in the other direction, took a few steps, and said nothing. Not for a while. No rebuttal.

For now, anyway.

It wasn't lost on me that she was apparently disarmed by my revelation that I was falling in love with this woman. A woman I was determined to pursue regardless of her approval or not. I knew my words had struck her hard, but my mother needed a reality check. It was past time she realized I saw exactly what she was doing, and it wasn't going to work anymore. It was past time I make it clear that I didn't need her permission. I wasn't asking. And I was finally establishing a boundary. Though I disagreed, I understood her concern for family legacy and reputation. This was the only world my mother knew.

As an elite, wealthy Black woman, twice Ivy League educated with a degree in medicine, it was almost expected that she would voice her concerns and disapproval about a "common" woman I was seeing. And she would express her maternal protectiveness over my future and my heart, layering her words in a classy, diplomatic tone that cut sharply beneath. Yeah, my mother was quite protective of me. She didn't appreciate any of the harm Claudia brought on.

Just as well, her subtle or not-so-subtle dismissal of the very idea of India pissed me off. More than a few beats passed. Nothing but silence between us. Our housekeeper returned to the kitchen to quietly inform my mother that dinner was ready to be served. And my mother nodded.

"Thank you, Helena," I told her.

"You're very welcome, Mr. Avery." She quietly left the kitchen, and moments later, my father came in.

"Hey Dad." I went over to my father for a quick hug.

"Hello, son. I didn't realize you were in here."

When we parted, I saw him glance over at my mother. Her back was still turned to me. She was leaning against a counter.

My father and I exchanged expressions. His eyebrows were up, and I nodded.

He understood.

"Mom and I had a chance to talk over a few things, and I expect the two of you will want to discuss that." He nodded again.

"I won't be staying for dinner this afternoon. I'm not in the best space right now." My father nodded at that, too.

I inhaled deeply, exhaling slowly. "Dad. I love you and Mom. So much. I truly do, and I appreciate everything you've provided for me. I see that everything you've built is about continuing this family's legacy. I understand that, and I respect it. But..." I looked into my father's expectant eyes. "That's not the same thing I want. That life isn't me. The galas. The circles. The politics." I sighed heavily. "It's never been who I am."

"And I don't want a wife who just looks good on paper. I want someone who sees me and loves me. That's India. She gives me that. You haven't met her, but..." I smiled, for the first time since I arrived here. I smiled really big. I saw the shift in my father's face and expression. Can't quite call it. Whatever it was. But I saw it. "If you met this woman... you'd see what I see."

I continued, "She's not from our world, but maybe that's the point. It isn't about appearances for me. I'm not trying to tarnish the family name; I want to live my life on my terms. Loving the woman I chose. The woman I love. And building the kind of future that I want to build."

My father gave a subtle nod. Typical. My mother was still standing by the kitchen counter, still hadn't turned to face me again. But that was fine. I'd made my point. Grounded in respect. Always respectful. That's one thing I wouldn't waver on. I acknowledge their sacrifices and the legacy they care so much about. I sincerely hope they can someday care just as much about the life I want for myself and the possibilities that come with it.

With nothing more to add, I said, "I'll talk to you later, Dad. Mom. I love you both."

I slipped through the kitchen door, headed toward the front door. Things hadn't quite gone as I expected. But I was glad it was over. I'd set some boundaries and made it clear I wouldn't be controlled or manipulated. Proud of myself for being emotionally honest. And for speaking from my heart about the woman I was falling for.

And. Maybe I was getting ahead of myself.

Yeah. I definitely was, but I didn't care.

I was almost at the front door when I heard, "Solomon? Where are you going?"

I turned toward the soft voice a few feet behind me. "I won't be joining you all for dinner," I said carefully, and I saw Noelle's brows dip in confusion, so I quickly added, "My mother and father can answer all of your questions."

I drove away feeling lighter and affirmed. All I needed was honest love and simplicity, not *performative* black excellence. I smiled the entire way, and when I arrived home eleven minutes later, I called India.

"Hey Artist Girl."

"Hi, Music Man. Home already?"

"Yeah." I sighed. "Things ended early." Deciding to skip the details. That was enough drama for the day. I just wanted to focus on talking to her.

"Hmm. You okay?"

"I am now."

"Aww."

"How was your day?"

"Low key so far. Went to church. Helped Ma cook dinner. You called at the perfect time. Just took a shower."

"Mmm. In bed with your sketchbook?"

Her light titter cruised through the line. "You know it. In bed with your guitar?"

"I would be. But… you're more interesting than my chords right now."

Her giggle was soft. And so cute. I knew her cheeks were warm, too.

And I was glad that our flirty banter had made its way back in this moment, as if it had never left.

This was just a phone call. No FaceTime. But there was something special about her tone when it was only our voices. I knew she was settling against her pillows and probably lying on her back. Her damp hair was likely twisted on top of her head.

"Your parents having a good day?" She knew what I was asking.

"They are. Thank you. Oh! Dad finally fixed the light in my shed," she chuckled sweetly.

We drifted into quiet comfort. Friendly and familiar. Words didn't need to fill every pause between us. It was perfect.

"Planning to get in a nap today?" I asked. India told me she loved naps but rarely got to take them. I knew Sundays were slower for her, and it was her only day off, which I was glad she was intentional about. She was always busy, always working.

"That sounds wonderful." Her cute giggle leaving her lips again. Then, "I could take the best naps in your bed. Wish I was there."

I closed my eyes. "I do too." I paused for a moment. "Don't forget about your open invitation." My voice was a little rougher now. "I feel close to you, Artist Girl. Even when you're not here."

I heard her exhale slowly, "Yeah. That's exactly how it feels."

We didn't press. But now, the silence carried a different weight. It felt… aching.

A humming ache.

"I like us like this," she whispered that.

"So do I," I murmured.

"I think about you a lot, Sol."

"Belle. You have no idea." My voice hardly audible.

There was a brief moment or two. We remained silent.

"That nap sounds like a great idea right about now." she laughed. "Can I call you in a little while?"

"You absolutely can."

A beat.

Then another.

Then another.

"I should let you sleep," I said, but neither of us moved to hang up.

"I'll call you when I wake up," she said softly.

"I'll be right here."

thirty

INDIA

Sol leaned down, his nose gently brushing my cheek. His lips pressed against my ear as he kissed me there.

Then he softly spoke, his voice trembling with restraint, "You alright, Belle?"

I nodded, but only just.

He had my eyes, mine blinking slow and heavy.

This was our second round, and I was blissfully satisfied. I wanted more, just like he did. But I was... fuck. I don't even know how to describe it.

He chuckled deep in his chest. "Tell me, baby... I want to hear you... Are you okay?"

That **baby** *got me every damn time.*

We only use it when we're doing this. Only then. But it was so sweet the way it flowed from his lips. Naturally. Like second nature. I can admit that I'd love to hear it all the time.

"Yes." My voice was laced with need. "Just take it slow. Okay?"

"Always." Sol's lips were back on my neck, pressed softly and tenderly. His tongue revealed itself as he moved over me, brushing a kiss to my temple. "Taking our time, baby. I'm not going anywhere. And this mouth of yours, these soft ass lips..." Kiss. "This sweet pussy, this little body. I'm gone take my time with you. Stretch you real slow. You ready for that, baby?"

My response wasn't instant. I needed a moment to compose myself. Sol just ate me out again. For the second time tonight. Past satisfaction. I'd just come again. That orgasm surged through my whole body, and I swear you could have knocked me over with a feather.

I was so turned on, totally distracted and getting worked up all over again.

Sol's words were something else. He'd been talking to me all night. Before. During. After. Especially during. Explicit. Descriptive. Dirty. Nasty.

Yet. Sweet as hell.

Tender. Respectfully. All at once.

And. Sol enjoyed talking to me. He'd be balls deep carrying on with his conversation, constantly asking me questions. He liked when I responded, and I was fine with that. I liked it too, and I didn't realize how much I did. But I was learning all kinds of things, spending time with Solomon. Most of all, I was learning about myself.

I haven't been the same since experiencing him. In any capacity. Mentally. Physically. Emotionally.

And side note: his playlist constantly blew my mind. He'd turned me on, pun intended, to DVSN. Their whole catalog was fire. "Excited" was on right now, whispering low. I loved this one. I'd asked him to run it back a few times when I heard it for the first time earlier.

"Can I be inside you, Belle?" He posed. "I'm hungry for you."

We've connected intimately so many times. Yet, he still asked first. Constantly checking in with me, making sure I was okay with anything he wanted to do. Those questions were woven into everything else. Questions, declarations, praise. Freely flowing from his lips.

And even when prompted, sometimes I was at a loss for words. Like right now. Just before he ate me out, he was having the time of his life playing with my pierced nipple. His fucking tongue doing all sorts of shit, making my nipples ache. In the best way. Something crazy was that I hadn't even realized how much my confidence had increased. I used to be so self-cautious about my tiny ass boobs, but those feelings were long forgotten. Sol made sure of that.

He kissed the piercing, sucking my nipple into his mouth. He was gentle. Always gentle, but firm enough. His tongue. Fuck.

"This was the sexiest surprise of all..." he told me, licking over the tiny gold hoop. "A sexy ass pleasant surprise."

I murmured at the pleasure he gave me. At the pleasure he found in me. Never have I ever. Man, I swear.

Earlier, during the first round, I was on top. For the first time. Briefly. His hands were on my thighs, then came up around my waist. I slowly rocked my hips over him. It was the way he looked at me. His eyes locked onto mine, but his gaze also swept over my body. And it gave me a feeling I'd never had.

"Look at you," Sol murmured, "My sexy Artist Girl."

Sol was always meticulous in everything he did. Took such care.

My nipples were very sensitive, especially the one that was pierced.

"You are perfect, Belle. You know that?" He shifted to my other side, kissing softly and licking my erect nipple. Though it wasn't pierced, it was peaked to capacity. I could probably cut glass. It almost hurt.

Yeah. It did. Hurt so fucking good. He rubbed his warm palms over both of my boobs. Always gentle.

"You used to worry about these, huh? Cause they're small."

These questions weren't meant to be answered. They didn't need to be. Though they were posed as questions, he wasn't really asking anything.

Sol was reminding me, making sure I never forgot how he felt or how he saw me.

His mouth returned to the pierced one. His flat tongue nearly covered the entire surface. He flicked my nipple again and moved to the other one, repeating the same. "I love your tits, Belle. Don't ever get it twisted." His voice was low, reverent, as usual. "They're beautiful and they fit in my hands as if they were made for me."

He kissed between them, moving down the center of my chest and generously planting the tenderest kisses. "They're the prettiest set of tits I've seen. Perfect. You were made just for me, Indie." His tongue traced the hoop slow and deliberate. "Yeah. I'm obsessed with this right here." He flicked it lightly with his tongue.

My hands were woven in his locs. I moved my body closer to him. "Ready to taste you again, baby. Learning you like a beautiful language. Wanna speak fluent Indie."

I moaned. Got damn.

He let out a faint chuckle. "When you think of me, you remember this baby. The way I saw you and how I loved every inch of this beautiful body."

Oh Sol. We're way past that.

"Indie. Baby. You hear me? That alright with you? My sexy Artist Girl."

"Please. Yes. Baby... mmm." That was all I could manage.

And then he moved, entering me inch by inch. The lighting was dim, but I could see he watched my face intently. That was his M.O., reading every movement, every twitch, every nonverbal cue.

His breath was quickening, but he held back. A low growl was caught.

"You feel like heaven." He loved to tell me that, and I loved to hear it. I was so happy he was happy. That he was so into me. That he enjoyed this. I did too.

His lips pressed to mine again. I had his tongue back, swirling around my mouth and dancing with mine. Faintly flavored like me from his earlier feast.

At some point he murmured, "You're so warm. Taking me so well. Baby... you're so fucking wet for me."

"Mmm." I managed. Yeah, all of this was for him. "You did that..." I'd found my voice. Somehow. "You ate my pussy, remember... ate me so good... got me wet as a damn faucet." I lightly tittered.

Speaking of which. Damn. Sol would eat me for so long. Oh my gosh. It was the sexiest thing.

He was eating me earlier, and he just kept going. He would've stayed between my thighs all night if I'd let him. His compliments steady flowing. Just like my essence.

Yeah. Sol was telling me his every thought. A play by play in real time. He loved my scent. The way I tasted. How wet I got.

Sol loved spreading my legs wide, pushing them apart. I was incredibly flexible I could do the splits, and that really turned him on.

Always saying something sexy.

"God, I love having this kind of access to you. You don't know what it does to me."

"I could take my time looking at you just like this, Belle. You're incredible. This view is unreal, and you have no idea how sexy this view is to me."

Yeah. Shit like that.

Also. He intently shared my progress, complimenting me on how long I could go now.

It was true. The first few times he ate me out, I would come so fast.

But according to him, letting him eat me as often as he did, I had built up some endurance.

He explained... in explicit detail, between licking and sucking and flicking and kissing... all up, around and inside my pussy that My sensitivity, arousal response, and orgasm timing have evolved. Now that I've experienced him and my comfort has grown, most of all, we've been communicating, we're intimately familiar, and I'm letting him please me so consistently." Yes. His words, not mine. His exact words. Not only was my mind blown, but I was even more aroused.

I agree.

Emphatically.

The sensations were overwhelming at first. In the best way. I'd never experienced them before. Nothing compares to having your clit licked just right. Your lower lips sucked with just enough pressure. Nothing like it. I realized that now. And it was incredibly pleasurable.

But the more Sol pleased me with his mouth, the more control I gained. I became more aware of myself. More confident in myself and in my communication with Sol. What I loved. What felt good. Of course, he asked a lot of questions. And he was great at pacing himself once we found the sweet spot. I knew exactly when an orgasm was building up. I knew how to edge them now too. But he didn't want that.

No. Sol wanted those the moment they were ready.

Yeah. I was okay with that.

I realized the connection we shared, the psychological comfort I felt with him, which was something I never experienced before him, translated into my mind-body connection. I feel comfortable with Sol. I feel safe with Sol. Rushing toward an orgasm isn't the goal. I enjoy the long sessions. We haven't had any quickies. Not yet.

I heard a faint chuckle from him. "Sol. You're so hard, baby..." I managed through a moan. "You feel amazing."

"Hmm. Love to hear that." His voice was deep and soft, sending vibrations through me. "That was all you, baby. The way you sucked my dick earlier." He groaned, then had a faint chuckle. "Been hard as fucking concrete ever since."

I bit my lip, moaning as he moved deeper, gradually taking long strokes. Making my body... sing? I don't know. My walls fluttered around him, wave after wave of pleasure with each gentle thrust.

My eyes fluttered shut.

"Indie. Baby..."

Yeah. I feel that way too, Sol. He was driving, but I moved with him, hips tilting to match each of his strokes. We had a nice rhythm. Slow enough, taking all the time we wanted.

His hand reached for mine. Instinctively, our fingers intertwined in seconds.

And he squeezed my hand, gently. **You good?**

I squeezed back immediately. **Yes.**

Fuck.

He pressed a kiss to the corner of my mouth. It was such a sweet kiss. He pressed another one to my jaw, lingered there, then moved down to my collarbone and pressed one there too.

"You're getting close, baby. I can feel you," he told me.

It wasn't a question. He knew.

Yeah. Sol knew my body inside and out. Knew every one of my curves. Knew each of my spots. My erogenous zones. He was so deep inside me.

And. I whimpered as he said, "You come whenever you're ready, baby..."

And I whimpered again. High-pitched, breathy.

"Sol..."

"Hmm."

"Baby... I'm going to come all over you."

"Please do. Help yourself… fuck…"
"Yeah…" I drew that out. "Sol. Baby. I'm going to…"
"I got you baby. Go head."

Yeah. Things were so intense. We were in love without saying it out loud. Since our conversation, my thoughts have been all over the place. Consumed. It's been harder than I thought it would be to act like this is casual. I'm already way too deep, and I don't even know how to slow down. I was still riding the afterglow of the last time Sol and I were together, both literally and figuratively. I'd been riding that wave like it was my lifeline.

Craving. Yearning.

I wanted him again. Like that.

But. I wouldn't call him. Not for that reason. Didn't seem right. Didn't feel right. As much as I enjoyed him in that way. We enjoyed each other. It was kismet. Magical. Passionate. But. I told him we couldn't be us. I saw how it crushed him. I can't get the image out of my head. It was subtle. But I saw it. And I told him I'd think about it. I suggested we slow down. He readily agreed. It's just like Sol to do that.

So. Slowing down. In my mind, that meant maybe not sleeping together again for now. Which would be difficult. Because. Shit. But. I care about Sol. And I respect him. It's easy to do. He's been so amazing. Solid. Respectful. Just. Everything.

But calling him back just for lovemaking? Hell no. I wouldn't dare. He's more than what he can do for me physically. So much more. I'll survive if I don't have sex. Maybe this is what I need to clear my head.

In other news, I decided I'm going to call Destiney's therapist. It was past time I made myself an appointment. I don't have insurance, so I'll ask about any cash pay discounts. I hope it's not astronomically high. Since Sol was kind enough to give me cash, I was able to take care of a few things.

The first thing I bought after paying all the bills was a bus pass, and one for next month. Took a load off my mind. I'd get that equipment eventually, but it wasn't a priority, and I couldn't do that right now. The money Sol gave was almost gone. But we were all caught up. We had groceries, and I had secure transportation that would last me the next few weeks. But I would get it.

Somehow. I hadn't looked into tattoo equipment until now. Not really. Simply because I knew I didn't have the money. When I left Sol's place last weekend, I looked into it for the first time and got lost in the rabbit hole.

The very expensive rabbit hole. Tattoo equipment can vary, like most things, depending on quality and whether I bought everything all at once or piece by piece. I had a list in my sketchbook, and it would range from about eight hundred to two thousand dollars for everything I needed. I was definitely leaning toward the higher end if I wanted to invest in quality equipment from the start. However, the tattoo machine, power source, needles and cartridges, inks, hygiene supplies, and miscellaneous items like gloves, ointment, ink caps, and skins, as well as a few bins to organize everything organized, would cost more than I expected. I figured I would add things gradually, which made the most sense. Once I finished a few more commissioned pieces, I could at least buy a gun.

"That looks dope Kam! Love the way that came out!"

Yeah. I'd been fantasizing, and that was a problem because I was shadowing with Kam. I was supposed to be paying attention, and for the most part, I was doing a convincing job. But I already knew all this stuff, with my eyes closed.

"Thanks, girlie. Your work will look better than this once you get started." She wrapped her client's arm in Saran Wrap after giving her aftercare instructions. She'd tatted a detailed sunflower, and it was amazing. The line work. The colors. It took a few sessions, and I was here for each one. It really did look phenomenal.

"You are gassing me up. Please stop! Although I wouldn't mind having a bigger chest, come to think of it… tell me more, Kameron!"

We both cracked up as I helped her clean her station. Returned the ink to the cabinet. Each station had its own sets. Placed her box of gloves there as well. Her antiseptic spray.

It was another Friday night at King Tattoo. Many customers were getting tattooed, pierced, or waiting for their turn. Music filled the wide-open space, layered with chatter, laughs, and the buzzing of different machines.

I'd been shadowing Kameron, or Kam as most everyone called her, for most of the day.

Most of my shadowing was with Kam, but I also shadowed Drew occasionally. Both were equally talented, having been in the game for decades and best to learn from, if I ever get the chance to apply it.

"Girl, stop. You know you're bad. You don't need anyone to gas you up." Kameron had OG energy, like an older cousin looking out for you. She's in her late thirties and has been tatting for nearly twenty years.

She's dope too. Calm and confident, covered in clean, beautiful ink. Her work speaks for itself. She has a loyal clientele that keeps coming back and referring family and friends. Kam stays booked and busy, always in demand.

She's tall too. Not as tall as me, but it was nice meeting another tall woman. It's something tall women would understand. She has a cropped haircut that fits her personality. Minimal makeup. Always in work mode, but she has a presence that commands respect.

I'll always appreciate Kam. When I started here, Kam took me under her wing. She told me she understood what it was like to be the new girl. From day one, she has been very generous with her knowledge and is quietly protective of me. She carefully reviewed my sketches and immediately offered tips for improvement.

I sighed softly as I sprayed the chair with cleaner and wiped it with paper towels.

"The big guy has to agree to that." I let it slip and cursed under my breath instantly. I didn't work in corporate America for long, but I knew better than to gossip about the boss to anyone. People will lead you to believe you can trust them, but they'll throw you under the bus at the first chance they get. And even though Kam was cool people, I knew better. Guess my frustration impaired my judgment.

She chuckled softly as she kept shutting things down. This was her last appointment for the night, and she was ready to leave. The shop closed at eleven pm on Fridays, and it was almost nine pm.

"King is particular," she casually said after a pause. "The fact that he agreed to your apprenticeship was huge. People come in here all the time asking. He doesn't do shit like that. He's very protective of his brand and his clientele." She took off her black rubber gloves and tossed them in the trash bin in the corner. "Keep showing up and doing your thing. He'll give you a shot soon."

"Yeah," I mumbled, trying to sound hopeful.

She had a point. King curated the clientele that came in and out of the shop. He had the talent, and only the best in Sac had chairs here.

But sometimes I wonder if King was holding me back.

I mean, I don't know. He did agree to my apprenticeship, but I'd been putting in so many hours. So many that I practically lived here. I'd only go home to eat and sleep.

But I'd been working these long hours, and it felt like I was just spinning my wheels. I didn't seem to be any closer to moving forward, and I didn't know how to interpret that or what to do about it. I've thought about switching to another shop. Something about this situation made me feel like I'd never reach my goal. Not in this lifetime.

But. The artists who worked here were some of the best in the game. King Tattoo was renown. But. None of that shit mattered if I couldn't get my license. Or any practical experience.

"Hey," Kam said. I looked up at her. "I'll talk to King when I come back Monday. As far as I'm concerned, you're ready to start. At least on some skins. And I'm willing to take the time to train you on that myself."

I smiled. Bright. "Thank you, Kam!"

She smiled in return. "You're welcome."

Kam zipped up her sleek black bag and stood to pull it onto her shoulder. "Any plans this weekend?"

I smiled again, "Yeah. Gonna meet up with a friend. Ride bikes."

Her eyebrows went up. "*Oooh*. Some friend. I don't think I've ever seen you smile like that!" she teased, laughing.

I shrugged. Yeah. That's what happens when I talk about Sol. He gave me the feels, and I couldn't wait to see him tomorrow. I saw him close to three weeks ago, and I missed him. Never really missed him the way I do now. I don't know… I guess it's because the last time I saw him, I told him I couldn't be with him. He poured his heart out, and I turned him down. My heart was soft for him, especially since I wanted that too. I wanted it so badly. I noticed that in the first few days after that conversation, things between us seemed just a little off. Maybe it was me.

Yeah. It was me. Hell. I don't know.

But. We've spoken since and got everything sorted out. I'm glad we're okay again. Sol is special to me. I appreciate his friendship, and I look forward to seeing him. Sharing space.

I'd love a hug too.

"Well. Enjoy your bike ride!" Kam offered. "And have a great weekend. Gotta get out of here. Get my baby. I'll see you Monday." She smiled, and that made me smile again. Kam had an adorable six-year-old son. She talked about her child all the time. She was such a proud, loving mom, and it was the sweetest thing.

"You do the same," I said. "See you." I followed Kam out of her station and back toward the front desk. I had another half hour until it was time for me to leave for the night. I'd float around, checking to see if anyone else needed anything.

Drew was off tonight. He mentioned his teenage daughter had something at school. Drew was a doting father to his one and only princess, his pride and joy. It was the sweetest thing. It reminded me so much of my relationship with my father. Drew had a radiant picture proudly displayed at his station of his wife and daughter. Both are equally stunning, both beaming in the bright sunlight. Drew spoke so kindly of his wife, whom I've had the pleasure of meeting a few times. She often comes to the shop to bring food for Drew. She's warm, kind, and gorgeous. A shining smile. The best part is that his wife is Trini, and it was so nice to bond over our shared Caribbean roots. She was born here but always reps Trinidad and Tobago. She cooks some of the best oxtails I've ever had. She once brought some in for Drew and was kind enough to share some with me, which I gladly accepted. I wasn't about to turn down oxtails!

I headed to Malik's station. I leaned over the wall. "Hey Malik." Malik was adding detail to a tribal design on a man's back. He appeared to be in deep concentration. Understandably.

"Hey India." He didn't look up. "You good?"

Yeah. Malik was cold. We're around the same age, maybe he's a year older. He had the cleanest lines. Malik was the epitome of fine line work. Black and grey was his specialty. I believe he's been tatting for about six years, and he's respected. He can do the dopest portraits, and his shading is unmatched.

He has a fiancé. And they have a baby boy who is about six months old, I think. He loves his little family. He also has pictures hanging at his station, and his son's name is tattooed on his neck. Malik keeps his head down; he comes in, gets to work, and then goes home. Always friendly. Always professional. No drama or flirting. Good, positive energy.

"I'm good. Yep. Just checking in before I leave. Do you need anything?"

Malik works quietly, with precision, nonchalant, and calm energy. He's a man of few words, but it works. And Malik is cute, dark, and muscular. He's clean-cut with a beard and covered in tattoos. Women love Malik; they notice him and try to flirt with him, but he doesn't entertain them.

Finally, "I'm straight, India. Thanks for checking. You have a great night."

"Thanks, Malik. You too."

I was already turning to walk away as quickly as I could. Malik was cool and all, but he was collateral damage. His station was right next to Shawni's. And Shawni is a bitch. Plain and simple. Shawni's in her early twenties, and she didn't waste any time letting me know she was watching me. I wasn't here for her, so I don't understand why she was so pressed. But I guess that's nothing new. She acted just like the girls I dealt with in high school. Sizing me up, offering backhanded compliments, and pretending to be friendly to gain my trust.

I know she's recently licensed. I think she's trying to earn her place and gain respect. She's the youngest person here, and it shows. Her overcompensating behavior is... tacky. Poor thing. She's craving approval, especially from King and Famita. I could tell that right off the bat. She walks in, and the men definitely fawn over her. She's stylish, with her nails always done in cute designs, and she's adorable, but she still seems to be figuring things out. I don't miss the days when I was so unsure of myself. She's friendly enough on the surface, but deep down she's jealous.

Yeah, I said it. I knew her type. She was always watching me. And the second she heard Fatima tell me that she'd be glad to show me how to pierce if I ever wanted to learn, she didn't waste any time telling me what she thought of that. She had an issue with Fatima's energy toward me. Her acknowledgment. Something I don't think I ever saw Fatima do with Shawni. I remember the day well. After Fatima said that, I went to the break room, taking a break and minding my own business. At that point, I'd only been here a couple of weeks.

I had my sketchbook out in front of me, working on some design. Kameron came in and looked over my shoulder.

"This is dope. Can I see?"

Kam flipped through a few more pages. She stayed quiet but gave a slow nod.

"Nice. Clean too," she said, handing me my sketchbook back. "You keep working; you have something."

At some point, Shawni came into the breakroom and caught that part. She didn't say anything, but I could see her looking from across the room. Longer than she needed to. That's when the comments started. Snarky stuff, disguised as playful. Yeah, she wasn't slick. And I'm not stupid. She was jealous.

A few days passed, and Shawni found her way to where I was. I was restocking ink.

"Kam in your sketchbook already?" Her tone was playful, but she had a smirk. "You been here five minutes. You special or something?"

I glanced at her keeping my cool. "She saw something she liked. I was glad to show her my work."

Shawni popped her gum loudly.

I wanted to knock it out of her smart-ass mouth. She didn't know me.

"Mmm." She had a fake smile as she said, "Guess some people get fast-tracked around here."

Yep. She needed her ass beat.

Another time, she asked me the age-old question I'd been asked my entire life.

"You Black... for real? You look kinda mixed."

I wasn't surprised by her question, and I'm darker than Shawni. So, I mean.

"Mixed. Afro-Guyanese and Indo-Guyanese."

She blinked. "Oh... that's different."

Well, that's relative. Back home in Berbice, there's a large community of Afro-Indo Guyanese people. Whatever. I kept my expression neutral. This wasn't the first, and it wouldn't be the last. At some point, Kam told me Shawni was still trying to prove herself. She also said Shawni's behavior had nothing to do with me. She had personal issues. That much was obvious.

I headed to the host station. I'd check in with Fatima and then get ready to head out. I was tired.

"Hey India. King wants to see you before you leave for the night," she glanced at her Apple Watch. "You're almost out of here. You can head there now," she offered.

"Sounds good."

When I entered Kingston's office, he immediately looked up from his laptop. He grinned, and that disarmed me. I wasn't sure what he wanted, but I'd never been called into his office before. I either go in willingly or chat with him when he's out on the floor.

"Am I in trouble?" I asked playfully.

"Everything's fine, Pretty thing." His voice smooth.

I smiled. Saying nothing.

"Sit down a minute. I want to check in with you."

I sat in one of the chairs facing his desk.

"You feeling good?" he asked.

I nodded eagerly.

He chuckled softly, looking me over. He wasn't discreet at all. He licked his lips and nodded. "Tell me more. Pretty thing."

I gave a sweet, closed-mouth smile. "I'm learning so much. Thank you again for the opportunity."

King leaned back in his chair, eyes fixed steadily.

And I warred with myself. This would be a great time to tell King how I'm feeling. How I felt about finally learning to use the gun.

But I didn't. Why? I don't fucking know.

"It's nothing. You're moving faster than I expected. Asking the right questions and picking things up quick." He waited a minute looking me over. He had a pen in his hand; he clicked it a few times. "I'm impressed."

A smile tugged at my lips. "Thank you."

He nodded once. Then, "You have everything you need?"

I sighed lightly.

Tell him, India!

"I do."

King nodded again. "Anything more I can do for you?"

Hmm.

I gave a subtle nod. "When can I start practicing with the gun?" I rushed out before I could change my mind.

He'd been spinning in his chair and then stopped. "You think you ready for that?" His voice was steady, unreadable.

I nodded eagerly. "Absolutely." I responded confidently without hesitation.

He nodded once. Again. Said nothing. Finally, "Aight. Come Monday. We'll start. Let's see what you can do."

"Thank you, Kingston," I said excitedly, trying to play it cool, though I was beside myself.

"Ain't nothing."

I stood turning to leave.

"Pretty Thing."

I looked back, and he slid a plain white envelope across his desk.

My brows furrowed. "What's this?"

"Yours. Open it."

I nervously picked up the envelope. As I opened it, I saw a check inside. Made out to me. For twelve hundred dollars. My eyes widened.

"Wh…But… this apprenticeship is unpaid."

King shrugged. "Says who?"

I said nothing, at a loss for words. Literally. I opened my mouth, and nothing came out. I stood there, in front of his desk, the check in my hand. Processing. I hadn't had this much money at once, without it already being spent, in a long, long time. Maybe it wasn't a lot to King or most people, but it was to me. Times had been so hard. Sol helped me without even knowing it. And now, this. Wow.

"Look. This my shit. If I wanna pay my apprentice for her hard work and because I appreciate her, I'm gonna do it."

I smiled wide. "Thank you so much, Kingston."

"You good." His smile lingered.

"See you Monday."

"I'll be here."

I turned to leave, feeling like a thousand bucks.

Literally.

thirty-one

INDIA

"You friend-zoned him? Girl!"

"Don't say it like that, Des." I shook my head.

"You did, though."

"Not like that."

Destiney peered at me deadpan. "So there's a way to do it? What does that even mean? Please explain."

I shook my head. Laughing despite myself. I didn't even know. I didn't even have an answer.

Things at the shop were hectic today and I was so glad to be off. When I left, I texted her to ask if she was up and if I could give her a call. Instead of replying, Destiney called me, and we shot the shit for a while. Per usual. Eventually she asked if I could spend the night. She was home alone in her big ass house and wanted the company. Micah traveled for work on occasion, so he was in SoCal for a few days. I readily agreed. I missed our impromptu sleepovers. Since they'd gotten married, those weren't really a thing anymore, which was fine. My bestie was a whole wifey and soon-to-be mommy, and I was so stoked for her.

Add to that, I was in my feelings too. My pathetic ass feelings. Feelings I brought on myself.

Missing my connection with Sol. I told him I couldn't be with him, and things got complicated after that. He said everything was fine. Then he gradually pulled away. I thought we were okay again, but then he started backing off again. I felt confused and I missed him.

This sleepover with Destiney couldn't have come at a better time. I'm glad we got to relax. Just like old times, we were eating, laughing, lounging, and chatting. Just enjoying each other's company.

Destiny moved into Micah's house after they got married, and it was a big, beautiful home. I love the high ceilings and wanted to paint them. I felt completely comfortable on their plush, oversized sectional in the spacious main living area. They have another living room, but this is where the TV is. It was on earlier, but we weren't watching. Eventually, we turned on a playlist.

Destiney was comfortably stretched out, munching on dried apricots. After she picked me up, we decided to stop for some snacks. We ultimately settled on making a charcuterie board, one of our favorite things to snack on.

We had the coffee table pulled as close to the couch as we could. Destiney reached over, grabbing another apricot and a cube of pepperjack cheese.

"Oh my gosh. I love this cheese, but I swear it's making me extra gassy." She looked at me, making a face. "I'm sorry. Just warning you Best."

I cracked up, waving her off, "Girl. We've bared all by now."

And then we both cracked up for a good while.

Yeah. Destiney is my sister. So much more than my bestie.

And I loved our girl talks. Absolutely loved them. She could be so silly.

I took a sip of cranberry juice, grimacing at the bitter taste. I've always found cranberry juice too bitter for my liking. I prefer blends like cran-mango, cran-apple, and cran-grape. But Destiney wanted straight cranberry. Apparently, the baby is making their specific demands.

"We have." She returned. Reaching for another cube of cheese and another apricot. "I need to stop, but I can't. I love the pepper jack with this dried fruit."

Destiney wasn't playing around. That's all she was eating.

The board had all our favorites, but that's all she was interested in. The rest of it was for me. We had pepper jack cheese, dried apricots, dried mangoes, almonds, sesame crackers, and green grapes.

"Oh! I just had an appointment the other day." She announced proudly. "Our next appointment is the anatomy scan, and we'll need to tell them not to tell us the gender. We decided we don't want to know. After what happened last time, we just want them healthy."

"Yeah. I hear you. That's all that matters in the end anyway. People get so caught up in all that, gender disappointment. Those TikToks are just plain embarrassing." We laughed. "How are you feeling?"

"Pretty good, most days. The morning sickness is about over with."

"You look amazing."

Destiney smiled sweetly. She really did.

"Thank you."

I nodded. "Yeah. You're glowing. Oh my gosh, you're so beautiful Best. You're so happy. I love this for you."

"Thank you. I am. And it's such a blessing, I just... thank you. I could cry. Don't go getting me all emotional. I'm pregnant."

We cracked up, and Destiney ate more cheese.

"Girl, you may wanna lay off. You'll be blowing trumpets all night."

"My husband will still want me."

I guffawed. "Girl, you're too much."

"He's so good to me, Indie. And super protective. Especially after everything you know. He tells me all the time just to grow our baby. Not to worry about this or that. I can hardly wipe my own ass without him asking what if I need help." She beamed.

"I'm like Micah *chill*. I'll holler if something's wrong. He didn't want to go to SoCal without me. But I insisted I'd be fine. He needed this time away." We laughed.

"Up Late" By Ari Lennox came on. I love this song. Shit, I love Ari period. We chilled in silence for a while.

"He wants me to have everything. You know, he had a smart toilet put in? Just because I mentioned seeing it on YouTube?"

"Wait. A smart... *toilet?*" I posed.

"I'm serious. And it's *smart!* It knows if you peed or pooped. Flushes on its own. Lights up when it's dark."

"Girl, stop!" I was rolling at this point. "Wow." I was still laughing. "Sounds smart, alright."

"Girl. I was telling him, just because I mentioned it, doesn't mean I wanted it. But I'm not mad. My husband listens. Then acts accordingly. He's amazing."

"Micah loves you Best. Honestly, that man will redo this entire house to keep you smiling. I love that."

"Me too. He's such a great man, Indie." Destiney beamed. "And I still don't know what the hell I ever did, but I'm so grateful. Way past grateful. And so blessed."

"Hey! Don't shortchange your amazingness. This relationship is two equal parts. Behind every great man is an even greater woman."

"Period!"

We high-fived each other, cracking up all over again.

"That's sweet. Thanks Indie." Destiney stretched out on the couch. Yawning. We were quiet for a moment. "Honestly, this is all thanks to you. You wouldn't let me give up. You wouldn't let me miss out. Reminding me that I had something great right in front of me if only I would open my eyes and see it. If not for you, I would have missed out." Her tone was sincere. "Now here we are. I have a whole husband who installed a smart toilet for me. And I'm growing our miracle baby. Thank you."

I smiled. "I couldn't let that happen, Best. You two were made for each other."

"You're so sweet, Indie."

"You're sweeter." I returned.

"No way." Destiney shook her head. "You're much sweeter. So sweet, I'm going to get a fucking cavity. Sweet on my own, then fucking with you and all your damn sweetness."

I smiled at that. "You're sweeter. Now stop it."

"You about to fight a woman with child?"

"Oh my gosh." I cracked up, and eventually Destiney did too. I grabbed a few grapes off the tray.

"Hrs & Hrs." By Muni Long crooned in the background. She was dope too.

"You know, Indie," Destiney began, "I feel like you don't believe you're deserving of happiness. But you are."

I creased my brows. "What?"

"You matter and you deserve happiness too."

I glanced at her. "Where is this coming from? What are you even talking about?"

"You know exactly what I'm talking about." When I said nothing, Destiney nodded. "Yeah, I've figured it out."

"Figured what out?"

"You. Your problem."

"Who says I have a problem?"

She looked at me deadpan. "Best. We all have problems."

"Yeah," I said hesitantly. "This is pointed, though."

"Damn right it is. Indie. You said a bunch of stuff about *you can't because of this and that*. But I don't think that's it. There are reasons and then there are excuses." She said, gesturing with her hands. Destiney was curled up on the couch now. Looking comfortable. I had my leg tucked under me. Feeling a lot like she did. This couch man.

"Brandon lied to you, Best. And it seems you've internalized the lies you've been told. You deserve love and to be taken care of. To be appreciated. Spoiled."

I shook my head and sighed.

"Why not? You're one of the most selfless people I know. You think of others, putting everyone and everything before yourself. Be selfish just this once. Sol cares about you. He wants to be with you."

I looked away. A small smile on my lips.

"You need to get out of your own way, Best. I'd hate for you to miss out on something so beautiful. Sol is solid. And the two of you together… two artists… *girl!*" Destiney shook her head.

And. I was intrigued. I'd never thought of it like that.

Destiney continued. "Yeah. You and Sol. Ya'll are ridiculous." She smirked. She sat up to take a drink of her cranberry juice. "Art is love in all its forms. As an artist, I can say this. India."

She waited for me to look at her. "Y'all got it coming out of your pores. I see it whenever I see you, whenever I talk to you. And when I see Sol. Micah said it was all over him when he saw Sol. You two aren't just falling for each other. *You're feeding each other.*" After a beat, "You don't run from that magic, Best."

"Hmm." Is what I gave her. But. Yeah. I was *so intrigued.*

Destiney said so much, saying so little.

She wasn't finished. "Think about it. He's been showing up for you. You said he gave you money when you asked for your own equipment. Offered it without hesitation. Insisted you take it."

"Yeah." I turned to my back, looking up at the high ceiling. "Said he wanted to invest in my dream. Said he believed in me." I sighed again. "That's never happened before… Brandon never… he would ask me when I planned to get a real job. Said this was only something I should do as a hobby."

"See what I mean?"

"I do." We chilled another moment. Then, "I have to be honest. I didn't even use the money for equipment. I spent it getting groceries and caught up on some bills. But since King gave me that check, I should be able to get something. I don't want him to ask about it, and I have to come up with a convincing story on the spot."

"Yeah. I mean. You can always tell him the truth." She sang that part. "I can tell you that Sol wouldn't have an issue with that. He would have told you to use it for what you needed. Not strictly what you *wanted.* There's more where that came from, too. Plenty more. Sol would take care of all that. I don't think you understand Indie. Sol is loaded. His money and long and lowkey."

I said nothing.

"Be his woman. Sol would take care of you like you wouldn't believe. And not just material things. But make no mistake…. I can see him opening an account for you."

I whined. "Des. You know I don't like talking about money." I was still on my back looking up at their high ass ceiling.

"I know. But this is about letting a man take care of you. A man who cares for you. Not some rando looking for a transaction. I get a weird feeling thinking about Kingston. My antennas went up the second you told me about that check."

"Really?"

"Yeah."

"Hmm."

"But back to Sol. He's falling for you. Just like you're falling for him. Will you give that man a chance already? He's showing up for you. Showing his love with receipts."

Destiney was grinning. Though I wasn't looking at her, I could hear it in her voice. "I'm not wrong."

"You're not." A few beats. "Best. It made me so emotional," I spoke softly. "I'm always figuring things out. Always making it work somehow. And then he lightened the load like it was nothing. Without making it an ego thing or making me out to be some charity case. No expectations either."

"Right. And then you went and friend-zoned him? Oh Indie!"

We laughed. But mine was weak. Wasn't hearty because wasn't shit funny.

"Des. Don't say it like that."

"You did, though! Poor Sol. I can't help but feel bad. Best."

"Yeah, I feel it." I sighed. "And the way he talks about my art Best. He believes in everything I speak about. My talent, my artistry, my dreams. I stopped dreaming at one point, but Sol rekindled that. You should have heard him raving about the mural we painted for Micah when we all were here for the party."

"Aww. What did he say?"

I shook my head. "He said, it was incredible. Alive. Love in motion. He said we really did our thing with it."

"And did!"

We laughed.

"Loved by You" by Mali Music played, and I closed my eyes. I love this song. It's perfect. Almost like spoken word poetry combined with amazing string instruments. Only Mali and Jaz could have created this masterpiece. I love both of them.

"But seriously. It was in the way he said it. Called it powerful."

"Hmm. That's so sweet. I don't think I ever told you…Micah was damn near in tears when he first saw it."

"Wow. I would have been too. It really is amazing Best. You had the vision."

"Yeah. Well, you helped bring it to life."

"We have a dope collab. Just saying."

"*Abso-fucking-lutely* we do!"

We fell out.

"Whenever I show Sol my work, he says something profound like that. He has such a way with words. Once I showed him a sketch, which was all it was; I hadn't even added any color, he said that I leave my spirit wherever I create."

"Aww. Girl. Oh my gosh! Marry him already!"

"It's the nicest thing anyone has ever said to me about my work. By far."

"Yeah. Sol speaks just like the artist he is. With passion and honesty. That man is a wordsmith."

I was fully stretched out on the couch at this point. I was on my back.

Destiney was too on the other end. She was on her side. Throw pillow propped behind her.

"Girl. You should hear him when he's *in me.*"

Destiney screamed. *"Girl!"*

We cackled.

When we settled down, "You're badass Indie. In all facets. Sol's just calling it what it is. And I love that."

"Thank you, Des."

"That's your man Indie. He's husband material. Sol is establishing safety. Building trust. Curating a foundation where you can dream. And land softly if you fall."

And let's not ignore the fact he's figured out your love language. He's executing that with precision."

I tittered. "Pretty sure I don't have a love language."

"Girl, stop. Of course, you do. Most people have a primary love language and often a secondary one. Things shift as we move through life's seasons and stages. We evolve. Experiences shape us... so on and so forth."

My eyebrows were high on my forehead. "Okay. *Iyanla!* Excuse me! When did you become an expert on this kind of thing?" I teased.

Destiney giggled. "I mean. I've been reading a lot and paying attention, being loved the way I needed to, and loving the man I have the way he needed me to. I took the time to do the work."

I nodded. "Okay then."

"Seriously. When couples actively learn and use their partner's preferred love language, they build the most fulfilling relationships. Better communication, better sex, top-tier empathy for their partner. All the above."

Hmm.

"That sounds amazing. But I haven't had the luxury of finding out."

"I know you, Indie." Destiney paused. Then, "Your primary love language is definitely *acts of service*. I think you've forgotten how good, thought-out gestures can make you feel."

"Yeah. I've become fiercely independent."

"Right. And you'd greatly appreciate being done for. Taken care of. Burdens being lifted. Deeds that help make your life easier. You're into that shit."

"I can see that." I returned, nodding with a smile.

"You're welcome," Destiney sang, laughing. "Now… your secondary one is tied… I'd say one is *words of affirmation*… you enjoy being told sweet things. Most women do. Not in a reassuring way, but in a way where we're still being seen. On days we don't feel as beautiful or sexy. And being encouraged and appreciated, even for everyday things that some people take for granted."

"Yeah." I smiled at that as well. No lies detected.

And it's a trip. Like, I'm so used to handling shit and getting it done mostly on my own. Letting someone take care of me, even a little, feels so… I don't know, like a foreign concept. But it feels safe too. *If it's him.* With Sol, I can say confidently that I wouldn't have to do everything alone anymore. Yeah. It's a great feeling to do so much and then be called out for more than your physical attributes. To be seen.

Destiney had a point. I mean, I stop traffic and turn heads. It's nothing new to be called beautiful so often. And, it was sweet, sure. But being exoticized because I'm mixed was played out. And being a brown girl with good hair, all that shit. I wanted to be seen for more than what was on the outside. Being told by other girls that I only got opportunities because of my pretty privilege was something I fought hard to disprove. So much so that it was exhausting.

But Sol affirmed me beyond his attraction. He often told me I was beautiful, calling me Belle as much as he called me India. But Sol called out a lot of other things, too. My thoughtfulness, kindness, intelligence, talent, and creativity. I admit it made me feel good, hearing all of those things regularly. Being affirmed by someone I care about so much was powerful. Wow. I guess this was one of my love languages.

"Now," Destiney continued, bringing me out of my thoughts. "There's *physical touch* and *quality time*, which I think overlap a lot. These are closely linked with words of affirmation for your secondary. And anyway, I know you love that too. Quality time means expressing love by fully focusing your attention on your partner through shared activities, conversation, and togetherness. Physical touch shows care through intimate, affectionate contact, like hugging, kissing, and sex. Yeah, you love that. All of that."

"Don't do me."

We laughed for a while.

"I know you, Indie. And I know Sol is handling himself. Handling *you*, Ms. Ma'am!"

"Yeah." I sighed deeply. "Girl. The last time we were together. Was... girl. I can't even... *He's sooo...* Girl."

Destiney roared with laughter all over again.

"Sol checks all the boxes, Indie."

"You're right."

"In all seriousness, we weren't created to do it all alone. And a man like that deserves happiness, too, Indie. You can be happy together."

I nodded. But I said nothing.

"Please give him a chance. Give yourself a chance. I want you happy."

And I smiled at my thoughtful best friend, who is so beautiful inside and out. She only wants the best for me, and the love and happiness she's been experiencing, she wants me to have that too. It might look different for me and Sol, sure, but still, she desperately wants that for me.

"Good and Plenty" by Alex Isely came on. And I closed my eyes again.

And I said nothing.

Neither did Destiney for a while.

Then, "I think you want to."

"I do want to," I returned, resolute, without pause.

"So be with him, India. He wants that too. It's simple."

I nodded silently but still said nothing.

"I'm serious. You can't let a man like him get away. You and Sol would be so amazing together. Two creatives getting tangled up like that. You'd be so in love, and you'd create that love every day. Multiply it even. Amazingness is bound to happen."

"Yeah, maybe that's why everything feels so raw."

"Hell yeah." Destiney signed. "Think about it. Indie. *Please.* Think about it. *For me.*"

I promised, "I'll think about it."

And I really did think about it. All night long, I did.

I was sleeping in a guest room, and the bed was incredibly cozy. Plush down comforter. Pillows were fluffy. And I felt super comfortable. But I didn't sleep much that night. My body buzzed like it was covered in static. And every part of me was still aching from my fantasizing. It never stopped. Honestly.

The aching or the fantasizing.

Lying in this bed at my best friend's house, I wouldn't dare masturbate. As bad as I wanted to. That wouldn't feel right. But I was intensely turned on. My mind drifted to all the places I couldn't stop thinking about, especially feeling Sol's lips and tongue all over me. I remembered the tender way he held me and could still smell his natural scent, tinged with his signature cologne. It was vividly strong, as if he were lying right beside me. I wished he was. I wish I could call him now and ask him to come see me, or even have him pick me up and take me back to his place.

That night, I woke up at one point and found Sol sound asleep. He's a beautiful man. I love his chocolate skin. His bone structure. His sharp jawline. His pronounced Adam's apple. Yeah. I watched him sleep for a while, as if it were the most beautiful thing I had ever seen. His arm was draped over my waist, claiming space even in his slumber. I loved that. It felt like I was his in that moment. And I wanted that. I want that. Yeah. Here I was, thinking about him, had not gotten a wink of sleep. It had to be after 1 am by now. Destiney and I stayed up talking, and eventually, she knocked out.

I put the food away and cleaned up the kitchen. By the time I finished, she had said goodnight and wandered upstairs. I told her I was heading to bed right behind her.

And after a quick shower, I've been lying here ever since.

Sol on my mind heavy.

I'm so glad we're back. At least, I believe we are. I'll be seeing him tomorrow. This back-and-forth after our conversation was frustrating, but I understood. After our talk, he seemed to become a bit… distant. And despite understanding, I wasn't sure how I felt about that.

When we parted ways, Sol acted like everything was fine. We were still fine. Nothing had changed between us. Our friendship was still strong. But over the coming days, he seemed… colder. He wouldn't text me.

Well, he wouldn't text me *first*.

By now, I was accustomed to *good morning* texts and *have a great Wednesday* waiting to greet me with the sun.

But. I hadn't received any of that. I would still text him, as usual. And he replied, but it would be short. One-word texts, or just a thumbs up, or lol. Shit like that. It didn't take long for me to realize the vibe had definitely shifted.

As if maybe he'd had time to really think about what I'd said. Sit with it. Ponder it. He began to pull away. A week went by. And another. And another. And he didn't ask to see me.

271

And then I realized that maybe he wasn't as okay with that as he initially thought. I knew I'd hurt him. I knew that full well. I was hurting too. I wanted to be with Sol so badly. And being away from him gave me space to think it over on my own.

And I couldn't blame him for hurting me or being upset. He was cold toward me. He'd been so good and consistent. Yet, I turned him down.

I didn't want to lose Sol or our friendship. And during those uncertain days, I was frantic over the possibility.

But, we were slowly returning to how things used to be. We'd started texting again, sweet and a little flirty. Not spicy, but that was okay. Focusing on our friendship was probably best anyway. I reached around in the dark for my phone on the nightstand, lighting up the room as I navigated to my conversation with Sol. I skipped over the unread messages from Brandon, and there were quite a few. He'd called me too. Still trying to get some. Brandon was seriously crazy if he thought... I really should block his crazy ass.

Sol and I had been texting throughout the day. And we'd said our goodnights an hour ago.

Me: Hey

I saw three dots almost immediately.

And I had a huge ass grin on my face as soon as I saw those dots. Yup. Grinning like a sprung ass fool in the dark. But I didn't care. I am so sprung.

Music Man: Hey Artist Girl. You girls good? Staying out of trouble?

Earlier, I told him I'd come to spend the night with Destiney since Micah was away.

Me: Lol. To be honest with you I'm a little frazzled. I'm kinda drowning right now. Can't sleep.

I double texted him. **Thinking about you.**

As soon as I hit send, I immediately wondered if it was a good idea.

For starters, we couldn't really do anything with that.

But at the same time, I was glad it was out in the open. I could always be vulnerable with Sol. It was wild because in the past few days, since we had started talking again, I hadn't been sharing these things with him. Not really. Not like before. But now, I wanted to tell him exactly how I felt, in explicit detail.

Hell yeah, I was thinking about him. And hell yeah, I miss him. And I knew I was wet for him right now. Right. Now. Knew it. I didn't need to check, even though I wanted to. And I wanted to check so bad. Wanted to confirm. Trust but verify. I wanted to handle that and tell Sol all about it. It was only for him. I think I was feeling bold because it was dark, late, I was in my feelings, and extremely horny for him. I thought back to a time we had to-gether.

We were tangled together. He'd just come undone, right after me. His M.O. I could feel the pulse in my throat as my breath steadied, syncing with his. Sol was still inside me, and he lingered as if he didn't want to leave. And I didn't want him to either. But after a moment, he slowly pulled out of me.

I let out a soft gasp when I suddenly felt empty.

He chuckled softly as he moved to his side of the bed, pressing a gentle kiss to my cheek on his way. "I didn't want to. But I need to use the restroom. Otherwise, I'd stay inside you all night. Until I fell out."

"Hmm. That sounds so good." I closed my eyes and curled my legs up. My body was aching and still humming. I was definitely sore. But in a satis-fied way. A, been loved right kind of way.

"Don't it." I could hear him pulling the condom off. He stood and went to his ensuite.

I heard the toilet flush a moment later, followed by the sound of the sink. Then he returned to the bed.

Sol looked at me.

Me. Not my body. And. I looked at him.

"May I?" He posed. And that's when I noticed the hand towel he was holding. "It's clean. Just wet it with warm water."

Wow.

I nodded. And he didn't waste any time. He sat on the bed next to me and gently parted my legs, wiping between them. Every move he made was careful, tender, and intimate.

"You good, baby?"

Shivering, I gently grabbed his wrist, guiding his hand to where I became too sensitive. "Yeah."

My phone illuminated.

Music Man: Same. But I can calm us both down. Let me swim next to you.

Damn.

Bypassing that… for now, I sent, ***Love hearing from you***

And I did.. Hella.

I miss him more than I can describe.

God, I missed him. I really wanted to see him. These past few weeks, we haven't seen each other or talked like we usually do, and it's been brutal for me. I wonder how Sol was faring.

Yeah. I just miss him. He wasn't even mine, and I miss him.

Music Man: Love when we can talk

I smiled at that. **Me: I wasn't expecting a reply. You're not tired?**

Music Man: Not anymore. You recharge me

We volleyed back and forth until I dozed off.

When I woke up the next morning, I had a few unread messages from Sol.

The last one made my heart swell.

Sleep sweet, my Artist Girl

My eyes focused on the 'my,' and just like that, my day was made.

thirty-two

SOL

I was hanging in my garage. I knew India would be pulling up any minute.

And I couldn't wait.

I missed her something serious.

I'd been intensely pinning after her the past few days, especially after not seeing her for a few weeks.

But I was right back in it now. Once I got over myself.

When India told me she couldn't be with me, I was crushed… but I told her everything was cool. And I thought it was. Honestly.

But then I thought about it. And thought about it. And thought about it some more. And I wasn't cool with it. Not even a little bit. I admitted to myself in the beginning that my feelings were hurt. And they were. But then I got frustrated. Pissed the fuck off. And I was cold toward her. A few weeks went by during which we didn't speak or text much.

But I was irritated. I knew all of this had something to do with Brandon. His clowning ass.

The two and a half years India gave him were beyond generous.

Yeah. Brandon was a fucking clown.

India is not the type of woman you mess over. Play with.

He fed her lies.

Lies she ate for breakfast, lunch, and dinner for more than two years.

She was never safe with him, and he gaslit her for not trusting him completely.

Clown shit.

It seemed Brandon ruined any chance I might have had. I was right here, prepared to show India how a man treats his woman. How well she can be loved, cared for, and how safe and secure she can feel. I had to figure myself out though. Quickly. Giving that situation so much energy wasn't best. I care about India, but it wasn't my cross to bear.

I could care but not carry.

Because Lord knows I had my own issues. India was the one who needed to do the work. She told me she'd called a therapist. I was so proud of her. I believe in therapy. Wholeheartedly. Therapy is life-changing. But I missed India. I desperately missed the way things used to be. The friendship we'd cultivated.

Me being cold toward her. My distance caused the energy between us to shift, and it was my fault. But once I was sick and tired of being tired of myself, tired of being frustrated and missing her so much, we finally had a chance to talk about it. Just a few days ago. And everything was back to normal now. I was ready to enjoy this beautiful sunny afternoon with India and couldn't wait for her to arrive. I had been eagerly anticipating her arrival.

We spoke yesterday. Just a quick phone call, but mostly texting throughout the day, which I loved. When she randomly texted me at 1 in the morning, I opened that message instantly. I thought maybe she was asking me to come over. Then I remembered she was staying at Micah's with Destiney. And as much as I wanted India, I wouldn't go there and sleep with her. Not at my boy's house. Never. But India had me hard as hell, telling me she was frazzled thinking about me.

Yeah. I would have loved to calm her down. I was feeling the same way. Just texting her had me hard as steel. I craved her: her taste, her scent. The way she felt around me when she let me have her. I was still thinking about the last time… how good she felt.

That lovemaking was… fuck. I didn't have the words. We hadn't talked about being together again… like that. And I didn't expect we would. She asked if we could slow down, and I knew that was one of the things she was talking about. And I could do that. I wanted a chance with India, and if she needed to step back from that, I was okay with it. Whatever she needed, I was willing.

I felt my phone vibrating in the pocket of my joggers.

Artist Girl: About ten minutes away

Me: Great. Looking forward to seeing you

Artist Girl: Same. See you.

Me: See you.

In true India style, she added a lot of emojis. She loved using the smiley face with closed eyes. And it suits her personality.

Yeah. I could hardly wait for her to get here. It felt like more than three weeks had passed since I last saw her. But I knew it was because of the shifting moods. The conversation we had brought it all back, though, and I decided I wouldn't keep giving that Bardon shit any more energy. Instead, I would focus on our friendship maturing forward. Whatever that looked like.

I didn't have anything more to do in the garage, so I decided to sit on my porch and wait. It was just after 11 am, and the crisp morning was already turning into a lovely day. There was a light breeze, making it a little cool, but nothing a light jacket couldn't fix. I was dressed casually and comfortably in black joggers and a t-shirt. I relaxed in the comfortable rocking chair on my porch, grateful for the quiet and the break. The winter semester was ending, but things were still pretty hectic. Seeing India would be a double treat. A break from all the campus chaos and a chance to spend time with her. Time I absolutely loved.

Contrary to popular belief, the last two weeks of the semester are just as hectic for professors as they are for students. In fact, they might be even busier for professors. Professors are busy catching up on grading, for example. Many students tend to turn in work that was due weeks earlier, often begging for partial credit because they aren't satisfied with their grades.

Office hours, which are usually empty all semester, become crowded with students who are worried they'll fail the class. Many send emails requesting appointments if office hours don't fit their schedules. And I understand. Many students work full-time or multiple part-time jobs. Many have children. Some are almost like children themselves and are the first in their families to attend college. Since I teach mostly non-STEM majors, they aren't cramming for exams but trying to absorb as much knowledge as they can for their term papers and presentations.

Of course, we're also grading the other assignments to keep gradebooks current and ensure students know where they stand heading into finals.

This semester, I'm teaching *Music Theory II* and *Intro to Composition and Songwriting*, which meet twice a week along with a lab session. I enjoy teaching both of these courses because I can connect with students who share a passion for something that means a lot to me as well. I've had students come in who couldn't read a lick of music but are phenomenally talented musicians. Those are my favorite students. They respect music at a fundamental level and yearn to master that aspect of it.

Music Theory is a challenging class, especially at the advanced level. I took it myself, so I try my best to foster an environment where students can learn not only music but also to be patient with themselves and feel comfortable expressing themselves and their art. I nurture that while being encouraging and never pretentious.

I also teach The History of African American Music, which meets once a week. This is a course I personally requested to be added to the music program about three years ago. It has grown to become one of my most popular courses. I teach it twice a year, but I have considered offering it more than twice due to its popularity. I believe every music program at every university should include a course like this. African American music is music that transcends generations, and like the African Diaspora, it has reached every corner of the earth, from spirituals to blues and hip-hop.

When I studied music and culture while pursuing my doctorate, my research took me all over the world to many countries and communities. I saw firsthand the globalization of Hip-Hop music. It haas influenced people who have never even met a Black person. It's as fascinating as it is mind-boggling. People who don't speak or understand English can quote entire rhymes from a Tupac record, word for word. Every grunt, every pause, every beat. African American music has impacted the globe. Every continent. Yeah. That fills me with pride as a Black man. As a people, we are resilient and powerful. World changers.

A silver sedan slowly approached, pulling me out of my thoughts. I looked up and saw an older man driving. He appeared to be Hispanic, but I couldn't tell for sure because he was wearing shades and there was a glare. That's when I noticed it was an Uber. I stood, walking down my walkway, and approached the car as it stopped about fifty feet in front of my house.

India climbed out of the back seat behind the driver, then she closed the door and was startled to see me standing there. The shock was evident in her expression. But she quickly schooled her features. I saw it, though.

The car made a U-turn, driving away.

"You took an Uber?" I asked immediately. "Why did you take an Uber here India? Didn't you say Mala would bring you?" My tone was steady. But I wanted answers.

"Uh…yeah… she uh… our plans fell through, so. It was just easier." She shrugged, standing on the sidewalk facing me. She looked off into the distance. Adjusting her tote, she quickly added,

"My dad's got the car, and I didn't want to bother him. Anyway. Here I am." She offered a smile now. But it didn't reach her eyes.

And I creased my brows.

"India, you could have called me."

"It's fine."

I remained rooted to my spot. Standing firm. My tone steady, I told her, "I would have come to pick you up. I don't want you taking an Uber to come here without telling me. Next time you need a ride, just call me. Okay?"

"Sure. Okay." She was nonchalant. A little too nonchalant for my liking.

And I knew there was more to this, but I didn't want to get into that right now.

So instead, I offered. "How are you?"

"Good," She chirped. I could tell she had something on her mind just that quickly. But something told me she likely wouldn't share. At least not willingly. It probably had something to do with her family. Something at home. That seemed to be the topic she was most guarded about. And I wanted to know. I wanted her to take the load off. Share with me. I was right here.

But I wouldn't press. Not right now.

I nodded. "Good. You look great." I took her tote off her hands. "Thanks for coming by." India was wearing black leggings, a yellow tank top with a light grey crew tied around her waist. Her curls were slicked back in a low ponytail. Her face was bare. No lipstick today. But she was gorgeous. Always gorgeous. Her freckled skin was vibrant in the early afternoon sunshine.

"Thank you. So do you." She stepped a little closer. We were almost touching. "You smell nice."

"Thank you. You smell good too." I returned. And she did. She wore the same scent every time I saw her. A coconut layered with faint floral notes. India always smelled lovely.

"Thank you."

I nodded. "Appreciate you bringing her." I lifted her tote for emphasis. It was heavier than it looked. I glanced inside, nodding again. "You brought the essentials. That's good. Got something I want to try. But we'll save that for after our bike ride."

She smiled. "Okay. And after the farmers' market?" she asked hopeful.

I chuckled. She was so beautiful. Her smile was bright. Her eyes twinkled.

"Sure. After the farmers' market."

"I can't wait!"

"Same." I chuckled again. I started walking back toward the open garage. India followed. "We can take this in the house before we head out. I'll get everything locked up. Did you need to use the restroom or anything?

"Nope! Ready when you are."

"Alright." Just as we crossed the threshold, I stopped, then turned to her. India was right on my heels, and she was so fucking close to me. So damn close that I could feel her breath on me.

So close I could kiss her lips. And I wanted to.

God, I wanted to. I wanted to kiss all over India.

"Artist Girl." My voice steady.

"Yeah."

"Can I show you that something I said I wanted to show you?"

"Sure." Her voice soft. Her eyes big in wonder.

"Okay. Hang on for a quick second."

I placed her tote on the counter in my garage, then stepped behind my Jag.

A moment later, I wheeled over a matte periwinkle bike with white tires, a white leather seat, and a large brown wicker basket in front.

I was sure to keep my eyes on India. I'd waited all day for this moment. I wanted to see her reaction. And it didn't disappoint. I watched her take it in. It wasn't flashy, but it was her. As soon as I saw it, I knew what I could do with it and that she would love it. Sleek, simple, yet sturdy and safe. India blinked a few times and said nothing. Confused, I think.

She looked at me. "Sol… whose bike?"

I propped it on its kickstand in front of her, leaning on my car. Hands in my pockets. "It's yours, Artist Girl."

She shook her head immediately. "No. It's not."

I chuckled at that. Then I went to stand beside her. Slowly, I put my arm around her waist. "India. This is yours."

She looked at me. Eyes on eyes. A faint smile tugged at her lips. Then looked at the bike. "I…Sol…"

"India. I wanted you to have something that's yours. Not shared or borrowed. Yours. The frame is used. Restored it. Painted it. Brand new seat and tires… added the basket." I smiled. "Will this do?"

"Are you kidding?! *It's perfect Sol!*" She fell into my arms. Hugging me tight. And I embraced her just as eagerly. "I've never had a new bike before. New to me. Not even when I was a kid. I'm going to cry. Thank you."

She spoke into my locs. Her voice muffled, but I heard her. And she was emotional.

"Sounds like you already are." I teased sarcastically

"I hate you!" She laughed into my neck.

"You love me, Artist Girl. What you talking about?" I rubbed her back. "You're so welcome, Belle."

She shook her head, laughing, but didn't refute what I'd said. Something I hadn't planned to mention, but it slipped out before I could stop it.

When we parted, I took a good look at her. Her expression was telling. India was grateful, overwhelmed, and excited. After I adjusted her seat, she strapped on her helmet and pedaled down the driveway, telling me to hurry up. I burst out laughing, and just like that, my whole day was made.

♪♥♫♥♪

It was a twenty-minute bike ride from my house to the farmers market. I visit the farmers market at least three times a month. There are quite a few within a reasonable distance, but this one's my favorite. In my opinion, a great farmers market offers a diverse selection of fresh produce and goods, unique and of high quality. It doesn't need to be large. In fact, I'm not concerned with big-ticket grocery stores at all. Even though I still shop at supermarkets, I prefer supporting local farmers and do so as often as

281

possible. I know this is a major part of their livelihoods. And I prefer eating farm to fork whenever I can.

I also appreciate the community. Northern California is rich in agriculture, and Sacramento is incredibly diverse. It's inspiring to see the local family businesses represented. I love the cultural diversity at this farmers market. We're lucky to have a variety of vendors from around the world proudly showcasing their regional flavors and seasonal produce. European, Asian, East Asian, Indian, South American, Central American, Spanish. Each of them friendly and eager to share information about their products.

I buy most of my grocery essentials here. Fruits, vegetables, eggs, herbs, and even mushrooms and honey. There's a Greek family that has been selling infused olive oils for nearly four generations. They offer a few varieties, but there are two I buy regularly. I already told the matriarch that I'll keep coming back as long as they're selling it. My favorite is an extra virgin olive oil infused with truffle and garlic; it's delicious, aromatic, and full of flavor. I use it weekly for most of my cooking. Whether roasting, in pasta, sautéing vegetables, or drizzling on sandwiches or salads. It's a staple in my kitchen.

There's another one infused with rosemary and basil, and that one is perfect for marinades and vibrant sauces. I love to rub it into chicken before slow-cooking it in the oven. It also makes a great marinade for roasted lamb chops. I like to make a bread dip now and then, and this is the perfect base. I usually add fresh herbs like oregano and thyme, along with minced garlic. I enjoy experimenting, so if I'm in the mood, I might sprinkle in some red pepper flakes too. I've added lemon zest and freshly grated Parmesan cheese before, which gave it a unique flavor profile I didn't expect. Just a pinch of salt and pepper to taste, and all you need is your favorite artisan bread! It's amazing.

"Sol! Oh my gosh! Look at those peaches! Is there room for just a couple of those?" India asked excitedly. She walked ahead of me to the tent of fresh produce, chatting happily with the woman wearing a big sun hat. "She can give us a deal if we buy four peaches!" India told me as I approached the shaded area. She looked at me, smiling.

"Please," she sang.

"Sure thing." I said, chuckling. I pulled a few dollars from my wallet and handed them to India. "Please keep the change." I said after the friendly woman handed over the bag of peaches. I placed the peaches in my large canvas backpack along with the other produce India wanted.

"These peaches are gorgeous! I can't wait to have one!"

"They are! You had a great eye for spotting them." This vendor was near the back of the market.

India already knew what she wanted, but we took a walk around before we bought anything. It's easy to buy from the stands you see first, but the ones near the back also have quality items.

We were walking side by side again, taking in the vendors, the sights, the scents, and people watching. It was a little quieter on this end.

Something smelled incredible, and I knew it was coming from the food stalls we were nearing. I checked my watch; it was nearly two o'clock in the afternoon.

"Getting hungry. Want to try something here for lunch?"

"Sure!"

I nodded. "Cool. What are you thinking? There are quite a few options. They make great tacos and burritos, and I know they prepare their tortillas fresh on site. They also have fresh home-made salsas, tamales, and empanadas. If you're in the mood for something different, there's a crepe station that offers both sweet and savory options, and those are really tasty. Korean barbecue..."

"Yum!" India walked a little faster, a pep in her step now. She glanced from side to side. "I'm the type to canvas the options and then decide."

I chuckled. "Fair enough."

In the end, India ordered a loaded gyro with fries and salad. I had a rice plate with chicken adobo. We shared a few vegetable lumpia that were perfectly fried, golden, and crispy.

I brought my insulated tumbler, so we had plenty of cold water to drink. We found seats near some picnic tables, and I could faintly hear music playing as we enjoyed our meal.

"This gyro is delicious! Maybe I should have started with this instead of those fries!" India said, taking a bite. "I love fries. They were hard to resist, but I worry I won't have room to eat much of this."

Nodding, I told her, "Yeah, they gave you so many, too!" I grabbed a few and tossed them in my mouth. "Whatever you don't finish, we can wrap up and take it with us. Good thing your bike has that big basket in the front." I winked at her.

Covering her mouth, she giggled as she took another bite. "Very true. Glad you had the foresight!" She chewed and swallowed. "And thank you again so much. I love my bike. Really. I love it." Her eyes were on mine.

"I'm so glad. And you're so welcome, Belle."

I held her gaze, giving her mine. Feeling such peace with her. Spending this time with India here had been so easy. So much fun. We talked a lot about what we saw. The variety of produce. We spoke extensively about parsnips. She hadn't known the name until today; she just assumed they were white carrots. That made sense, as the vendor had purple carrots and yellow carrots for sale in addition to orange ones. But it was adorable. India said she hadn't tried them before and asked me to describe the taste. I shared that parsnips were just a little sweeter than carrots but had a nutty flavor. She was intrigued, so I bought a couple, and I offered to cook her some.

We talked recipes. We planned to try out a few new ones together, and I was excited. India told me she was eager to get back into my sexy ass kitchen, and I told her she could come in whenever she felt the need. Yeah. We'd been having a great time just being together. No pressure. No rush. Just the two of us. We didn't hold hands or anything. We weren't touching, but we were close. Sitting near each other, sharing water and space. And it felt so natural.

"Solomon! My boy!" The enthusiastic voice of an older gentleman snapped me out of my thoughts. When I looked up, Rick was approaching our table. He had a guitar in one hand and a clear plastic bucket in the other, with a few coins clinking at the bottom.

I smiled wide. "Rick! Nice to see you!" I instantly stood to hug him.

Rick was a guy who visited the market as often as I did. Over the past few years, I've seen him nearly every time I come.

Rick is the kind of guy who talks to all kinds of people, makes them laugh, and helps you forget your worries. Very friendly and always positive, he offers a smile, a prayer, or a friendly conversation. I'd say Rick is in his late sixties. Also, Rick is a veteran who always has a story to tell about his time in combat, living overseas in Germany and Japan. He lost a leg and walks on a prosthetic, but that didn't stop him. He was still getting around.

Rick has a heart of gold.

One day, Rick was playing his acoustic guitar near the food stalls. People tossed coins and dollars at him as they walked by. Some would stop nearby to listen or take a seat. Rick has a great voice, and he could really play that guitar!

We talked about music and shared a few things. I noticed his guitar wasn't in the best shape, so I offered him an acoustic guitar I no longer used that was like new. He begged me not to, but I insisted. Rick agreed to take the guitar on the condition that we play together sometime. I gladly accepted, as it would be my honor. However, it hasn't happened just yet.

He told me, "Always great to see you, man!"

"Likewise." The moment we parted, I asked, "How have you been?"

"Oh, you know. I'm 'round here," he cracked up. Typical of Rick. Always finding joy in the everyday. He took a seat at the table, looked at India, then glanced up at me.

"You got married since I saw you last?" He had a smirk, and I knew Rick was teasing me.

"Rick, I saw you two weeks ago." I let out a small chuckle.

He shrugged. "What that 'posed to mean?" His tone serious. He looked at India. "You're beautiful!" He looked up at me, "I'd marry her if you don't want to."

I laughed, shaking my head. Taking India's hand in mine, the first time I'd touched her all afternoon, I offered, "This is India… *and she's mine.*" I took a subtle glance at her. I didn't want to make her uncomfortable just to joke with Rick. But it felt so natural at the same time. "India is special to me." I rubbed her soft hand gently. "She's someone I'm so blessed to have in my life." She looked at me, smiling, and it reached her eyes.

And I signed in relief. That could have gone one of two ways.

By now, Rick was totally facing her. "India." He stuck his hand out. "Patrick Weston. You're a lovely lady. Pleasure to meet you."

"Nice to meet you, Mr. Weston." Her hand never leaving mine, she used her other hand to shake his.

He shook his head, saying, "Call me Rick. Yeah. You're a beautiful lady." He leaned in, lowering his voice, "I'm old, but I can keep up with you, Miss India..."

India guffawed. And I lightly chuckled.

"Come on Rick!" I shook my head.

"I'm joking with y'all." He finally chuckled too.

"India. Rick is pretty good at that guitar," I offered. "You mind playing us something?"

Rick shook his head. "No, Sol's the guy. He taught me a few things. Some of the very things I play while I'm here."

"Oh no. You didn't need me; I was just making a few suggestions."

He waved his hand dismissively, "Man you're being modest!" He turned to India again. "Have you heard him?"

"Play guitar? Sure. A few times."

"No, have you heard him sing?"

"Sing?" India knitted her brows and looked up at me. *"He sings? Sol, you sing?"*

I shrugged. "Now and then."

"Really? Wow! No, I've never heard him." India looked at Rick then back at me.

Rick stood, handing me his guitar. "Bless the lady with a tune, man. Bless us all!"

"Oh, I couldn't, Rick."

"Sure, you can. Come on, I haven't heard you in ages. You owe me one. Give us a good one, and we'll call it even."

"Yeah Sol. Please." I took the guitar but hesitated. Rick was saying something else, but I couldn't hear him. India's sweet voice floated above all the noise around me.

I looked over at her, taking in her bright eyes and her beautiful smile. I couldn't say no to her.

"Alright. I'll do a little something."

"That's my guy!" Rick said with a wide grin. As I stepped away from the tables, I heard Rick whisper loudly to India, "You're in for a treat!"

I chuckled to myself. Rick had blown my cover, but I wanted to keep India around, so I guess she would have found out about this eventually.

I placed Rick's bucket on the ground in front of me. Then I started playing a few chords to warm up my fingers. I preferred using a pick, but this was okay. I hummed a few notes to warm up my vocal cords as well.

I glanced up at India. Just that quickly, Rick had her engaged in a chat. And that was funny. Rick didn't need much time to start sharing his stories. I knew that once I started singing, he'd be quiet.

I kept playing a few chords and noticed a crowd starting to gather. I thought about what I should sing, then eventually strummed a familiar tune. I've played in many different places: high school gyms, symphony halls, churches, outdoor amphitheaters. Played for many people and just a few. Played in grand arenas with tens of thousands of people. And that was all good. Definitely a blessing. But I love casual settings like these the most.

The gentle murmur of the small crowd. Babies crying. Toddlers laughing. The brave people who stood from their seats to dance. The ones who sang along. You could see heads nodding; you could hear the tapping of each foot. Being closer to the crowd was something I loved. The couples sitting close, listening, intimately wrapping themselves in the melodies and lyrics, and segueing into their own private moments that were sure to come later.

Yeah. It was all a vibe. And here I was, doing my thing with a borrowed acoustic guitar. Rick put me on the spot. I knew India would have questions. She knew I played, but I hadn't mentioned I could sing. But here we were. Here I was. Crooning.

"My Cherie Amor."

Singing to her. *Directly.*

I adored her. I realized a while ago that my heart was beating for her. I'd told her so. And I absolutely wished that she were mine. But did she know that? Could she tell?

Either way, I sang my heart out. When the cheers and applause erupted, I found her eyes; she was already looking at me expectantly, and I held them for a moment.

I gave her a wink. Her smile was warm, sweet, and beautiful, and I wanted to keep it there.

"Thank you so much."

Yeah. That was to her. And for her.

thirty-three

INDIA

"Will this work?"

"It's perfect, Sol!" I fell into his arms, hugging him tight. Sol embraced me just as eagerly, just as tenderly. "I've never had a new bike before. New to me. Not even when I was a kid. I'm going to cry. Thank you."

"Sounds like you already are," he teased sarcastically.

"I hate you!" I laughed into his neck.

"You love me, Artist Girl. What you talking about?"

I sure the fuck do!

I stirred slightly, blinking slowly. Then I rolled onto my back, gazing up at the ceiling fan's slow hum. Sol's bedroom window was slightly cracked, letting in a cool spring breeze. The sun was starting to set. I looked at my watch. It was past five in the evening.

I couldn't believe I'd slept so long.

We got in from the Farmers Market just after three.

I was juiced about the things we got. And Sol was so sweet. He'd put everything in his backpack, and I knew it had to be extremely heavy by the time we left. He said he would drive us next time so I could get a few more things if I wanted to.

But I got some heirloom tomatoes, of course. I loved the colors and varieties to choose from. I was so glad they were locally sourced and organically grown. Sol was kind enough to help me decide which ones to get. I admit I was a bit overwhelmed. There had to be close to a dozen varieties at the market. In the end, I walked away with three different tomatoes, two of each. Sol insisted we could come back another weekend, and I planned to hold him to it.

I got two Cherokee Purple, the most visually striking, in my opinion. I love their deep burgundy color. Some were pinkish purple, and this one was the most versatile for cooking. I also picked up two Amish Paste, a bright red tomato that's meaty and great for homemade sauces. Additionally, I got two Brandywine, a beefsteak variety. They're perfect for slicing and delicious on sandwiches and burgers. Sol said these have lower acidity and a slightly sweet flavor. The Brandywine was big too! Some looked about three pounds! I also found a yellow one and another that was an ombre with black at the top and deep red at the bottom. There were pink and red ones too.

Got some big peaches that looked so beautiful and perfect. Almost too pretty to eat. But make no mistake, I planned to eat them. A few avocados, some mangoes, and some goat cheese too. A sweet family sold it freshly made, and I was won over when I tried a sample.

Sol suggested I try some chili-infused extra-virgin olive oil and got me a bottle. He was a regular there and talked with the family for a while. They were the kindest people I've met in a while.

An Afrocentric woman was selling herbal tea blends. I loved her energy. She had tea leaves, mugs, and even teapots and infusers. I decided I'd get something I could share with Destiney. I love tea, but I don't know anyone who loves tea as much as she does. I had such a hard time deciding but the owner was helpful and extremely friendly. Ultimately, I chose a blend called *Viv's Destiney*. I got such a kick out of that, I took a picture and sent it to Destiney. It smelled amazing, first of all and it had such a unique blend. It was a white tea, with hibiscus, ginger, cinnamon, maccha, and dried apples. It smelled delicious dried. I bet it smelled heavenly once it was steeped. I could hardly wait to try it. But Sis was *dope*. I followed her on the gram immediately. She also sold incense, and I got some of that, too.

Yeah. I had such a great time. Not just because I was at the farmers market but because I was with Sol. It felt good. It felt natural. We weren't hand in hand until the end, but this was perfect. I could spend every moment in his company.

And I loved this market! I couldn't believe all of the vendors. There were offerings beyond just fruits and vegetables. I saw beekeepers selling honey, fresh pasta, and bread for sale. One stall offered at least eight different kinds of rice. I love rice, and I was enamored with what I saw. Of course, there were long-, medium-, and short-grain varieties like those in Western supermarkets, such as Jasmine, Calrose, and Basmati. But there were many others too: Calusari Red Rice, Himalayan Red Rice, Egyptian Black Rice, Indonesian Black Rice, Kokuho Rose Rice, and Golden Parboiled Rice. I also saw lots of different legumes and lentil varieties at another stall.

Rice and lentils were pantry staples for us, affordable and something we could stockpile. We had plenty of that at my house.

Sol mostly let me lead the way. Never far behind and right there to offer insight and answer questions. When I couldn't decide, he let me get both if I wanted. That was incredibly sweet.

And maybe coming here wasn't a big deal to most people, but it was to me. I was beside myself. So excited.

It had been years since I'd been to a farmers' market here.

Back home, most everyone did their shopping at the market, but it was different.

They were affordable number one. And the vendors were trying to sell enough to provide for their families.

Honestly, I avoided the farmers' market here.

As much as I love the ambience, the organic farm fresh produce, and the locally and sustainably sourced products… this was a luxury we didn't have. Not really.

The last time I went to a farmers' market, I remember not having much to spare. Just enough to maybe buy a little something. Today, I had planned to buy my own things since I had a few extra dollars for once. But Sol wouldn't hear of it. He wouldn't let me. When I went to pay for the tomatoes, he told me I wouldn't be spending a penny there at the market. And he meant it. Sol got me anything I asked for, which I wasn't used to.

Another reason I avoided them was that they reminded me so much of home.

There's a lively market in the heart of Guyana called Port Mourant Market, and we would go there several times a week. Sometimes every day, even. My grandmother would sell goods there, and my cousins and I would help out after school.

That was a market like no other. A lively atmosphere, colorful stalls, and a wide variety of fresh fruits and vegetables. Fresh fish. Spices. All sourced locally.

The freshly cooked street food is what I miss the most. There were so many delicious options. I can still smell the fresh traditional Guyanese dishes. But there were also other Caribbean, African, and Indian dishes.

Local artisans would also have homemade crafts for sale.

Of everything we bought today, the only thing Sol got for himself was some fresh lavender and rosemary from a herbalist. I loved that stall, by the way. Such heavenly scents wafted through the air. Some reminded me of a spa, while others I knew would enhance the flavor of savory dishes like roasted potatoes. My mouth watered just thinking about it.

When we got home, we entered the kitchen through the garage, and as we started unpacking the produce, Sol said, "Not ready to take you home yet, Artist Girl. Is it cool if you chill with me a little longer?"

I smiled at that. "Yes!" I replied quickly. That made two of us. I wasn't anywhere near ready to go home either. Then I laughed, "I need a nap, though! Can I lie down for a while?"

"You're welcome to lie on my bed. I'll hang out up here. Holler if you need anything."

I figured I'd take a quick nap, but I ended up sleeping for hours.

And it was easy to do. For starters, Sol's bed is unbelievably comfortable. His linen smelled fresh but masculine. I wrapped myself in a navy-blue quilt he had folded at the foot of his bed. I could smell him all in that quilt, and it seemed I was out in minutes.

I smiled, thinking about the way Sol sang to me earlier.

I got the feeling he was singing to me. And. I got the feeling I was right. I loved that.

Sol was talented at playing the guitar, and I had heard him perform many times. So when he started playing, I listened intently. He began to nod his head, closed his eyes, bit his bottom lip… and it was adorable. Well. No. It was sexy. I'd never seen him play the guitar live.

He kept playing, and I couldn't place the tune at first, but then he started to sing.

And I melted.

"La, La, La, La, La. La…"

"My Cherie Amour." By the incomparable Mr. Stevie Wonder.

All of Stevie's songs were amazing, but this song was a masterpiece.

This was my first time hearing an acoustic version. I loved it.

And Sol sounded incredible. His voice… it was angelic. It was smooth. It was soulful. It was… wow. I couldn't believe I didn't know he could sing all this time.

It seemed like all the lively chatter in the area suddenly went silent. We were all in a trance.

Many people dropped dollars and change by the handful into Rick's bucket. Rick offered in vain for Sol to keep the money, but Sol refused to take it.

And Rick was like a goofy grandpa. I laughed thinking about his jokes. He was hilarious and had so much to say. He would have told me his life story if we'd had time.

After I used the restroom, I made my way to the living area in search of Sol.

As I walked down the hallway, I heard him playing the piano, and by the time I turned the corner, I recognized the song.

"It Never Rains in Southern California." Tony! Toni! Toné!

Wow. I love this song.

I padded toward the couch and quietly took a seat. Sol's back was to me as he sat playing and singing at the upright piano. The song typically has a moderate tempo, but Sol had it slowed down a bit. It almost sounded like a ballad.

"See you when I get there…"

Yeah. This was a '90s classic. And Sol sounded so good. Singing about the longing and anticipation of being reunited with a love you haven't seen in a long time.

The yearning. And the metaphoric backdrop of escaping someplace with no proverbial rain. No negativity.

Songs like these take me back to simpler times. It reminds me a lot of young love when it was new. And pure. Innocent. Free.

For many of us, that was a lot like our first love.

I clapped my hands lightly as Sol ended the tune. *"Bravo!"*

He turned in my direction, still sitting on the piano bench. Greeting me with a warm smile. "Hey, Sleeping Beauty. Didn't realize you were in here. Feeling refreshed?"

"Definitely. I loved being greeted with another serenade, too."

"Another?" He said teasing, his brows high.

I cut my eyes, then in a flirty tune, just a tad sultry, I said, "I know you were singing to me earlier… or is there someone else you adore?"

"What if there is?"

"Oh, that's cute." I giggled. Playing along, "You tell her your heart's been beating for her, too?"

He held my gaze. "Jealous, Artist Girl?" he sang, crossing his arms. "Imagine that. You won't let me have you, but you're worried about me adoring someone else." He nodded. "I see." Sol had a flirty chuckle and an excellent point.

And… maybe I was… *was I?*

No. I don't get jealous.

Shit.

I was in my head now. I had to be honest. The thought of another woman getting Sol. Having Sol's attention… his time. His energy.

The thought of that did make me feel something akin to jealousy.

But that's crazy. And he's not wrong. He wanted me.

And I said no.

And… I guess I don't want anyone else to have him.
Eww.
That shit is childish as hell.
And selfish.
I'm mature enough to admit it.
I rolled my eyes. Pissed at myself.
Frustrated too.
"I see you in your head over there," Sol said, bringing me from my thoughts.
I looked at him, still sitting on the bench. A sincere smile adoring his handsome face.
Me? My confidence from moments before was shot to hell. Ugh.
"All joking aside, I was absolutely singing to you. Artist Girl."
A smile lifted from the corner of my mouth. Couldn't help myself.
"You're the *only one* that I adore. You're the only one my heart beats for. I truly do wish that you were mine." My smile grew.
And, Sol. His expression was hard to read. He didn't seem upset. Not really sad either. Just… down maybe. I couldn't quite pinpoint it.
"I feel the same way you do." I offered.
He smiled. "Yeah?" He turned on the bench to face me.
"Mmmhmm. There's no one else." I told him. For what it's worth, I hope that made him feel better. Feel validated, maybe. It was the God honest truth.
Then, seemingly out of nowhere, "Does Brandon still have access to you?"
I looked into his eyes. That question caught me off guard.
And even though I knew precisely what he was asking, I said, "Are you asking if Brandon and I are still having sex?" My tone measured.
He held my gaze. After he said nothing, I asked, "So now who's jealous?"
He chuckled, shaking his head.
"The answer is no." I looked into Sol's eyes again. "No one has access to me. Not even Brandon." I stated.

I saw him exhaling slightly. And before I could stop it, "No one aside from you."

He looked at me, and I swear there was a shift. I'd awakened something in him.

Something primal for sure. I was confident I had because I'd awakened that same feeling in myself. I couldn't help but wonder, "Can he say the same?"

"I certainly can."

I froze. My eyes were as big as saucers, I'm sure. "Damn." I chuckled despite myself. "Didn't realize I said that out loud…" I shook my head, still chuckling. Mortified too for some reason.

"Well, why not?" Sol waited for me to look at him. "We're friends. You can ask me anything, Artist Girl."

I slightly shook my head. "It isn't any of my business, first of all."

"But you still wondered. That means you care."

"I do care."

"Well, let's set the record straight. No one has access to me either. Only you. Whenever that becomes a thing again. If it ever becomes a thing again." He sounded a bit somber when he said that last part. "You wanted to slow down. And I've been having a great time chilling with you. No pressure. No rush. Just us. Anything more can wait."

I nodded in agreement. Though I'd been consumed with vivid thoughts.

Dirty, nasty, wild images. Constant flashbacks from our time together, those weeks ago.

The very couch I now sat, was where I'd sucked Sol's hard ass dick for the first time. And he was so hard.

At the other end of the couch, right beside me, was where I'd climbed up his body. *Fuck.* I climbed Sol like a fucking tree and put my wet ass pussy on his face.

Yeah. The crazy thing was that those same thoughts existed in the inverse. In an alternate universe, these thoughts were so incredibly intimate, beautiful, and passionate. Perfectly paced. Tenderly expressed. Every caress gentle. The ultimate act of becoming one and transcending the physical.

"Where'd you go, Artist Girl?" Sol had risen from the bench and came over to the couch, standing in front of me. He wore a smirk.

I tittered. "Nowhere. I was right here, actually." I shook my head, still chuckling at the insider. This was crazy.

"You in the mood for some dinner?"

"I can eat. Definitely."

"Cool. I've got some sirloin steak marinating. I was thinking beef kabobs with roasted parsnips and carrots. A green salad?"

"Oh yes! That sounds delicious. I'm helping you, though!" I jumped up and announced excitedly as Sol turned to head back toward the kitchen.

"You don't have to. You're welcome to relax. No biggie."

"Sol. Please let me help. It's the least I can do. You spoiled me today. Took me to the market. Sang to me. I even got a new bike." I had a megawatt smile.

"You've got a point."

We entered the kitchen, and Sol immediately turned on the lights.

He took a few steps toward the kitchen table, then turned and handed me a bouquet of orange roses.

My jaw dropped.

"Sol… where did… when? *These are beautiful!*"

He chuckled. "Not as beautiful as you, Belle. But they're lovely for sure. I saw them when I went to the butcher. Went while you were asleep."

I couldn't believe how beautiful they were. Lush with long stems.

"I've never seen orange roses in person." They were a vivid orange, too.

"They're not very common, so I knew I had to get them."

"Thank you. What does an orange rose signify? I know each color has a meaning."

Sol took his time answering me. "Fascination. Gratitude. En-thusiasm. Pride… *Passion.*"

"Wow. Really?"

"Really."

"I love all of that. Thanks for these, Sol."

I'd never gotten flowers before. Never. Brandon and I talked about it once. I subtly mentioned that he'd never brought me any flowers, and he went off on a tangent about how flowers are a waste of money. I never mentioned it again.

Yeah. Sol was batting a hundred, home run after home run. And these weren't grand gestures at all. Not at all. But they meant so much to me. It was the intent. The thought.

That's what had my heart squeezing.

"You're very welcome, Belle. Nothing at all."

Oh yes, it is. Sol. You have no idea.

He pulled two black aprons down from the hook near his fridge and handed me one. I pulled my hair up in a bun on top of my head. Then I washed my hands at the sink after he did.

After rinsing off both of his cutting boards, Sol pulled a few bunches of fresh parsley and a few garlic cloves from the fridge.

"We'll make a chimichurri sauce to go with the grilled steak."

"Okay."

"Ever had any?" He asked as he rinsed the parsley under the water.

"It's been a while."

"Ever made any?"

"Never."

"Okay. It's pretty easy. We'll need this garlic and parsley minced finely. I don't have a food processor, so we'll need to do it by hand."

"I can do that."

"Okay." Sol went to his knife block. "This one should work well for that."

"Thanks."

"Thank *you*. Once that's minced, we'll add some red wine vinegar, olive oil, and dry oregano." He went back to the fridge, then came to stand beside me at the other cutting board. "I've been marinating the steak for the past couple of hours. I'll work on threading the skewers once I chop these red onions and red bell peppers."

"Great."

"Do you want anything else on the skewer? I've got some mushrooms and some zucchini.

"Oh, zucchini would be great!"

"You got it."

In no time at all, we were both at work prepping the veggies. I knew this food was about to be fire. And I was so impressed with Sol's knife skills.

It's great that I know how to handle knives safely. Sol had very sharp blades. It was a great set. And I would have cut my whole finger off if I weren't careful. Nice cutting boards, too. I noticed that the last time I was here.

"So you have two cutting boards and two aprons? You been cooking with another woman?"

As soon as it came out, I sighed in frustration. I have no idea why I asked that.

"This again?" Sol chuckled, shaking his head.

"I want to know," I replied. Stupidly. I was on a roll now. "Tell me. Have you had other women here wearing this apron and cooking in here with you?"

I kept mincing.

"Why continue down this road? You know you don't want to know that India."

"Yes I do." I dared.

He'd stopped chopping the bell pepper to look at me. And I kept mincing, only stopping to transfer to the bowl beside me, and continued again.

And Sol waited a few beats, then, "Yes. I have. I've had other women here. In this house. In this kitchen. In my bed too." A beat, "Slept with them."

I was still mincing, but I'd slowed down.

"Got the info you wanted?"

I sighed lightly. My mood was ruined. And I said nothing. In my peripheral vision, I could see Sol shaking his head. And I kept chopping the herbs. With a funky ass attitude. And it was utterly silent.

"Alexa, start my mood playlist," Sol said after several moments. And thank goodness. The silence was growing awkward. On my part anyway.

Sol kept chopping. And he said nothing. He'd said enough. Said everything I wanted to know. But nothing I wanted to hear.

I sighed again. Frustrated with myself. All over again. Me and my freaking mouth. At this point, I was past frustrated with myself. Honestly.

"Fragile" by Raheem DeVaughn and Malik Yusef played, and I let myself get lost in the lyrics.

They were deeply written, emotionally expressed. Touching me directly where I needed it. A man was singing about handling a woman's heart gently. Understanding it needed TLC, he promised to be fragile.

And he proclaimed from the depths of his soul that she could place all her trust in him. That he would be the best man he could be, loving her with all that was required of him.

Damn.

I already knew Sol would be gentle with me. He understood my heart was broken. Shattered. In a million pieces, and he had been handling me with such care.

I'd asked that we slow down, and he was more than willing.

And I was fucking shit up with my mouth.

I kept mincing. I was good at this; I knew how to finely chop herbs with my eyes closed.

At least I was good at something.

I saw that Sol had pulled the sirloin from the fridge and began threading the meat and veggies onto the metal skewers. I could smell the marinade from here. It smelled delicious.

I signed.

"I'm about done mincing. How much vinegar and olive oil should I add?" My voice small. So small I hardly recognized it.

Sol turned to me. Gave me his eyes. And they looked… *soft*. Tender and warm. Like he cared.

He knew exactly what this would do to me. And he tried to avoid that.

I thought maybe he was angry with me. But his eyes told a different story.

"I'm sorry, Sol," I told him immediately, sincerely. "I put my foot in my mouth, and I'm sorry." I shook my head. "I didn't mean to ruin the mood. I just… I don't know why I'm being so… dramatic. I just…" I exhaled a frustrated breath. "You're such a great guy. Such a cool person. The thought of you with someone

else is… it's doing things to me. I don't even know what it's doing. But. It's putting me in my feelings for sure."

Sol nodded. Saying. Nothing.

I put my head down.

"Indie." He waited for my eyes. "All of that was before you.
We've both seen other people. We aren't virgins."

"I know."

"You're the one here now. *You. And I want you!* You know
that."

I nodded. "I know. And I want you too."

"But you won't even try."

"I told you I can't."

"Okay." He took a deep breath. "India. Let's not ruin the
lovely day we've had. Let's just enjoy each other's company.
Okay? If you know those things get you in your feelings, don't ask
about them."

"Okay."

♪♥♫♥♪

"Alrighty Music Man. Ready?"

"You mean like in Titanic?" Sol joked.

I was rolling.

I moved closer to him. Sol was sitting on a stool in the middle of his living room.

"Thank you for agreeing to be my muse," I said, grinning.
"Give me a few minutes, and I'll turn your world upside down."

Sol thought that was so funny. "Is that right?"

I was right in his face. Close enough to kiss his lips. His kissable ass lips. I stood between his legs. Moving his arm just so, guiding him gently to turn toward his lamp, I'd moved it closer to
where he sat so that I could get the best lighting.

"No pressure, Music Man," I told him, winking. "Just know I
have plans to leave my mark on you."

"I'm all yours, Artist Girl."

After dinner, we relaxed in his music room and listened to
music.

His mood playlist was still going as we headed to the living room. It had so many great songs, including more from Raheem DeVaughn, Bryson Tiller, Brent Faiyaz, Isaiah Falls, Odeal, and Lucky Daye.

"A Muse" by DVSN came on, and I smiled wide. Everything was falling into place so perfectly.

That's when I was brave enough to ask him if he'd be my muse. I wanted to draw him. I desperately wanted to. I was so inspired.

Today was a day full of so many emotions.

And Sol readily agreed.

He removed his shirt before taking his seat, and once I had the lighting adjusted, I handed him his guitar.

I took a few steps back and sat on the couch. My sketchbook rested on my knees.

I'd sketch him out for now, and I planned to add watercolor later, but I was feeling so inspired. I'm glad I had my tote.

Yeah. Today was filled with so many great moments. I loved being with Sol.

Dinner was delicious, by the way. Those beef skewers were grilled to perfection, with just the right amount of char. The chimichurri sauce took it to another level. I still remember the recipe; it was pretty simple. The most tedious part was finely mincing the garlic and parsley. Sol roasted a few potatoes, carrots, and parsnips, seasoned beautifully with some olive oil. We also had a small salad, too, with one of the Brandywine tomatoes and a sprinkle of goat cheese.

Yum.

Sol is an excellent cook. He knows his way around the kitchen. He has all the latest appliances too. Beautiful pans and plates. Yeah. Sol had the finer things. He was quiet, but the wealth was obvious. I was starting to notice it more.

"You want me to stay completely still? Like a statue?"

I chuckled, sketching away. "Not completely still. Fear not, Music Man. I work pretty quickly. I've drawn from live models before. But I'm not Michelangelo, and you're not David."

"Oh, you mean you want me completely naked for this? Standing here with my junk out?"

We both cackled, and I shook my head. Yeah. Sol was the perfect model. His abs were solid, and his muscles were well-defined. I love his chocolate skin and tattoos. Once I've finished painting this, I plan to frame it and give it to Sol as a gift.

"Cool," he sat naturally with his hands in position as if he were about to play something.

I looked at his tatts. "Tell me about your tattoos."

He had a lot of script tattoos, and I was curious but never asked.

"Which one?"

"Hmm… the one on your forearm."

"You don't choose your family. They are God's gift to you, just as you are to them." A quote by Desmond Tutu. "

"Wow, I love that."

"Yeah."

I continued sketching.

"Still searching for my people. But I know something will happen. I've got faith, you know. And I'm not giving up. In the meantime, I'm grateful for my adopted family and chosen family."

"That's a great perspective. And perspective is everything, isn't it?"

"Certainly."

We didn't talk much for a while, which is typical when I'm in my creative zone. But this was different. It was the first time I'd ever drawn with Sol in the same room. I was so aware of his presence and energy. Then Sol gently picked at his strings, hesitantly, almost like he was afraid he'd disrupt something.

I looked into his eyes, and he was already gazing at me. "Will it be alright if I play you a little something while I'm sitting here? I can't help myself." He laughed. "Don't want to disrupt your rhythm, Artist Girl." His grin was wide and contagious.

"Sure," I laughed. "Go right ahead."

Sol played a few smooth chords at first. They were soft, slow, and soulful, but unfamiliar. He kept playing, gradually picking up the beat, and the sweet tune enveloped us. Yeah. He continued strumming that guitar, and I kept working, nearly finished. Then he started to sing again. I had no idea what this song was. Can't say I've ever heard it. But I loved the lyrics.

Sweet baby Jesus
It's nice to meet you
I like your little style
I like your little glow
Had to come around
To show you what I know
Ooo pretty mama
You're badder than karma
So bring that ass around here
I'm tryna make it so clear

Cause baby tonight
It's Rainin' in LA
Let me inside
And watch what we create
Baby tonight
It's Rainin' in LA
Let me inside
And watch what we create

Ooo baby mama
Be my baby mama
Let's have a couple kids
18 years I'd do the bid
Ooo we like chakras
This energy around us
The type of shit that you can't create
The type of shit you just can't erase

Baby baby baby
I would die for you
I would run away and start a life with you
I ain't even really gotta lie to you
Baby baby just wanna vibe with you
Baby baby baby
I would die for you
I would run away and start a life with you

I ain't even really gotta lie to you
Baby baby just wanna vibe with you

Been looking for a partner
Someone to build a life for
If you didn't wanna
Tell me what you holla back for
I'm ready and I'm willing
To give you all the attention
Everything you been missing
Something cool just to mix with
Ooo baby I'm different
Listen to what spitting
Ooo baby get lifted
Baby baby get lifted

Cause baby tonight
Its Rainin' in LA
Let me inside
And watch what we create
Baby tonight
Its Rainin' in LA
Let me inside
And watch what we create
Let's just get high
Let's just take time

At some point, I stopped sketching. I knew because I dropped my pencil. The clatter on the wood floor snapped me out of the spell I was under.

What the hell... the song and those lyrics surrounded me like a warm blanket and settled somewhere in my chest.

Deep in my chest.

What. The. Hell.

My brows knitted, then immediately went high on my head.

I looked at Sol.

He was already watching me. He'd ended that song and had been taking me in. Apparently.

While I was trying to gather my bearings.

He approached the couch, and I sat up straighter. He leaned his guitar against the coffee table.

"May I have a look?"

I handed him my oversized sketchbook without saying a word. Sol could have whatever the fuck he wanted from me.

I cleared my throat. "Sol. That was… you're amazing." I could barely speak.

"So are you."

I cleared my throat again. "Thank you." Much clearer now.

He nodded. "Wow. This is incredible work."

"Still need to paint it with watercolor... but thank you. You're a great model."

"It was easier than I thought."

I began to put my various pencils away. Moved the lamp back. The stool.

"We host an annual spring benefit for the Music Academy to raise funds. Auctioneers will be present. I'm happy to pay you for your time and any supplies needed. Do you want to donate a piece of your art to the auction? You can write off the amount on your taxes as a charitable contribution."

"To be auctioned? Wow. Sure. Not sure how much you'd get but I'd be honored to do that."

Sol nodded. "Oh, Belle, big spenders come out to these events. You'll get some great offers. You could even network and get some of your work in a consignment shop or something. Or get more commission requests. Believe me. You want to be in the room."

"I believe it," I said with a smile.

"You should come to the benefit. It's always a great time. The kids play live music. Lots of food and refreshments. You'd enjoy yourself." Then, "Plus, I'll be there." He shrugged playfully.

I laughed. "That would be dope. I'd love to."

"Great."

♪♥♫♥♪

I got in from Sol's around eleven thirty. Ma, and Daddy had gone to bed hours earlier.

I took a shower, then I laid on my bed, trying to wind down after such an eventful day.

But I couldn't sleep, just like the other night.

No, this was worse.

I couldn't sleep, because my mind was on Sol heavy.

Per usual.

But there was more.

I wanted more, but not anything sexual. Not right now.

I wanted Sol. I wanted us.

If he was on a mission to woo me. Win me over, or convince me to give things a try. Talk me out of my flimsy ass decision and my paper-thin excuses…he'd succeeded.

Ten times over.

I tossed and turned as I scrolled through all the pictures I'd taken today.

The market. Sol playing music there.

A silly moment we had walking under an archway of flowers. There were a few flower farm vendors, and the flowers were gorgeous.

I smiled to myself, thinking about the roses Sol gave me today.

Those were breathtaking. Ma would have a million questions for me when she saw them. This time, I planned to be honest with her and tell her everything I'd been holding back.

Everything.

Last weekend, she had a handful of questions, and I answered them with just enough information without revealing too much.

She knew I liked Sol. She knew I cared about him. And she knew I was scared. I didn't need to tell her. As usual, she understood.

"When I married Daddy, I was scared. But I took the chance. My Indie, you're the best thing to come from that. And I want that for you, too. You're still young, and you deserve love and laughter. A family. Not all caregiving and sacrifice. Daddy and I won't be here forever."

"Don't say that Ma."

"It's the truth Indie."

I said nothing. Then, "What if it's not the right time? I don't feel like I'm ready."

"If you wait for the perfect time, love will pass you by. You, my baby girl, deserve to be loved fully. Not someday. Right now."

Ma had a point. I wondered if that ship had already sailed for me. And the way I behaved at Sol's house earlier was evident. My fucking blunder. I was so embarrassed. Even now, I think about it. I believe my insecurity is showing. Amir cheated on me. And Brandon was a gaslighter.

But Sol isn't them. And I appreciated Sol helping us out. The help up. Though he didn't know. We were down pretty bad.

And the way he sang today was incredible. Each song was different from the others, but that last one was something else. I asked him if he had written it. He sang it with so much soul, passion, and conviction.

It was as if the lyrics flowed directly from his heart. But he told me about Reggie Becton. The song is called "Raining in LA." I added it to my playlist as soon as he told me.

Dad texted me earlier with updates on the car, and there were a few more issues to sort out. We had a mechanic come to look at it, and he kept finding more problems. I was really frustrated; I sighed at the news. That money King gave me was practically gone. I decided I'd give Dad the rest of the money I had left to put toward the repairs, which was most of it. I was also looking for a tattoo gun and had narrowed it down to a few options, but I hadn't bought it yet. Still, the car was the priority, and that money needed to go toward fixing it. In the meantime, I always had my bus pass and my new bike. Maybe I'd ask Sol to bring it over, and I could ride it whenever I needed to go somewhere. I'm so glad that basket was in the front; there was plenty of room for the few things I'd need to bring with me.

And speaking of King, Destiney had me thinking about that situation again. My Spidey senses were tingling too. I appreciated the check, but something didn't sit right. Even though King agreed to let me start with the gun on Monday, deep down I felt like King was trying to drag this process out just to keep me around. Yeah. I hadn't told Destiney this, but I think that's exactly what was going on. Still, I had a plan. As soon as I got my license, I was out of there.

A text came in. I assumed it was Destiney. We'd been texting a little here and there. I'd sent her a few pictures. And she was back in her happy place because Micah would be home tomorrow. But I figured she was knocked out by now. It was close to 1 am.

It was Sol.

Music Man: You okay?

Me: Yeah. Why?

Music Man: Cuz we're always vibing. So tell me the truth. You really okay?

I replied in nanoseconds. **No. I miss you.**

Sol replied immediately **Music Man: See. Vibing. I've been missing you too Belle**

Fuck me man. I wanted him, and I wanted to see him.

And I wanted to be with him.

Right. Now.

Before I could type a response, my screen filled up with his face.

"Hey." His voice was totally relaxed.

"Hey."

"Couldn't sleep?"

"No."

"Me either."

"I had a great time today. Thank you again." I told him. For the umpteenth time.

"Thank you so much for joining me. I had a great time as well."

A beat.

"Sol. I want to tell you something. But. I want to tell you in person. I know it's late… are you able to come here?"

"Yes Belle. I can come to you whenever you need me."

I smiled at that.

"Okay. Drive safely. Please tell me when you're here."

"I'll leave right now."

Sol called me a few minutes later, and we talked for a bit as he made his way over. My heart was bursting; I felt all the things.

I was nervous about this. But excited too. More excited than anything else I felt.

Back in my bedroom, we were lying in my bed. Sol was on his back with his arm around me, and I was cuddle close to him, where I felt most at peace. I couldn't go anywhere else and feel the way I did right now. It was still, dark, and quiet.

"Sol. Can I tell you something?"

"Please."

"There's something I wasn't honest with you about."

"Hmm." A beat, "Tell me more."

I took a breath and slowly released it, deciding to bear my heart, my soul, and for the first time in my life, I think, ask for what I want. And think of me.

I found his hand in the darkness and threaded our fingers.

"I want what you wanted."

He waited a beat, which made me nervous. But that was the way Sol moved. He took his time. With his words. With his actions.

With me.

I knew I didn't need to explain.

"You want what I want?"

I spoke with bated breath, "You still want that?"

"Yes, Belle. I do... You saying you want that too?"

"Yes."

There was a pause, and I think we were both processing, making sure we heard what we thought we'd just heard. I was so damn nervous. But sincere. I knew he could feel that, and he was caressing my fingers, keeping me right here in the moment. I love the way he did that.

"I thought I was protecting myself. But I was pushing you away in the process," I said. "Pushing away what I really wanted all along," I sighed. "Sol?"

"Yes Belle?"

Frantically, I pressed, "I want to be yours. I want to be with you. I wanted it then, and I still want it now. I wasted too much time fighting it. But I'm not going to fight it anymore." Slowing down, I said it again, "I want to be with you, Solomon."

"India." My name slipped from his lips in a soft whisper. It was incredibly sexy.

"Yeah."

"Thank you for sharing your heart with me."

I smiled. "Always."

"So, you want to be mine?"

"More than anything."

"Then let's do it. We're making this official. Right now."

A silly giggle left me, "Okay." I sighed in relief. Suddenly feeling… *serendipitous.*

But just that quickly, I revealed, "I'm scared."

"Me too. Honestly. But I still want this. I've wanted this for so long, and I'm so glad you're giving us a chance. We'll be fine, Artist Girl. Let's keep taking it slow. Anything you need to feel comfortable, I'll do it for you."

"I just want to be with you. I want you. And I want to be good to you. I don't even know how. Or if I can. I don't know anything." I laughed despite myself, growing emotional. "I just know I want us. I want this. Sol."

"It's alright not to know. It's okay. We can figure it out together. I'm right here with you, Indie. I want this just as much as you."

"Okay."

A beat. Then, "You're really officially *mine,* Artist Girl?"

"Yes. Officially."

"I love the way that sounds."

"Me too."

thirty-four

SOL

"Is this okay, Belle?"

"Yes."

I continued to push into her. Slow. Patient. And her breath caught.. "You sure this is okay baby?"

"Yes."

"Alright."

I continued pressing into her. And I watched everything. Every. Thing.

I watched her tight opening stretch around my fingers. I watched her receive me, drawing me in like she'd been waiting for me all her life. Her delicate hand was around my bicep and my eyes were locked on her. Her eyes, which had fluttered shut at the moment. Her mouth hung slightly open. Until she bit her bottom lip. Her legs were spread wide just the way I like to see them. India is so damn flexible and so fucking sexy.

"Mmm… even your fingers fill me up baby." India gripped my bicep tighter.

I dipped low kissing her inner thigh. One then the other. I left a trail of kisses back to her center as I continued to bring my fingers in and out of her slick pussy. She was dripping for me. Glistening.

I just finished pleasing her. We both worked overtime to keep our voices quiet, and I took my time eating her pussy. Licked her. Sucked her. She's so pretty down there. So sweet. She tasted so damn good. And she came all over my tongue.

Yeah. She was so sweet, as sweet as honey. All that water, all those mangoes. India drove me wild.

"You're really mine now baby? My Artist Girl officially?" I asked her for the second time tonight.

"Yeah." She moaned. Her soft voice pressed with need.

I looked up at her and she nodded, trembling too. I gently pulled my two fingers out of her, licking them clean.

"Mmm. I love the way you taste, baby. *Fuck!*" I managed to keep my voice low.

I slowly pressed my fingers back into her and she inhaled as she received me. Then moved with me, her hips tilted slightly, meeting my strokes.

"I love the way you feel, baby." She whispered. "Are you really mine?"

"Always." I told her without delay. "I've been yours, Belle."

Indie and I spent the day together. And as it turned out it was one of the best. Definitely one for the books.

She got home late and eventually called me asking me to come see her and that she wanted to talk to me. By then it was super late. But I came.

And we talked.

India poured her heart out, telling me she wanted to be with me, and it was music to my ears. The best thing I'd heard in a while, the very words I'd been waiting for.

After we made it official, she let me hold her. And she let me kiss all on her. All over her.

Then she asked me to taste her. And I was much obliged.

I had two fingers inside of her now. And as I moved inch by inch I watched her face. Reading her every move. And my own voice was growing heavy and ragged. She was turning me on so much. Especially knowing she was mine now.

"You are warm, baby. Mmm. I look forward to being one with you again... putting my hard dick back inside of you." I knew my voice would carry so I kept my volume low. "Would you like that, baby?"

"Yes… I would." She bit her lip, holding back her moan, and she continued to move with me as my fingers continued to penetrate her. I adjusted my angle, sliding my thumb over her clit and circling it. Slow. Gently. Her mouth parted slightly, and she softly jerked.

I chuckled softly. Whispering, "Yeah. You got one more for me, baby."

She whimpered.

"One more." I kept working her clit, using my other hand to penetrate her. "Give it to me, baby. I got you." I dipped low and licked her, too. Soon after, her walls fluttered around me, and she was coming around my fingers again.

Silent but wrecked. Her legs were shaking. Her back arched. And she was still moving her hips.

I moved up her body, and pressed kisses everywhere. Settling between her legs.

India's legs wrapped around me, locking her thighs around my waist. Instinctively.

I pressed kisses to the corner of her mouth.

Her jaw. Her collarbone.

"Lay on your back," she whispered. "It's your turn now."

My chuckle was faint. But I did what I was told.

India moved low on my body and took my hard dick in her mouth. Sucking me so damn good.

"Fuck." I couldn't help myself, but I kept my voice soft. It was deep in vibration, not volume.

I found her hand in the dark and laced our fingers tightly together. Her other hand was securely around me as she sucked me deep and sloppy. The slurping sounds she was making. The moaning she was doing. Yeah. That shit was sexy as hell.

"You missed me that much, baby?" I posed it like a question. But I didn't even need to ask. India was showing me something. "Shit, Belle."

She moaned but kept doing what she was doing.

And that quiet intensity. The same intensity I felt while pleasing her with my mouth. Set the entire atmosphere. We needed to stay as silent as possible, and that only heightened everything. Every breath. Every touch. The eye contact. The weight of each shared whisper. Yeah. It turned this into something so intense it amplified the heat. We'd gotten pretty good at this, even though it had been a while. We'd learned how to communicate with nonverbal cues. Reading moaned exhales, kisses, straining to stay quiet yet burning to connect.

When I had my tongue on her, my lips on her, I was reading her. Asking questions with my hands, my mouth. And she answered with her breath, her grips, her arches, her kisses.

All of it.

"Belle..." I pressed. "Getting close, baby."

India quickened her pace, moving with me. And that did something to me. I lifted slightly, and she understood. Seconds later, I released in her warm mouth, and I cursed softly under my breath.

"Come here, baby." I pulled her close and wrapped my arms around her. "You're something else," I whispered into her neck, kissing her there.

India held me as tightly as I held her.

Breathless, she whispered, "I'm yours."

thirty-five

SOL

"Don't overthink it. Just feel. Whatever you feel, write it down. Don't worry about it rhyming or sounding perfect. For now, focus on your feelings and just write. And don't erase. Maybe cross it out, but leave it visible so you can review it later. It might be useful later."

The spring semester was in full swing. I had a brand new schedule and new students to get to know. At the moment, we were about halfway through my ninety-minute Songwriting and Composition class. We meet twice a week. The lecture is on Tuesdays, and the lab is on Thursdays.

During the lab, students write and compose freely, exploring different genres.

This was a class I enjoyed when I was a music major, specifically during undergrad. Things aren't so rigid.

If a student continues with graduate or doctoral studies, the environment definitely changes. However, at this stage, it's more about learning, making mistakes, and having fun.

Songwriting and composition require patience with yourself and confidence that you can make it happen. Also required, not optional, is creativity, technical skill, and emotional insight. There's no way around it.

I tell my students on the first day of this course that everyone in this room is a creative. Even if they're unsure how to tap into that. And within just a few lab meetings, most of them fall into step. It's amazing to see them thrive once everything clicks. I've received consistent feedback from my students about how much they appreciate and enjoy the creative environment.

"I'll try that. I've been stuck, and at this point I'll try anything." My student managed to laugh, which was music to my ears. Pun intended. She was wound tight when she came asking for help, but I'm glad we could turn that around. "Thank you, Professor Avery," she said as she returned to her seat.

"You're very welcome. Glad to help."

This student was perseverant and enthusiastic. She always arrived with a positive attitude and was ready to work until the end of the class period. She had a lovely singing voice and shared with me that she was taking this class to learn more about writing original music. She's one of my non-traditional students. Much older than I am. If I recall, she mentioned she has grandchildren. I appreciate her hard work. That's the beautiful thing about teaching in community college: the opportunity to meet many different people from diverse backgrounds. Not only do they make my job interesting, but they also make it rewarding. That's what it's all about, as far as I'm concerned. I love teaching and music.

Some students were seasoned musicians, others were emerging and exploring their developing musicianship. Either way, there was room for them here.

There were no exams, no midterms, no papers, and no final exam. In this course, students submit an original composition as their final.

Songwriting and composition can be frustrating for sure, especially if you put too much pressure on yourself. Some students are very ambitious, which is a great thing, but sometimes they stumble and fall. There's also a lot of comparison. Some of these students are naturals; they can write a song in a single 90-minute class. Others struggle to produce just one measure of music and lyrics in an entire semester.

I've always told them not to compare their work or skills with anyone else's. I do this in all my classes. This is very much a personal journey. Unless they are co-writing a song, but that's not the goal of this class, nor should it be their focus.

The objective of this class is to learn the fundamental con-
cepts of songwriting and composition, not for any particular instrument.

By the end of the course, students should be able to identify
what makes a song. The beginning, middle, and end. Identify the
bridge, vamp, and chorus.

Apart from that, students should understand song structure
because it's essential for creating cohesive music. I teach them that
in music composition, the structure of a song involves different
musical elements. First, the melody. Then, the harmony. And finally, the rhythm. These three elements are arranged cohesively
and, in theory, produce a piece they can call a song.

Students submit their song at the end of the semester. They
are free to choose the genre. The only requirement is that the song
must be at least sixty seconds long.

Now, I don't grade them based on quality at all. Instead, they
are evaluated on their class participation and their ability to identify the characteristics. They're not required to perform the song,
which many students prefer not to do. In a course like this, that
might be surprising, but not everyone enrolled in this course as-
pires to be a musician. Some people simply want to fulfill their
general education requirements. Similarly, someone taking an in-
troductory theatre class might not necessarily want to act. Acting
classes are excellent for building confidence and improving public
speaking skills.

But hearing the original music is my favorite part of all, and I
give extra credit to anyone who wants to perform their song for
the class.

Some students upload videos of themselves performing their
songs on YouTube, and we watch them in class. Or I'll watch
them separately. I've adapted to many requests.

I had a few tabs open on my laptop. A few different things
had my attention.

Moments before my student approached me with her question, I'd been reading an email I received from a community college in Modesto, about an hour south of me. I hadn't applied
there, but networking between community colleges isn't unusual. I
read a few years ago that California has the largest number of

community colleges in the nation. In California, there are roughly 115 community colleges and 73 districts, serving more than 1.8 million students annually. Or something like that.

As a presumed native Californian (the jury was still out on that), an academic, an educator, and a lifelong lover of learning, I feel extremely proud. The entire philosophy surrounding community colleges is something I have always admired. I understand that college isn't for everyone, but for those who want to attend, community college is a great starting point. Equally important is the equity and accessibility it provides. In-state residents can enroll in courses for free or at very low cost, and tuition is covered for eligible students with demonstrated need. This has opened a path to higher education for many who might not have had one otherwise. Community colleges are especially vital for marginalized communities and students from low-income backgrounds, giving them an opportunity to reduce their educational gaps. I'm just grateful to be part of that.

I read the email carefully as I sat there. I didn't plan to leave Sac City College for another community college, at least not permanently. However, I was willing to teach an online course if my schedule permitted. I was also open to an in-person summer term. I've moved to temporary housing in other cities a few times to teach courses.

I would do it again if we can reach a mutual agreement.

Humbly and respectfully, I recognize that I am in demand due to my interdisciplinary research interests and publications. My scholarly dedication to diverse African diaspora communities, along with my expertise as a musician, conductor, composer, arranger, and educator, has opened many doors for me. Most importantly, my hard work and commitment to the field of music education stand out.

I've heard back from a few of the universities I applied to, but none of them felt like a good fit, for one reason or another. This round of applications was to universities in Central California, just south of here. Depending on where you live in California, it's sometimes called The Central Valley. Sac is on the border of what's considered Northern California. These universities are in Stockton, Stanislaus, and Merced. The drive would be less than two hours with traffic. Another one I applied to is out in Fresno, which would mean a commute closer to three hours on a good day.

I'd have to seriously consider that. I'm not a fan of long commutes. I got spoiled living so close to Sacramento City College, so close I could ride my bike, weather permitting. And I often did. It took about twenty minutes. When the weather was bad, the drive was less than twelve minutes.

Even though these universities were within commuting distance for me, signing up for one had to make sense. One thing to consider was that I wouldn't need to be on campus every day. It would be at most three days a week. But. Still. That was the main point. If I was going to leave Sacramento, it needed to be worth it.

It had to feel like a good move, especially on an emotional level. The salary offered was less important.

I was doing just fine with my salary here. My various passion projects are bringing in different streams of income. I hadn't touched the money my parents set aside for me. I still hadn't touched the small fortune my parents deposited for me.

That money was mine. It had been put into an account when I was just a child and had been earning interest all this time. But yeah, it was mine. All of it… on the condition that I earned my master's. I graduated from college with a master's and didn't owe a penny, all thanks to them, which was the only thing I agreed to accept. That was a deal we made. Initially, I didn't even want to go to college, but they agreed to cover my tuition and expenses. I paid for my doctoral studies myself.

But accepting that money as a graduation gift… I knew there was more to it than that. I had the foresight to realize that accepting that money meant agreeing to everything else they expected of me. I had enough sense to understand that accepting their money came with conditions, and I didn't want to owe my parents anything. Literally or ethically.

For example, if I had taken just a penny, they'd have that over my head, and things like marrying Noelle wouldn't be a request; it would be a requirement. In so many words.

But I knew better. Because I probably still wouldn't have wanted to marry whoever they'd chosen for me… and if they decided to cut me off, it wouldn't have taken food from my mouth. It wouldn't have disrupted the life I live. Not even a little bit.

I'm completely self-sufficient. My life is low-key and simple. I drive a Jag, but it's nearly sixteen years old. My house payment is the only debt I have. I bought this house on my own about five years ago, and I plan to pay off my thirty-year mortgage in fifteen. So far, I'm on track to do that. I make a conscious effort to live below my means, for sure. I save my money. I don't vacation much. I haven't been on a leisure trip of any kind in nearly three years. My parents go on trips, both domestically and internationally, multiple times a year, and they invite me along, especially in the summer. But I've passed on the past couple of trips. And speaking of which, I've thought about that too. I haven't applied to any schools, but I've received offers from universities out of state. However, I needed to be sure it was a smart move, especially if I were to relocate.

At the time I applied to those, India and I weren't a thing. But now that we've started a relationship, I consider her, too. I mean, I definitely see a future with her, even though I hadn't allowed myself to think that far ahead with anyone since Claudia. But with India... my kind, beautiful, passionate, talented, and sweet Artist Girl, I'd passed go and collected my two hundred dollars a long time ago.

Yeah.

We haven't talked about marriage yet, but I wouldn't mind it. India is definitely marriage material, and I was absolutely falling in love with India. We hadn't shared those feelings with each other yet, but I knew the moment was coming. I also knew that would start a conversation. A conversation I was perfectly fine having.

Speaking of trips, India will be celebrating her twenty-eighth birthday here pretty soon. End of May. I never made my birthday a big deal, but I thought about taking India somewhere, maybe for the weekend. We wouldn't go far, as I knew she wouldn't want to leave her parents for too long. But a staycation would be a nice gift for her.

I thought about taking her to Napa. Wine country is beautiful in spring, and it's a quick drive from here. I considered Bodega

Bay or maybe even Lake Tahoe. Each of these places is a short drive from Sacramento and would be excellent choices. It really depends on what she wants to do. I knew she'd enjoy each for different reasons. I planned to ask her about it. I also knew she wouldn't agree right away, but I'd work on convincing her. If I needed to bring in Destiney as a reinforcement, I would. India deserves to do something for herself, and I saw no harm in taking a long weekend for her birthday.

I returned to a document I had opened. I've been reviewing the final program for the Music Academy Spring Benefit. This year's theme was "Keys to the Future: Every key a chance, every note a dream." Pretty exciting. It captured what the academy was all about: providing opportunities for the underserved and sharing the gift of music. We had secured our keynote speaker, and only a few loose ends remained to be finalized. I felt pretty good; we had a couple more weeks, and I didn't doubt we'd have everything squared away by the end of the month.

The grant we submitted weeks ago had been approved, and we'd secured a significant donation. Now that those funds were in place, we knew our goal for the benefit. I had a committee assisting with planning. Some worked to secure donors, whether anonymous or not. Others helped with the catering. We secured our venue, and a few members assisted with decorations. We will also have some vendors attending.

The kids would be playing at the start of the benefit partly so they could show what they've learned, but mostly so we could show the donors how their money was being used. The kids wouldn't be on the hook the entire time. The benefit would run most of the afternoon, and they wouldn't want to be stuck sitting in chairs strapped to instruments. The benefit was for them too, and they wanted to run around, hang out with their friends, and enjoy the festivities.

The benefit was a blast every year, I dare say. I was so excited that India would be there. She'd enjoy herself, for sure. But I was especially thrilled that she'd be with me. Be right by my side. My date.

We'd made things official a few weeks ago, and everything was going so well between us. I think back on the conversation we had that night, and I can't help but smile wide every time I do. I was so proud of her for being brave and sharing her heart with me, and for following her heart and thinking about what she wanted and pursuing it.

I still hadn't met her people, and I asked her when she thought that would happen. She said it would be pretty soon. Although she was confident in us, she didn't want to introduce anyone too soon. Especially since it hadn't been long since she and Brandon ended things. Out of respect for them, she wanted to wait a little longer.

I could understand that, I suppose. It made sense. She was with Brandon for over two years, and things didn't end well. It's been a few months, and not wanting to introduce another man too soon makes sense.

But I looked forward to that happening, and I had told her so.

On the flip side, I had to admit that I wasn't too excited about bringing her to meet my parents either. I wasn't sure it would go over well, and I am very protective of India especially when it comes to my mother. Not as worried about my old man.

We haven't spoken either. My mom and I, that is. My father and I have had occasional conversations. In fact, we just spoke yesterday afternoon, but he called me to share my mother's good news…

And my mother was the queen of guilt-tripping. She'd been doing that quite a lot lately.

Indirectly.

She liked to have my father call and guilt-trip me about not coming to dinner on Sundays. He explained that my mother hasn't been herself since I was there last. And she liked to remind me how much I humiliated her in front of Noelle, and that Noelle went home telling her mother that I left abruptly without speaking to her. And Noelle's family might no longer want to go through with the marriage. I probably ruined this for her. Her, as in my mother. Yada, yada.

And I couldn't believe the tomfoolery. It was hilarious. Really. I remember saying to my father, *"Are you serious?"*

He said nothing, of course.

And when I said nothing, he added something like, *"Well, your mother wanted you to know. I'm just the messenger, son."*

And I said, *"But you actually called me to tell me that? None of that sounded ridiculous to you?"*

He said nothing.

Then he doubled back about *"How somber things were around the house because my mother was so upset."*

And I sighed. That wasn't my problem either.

And I told my father that my mother hadn't called me. She hasn't apologized.

Then he said, *"Maybe she planned to apologize when I came to dinner."*

And I shook my head. Finally, I said, *"If she wants to sit down and discuss this in a respectful way where she isn't telling me what I'm going to do or who I'm going to spend my life with, then we can do that. But only then will I agree to come to dinner. And the second she tries it again, I would leave."*

Then my father suggested, *"Maybe I should bring India to dinner with me. And introduce her to them."*

And I did consider that.

But I thought better of it.

I hesitate because I know my mother is still upset about my declaration. And I wasn't eager to walk into a situation where India was an outsider, and God knows what could come out of my mother's mouth.

No. I didn't think that was a good idea. So, I told my father that *"My mother and I needed to settle our differences. Respectfully. **Only** then would I bring India to meet them."*

He appeared to understand and didn't disagree, but he wasn't the most expressive person either.

After my talk with my old man, I reflected a lot on everything. The song and dance he and my mother were putting on. The optics of it all. I knew my mother was the one pushing him to call me and guilt-trip me. And just like she expected and I knew he would, he called parroting her delusion.

Yeah. Delusion is exactly what it was.

She couldn't admit her culpability at all and refused to accept any accountability either.

I'd already admitted to mine. Had even apologized. Stayed re-spectful. Always respectful.

If he'd just called and said, *"Your mother misses you, and I'd appre-ciate it if you did me a solid and came to dinner on Sunday. Perhaps you two can have a conversation. I'll encourage her to listen and try to see things from your perspective, and I'll make sure she doesn't cut you off, belittle you, or dis-respect your feelings, as I know you wouldn't do any of those things."* I would have agreed to come, with no hesitation.

But nah. My father was the type to let my mother tell him what to do. Be walked all over. Bossed around. Controlled. She was probably right there when he called me. I rolled my eyes.

Hey, it wasn't my problem. She wasn't my wife. What works for them is what works for them. I just know I didn't want that. I wasn't about to be "yes, deared" to death. Just like I wasn't going to control my wife. Whenever that happened, we wouldn't handle each other that way.

And although I've never felt like I belonged, I've lived it for the past thirty-four years. I understand her position. I don't be-lieve this is something she can accept overnight, nor do I expect her to.

But I require respect. Demand it.

Respectfully.

Just because she's my mother doesn't mean I have to accept her belittling and condescending attitude. I've tolerated it long enough that I decided I no longer want to. I would be furious if she said anything unkind to India. And that's the truth... she's a loose cannon now. I can't trust her to behave around India. Not right now anyway.

And. My mother is a kind woman. She's brilliant, I might add. As a second-generation Stanford alumna, she became a well-re-spected OB-GYN and worked at my late grandfather's medical practice. They shared a passion for equitable healthcare for women of color. The practice was so successful that they opened multiple offices across greater Sacramento. Later, my mother tran-sitioned into hospital administration and eventually joined the boards of several nonprofits and foundations.

Her passion and drive are unmistakable. Since I was a child, I've always known that about my mother. Her heart lies in equitable healthcare, and she loves giving back by helping marginalized communities. I remember often traveling with my mother when she went overseas for mission work. In places with limited resources, I saw it firsthand. I went with her to Haiti and Nicaragua. She would hire a teacher to travel with us so I could continue my schooling. Even though my mother has been retired for many years, she and my father still donate tens of thousands of dollars annually to many organizations.

And I suppose that's where I get confused. To give so much of herself but still be so caught up in the optics in these elite social circles... I didn't get it. But the fact of the matter is that it isn't my problem, it's hers.

And a forced arranged wedding would just be a spectacle. An opportunity for her to spend unnecessary money to impress people she doesn't even like. People I wouldn't even want at my wedding.

Their energy isn't wanted.

My father told me she'd need some time. I still remember his words that day when I told him I was seeing someone, as we spoke privately in the backyard.

Yeah. He saw the writing on the wall.

But India, being mine, finally and officially had me in heaven.

We'd been spending time together, which was tricky. Some days, she couldn't be away for too long, but we'd been making it work.

I saw her the very day we made it official, in the daylight. And the kiss we shared felt so different now that we were official. Those lips were mine. Those soft hands I'd captured. Her tongue.

Yeah, that was all mine.

We've orally pleased each other. But I haven't been inside of her again. Haven't made love to her again. Not yet. But this was just fine. Things were progressing just as they needed to. We'd get back to that.

She'd been back twice to ride bikes. She loved her bicycle, and I was so happy for her.

I bought that frame online, and it was sitting in my garage, collecting dust. I got it because it was nearly free, and I knew I could eventually find a use for it. I'm glad I discovered the perfect purpose for it.

We tried a couple of other recipes. We had Bolognese with fresh pasta one evening, which was delicious. Another night, she taught me how to make cook up rice and peas, fried plantains, and jerk chicken.

India can cook her ass off.

We made everything from scratch, starting with dry dark red kidney beans and a homemade jerk sauce. India spoke at length about this jerk being a Guyanese style, and I naturally asked her about the difference. She explained that the core ingredients are similar, but Jamaican jerk is mostly known for its fiery flavor from scotch bonnet peppers. The Guyanese style, she mentioned, is a bit sweeter because many Caribbean islands tend to favor sweeter or more citrus-infused marinades. There are also different cooking techniques. Jamaican jerk is traditionally grilled over an open flame, but when we made jerk chicken, she cooked it on the stove.

It was delicious.

And yeah, India can cook her ass off. She promised to fix us chicken curry soon, but not until I built her a stove in the backyard. Something about my house smelling like spices for a week, if not.

That made me laugh. But I told her I could get a small propane stove to put on my patio for her to use. She said I was being fancy and mentioned that they had one her father made from cinder blocks.

And my Belle can eat too! I love how comfortable she is eating in front of me. She isn't shy. She cleaned the chicken to the bone. I enjoy learning more about her heritage and her culture each time we break bread together.

She painted and framed the sketch of me, and it's proudly hanging in my living room. I see it as soon as I walk into my home. And I notice it every time I leave, especially when I go through my living room. Yeah, I love having her art on my wall.

She's my favorite Artist Girl.

I decided to check my email again. I'd been waiting for a few more responses from my various auxiliary heads about the benefit, and I asked them to get back to me by the end of the week. Since it was Thursday, they still had time.

I scanned through my emails, not noticing anything that stood out until I saw something that stopped me in my tracks. It was from a former student. The name was familiar because he's reached out a few times before, which wasn't unusual. Many of my students stayed in touch with me after they left Sac City. I loved receiving updates from them, whether it was about marriages, birth announcements, or pictures from their university graduations, even beyond undergrad. Some also shared their music achievements.

But it was the subject line that made me pause. The subject line read, "Saw your twin in ATL." I clicked on the email and opening it immediately.

Hey Dr. Avery,

Hope thing's are solid! It's been a while. Super random thing, but I just got back from the AfroFuturism and Sound conference in Atlanta, and there was a DJ there. He was dope and did both a panel and a set. His name is Samuel. Unfortunately, I didn't catch his last name, but he looked exactly like you, and I mean identical. The dreads, the voice cadence, and he seemed about your same height too. He even plays the keys. He had an East Coast vibe, but it messed me up, and I swore it could have been you. I didn't talk to him, didn't want to seem weird, but I thought of you. They posted a video of his set on the conference's Instagram. Check it out, and if nothing else, you should follow him, he's dope!

Be well!

Deon

I sat down, trying with all my might to catch my breath.

At the same time, I was trying to click on the hyperlink. My hands were shaking; I was so overcome. With what I couldn't explain. I'd been searching for so long, I didn't think the day would come.

And. It didn't necessarily mean much. But the idea that it did had me beside myself. This was the closest thing to anything I had ever received. A name. A face. A possibility.

I mean, they say we all have a twin. But what if it's my actual twin. My brother?

This is crazy.

Sometimes, I wondered if things not working out were God's way of blocking them. I'd been up late, lost in the rabbit hole, reading message boards and forums about people meeting their birth families and things not going well. Some people didn't want to be found and weren't shy about it when you came knocking.

I finally managed to click the link, and it loaded slowly. My heart was beating the entire time. Pounding. In anticipation, hope, and possibility. I could almost feel it pounding in my throat.

Then I saw him.

And it could have been me. I swear it could have been me.

He looked just like me.

How is it not me, was the question.

But I saw him.

Behind the DJ booth. Using his left hand predominantly.

He's a lefty, just like me?

He moved just like me. It was like watching myself.

"Ya'll look amazing tonight! Thanks for grooving with me, ATL!"

Yeah. I could hear the East Coast flare, but it was my voice at the same time.

And he laughed; he smiled. Just like me. It was… crazy. It was a mind fuck. It was… wild.

Bizarre.

Insane.

Inexplicable.

I think I stopped breathing, watching this person. His hands, his posture. I felt like I was in the Twilight Zone, observing my doppelgänger from the outside.

And… the lively classroom commotion…the music, the movement, the spirited chatter and interaction, the laughter. I couldn't hear any of it. My focus stayed on the clip.

My twin brother.

And I knew it wasn't official. I knew there was a chance he was just a stranger, with no relation, and an uncanny resemblance. But I felt something. Something I can't explain. But there was a connection.

The clip ended, and I watched it again.

There you are. I've been searching for you, and there you are.

I grew emotional.

After the video ended for a second time, I zoomed in to get a close-up.

Wow.

I did a quick Google search about the Afrofuturism & Sound conference in Atlanta. I had heard of the annual conference, but I had never attended. It's definitely something I would love to go to someday.

The conference was exactly a week ago, over three days. It appeared a time was had, and it was right up my alley. Something akin to a fusion of the Essence Fest and a Comic Con. All things music for music lovers.

The event flyer and website were up, and I clicked on the panel of scheduled guests.

And there it was. A headshot and a bio.

I clicked on the photo that easily could have been me.

"Samuel Haman. A devoted husband, jubilant father, passionate musician, and prolific music educator. Samuel graduated from Morgan State University. He currently lives in Columbia, Maryland."

Wow. He's on the East Coast. I wondered how we ended up so far apart.

I wondered if he knew about me or if he'd ever searched for me.

I had so many questions.

I picked up my phone texting India.

Me: I think I have a twin brother.

I saw dots but didn't wait. Quickly navigating to the event site, I sent a screenshot of his bio page. Then shared his IG link of him performing.

And she replied **OMG!!!!**

Yeah.

My sentiments exactly.

thirty-six

SOL

Can you get away Belle?

Artist Girl: Yes

Me: Okay. I want you ready. I'm coming to get you. Be there in twenty

Arist Girl: I'll be ready baby

As soon as class ended, I rode my bike home from Sac City, then immediately jumped into my Jag once I pulled into the garage. Didn't even go in the house.

Yeah. I was feeling extra good right now.

I'd seen my brother.

My. Brother.

I passed the I-5 N freeway entrance, heading down Gloria Drive. The freeway would have taken about fifteen minutes tops, but taking the scenic route to India's at 8:30 on a Thursday night would be roughly the same amount of time.

I planned to pick my woman up and grab some junk food. I try not to eat that stuff too often. Honestly, I rarely eat it. But tonight was different, and I was in the mood. I needed to be close to her. I was feeling good about this possibility, and I wanted India to get the residuals.

I was in a great mood. Too good to spend the evening alone.

And it was wide open. I was off tonight from HomeGrown.

Gloria Drive took me to Fruitridge Road, and I wondered where we might go. Sonic sounded good. We could grab some greasy burgers, onion rings, and maybe a milkshake or two. A perfect way to celebrate this occasion.

And I knew that none of this was guaranteed.

But just the thought of it was taking me so fucking high. I smiled wide as I drove. This was the first significant thing I'd gotten since I started my search over a decade ago.

I wanted to talk with Samuel and hear his life story. Even though we didn't grow up together, it seems we have a lot in common.

I couldn't wait to learn more about him.

He's a married man, which I loved to see. I wonder how long he's been married and where he found his wife. I wonder how old his child was. Or children.

I wondered how long he's been on the East Coast.

His bio said he's an educator. I wondered where he taught music because music was clearly a passion of his, and I love that too. Not everyone is lucky enough to pursue their music. Unless you make it big, this industry is a hustle, even for someone with extreme talent. It takes your name being mentioned in rooms, someone putting you on, invitations, introductions, hunger, and passion.

I wondered about the family he was adopted into and whether he had adopted siblings.

Siblings must have been cool. I grew up as an only child, and I often wondered how things would have been if I'd had siblings.

If I were to become a father, I would want at least two children.

As I made my way to India's, I thought about all those things. And for every positive thought, I kept reminding myself that none of it was official.

But I couldn't contain my excitement. He looks just like me. He has to be my brother.

I recall mentioning to my parents that I wanted to find my birth family. And. Well. My mother was less than enthused.

It was a Sunday, and I was over for dinner.

She went radio silent, which isn't typical for her.

Eventually, she asked me one question. "Why?" Tone even.

And I responded, "Why not?" Her question caught me off guard, and I maintained an even tone, but I was appalled. My flabber was ghasted.

She didn't have much of an answer.

Later, I recall my father telling me my mother felt I was looking to replace her. And that she always felt inadequate, being unable to bear children of her own. Which I of course refuted immediately.

I could never replace the woman who raised me. Biological or not.

But she couldn't understand. And honestly, I don't believe anyone who isn't adopted would understand. Finding your people, your biological origins... It's like the last piece of a puzzle. A missing piece. It's a personal journey. I needed to know this other part of myself. This had nothing to do with either of them.

But they couldn't offer me much. It was a closed adoption, so there wasn't much information available.

My mother never encouraged me. Didn't offer her help.

Didn't ask how the search was going.

My father didn't really either. There was one day I mentioned submitting a petition through the court to open sealed records, and there was a weeks-long waiting period. Then, I was visiting one afternoon, and he asked if I'd heard anything, and I said not yet.

And that was that.

After several weeks of waiting, I received a notice that the request was denied. The judge didn't provide much of a reason, just something generic like "public interest in the records is not compelling enough to warrant the disclosure of the sealed information."

I about fell apart getting that letter after waiting so long.

It would have been nice to have access to non-identifying information at least.

I didn't bother updating my father, and he didn't ask. We never discussed it again.

So, I didn't plan to tell him about this lead. Not yet, anyway. Maybe once I had more information. Once everything was confirmed, and I prayed sincerely that it would be soon.

Fruitridge Road led me to Martin Luther King Jr. Boulevard, and I smiled even wider. I'd see my baby in just a few minutes.

It was just about dark when I turned down India's block. It was lively for a Thursday evening, which was typical in her part of central Oak Park. Most of the urban bungalows I cruised past had a few people sitting out on their porches. I weaved through a few teenagers in the street tossing a football back and forth.

I came to a stop but left my engine running and sighed lightly.

I never liked this. I probably never will.

I wanted to step out of this car and knock on the door like a gentleman does.

Look into Mr. Rampersaud's eyes. Shake his hand. Assure him I will look after his daughter and give him my word that she is safe while she's with me. And that I will bring her back to him.

And I started to.

Yep. I was moments from shutting off the car, unbuckling my seatbelt, and doing just that.

But. I was in such a great mood that I decided not to.

Though I intended to remind India once more that I wanted to meet her parents.

I longed to meet the people responsible for the greatness she embodies. Two exceptionally remarkable individuals who clearly imparted the very best of themselves when they came together.

Her Ma and her Daddy raised a queen.

More specifically, they raised a catch. I'd told India that with conviction on more than one occasion.

Yeah. A catch I didn't intend to throw back. I was her Music Man now for real. She officially agreed to be my Artist Girl, and I now have the privilege of showing India how it's done. And I intended to do just that.

I planned to be all in, and so far, that's exactly what I've been doing. All of that reservation stemming from you know who, a name I decided I would no longer give life to, was no longer relevant the moment India agreed to let me be her man. Not consciously anyway.

And since we'd made it official and had been spending more time together, I realized my desire to meet her parents had grown tremendously. I'd been picking her up more often over the past couple of weeks, and I had an intense desire to meet the people I'd come to respect greatly based solely on what she'd shared.

Two people who, if it weren't for their union, India wouldn't be here.

But. India wasn't ready to introduce us, so I would keep doing my best to wait patiently.

The silver lining is that I finally have her now, and I love having her.

And when she was ready for us to be intimate again, I couldn't wait to be with her once more.

So yeah, I stayed in my seat, remained in my car, and pulled out my phone to text her that I was out front. She said it would just be another minute.

I kept my eyes on her front door, and as she emerged, my smile was back, wide as ever.

India was dressed in dark jeans and a lavender crew neck sweatshirt, with white high-top Converse. Her hair was wild, her face bare, glowing in the early evening. Her eyes shone brightly. She smiled as she approached me. She's so beautiful. As she descended her walkway, I got out of the car and walked around the hood to meet her, wrapping her in my arms. Our lips met immediately, brief but tender, as we exchanged kisses.

"Hey, Indie."

"Hey Sol."

I pecked her a few more times. I loved that I could kiss her all the time now.

Now that she's mine. I love her lips.

I opened my trunk. India had her tote and a backpack.

"Packed a bag. Can I stay the night since you don't have class tomorrow?"

"Of course you can, baby."

"Okay."

I closed the trunk and opened the passenger door for her. When I was back in my seat, we both leaned into each other over the console. She gave me her tongue, and I went all over the place with mine. Deep in her mouth, on her neck. I gently grabbed her hand and kissed her fingertips. Then we reconnect our lips again, and India was kissing me just as passionately as I was kissing her. India's a great kisser.

"Mmm. You better stop all this kissing you're doing," I murmured. Just a breath between us.

"Or what?" She kept us closely connected and immediately got back to it.

"Or… you'll have me begging to finish what we've started." I gently held her face in my hands, deepening the kiss like never before.

"Who said you had to beg?" She said, around bated breath, several moments later.

Say less, Belle.

We kept kissing. Then her phone started to ring.

But we kept kissing.

I was ready to get her out of here. Get out of this car. And these clothes. Get her in my bed. And get inside of her.

She silenced her phone, only for it to ring again.

She reluctantly broke the kiss. "Let me see who it is. It may be my mom wondering why we're still sitting in front of the house."

We laughed.

"It's Destiney. We were just on the phone when I told her you were here to get me."

I pulled from the curb as she answered the phone on speaker.

"Best! You're on the speaker. Just got in my man's car!" She looked over, and at that exact moment, I was already looking at her.

I winked and she smiled big and bright.

"Hey Sol!"

"Hey Sis."

"Girl. I had to call you twice. Ya'll were already going at it?" The girls cracked up. "Speaking of which, Micah and I are lying here chilling, and I'm hungry. He's about to make me some French toast. He can make some waffles and fry some chicken, too. Want to come by? Oh wait. We should all go get something. I've got a sweet tooth, and we don't have anything sweet in this house…Ooh I know! Let's go to Keisha's!"

India squealed in her seat. And I heard the same squeal coming from her phone.

"Can we, baby? Please?" India pressed.

I laughed; these two were conspiring. But it was all good. I was thinking the same. I didn't really want to go home. Too excited. Chilling with my woman, my best friend, and his wife sounded perfect.

"Yeah. I'm cool with that."

"Micah, can we go too right? I want a slice of their key lime cheesecake!"

I couldn't hear Micah in the background, but moments later, Destiney said, "Great! We'll be there in like twenty."

"Cool. We'll head straight over. Please leave now and don't get any ideas."

The girls giggled, and Indie hung up.

"Have you heard back from him yet?" India asked.

"Not yet. I hope soon."

She nodded. "Me too."

As soon as my class ended earlier, I called her. I could hardly contain myself. Since learning about Samuel less than an hour earlier, I was ecstatic. Very emotional, nearly hyperventilating. India managed to calm me down while celebrating the possibility of it all with me. And we talked about reaching out somehow.

I searched for Samuel on social media, of course, but he didn't have much presence there.

There was a Facebook. But the page had very little activity, and the settings we so I was unable to send a message. And I understood. He's an educator. Most teachers weren't active on social media. Or if they were, they used an alias.

I looked on IG. The AfroFuturism event hadn't tagged him, so I searched for his name. A page came up, and though it wasn't private, he didn't post on there much. There may have been a dozen posts total, and the last one was from several weeks ago. But I messaged him there.

I also did a Google search, hoping he might have a LinkedIn profile. But I didn't find him there.

I took MLK boulevard back toward Broadway. Keisha's Diner is centrally located in the heart of the city, but more specifically in the Arden-Arcade area of North Sacramento, near Arden Fair Mall.

It would take fewer than fifteen minutes to get to Keisha's on the freeway from India's house. Since Micah and Destiney are coming from Elk Grove, we'll probably arrive a few minutes before them.

I stopped at a red light, and India leaned over, pecking my cheek. "Hey you." So sweet.

"Hey baby. I gently caressed her inner thigh with my right hand.

And India kissed my cheek again, then leaned over, kissing the corner of my mouth. "We were interrupted. And I wasn't finished." she said, kissing me again. I turned toward her, connecting our lips. "Missed you." she offered, which was nearly swallowed, but I heard her just fine.

"Missed you more, baby…missed these too."

And our lips remained connected.

A blaring horn behind me jolted us apart, and she burst out laughing at me, adjusting herself in her seat.

I chuckled deep, shaking my head.

"I love that I get this baby now. Full time." she told me as she took my right hand with her left. We intertwined our fingers. "Love the way it sounds."

"Love saying it. Love that things are official now. I would only get to say it when I was balls deep. So…" I glanced at her quickly, then focused ahead as I merged onto CA-99N from 12th Avenue.

We both cackled and rode in comfortable silence, "Tell Me" by Usher whispering in the background.

"I wanna tell you everything, baby," India said. "I'm glad things are official, too." A beat. "There's more to you. Just like there's more to me. I know our conversations will grow even deeper. We've talked about so much, but there's still so much. You know?"

"Yeah. Yeah, definitely."

India pulled out her phone. "Okay, just googled deep questions to ask your significant other."

I chuckled. She's so much fun. Keeps me on my toes. Keeps me guessing. And she's so interested in me. Even more so now it seems.

Now that we were us.

I shared those same notions. India was by far one of the dopest people I've met in such a long time. And she was all mine.

"We both have to answer honestly, okay."

"Of course."

"Okay. I'm gonna scan these. I want a juicy one…" A beat. "Hmm, okay, here's one. When's the last time you cried?"

"The last time I cried?" I thought about that. "Well. I don't cry much. Not that I suppress it, but I don't cry a lot, you know.

But I got pretty emotional earlier today, learning I may have a twin. A brother. And seeing him in that clip."

"Of course. I would have too."

"Yeah." We'd passed through downtown Sacramento and continued onto I-80 East. The Capital City Freeway. And the freeway was wide open. We'd be at the mall in another ten minutes, easy. "Can I tell you something else?"

"Of course!"

"The Music Academy usually hosts a Holiday Dinner; we partner with a few other organizations, and anyway, the kids get presents, most of which are donated unwrapped. We have a fancy banquet for them, a Santa Claus will come, they can play games, have a Christmas dinner, there's a raffle, and we've been blessed to donate brand new bicycles. Electric Scooters. Video game systems. Laptops. iPads. Gift cards."

"Wow."

"Yeah, that's always a great time for everyone. It's all about giving back, you know."

"For sure."

"But I get emotional. Every year, and it never fails. When those kids tear open those presents… they're so grateful. And so happy. Some of them may not have gotten anything for Christmas otherwise."

"Yeah. That would make me emotional, too. I didn't grow up with much. Though I had everything I needed… the extra things weren't so frequent. And do you know what's interesting… when I was living in Berbice surrounded by a tribe of family. Cousins galore. We all lived together in the same area, houses close by, always sleeping over cousins' houses or them sleeping over my house. I was so happy. Loving life, it was simple. And… it wasn't until we moved back here that I was made aware that we didn't have a lot. Kids liked to remind me." She laughed, shaking her head.

"I didn't wear the same clothes or shoes that they did. I didn't have the latest technology or whatever. Couldn't afford to go to the movies every time my friends wanted to go or to the mall." She shrugged. "That's why I threw myself into art. I knew it was something I was good at, and that made me cool, I guess. I did everything art. Volunteered around campus to paint posters for the student government. Entered art contests. Submitted my work every time I heard about something. And once I got my footing, people seemed to forget about everything I didn't have. Of course, the way I look isn't something they let go of. But I hid myself away with the art geeks."

We both laughed at that.

"Glad you found your tribe. I'd imagine art geeks are loyal. The band geeks certainly are."

We laughed all over again.

"But I get it. And you know what's funny? Even having the latest of everything… kids will still find a reason to pick on you."

"Hmm."

Man, fuck them kids.

"You have to answer now," I said to India as we were exiting the freeway. We'd take Arden Way straight to Keisha's Diner. About four minutes.

"The last time I cried. Hmm. Some weeks ago." She sighed. "I was frustrated. Money was tight. Well, we didn't have money, so the lack of money was just getting to me…" She laughed. "I was in my room, looking through some of my paintings. I figured maybe I could sell some to get us through till Daddy got paid. He's only able to work a few shifts a week due to his arthritis. It's been worsening. And I found this business card…" she sighed again, glancing out the window. "I took a pole dancing class when we went out for Destiney's bachelorette party, and the instructor. She took an interest in me and complimented me all night. Told me I was a natural, and before we left, she passed me a card and said she owned a club and could get me on the schedule. Told me I'd make unbelievable money, that I was sexy, had the look, and I could work that pole, and I'd be a favorite."

My eyebrows had to be at my hairline. But I said nothing.

"And I wasn't offended. Not really." She laughed, but it was an empty laugh. "Kind of shocked, I guess. But all the girls told me I was a badass, and I was just having fun. We all were. But… I kept the card. I figured, maybe if I really, really needed it, I could use it."

"Have you?" I asked just as we'd pulled into a parking spot. We got one right in front of Keisha's, facing their large windows. I killed the engine.

And India turned to look at me.

"Would it change anything if I had?"

"No, Belle," I told her immediately. "Wouldn't change a thing."

She smiled sweetly. Closed mouth, but it was beautiful and sweet. And I swear, I cared for her even more now that she had been vulnerable enough to be so transparent with me.

"Don't forget you don't have to carry anything by yourself anymore. If you ever need anything. Please don't hesitate to let me know."

"I know."

"Good."

She sent Destiney a text letting her know we were here, and we'd get a table for the four of us.

Before we got out, I said, "Can I have a kiss?"

"You may."

We kissed passionately. It turned sloppy. And nasty. And in no time, smacking sounds were all I could hear, woven in with our moans. India was leaning over the console. Damn near in my lap. My hands were beneath her sweater, rubbing up and down her warm back. Glad my windows were tinted. I'd take her right here, right now.

Out of nowhere, we heard pounding on the window.

"Hey, kids! I'll give you a few minutes to get yourselves decent, then I'll need you to step out of the car, please." Micah's clowning ass.

I could hear Destiney cracking up laughing, blowing his cover. "Leave them alone, Micah! They're making up for lost time."

India and I were rolling.

I got out of the car, rounded the hood, and slapped hands with Micah. "My boy! What's good dude!"

"Shit! You're the one needing to give me some updates."

I chuckled easy. "Right. Hang on man." I stepped over to the passenger side and let Indie out. She and Destiney embraced and fell right into their chatter. I'd given Destiney a side hug just before they followed us inside.

I could smell the savory entrees and scrumptious desserts as soon as we crossed the threshold.

Keisha's Diner is black owned, and they deliver just what you need to hit the spot.

Whatever you have a taste for, you'll find it here. The word "diner" doesn't truly capture their exceptional service and superb quality. They serve breakfast, lunch, and dinner. All day.

This was a great call; I'm glad Destiney suggested the place. I haven't been here in a while.

They're open early, and they stay open late. There's always a decent-sized crowd. Thankfully, they weren't too busy for a Thursday evening, and our host seated us immediately. There was low chatter from the scattered patrons. And I could hear music floating beneath the chatter.

We all settled into a booth. Micah and I were across from each other. The women climbed in beside us. India, next to me, Destiney, next to Micah. And they were still carrying on with their conversation. I heard mentions of plans this weekend. But I missed the details.

"Hey there. So glad ya'll came to Keisha's. Any drinks to start you all tonight?" A younger woman politely asked us, likely in her early twenties.

I didn't know this young lady, but based on her familiar smile, she was likely one of Mrs. Keisha's granddaughters. Keisha's is family-owned, and the diner has been in business for more than thirty years. Once upon a time, her daughters were waiting tables. Back then, Mrs. Keisha would be here, there, and everywhere, running a tight ship. She'd be back in the kitchen, or handling the front of the house, even running orders. A smile on her face all the while. Greeting everyone warmly and treating all who dined here like family. She ensured everyone who worked here maintained that same expression. I'd like to think that's the reason this place has been in business for so long.

She's slowed down just as little as she's gotten older, and her children and grandchildren have taken the mantle. But knowing Mrs. Keisha, she still comes by once in a while to make sure everyone knows she's still the boss. She's no-nonsense but sweet as pie.

"Can we have hot water for tea, please? And water with lemon?" Destiney asked.

India nodded, "Same. I'll have tea. And water for me too, please."

Micah and I both ordered hot coffee and water.

Our server promised to return with the drinks and to take our orders. After thanking her, the women went back to their engrossing conversation.

Micah and I looked at each other, exchanging glances, then cracked up laughing.

The women didn't even notice. But that was to be expected. And it was all good. I would worry if they weren't deep in conversation with one another.

I browsed the menu, trying to decide on what I wanted.

I love the breakfast here. They have omelets, breakfast burritos, and fluffy pancakes. I was seriously considering the Eggs Benedict. They were delightful. But the entire breakfast menu is. Flavors are top-notch.

"So, you got your girl?" I looked up, and his eyebrows were high. A wide grin. I chuckled light. Micah was ready to lay into me. And I didn't mind. I was ready for it.

Nah. I didn't mind it at all. I smiled just as wide as he was before I could even respond, and Micah thought that was so funny.

"Yeah. Got my girl." I glanced at her, then looked back at the menu. Trying to play cool.

"Man! Get out of here! You don't have to play in my face. I know you sprung. I know you've been sprung!" Micah was rolling.

I joined him. He wasn't lying.

We looked at the women, and they looked at us. Quizzical expressions. But quickly returned to their chatter. They'd stopped their chatter long enough to put in their drink orders a moment ago, and that was the first time they had since they embraced in the parking lot. They never missed a beat. I loved that India had Destiney.

"Man. I'm on a fucking cloud, Mich!" I shared.

"I see that!"

We laughed.

"You two look great together. And I'm happy for you. Just take care of each other, man."

I nodded. "She's pretty special." I placed my hand on her thigh and looked over at her. She wasn't far. Never far when we were in the same space. Always on me. Always near me. Something I loved so much. And India looked at me, smiling back. "No doubt about it."

We'd both returned to our menus.

Lunch here at Keisha's offered everything from soups and salads to fish and chips, tri-tip sandwiches, steak salads, juicy char-broiled chicken sandwiches, and burgers with all the fixings and plenty of fries.

For dinner, they rotate their menu offerings. Tonight, there was brick-oven pizza with plenty of toppings to choose from, wood-fired rotisserie chicken and pasta, gumbo, roasted Mediter-ranean vegetables, seasonal grilled salmon, and pork chops with creamy garlic mashed potatoes and a gravy simmered to perfec-tion… so flavorful. That gravy would seriously melt in your mouth. It's so good you'd want to take it home by the gallon. You can't find a gravy like that anywhere else in Sac. I've looked.

All I know is, Mrs. Keisha better not ever let that recipe die. I hope it's written down and locked away somewhere. And I hope she taught every surviving member of her family how to make it. She should really bottle it and sell it.

Our waitress returned with our drinks and took our orders. She promised it wouldn't be too long before we got our food.

Micah and I got caught up. Shot the shit. I was bursting with the news I had, but I wanted him to go first.

He told me about his quick business trip. He's been acting as Interim President of his division for the past several weeks, as his boss had to take an unexpected leave.

He mentioned receiving acting pay for his additional duties, but he didn't like the added pressure or responsibility. I could un-derstand that. It wasn't always about the money. Especially in this new season he was in. He said it would only be another month and that he was doing his best not to let it all consume him.

And I encouraged him. Told him he was doing a great job and to hang in there. And to speak up for himself immediately if needed. But knowing Micah, I'm sure he had that under control. Micah was all about self-advocacy.

And I was so very proud of Micah. And I've always been so proud of him.

My boy was doing his thing in the corporate world. At thirty-five, he's accomplished much, with no signs of slowing down. He works in Mergers and Acquisitions, and he can negotiate some of the best deals. Fair deals. Still saving the company hundreds of thousands of dollars.

The best part is that Micah's so humble about it and doesn't hesitate to acknowledge anyone who helped make it happen.

"You doing alright, Belle?" I gently squeezed her hand. My hand was on her lap, and we'd threaded our fingers under the table.

I checked with India when the ladies finally paused for the cause.

Destiney asked Micah something, and they'd been going back and forth for a few.

"Yes. I'm perfect. Getting hungry. Hella excited about my Gourmet Mac and Cheese." She was so cute, smiling at me, flirty.

"Oh, you'll enjoy that. Have you tried it?" It was, in fact, gourmet. Made with three cheeses: smoked Gouda, Swiss cheese, and white cheddar.

"A while ago, and I loved it. Got a side of garlic fries too."

I nodded. "Now that will be tasty. No meat tonight?"

She shook her head. "I don't eat meat when I'm out with Des. It's just a thing I do."

"I see," I recall Micah mentioning that Destiney is a vegetarian.

"She calls me a flexitarian." she giggled again. "I kinda like it."

I chuckled at her. "It's certainly fitting. You can go without meat and not give it a second thought. Then you can devour an entire plate of baby back ribs like I wouldn't believe." I said in jest.

We both burst out laughing.

"Hey! Don't make me look like a pig!"

"Never that, Belle." I was still laughing. "You're so cute, Artist Girl." I leaned over, planting a tender kiss on her cheek.

Well. It was closer to her mouth.

"Mmm... One more baby. Right here." She lightly tapped her lips. They were pressed into a closed-mouth smile. Her lids were partially lowered.

"My pleasure, baby. As many as you want." I leaned in, giving her soft pecks a few times. Closed-mouth kisses... but the kind you don't pull away from. You remain close. Lips remain connected. No more than a breath separates you. Puckering is all the movement needed to land these kisses.

And.

They're loud... ish. The smacking noises.

At some point, my eyes were closed. I'm sure India's were too.

And by now, both of our mouths were open.

Yup.

"Umm... uh... ma'am... your seasonal chef's pizza..."

Someone softly cleared their throat.

"Sir... your grilled salmon sandwich."

"I mean... we could just put it on the table." The female voice offered.

"Okay."

I felt someone reaching over me. I opened my eyes, and there stood two runners.

A younger girl and a young man. Maybe late teens.

I looked at him, and he was holding my Eggs Benedict, looking embarrassed.

Almost like a kid walking in on his parents.

I bit back my laugh and looked at Micah. He shrugged with a guilty expression, and I could tell he was trying to hold in his laugh too.

Yeah, that kid looked mortified.

Evidently, they'd been in make-out mode too. At the same time, we were. Since soft-spoken, unfamiliar voices were running the food, neither of us realized they were there for us.

"Thank you!" Destiney shrieked. "She pulled her pizza close to her, then she pulled out her hand sanitizer.

"Yummy! Thank you!" India had a hearty serving of mac and cheese and a large basket of crispy fries in front of her.

Mr. Bashful had since placed my Eggs Benedict in front of me. Yeah. I couldn't wait.

"That's everything. Thank you, man. And here's a tip for both of you. Sorry about that," Micah chuckled. He had what appeared to be an Italian pasta salad next to his sandwich. He'd since reached into his pocket and handed each of them a crisp Jackson. "Keep that for yourself. Our server will still get her tip."

They thanked him and walked away, all seemingly forgotten.

And we all cracked up.

"Man. I swear!" Micah was rolling. "We're in our thirties…" He nodded at me. "The women are in their twenties. And we out here behaving like teenagers."

We all laughed even harder.

"I love it though." Destiney offered. "I'm so glad you two are together! Finally."

"We are too," India replied. Smiling back at me.

"Yeah. Been juiced and squeezed ever since." I said with a smile.

Everyone laughed all over again.

"Let's pray. This food looks too good, and I can't wait any longer." That was Micah.

We bowed our heads, and he blessed our food.

Thanking God for another day.

Thanking God for the fellowship.

Then, blessed our friendships.

Blessed the child growing in his wife's belly.

Prayed we all made it home safely.

And we agreed in Jesus' name.

I was the only one with breakfast. And yeah, this Benedict was… harmonious.

The eggs were perfectly poached. The English muffins were crisp on the outside with a firm texture and soft, airy insides. The hollandaise was golden, smooth, creamy, and rich with a tangy flavor. It complemented the richness of the eggs perfectly. I had crispy breakfast potatoes on the side, which were ideal for soaking up the hollandaise sauce.

The women were back at it. Chatting away again.

Her garlic fries were in the middle of the table. There was so much India offered to share with everyone.

Micah asked me if I had received any promising offers. We discussed this from time to time. I confided in him about the mounting pressure I had been feeling from my dean.

And I gave him a rundown on the latest. He knew I wasn't actively looking, but he still offered kind words, saying the right one is out there and will come along just when I'm ready for it.

I appreciated that. And received it too.

That's when I decided to share my news with Micah.

"Mich, one of my former students reached out today. He was in Atlanta last week for a music conference. And there was a DJ there, that he swore was me. The man looked just like me."

That caught Micah's attention. He looked up, pausing mid-chew.

"At a music conference in Atlanta? And it wasn't you?" He looked a bit confused.

"No. It wasn't me."

"Okay. Where is this going?"

I pulled out my phone. "He linked a video of the guy. And… he may be my brother. My twin. He looks just like me. Talks like me. Laughs like me. He's a leftie too." I turned my phone toward Micah and pushed it across the table to show the clip.

Micah's eyes had widened. "You sure this ain't you?"

I chuckled. "Crazy, right? I definitely wasn't in Atlanta last week. And I'm a lot of things, but I'm no DJ."

Micah picked up my phone and turned up the volume. "Wild! He sounds just like you, man!" He replayed the clip. "Who is this?"

"His name is Samuel Haman, and he lives in Columbia, Maryland."

I picked up my phone and went to his bio page. I showed it to Micah, too.

"If he isn't your twin, he's definitely your brother."

"Twin? Brother?" Destiney asked, her brows knitting together. "Can I see?" She had stopped the conversation she was having with India about whatever they were discussing.

Micah handed her the phone. "Oh my gosh!" she gasped, covering her mouth. "Sol! He looks just like you."

"He does." I nodded.

India said, "Right! Let me show you the IG video. This shit is almost scary."

The girls carried on chatting again.

"What's the plan? You gonna reach out? We need some answers." Micah knew I'd been searching for my birth family. We talked about that all the time. Especially lately. Since I'd been back on the hunt.

"I already have. Been watching my IG like a hawk. Messaged him earlier. I even turned my notifications back on."

Micah nodded. "I know you still don't know for sure. But… how you feeling?"

"I can't even explain it. Excited… nervous. Intrigued. He seems like a cool guy. I just want to hear his voice. I want to talk to him. Get the official confirmation and meet him. His wife. His kids."

"Yeah. For sure. I'm excited for you! I want everything to work out for you, man. I pray it does. Keep me updated. And please let me know if there's anything I can help with. Not sure what, but I'm around."

"Thank you."

♪♥♫♥♪

I unlocked my front door. India stepped in ahead of me. I closed and locked the door behind us.

It had been a long day. Long, but it ended on such a high note. India sat on the small foyer bench just inside the front door and took off her shoes. She never wore shoes inside when she was over. Ever.

I never made it a big deal, but she told me, "She wouldn't dare do such a thing. She's Indian and Guyanese." She also explained the cultural significance of removing shoes before entering homes. It's customary because "outside shoes" are seen as unclean and impure. When you take them off before entering your home, you're showing respect for its humility and cleanliness. Since then, I haven't worn shoes inside either.

She took the desserts we'd gotten wrapped to-go from Keisha's and headed toward the kitchen.

"I'll meet you in your room, baby. I'm going to put these sweets in the fridge."

Yeah. I noticed the case of sweets on the way to our table, and I had already made up my mind before we even ordered dinner. The food there was amazing, and we all left full, but the highlight of the place was their desserts. They made them fresh in-house every day, and they were award-winning.

Visually appealing.

Delectable. Scrumptious.

Cakes, pies, tarts, and Napoleons.

"Sounds good, baby." I carried her backpack and tote. Once I took off my shoes, I headed down the hall.

I'd gotten a slice of Kahlua cake, and I could barely wait to enjoy it tomorrow. I couldn't eat a single thing more tonight. Not one iota.

India had a few things. She couldn't decide, so I told her to go ahead and get whatever she wanted, and we could share.

She drooled over the caramel pecan cheesecake and grabbed a slice of that. She also took a slice of fruit basket cake, a caramel walnut bar, some petit fours, and a few mini cannoli's. We'd have a field day with these tomorrow.

We'll definitely go for a bike ride tomorrow or sometime this weekend. Need to burn off some calories.

"Thank you for dinner," India told me as she entered my bedroom. It was dark in here aside from the light flooding in from the hallway. I didn't bother turning on the light in here. I knew we'd be falling out soon. We were both tired. The ride back was pretty quiet. We just cruised, hand in hand, enjoying each other's company.

India immediately moved to my side of the bed, slipping into my arms. Hers wrapped around my neck in seconds. We kissed.

"You're very welcome, Belle. Thanks for hanging out with me. That was our first time eating at a restaurant together."

"It was, wasn't it?"

"It was. Looking forward to many more of those."

"Me too, baby."

We were standing close, embraced. Still. Breathing each other in. My inhale was her exhale. And hers mine.

"That was thoughtful of you to treat Des and Micah."

"Oh, that wasn't nothing. Mich and I go back and forth. It was my turn."

"You two are pretty close, huh?"

"Man, Mich is my brother."

"I love that."

"You and Destiney have a great friendship."

"We do. I couldn't be more blessed to have met her."

"Absolutely."

I caressed India's back, moving lower. I could feel her moans.

"Mmm. I love this song."

"Comfortable" by H.E.R. I'd turn on some music when I came into my bedroom.

"Yeah. She's dope. All her songs are fire."

"That was funny when we all got caught making out," she lightly tittered.

"It was!" I chuckled deep.

"I'm off from the shop tomorrow."

"Are you?"

"Yeah, we've got plans."

"Do we?"

"Yep. There's a fight tomorrow, and Daijah and Julian are hosting. Daijah asked us to come. Everyone will be there."

"Everyone?"

She giggled again. "Everyone, as in Daijah and Julian. Des and Micah, of course. Mal. Ella."

"Oh, the crew you mean?" I chuckled again, kissing her cheek. "Micah calls us the crew. So next time, say that and I'll know exactly who you're talking about."

"Okay."

We stayed where we were, but we had started to sway. "Love Again" by Alex Isely was crooning now. I was still caressing her back. I'd gone beneath her sweatshirt again.

Her skin felt incredibly soft. She smelled wonderful. My nose was pressed against her neck, and I'd been kissing there, including under her chin too.

"That worked out perfectly. I'm off from HomeGrown again tomorrow. Instead, we play on Sunday for their Anniversary Soiree, celebrating their fourteenth year in business."

"So we've got plans Sunday evening too."

"Yeah. They usually do it pretty big. Micah knows, but I'll mention it to the other guys tomorrow. You can invite the ladies. It would be cool if everyone could come out. It'll be a great time. I'll have a VIP section reserved for you all."

"That sounds dope. Thank you."

I nodded.

"I'm tired, baby," she yawned. "If we weren't standing here, I would have *been* sleep!"

"Me too."

We laughed.

"Ate so much it's knocking me out."

"It's been a day. How about we call it?" I offered. It was after eleven at night.

"Let's." Her voice relaxed and slowed, carrying a sultry tone.

And I knew it was everything. All the things.

The closeness. The music. The… slow dancing we were doing.

The hour being far spent. The sexual tension that had been steadily building.

Yeah. It was all of that.

I gently guided India's chin, bringing her lips back to mine. And I captured them kissing her tenderly as if I hadn't been kissing her lips all night. And she kissed me back. Parting right away, we deepened the kiss in seconds.

"We can shower in the morning. Let's lie down, baby," I offered, murmuring against her lips. I held her face gently with both my hands, but I didn't let her go.

She hadn't let me go either. Her arms remained securely around my waist.

"Sol."

"Yeah?"

Her eyes were closed, but now they were wide open again. She looked at me confidently. She didn't look away as I held her gaze. Her beautiful dark brown eyes were full of wonder and vulnerability.

"I know I said I wanted to take things slow. And we have been, and thank you for doing that for me. For being patient with me. I needed to figure my life out."

"You're so welcome, Belle."

"Sol. Can we start again? I'm tired right now..." She giggled, blinking slow and heavy. "But... soon? Like tomorrow... or something? Or whenever the time feels right? Can we... will that be alright with you?"

Mmm.

"Indie. Baby. I'm ready to make love again as soon as you are." I gently caressed her cheeks with my thumbs. "No pressure. No rush. Just us."

She smiled at that.

"I mean it, Belle. I'm not going anywhere. I'm waiting, patiently for you. But you should know you're still my guilty pleasure. I look forward to being one with you again, whenever that may be."

"I'm your guilty pleasure?"

"Oh, Belle. You have no idea. I get so undone for you, baby. When you let me touch you. When I get a taste of you... Thinking about it right now... I'm waking shit up."

We chuckled.

"We can keep taking our time. But I'm ready for you again. Whatever you need."

"Hmm... so... if I were to grab him, would he know what time it is?"

"He'd know exactly what time it is."

She nodded. "Cool."

My chuckle was deep.

"Let's lie down, baby, before we collapse."

"I know, right? I was leaning on you for support," India said as she moved to her side of the bed. She rummaged for her toothbrush. "I'll be back. Going to brush my teeth."

"I'll be right here."

thirty-seven

INDIA

"He said, make love! And here's the thing... I know people like to toss that around. But do you think that means he actually loves me?"

"Yeah. People definitely toss that around. But in this case, it could! I get the sense that Sol is the type to mean what he says. Based on what you've told me about him."

"He absolutely is."

"Well, there's your answer."

"Yeah..." I smiled at that.

Sol was taking a shower in his ensuite. We were getting ready to head out to Daijah's house. I'd taken mine right before him. And I called Mala while I got dressed.

"That's a good thing, right? You don't sound uber excited," Mala posed.

"Yeah! That's freakin' fantastic!"

"But?" Mala's tone was flat. She knew me and that I was overthinking; my mind was working overtime.

I cracked up. "Don't do me, cousin!"

"Don't do me, cousin!" she teased, mimicking my voice.

We both cackled.

"I'm curious why he hasn't mentioned it yet. Our chemistry is intense, and our bond is powerful. The sexual tension between us is off the charts. Now that we're official, everything feels even more heightened. Although I've only known him for a short time in the grand scheme, I can tell he's starting to fall for me, just like I'm falling for him."

"Yeah."

I shimmied into my black, destructed, high-waisted skinny jeans. I could still hear the shower. "I know he feels it like I do, so when he said that, I was like... kinda sorta thinking that would follow. And cousin… he said some sweet, lovely things. The moment was almost perfect. He was holding me close. We were dancing slow. Right here in his bedroom. He said so much. Made me feel so special. But not that."

"You didn't either."

I stilled my movements. I had Mala on speaker as I carefully pulled my shirt over my head. I'd already brushed my hair back into a low bun and slicked my edges. I wasn't trying to mess up my baby hairs. Once my shirt was completely on, I stood there for a moment. She said a lot without saying much at all.

"Touche. My. Touche."

"I know I'm right." she cackled. "You could have said it just like he could have. And let me remind you of something, cousin. So far, you're the one racking up the… *little white lies.*"

"White lies? What are you talking about?!"

"Oh, I'll explain myself. Gladly. First, you used the money he gave you for tattoo equipment to pay bills. And I'm not saying that was wrong. You did what anyone responsible would have done. We're all out here trying to survive." Mala suddenly cracked up. "I'm sorry, cousin. I was thinking about that tweet. It had me rolling, but it's true. *Adulthood is the worst hood.*"

We cackled. "Girl, you ain't lyin'."

"Then there's the car situation. Instead of telling him what's going on, you've been taking Ubers, walking, and riding the bus. If Sol knew, he'd help you out. I know he would, especially now that he's your man."

I said nothing.

"This next one is a free space on your bingo card. I think you should tell him about Kingston, specifically about him wanting you sexually and about him giving you money. None of that feels right to me."

"Yeah," I mumbled. "Me neither."

I hadn't told Destiney or Mala, but King gave me another fifteen hundred last week.

And even though I didn't really feel right about accepting it, I did anyway. For the first time in a while, I had a comma in my account. After paying the bills, that was rarely ever a thing for me, and I was glad I could breathe easier, even if just for a moment.

But there was always something. A medication. An unexpected expense. Another issue with the car. Money was fleeting. Still, it felt good to be free from that pressure for a little while longer. I was clearly chasing that feeling, which led me to accept King's money. Money I knew deep down was conditional. I was anxious as hell thinking about what would happen when the other shoe dropped.

"Destiney said the same thing," I offered.

"Yeah. You need to move on from that shop, cousin. I feel like something is going to pop off over there. If Sol knew, at least, maybe he'd visit. Stake his claim. Check in on you. Niggas are less likely to try women if they know you have a man."

"Hmm." Was all I had.

For what it's worth, things have been going well at the shop. As promised, King let me start tatting on skins, and I was progressing rather quickly, according to Kam and Drew. I'd been working with both of them, and they each said I'd been doing well. I was one step closer to getting my license, and I didn't plan to stick around after that.

"I'm saying this in love, cousin... you've been lying by omission, not being transparent. Let's call it what it is. Maybe you didn't have to tell him everything before you two were official, but you were friends. And friendships deserve honesty. Now that you're official, you don't want to start with lies between you. Half-truths aren't whole truths. They're untruths, no matter how you spin it."

"You're right. I need to talk to him."

"Please do, cousin. A-SAP! And tell him everything. You'll feel better."

"Yeah." I heard the shower cut off. "I gotta go, cousin. But I'll see you Sunday, right?"

"Yep. I'll be there. See you! Have a great time. Tell Des I said hey!"

"I'll tell her! Love you, cousin. Later!"

"Love you more! Later!"

I looked up when Sol emerged from the ensuite. He'd dried off in the restroom, so he came out shirtless in his boxers.

"Hey you."

"Hey. I was just talking to Mala. I invited her to HomeGrown Sunday. I hope that's alright."

"Of course it is, baby."

"Thank you."

I was putting on my accessories. I wear a single gold figaro chain around my neck. I also have an old-school Casio Illuminator watch that I love. I've had it for years, and I wear it almost every day. Everywhere. They're built to last for decades. It's simple, functional, and, most importantly, affordable. If something happens to it, I can replace it with no problem.

But I love this watch. It's a classic sports watch design with a square face. It's a man's watch, so it's oversized for my delicate wrist, but that was the point. It's teal, with a large digital display showing the time, date, and day of the week. I use the alarm on it too. And that little shit is small but mighty. Very old school. People my age don't wear these watches. Everyone seems to have an Apple Watch. But not me. This watch is just fine. Perfect for daily wear. There's an orange LED light for checking the time in the dark. It's made of resin, so it's water-resistant, which is perfect for me as an artist. I remove it when I shower, but that's about it. I can wash my hands and the dishes without worrying.

"You think she'll invite Lorenzo?" Sol asked, bringing me back from my thoughts.

I looked up and he had a silly grin. I grinned too. "I didn't ask her. But she hasn't had anything to report, so maybe?"

Sol nodded, pulling his striped black and white polo over his head. "I wouldn't mind seeing Zo. He's cool. He transferred from Sac City at the end of last semester, so it's been a while." He'd already pulled on some dark, washed jeans.

I sat on my side of the bed. I was ready to go.

"You look great, baby," Sol told me. "And you smell lovely."

"Thank you."

I wore my black, distressed high-waisted skinny jeans with a fitted, canary-yellow graphic tee. A deep scarlet hibiscus covered the entire front of it. This is one of my favorite shirts, but I don't wear it often because I want it to last. I've been searching for another shirt like it, and if I don't find one, I might have to make one. I could airbrush it or something. But this shirt represents two of my very favorite things in the entire world. Yellow is my favorite color, and hibiscus is my favorite flower. Like ever. Especially the Hibiscus Summerific 'Cranberry Crush'.

I remember staying up one night reading about hibiscus plants in general. There are over 200 species of hibiscus worldwide. They come in a variety of shapes, sizes, and colors. They're stunning. Someday, I plan to paint an oversized canvas of hibiscus flowers arranged in a rainbow of colors.

But the Cranberry Crush is so me! I love the deep scarlet red flowers, and we have a lot in common. This plant usually blooms in mid-summer; it loves the sunlight and the water, which results in larger flowers, lush leaves, and vibrant foliage.

That's me too. Even though I'm a spring baby, I love late summertime as well! And the water. I am a water baby.

My hair was pulled back in a low bun, and my face was bare, as usual. Aside from a cute lipstick I'd just picked up called Red Dahlia, which was a shade of red I loved. Best eight dollars I've spent in a while. I'd just bought it when I was at Walgreens a few days ago. Yes. I'm the girl who buys drugstore lipstick, and I'm not ashamed. It's what I can afford, and it works for me.

"I'll just be a few more minutes," Sol offered. He left the bedroom as I gathered my belongings.

He'd be taking me home on the way back. It was about four o'clock now, and it'd be pretty late when we get in tonight. Daijah and Julian bought a house out in Marysville, about an hour north of Sacramento. We spoke a few times earlier, but I needed to check in on Ma and Daddy. I have to be at the shop by noon tomorrow. But we'd get back together on Sunday.

"That's fine."

"Cool."

I loved spending time with Sol today, just like I always do. We slept in, which was really nice. When we woke up, we had oatmeal and fruit for breakfast. Afterwards, we went for a bike ride. Sol knows the American River Trail like the back of his hand, and he lives near a spot I'm starting to love. He's taken me there a few times. It's very... zen. Close to the water, with lots of trees, big rocks, and fresh air. Quiet, with just a few people coming and going. Perfect for photos too. It's just a chill place to be. Yeah. I love being out there. We hung around for a while. Spent time at the water, walked, talked. A lot.

On the way back, we stopped for Jamba Juice and then grabbed something to-go from a Teriyaki place for lunch. Once we got home, we ate and took naps. Yeah, it was a great afternoon. I knew we'd enjoy time with the crew once we reached Marysville. I'd also been thinking about what I told Mala earlier, and I found myself thinking about it again for some reason. Maybe he's just waiting for the right time to tell me. I'm definitely falling for him. Been.

And I thought a lot about what I told him, which led to his initial statement. About being ready to resume our intimacy. Our lovemaking. Whether spoken aloud or not, that's what it had been. That's what it would be. I knew it would be beautiful.

Yeah. I'd been thinking about that too. We hadn't yet indulged in each other again, but I knew he wanted to make sure we were ready. And that was fine. I'm glad I told him I was ready for him again. And I was so ready.

Of course, I'd thought about everything Mala laid out. And she laid it all bare. She read me like a damn book. I appreciate her for holding me accountable and calling me on my shit. None of what Mala said was wrong. Not a thing. There was more too. Something told me it was going to come up soon, especially since Destiney and Micah are expecting. Daijah and Julian are expecting their first child, too. A baby girl.

It's so sweet that Destiney and Daijah are sharing this season. I was ecstatic for both of them. Destiney already asked me to be her baby's godmother. I was so honored and agreed immediately. This little one is already so blessed. They will have two godmothers because Daijah and Julian will also be godparents.

I decided I'd take Mala's advice and discuss everything I had been holding back with Sol.

I headed to the living area with my backpack and tote bag. Sol was coming my way and met me in the hallway.

"I was just coming for you. Ready, baby?" he asked, taking my bags and slinging them over his shoulder.

He kissed my lips tenderly where we met. He'd been kissing me all over, all weekend. And I loved it. Responding in kind.

"I am."

We stood there kissing a moment longer.

I eventually told him, "We should hit the road. It's an hour drive."

He chuckled deep. "You're right."

We left through the garage.

After Sol opened my door, he put my bags in the trunk.

I figured we could talk on the drive over.

We had an hour after all.

thirty-eight

INDIA

"Alright, birthday girl. I've got a proposition for you."

Sol caught me off guard with that one.

I looked to my left. "Birthday girl?"

"Yeah. I mean. Almost," he chuckled. "We're celebrating your birthday at the end of next month, so maybe I'm a bit premature, but… almost." He gave me a silly grin, rubbing my inner thigh with his right hand.

I giggled. "Yeah. You've got a point." I softly rubbed the top of his hand with mine. "What's your proposition?"

We were on the road heading to Marysville The radio was on, but playing softly. Something old school, I think Mint Condition.

I looked over to see Sol nodding. "So. I was wondering if you can get away for a few days. I'd love to take you on a quick getaway. A staycation." My eyes widened, and he quickly added, "We won't be far. No more than a two-hour drive wherever we go."

I considered that. I could take a few days off if it wasn't a far drive. Plus, I always had Mala and Aunt Gloria to check in with Ma and Daddy if I needed them. How thoughtful of Sol to already think ahead. He knew I might hesitate, and he was steps ahead. I haven't been away in so long. Honestly, a few years. I just haven't had the extra money. I could really use a getaway. A trip with him would be perfect.

"You send me" is the song. I like this song.

"I'd love that, Sol. Thank you." I squeezed his hand, which was still on my upper thigh. His hands were large, warm, and very close to that sweet spot. "Where are we going?"

"That's totally up to you, baby. Anywhere you want to visit works for me. I was thinking South Lake Tahoe. If you want to see wine country, I can take you to Napa."

"Both of those places sound awesome. Never been to either."

"You don't have to decide right now. Take your time to think it over. Just let me know soon so I can make the arrangements."

"Okay! I'm so excited, Sol. Thank you."

"You're welcome, Belle."

"This will be a hard choice!" I laughed.

"Well. They're different, but both would be a great time. Let me know your top choice, and later I'll take you to your second."

"Why are you so good to me?" I held his hand, threading our fingers together. "Sol. I swear… you're so good to me. You're so thoughtful. Thank you."

"You're good to me. So good to me."

When I looked over, he was smiling. I smiled too. I've been smiling so much since coming to know him. And if I didn't know any better, I'd say he's going out of his way to ensure that I was. It's certainly working.

"What days were you thinking? Depending, I might have to reschedule my therapy appointment."

Sol nodded. "A long weekend, maybe? If that works for you."

"Yes. I go to therapy every other Wednesday."

"Good stuff. How's that going?"

"Really well. Thank you! I should have gone sooner. She's incredible."

"Great to hear."

"Have you gone?"

"To therapy? Sure. When things ended with that other person, I needed to talk about everything I was feeling. When I started searching for my family, it was a lot of stop-and-go, and it took a mental toll on me. So I needed tools to process that, along with sorting through the questions: Why didn't my mother want me? Who is she? Where is she? Does she ever think of me? Wonder how I'm doing? The possibility that I could walk right past her without knowing it. All of that affected me for a while until I got the help and did the work."

"Yeah. For sure. I'd have the same questions."

A beat. "Now that I know of Samuel. I may need to go back. It's a lot you know. Processing this new reality. If that's even…"

"Oh Sol. He's your family. We don't know for sure, but how can he not be? You look identical." I placed my right hand on top of his. His hand was between both of mine now, and I rubbed them softly. Caressed them. Comforting him. I knew this had him all in his head.

And it was no surprise. He finally had something after years of nothing. He finally had something. But he had a valid reason to be worried. In my view, the chances of them not being related were low, but it was still possible. And that's granted, Samuel was willing to talk with Sol. He didn't have to. They were practically strangers. And you never knew how people would react or be received. We needed that to happen before we could know anything for sure.

"I want so much for him to be. And for him to want to know me as much as I want to know him."

"I'd like to think he does." I was still rubbing his hand in mine. "I believe he's wondered the very things you have. These are your prayers being answered, baby."

"Thank you, Belle. I'll keep you posted every step of the way." He gently squeezed my hand. Then he sighed. "I'm a bit nervous because I still haven't heard anything."

"Try not to worry. Maybe he's not very active on social media. You said he doesn't post often. Plus, the conference wasn't very long ago. He may be getting settled in after traveling home," I said. "I get it, though. You've waited so long."

"I have. Thanks for caring so much. You gave me the push I needed to restart my search. And although this was brought to me, the fact that you wouldn't let me give up means the world."

"I'm glad I could, baby. And. For the record… you're the cuter twin." I was partly joking, but I knew Sol could use the laugh.

Sol chuckled at that. *"Say whaaaa?!* You think I'm cute, Indie?"

I cracked up. "You know I think you're fine as fuck, Sol." I leaned over, planting a sweet kiss on him. "My man looks damn good. You ain't know?"

He beamed at that. "Means a lot coming from you. You're fucking beautiful. Belle." He briefly glanced at me, then he returned his eyes to the freeway ahead.

There was a bit of traffic on the way out of Sac. Especially when we drove through Natomas, but it's been smooth sailing ever since.

"My woman is bad."

"Aww baby. Thank you."

"You ain't know?"

I cackled.

"I'll never forget the first time I saw you. I couldn't believe how stunning you looked, without even trying. Long and beautiful, like a porcelain doll. Not a stitch of makeup. All that hair is yours. You had an air of grace and royalty about you. Your vibe radiated across the room. I caught a glimpse of you at the bar before I knew you were there with Mich and Destiney. But when he introduced us, I was floored by how dope you are. We talked for five minutes, but you were so easy to chat with. I could have talked to you all night. I knew I wanted to get to know you better. And I knew it would be more than just a fling."

I was smiling so big, and Sol chuckled. "When I was on stage, I couldn't keep my eyes off you. I stared at you all night." He glanced at me quickly. "I still remember what you were wearing."

Wow.

"Do you really?"

"Really."

"I remember the evening well. I remember seeing you, meeting you, and hearing you for the first time. You're so talented. When we spoke, I felt such a comfortable vibe come over me. Your energy put me in a chill mood. You had this swag. This

BDE. I loved the way you looked. I thought you were very hand-some. Loved your tatts. Your smile." I was turned in my seat now, facing him. "I could see you checking me out. I was intrigued. Checking you out too. I had a crush right away."

"Same."

I kept admiring Sol as we cruised down CA 99 North. We had roughly 30 minutes to go.

"You don't think I'm for real, do you? I still remember what you were wearing." He smiled wide. "Did you and Destiney take any pictures that night?"

"I'm sure we did."

"Bet. Pull it up. I can tell you exactly what you were wearing."

I went through the photos from that night. It took a minute because it was a few months ago. I also kept my phone out of Sol's sight.

"Okay. Found 'em!"

I have a picture we took when we went to the ladies' room. There were full-length mirrors on the walls, and we took a photo standing right in front of one near the door.

"Excellent. Before I tell you..." He glanced at me briefly. "What do I get if I'm right?" His voice dipped an octave.

"What do you want?" My tone had taken a sultry dip, too.

"Hmm." A few beats. "I need to think on that. But I know I'm going to be right."

"We'll see. This includes accessories."

We laughed.

"I'm agreeing to something undisclosed. Gotta up the ante."

"That's cool. I know those too."

"Okay. And just for shits and giggles, what do you want if I'm wrong?"

"You scared?"

"Nah. Curious as hell though… I know you want something from me." His tone still carried that deep octave.

Turning me the fuck on.

"I know I can ask for that *something* anytime I want it… If I wanna be a lady about it. And I know I can take what I want… If I wanna be a freak about it."

His laugh was deep. And sexy.

"Okay, Belle. I hear you. You're not wrong."

"I know this."

"Mmm." He chuckled some more. Then, "You are so sexy, India. Fuck."

"You're sexy too, baby. I'm thinking you're hard right now. Am I right?"

"Oh yes. You're right... what else you thinking?"

"About maybe touching you. Jerking you."

"Mmm. That so?"

"Yeah. Would you like that, baby?"

"I would like that very much."

I looked down and saw his prominent erection. I knew the massive middle console in his Jag wasn't a problem. My arms are long, and Sol had lots of space in front of him. His legs are long, and he was sitting farther back from the steering wheel. I reached over with my left hand, grabbed his belt buckle, and, after some maneuvering, undid it. Then I pulled down his zipper.

"You sure we'll be okay? This won't distract you too much?"

"I promise we'll be okay, baby," he reassured.

"Okay."

I slipped my hand through the hole in his boxers and found him standing at full attention. And Sol hadn't lied. He was rock hard. Shit was so sexy. I had a good grip on him and moved my hand up and down. But his dick is so big, there wasn't much space, so I knew I needed to free him from these confines.

"Baby."

"Yeah?" His breath bated.

"I'm going to use my other hand to pull your boxers down, so I need to lean over a little."

"You're good baby."

Once he was free, I stroked him up and down. The tip was oozing precum. I rubbed my thumb over it, working it into my hand job. He kept leaking too.

I wanted to taste it.

"You like that, baby?" I asked, still holding on tight and stroking him slow.

"I sure do... *mmm.*"

"Can I keep going?"

"Absolutely."

Once I found a good tempo, I picked up my phone with my right hand.

"Sol, baby. Don't leave me hanging…" I began. "I'm still wondering if you really do remember what I had on that night."

His chuckle transitioned into a moan.

A sexy ass moan.

"Belle. You were wearing a white blouse. Flowy. Had buttons and a collar. Light-washed skinny jeans. Big gold hoops. Red pumps. A black blazer... And a sexy, deep red lipstick. That gold chain you love to wear. Your watch."

He said all that while I was stroking his dick.

I maintained my tempo. Sol liked that. Moaning and praising. Expressing his pleasure.

I was into it too.

I looked at the picture.

He nailed it.

"Wow." I continued what I'd been doing. Sol was so fucking hard. Thick. And heavy. With some angry-ass veins. "You're *good*…" I drew out the word. "Now, I want to lick you like a lolli-pop."

"You do whatever you want to do. Belle."

Yeah. We could talk later.

♪♥♫♥♪

"Mala! *Over here!*" I waved, getting my cousin's attention.

She waved back as she weaved through the tables and crossed the dance floor, making her way over.

Destiney, Daijah, and I were hanging out in the VIP section, relaxing in a huge booth. Sol got us the booth and a few tables up here. But this booth was so big that we had plenty of space.

Julian and Micah went outside a while ago to check out the other festivities. I'm sure they'll be back to check in soon. They're too protective to go too far for too long. Especially right now.

"Hey! Glad you could make it." Once Mala scooted in next to me, we hugged.

"Me too! This place is poppin'!"

Daijah was at the other end, across from me. Destiney right beside her.

"Right! Glad Sol could get us seats up here." The VIP section wasn't as packed as the floor, but there were quite a few people up here.

Mala got caught up with Destiney and Daijah. She also ordered a drink when our server stopped by. We had plenty of appetizers on the table to share.

I'd been having such a great time.

It was just after seven in the evening now. Sol picked me up, and we got here about four for sound check. They opened the doors at five. Everything was in full swing by six.

And this Anniversary Soiree had such a great turnout. There was always a decent crowd at HomeGrown, but tonight it was packed.

The VIP section was up on a platform, and we could see everything out on the main floor from here. And it was standing room only, damn near. Every seat out on the main floor had an ass in it.

Yeah. This place was packed.

The dance floor was packed with patrons moving close Each of the full bars on either side of the dance floor had a crowd gathering around them. Many people stood around the high tables near the back of the lounge. The patio doors were open, with a steady flow of people coming in and out. There were just as many people outside as inside. Sol came through, and these were great seats. We could see the stage without any obstruction, too. The stage was at the front of the house. VIP was about halfway back.

Smoke had everyone grooving. The lead had been belting all night, driving the ladies crazy. And dude could sing! The band was jamming now, playing a seamless string of instrumentals. They were all over the place with it, blessing us with incredible covers and impressing the crowd with their skills, talent, and love for the music. They played so well together. The songs were familiar, but Smoke was improvising and infusing their own interpretations and unique signatures.

Yeah. They were cold, making the upbeat songs extra funky. The ballads felt extra smooth, and they got deep into the groove with the mid-tempos. The vibe in here was insane. The lighting was dim, the chatter lively but quieter than the music. Everything was layered just right and textured perfectly. Each musician was emotionally connected to every note they played.

You could see it on their faces.

Rhythms were smooth and rich.

Soul-infused.

Filling the space with everything from Neo Soul to Hip Hop and R&B.

It was amazing.

I had a glass of red wine in front of me. I'd been sipping it slow all evening, and somehow my glass stayed full. I'm sure Sol made that happen. Our attentive server checked on us often. Until Mala arrived, I was the only one drinking, which was fine. My bestie and her sister were growing babies. Daijah's belly was so cute. When I saw her last night, it was the first time I'd seen her in quite a while. She's about the same height as me... no, actually, Daijah might be a little taller by an inch. But she's all in the front. When I went to hug her, I had to hug her up top!

The crowd went wild when Smoke segued into *"Leave the Door Open"* by Silk Sonic.

"This band is smooth!" Mala said. She'd begun grooving in her seat.

"Right! They've been showing out all night, too."

They'd been jamming for quite a while. They'd played "Doo Wop (That Thing)" by Lauryn Hill, "Superstition" by Mr. Stevie Wonder, "I Wanna Be Your Lover" by Prince, "Sweet Love" by Anita Baker, "Rock with You" by Michael Jackson, "Cranes in the Sky" by Solange, and "Bag Lady" by Erykah Badu.

Yeah. They had everybody covered.

Right before Silk Sonic, they'd been playing "Break You Off" by The Roots. I love The Roots.

Yeah. Smoke is bad ass!

The bass player Joe proudly introduced me to his wife, Ava. She stopped by briefly, and during their break, he and Sol came over to say hello. Ava and I got a chance to chat, and I invited her to join Daijah, Des, and me. But she didn't plan to stay too long. She cracked me up, saying, *"She'd leave all this to the younger folks."*

Ava and Joe are in their early fifties, I believe. And they both looked damn good for their age!

And Ava was dope as hell. Like a cool ass auntie.

Then Ava told Sol, right in front of me, *"To be sure to bring his wife by so we can break bread together."* Then Joe cosigned, saying, *"We could talk more about being grown folks and handling grown folks' business"* or something.

Joe and Ava made sure to give Sol a pointed nod and a knowing smile when they said that, and Sol nodded in understanding, smiling all the while. Clearly, it was an insider. I'd have to ask him what that was about. I could tell it was all in love. Sol told me he's known Joe for nearly fifteen years.

"HomeGrown! It's that time!" The lead singer said into the mic. "Sorry to say this, but we've come to the end of our set!" Cheers and applause erupted all over the place. For a while. A good while.

"Ya'll are too kind!"

The crowd wouldn't stop cheering. Eventually, everyone began to request an encore.

"Oh, y'all want one more?"

The cheers erupted even louder.

"Y'all hear that, fellas? They want one more!"

The crowd continued to clap and cheer.

"It's a special occasion, no doubt about it. We can do one more for y'all. We tired so it'll be something mid-tempo. Is that alright?"

The cheering continued, and he turned toward the band, saying something to his bandmates.

"Tell you what… If we play y'all one more, I need everyone on their feet for this one! This is a celebration. Black joy personified! Can ya'll do that for me?"

The crowd cheered and clapped, and the drummer counted them in.

And the second Joe came in with that unmistakable bassline, the lead guitar played that familiar riff... the crowd really erupted.

And the lead singer was back in the mic.

"Whoa Whoa ho!... You make me happy! This you can bet!..."

"Before I let go." Frankie Beverly and Maze.

Yeah. This was the perfect encore choice. It's celebratory. Communal, and it's the kind of tune that pulls everyone out of their seats. You couldn't help but move when you heard this one.

Such a classic feel-good song. A song we were sure to hear at every birthday party. Every family reunion. Cookout. Wedding reception. Even a repass if it was in someone's backyard.

I saw Sol grooving, and his saxophone playing was irresistible in this one. He's been shining all night, honestly.

Yeah. The band kept grooving, and when they hit that iconic hook, each member got their moment to shine. I looked out into the crowd. Everyone was clapping, swaying, singing, smiling, and dancing. Folks by the bar were two-stepping, and I saw a group doing the electric slide in a far corner.

And of course I would. How could you not, hearing a song like this in a place like this?

In a sea of melanated faces.

With melanated energy.

Having a great ass melanated fucking time.

He was right. This was BLACK JOY PERSONIFIED.

At a black-owned establishment.

Something our ancestors could only have dreamed of.

And the band eased into it, smiling through their fatigue and playing like it was the first song of the evening, aiming to satisfy the crowd. It felt like a warm embrace, bridging the musicians and the audience. Yeah, I was so glad to be here, and I'm so happy so many people came out to celebrate.

"Alright, y'all. DJ Sho with the Flow is up next! Be easy!... You can still groove with us! Stay awhile... We'll be here!" the lead singer offered, then introduced each member of the band. I always love that part. "Love y'all, thanks for always showing Smoke so much love! We play here every Thursday and Friday night! Seven sharp! Right here at HomeGrown! I'm Carlton, Fresh Mosely! And we're Smoke! See y'all next week!"

After some applause, a man I know as the owner came on stage. The band started to quiet down, but they were still grooving. They'd probably wait for him to finish what he needed to say before they packed it up for the night.

"I know some of ya'll are about to head out. But I wanted to be sure I came up to thank everyone for coming out and celebrating fourteen years of HomeGrownSol!"

The crowd cheered.

"So, thank you! From the bottom of my heart! Thank you!"

"And I guess I should introduce myself to those of you who don't know. I'm Tim. And where's my wife?" He looked into the crowd. "There she is. Come on up here, baby. I want everyone to see you… This is my lovely wife, Janelle…"

The crowd clapped and cheered again.

"A lot of people don't know who she is because she's usually in the kitchen throwing it down! Making y'all's taste buds go bananas!"

We all laughed.

"My wife is such an incredible cook. That's actually why I married her."

We all fell out. Even Janelle.

After we settled down, "No. But seriously. She was self-taught, but a few years ago she decided to attend culinary school to formally learn the skills and techniques to further elevate her food. And when she finished, I was so proud to call her Executive Chef. Janelle loves to do this, and her heart and her passion for good food go into every single thing you all come here and enjoy… come on, y'all! Help me thank her!"

Cheers went up again, and someone presented her with a beautiful bouquet of red roses. They hugged, and he said something to her that none of us could hear. She cracked up laughing again. Meanwhile, Des, Daijah, Mala, and I were over here swooning. A low chorus of *"awwws"* came out in unison.

That was so sweet. I love seeing a man love on his woman. I've formally met both Janelle and Tim, and they're some of the coolest people in the world. To be hugely successful and stay true and dedicated to your passion, while giving so much without losing your moral compass... It's truly amazing.

I've learned that they offer this space as a venue for indie artists to use regularly. They host art shows and showcases, poetry nights, and benefits often free of charge for a good cause.

Sol mentioned that Janelle has donated delicious, freshly prepared food for memorial services or for women's and children's shelters. Setting it up like a fancy dinner. The whole shebang. Servers, setup, and cleanup. He told me she'd been hired to cater the upcoming Music Academy Benefit.

"I got one more thing to do and I'll be out of your way…" Tim continued. "I'd like to thank my good friend and brother, Dr. Solomon Avery, *the Sol in HomeGrownSol.*"

Get out of here. Really?

The crowd cheered. Especially the ladies. I could hear them.

My eyes grew wide. My lips parted.

I looked at Sol, who was still grooving on his sax. He froze mid-breath. Clearly taken by surprise.

It was adorable.

"It's pronounced *soul.* But it's spelled S-O-L after him. He's so humble; a compromise we came to was that I couldn't tell anyone. It's the only way he could get me to agree. I know I've blown your cover, man."

Tim cracked up, and I could see that Sol was falling over laughing, too, shaking his head.

"Oh my gosh! Indie! Did you know that?" Destiney asked eagerly. I looked over and all three of them were curious.

I shook my head. "Sure didn't, but that's *sooo…* wow. What an honor."

"For sure!" "That's amazing!" Mala and Daijah chimed in.

"Come on over here man. I got something for you."

The crowd cheered as Sol removed his sax and made his way to the front of the stage. "He likes to hide in the back behind his sax. And he's cold on the sax. But Dr. Avery can play every instrument on this stage." The band members all nodded in agreement. Clapping with the audience. Laughing. Smiling.

He can sing too.

"I want to present you with this award of recognition and appreciation. Only a few people know this, but… he was the one who put this house band together. Smoke was all him. I shared my vision of what my wife and I wanted to do here."

"We wanted a place where people could come, enjoy good food, and hear good music. And Dr. Solomon Avery understood the assignment. Smoke is the smoothest band around. People come for the food, but they come back for the music. I sincerely believe that part of the reason we're still here is because of that. Thank you, man."

The crowd went crazy.

And Sol nodded, brought his hands together in front of his face as if he were praying. And bowed his head in regard. Respect. Expressing his own appreciation.

And it's just like Sol to do that.

A small plaque was handed to Sol, and he hugged Tim and Janelle, who still stood proudly beside him. They posed for a few pictures and a few more with the rest of the band. I took some with my own phone.

What a moment.

The band started to pack up. The DJ announced he'd be up next. There are a couple of dressing rooms in the back, and Sol would probably change his shirt before heading back up here. And I couldn't wait. I missed him, and I was ready to spend the rest of the night in his arms. We might dance, maybe. I knew the DJ would get us right. He's probably going to play a few dance tunes, but some slow jams are sure to be in there too. Or we could relax up here in this booth. Vibe and groove from our seat. He might be tired. They played for an hour and a half.

"I have to pee, cousin. Let's go to the ladies' room." Mala brought me out of my thoughts.

"Girl, me too, actually. You know how it is once you start drinking."

"Try being pregnant. You'll have to pee every five minutes. I need to go too," Daijah said

Destiney laughed. "Oh, I feel that. And I'm not even as pregnant as you, Day!"

We headed toward the VIP section exit as Julian and Micah were making their way back.

"Headed to pee," Daijah told Julian.

"We're coming too." He grabbed her hand, helping her down the three steps, and they headed toward the restrooms.

"Yeah. We'll walk you ladies. It's a different vibe back there." Micah offered. He helped Destiney, too. Their hands remained embraced as they walked ahead of us, following Daijah and Julian.

Mala and I linked arms playfully and followed. The restrooms were near the back of the lounge, close to the back door. The space was dimly lit, but I could see how everything came together so nicely. HomeGrown went all out, and this was such a wonderful occasion. There were black tablecloths and black-and-gold centerpieces on each table. A black-and-gold balloon arch led to the front entrance. A few balloon towers sat throughout the lounge. Tonight, there was a guest chef and a featured menu. And I was glad Janelle could get a night off and enjoy the festivities.

"You look cute!" I told Mala as we weaved through the clusters of people to get to the restrooms. I had to speak a lot louder than I did in the VIP section.

Micah looked back, giving a thumbs-up, and I returned the gesture, smiling wide. He was only a few steps ahead. He's pretty protective of me. All the men are.

Just before Mala arrived, Malachi and Ella came out. They couldn't stay long since they found out at the last minute and had prior plans, but they still wanted to support Sol. I had a chance to catch up with Ella last night at Daijah's, and Ella is the folks. I love when we get to chat. And she's such a sweet sister to Destiney. The ideal sister-in-love. She really couldn't be more perfect. Malachi is the coolest big brother ever. He's all of our honorary big brother. We told him that, and after cracking up, he said he didn't mind at all. He takes his job quite seriously.

"Thank you! I try. You look good too, cuz!" She leaned over, telling me. The DJ started spinning, so it was a bit louder now. Being closer to the crowd meant we were competing with all of their voices, too.

"Thank you!" I told Mala. I kept it classy and simple tonight. I wore a black halter dress. I wear a lot of yellow, but I love a sexy little black dress now and then. My hair was wild and free. Barefaced. No lipstick tonight. Sol kept complimenting me over and over. It's satin and chic, and it fits like a bodycon. Close to my skin. My boobs are small, and since the back is out, I didn't need to bother with a bra. Black pointed-toe loafers. I wasn't in the mood for heels tonight.

The lights were dim in here, but I could see that Mala looked good. She was wearing a high-waisted burgundy leather pleated mini skirt. Very mini, stopping at the upper mid-thigh. Mala has long, slender legs; I believe she's about 5-7'. She paired it with a white fitted long-sleeve V-neck shirt that she tucked in, along with cute grey wedge booties. Yeah, Mala looked good.

And I peeped the men checking for her.

I'm no longer single, so that's exactly who they were checking for. I carefully avoided making eye contact with any of them. That's a frequently misunderstood signal. Just because I smile doesn't mean I'm interested. I smile at everyone. All the time.

Julian and Micah were waiting for us when the four of us came out of the ladies' room. I pulled my phone out of my purse when I felt it vibrate.

Music Man: On my way to you, baby. Got held up talking to a few people. You good?

Me: Yeah. J and Mich are here with us ladies. We're near the back door. May go check out what's on the patio.

Music Man: Bet. Stay with the husbands

That made me laugh. Destiney collectively called the men, *The Husbands* because "it was just easier." Or something. I was laughing hard when she said that. She loved to give people and nearly everything a nickname. But they were husbands. All of them. Except for Sol. And Sol said that everyone in Smoke was married, except James, the keyboard player, who was engaged.

We headed outside to a large covered outdoor patio. This was my first time here, and it was nice. I bet it was incredible coming out here during summer evenings.

There were lots of tables and chairs. Most were free now, as many people had started moving indoors. It was cooling down a bit as the hour grew later. Several heat lamps were visible. We ladies found seats at a table right between a heat lamp and an electric fire pit. It was perfect. The men hung out a few steps away and continued chatting about something. I could hear music playing from some speakers. Different music from inside. Off to the side were giant Dominoes, Jenga, and an oversized chess game. A makeshift minibar with pizza and wings was for sale if you didn't want to order inside.

"This was so much fun. I'm glad Sol mentioned this," Destiney said.

We all agreed.

"Yeah, and that band is freakin' *hot!* They sound better every time I hear them." That was Daijah. She was rubbing her belly.

"I know!" Mala chimed in. "And Sol is the one who put the whole band together! Girl, your man is beyond talented! He's not normal!"

We all laughed.

"Thank you. Yeah, he's incredible. Really. And ladies… get this. I found out he can sing. *I mean sing!*"

"Damn for real?" Mala posed

"Girl! I'd have him singing everything! *Don't talk to me. You got something to say, sing it nigga!*" Daijah had us all rolling. "What can he not do?"

I shook my head. "I don't even know. And he's so handy. I was surprised. He built me a bike!" I pulled my phone back out and showed the pictures to Daijah and Mala. Destiney had already seen them.

"Damn, cousin. What kind of juice you got, having a man build you a bike and singing to you?"

We all laughed. "He got a brother?" Mala teased.

"He may." Mala and Daijah looked surprised.

"One of his students saw a guy in Atlanta who looked just like Sol. I mean identical. And he's a musician too. Sol reached out to him on IG. And we're waiting for him to respond. But girls, I'm telling you. There's no way he isn't."

"Oh wow, that would be amazing."

"Yeah. And sorry he's married."

Mala laughed. "Figured as much."

"What's going on with *Lorenzo?*" I sang his name.

"He's cool." She shrugged. "I haven't seen him in a minute. But he's cool. Just hella deep! I feel like I'm not black enough when I talk to him or something."

We all laughed.

"Like Dr. Umar Johnson?" Destiney offered.

"Noooo." Mala, Daijah, and I were cackling. "Not like that. But just deep. I'm into it. I think… Just gotta take it in doses."

"Hey Artist Girl." I turned around, and Sol was right behind me.

"Hey!" I stood immediately. Falling into his arms.

The ladies greeted Sol, too, complimenting him on the great show.

"I missed you," I told him, embracing him again.

"Missed you too, Belle. Having a good time?"

"I am. I've had a great night. Thank you. You guys killed it tonight!"

"Thank you baby."

"What's happenin'! How ya'll doing?!" I looked over my shoulder, and I could see Micah slapping hands with his cousin, Ray. I've met him on a few occasions. Julian dapped him up as well.

"Excuse me for one second, baby. I'm going to say hey to Ray. I'll be right back."

"Okay."

The men were just a few steps away. I pulled my phone out, looking back at some of the pictures we took tonight, back in the VIP section.

"Hey ladies. *Say cheese!*" I snapped a quick one of the three of them still sitting and chatting at the table. As I lowered my phone, I saw that Destiney's smile faded instantly. She was seated closest to where I stood.

I raised my brows. But before I could react, I heard a familiar voice close to me.

Much too close for comfort.

"So this is where you've been hanging out?"

I turned around. But I knew who it was.

Brandon.

"Had I known that, I would have come looking for you a long time ago."

I said nothing. And my face remained expressionless. By now, Destiney was making her way over. I could see her approaching in my peripheral vision. And the other ladies. I could hear each of their chairs as they scooted back to stand up.

I ignored Brandon, attempting to step around him. But he moved, blocking me. I stepped to the left instead, and he stepped to the right. The men were just behind him. A few feet away.

"Sol," I called.

"India, don't you hear me talking to you?" His voice cold. Stern. Upset.

But that wasn't my issue.

I still said nothing and kept walking around him, even though he was trying to block my path.

Then he grabbed my arm.

"You're ignoring people now, India?"

"Don't touch me, Brandon." I snatched my arm away. "Please leave me alone." I kept my cool, knowing he wasn't going to do anything. Brandon was all bark and no bite.

"Oh, now you wanna talk?"

"No. She doesn't. She asked you to leave her alone. I'd keep your hands off her, too, if I were you."

Sol calmly stated. Calm as a still lake.

Brandon didn't seem to notice Sol. Or even hear him. He paid him no mind. Maybe he was ignoring him.

That was a mistake.

"You're not taking my calls, you won't reply to my messages. You too good to talk to me now or something?"

I'd made my way to the other end of the patio. Where the other ladies were. The men standing right in front of us.

The four of them shoulder to shoulder.

Micah. Sol. Julian and Ray.

The rest of the people on the patio watched with intrigue. Yeah, these men had this under control.

"The lady asked you nicely. I won't be so accommodating." Sol's hands were still in his pockets.

"*Man move!* India! I'm trying to talk to you. You can't just blow me off like that. I need to talk to you!"

The men remained where they were. "I'm not going to tell you again. She doesn't want to talk to you. It's best you leave her alone man. In fact. Just leave. Head on out of here. Drive safe."

"This doesn't concern you!" Brandon shot. "Mind your business."

"Anything concerning my woman concerns me. Now, she asked you to leave her alone. I suggest you move aside, my man."

"Your woman?" he seethed, then he laughed. "Oh, this nut got you thinking you're better than somebody or something?"

I still hadn't said a word more. And I wasn't going to.

Sol stood ten toes down. "I need you to leave. Now. This is a place of business. You can't behave like a grown man, you don't need to be here."

I could see that Brandon's fists were clenched. As if he'd swing any second.

I didn't want them fighting, but I knew Brandon's ass was all talk.

"Man, get the fuck outta my face! I'm not taking orders from you!"

Brandon tried to push through the wall of men, and Ray sprang into action.

Grabbing Brandon's arm, he quickly twisted him around and pushed him against the wall. Briskly. Roughly.

Yeah. It happened so quickly. We ladies were shocked. We'd each covered our mouths. Eyes wide.

Ray had him pressed against the wall. His face pressed in what had to be cold ass concrete. His arms were forced behind his back.

"You don't touch my family. You don't come near their women either. We're all having a good time, and you won't ruin it. Get the fuck outta here, man." Ray was cool as a cucumber. "I'm going to let you go, and you get the fuck gone. You understand me?"

Ray forcefully snatched him off the wall, and Brandon was huffing and puffing. He adjusted his clothes. Brushed himself off.

Then cut his eyes at me.

"You don't contact India again. Ever. She's mine. You fumbled her, and that's your problem." Sol said. "Please leave. And leave her alone."

When Brandon didn't move fast enough, Ray said, "Get gone, man!"

Brandon meandered out of the patio area.

"So that's Brandon?" Sol asked me.

I nodded.
Sol nodded too.
"He knows you're mine now."

thirty-nine

SOL

"You nervous?"

"No baby. Not at all. Why?"

"You're trembling."

India smiled bashfully. "That's excitement."

"Excitement." I parroted, smirking. She's so cute.

I dipped low, capturing her lips. Kissing her.

Tenderly. Gently.

"As hard as I am, I can't imagine you're more excited than me."

We were in my bed. India was settled on her back. I was settled between her legs. Resting on my forearms, I balanced my weight. We'd been talking about the fantastic night we had. Kissing in between. Taking our time. I knew tonight was the night we'd be one again. The stars have aligned. Everything felt right. Everything felt perfect. And that was always the case. Every damn thing felt right with India and me.

We got in from HomeGrown a little while ago. It wasn't super late, after 9 in the evening. But we were at HomeGrown for a few hours, and it had been a very long day. I appreciated seeing the crew. It was dope, they all showed up for me.

I loved playing with my boys, too. And Smoke delivered. We grooved together like we never had before. The energy was high, and the crowd was into everything we did. Performers feed off that energy. And many people don't realize how much an audience can directly impact a show. But it can. The call-and-response, back-and-forth. The singing along. The dancing. The cheers and applause.

Tonight, everything was on point, and the audience was rocking with us from start to finish. And every member of Smoke handled their business. Especially my boy Fresh. Not only is he a great singer, but he's charismatic as hell. Tonight was no different, and he handled business. Fresh can work any crowd. Any day.

And. Aside from the minor situation we had to handle with Brandon the Clown, it was a great time.

Indie and I talked about it a bit more on the way home.

Apparently, he'd still been reaching out, and she said she'd been ignoring him. They'd slept together a couple of times after they ended things, before she and I started seeing each other.

Sounds like he'd been trying to spin the block again, and she left him on read.

Eventually, ghosting him.

Perspective is everything, and it all made sense after that.

I now knew precisely why he was so pressed to talk to her.

India had the kind of pussy that would make a man lose his damn mind.

And that clown was *pressed*.

Pressed and stressed. It was almost pathetic.

Don't be *that* guy. Don't *ever* be that guy.

Grabbing her the way he did was a punk ass move. And incredibly stupid.

But. Now that I've experienced India… I almost can't blame him.

Almost.

Being cut off from accessing her is like cutting a man off at the knees.

I mean. I'd almost expect some young cat to act out. When you first start getting some, it's unlike anything else you'll experience.

But we're grown men. At this point pussy shouldn't have you so whipped. Least of all, clowning in public, in front of people with cell phones in their hands. The way cancel culture has ruined people. He should be handling himself with decorum.

Fucking clownin' ass. India blocked his number while we were in the car.

And hell yeah, dude was a clown.

For a few reasons.

He had India for more than two years.

You don't fumble a woman like her. Ever.

He's been a clown, but he was a clownin' for real, trying to come at a woman with a four-man army. Men who are each more than six feet tall. Men who clearly keep their asses in the gym. And his ass was by himself. Yeah. Clown shit. But the situation is handled. Brandon knows what it is now. He knows *who's* she is, too. And he can get his clownin' ass on somewhere.

Also, Cousin Ray is with the shits. That didn't take me by surprise. I've known Ray as long as I've known Micah. His cousin is a year older than us. Malachi is a year older than Ray.

But yeah, Ray been with the shits. His timing couldn't have been better. Showing up late as hell. He was just in time, though.

Yeah. We had a good time, nonetheless.

"I don't know. I'm pretty excited. Anticipating." India spread her legs wider. Her lids low, she dared, "You should feel how wet I am."

I raised my brows.

We'd been kissing. Talking nasty and talking normal.

Then talking nasty again. Flirting. Laughing. Chilling. We hadn't explicitly said it, but the energy between us did. I knew what she wanted because I wanted the same thing. It was nearly dark in my bedroom. I had a nightlight across the room, near my ensuite. And it was bright. Bright enough for me to see India. Her beautiful face. She's incredibly beautiful. Her lids were low. Her voice relaxed after the long day. Every word that left her lips was smooth as a lullaby. Her wild hair fanned behind her on the pillow. Yeah. I could gaze at her all night. We also had music playing, as usual. "Always Forever" by Bryson Tiller was on now.

"I'm so slippery I can feel it running down my ass." India tittered. Surprising me.

"Oh yeah?" My brows high. I chuckled deep, dipping to kiss her lips again.

"Yeah."

"I'll take care of that for you," I offered playfully.

"What do you mean?" She teased. Flirty.

"You know what I mean. Nothing's going to waste. Every drop of your honey is precious, Belle."

"You'll make it worse by saying shit like that." Her long, slender, delicate fingers grazing the hair on my chin.

"That's what I want." I kissed her lips again. "Nothing's going to waste."

Still teasing me, she said, "You'll make it much worse if it means what I think it means."

"Worse for who?"

We tittered again.

India rubbed her hands across my bare chest. Down my biceps. Back again. Her hands were so soft.

I didn't put a shirt on after my shower, only boxers and basketball shorts.

India was dressed in a cropped T-shirt and black boy shorts. She looked so good. India had legs for days. After her shower, I watched her intently as she did her skincare routine: her face, her body, her hair. Layering natural shea butter, she used it from head to toe.

India took incredibly great care of herself. Her toasted cinnamon skin was always supple and moist. Soft. Warm. Inviting. Always. And she smelled heavenly, as usual. A lovely coconut layered with a light floral scent.

She had her long legs wrapped around me again, this time a little tighter. She was like a furnace between her legs, too. Fuck. My dick was extremely hard. She knew it. She felt it when I pressed my body against hers. And she was feeling it right now. I gently laid my body on top of hers a moment ago.

She was still in her boy shorts. I was still in my basketball shorts. But nothing was hidden. Her heat or my hardness. I knew the moment was here; I knew we'd go all the way again. But I was never one to assume. I planned to ask her if she was ready before making any moves like that.

I surveyed India's body from head to toe. I'd been admiring her all evening. When her look came together earlier, I was so pleased with everything I saw.

The black dress she wore was alluring, accentuating her every line and curve. It was long, reaching just above her shins. Her shoulders were bare, revealing her long neck. Her hair was wild and free, which I love.

And India has a strut. She didn't even wear heels tonight, but... she has this captivating walk. Still. Where she commanded any room she entered. Without trying and just being. Not imposing. No. In an alluring way. In an intriguing way. I noticed the men noticing her. Especially when she was on my arm. But it comes with the territory. It didn't bother me.

"I could get lost looking in your eyes, baby," I told her. I lay beside her and pulled her into my arms. Now we were facing each other. Eyes on eyes. Side by side. I kissed her forehead.

"I could too, baby. I love staring into your dark brown eyes. They tell a story. They sing a song. There's depth. There's soul. Safety. Comfort. It's endless. I could look into your eyes and just... wander... get lost in them. And I know I'll be safe."

"You'll definitely be safe. Anything you do involving you and me, you'll be safe. Feel free to fall... I'll catch you, Belle."

"Oh my gosh. Sol. I can't even..." She laughed, and it was so sweet. I love her laugh.

I wrapped my arms around her a little tighter. She held onto me, nestling into me. Our legs tangled, and we just chilled for a bit.

"Miami" by Odeal & Leon Thomas lulled us for a few beats.

"Sol."

"Yeah?"

"I'm there already."

Hmm.

"Where?" I held her eyes again.

"I've... I've already fallen."

I slowly reared my head back. Just a little. Never breaking our connection. We looked at each other. Eyes on eyes again.

"What are you saying, India?" I knew exactly what she meant because I felt the same. But never one to assume, I needed her to tell me.

She held my gaze, confidently saying, "I've fallen in love with you. Solomon. I'm in love with you."

"You're in love with me, Belle?"

"I am," she nodded. *"I so am."* She laughed. "You're so easy to love. And you're so good to me."

I held her beautiful face in my hands. "I'm in love with you. I love you too, Indie." I softly kissed her lips. She kissed me back, but the kiss was brief.

She playfully asked urgently, "You're in love with me?" Her sweet giggles surrounded us. "I get the feeling you've been keeping this a secret from me."

"No idea what you're talking about."

She kept giggling. "Sol! You're in love with me and never told me?"

"Indie. I think I can argue the same point." I nodded my head toward her, my eyebrows raised.

She nodded as well, saying nothing. I knew this was the moment. Right now. I could feel it. Her desire radiated from her like pheromones. Her body was calling me.

I'm right here baby. I want you too.

"Let's do this right. Confess our love. Then… let's make love. Does that sound good, baby?"

"Yes." She smiled sweetly.

I nodded. Smiling too.

My eyes never left hers when I said, "I love you. India Rampersaud."

Her sweet smile blossomed into her dazzling megawatt smile.

"I love you, too. Dr. Solomon Avery."

"*Mmm.* That sounds so good, baby."

"It does. Like a sweet song. Like a vivid painting. I can hear the colors, I see. It's… superlative… it's… marvelous. A masterpiece! In color and in frequency." She laughed, becoming emotional.

"That's… wow. That's so dope, Artist girl."

"It's the best way I can describe it. I'm so in love with you, baby. I'm feeling so inspired at the moment." She giggled. "I could paint my ass off right now!"

"You are fascinating." I gently held her face in my hands. "I love you too. I really do, baby. So much."

A beat.

"I've been waiting patiently. And I can keep waiting. I want you… But I can keep waiting, baby," I told her.

"You don't need to wait anymore. I've been wanting you so bad, baby. Like right now. Sol. I am aching for you. My goodness."

"I've been wanting you too and thinking about getting back to the sweet love you give me, baby. I'm so hard, it's starting to hurt", I chuckled softly.

"Let's put each other out of this misery." India leaned into me, and we kissed passionately for a while.

"I swear Belle. There's magic when we kiss."

"Yeah."

Her hands were all over me. Mine. All over her.

"There's magic in your fingertips. Every surface you grace. You make breathtaking art with these." I captured her left hand with my right. She had a sweet smile for me.

"Indie." I pressed her fingers to my lips.

"Yes." Her lids low.

"Been taking care of yourself while I've been away?"

"Yeah."

"When was the last time you played with your pussy, baby?"

"Last night."

"Mmm," I swear I grew even harder in my boxers. That was some sexy shit.

I discovered that India is incredibly sexual, but not in a promiscuous way. There's a distinct difference. India is very connected to her body and deeply aware of herself. Honestly, it blew my mind. Yeah, that shit is so fucking sexy. We discussed this openly. I never wanted her to hold back with me, hide anything, or be shy about anything.

"It isn't the same," she said. "I've replayed the last time we made love so many times. Too many to count."

"I have too."

"Mmm. Can you imagine?"

We laughed.

"I'm ready to taste you, Belle. Would you like that too?"

"Yes, baby. I'd love that. I've missed it."

"Mmm." I kissed her lips again, pressing my body close to hers. "I can't wait to lick you," I whispered in her ear. I knew she loved that. "You like when I lick your pussy, baby?"

"Yessss." She drew the word out.

Yeah. It was time. I wasn't going to make her wait a second longer.

"You really got me hard as hell, Indie."

"I can feel you, baby."

I'd been brushing against her, losing my damn mind. Damn near losing control.

I felt like a kid in a candy store, but I'm a gentleman, ladies first. It's always ladies first.

I pressed another gentle kiss to India's lips, then leaned back on my hunches.

"I'm going to take these panties off, baby."

I gently hooked my fingers on each side of her hips, holding her gaze the entire time. The desire between us, the fire, the connection. The longing. It was thick in the atmosphere. India lifted her hips as I pulled them down, and when I had them completely off, she spread her legs. Instantly. Like instinctively. I chuckled,

"Look at you, my sexy Artist Girl."

Even in the low lighting, I noted how slick and glistening she was. Her clit plump.

Fuck.

Yeah. Her legs were spread wide. I caressed her inner thighs, growing even stiffer.

"Oh, Belle. You have no idea what this right here does to me. You look so good. And I can smell you, baby."

She watched my every move with low lids.

I moved closer, "Can I taste you, India. Please?"

"Yes, please," she breathed softly. "Taste me. Touch me, baby. Please touch me. Everywhere."

"Okay." I chuckled. "I sure plan to."

forty

INDIA

"Okay… that doesn't make any sense. I thought you fixed the radiator last time."

"Nope. That was the alternator."

"What did you fix before that?"

"The clutch."

I said nothing, but it was written all over my face.

"You need the clutch to drive this car, ma'am. It's a manual transmission."

I sighed. "What exactly do you need to fix now?"

"It's likely the fuel pump."

"Likely?"

"I'll need to get under the hood and take a closer look."

"Fine."

I was at the mechanic with Daddy. I asked to come along because I needed to talk to this guy myself. It seemed he was taking advantage of my father. We've paid him so much money, and the car keeps giving us problems.

"I'll also mention the transmission is failing. That'll need to be replaced eventually."

I sighed, feeling exasperated, frustrated. Damn near in tears.

This mechanic was making so much money off us, and we didn't have any more to give.

He stood there smug. Eyeing me, smoking a cigarette, and giving me the ick.

The money King gave me last week was as good as gone. This job would run us a few hundred dollars. I'm grateful I had it, but this was getting to be ridiculous.

And my mom needed laser surgery. The specialist she's been seeing said Ma would be a good candidate, and it could prevent further vision loss. But the procedure would be expensive. We would be responsible for the remaining thirty percent if she decided to go through with it. And she wants to. Preserving her remaining vision is very important to her. Which I completely understand.

Dad and I left after making our appointment. The plan was to bring the car back in the morning to get the fuel pump replaced. We drove away, and I could see my dad watching me out of the corner of my eye.

"What?" I glanced quickly, then shifted my focus back to the road.

"You know, you look just like Ma. And it's more noticeable as you get older. Same smile. Same eyes. When I see you, it's like I'm looking at her all over again."

"Aww. Thank you, Daddy." I beamed. "That's certainly a compliment." My mother is by far one of the most beautiful women I've seen. I've always noticed the long stares she gets when we're in public. Since I was a child, the men and women have been captivated by her. And it's so sweet that I get to look just like her.

"You've made us so proud. Your light. Your kind spirit. You're beautiful inside and out, baby girl."

"Thank you."

He nodded. Then said, "Thank you for coming, Beta."

"You're welcome, Daddy. Of course."

We rode in silence a little longer.

"I didn't want this for you, baby girl. I'm sorry if I need too much."

My head snapped toward him, swiveling. "Daddy, what are you talking about? You don't ask for too much at all," I told him sincerely.

"You do so much," he said softly. "You look after Ma and me. And I worry about you being so busy. Or tired."

I smiled, though it was faint. I've been mentally tired. For sure. Physically too. But family was everything. My parents were all I had, and I was all they had. "We're a family. I wouldn't have it any other way. Someone's got to take care of things."

"Is someone taking care of you?" he asked after a pause.

I paused too, hesitating and feeling a bit shy. I looked over and saw a smile. I let mine spread wide. That was all the response he needed.

Nodding knowingly, he said softly, "Let him care for you, Indie. He's making you smile. A smile I haven't seen in a long time."

"He does. And it's so sweet, Daddy," I sighed softly. "I just don't want to let anyone down. I want to be good to him and still be here for you and Ma."

"You won't let anyone down. A good man would stand beside you. Help you without noise. And loving such a man wouldn't mean leaving us. It means building your own life."

My smile spread wider than before. Somehow. He was describing Sol perfectly. Sol is a good person. A good man. A good fucking human. I'm juiced as hell that it's me. Way past grateful. Yeah. God was smiling on me. And the way I've been carrying on. I was on a damn cloud. High as hell, and I had no desire to come down. Not anytime soon. I'd been floating every damn where. Physically there… but mentally somewhere else.

I'm so in love and happy, feeling good as I settle into what we're doing now. I'm even more delighted that I came to my senses before he moved on. Sol is definitely a man with options, but I've been feeling so good. I've been able to relax and just exist. The voices of doubt have quieted down. My worries, though they haven't disappeared, are less frequent. My fear of letting people down lingered and was louder some days for sure. But it wasn't as overwhelming as before. Daddy's words of wisdom certainly helped.

What my father shared was exactly what I needed to help me start letting things go. Sol had already come in and taken care of most of those thoughts. Reassuring me and helping me relax and enjoy what we were building. I didn't realize it, but in hindsight, that's precisely what he was doing.

He never made any declarations that he would. But his simply being here… *absorbed* all of that.

And. About two weeks ago, Sol and I confessed our love for each other.

Aloud. In person.

And. We made the sweetest love we ever could have made. Like. Ever.

It was emotionally layered with tension and a longing we shared. Exhilarating. After we waited for so long. We longed in tandem, and we verbally expressed that we'd longed to be connected again. To be intimate again. At the right time. In the right moment. And that moment couldn't have been more right. It was so right. Everything was so right. After we agreed, we would slow down. Take our time. *No pressure. No rush. Just us.*

I loved that, from the first time Sol ever said it. It summed up everything in just a few simple words. But agreeing to slow down… spend time together, talk, cook, laugh, create art. All of that. As our hearts aligned, our love grew throughout the process. We had fallen in love while focusing on our friendship. Looking back, I see how we've grown both as individuals and as friends. Rebuilding something new.

Being in love *while* love making was… mind-blowing. Heart-stopping. Soft. Slow. Sexy. All the things. Everything Sol did to me was just … fuck. I don't know anymore. I was pleased beyond satisfaction. Riveted. And I was still buzzing two weeks later.

Yeah. Foreplay seemed to go on forever. Thinking back on that had me rousing in my thoughts, now saturated with his intoxicating touch.

Several weeks after the last time we made love, a time still so fresh in my mind. There were weeks… no… there were hours of talking. Likely thousands of texts between us. Sharing in the silence. The desire not just to be one again but to be together. To be us. Until finally we were. And then in the waiting to be together again intimately.

And that night, it finally happened. We talked for hours before going there. Talking was something we were so fucking good at. And we talked. And talked. And talked. Tension built between us. Our bodies ached with desire. But it all felt perfect the way it unfolded. All of it.

We arrived back from HomeGrown, got ready for bed, and laid in Sol's bed. We discussed the evening highlights, wrapped into each other, and my legs tangled in Sol's. Laughing. Cuddling. Holding hands. Kissing too. Lots of kissing. The space between us felt electric, and the silence was full without us speaking a word. Music played softly, setting the mood, while the low lighting cast a gentle glow across Sol's bedroom.

Damn.

"I remember telling you that you were dangerous when I first met you."

"Yeah. I remember that."

A beat, "You're still dangerous. More so, actually."

We laughed easy.

"Still don't know what makes me dangerous?" I teased.

"Oh, Belle." Sol's large hands explored my body, kneading and caressing my flat stomach, my upper thighs. My back.

My skin awakened, and thirsting for his touch.

"You know you're beautiful," he began. "And it keeps hitting me. Each time I see you. Each time I look at you…"

"You always say that, baby. Thank you."

"I'll keep telling you. It's true. But you're so much more… and… you've turned my whole world inside out, baby. It isn't just in the way you look. It's in the way you move… it's unlike anything I've ever seen. The way you laugh. Your spirit. Your vibe. And then you look at me in a way I can't describe. Doesn't matter if you're pissed at me…" He laughed. "Or curious. Or frustrated. Or juiced to share something with me… you're magic, baby." He gently held my face in his hands. We were eyes on eyes.

"Damn Sol. That's the dopest thing anyone's ever said to me."

"I meant every word."

"You make me feel so safe. I've never felt so safe before. Especially tonight. You protected me. And it isn't something I take lightly."

"You can trust that I'll always keep you safe, India."

"That means the world. And it's fueling my desire… for you. Only for you, baby." I revealed. "It's like I want you even more. And I want to give to you. Everything I can give you. Please you too."

He held my gaze, and at some point, he captured my lips. He'd been doing that all night.

But this kiss was unlike the others.

It had this commanding… aching tenderness, along with a deep hunger.

"I love this. Being with you. Being close to you. I love this so much, Belle."

"I do too baby."

Eventually, I ended up completely naked in Sol's bed.

That was foreplay in and of itself. He removed my t-shirt and my panties like he was unwrapping something so fragile that it would break if he moved too quickly.

When he touched me, it was as if he honored every inch of my skin. He called me sacred. He called me sexy. He called me precious. And beautiful. Speaking in French some of the time. It made no difference to me; it all sounded good. Sol took his time brushing my sensitive nipples with his fingers. Brushed them back and forth, a few times. Damn, I liked that. A lot. I moaned through shallow breaths. He'd woken them up, teasing me like he was doing, and my nipples were begging for attention. And they were taut, stiff peaks.

"I like that too, baby. I told you I'm obsessed with these." He continued lightly dancing his fingertips over my perked nipples. "They're so perfect, so pretty, kissable, lickable..." His moan resonated deep in his chest. "Don't you think otherwise. Ever."

I looked up at him, feeling such relief that I had moved past that. That my bare chest in front of him didn't make me feel insecure. I had let go of that. Finally. And I loved being able to tell him so.

"Baby. I used to feel inadequate, but not anymore. I feel like I'm enough, and I can sense your desire for me."

"You are baby. You are. And I do. Always."

Yeah.

When we were finally one again, it was as if we'd rediscovered one another. We moved together to the beat of a rhythm only we knew. Slow, but certain. Everything was confirmed. The very moment Sol entered me. Stretching me slow and filling me to the hilt. Gently moving his hips. Thrusts so gentle they hurt so good. This was the real thing. And the time we took to slow down before coming together again was just what we needed. The love we made was gratifying. The words spoken and unspoken had me blissed the fuck out.

Sol moved with intention. Asking me what was on my mind. Listening intently to everything I managed to utter and conversely, telling me what was on his. And I surrendered to all of it. Let it all go for him. I was helpless. Couldn't have resisted if I wanted to. And I didn't. This was love.

For real love.

Unlike the love I'd experienced before. I expressed my love and pleasure boldly. Sol gave me all the room I needed. Encouraging me to take my time. That he wasn't going anywhere, and we had plenty of time. I kissed him deeply. Boldly, too, while letting go and allowing myself to feel everything. Everything I'd desired to feel, and everything Sol brought out of me.

My love for him. My desire for him.

The ache I had to fulfill his desires, too. And how much I missed him. The delight I had in pleasing him again. In this way. Having the honor of pleasing Sol period. A man like him. Of his caliber. His stature. A man *who wanted nothing more than to please me, too. From head to toe. And content, I felt that we waited for the right moment.*

Yeah. All of it was… euphoric.

"Sol."

"Yeah?"

I'd come for the second time. I was already in ecstasy… spellbound. Entranced. Feeling a sense of intense gratification. My head rested on his chest. Being lulled to a blissful high by his steady heartbeat. His arms wrapped securely around me. Our legs tangled.

"I never knew I could love you this deeply already. I'm intrigued. But it's scary too."

"Hmm. I feel the same. But it doesn't have to be scary. We're in this together. You and me, baby. This is real."

"Can we build something lasting, baby?" I asked, surprising myself. After things with Amir and then Brandon, my thoughts about something lasting… were distorted.

I didn't think I was capable or deserving. But here I was. With Sol, I couldn't help myself.

"Something like forever?" he asked.

"Yes. Something like that would be amazing with you," I returned.

Sol planted a sweet kiss on my forehead.

*"I want that too, so let's create it together. Trust in us, baby. This is our relationship. **Ours**. We can make it as beautiful, meaningful, and special as we want. Does that sound good to you, my Artist Girl?"*

"Yes. That sounds perfect, baby."

♪♥♫♥♪

After Dad and I got home, I checked in with Ma and then went to my bedroom. I decided to lie on my bed and try to relax for a while. Calm down. I still had an attitude about that mechanic. His ego pissed me off. And maybe I'm reaching, but sometimes it seemed like people didn't treat my dad well because of his Indian accent. They talked down to him, as if he weren't intelligent. I should have gone down there with my father a long time ago. I know how to turn my voice on.

Mr. Mechanic looked surprised to see me walk in and appeared visibly disarmed when I began asking questions and demanding clarification. I also pointed out his tentative language.

Sir, you're a certified mechanic, and I need you to be more confident about what you're telling me regarding this damn car. He probably thought that since he had been giving my immigrant father the runaround, I would fall for the same okey-doke. He couldn't have been more wrong. People are insulting, dismissive, and can be racist, prejudiced, or judgmental. It made me so angry.

As I lay there thinking about it, I grew even more upset. Ma has an accent, too Caribbean. And although hers isn't extremely thick, it was like once people heard a trace of it, they liked to categorize you. People who speak with foreign accents here in America are part of a marginalized community. Especially Black and Brown immigrants. That's the truth. And it's one of the reasons I'm so protective of my parents.

Mr. Mechanic quoted us something close to three thousand dollars. So that transmission would have to wait a bit longer. Thankfully, it was still drivable. We'd just have to avoid the freeway. The occasional stalling has made me much too nervous.

Our 2003 Toyota Camry had been good to us, but I wondered if it might be time to let it go. By the time we pay for all these repairs, we could have replaced it. It was old, but it had been so dependable. I also wondered if it was worth fixing since it's a Toyota. And she had several personality quirks we've learned to live with.

The clutch was worn, and it was nice finally getting that fixed because in traffic, it would shudder if we shifted too quickly. The AC is temperamental. Even after a recharge, it doesn't always blow cool air. Summers can get pretty hot here in Sac, so that was always a hassle. We make do. I just keep the windows down, and I keep a fan in the glovebox. I can clip it to the vents if it ever becomes unbearable. And yeah, these warm Sacramento summers have faded the hood and roof of the car. Other than that, there's no other cosmetic damage.

Speaking of the windows, they're manual, and there's one in the back that doesn't roll down more than a few inches. But we've gotten used to that. It's better for it to be stuck up than stuck down. A new issue is the check engine light coming on randomly and then going off just as randomly. The mechanic said it's probably a sensor problem, and unless it starts blinking, everything is likely fine.

And one frustrating issue is a slow leak in the power steering fluid. We have to top it off every few weeks, but other than that, we're keeping it running. Always making it work.

But yeah. We had the alternator replaced a few months ago. And even though it was money we really didn't have, it made the car reliable again. Not knowing if the car would start was stressful as fuck.

I felt my phone buzz on my bed beside me.

My Music Man: My Artist Girl

I replied immediately.

Me: Hey baby

My Music Man: Hey. How's it going?

Me: It's going.

My phone rang in seconds.

"What's going on with you, Belle?" His voice held concern.

I smiled at that.

"What makes you think something's going on?"

"I know you."

"Do you?"

"I do. Now. Let me know what's going on."

I hesitated for a brief moment. Sighing lightly. "Car issues, and I feel like this mechanic is giving my dad the run-around. Dad keeps taking it in, only for something else to go wrong. And we keep spending money we don't really have."

"What's the issue with it now?"

"He mentioned the fuel pump. He said eventually the transmission will need to be replaced. But we just got a lot of other work done on it. I feel like he's taking advantage of my father, as if he can talk over his head." I started to get emotional. "My parents are often discriminated against because they both speak with accents. But it's the only car we have, and we need to get it running well."

"I see."

And then I did it. I began to cry, quietly at first. But I blew my cover once I sniffed.

"Artist Girl. We'll figure this out." His voice held even more concern. "You hear me? We'll figure this out."

"Okay."

A beat.

"India."

"Yeah."

"I'd like to come take a look at the car, if that's okay with you."

"Alright." I didn't hesitate at all that time. "You know where to find us."

"I'll see you soon."

"See you baby."

"I love you."

"I love you too."

♪♥♫♥♪

"He's handsome, baby girl. Why hide such a handsome man? And so tall. And so kind. Great with his hands, too." Ma nodded toward the front door.

She removed the large pot from the heat. The dish was ready, and it smelled delicious. I couldn't wait to have some.

"He is. And I should have brought him around sooner. But I'm glad you could finally meet each other."

Sol was at my house within 15 minutes of us hanging up. When he arrived, he came to the front door, dressed casually with a bag of tools.

He met my parents, and they met him. Officially.

I beamed with pride introducing them. Proud of all three of them. After introductions, Sol followed Dad around to the driveway where the car was parked. Ma and I went back to the kitchen. We'd been cooking, and naturally, she said he'd be joining us. Not offering but insisting. I knew agreeing to letting Sol come here to look at the car meant he'd be meeting them.

I was okay with that. Perfectly fine with that. The three of them wanted to meet. I'd been asked that question from all directions. There was no time like the present.

And I knew Sol was handy, but I didn't know he knew so much about cars. At this point, nothing about him should surprise me. Sol and Dad got to work looking under the hood, then jacked the car up to check out a few things underneath.

"Daddy and I knew he was a keeper. We noticed you're lighter these days. Your spirit. Your smile. We knew he was a good one, my Indie."

I smiled wide, looking over at her. "Yes. He sure is, Ma."

I was standing beside my mother, flipping roti. I had two left to make. Hopefully, by the time these were ready, the men would be headed inside. Everything else was done. They'd been out there for quite a while. The sun was beginning to descend, too.

It had been an otherwise uneventful Monday. I was off from the shop, so I planned to work on the art piece I would donate to the Music Academy Benefit two weeks from now. Never got around to that. Instead, I was making Roti for my man to enjoy with my family during our first meal together.

That had me excited.

"My goodness. It smells great in here!"

My smile tripled hearing Sol's voice as he entered the front door. It was just off the kitchen.

"Thank you. There's a restroom behind you there. Please wash up and join us. The food is ready." Ma told him.

"Yes ma'am. Thank you!"

Sol winked at me just before he turned and headed down the hall, and it made me feel warm inside.

I'm sure I blushed too. I felt my face grow hot.

I took the plate of rotis to the table. Then I placed the main dish on a trivet. Ma brought a few plates down from the cabinet, just as my dad came up behind her, slipping an arm around her waist. He pressed a kiss to her cheek and whispered something low. They quietly carried on back and forth, and I continued setting the four places. I heard Sol emerge from the restroom a moment later, and I looked up just as he arrived at the entrance to our eat-in kitchen.

My megawatt smile returned. "Come on in," I told him. "You're sitting right next to me!"

"Alright."

We each took our seats. Ma and Daddy sitting directly across from Sol and me.

We grabbed hands. Then Daddy prayed for our food.

"Solomon. This is fish biryani. Has India made this for you yet?" my father asked pointedly. My mother had just placed a plate with the layered confection and two fresh rotis in front of him.

I was making Sol's plate. Gently placing it in front of him, a moment later.

He looked quite pleased with what he saw. Inhaling deeply. "Not yet, Mr. Rampersaud. *I wish!*"

Ma and Daddy laughed for a while. And I shook my head.

"Well, you'll have to put in a request. I'll send you home with some in the meantime. Yeah?" That was Ma.

"Only if there's enough."

"There's plenty. Not to worry," my father assured.

Sol tore a piece of roti and started eating his biryani. "This is delicious!" He looked at me, then at Ma. *"Wow!* This is my first time trying fish biryani. I love it."

We thanked him in unison.

He's gotten pretty good at eating with his right hand, which made me smile. Ma and Daddy wouldn't have held it against him if not, but I'm sure they noticed and were impressed too.

We continued eating, and I paused for a drink of water.

"No one will judge you if you need a drink of water, Sol. This has a moderate spice, which might be a little higher on the heat scale for you," I teased with a smile.

Fish biryani is a layered rice dish that combines fish, fragrant rice, and a harmony of South Asian spices. It's made with firm fish; we used boneless red snapper fillets and cooked them with a ginger-garlic paste, turmeric, and red chili powder. The basmati rice is layered with green chilies, mint leaves, coriander leaves, fried onions, and a drizzle of saffron for a vibrant color. The moderate spice level isn't much for us since we have a higher tolerance.

Sol nodded, chuckling. "It's pretty spicy." He took a drink, and we all laughed.

"The roti helps with the heat. We have a mint yogurt too."

I went to get the yogurt from the fridge. Giving it a quick stir, I gave some to Sol.

"It's plain yogurt with minced mint leaves, lemon juice, and a few other fresh spices mixed in. It offers a cool, refreshing contrast to spicy foods."

Sol nodded enthusiastically, thanking me. He swallowed the food in his mouth, and before taking another bite, he said, "India's made many things for me to try. And I learn something beautiful about her Indian and Afro-Guyanese heritage every time. I love that India's so proud of her culture. And she's a great cook. Everything she makes is my favorite. I can't decide because she'll make something else, and I'll love that dish just as much as the last one."

Both of my parents beamed.

That made me smile too.

"Yes. Thank you. Our Indie is a great cook. She's been in the kitchen with me since she was a tiny girl. So small she would stand on a chair to see the pan at the stove," Ma laughed at the memory.

I remember that too. I've been in the kitchen for as long as I can remember.

"She's learned to make dishes from both cultures because that's something we were sure to teach her. We wanted her to know both sides. They're each a part of her." Daddy said.

"I love that. It's beautiful to know your roots. And a blessing too. I'm adopted, and I've wanted to know where I'm from for so long. Learning so much from India has been welcomed and appreciated."

My parents nodded. "We pray you can get the answers you're searching for," Daddy offered.

"Yes. Don't stop searching. The blessing is on the other side of your faith," Ma added, smiling warmly.

"Thank you. I pray the same. It's been a long road, but I'll keep that in mind."

forty-one

INDIA

"So, what are the damages?"

"Well. I can fix the fuel pump; I need a few parts from Auto-Zone."

"You can?"

"Yeah. That's not a complicated job. I've done it a few times."

We were sitting on the couch in my living room, close to each other and holding hands.

Ma and Daddy went out to the patio to enjoy a cup of tea and the cool evening. They'd be heading to bed soon. We enjoyed dinner and had such a great conversation. Ma and Daddy asked Sol so many questions. They were so interested in him. And he, them. He had just as many questions of his own.

When I shared that Sol is a music professor and earned his Doctorate in Ethnomusicology, he passionately talked about his love for music and its connection to culture, as well as his travels during his research as a doctoral candidate. He smoothly segued into sharing stories from his childhood. As I listened, I learned a lot about his parents.

I learned things that fascinated me. The extensive travel they did as a family for his mother's mission work, spending months each year in underdeveloped countries. They helped and cared for women and girls with little agency. I bet she and Mala could talk for hours about this stuff. I was so inspired listening to Sol. He proudly spoke of his mother's passion for women's health. Even here in the U.S., right here in Sacramento, she worked to establish accessible reproductive health for black women.

Then he spoke about his father's philanthropic efforts, sharing that his father was a retired judge but had worked as an attorney for many years, focusing on exonerating the wrongfully convicted who lacked proper legal representation. Specifically, those incarcerated as teenagers or in their early twenties.

Shit. Both of his parents are humanitarians as far as I'm concerned. And I realized why Sol had the kind of heart he had. He gives back so much. It's innate. Second nature. And I would have known this sooner had I asked. He spoke openly about it.

But I can admit that I consciously kept the conversation about parents superficial. I realized that the deeper we went, the more interested I would be in meeting them. And surely, his interest had been piqued a long time ago. Sol told me several times he wanted to meet my parents. Even before we were official, and it was no wonder. I carried on about Ma and Daddy. I almost couldn't help myself.

Deciding that I wouldn't introduce them just yet, I didn't ask him deep questions about his parents. Attempting to hold off as long as I could. I suppose. I wouldn't do that to him, knowing I wasn't ready for him to meet my parents. But. Now that he has, and things have gone so well… and I've learned the things I've learned… I'd love to meet Sol's parents, too. I'd be honored to meet them.

I bet they're amazing. I bet they're smart just like Sol. Biology be damned. He was nurtured by these people from birth. And they raised a gentleman. A giver. A leader.

A lifelong learner. A teacher. A gifted, soulful, *passionate musician.*

A husband.

Yeah.

I bet they're black excellence. Well doing. Good-hearted. Kind and giving.

I know his parents speak French as well.

Yeah. I wanted to meet them. Desperately, I think.

"You're pretty handy for a musician," I teased. Leaning in slightly, I kissed his cheek sweetly. "Thanks for saving the day. I was about to lose it." I laughed despite myself.

He leaned over, kissing my cheek. "I'm glad we could take care of it. Call me anytime. For anything. We'll always figure it out. You hear me, Belle?"

"Yes. I will. Absolutely," and I meant that shit. Sol made me feel so much better. After dinner, Sol helped me clean the kitchen. Insisting with my mother, it was the least he could do after sharing such a delicious meal with us. She packed him a hearty Tupperware of biryani too. He went on about how excited he is for lunch tomorrow.

"When I took the car for a quick spin, I told Dad we might want someone else to check the transmission more closely. It does seem to be slipping a bit."

I nodded. Saying nothing. Sighing heavily, I asked, "You think it's worth fixing? We'll need to decide on something soon."

"Well, it's a Toyota. For an '03, the miles aren't too high. Depending on the engine's overall condition and whether we can confirm the transmission is in good shape, I'd say so. That can be a tough call, but a good buddy of mine is a certified mechanic. He's got a shop out in West Sacramento. I'll call him in the morning and ask him to do a complete analysis. We'll see where we land."

"Hmm. I'm no mathematician, but I'm pretty sure that'll be cheaper than buying a newer car." I chuckled. "Nickels and dimes are cheaper than monthly car payments in the hundreds. Then there's the upkeep. Insurance."

"Oh, absolutely. Taking good care of a faithful car makes the most economic sense. I don't think she's too far gone. But he may have to keep it for a few days, so I'll pass you my Jetta."

My head snapped in Sol's direction. But I said nothing. Not at first. I was at a loss for words initially. Feeling incredibly grateful. Yet... I was still trying to grasp the idea of him being here for me, instead of obsessively trying to figure it out on my own, and accepting that I didn't have to do that anymore. My fierce independence was a habit that was hanging on tight. Sol is solution-based. He's already thought about it and handled it. He was simply informing me.

We didn't ride in his Jetta, but just a few times. It was an older model too, but ran great. Sol had a bike rack on top, and we took the bikes up to Folsom recently to ride some trails out there.

"Thank you." I found my voice. "But. Are you… are you sure?"

"Positive." We were still holding hands. He continued caressing my fingers in his. "I hardly drive it. I have my Jag. I hardly drive that either. I'm on my bike mostly. You know that." He looked into my eyes. A warm smile on his handsome face. "It's just sitting there. I start it up now and then, but I don't need it. You can use it. I trust you." He winked.

And. I grew warm inside. Then. I felt a pulse forming below. Yeah.

"Wow, thank you so much, baby. This will really help us out."

"You're welcome so much. I got you. You can use it for as long as you need."

I leaned into him, damn near in his lap, and planted a sweet kiss on his lips.

"You're getting me excited, Music Man," I murmured, sultry. Low. "Taking care of me like you're doing…" I kissed Sol along his jaw a few times. Then, I trailed my tongue down his neck. Scattering kisses there, too.

"Hmm. That so?"

"It is." I fully climbed into his lap. Straddling him. "They're going to head to bed soon," I whispered in his ear. "Then we can go to bed."

"Mmm." It was deep in his chest. The ones I love. I can feel them just as much as I can hear them.

I'd begun to grind into his lap. And I could feel his hard dick beneath me. He sat back, settling into the couch and getting comfortable. His moans were faint, but deep as hell and so fucking sexy. He slowly brought his hands up around my hips. Holding me gently as I continued gyrating into him. He growled. Moaned. Actually, I don't even know. He did something. It was a carnal sound. The kind of noise a grown ass man makes when he's being pleased. And. It wet my panties even more. Instantly.

He firmly held my hips, stilling my movements. *"Artist Girl…"* His voice urgent. I opened my eyes to find his gaze already trained on me. He rubbed the back of his neck; his other hand remained at my hip. Anchored to me.

"Yeah?"

"Can I tell you something? Please."

"Of course." My brows furrowed now.

"Okay… When we first started…" he trailed off, looking away. Then his eyes returned. "Those times we were together… here. It's been on my mind. But it's not because of you. And I don't want you to think that. But I don't feel right making love to you here. I respect your parents too much. Your home. You." He reached for my hands, capturing them and threading our fingers.

"Okay," I said gently.

"I want us to be free to express ourselves and share everything we want to. But not here. It just doesn't feel right. It doesn't mean I don't want you, Belle. You know that, right?" Before I could answer, he brought my hand forward and placed it on his hardness. He was even harder than he was a moment ago.

Damn.

"I want you bad. But we keep it sweet when we're here. Kissing you is all I can handle. Anything more, we go to my place. That cool with you, baby?"

I could respect that, and I appreciated the respect he showed to my parents and me.

"You're setting ground rules now?" I teased, smiling wide.

Sol grinned. "I'll take that as a yes. And I'm simply respecting the temple. And it's integrity. Yours and theirs."

"I understand. And I can rock with that."

I climbed off his lap, standing to my feet.

"How about I take you to my art shed. Want to see it?"

"I'd love to."

"Follow me."

It was dark outside now, about eight-thirty in the evening. The backyard was completely silent. Sol had a few brief words with my parents, thanking them again for their hospitality and wishing them a restful sleep. They thanked him for joining us, told him he was always welcome, and expressed their gratitude for his help with the car. Then Ma and Daddy headed to bed, and we followed the stone path leading from the back patio to my shed.

"So. This is where all the magic happens." I pulled the string, illuminating the shed with one of the lamps I had in here. Sol crossed the threshold behind me, and as he took in everything he saw, I tried to hide my smile. Suddenly feeling shy.

I watched as his eyes swept the shed. A smile lifted at the corner of his lips.

"You weren't joking." He kept walking into the shed, past me. Sol looked up, then glanced behind him. Then looked beside him. At the ground under his feet.

I saw him as he explored my shelves. His eyes lined the rows of sketchbooks and canvases. A corkboard covered with inspiration, quotes. Tubes of paint, jars of paintbrushes, illustration pens, and pencils. A dozen more empty glass jars were stacked neatly in a corner. Whenever we finished a glass jar, I washed it out and brought it out here. An artist can never have too many glass jars of any size.

"India…this is… *breathtaking.*"

"Thank you." I walked all the way inside. "It's a little messy in here. Wasn't expecting company." I chuckled. Well, kind of. I wasn't just shy. Now I was feeling something like… uncertainty? Wondering why I even invited him out here. This wasn't anything fancy, far from it. I've seen some breathtaking art studios. This wasn't that. As proud as I was of my art shed. I'd never really shown it to anyone before. It was just a place I came and created.

I realized Sol was looking at me as if I'd said something outrageous. "This is yours."

And. That did something to me, in the best way. His words hit me in my chest, and I smiled wide. He walked toward me as I leaned against my worktable. I often worked from here; if I weren't painting at an easel, this was where you'd find me. I had a paint-splattered stool pulled up close to it.

"You said your father built this for you?"

I smiled in nanoseconds. "Every square inch."

I looked around as if this was my first time in here.

"He laid the foundation, installed the flooring, wired everything himself, and put in a sink so I wouldn't have to use the water hose. He built all these shelves. My worktable." I ran my fingers across the smooth wood. "Sanded the wood himself. Walls are insulated, so I don't burn up in the summer or freeze in the winter." I laughed. "Even has roofing to keep the rain out. My favorite part of all is this big window. Since my dad builds houses, he told me that in the U.S., south-facing windows are the best because they get the most sunlight throughout the day. He made sure to get me the biggest window he could find so I'd get as much natural light as possible for as many hours a day," I said.

And just like that, the space felt… fuller. This was the only place I could truly call mine. Yeah, my whole heart lived here, in a space my father built just for me. Everything about it is directly from his heart.

"This is phenomenal. Your father is extremely talented. You can see the love here. His love for you when he built it, and the love you have existing here."

"You think so?"

"I do." He nodded, turning to meet my gaze. "I can feel it. The love. The creativity. It's very much alive here."

"You really get it Sol." I took a seat on one of the upside-down paint buckets. Sighing in content. I didn't need a fancy art loft with exposed brick. Not right now. This would do just fine. This art shed in the backyard of my childhood home, with the essence of my father's hardworking hands in every crevice, was precisely where I was supposed to be.

Sol took a seat on one of the other buckets, moving it beside me. "Some of this art stuff goes over my head. I don't know it quite the way you do." He chuckled easy. "However, I know what it means to have a passion for something that fuels your soul. And having a space to come and feed that passion is important. This is that place for you, Artist Girl. How blessed you are."

"Aww. Yes. It is. For sure. And I am."

I was feeling extremely emotional now. The shyness and uncertainty I felt moments before had dissipated. And Sol saw me.

Yet again. He saw me.

Sol saw me.

In all of my… *commotion*.

The artist who painted until my eyelids grew heavy and my fingers cramped.

The doting daughter who loved her parents fiercely.

The woman who loved with such intensity. And simply wanted that love reciprocated.

He saw me. Beyond what was visible. Past the physical. Despite my chaos.

My disarray.

And he didn't run away, make me feel bad, or demand I figure it out.

He was still here, right beside me. Not trying to fix me. Or take me away from the people who mean most to me.

Yeah.

"Want to stay a little longer? I was just about to work on something."

"I'd love that, Artist Girl."

♪♥♫♥♪

"Hey India. You've got a walk-in."

The next day, I was at the shop working on a skin. I had my own station now that I'd been doing more of that. It wasn't decked out with anything personal, like the other stations, but it was nice having my own space. I kept it clean. Everything tidy and in its place. That had been drilled into me while I shadowed. And I kept my supplies stocked. I didn't expect to use them anytime soon, but I was ready if I had to be.

The shop was pretty busy for an early Tuesday evening. I noticed more people coming in for new ink as the weather got warmer. The shop was crawling with people. Their chatter floated over the buzzing of the machines and the music.

I looked up at Kat, feeling surprised and confused.

"A walk-in? Me?"

"Yes. *You.*" Kat gave me a pointed nod as she leaned over the wall of my station.

She wore a mischievous grin, so I couldn't tell if she was joking. Deciding to humor her, I played along.

I turned off my machine. "Okay." I placed the gun beside me. "What is it?"

Kam's smile widened as she walked around the wall and entered my station. She leaned back against it, still grinning.

"Faith. In script on the wrist."

And I said nothing. But I processed that. I could do that. I think…

406

"India. You've been killing it on your practice skins. You can do that in your sleep."

"And she wants me?" I asked, for some reason. This is the moment I had been waiting for, yet my heart was pounding. I wasn't sure if I should be bursting with excitement or scared shitless.

"She's a walk-in, and this is her first tattoo. That means she's looking for an artist. That's you," Kat explained.

And it clicked. Kat was giving me a chance. She could easily have intercepted this client or taken her to another station. She came looking for me.

"You can handle one solo. And I'll be right here. But you got this."

I smiled. "Thanks, Kam."

"You're good. Come meet her. She's chill and a little nervous. Since I know your ass is nervous too, you two are perfect for each other."

We both chuckled. I followed Kam to the front to meet my first client. She was a sweetheart. A cute, chocolate-skinned girl in her mid-20s. She looked pretty nervous. She talked about placement, sizing, and font. I didn't tell her she was my first tattoo. Instead, speaking confidently and calmly, I assured her it would look amazing, and I'd make sure she was as comfortable as possible. Unfortunately, tattoos are painful. But my steady hand would help alleviate some of that.

And *faith* was a gift to herself for passing her NCLEX exam. She'd graduated with her BSN and was now officially a Registered Nurse. I congratulated her. I know that was hard work. And with a kind smile and warm eyes, I assured her she was in great hands.

She followed me back to my station. After I prepped the stencil, I placed it on her wrist to ensure it was exactly what she wanted. Once I received her confirmation, I put on my gloves. Kam sat nearby, winking and smiling like a proud mother watching her child take their first steps.

"Alright, nurse. Let's get this masterpiece on you!"

It wasn't until I connected the machine to her skin carefully. Steady. Precise… that something ignited in me. Everything clicked. It was like a fuse lit; a spark was kindled. And I did what

I'd been preparing for all this time. I took my time, but since there were only five letters, it didn't take too long. The highlight was when I wiped her down and let her see it. I was so emotional. She was too, telling me it was perfect.

I glanced at Kam, mouthing "Thank you."

Later, while I was cleaning up, Kam told me I was officially a tattoo artist.

And, yeah. That felt so damn good.

♪♥♫♥♪

"Kam said you did your thing."

I beamed. "I did. It looks great."

King nodded. "Look at you. Soon you'll have your license."

It was about time for me to head out, but King asked me to stop by his office before I left.

I closed the door behind me. I figured this would be quick, so I stood instead of taking a seat.

King rose from his chair, walking around his desk. He moved close to me. I turned toward him, his face just a whisper away from mine. His desk was behind me, and he stood in front of me.

What the…

"Kingston…" I said slowly, measured. "What are you doing?"

"I won't hurt you, Pretty Thing."

I took a few breaths.

"But I'll be honest. I'm almost ready to cash in on my investment."

My blood ran cold.

"Wh-… what are you talking about?"

"All the time you've been spending in here learning the game. In my shop. Using my equipment. Access to my clientele. I've passed you close to five Gs already. You know I been wanting you. I'm ready for something, Pretty Thing. Been ready."

"Kingston… you never said this was a part of the deal." I tried to play it cool. I didn't want to let on that I was extremely nervous. Extremely unformattable. I didn't think King would do anything drastic. But he was too close for comfort. And I couldn't show all of my cards. He could play on my fear as a power move.

408

He chuckled low, and it made me sick.

"I needed to say it?" His tone was incredulous. "We grown, Pretty Thing. What grown people you know give that kind of money away for free?"

"Come on now. Had you told me, I wouldn't have agreed. This is how you do business?" Still attempting to play it cool. Though my heart was doing somersaults in my chest, I replied as confidently as I could.

He'd spread my legs and was standing between them now. His hands on either side of me, gripping his desk.

"Why you playing with me? I know you want me too."

"You have Fatima."

"Fatima don't run me. I can call her right now. She'd want to watch. She been telling me how bad she want you her damn self." He cackled. As if that was the funniest thing he'd heard.

Thinking quickly, I offered. "It's not the best time, King. I'm on my period. I'm bleeding. Just started today."

His demeanor changed. His body laxed. "I want you, India. Don't want to wait much longer."

I nodded. "Yeah. Mother nature has no chill." I shrugged, smiling sweetly. The sweetest smile I could muster.

King took a few steps back, putting space between us again.

It was subtle, but I sighed in relief.

Adjusting myself and maintaining my composure, I offered, "I should get back out there."

He turned and headed back around his desk. "Aight."

I casually dipped out, heading back toward my station. I would get my tote and leave. No plans to speak a word to anyone. I didn't need to pass Go and collect $200 either.

I couldn't stay at King Tattoo for another minute.

I would leave right now and never come back.

I was so uncomfortable and anxious; I'm grateful I could keep it together enough not to draw attention to myself.

I'll find another shop.

And I'd still get my license.

This was only a detour.

forty-two

SOL

I'd finally met India's parents, and I was overwhelmed in the best way.

Her dad and I spoke at length about so many things while we worked on the car. Mr. Vijay Rampersaud is a man of valor. And strength. The dedication he had for this family, both nuclear and extended, was truly admirable. Family and faith are very important to him.

His wife is his heart. His daughter is his heartbeat. He spoke of his humble upbringing, his journey to America with his new bride, and the dreams they had for their future family.

I listened intently and in awe as he shared about his profession as a contractor. Building houses from the ground up. His working hands built a multitude of homes all over greater Sacramento and beyond. Numbers in the tens of thousands. He did it for decades. At one point, he co-owned a contracting business that secured contracts with the city, the county, and the state. He did good work. Trusted work. Sought after for many years. And he gave jobs to many men who just wanted a chance to feed their families. He spoke about hiring men who had served time in the penitentiary and couldn't get work anywhere else, or immigrants who needed a hand up getting on their feet, which he could relate to directly.

What a man.

And his Indie. His baby girl. She's his world. He beamed with such pride speaking of his one and only. How talented she is. How selfless she is. Yeah. And I knew this full well. But I loved to hear it from him.

I told Mr. Rampersaud how much India means to me and how deeply I love and care for her.

How fortunate I am to have met her. How kind she's been. How sweet she is. How well they raised such a woman. I told him India was a queen and a catch. A woman who would make an incredible wife. I hadn't planned to go down that line, but it was easy to do. And I believe it would have been a question Mr. Rampersaud had for me.

He'd seen his Indie heartbroken too many times. And, I suppose, as her father, he would want to know my intentions with her. And I shared them honestly and openly, man to man. I held nothing back. I shared that India is precious. And so special to me. Her heart was in my possession now, and I planned to take great care of India. I wanted a future with her. She told me she wanted to build something lasting, and I want the same. I realized a while ago that I wanted that with her. When she brought that up, I readily agreed. I assured Mr. Rampersaud that I had only the best intentions for India. And I wanted to continue to get to know them as our relationship grew.

And her mother.

Marva.

Her mother is stunning.

A regal Afro-Guyanese woman with a gentle, feminine aura. Carefree and playful too. I can see where India inherited her sense of humor. And India really resembles her mother. I love seeing children resemble their parents. Maybe because I'm adopted and I don't look like my parents at all.

Yeah. India looks exactly like her mother.

When I looked at her, I saw India about twenty years older.

And her mother looked fantastic. Vibrant, with warm brown eyes and an ever-present smile. They could have been sisters. India is just a shade lighter and much taller than her mother, but they share the same mannerisms.

And I noticed India's accent came alive as she continued speaking with them. She always had it, which I found adorable, but it became much more pronounced during their conversation. They spoke Guyanese Creole, an English-based language, so I understood a lot of it, but not everything. India told me some time ago that Guyanese Creole draws on African, Indian, and Indigenous languages and is widely spoken across Guyana.

I was fascinated by her and all of it.

Mrs. Rampersaud's Caribbean roots are strong, and she spoke in a rapid cadence. When India spoke with her mother, she matched her mother's rate of speech without missing a beat. Everything: her timing, stresses, and inflections flowing like backbeats.

Then she would talk with her father. And she's such a daddy's girl, by the way, which is so cool. With him, she slowed down. Just the way he spoke. Easy. Unassuming. Measured speech. Taking his time. Her father's native language is Hindi, and India knows many words and phrases. He affectionately calls her *Beta*, a term of endearment meaning "child."

She told me that Indo-Guyanese speakers like him usually use different expressions with slight Hindi influences, and their speech can be more melodic in some places or more clipped in others. Yeah. I was so into it. I liked it. I was reminded, once again, how deeply rooted she is in her heritage. Her culture lives in her spirit. Seeing India in her element and hearing her code-switch like that. Naturally slipping into Creole phrases and intonations. I was entranced. Mesmerized. That shit was seducing. Yeah.

I spoke with her parents over dinner and shared my life story. They were pretty interested in learning about me, so I spoke openly. Sharing that, I always longed for cultural connections. I was always curious about my roots. So, studying ethnomusicology was the perfect field for me. It was therapeutic in a way. I learned about music, my first love, and was able to further explore culture and history, which helped my healing journey. I never knew whether I would ever find my family, so in a way, this fulfilled that dream.

That dream. I've thought about it too. I have many times. I can admit that maybe that's what initially drew me to India. She's extremely beautiful, of course, but her deep connection to her heritage stands out. She's so knowledgeable about her roots, proud of both sides. As I've gotten to know her and fallen in love with her, she's started to feel like the home I've always longed for.

Then they asked about Ethnomusicology as a discipline.
What is it? What does an Ethnomusicologist do?

It's always welcome when I receive those questions. Though Ethnomusicology is a long-established discipline, most people don't know much about it, and I often get this question.

But I was more than happy to share.

I told them I studied music within social and cultural contexts, and I also examined the intersection of music, anthropology, and history. The goal is to better understand why people make music, what it means to them, and how it reflects their identity, beliefs, and community life.

As a music professor who is also a full-time musician, I believe it gives me the technical skill to teach with credibility.

At some point, I mentioned visiting the Caribbean during my doctoral research and that it was one of my favorite places. I traveled a fair bit doing fieldwork during my doctorate program. Exploring global musical traditions in their natural element was required for my thesis, and they inquired extensively, deeply engaged as I spoke passionately about something I deeply revere.

And. That meant the world.

♪❤♫❤♪

Me: You home Artist Girl?
Artist Girl: I am
Me: Coming to you
Artist Girl: Okay

And... I didn't mean to show up like that, but it was hard to stay away from her. After seeing her the other night, in her element, with the people who made her. I thought about the way she looked at me and the kiss she gave me when I left. It was sweet, and it lingered.

India started working on something after she took me to her art shed. And I loved that quiet with her. The stillness felt full and ripe with creativity. And even in silence, it wasn't empty at all.

Yeah. I wanted more of that with her.

So, I went to her. Bearing gifts. I had flowers for her mother. A bright mixed bouquet. Brilliant hues of reds, blues, yellows, and greens. Combined with lilies and daisies. Tulips. Peonies and sunflowers. I was so appreciative of the food she sent home with me.

After shaking her father's hand and speaking with him, I followed Indie to her art shed.

I had my acoustic hanging on my shoulder. I loved being back in this space with her. The sacred space where the magic of her creativity came alive. She sat on her stool, barefoot in paint-splattered overalls, a faded yellow spaghetti strap underneath, her hair piled on top of her head in a messy bun… and she saw that I held a rectangle-shaped velvet box. And. Her eyes lit up as I handed it to her. Yeah. They lit up even brighter than usual.

"What's this?"

"It's for you."

"What is it?"

"You'll have to open it, silly."

I took a seat on a bucket and tuned my strings. I didn't know what I would play, but I knew I wanted to groove with her. Get lost in this sacred space of creativity while she worked. I knew I wanted to be near her while she worked. I started strumming softly. Thinking about the way my chest ached when I left her the other night.

"Sol. This is beautiful. Thank you!" She came to hug me, and I gently set my guitar down beside me. I wrapped her in my arms. "I love this! Thank you!"

"You're so welcome, my Artist Girl."

It was a Pandora charm bracelet with a few charms that suited her personality, leaving room for more if she ever wanted to add them. A paintbrush, a hibiscus flower, a sun, a palm tree, and a cursive I.

Then I reached into my pocket and pulled out a smaller box. I opened it. "Can we add this to the chain around your neck, baby?" It was a gold painter's palette pendant. On the back, engraved, "Always My Artist Girl."

"Oh, Sol!" she hugged me again. "You just keep spoiling me!"

I held her close. "I know you always wear your chain. Now you'll always have a piece of me with you."

She threaded the charm on and then returned it to her neck. It looked great on her. The painter pendant wasn't huge but large enough to make a statement, slightly smaller than a quarter.

Elegant and perfect for her daily wear. I went to a jeweler and had it custom-made. This was solid gold, with no fillers or plating, ensuring it would be long-lasting and timeless.

She smiled at me. Warm. Reaching her eyes.

"You're too good to be true." She was emotional, returning to my arms.

"I'm true baby. You can trust in us."

When she returned to her easel, I went back to strumming some soft chords.

India mixed a few colors, dipping her brush in water. She moved with such fluidity as she approached her easel. She glided across the canvas. And. I watched her in awe. She painted as if it were second nature. And to her it was.

Meanwhile, I kept playing a soft rhythm. Mellow and sweet. And. I got lost in it. Closed my eyes, let the music take over. I wanted to wrap her in the melody without disturbing her groove. Eventually, I glanced up and saw her pretty brown eyes on mine. She was still. Hadn't painted much more than what I saw moments before. She looked at me. Saying nothing for a while and looking into my soul.

I held the same depth as I looked into her eyes. But. My goodness… she was looking at me. And without speaking a word, I knew she understood everything unsaid. We shared that understanding. It was like our own language.

"Sol. You are amazing," her voice small, just above a whisper.

She was so beautiful. Standing there. In awe of me. And full of wonder.

Fuck. I wanted to kiss her.

I wanted to make love to her.

I wanted to remind her that I was completely hers, and she was completely mine. And that she drove me wild, the way I constantly desired to have her.

By simply being my sweet India.

I wanted her so much.

And I love her.

So much.

I kept playing. Then, "You're amazing, Belle. And I mean that."

And I kept playing. For her.

India was incredible. The most incredible woman I've ever had the pleasure of knowing. She was so grounded… so humble. So fucking dope. And so high. All at once. I knew we were building something remarkable.

Monumental. I knew we weren't just passing time. This was the real thing. I kept my eyes on her as she painted. And as much as I wanted to go to her and kiss her, I didn't. I knew I'd get the chance again. It was fine. It was perfect. I continued to play for her as she continued to paint her masterpiece.

And we didn't speak much. Just let the creative juices flow. And the room remained void of conversation, which was fine. It was perfectly fine. The unspoken space between us was the loudest energy I've ever felt in the best way.

Ever.

Yeah.

Later that evening, I was back home again, lying in my bed and thinking about her. It was late, close to midnight. I was sure India was already asleep. She seemed a little quiet today; even though we were deep in our creative zones, she said she was just a little tired. But I was wide awake, so I sent her a voice memo. We still exchanged those, and I loved getting one from her whenever she sent it.

"Indie. My Artist Girl… have you ever had a moment so profound that it settles into your soul? That's what tonight felt like. When I came to see you and you let me watch you paint that masterpiece. It was… nothing short of amazing. Thank you for letting me be a part of that. I was so fortunate to play next to you. Text me when you're up. Sleep sweet. My Artist Girl."

But I still didn't go to sleep just yet.

Couldn't. My mind was much too busy. Occupied. Swarming with her face. Her sweet kisses. Her laugh. I was consumed. And. So in love with this woman who had come in like the calmest whirlwind and changed my life. Changed so much. And gave me the push I needed to keep searching for the other part of me.

That melody I played for India earlier came to me right then. It was a string of chords that seamlessly worked together somehow. Though it was something improvised and entirely off the cuff, it was stellar, I dare say. It gave me a delightful feeling. It reminded me of her… of home. Of peace. Of serenity. Of everything new and exciting yet so very familiar and close.

I got up and grabbed my acoustic.

When I walked in the door earlier, I had the mind to record myself humming that melody in my voice notes app. That app was always handy, and I used it anytime a tune came to me, which happened at the most random of times. Creatives of any kind can understand that.

After fetching my acoustic, I went to my music room. Since I was wide awake, I sat there picking through the chords on my guitar and put words to it.

I worked on it for a while. More than an hour.

I went back to my bedroom to try and get some sleep when I saw three missed calls from India. One of them was just ten minutes ago. There was also a text.

Artist Girl: Sol. I need to talk to you

I called her immediately.

♪♥♫♥♪

"Did he touch you, baby?"

"No."

"Okay."

I took several calming breaths. India shared that yesterday, the owner of the tattoo parlor implied an expected sexual favor. And she walked out of the shop.

I wasn't as angry now that I knew he hadn't made any physical contact with her. I'm glad she could walk out of there before anything else happened.

"Are you alright, Indie?"

She paused. "No. There's some things I haven't been honest about."

My antennas went up. "Okay," I told her gently. "Then, let's talk about it."

She took a few beats. "He's given me money. Lots of money. That's what this is all about."

Hmm.

"Was this before us, Indie?"

"Yes. Before us."

"Okay." A beat. "How much money?"

She paused. Then, "We needed it. We were so behind. Bills were past due… the car… it was as if he knew exactly when I needed it and I wouldn't turn it away."

"How much money, baby?

"About five thousand."

Wow.

"Five thousand dollars?"

"Close. And not all at once. I was there for months, and it was over three different occasions. First was twelve hundred. Then, fifteen hundred. Then eighteen hundred."

"I see." A beat. "That's serious money, India. Why take money from a man you don't plan to do more with? That kind of cash comes with conditions."

"I know. But I was desperate. I just… it was stupid."

I said nothing. I was trying my damndest not to get too upset.

"He's been calling me. Since I left the shop, I haven't been back. I'm scared. I don't know what he's going to do to me. That money is long gone." Her voice grew urgent. She was emotional now, too.

It was all making sense. That's why she'd been so quiet today.

"Block his number. Right now."

"Okay."

I continued. "He won't do anything to you. Alright. He won't bother you." She'd begun to cry. "Indie. Baby. Nothing will happen to you, okay?" I spoke with care.

"I knew better. I wish I hadn't accepted the money. "She said once she'd gathered her bearings.

"Hey. Don't beat yourself up. He gave it to you of his own free will."

She sniffled. "Sol."

"Yes."

"The money you gave me for equipment. I used that to pay bills with. I never bought any tattoo equipment. I used the equipment at the shop."

I said nothing.

"I've been keeping things from you. And I'm sorry. I'm so sorry." She started to cry again. "You're such a good man, Sol." There was a pause. "I haven't been good to you… will I lose you?"

Her cries grew in volume. And it pulled at my heartstrings. I wanted to hold her. Dry her tears.

I wouldn't kick her while she was down. Not at all.

And I had to be honest. This was tough. She came to me in desperation and… I could admit that it didn't make me feel good. The shit stung. *Like hell.* And her accepting money from a man. That had me feeling some type of way. It pissed me off. Despite it being before we were official. But. I was in her life. We were sleeping together. And we weren't fucking. She didn't need his money. Not a red cent. Taking money from a nigga was *absolutely* conditional.

I sighed again. But she came to me, nonetheless. And. Now. *Right now…* she's still mine. I'm still hers. She'd calmed down a little.

"We can fix this, baby," I gently told her.

"We can?"

"We can. But starting right now, I need you to be honest with me. Completely and transparently. Always. Alright?"

"Alright."

"Is there anything more I should know? I'm right here. And I'm not walking away from you. But we need to start fresh with a clean slate."

"No, baby. There isn't."

"Are you sure?"

"Yes. I'm sure."

"Alright. We'll find another shop for you. And we'll get you your own equipment. Alright?"

"Alright."

"As for Kingston. He won't bother you anymore. Consider that situation handled."

"I won't ask." she lightly tittered, and I was so glad to hear it.

"All better now, my Artist Girl?"

"Yeah. Much better. Thank you."

"Good."

"Why are you like this?"

It was my turn to chuckle. "Great question." A beat. "This is me. And. I guess because I love you so much, I want you to be okay. I want us to be okay. You're precious to me, Indie. And now that I'm here, let me in. Let me be here for you. Tell me what you need. You don't have to figure things out on your own anymore. Alright?"

"I love you too, Sol. And I will. I promise you, I will."

♪♥♫♥♪

"Call me."

Two simple words.

But they were so much more than that.

Two words weighed. In promise. In possibility.

I was at Sac city. Hanging out in my office. Thursday was my long day.

The longest day of the week for me.

I had three classes, then I played at HomeGrown. I had one class left before I could head out. These were my office hours, but no one showed up, which wasn't unusual.

Typically, students only came to office hours right after an exam because they hadn't done well, or at the end of the semester when they were afraid of failing.

Although students rarely attended office hours, it was still required that I be available for them.

When I teach virtually, I hold office hours via Zoom, and students often drop in for questions. Sometimes a former student would stop by to say hello. Other students wouldn't have questions but would come just to chat for a few minutes. I didn't mind that. With online courses, there was a discussion board where students were required to post responses to prompts, so this was a good time to check those.

So, most of the time, I spent office hours preparing my lecture for the next class and reviewing my slides. I made sure the homework assignment was in order. If I needed copies for the class, I took care of that. I also caught up on grading. At the community college level, we weren't provided with a teacher's assistant, so I was responsible for managing all of that myself.

During my doctorate program, I used office hours to catch up on some of my own assignments whenever necessary. That time was always helpful and appreciated.

Throughout all of that, I always kept an eye on my email, which is what I was doing now.

I was reading over an email from Monique Crocker, who has been my right hand and all things event coordinator extraordinaire for the past few years. Monique is a savvy fifty-year-old woman, and nothing and no one will stop her from delivering the best event you've ever seen. She's organized, resourceful, dependable, responsive, and determined. She gets the job done. She truly does it all.

She performs great under pressure as well. Sometimes things fall through at the last minute, or we need to pivot or make adjustments. She steps in and saves the day without missing a beat. I'm incredibly grateful to have her on my team.

Her email included the final event details for the Music Academy Benefit for my review and follow-up on a few questions I'd asked her. I read her email carefully, making a mental note to respond when I had a few more moments. I glanced at my watch; class was scheduled to start in the next fifteen minutes. With the last ten minutes of office hours remaining, I planned to use the restroom and then head to class. Today, I'd be in the music lab.

I thought about it. Since I had at least five minutes to spare, I decided to go ahead and email her. The event was exactly one week away, and I wanted to confirm that everything was in place. Everyone delivered as promised, and it was expected to draw a great turnout. India was very excited to be part of it. She'd finished the piece she planned to donate to the auction. I watched her paint most of it in real time, and I was spellbound.

I sent Monique the email, and I went to close my laptop to pack up, but something in my inbox caught my eye.

It was from Samuel Haman. The subject line read, "Call me."

My heart rate immediately increased, but I managed to quickly open the email that came about a half hour ago.

Solomon,

First, forgive me for the delay. I don't check my social media often. But as soon as I got your message, I looked you up. I'm so glad you reached out. I've been searching for you for a long time.

I would love to talk to you. Please call me anytime. Looking forward to hearing from you.

Sam Haman

I hated that I had class in ten minutes. I wanted to talk to Sam. I considered canceling class so I could call him now instead of later. Maybe I'd let them out early tonight, then Sam and I would have time to chat before my gig at HomeGrown.

I was so happy. Happy wasn't big enough. I was… elated. He had been searching for me and was looking forward to talking to me. Wow. I pulled out my phone and started composing a text message.

Hey Sam. It's Sol. Got your email. I have a class about to start, but I'd love to call you afterward. Should end in the next hour.

As soon as I sent that, dots appeared.

Hey Sol! Totally fine. Looking forward to it. Have a great class.

I was beside myself. I was way past excited.

This was about to be the longest sixty minutes of my life.

forty-three

SOL

"Our mother was just a teenager. She named us, then left us at the hospital when she was discharged."

"Wow."

"Yeah. And honestly, I can't blame her. She was probably scared and alone. An unwed teen with two babies. One of us in the NICU, even. She likely didn't have much support. It must have been overwhelming for her."

I was talking to Samuel, and I had been for over an hour. Minutes passed like seconds.

And today, after years of nothing, I barely managed to get through the last thirty-six hundred seconds to talk to him. Speaking of seconds, I felt each one as they dragged on endlessly. I was overwhelmed. I could hardly wait for class to end so I could call my brother. I had my bag packed so we could all leave together. Then I headed back to my office and called my brother as soon as I could. I planned to go straight to HomeGrown from there. It was fine. I'm glad I drove today because I had a few clean shirts in my car. I could change and freshen up in the dressing room there.

When I finally called him, it rang once before he picked up. That one ring was enough for a lump to form in my throat, and I couldn't speak for a second or two. But Samuel seemed just as excited as I was, asking if we could connect on FaceTime. I agreed, of course, my heart pounding. I was so glad he asked. Not sure I may have. Then I saw him, my same face looking back at me.

Same eyes. Same jawline.

Samuel.

In real time. That shit was bananas.

He was smiling so wide. It reached his eyes.

And he laughed, and kept on laughing for a long time. It was a joyous belly laugh that was contagious. I laughed too. First nervously, then becoming more emotional laughing all the while.

And when we gathered ourselves, Sam said, "Yo! You look just like me! Damn this is crazy!" His wide grin remained.

"It is! Wild man." I finally found my voice.

"Yeah! I always felt so alone in the world. But look at you man! Look at you!"

I shook my head in awe of everything before me. "I didn't even know you existed. But… at the same time… It's as if I've missed you my entire life."

Yeah.

"Were you born April sixth?"

"Yeah. Just turned thirty-five."

"Me too! So, we're twin brothers."

Yeah. We talked about getting a DNA test just for principle. But. I felt it in every fiber of my being. Sam and I are twin brothers.

I had so many questions for him. And he shared. Asking me the same. I quickly discovered that we had starkly different childhoods.

"So, where'd you grow up?"

"Del Paso Heights. Graduated from Grant High School."

Grant High was on the north side of Sacramento, and Del Paso Heights... is the hood. He continued. "I went to a lot of different schools. Got expelled from a few. I was a troubled kid. Honestly. Fought a lot. No direction. No purpose. Just angry."

"I see. I don't get the feeling you're like that now. How did your parents get you to buckle down?"

"I didn't have parents. I was never adopted. Stayed in the system till I aged out."

"Oh man! I didn't realize…"

"It's alright man. Don't worry about it. Everything worked out for me."

I felt awful. Honestly, I really did. Sam never had a family of his own, and I can only imagine how tough that must have been.

"I was in over twenty foster homes. They ran out of places to put me. No one wanted to deal with me. Troubled teenage boys are the hardest to place. Eventually, I ended up at a group home. And that was my last stop. There was nowhere else for me to go from there. Thankfully, things were a little better, and I graduated on time."

"Love to hear that. Wow."

Perspective really is everything.

I wanted to take back everything I ever complained about, everything I griped over. Talking to Sam and hearing his story made my grievances seem so trivial. So insignificant. I at least had parents who loved me. They were overbearing and insufferable, sure, but they loved me like their own and would do anything for me. I had so much. He had no one. Shifting gears, I asked, "How'd you end up on the East Coast?"

"After I graduated high school, I joined the Navy and eventually got stationed out here."

"Are you still in?"

"No, I got out after five years."

"Thank you for your service."

We chuckled. "Thank you. Had I not joined the service, I'd be in prison or dead by now. It was one of the best things I could have done… leaving was probably the second-best thing I could have done."

I laughed at that.

"You stayed out there. You like the East Coast?"

"I love it. The change up. It's a lot different. Ever been out this way?"

"Matter of fact, I have. I was in Baltimore about two years ago as a guest lecturer in residence for the summer terms at Coppin State."

"Coppin? That's like thirty minutes from me!"

"Wow! I can't believe we were so close to each other. I could've walked by you in the grocery store or at the gym."

"No kidding! You were here the whole summer?"

"Yeah. Just about. And right before I left, they had a summer concert series, and I was on stage with my sax."

"You're a cold musician, man! I devoured your IG!" Sam told me.

"You're a cold DJ! And don't act like you can't play that piano, man! You don't have much on your IG, but I saw what I needed to!"

We laughed.

"How long have you been playing?" He asked.

"Hmm. Piano since about high school. I learned violin as a child. I still play it on occasion. Then picked up the alto sax in junior high. Acoustic, I started around twenty."

"You play all those well?"

"I'm probably best at violin. Just because I played it the longest."

"That's dope man."

"You play other instruments aside from the keys?"

"Yeah, percussion. That's probably my favorite. Got a cool set. Play a little trumpet. That was my first instrument."

"Nice." I smiled, loving everything we had in common.

"Yeah. Imagine that. We're both musicians."

"Yeah. And you're a teacher too?"

"Part time. Yeah. I teach piano at a music school. Something I enjoy doing on the side. I teach people of all ages. Solomon, it's dope that you're a professor. *A doctor.*"

"Thank you. Music is my first love."

"I get it. Music has been good to me, too."

A beat. "Can you sing?" I asked.

"Can you?"

"I asked you first, bro!" I laughed.

Sam cackled.

"I can sing. But I don't. Not really. Do you?"

"Not a lot. Been singing much more lately, though," I shared.

"Oh yeah? Tell me about her."

"Get out of here man!"

We cackled all over again. And I told him about India. Told him how special she is. How much my life has changed since knowing her. And told him she encouraged me to keep searching for him. Yeah.

"You're married. Tell me about your wife."

He smiled. "She's pretty dope, man. My prime rib. Not my spare rib!" We both cackled. "I met her at a football game. Morgan versus Bowie. I was with my boys. She was with her friends. They walked past me, and I noticed her immediately. Stopped me in my tracks."

I nodded, smiling myself. I understood. Precisely.

"Nice. How long have you been married?"

He smiled wide again. No. Much wider than last time. "Eight years. She's been the best thing to happen to me. And she made me a father. Gave me a beautiful little girl. Everything changed for me after that."

"Wow. I love that for you, man."

"Thank you. Any kids?"

"Not yet. But I wouldn't mind it." A beat. I asked him, "Did you go to an HBCU?"

"Morgan."

"Home of the *Magnificent Marching Machine*. Legendary."

"Yes sir! My wife went to Bowie. Twice. She's very proud of her alma mater. I rep both."

"That's what a good husband does. Bowie State. *Symphony of Soul.*"

Sam chuckled. "What you know about all that Cali boy?"

I laughed too. "When I was at Coppin, teaching music, I may have picked up a thing or two."

We laughed.

"Did you go to an HBCU?" Sam asked.

"I didn't. Wish I had. I earned my undergraduate degree at UCLA and then chose Berkeley for my master's and doctorate. Berkeley has a world-class ethnomusicology program. It would have taken some serious convincing to go anywhere else."

"I hear you. Those are great schools, Sol!"

"Thank you."

I talked with Sam until I had to leave. And if it weren't for the show at HomeGrown, I'd have kept talking to him. I knew I needed to let him go anyway, given the three-hour time difference. We had plans to catch up again soon. And once our DNA was confirmed, we'd meet each other. Sam hadn't been back to the West Coast since he left nearly eighteen years ago, but said he was willing to come out this way. Honestly, though, I'd rather visit him. He has a family I'd love to meet, and I planned to ask India to come with me. I need her with me. Besides, she's never been to the East Coast, and I'd love to take her there.

And Sam shared all he knew about our origins. He knew everything I didn't. We were born to teenage parents. And he knew we were abandoned at days old. It turned out that Sam was the smaller twin and needed more time and more care, so he was in the NICU for several weeks.

I was amazed and fascinated by Samuel. He's been through so much, never adopted, aging out of the system with no family to call his own. I was so proud of him. He made a life for himself despite all the odds stacked against him. He seems to be a great person with a great heart, a good head on his shoulders, and a beautiful family he beamed about.

I loved talking to him. It was a feeling I'd never known. He's so chill. So dope. Someone I'd want to be friends with. And the fact that he's my brother made me feel really good inside. I felt so refreshed. So excited to get to know him better and meet him.

Sam and I discovered so many commonalities. But we're pretty different at the same time. Off rip, I noticed that Sam was considerably more outgoing than I am. I'm much more reserved. We balance each other out, that's for sure.

And he's been searching for me too. He knew he was born a twin, but he couldn't find me. He'd searched for me. I told him that my student saw him last month in Atlanta and reached out to me. Yeah, it was nothing but God, in His infinite wisdom and divine timing, who led us to each other.

I was happy to find out that Sam is a man of faith too.

Yup. All kinds of gratitude.

♪❤♫❤♪

"Well, hello there! Welcome to King Tattoo and Piercing!"

The petite, light-brown woman greeted me enthusiastically as I approached the host desk. She didn't hide her flirtation either.

I'd say she's in her early thirties. Very well put together and dressed borderline provocatively.

She's bad. I'll admit that. But no. Hell no.

No way.

I have a woman. A woman who doesn't compare. In a class all her own.

And I was here to ensure she was left alone.

"What brings you in?" she asked, flirty. "Here for a piercing? I'm the only piercer here. I can take care of you. If you want ink, I can check and see who's available depending on what you want to get done today." She spoke confidently, her voice alluring.

And a sexual energy seeped from her pores.

That shit flowed.

Percolated. Loudly. It was loud as hell.

I didn't know her from a can of paint, but it was the most evident thing about her vibe.

Unmistakable.

Women try to play like they're not down for shit, but men know what's up. Instantly. Not that it mattered. Because it sure the fuck didn't. I'm in love with India Rampersaud. She's my impetus for coming in here today.

When I said nothing, the young lady sashayed around the host desk, stopping in front of me. Much closer than necessary.

Facing me, even though I didn't turn to face her. Nope. I hadn't moved.

I knew her type.

She was the type of woman to get precisely what she wanted from any man who fell for the allure of an attractive woman. There's a sucker born every minute, too. Namely, thirsty men who didn't get attention from attractive women. A man like that would be a goner fucking around with her.

But she isn't the type of woman who'd get my attention. She isn't my type. Period. Not even a little bit. I bet she got all kinds of shit out of the men who started stumbling and tripping over their tongues dealing with her. Irresponsible Uncles. If I were with that shit, she'd handle me like putty in her hands.

But I wasn't here for her.

Still facing the host desk, I got straight to it.

"I need to speak with Kingston regarding a business matter. Is he available?"

Seemingly disarmed and clearly embarrassed, she quickly took a few steps back. "Oh! I didn't realize you were here for business. I'm Fatima. Co-owner," she offered. "King should be in his office. I can go back and check." She scurried toward the back of the shop.

"Appreciate it."

I took a moment to look around.

It was nice in here. Very nice. Modern. Bright. Dope golden light fixtures and stylish décor. I loved the surround-sound system blasting hip-hop music.

The music layered in was the buzzing of the machines and the soft chatter of a few patrons. It wasn't slow, but not super busy either. I'm glad the place wasn't too busy. I wasn't trying to embarrass anyone. Just needed to set a few things straight. After all, he hadn't attempted to take India's dignity in front of anyone. Which low-key made me angrier the more I thought about it. He had her in his office, disarmed and unassuming. Trusting him in an enclosed space where she was alone and vulnerable.

I wondered what would have happened if she hadn't managed to get out of there. But she did. Unscathed. And thank God she did. I didn't owe this fool any kind of courtesy either.

"Here he is." The woman I now knew as Fatima spoke. I could hear them approaching me from behind. "What did you say your name was?"

I turned to face a dark-skinned gentleman. He was long and lean, but muscular. Tatted all over. I could see it crawling up his neck. And out of his sleeves. The woman was more than a foot shorter than he was as she stood beside him.

"I didn't." I stood to my full height, shoulders back.

Yeah. He was tall. But I had him by a few inches.

He cut his eyes instantly. "I know you or something?" His tone was as cold as ice. That was fine.

"You're about to." He raised his brows. It was subtle, but I caught it. "I'll make this quick. India Rampersaud won't be coming back here." His demeanor shifted. Not so subtle that time. And that was fine too. "She's not interested in anything more with you. Please don't attempt to contact her again. If you see her on the streets, go the other way. Don't look at her. Don't even think about her." I reached into my pocket and retrieved an envelope. "Here's your money." I placed it on the host desk beside me. "This ends right here, right now. If it doesn't, you'll have bigger problems."

I didn't wait for a rebuttal because frankly, I didn't give a fuck what he had to say.

With nothing more to add, I turned to leave.

♪♥♫♥♪

I got in from HomeGrown exhausted. It was about nine-thirty in the evening.

We had a great show, but I was wiped out.

I called India before I left, and we talked on my way home. I told her all about my conversation with Sam, and she was so excited for me. When I asked her to come with me to meet him, she agreed immediately. I told her I'd take a quick shower and call her back.

I placed my bag on the bench near my front door, then sat down and took off my shoes. I had a stack of mail on this table that I needed to sort through. I didn't usually let it pile up too much, since most of it was junk anyway. Most of my bills were sent electronically. For anything else important, I would address it right away and wouldn't even leave it in this pile.

I remembered I had a few pieces of mail from my box at Sac City. Snail mail isn't as common these days, but I still received correspondence there now and then.

I reached into my bag to grab the three envelopes, quickly scanning them. One was an invitation to contribute to an academic journal. I'd look at that more closely later. I receive those often, and I consider each one. Though it's time-consuming and sometimes daunting, I try to contribute to academic journals as often as I can. Working with fellow researchers and fostering meaningful collaborations are essential to me, especially in music.

Another was an invitation to a two-day music workshop hosted at American River College. ARC is a sister college in the same district as Sacramento City. The entire department was invited to offer a hands-on learning experience as clinicians. I'd have to check my schedule and see if I could commit to that.

The third envelope halted my movements.

It was from an international university. Addressed to me.

Ruth Pearl Batiste School of Music
Caribbean Conservatory at the University of Montreal
Office of the Dean

Dr. Solomon Avery
Adjunct Professor, Department of Music
Sacramento City College

Dear Dr. Avery
The search committee was deeply impressed by your teaching philosophy,
your scholarship in diasporic sound traditions, and your commitment to access

*and equity in music education. We believe your presence at **Ruth Pearl Batiste School of Music** will enrich our program and challenge our students to approach music with deeper awareness, curiosity, and intention.*

*It is my distinct pleasure to formally offer you the position of **Assistant Professor of Music (Tenure Track)** in the Division of Contemporary Music. Your reputation as an educator, composer, and community-centered musician precedes you.*

The position includes:

A starting salary of CAD 122,000 annually, plus full benefits

A CAD 10,000 research and creative activity fund (renewable)

A reduced course load in your first year to support your transition and creative work

Relocation assistance and housing allowance if needed

*This appointment is contingent upon final approval by the university's Board of Trustees and the completion of standard background checks. A formal contract will be issued upon acceptance of this offer. We kindly ask for your response by **Aug 1.***

*We sincerely hope you will join us in shaping the future of music and musical thought at **Ruth Pearl Batiste School of Music**. Please don't hesitate to reach out with any questions.*

Best,

Dr. Calvin Lymos

Dean, Ruth Pearl Batiste School of Music

Caribbean Conservatory at the University of Montreal

I stared at the letter for what felt like forever and read over it many times, just to make sure what I read was really what I thought I read.

What the hell. I hadn't applied to this university, but I'd heard of it. It was a well-known music school, the largest in Canada.

Canada.

That Canada.

Yeah. I'd read it a few times, and for some reason, it still didn't seem real.

They want me. My name was at the top. Right there in black and white.

I was extremely humbled by that.

And the offer was almost impossible to refuse. Almost.

A tenure track. Full benefits. Renewable research funds.

I sat back on the bench, breathing in and out, letting the weight of this settle some.

What a day I've had. God really has a sense of humor. This letter in my hand encompasses everything people in my position work towards. For years. It was the very thing my dean has been nudging me towards.

And something my parents have invested in since I was a child. My private music lessons. My private education. Learning French fluently. I would be qualified to teach in English and French. Montreal has a huge French-speaking population.

It all seemed worth it now. Being the only black kid in a sea of faces, nearly everywhere I dwelled. The opportunity to teach at an international university on a tenure track was a dream come true.

And. I should be ecstatic.

And I am.

But.

My students at Sac City. They need me. And I need them. They're a part of my purpose. They came to class hungry to learn. They were honest, keeping me sharp with their questions and coming to class to better their circumstances, not for prestige. These students have my heart.

But.

Caribbean Conservatory at the University of Montreal.

They want me.

Me.

I closed my eyes.

This wasn't the first time I'd been approached. I didn't think it would be the last. But. I've never received anything that seriously had me considering, actually taking the offer. I liked it here. The freedom and the pace of it all. My simple life. Biking to campus. The familiar faces. The community feel. I could breathe. I could teach classes in the daytime and head to HomeGrown to jam in the evening.

HomeGrown.

I'd be leaving Smoke.

But this was a once-in-a-lifetime opportunity.

I looked at my phone. India was on my lock screen. I love this picture of her. It was a candid shot of her laughing at something, her chin up, eyes squinted. Her hair wild.

She's my favorite song.

I exhaled.

I had a lot to think about. I had decisions to make.

All of which considered her.

forty-four

INDIA

"You can dance your ass off, Belle. I had no idea."

"I try." I shrugged, giving Sol a flirty grin as I took a sip of my pineapple mango white sangria.

"Yeah, you surprised the hell out of me working your hips like that. Those were dancehall moves." He gave me a pointed nod, drinking from his brandy and Coke. "Caribbean, proud, that's for sure."

Sol and I were enjoying dinner and drinks at a place called *Streetlights*. They had a DJ spinning some of the best music I've heard in a while.

Sol and I chilled. Had dinner and a few drinks. And grooved to the music. I didn't plan on dancing, but when the DJ played "Go Go Wine" by Vybz Kartel, I couldn't resist. This was a dancehall throwback with an infectious hook, and when this came on, you didn't sit through it. Like ever. So, I got up to dance and asked Sol to join me. I'm glad he didn't leave me hanging.

"What you know about dancehall?" I asked him. Teasing.

"I been around."

We laughed.

Now I was curious. "Been around where?"

"I traveled a lot during my doctorate, remember. I spent a lot of time in the Caribbean and in the club spaces. Seen it with my own two eyes. Dancehall is on another level entirely. Especially in the Caribbean."

"Yeah. You're right about that." I took another sip of my sangria, loving how it had just the right sweetness. Cool and refreshing after dancing for a while. "You're not a bad dancer yourself. You surprised the hell out of me, too."

Sol chuckled. Taking a page from my book, "I try."

My smile was easy. With Solomon, they always were. "I still can't believe I've never been here. I'd never even seen this place. Thanks for bringing me here."

He smiled too. "It's a tiny place. A lot of people don't know it's here. But I love these spots. Intimate setting. No room for a large crowd."

This little jazz club, Streetlights, was literally five minutes from my house, on the corner of Broadway and Seventeenth. Sol said he played here now and then. Sometimes solo, sometimes with another band. They had a gig coming up, and he'd be sure to give me details. I'm excited to hear them.

I got a text from Sol earlier, asking if he could take me out. Spontaneously.

Which I loved. It was so sweet and right on time.

Music Man: You free tonight? I need my favorite artist's opinion on something.

A moment later, another text came in.

Music Man: Also just want to see you.

Me: Yes I'm free. And I want to see you too baby. I always want to see you. When are you coming?

Yeah. I wanted to see him too.

I always want to see him.

He didn't reply, but called me instead.

"Streetlights. It's right up the road from you. And I'll need your opinion."

"On what?"

"This place is slept on, but in my humble opinion, they have the best barbecue in Sac. Wanna know what you think. Oh wait…will you be having meat tonight?"

I giggled. "Oh yes! That's going to hit the spot!"

"Excellent. I can pick you up around six. How's that baby?"

"Sounds lovely." I offered. Already sold. I love barbecue. Any barbecue. Caribbean barbecue. Korean. Mongolian. But the kind you'll find at a cookout is my favorite. I don't get to enjoy it as much. I couldn't wait either.

And I loved seeing Sol. Anytime I could. I really loved that.

He asked me to pack a bag too. Telling me he wanted to keep me for the night. And I readily agreed to that, too.

We each ordered a barbecue platter. It came with two meats, three sides, and a drink. I got chicken wings as both of my meats. On the side, macaroni and cheese, greens, and potato salad. Sol got ribs, a hot link, macaroni and cheese, greens, and spaghetti.

We also ordered drinks from the bar. And we danced.

We'd been having such a great time, too. I loved this place, and I planned to come back. The food was so good. I'd have to get some for Ma and Daddy to try soon.

"You play here too in another band? Sol, when do you sleep?" I lightly tittered.

He smiled at that. "I get plenty of sleep. I could ask you the same question, Belle."

"Touché."

"I'm so glad you could come here with me and enjoy your-self."

"Me too baby."

Yeah. Sol was being modest, but he can dance too. He stayed close to me; my hips nestled into his like a big spoon and a little spoon. And he grooved with me. Moved with me. Held me tight, but I was free to move. And. Damn. He smelled grown, and he looked sexy, and it immediately got me going. He wore all black. A loser fitting black button-up. His arms were out, revealing his muscles and ink. Black slacks.

When we returned to our table, Sol gently took my hand into his and didn't let it go. Not that I wanted him to. Our fingers were threaded now and tangled and warm.

When we arrived earlier, I took a look around, and it was pre-cisely as Sol had described.

There was a decent-sized crowd. A lot of couples. Dimly lit.

Streetlights is shabby but clean and comfortable. And. There was something charming about the place. A homey feeling. Like you knew you'd get good food and have a good time.

There were only a few tables. Maybe eight. Mini lanterns were at the center of each table. Closer to the stage where we were sitting, there were a few sweetheart tables. A bar at the farthest end. A few tall tables near there. A couple of pool tables as well.

"Can I get you anything more, sweetheart?" I looked to my right at the middle-aged black woman wearing a warm smile, perhaps in her early fifties. She'd been taking care of us tonight. "Maybe some dessert? We have banana pudding, peach cobbler, red velvet cake, lemon pound cake, and 7-Up cake."

She looked at me, then at Sol, and then back to me, giving me a wink.

"Feel free to order something. Anything." Sol told me.

"Thank you." I thought it over for a moment. I was very full off my barbecue, which I hadn't even finished. I'd be packing it up to go. But I appreciated the gesture.

I appreciated everything about Sol.

"Maybe we can get something to share?"

"Sure. Whatever you want." Sol offered.

I looked back at the woman; she'd given Sol a knowing expression.

"Which one do you suggest, ma'am?"

"Too young to be anyone's ma'am! Call me Auntie Machel. Or Auntie." She winked again.

Sol and I chuckled at that.

"Banana pudding is my favorite. You'll enjoy that."

"Perfect. We'll take one to share, please."

"I'll put that in for you right now."

"She's funny. And so sweet."

"Oh yeah. Auntie is amazing. She's been here for as long as I can remember. Treating everyone like family. Her father opened this place when she was just a kid. She told me investors have approached her over the years to buy the place. Throwing her ridiculous amounts of money to walk away, but she won't hear it. And I'm so glad. This place would lose its charm if it's commercialized."

"It totally would." It wasn't fancy, but that's what gave it that something.

That's the thing too. This portion of Oak Park off Broadway was going through intense gentrification. Both the residents and commercial businesses. My parents were approached about selling our home, too. But they've been steadfast. I commend Auntie Machel for staying put. I know those offers are enticing.

Sol kissed my hand. The one he never let go of. And I was okay with that. The kiss, and that my hand was still securely in his.

"Thank you for coming out. You're a sight to behold."

"Thank you, baby. I'm glad I could be here with you. I love being with you."

I was wearing a bright marigold halter dress. It was long and sleek, and he was right. Very sexy. I had my shoulders out. And damn proud of myself. Once upon a time, I was so insecure about my shoulders. I never wanted to expose them because I was teased relentlessly for them. They're thin and pointy but broad as hell. Kids would call me "coat hanger." Mean shit like that. I also have a long ass neck, got teased about that too. "You look great yourself," I replied.

"Appreciate you." He kissed my hand again. The most tender of the last three he'd sweetly planted, and my heart squeezed. Sol had been kissing my hand all night.

And. The fact that PG hand kisses could have this effect on me was wild. Who knew. But it was no wonder. Sol's been doing his thing, handling me. Spoiling me. Making me feel lighter. Taken care of. Loved and appreciated.

And. I'd felt an immense relief now that I'd told him everything. And I mean everything. And I hated that it needed to come to that for me to be transparent. But we were starting fresh, and I wasn't going to let that happen again. Ever. Next time, I would tell him first. Always.

Sol didn't deserve anything less than that.

But damn. My man's been taking such good care of me.

We got the car back from the shop a few days ago, after the mechanic kept it for about a week. It was good as new when we got it back. Better actually. A new transmission. New spark plugs. New brakes, new rotors, new tires. The back window was back on track and in working order. The AC blew cool air as soon as we turned it on. Even the outside. The sunspots were touched up. It was washed, waxed, and detailed inside.

I swear she shone like it was new again. His friend did excellent work. She ran smoother than she had in a long time. And the craziest part? Sol took care of all of that for us. Yup. All that work done to get the car running smoothly again didn't cost us a penny. We were so appreciative. I was nearly in tears.

And then Sol said that I could keep driving the Jetta and that he wasn't in any hurry to get it back. Telling me I was free to use it and that he didn't need it, except when we wanted to take the bikes somewhere. Yeah.

"This DJ is hot!" I offered a moment later. He'd been playing everything. Hip Hop. R&B. Rap. Reggae. Afrobeats.

"Yeah, he is."

Eventually, our banana pudding came out. it was already in a to-go container for us. Auntie knew we may not have much beyond a taste of it. She was right. A small bite was all I could handle, but it was delicious!

"You know. I was thinking…"

I looked up at Sol expectantly.

"They have an open mic here. Maybe we can come check it out."

"Sure! Like Poetry?"

He nodded. "People sing too. I was thinking *we* could sign up to perform?"

My brows knitted instantly.

"I'm no singer or poet, Sol!"

He chuckled easy. "Relax, Artist Girl." He squeezed my hand gently. "I was thinking, you could paint while I play music on my acoustic."

I smiled as I thought about it. "Yeah. That would be dope!" I'd love to do that. We've done it a few times already in my art shed. And Sol and I have an ethereal chemistry.

"Yeah, it would be. "

"Let's do it!" I gushed eagerly. Giddy with excitement all of a sudden.

"Someone's anxious!" He chuckled again. "I'll check the schedule and see when the next one is."

"Sounds good."

♪♥♫♥♪

"No touching."

Sol cackled.

"You aren't playing fair."

We got in from Streetlights, and after we were showered, we got ready for bed.

Honestly, though, getting dressed was a waste of time. We'd rid ourselves of our night clothes almost as soon as we put them on. Now. Right now… both of us were naked from head to toe.

"And you are? You've done nothing but show off. Spoiling me. Taking care of me. It's your turn, baby."

"My turn?"

"Yeah."

Sol was lying on his back. I'd straddled him for the past several minutes, I had his hard dick in my hand. And he was hard. *So fucking hard.* Stiff as a steel pipe.

"I'm pleasing you, baby. Taking good care of my man for taking such good care of me." I continued jerking him. Both hands. "You are hard, baby."

"You do that to me." He groaned.

"You like this baby?"

"I sure do. *Mmmm…fuck.* Yeah, I like that."

I moved down and took his hardness into my mouth. He growled at that. Using both hands, I twisted and pulled as I continued sucking. Then I felt his hands gently cradle my face. I brought my eyes up, and his were already trained on me. Then slowly, I removed his dick from my mouth.

"Nope. I said no touching."

"Oooh, I don't know if I like this game."

"Who said it's a game?"

He chuckled, moaning too. "You're playing with me, baby."

440

"Put your hands behind your head." He did. "You just enjoy right now." I resumed licking him, sucking him, and trailing my tongue all over his shaft.

He groaned again, "Show me something, Indie… I like everything you do to me. Belle, you are so fucking sexy… sucking my dick like that."

"Mmm… I like it too." Yeah. I sucked him for a good while.

"I want you inside of me, baby," I murmured. "…Gonna climb on top of you, okay."

"Go head baby."

Leaving my feet flat, I eased down onto him. Slow. Sol had hella girth. He's a shower and a grower. He stretched me out as I lowered myself, and both of us sighed in contented relief. And for a minute, I didn't move. I needed to adjust. Sol stretched me out, filling me like only he could, and I'd never been on top like this before, with my feet flat. It's definitely deeper this way. I reached for his hands, bringing them around me, and in seconds, Sol's hands were firmly holding my hips. Then. Finally. I began a slow ride.

And Sol started meeting me upward. Stroke for stroke. "This so good, baby. *Mmm*."

"Hell yeah, it is." I ground into him, working my hips slowly.

"You good baby?" Sol's arms came around my waist. Anchoring me tighter. Still meeting me for each stroke.

Yeah… just…" I threw my head back, kept gyrating my hips, and slowly rode myself into oblivion.

He chuckled deep at that. "Go head, baby, get what you need."

I picked up the pace, just slightly, my feet still planted. This was a great tempo for what we needed to accomplish.

"*Fuck Indie…*"

"You feel so good," I managed to tell him. I was still swirling my hips. My head still back. My fingers threaded in my hair.

"*Mmmhmm*… that's beautiful, baby… look at you."

When I woke up the next morning, Sol was kissing my forehead. He had to head to campus but whispered that he'd call me when he was done and told me to go back to sleep. Telling me I could stay as long as I wanted.

And I did. I slept another hour or so. Took a shower. My body ached in the best way, and the hot water helped. I tidied up the place. Then I locked everything before I headed out. I had lunch plans with Destiney, and I smiled the whole drive.

With Sol I felt so sure. I knew I wanted to continue building this thing we'd been building. I'm so glad Sol wants that too. And even though there were a few things we still hadn't talked about, I just felt sure.

That it would all work itself out.

Sol loved me through everything I was still trying to figure out. Things with Ma and Daddy could be unpredictable, but Sol didn't demand anything more than what I could offer. He loved me through it.

His words and his actions continued to solidify my certainty in him and in us. I was finally beginning to let all of my self-doubts go. I hadn't even realized when it happened. But. Sol made it so easy. I doubted so many things before him. I doubted that I was deserving of a lasting love. I doubted that I could find that love. I doubted I had room in all my mess and all my chaos to maintain it. Yeah. Sol dispelled all my self-doubt by speaking intentionally. Honestly. Meaning every word he said to me. And any quiet between us was full of truth and trust.

And. Now that I've experienced something real… I wasn't afraid to hold on to it. I'd been waiting, and it was here now. Finally. I wasn't running from the possibility of anything with him anymore. I'd left all my caution to the wind. Yeah. I smiled all the way to the restaurant, thinking about how sweet things are with Sol. When we're together, there's a softness he has with me. I love the way he handles me. I love our quiet moments together. We're quite affectionate. I'm always touching him, and he doesn't mind at all. I love it when our eye contact lingers. I love holding hands. I love his kisses. Love kissing him.

"Girl, you are glowing! You got some before you came! Didn't you?"

I laughed that off. Partly embarrassed, but I didn't deny it.

Destiney didn't need me to. She carried on, "*Best!* You're looking moisturized, hydrated, and happy."

"Oh my gosh." I shook my head, laughing. Couldn't help myself.

I didn't gush or overexplain. Destiney already knew.

I took my seat in the booth across from her. She was already seated, sipping from a teacup.

"Hey girl, hey! I already ordered. I needed them to get that going as soon as possible. Panang curry for you, spicy eggplant basil for me. And of course, a side of mango sticky rice. You know I got you."

We'd met at our favorite Thai spot. It was in South Sac, not far from where Destiney grew up. A little place off Fruitridge Road. We've been coming here for a few years. The food here is bomb! And not overly expensive. And you get a lot for your money. More bang for your buck. Some places were so outta pocket. Overcharging for appetizer portions.

"Yeah, you're thoughtful like that. Thank you Best! And good to see you. You look great. You're the one glowing!" Destiney had begun to show a bit more, and her belly was rounding out beautifully.

"Thank you! You look all floaty. Like you've been up in the clouds."

"I sure have been!" I giggled low. Sitting back in the booth, getting comfortable. I looked off for a moment. This place had a moderate lunch crowd. There was low music playing. I couldn't wait for my food.

I love the fragrant smells in Thai restaurants. I love Thai food, period.

"Best. Sol's been… amazing." I continued. "I thought I was in love before, but this is… I can't explain it. And he's been taking such care of me. I told him about everything at the shop. About the money. Everything. He told me not to worry about it. To consider it handled. And I trust him. Implicitly. I've never felt so safe before."

Destiney smiled wide. "That's what it's supposed to feel like. Passion with protection. Desire with care."

"Yeah. That about sums it up." I nodded slowly, looking off again. "And. It seems I'm learning myself all over again. With him, I've been able to let go of so many things and just exist for once."

"That's love, Best. So much more than the butterflies. I'm so happy for you!"

"Thank you. He met my parents. They adore him Des. Oh my gosh."

She gushed at that. "Of course they do! Sol's such a great guy."

"Yeah. He helped us get the car running again. Took care of everything."

Destiney nodded her eyebrows high.

"Oh, and he had me order my equipment on his laptop." I laughed. "Had me do it right in front of him." We laughed. "Everything should be arriving soon. But he wasn't playing around this time. He wanted to ensure I have my own shit. And he insisted I got everything I wanted. Not just the things I needed. And even though it was awkward, Sol was so sweet about it."

Destiney nodded slow. Smiling all the while. "That's so sweet! Have you found another shop? How close are you to getting your license?" She sipped again from her cup of mint tea. She ordered me a cup as well, and I began to drink mine.

"Not far. And I did find a shop that looks promising. I talked to the owner yesterday. She seems cool. She asked me to stop by when I can. I'll probably go in first thing tomorrow."

"I'm sure that'll go well, but let me know. I'm just glad you're no longer at King's."

"Same." I nodded. "So glad that's over with." I'd brought Mala up to speed about everything, too. She felt just like we did. Yeah. So glad that was done.

When our food came out, we dug in immediately. We had about an hour until we needed to be at a Zaffre meeting.

"I hope I can meet Sol's parents soon. I wonder if they'll be at the benefit next weekend." My Panang curry was delicious. A golden color with tofu and veggies. Medium spicy, full of flavor, taste, and textures. I had vegetable fried rice on the side. I love Thai-style curries, and Panang is my very favorite. I love the onions, the bell peppers, and the coconut peanut sauce. Gave it the perfect sweetness, which married so well with the warm aromatic spices. I needed to learn how to make this.

"They may be." In addition to her basil eggplant, Destiney also ordered drunken noodles. She hadn't mentioned that. I'd let her rock. I wouldn't give her a hard time, even though it was always in jest.

And I planned to treat her to lunch this time. I was so glad to be able to do that. Sol had been handing me cash here and there. I mentioned Destiney and I had lunch plans, and he gave me money. Saying it was his treat. But he gave me much more than I needed. I'm sure that was by design.

"Yeah. I hope so."

"I'm sure you'll meet them soon."

"You think they'll like me?" I asked. Somehow, that left my lips without permission. And. I wasn't sure how I felt about that. I don't think the thought ever crossed my mind until now. But it had for some reason.

"Of course they will, Best." Destiney offered. She'd stilled her movements. Mid chew even. "Why wouldn't they?" She asked with care.

I shrugged but said nothing.

"Indie. Don't do that. What's not to like? You, my friend, are *amazing*. And you've made their son so happy. Of course, they'll like you. They'll love you."

I nodded. And smiled too. Still saying nothing.

After a moment, "I get it. Girl! I was *terrified* of meeting Micah's parents. But not because I didn't think they wouldn't like me." She paused for a moment. "Indie." When I met her eyes, she said, "You're a good person. You're sweet. You're warm. You've got great energy. Parents have discernment, and they'll see that. You'll do just fine. His parents will adore you, Indie."

"Thank you." I smiled at that.

Destiney smiled too. "You're so welcome, Best."

We ate in silence for a moment longer.

"And thank you for ensuring I wasn't an idiot. To think I could have missed out on this." I laughed. "After all of that. After everything… here I am. *So freaking in love.*" I laughed again. I couldn't help myself. "Sol and I couldn't have met if not for you and Micah. And I've loved watching you and Micah. And now there's this precious little one coming. I'm so happy for you, too. It's all been so beautiful."

"You trying to make me cry?" She teased. "I'm pregnant!"

We laughed. Both of us emotional for different reasons. And I loved that.

Then Destiney said, "Well. Now you get your own kind of beautiful."

And. I liked that.

A lot.

forty-five

SOL

"I got something in the mail. Day before yesterday."

My father looked over at me. His brows high. "A bill or a blessing?"

We both tittered. He always landed those, right on time.

I was at my parents' house. First time I'd been here in a while. Several weeks. Several.

I arrived unannounced. But I'd never had to call first. I had a key to my childhood home, and I could come and go as I pleased. When I arrived, only my father was home. He told me that my mother was out with my aunt. She'd only just left shortly before I arrived, and she was expected to be out for a while. They had spa appointments and lunch plans, and knowing them, maybe some shopping.

Dad and I were sitting in their sunroom. It was a lovely early spring afternoon. The bright sunlight slanted across their pristinely manicured back lawn.

My father was in his chair. Comfortable. Had a glass of scotch. His go-to. A book beside him. He reads quite a bit, namely anything non-fiction, law, and justice. He's got quite a collection of law books. Though my father has been retired for a few years now, he still contributes legal writing and thought pieces on occasion. Remaining abreast and adhering to ethical practices, along with honesty and integrity, are vital in legal writing. One mustn't omit any important facts or misrepresent anything.

I'd been here for close to an hour. It was nice to see him. We'd still been speaking on the telephone regularly, but he hadn't given me the third degree about my mother. He hadn't been relaying any messages either. I'd been asking about her, still, and he was glad to tell me she was doing okay. Mostly. I asked about her today. My father and I caught up on a few things. Neutral topics mostly. And I'd been holding the news.

Both sets of news. Samuel and the international offer. I'd kept Micah up to speed. Of course. But. I hadn't shared either of these things with my father. And. I guess I didn't know why. Not really. With Sam, maybe I was waiting for things to be official first. Which. I suppose it made sense. Despite my feeling like that was only a formality.

But this stuff with the university. I think I was letting it breathe. Maybe balancing the weight of it all on my own. Sharing it with him would mean I was considering it. And I am.

But I was considering *her* too. My angel. My Belle. My Arist Girl. My favorite song.

I wanted to accept. And. I wanted her to go with me.

And telling her this… I knew things would get complicated. I didn't have to tell her to know that. She wouldn't want to leave her parents. I wouldn't expect her to. Nor would I want that for any of them. But news like this wasn't something you sit on long. You'd share it, especially with my father.

The Honorable Leonard Avery.

I cleared my throat. Sitting forward in my chair. I sat right beside him. I put my elbows on my knees. Then I chuckled when I thought about it. "A little of both. Maybe."

"Oh?"

I waited a moment.

"I received an offer from a university in Montreal, Canada. Full-time faculty. Tenure track."

That got my father's attention. Just like I knew it would.

He sat up for himself now. Moved his glass of scotch to the small table beside him. *"Canada?"* He said that slowly, as if he hadn't heard me correctly.

I nodded. Saying nothing.

"That's incredible son! That's what you've worked toward. All these years. And you'd establish a legacy. You'd be set."

Nodding again, I said, "I know."

"You're thinking about accepting?" Though posed like one, it wasn't really a question. My father knew me. I wouldn't have told him if I weren't.

I took a heavy breath. "That's the part I'm trying to figure out."

My father said nothing. But I could see him looking at me in his peripheral vision. Studying me. Which was his M.O., he wasn't a man of many words. He was more of an observer. Quite selective about what to speak on. Not the most expressive either. He leaned back in his chair again.

After a long moment, "One thing about you, Solomon… you've never been the type to chase something simply because it shines. You're hesitating." He paused. "If you're hesitating, there's a reason."

"There's a few reasons if I'm honest."

My father gave me space. Saying nothing. Nodding slowly, encouraging me to continue.

"I'm so passionate about what I'm doing now. My students. The pace. I have room for my other passion projects as well."

My father nodded again. "You've always spoken in such esteem about community college."

"There will be a significant difference. In the setting. With the students. The administration. But at the university, so many doors will open. I'll have funding, and I can do research. Build something long-term, like you said. Legacy."

Interestingly, *'legacy' in this context sounded like a good* thing.

He nodded once. Sipped is scotch again. Surprising me, he posed, "And what about your sweetheart?"

And I smiled at that. Because of course I would.

"India is a big part of why I haven't jumped already." My smile was faint now. "Her life is here. Her parents. The community she's a part of. Her art. Her closest friends. She's deeply rooted."

Gently, my father said, "Your heart is deeply rooted in her."

"Yeah." I returned immediately.

"Well, son. Whatever you decide, it must be something you can live with. Tomorrow. Ten years from now, you want to wake up every day free of regret. If Montreal is what you want, we'll celebrate that. If it isn't, we'll still be proud of you, son. But Solomon. Don't hold yourself back. You're destined for greatness, and you have so much to offer. Too much to play small." He spoke with calm certainty. "Whatever decision you make, make it with both hands."

As I let my father's words settle, I don't think I realized how much I needed to hear them. And that was just like my father. He spoke his own language. He had his own idioms. But they always worked. They always made sense. And I understood precisely what he meant. I'm so glad I came here and shared this. I was so grateful for his insight. His wisdom. And our relationship.

"Thank you, Dad."

I spent another hour or so with my father, and when I left later that afternoon, I thought about something. I wanted to speak with my mother again. Meeting India's parents made me realize that. We had a different dynamic than she did with her parents. Sure. But we had a good relationship. I thought about Sam not having any parents at all. And. I was more compelled to fix this.

I'd already apologized to my mother. I'd already moved past that. I'd already forgiven her, despite her not apologizing. But I realized she was insistent that I was the one who needed to fix it. And, though I didn't agree with that, for the sake of our relationship, I was willing to reach across the aisle. I wanted to call a truce. Address things. Talk through them. Smooth things over. I would even come to Sunday dinner again. And after our conversation. I would be glad to bring India to meet them. Yeah. That's what I planned on doing. India and I were building, and restoring the relationship with my mother to a healthy place was a step in that direction.

But yeah. I'd shared everything about Sam and the job offer with Micah. I saw him some days ago. We got to play ball and catch up. We took a break, and I leaned against the railing of the park bench. As I took a swig of water, I admired my friend. The man. The husband. The future father.

"Mich.. You look great. Settled."

"Is that code for tired?" He took a seat on the bench and drank some of his own water.

We cackled.

"Man get out!"

We laughed some more.

"You wear marriage so well. Soon you'll have a little one. You were built for this."

Micah nodded. Beaming at that. "Thank you man. Indeed. I can't believe it sometimes. Everything I prayed for. God orchestrated. And this is so much more. Destiney is all that and more. Exceedingly and abundantly."

"Amen. Love to hear that. You two make it look easy. You make it look beautiful. You're an inspiration. First, Malachi and Ella. Now you two."

Micah chuckled. "Mal and sis are the O.G.'s. But we're trying."

Micah's older brother, Malachi, and his wife, Ella, are high school sweethearts. They were married young. Like I think at twenty and twenty-one. They've been married seventeen years now, and they have two teenagers. They were doing it. Inspiring us all.

Micah continued. "Most days I don't even know what I'm doing." He laughed. "But Destiney makes it easy. She's easy to love. Takes great care of me. I just try to make her happy. We make a good team."

I nodded. I could see that. "You know Mich. Seeing you two… it gets to me. In a good way."

Micah's brow was up instantly. A grin teasing at the corner of his lip. "And how do you mean exactly?"

We laughed. And. I took my time answering. I do my very best to speak with intention. Every word. I don't toss shit around flippantly. Ever. Words are powerful. If I speak on something, I mean it. And I was speaking with my best friend. Someone I knew

I could speak candidly with. Transparently. Honestly. I knew I could give Micah the unfiltered truth.

I stood up straight from leaning against the bench.

"India. She's it for me. We're building something. And we're taking our time. And it's soon. We have some things to talk about…But. I don't desire to know what else is out there. My heart is with her. *Been*. She challenges me. She wouldn't let me give up searching for my people. She holds space for everything I'm trying to figure out."

Micah nodded in understanding. Letting me rock.

"The certainty I feel with her. The safety." I laughed. "I didn't even know this kind of love existed. And… here I am. Relishing in it. I love life with India. Her parents are… amazing. And when I'm with her, all I see is a future. A real future. Not something wishful."

Micah let his smile spread. It reached his eyes. Nodding, he said, "That's exactly how you know. And now, you start planning around it."

"Yeah. I've been hit with a dilemma. And I'm trying to be careful with how I approach this."

"You're talking about the gig in Canada?"

"Exactly. I haven't told her yet. I'm waiting for the right time."

"I hear you man. That's a significant thing to discuss."

"I'm nervous. This could break us."

A few beats. "Well, you don't know that. She may appreciate a ticket out of here."

"I just know she won't want to leave her parents. She's protective of them. She takes care of them with no complaints."

"Oh yeah. India's been through a lot."

"Yeah. She's selfless. Showing up for everyone else. And I've been trying to show her that she doesn't have to carry everything on her own. Not anymore. I'm in her life now."

"She's fortunate to have you. And you, her. India is one of a kind. She means a lot to Destiney."

"Destiney means a lot to India. Who knew we'd end up in love with two best friends?"

We chuckled easy. Continuing, I said, "I see myself loving India and committing to her for the rest of my days. I want that. I know that's what I want. I feel like she wants that too. Our synergy is unreal. I also know I want to accept this offer." I sighed. "This little… *detour* has thrown me off. Yet… somehow, I know it will work out. But how?"

"You continue to build your future with her. Piece by piece. Have patience with yourself. And with her. I'm sure you can figure this out without losing either of these things. You want each of them bad enough, you'll find a way. No doubt in my mind."

"Yeah… We have to talk about it. And we'll keep building this beautiful thing. But eventually I want to marry India."

Micah jumped to his feet in haste. "That's what the fuck I'm talking about!" He slapped me on the back. "You'll know when it's time, whenever that is. You'll know. And I can't wait to hear all about it, man!"

That sounded so good. I had a few things I needed to discuss with India. And I would when the time was right.

I had all our accommodations booked in South Lake Tahoe. We leave exactly three weeks from now. The benefit was next weekend, and we'd go out to Tahoe the following week. I looked forward to getting away and celebrating with India. I'm glad she'll be able to get away and enjoy herself. Be pampered. Be cooked for and catered to. No chores. No work. Just enjoy the ambiance. And leave the rest to me. Or the staff.

I found a lovely Airbnb right on the lake. It was just about a two-hour drive from Sacramento. It would be gorgeous up there during the spring. And. We'd only be gone a few days, but I wanted her to enjoy herself. And not worry about her parents. Or anything for that matter.

Yeah.

Then I could talk to her about continuing to build our future.

What I envision for us. Find out how that looks for her and confirm what she needs from me.

Because I need her to agree. I want her. I want us. So much. That's all I want.

And then I can tell her about the offer in Montreal.

A move I didn't want to make without her beside me.

Didn't even want to consider it.
Nope.

forty-six

INDIA

"Trying to sneak away, Belle?"

Sol's voice pulled me from my thoughts, and I smiled as he approached and stood beside me. He gently wrapped his arm around my waist and drew me closer. "Are you alright?"

"Yes, baby. Just collecting myself," I giggled nervously. "This is kind of a lot."

"You look great. You're doing fine. And you belong here with me, baby."

Sol kissed my forehead, and my eyes fluttered shut.

Today was the annual music benefit. It started about an hour ago, and I stepped out onto the terrace to enjoy a moment alone. It was early evening, so the sun was still shining but beginning to set. The colors cast by the sunset were beautiful.

We were at a venue near Garden Highway, close to West Sacramento. It was a nice venue too. State-of-the-art and spacious. Very nice. High ceilings. Open concept. French double doors everywhere.

And the venue was buzzing with energy. So many people came out, and I was so proud of Sol and his team. They'd pulled off something truly incredible. I don't know how much money they aimed to raise, but I'm sure they'd gather a good amount of cash by the time this was done.

The kids performed a few selections at the start of the program, and they did an amazing job. I've never heard young kids play music so beautifully in a concert before. It was impressive to see. Flutes, trumpets, tubas, clarinets. Some were as young as fourth graders.

Sol was the guest conductor for their final piece. Their regular conductor said it was a work that Sol arranged and interpreted, especially for tonight. When Sol stepped up to conduct, I was impressed all over again. Yeah. Sol just doesn't cease to amaze me.

After the kids played a few selections, a jazz trio set up, filling the space with lovely tunes. The trio were friends of Sol's, and they sounded great.

Layered into the music were lively chatter, clinking glasses, and laughter as people moved about the space. There were refreshments and heavy appetizers. And Janelle from HomeGrown came through. There was literally something for everyone. The bougie rich people who came with their checks. And for the kids who came to play their instruments to seal the deal.

Teriyaki meatballs. Avocado and tomato bruschetta. French dip sliders. Jalapeno popper wontons. Mini grilled cheese sandwiches. Veggie potstickers. Rotisserie chicken taquitos. Antipasto skewers. And a few other things. There were homemade sauces to go with each of them, too. That guacamole was so good. I could have eaten that by itself. I love guacamole.

Yeah. Janelle showed out. And these were like fusion versions. I didn't try everything. But the things I tried clearly had a personal touch. There were sweets too. Brownie bites. A cookie platter. Cake pops.

The display was impressive too. She'd brought a few servers as well, and they were friendly, hospitable, and helpful. Janelle had a stack of cards near the setup, and so many people grabbed one that she had to refill it a few times.

"You're the masterpiece in here tonight," Sol murmured close to my ear. Still holding me tight. "As soon as this is over, I want some of you."

"Mmm. We can work that out."

Sol rubbed up and down my back as I leaned into him.

"You look stunning, baby."

I tittered. "Sol. You've only told me that a dozen times by now. But thank you. So do you."

I wore a soft cream linen dress that was perfect for this early spring evening. It wasn't too formal because this wasn't that kind of party, but it was comfortable and dressy enough. I wore dangly beaded earrings, a gift from Mala, who brought them back for me from Berbice. They were yellow with turquoise accents, very cute. My hair was pulled back in a neat, low bun on my neck, sleek and controlled, with every tendril in place. I liked the look with this dress and these earrings. I wore some khaki wedge heels, and everything came together nicely.

Sol told me so several times by now.

He looked great too. He wore a stylish, slim-fitting, light grey two-piece suit, a white button-up underneath, and a burnt orange tie. Brown dress shoes.

Yeah. Sol looked great. And comfortable. And so natural as he worked the room. He'd been talking to so many people. And he proudly introduced me to most of them.

His assistant, Monique Crocker, helped pull this off. She was extremely sweet. A few of his colleagues from Sac City came. Met a few of them. I met his dean. Dr. Whittaker. He was wonderful.

A few of his bandmates from Smoke were here. Joe and his wife, Ava, hung out with us for a while. We got to chat, and Ava had me laughing the whole time. Later, we exchanged numbers. She reminded me she wanted us over for dinner, and I told her we'd make it happen.

James, the keyboard player, was here with his fiancée. She was so kind and radiated with the unmistakable glow of pregnancy. She said she was about seven months along, and this was their first.

And I didn't know what was in the water, but there seemed to be quite a few pregnant women as of late.

"There you are, Solomon. Great benefit."

Sol and I turned back toward the open French double doors, and there stood an older man dressed in a black suit. He had salt-and-pepper hair and a neatly trimmed salt-and-pepper beard. He wore a kind smile.

"Hey! I didn't know you would be here." Sol took a few steps to meet him halfway. "Nice to see you." They embraced one another.

"India. Baby." He reached back for me as soon as they parted. "Please meet the Honorable Leonard Avery. My father."

My eyes were wide, and I smiled even wider.

"Hello! Very nice to meet you!"

"Pleasure's mine. Please call me Leonard."

"Oh, I couldn't. I hope Mr. Avery will do."

"It will do just fine."

We had a friendly hug. And Sol returned his hand to my waist. Pulling me close to him.

I saw his father give him a knowing expression.

"So, you're the famous India I've heard about. What a beauty you are."

"Thank you. All good things, I hope."

"Only good things. You mean a lot to my son, and that means everything to this old man. He's my pride and joy."

In my peripheral vision, I saw Sol nod sincerely. That made my heart squeeze.

"I've heard quite a lot about you, too. I'm so glad we're finally meeting."

"Absolutely. As far as I'm concerned, you're family now. Lots more to come."

I grinned like a Cheshire cat. "Looking forward to it."

"Is Mom here?" Sol asked his father.

"Yes, she's in there having a chat with a few ladies. She stopped along the way, and eventually I kept walking."

We laughed.

Mr. Avery offered, "We can back head inside and find her if you like."

We hardly crossed the threshold when Sol's assistant came around the corner.

"Hello, Judge Avery. Nice to see you!"

They exchanged pleasantries.

"Dr. Avery, you're up in the next few minutes. You'll be introducing our keynote speaker."

"Right. Thank you, Monique. I'll be right there."

Sol turned toward me, gently kissed my cheek. "I won't be away too long. This will only take me a moment. Will you be alright?"

"Yes baby. I'll be fine."

"Okay."

Sol walked ahead of Mr. Avery and me.

Once we returned to the reception area, Mr. Avery said, "I can see my wife. I'm going to get her so that by the time Solomon is finished, we can all meet each other."

"That sounds great." My voice was a bit louder because the noise level was significantly higher in here. There were a lot more guests here than there were when I went out to the terrace. Yeah. This was almost a sensory overload. I like people and I'm outgoing, but I don't particularly enjoy large crowds.

Mr. Avery and I went in opposite directions. We'd meet again; the place wasn't too big, so it would be easy to find him. I headed toward the back of the venue just as Sol made his way to the podium on stage. I'd wait here until he was finished.

Sol welcomed everyone who arrived since he'd last been on stage and introduced himself. Then he covered housekeeping, such as where to find restrooms. After he reminded everyone to enjoy the plentiful refreshments and appetizers, he spoke about the silent auction and raffle.

That reminded me. Since I hadn't gone over yet, I could take a quick moment to go check it out. There was a setup in the furthest corner with all of the donations. As I neared the table, I could see that there were some great items for auction.

Three-night vacation packages, a cruise voucher, a few themed gift baskets, fine wines, brewery tours, date night tickets, event tickets for concerts and Broadway shows, signed memorabilia, country club memberships, professional photoshoots, and spa day packages. I saw a Chef's Tasting Menu for two donated by executive chef Jannelle. That would be really cool. Speaking of Jannelle, I saw her husband, Tim, helping out at the food table. Those two are so awesome for so many reasons. Such great people. I also met their daughter, Naomi, who was here helping out as well, and she's such a sweetheart.

I felt my phone vibrate. Pulling it out of my purse, I saw it was a text from Destiney.

Des the Best: In route! Sorry Best. ETA 6:18pm. Luv ya!!!

I laughed. She's so funny. She said they were running late, but their ETA was in about 7 minutes. I'm glad they'd be able to support Sol, too. I know Micah wouldn't miss it.

Sol was still on stage talking, so I turned my attention to the table and saw my original artwork on display. I was very proud of it. I noticed that it already had a few offers, but I didn't check the amounts. All the money was going straight to the Music Academy.

It was a large piece, the canvas measuring 18x24 inches. It was unique because it was a bit more abstract than what I usually create, but I must say it looked fantastic. Everything I did with this turned out well. I started painting it the day Sol came by to look at the car, and we went into my art shed. That was the first time he saw my art shed and the first time he saw me paint anything live. I felt so inspired. I finished it when he returned unannounced with his acoustic.

Yeah. This piece was special. I used blues and gold, and I called it Heritage (Indigo & Ochre). Sol insisted I write a short artist bio about myself, and there it sat beside my canvas, along with a small picture of me and my social media handles. Sol was also insistent on this, too, as he knew people would want to contact me for commissioned work. I appreciated him for putting me on.

"It's you, isn't it?"

I looked to my left, and there stood a woman who seemingly came out of nowhere. Maybe I just didn't notice. I was wrapped up. Reminiscing on the day we created this masterpiece. I'm saying we because it was a concerted effort.

"You." She pointed to the tiny picture of me. "The artist. Are you India Rampersaud?"

"Oh!" I giggled, nervously and embarrassed. "Yes. I am. That's me." I shook my head. "I had to think for a second."

"It's alright," she smiled warmly, and I already felt better.

"Noelle Baker. So nice to meet you," she gushed, offering her hand, which I shook. "This is magnificent. I already placed a bid on it. I was just coming to see if anyone else was trying to take this home. This is mine."

Aww. 'Magnificent' is a new one. That's so nice of you."

"Well, I love art, and it's one of a kind," she shrugged. "It's the only thing here that interests me."

And, side note, this girl was *gorgeous*. Light brown skin with a flawless complexion. She wore makeup, but it looked natural. She had skill. Not overdone or overly dramatic.

She wore a lavender chiffon cocktail dress with an asymmetrical skirt that flowed gracefully with every move. The V-neckline showed the delicate pearls she wore. She was almost too dressy for this event. Almost. But she looked lovely. Manicured nails. White lace-up heeled sandals. Her hair was neatly pulled back in a sleek ponytail. Her full black hair fell to her mid-back. Her understated ponytail was simple yet elegant and worked so well with her diamond drop earrings. Those bad boys looked real. I mean *authentic*.

And expensive. Those pearls around her neck were probably real, too. She must be one of the wealthy sponsors. She looked extremely young, though.

Des the Best: Parking.

Perfect.

"So, are you a mom of one of the kids? Or…?" I wondered aloud. I guess we could kill another minute or two while we stood here. Sol was still on stage, but it sounded like he was wrapping things up.

I turned to face him just as she said, "Oh no! I'm here to support my fiancé. He's the one who put this whole thing on."

She had to be mistaken. Or maybe I was mistaken. Sol hadn't mentioned anyone else working with him besides his assistant.

"Oh?"

"Yeah." She smiled brightly. Facing the stage, "The guy up there talking. Dr. Solomon Avery."

My blood ran cold, but I kept my composure.

There had to be a logical explanation.

"Solomon is your fiancé?"

She laughed. And for a brief second, I sighed in relief.

Then, "Well… kind of. Basically. Our families are old friends, and we were promised to each other. We've been dating for a while, and we're going to be married soon."

I nodded, saying nothing. Suddenly, I felt sick. Disoriented. *Stupid.* I wished the ground would open up and swallow me whole.

"What about you? How do you know Solomon?"

The room filled with applause as the keynote speaker stepped onto the stage. I moved toward the entrance and saw Destiney and Micah approaching.

Destiney walked a few steps ahead of Micah.

"Hey Indie! Girl, I am so sorry! We… Best? *Are you okay?*"

I was crying now. Tears were flowing down my face rapidly. I'd been wiping my eyes, but it was no use. I couldn't keep up.

"I just met Sol's fiancé." I saw Destiney's jaw drop. Her eyes were as wide as saucers. "Please get me out of here. Please." I managed.

forty-seven

SOL

It all seemed to happen in slow motion.

When I went up on stage, I had one job: to introduce our keynote speaker.

When I stepped on stage, I saw how much the crowd had grown since I did my welcome address about an hour earlier. I would have been remiss if I hadn't welcomed the newcomers and introduced myself. This year's benefit has been the biggest yet; so many people came out, and I knew we'd meet and even surpass our goals for the year.

I was so proud of the kids. How well they performed. They'd been practicing, and all their hard work paid off. I knew we'd gotten the buy-in on that strength alone.

The food looked phenomenal. Janelle and Tim are always so kind. They believe in the program and always want to give back in some way. They donated most of the spread tonight, and everything tasted delicious.

The jazz trio were friends of mine. And they were superb! They had us all grooving to their easy listening.

There were cocktail tables set up. A few more tables for people to sit down. Each table was covered in a black satin tablecloth, with purple music note centerpieces and black-and-silver music note confetti scattered on top.

Monique had done such a great job. I was sure to thank her many times.

It was such a great evening.

India was here with me, looking amazing and making me feel even better. Yeah, I loved introducing her to everyone, bragging about her and the fantastic artwork she'd donated to our silent auction. I guess I got caught up in it all. If I hadn't, maybe I would have gotten off stage quickly enough to intercept whatever it was Noelle said to India. It was unclear why Noel was here in the first place. But yeah, I swear it all seemed to happen in slow motion.

From the podium, I saw India in the back of the venue. Just after I mentioned the silent auction, she headed that way. I kept talking. A moment later, I spotted Noelle. Confused, I watched her walk toward the silent auction as I kept speaking. Mid-sentence, I started to lose my resolve. I knew this might turn out badly. I spoke quickly, trying to get my ass off that stage. Yeah, I knew things wouldn't go over well.

And it didn't take long.

I saw them exchange words. I saw them shake hands. Then, Noelle said something that had them both looking in my direction, and shortly after, I saw India heading toward the exit, visibly upset. I couldn't get off that stage fast enough. As soon as I did, I headed toward the exit I saw her leaving from. I had blinders on too; I needed to get to her quickly. I weaved through clusters of people dressed in semi-formal attire, dancing, laughing, mingling, and vibrantly chatting over glasses of champagne. They indulged in the appetizers, networked, and had a great time.

A few people stopped me to make small talk, and I kept it as light as I could. I needed to get to her to check on her. I don't know what Noelle said, but I had a vague idea, and that made me extremely nervous. Frantic.

Another thing, I might have even seen her wipe her eyes. The thought of seeing the woman I loved crying made me angry. I didn't want that, especially when I couldn't comfort her.

When I reached the exit, I didn't see her sitting outside and wondered where she might have gone. We drove here together. I turned around to head back inside. I passed people, all unaware, and kept my trained expression, not revealing that I was feeling frantic. Concerned and anxious.

None of which I should feel as a host of tonight's event.

I'm so glad I didn't need to go back on stage for at least another hour. Maybe I wouldn't go back up at all. I was going to thank everyone for coming and all of that jazz. But I could always have Monique do that. She's great at public speaking. She can work any room. Yeah. I'd find my baby and we'd go home. We were done here.

I headed back toward the terrace. Maybe she slipped back inside while I was held up talking to someone.

"*Solomon*! There you are, honey."

I turned around to see my mother waving excitedly. She was standing by the bar we had set up, holding a tall glass of red wine.

She looked lovely tonight in a rust-red silk gown, which was very fancy for this event, but my mother was the type to always dress to the nines. She didn't pay any attention to a dress code. In a room like this. Full of people like this. I wouldn't expect anything less. My mother carried on with her animated conversation, talking to a group of women. Standing beside her was the woman she wanted for me. Smiling sweetly, perfectly poised.

Perfectly *wrong*.

I crossed the room. Slowly. And that's when realization hit me. Now I was angry. I neared the bar, and I could see my father coming from the other direction.

This was great. I could use some reinforcements. I just hoped he rose to the occasion for once. My Anger and heartbreak were boiling up quietly. I knew I would remain respectful. Keep my composure. That was a non-negotiable. Besides, there were too many people watching my every move. These rich people tend to be nosy. Especially the women. Reputations were at stake. Apart from that, I wouldn't create anything that could be spun into a scandal.

I had a subtle eye roll. Noelle looked comfortable. As if standing beside my mother was where she belonged. Yup. She's the type that would sense something's the matter but remain where she was anyway. Polite to a default and… awkward.

Good grief.

I would need to pull my mother aside.

"Hey there, son. I was looking for you." My father had a look in his eye and subtly nodded once toward Noelle.

I nodded too. Just as subtle. My father had no idea Noelle would be here. And I figured as much.

Mom and Noelle were talking now. And when I reached them, calm and cold, their conversation faltered. My mother got the hint and wrapped up her conversation. Perfect timing.

Noelle smiled at me politely, but I didn't have anything for her. I'm sure she sensed my mood.

"Mother." My tone pressed, my words cutting through the surrounding chatter. "I need to speak with you. Privately."

My mother looked up with a pleasant smile. Her voice sweet. "Hello, honey. We can talk later on. Why don't you say hello to Noelle? Doesn't she look lovely tonight?"

I inhaled slowly. Deeply. Trying not to lose it.

Thinking quickly on my feet, I spoke in French.

"Mother. Please. This can't wait. We need to talk privately. Right now."

My mother blinked at me. A bit startled, likely. We haven't spoken in French for a long time. A few years. When I was a child and learning the language, I was required to speak only French with my mother. She speaks French really well. Almost as well as a native speaker. My father's French isn't so great, but he's fluent. I noticed his demeanor shifted, too.

And Noelle. She looked at me and then at my mother.

I knew she didn't speak French at all, and I knew she didn't understand anything I said, but she'd likely picked up the weight of it. The energy had certainly shifted.

My mother, attempting to maintain her poise in front of Noelle, responded in English. "It's alright, honey. We can talk later. Now isn't the time..."

I didn't even let her finish. Still speaking French, my tone firmer now, *"Now, mother. Please. I'm not here to humiliate anyone. Including Noelle."*

I'm certain something in my expression gave her pause. My mother's smile faltered. She spoke quietly, almost as if her responding in French was a subtle surrender. *"Alright. Let's go."* Turning to Noelle, she said, "Please excuse us for a moment."

My parents followed me down a hallway. The laughter and jazz music echoed behind us. Once we were a reasonable distance from prying eyes and ears, I turned to find my mother looking at me, just like nothing was wrong. I rubbed my hands over my head. My jaw was tight. The air between us thick with tension. Yeah. The tension followed us like a shadow.

"You invited Noelle here? *Really?* After everything I told you?"

"Solomon. Honey. Our families have known each other for years. Of course, I would invite her. I thought…"

"No. You didn't think. *You planned.* You knew what Noelle being here would mean. And you knew what it would do to India and to us!"

My mother looked startled for a moment but quickly composed herself. "Son. You're caught up in your emotions, and I'm being practical. That girl…"

"Her name is India." I cut in.

"Alright. India. She's lovely. But she isn't from this world. You'd be miserable. Her too. I'm thinking of what's best for you," she said defensively. "I'm trying to keep things civil. You know people are expecting..."

"You mean *you.*" I stepped closer to her. I kept my voice down, but it was sharp now. We were going in circles. I swear we already had this conversation. More than once. "What you're doing isn't civility. It's control. You invited Noelle here to make India feel inadequate. And you did it with people around." I was angry.

My mother's face tightened, though she remained composed. "I was showing you your options. You've worked so hard, Solomon. I'm trying to protect you from making a mistake."

"The mistake you've made tonight was thinking I would let you hurt the woman I love." My voice broke slightly. "She left here in tears." I exhaled. "Do you know how small that made me feel?"

Her demeanor shifted, but she said nothing.

"You're not concerned with what's best for me. You want what's comfortable for you. But I'll tell you what's best for me; She is. You haven't even met her." I shrugged. "Given her a chance."

She still said nothing.

I continued, "You make me feel like I have to choose. And hurting her the way you have hurt me."

"I didn't mean to hurt her or you. I just thought seeing what life would be like with someone who understands this world…"

"This world wouldn't mean anything if I were unhappy."

My mother's eyes were wide.

"India makes me happy. She keeps me grounded. She makes all of this mean something. If you refuse to see that, that's fine. But don't put me in that position again. And don't make me have to decide between you and her." I paused. "I love India. And we're building a future together. I'd like to marry her someday. She makes me want to be better. Not simply fit in. If you want us to have peace, you'll need to accept that. She's the woman I've chosen, and that isn't changing."

That got her attention.

"Son… how could… *love? Marry her!?* We hardly know her!"

"Claudine! That is enough!"

My father finally spoke up. Finally, his voice boomed in the hallway, startling my mother. And me. He never had much to add. If he did, he would be cosigning with my mother.

Not this time.

"Solomon is an adult. He has the right to choose the woman he wants to spend his life with. She's a wonderful woman. And she's the one making him smile. I haven't seen him smile this way in a long time. And that's all I want for our son."

The muffled music filled the heavy silence that hung in the hallway.

I looked at my father. His kind eyes smiled back at me.

I looked at my mother. Her chin trembled. I saw her nod. Then softly she said, "I crossed a line. I'm sorry."

My eyes were wide. But I remained silent.

"India really loves you, doesn't she?"

A smile spread when I said, "She does. And I love her. So much." I sighed lightly. "Enough to walk away from all of this if I had to. It isn't worth having without her."

"Wow. That's… Son, that's beautiful."

I found my mother's eyes on mine. And they were shiny. Glistening with unshed tears. Her expression was soft. I could see the fight draining from her eyes.

"It was never my intention to hurt you. I just want to protect you."

"I understand. But sometimes your protection is like control. And I don't need protection from love. India understands me more than anyone ever has. You see differences, and I see balance. You see a risk, but I see home."

Her tone uncharacteristically softer now, my mother asked, "When can I meet her?"

♪❤♫❤♪

Checking my GPS, I was eighteen minutes away from Micah's house. Micah texted me while I was talking to my parents, but I didn't see it until afterward.

He let me know that India was at his house. He and Destiney arrived at the benefit, just as India was walking outside in tears. And Micah drove them all home.

I appreciated him being there for her while she was so upset. And I appreciated Destiney, too. I'm glad India was somewhere safe, especially since it was dark outside now. And cold.

I cruised down I-5 South. From Garden Highway in West Sacramento to Laguna Boulevard in Elk Grove. My windows down. The cool spring night air blowing in my face. Trying to get to her as soon as I could. Without getting a ticket. The freeway was nearly empty for a Saturday evening. It was close to nine in the evening. I'd tasked Monique with closing out the event and wishing everyone a good evening. I had something pressing to tend to. I could hardly wait to get to her. I had some apologies for her. Some explanations. Some reassurance. And anything else she needed from me. Because I needed us to be okay.

I was glad to have finally gotten through to my mother.

What a change in events tonight was.

I didn't expect that at all. My mother's apology. Her being damn near in tears. Her asking to meet the woman she insisted wasn't good enough for me. I knew I wanted to resolve the division with my mother, and though it didn't quite go the way I expected, I'm glad she realized she'd gone too far. And she was willing to hear me. And listen to understand.

And my father. I appreciated him speaking up for me and having my back.

And Noelle wouldn't surface again. Literally or figuratively. Yeah.

Now all I needed to do was fix things with India.

♪♥♫♥♪

When I arrived, I texted Micah to let him know I was outside. I didn't want to ring the doorbell and alert India that I was there. I called her once when I got in the car, but she didn't answer. Still, that was fine. I prayed she'd be willing to hear me out when I saw her.

"Hey bro. Thanks again."

Mich and I had a quick embrace.

"Of course. She's upstairs, first door on the left."

The lights were off in Micah's house, but their television was on. Illuminating the downstairs living area. Micah returned to his seat on his sectional, where Destiney returned to lying her head in his lap with a throw blanket over her.

Destiney waved at me as I walked past them. I believe she knew there was more to be considered, and I was glad that I wasn't in the doghouse with her, too.

I went up the stairs and hesitated when I reached the door to the guest room where India was. After collecting myself, I knocked gently. The door opened slowly. The hallway was dark, and it was dark behind her, but I could see her clearly. Her eyes were red and puffy. Her shoulders sagged. And my heart broke all over again.

"Artist Girl. Hey."

467

"What are you doing here?" she asked. Her voice low and tired.

With a sincere sense of remorse, I replied, "I'm here to fix what I should have protected."

forty-eight

INDIA

I didn't say anything. Not right away.

Sol left a reasonable distance between us. But it seemed like the Grand Canyon. And the silence between us ached and dragged.

I could hear the sincerity in Sol's voice. And despite the hallway being dark, I could see it in his eyes. They were trained on me. Soft and full of warmth and care.

Stepping closer, he said, low and measured, "India. Baby. Can I come in and talk to you? Please?"

As Sol patiently waited for an answer, I regarded him.

His hands remained at his sides, his body language open. He'd slightly leaned forward, still giving me space. When my eyes were back on his, I could see that he was hurting too. For us. And for me. We didn't even need to express it verbally. Our synergy has always been intensely kismet. But we needed to have a conversation. And I was willing to hear him. We needed to acknowledge our feelings. Both of our feelings. But. This was uncharted territory for us. We'd never been in this situation before.

Yet here we were. And it was worth talking through. I knew there was more to the story. Both Destiney and Micah insisted there had to be. Reminding me of something I already knew. Sol isn't the type to be out here playing games. Especially no shit like having an alleged fiancé. And the fact that I didn't know that woman, whoever she is, I could have asked Sol about it, instead of rushing off.

I'm glad I didn't cause a scene. That event had a lot of people in high places with deep ass pockets, power, and prestige. Ruining that for Sol would have been incredibly selfish of me. Not to mention the losses the music academy could have faced.

And Destiney knew I didn't want to go home, so she offered me one of the guestrooms. The same one I slept in last time I was here. Their home is huge, and Destiney reminded me that I always have a room here should I need one.

I'd come straight up here and cried my eyes out. I saw Sol's call earlier, but I wasn't in the right headspace to answer it.

But. Still. I felt as if there was something Sol hadn't told me. *Wasn't* telling me.

And *that* was what hurt.

Yeah. We needed to have a conversation.

"Yes. Come on in."

I stepped back, opening the bedroom door wider for Sol to enter. Once he crossed the threshold, I softly closed the door behind him. The room was dark. I hadn't bothered to turn on the light when I came in earlier. Still don't really need it now. So I wouldn't bother. The moon was bright enough for some light to shine through the thin drapes. So, we were able to move around without worrying about stubbing our toes or running into anything.

Sol stood against the wall across from the queen-sized bed and then slid down to sit on the floor. I sat on the floor too. Facing him. My back against the bed.

I couldn't see his face clearly, only his dim profile. He was looking out of the window. The energy between us was palpable. I could feel everything. The tension. The love. The aching. And the urge we both had to get this figured out.

"I had no idea my mother invited her. It was too late by the time I realized what happened." He offered. His words were gentle.

And. There was a long pause. A long, heavy pause.

"Sol. I don't think I fit. I don't dress the part. I don't belong in your world."

I heard him take a low breath.

"My world?" He sighed heavily. "That isn't my world. That's theirs. Their money and their expectations. Not mine. I don't subscribe to that."

"Your mother has everything planned for you, with a perfect woman to go along with it. Far be it from me to interfere. I'm just…"

"India. Please. Don't even finish." His voice was gentle and firm. "You aren't *just* anything. We've come too far for you to think otherwise."

I said nothing. I twisted my fingers in my lap.

"India. My beautiful Artist Girl. You're the one who makes me laugh when I forget how. The one who speaks to people as if they matter. The one who saw me for who I am. And all that I am. Not what I have."

"Who is she?" My tone curious. But my voice was small. So small it was almost lost in the darkness.

"No one."

"Sol."

"I'm serious, India. She's no one. Except a woman, my mother wanted me to marry. But I don't want to marry her. And I've told my mother this many times." His words were so gentle.

"She said you've been dating."

"We *did* date. I haven't dated her since before we've been us, India."

"Are you sleeping with her?"

"No. I've never slept with her and never kissed her. Nothing. Just a friendly side hug out of politeness. I'm not interested in her in that way." A beat. "I didn't mean to lie to you by not telling you sooner. But. I guess I didn't think you wanted to know."

I laughed. It held no mirth. "I didn't think I did either." Another beat. "Are you sleeping with anyone?" That question wasn't planned, yet it came out.

"Not since you and me. There was someone I would see once in a while. But since you, I haven't seen her. Especially now. We're exclusive India. There's nothing out there I want."

Running it back, I said, "It hurt to hear that from a stranger. I wish *you'd* told me that."

"You're right. I should have told you a long time ago. And I regret that so much. And I'm sorry. I'm so sorry."

I said nothing for a while. Then, "She's your mother. You only get one. I don't want to come between you two."

"What do you mean by that?" His tone held an element of urgency.

"I'm sure there's a reason your mother wants her for you. And… I mean… I saw it myself." I'd grown emotional, and a tear slid down my cheek. "I'll never be like her. I don't fit into your world, Sol. Someone like me doesn't belong with someone like you." After a beat, I declared, proudly, "And even if I could change. I wouldn't."

I wiped my eyes. Crying quietly. The space between us grew even quieter. So quiet we could faintly hear the television downstairs.

"You do belong with me. You fit into my world perfectly… because when I'm with you, that *is* my world. Everything else is just noise."

I listened to Sol continue with his heartfelt reassurance, processing everything. I wanted this to work. I wanted him, and I wanted us. But family was everything to me. And I never saw myself building with a man whose family didn't care for me. Building with someone would mean being part of their family, just as they would be part of mine. My fear of dividing his family was stronger than my desire to be with him. And that wasn't something I was willing to be a part of.

"India. I don't want you to change. I fell in love with you *because* of who you are. The way you see the world. The way you move through it. I've missed something so profound before you came along. You're the woman I want, India. And I've told my mother that. As much as my mother's feelings matter, I won't let them define my future. I don't need her approval or anyone else's to love you. You belong with me. Artist Girl. You have my heart, and that's not something I give easily."

I processed all of that. Smiling weakly, though he couldn't see. My heart squeezed at his words. He still wasn't finished.

"I want something real. And that's what you give me. India. When the time is right, I want to marry you, baby."

"Sol." My voice still small. Aching. Almost pleading. "All of that sounds so beautiful. And so sweet. And I know you mean every word… but you mother… Sol… I can't… she's your family, and you can't fix this with your words. As sweet as they are. You just can't."

"She wants to meet you," he cut in. "She wants to meet you and get to know the woman who loves me. The woman I love with my whole heart. The woman who made me want a family of my own again." Sol's voice was softer now. And it broke with sincerity. "I told her tonight that you're the woman I love and the woman I chose. And that she crossed a line."

"You did?" My eyes were wide.

"I did. And though I can't change what happened, I can make sure it never happens again, Belle." I said nothing. "She wants to meet you. And she wants to apologize to you. And get to know you. When you're ready… if you're willing to give her that space, she can show you she's sincere." A beat. "And do you know what, I believe you'll be the reason my mother learns what real love looks like."

Wow.

I didn't expect this, but I was so glad to hear it. And. Hearing Sol pour his heart out, defend his love for me. And then hear him say he wanted to marry me. I wanted that too. And…I'd been harboring that. Almost afraid to bring it up. Just because of what happened before. But. Hearing him say that just did something to me.

After a pause, I offered, "Sure. I'm willing to meet her. And I'd love to get to know her, too." And I did. Genuinely. Even though his mother and I haven't officially met, we could start again.

"Thank you for doing this." Sol offered.

"Thank you for loving me," I told him. "I love you too, Sol. Fiercely. Never have I ever loved anyone as much as I love you."

We were still sitting in the dark. We still hadn't moved.

"Oh, Belle. I do. With everything within me."

A few moments passed.

"That's weird, though," I revealed. Couldn't help myself, and it was out now. "Like. It's bizarre. It weirds me out that your mom has convinced that young lady that you've been promised to her. And she's walking around believing as much. Especially when you haven't even verbally confirmed that. It's all so weird. My family is unique, and we've got our issues. But… baby. This takes the cake."

"I'm adopted, remember?"

We cackled.

"Sol."

"Indie."

We'd spoken at the same time, and that had us laughing all over again.

"Yes baby? You go first."

"Okay." I crawled over to him in the dark, then sat against the wall next to him. Our shoulders touching. Both of us reacting to each other's presence. I could feel it. My heart fluttered as we grabbed hands in the dark. A flutter I welcomed. Feeling closer to Sol than I've ever felt, I asked him, "Can we go home, baby? And maybe make love too?"

I longed for him.

Goodness. I longed for him so. Right now.

My half-spoken… alluded thought. Well. It was posed like a question. It wasn't quite an admission. But. Sol understood. He didn't need the entire thing. Just a hint of my inner longing was plenty for him.

My fingers and his fingers. They were making love right now.

Tangled. Emersed. Captive in each other.

His touch had me intoxicated. Drowning. Deep in my desire.

I was in fucking *heat.*

And it lingered as I waited for him to oblige me.

He chuckled easy. And it flowed lightly from him, like a sweet melody floating from a music box. It was so cute. Had me smiling from ear to ear.

"You're reading my mind, Belle." Sol brought his hand up around my cheek. Gently rubbed his thumb over my bottom lip. He moved closer. I felt his breath on my lips before the gentlest kiss came. It was slow. And I felt his heart racing just like mine. He murmured against my lips, "You can't just whisper that and expect me to be able to behave." Sol gave me another sweet kiss, which landed on the corner of my mouth. As he lingered there, we shared warmth. Breathing in sync in no time.

I leaned in, kissing him on the cheek, and using my free hand, I gently turned his chin toward me, connecting our lips again. I felt an enormous relief now. Unsure if I should even speak it aloud. That. And the fact that I missed him so much that quickly. My emotional honesty revealed itself when I was here. Alone in the dark. Crying. And. Unsure.

When Sol arrived, I wasn't expecting him, but I wasn't surprised either. I know him, and I was hoping he would come.

So grateful he had.

With no choice but to let my guard down.

And now all was well again.

"You're impossible. You know that?" He murmured.

We'd still been kissing. Pecked a few times at first, but when we both parted, and our tongues began a slow dance, things grew intense very quickly.

Breaking the kiss, he said. "Let's get out of here, baby. No way I'm making love to you in my boy's house!"

forty-nine

INDIA

"Turn around baby."

"Why would I do that?" I teased flirty. Looking over my shoulder. I wanted to say something clever, but that was all I could come up with.

And meanwhile, Sol was looking at me like I was a whole meal he wanted to devour. At the same time, it was the sweetest look. And in true Solomon fashion, it was a look of reverence. Yeah. It was both of those, all at once. No one looks at me the way he does. Ever.

I took the steps from the outdoor patio, sauntering near the king-sized bed in the center of the main bedroom. Leaving the grand French doors open behind me, letting the bright sunlight flow in, and casting a warm glow all over the room.

Sol was propped on his elbow, lying on his side, watching me as I neared him. He was shirtless, his naked bottom half covered by a white sheet.

We were in Tahoe, enjoying the stunning view and each other's company. The main bedroom was exceptional: visually appealing and incredibly comfortable. The décor featured whites and beiges, with subtle accents here and there. And I must say, those linens were divine! The sheets were probably 500 thread count or something similar. I didn't really understand what that meant, but I knew it indicated higher quality. These sheets were resort-quality, penthouse-suit level. The plush down comforter and the impossibly comfortable pillows matched that standard.

We drove up yesterday. Left mid-morning, and Highway 50 brought us right up here. The drive was easy. Not much traffic aside from a slight delay in Roseville. We had the windows cracked just a little; the wind was chillier up here, but it was a lovely drive.

We stopped at Apple Hill on the way out and got a slice of fresh-baked apple pie and coffee. Apple Hill is about thirty minutes East of Sacramento in neighboring Placer County. Lots of apple orchards with scrumptious apple pie. Apple fritters. Apple ciders. Quite a few people visit Apple Hill in the fall and winter.

We arrived just about one o'clock in the afternoon and settled into our Airbnb. It was a charming two-story cabin and quite spacious. Sol surprised me with a bottle of champagne. And we toasted to us.

To our first trip.

My birthday.

Our love. And everything we'd been building.

We hung out in the house for a while. Relaxed.

Later, we had a Mediterranean lunch at a lakefront café right by the water. They had grilled fish that was so delicious. After lunch, we strolled through the shops and found a lounge. The vibe was chill, so we had a drink and had a fantastic conversation. I loved that. We made it back to the Airbnb and decided to rest. I took a nap. When I woke up, we got dressed and went out for dinner.

Just before we left for dinner, Sol surprised me with "one of my birthday presents," he said.

It was in a flat slim gift box. A yellow ribbon was tied around it. And when I opened it, my flabber was ghasted.

It was a Tissot Lovely Automatic Diamond watch. My jaw was on the floor. It was gorgeous. And Sol was so sweet. I can still hear his words and his voice when I opened it and put it on. Thanking him all the while.

"Belle. I wanted to gift you with something that will remind you of us each time you look at it. And remind you of the time we've spent… and the time ahead. You are so special to me, baby. This is a token of that. For our journey together and for all of the time we will share. I love you, India."

"Oh, Sol! I love you too! And I love this watch. Thank you!"

I wore it to dinner. I planned to wear it all the time.

It's a timeless design. Yellow gold and elegant. Swiss-made quartz movement. A round pearl face with diamond markers at 12, 3, 6, and 9 o'clock. A bezel set around the circumference with another forty tiny diamonds.

Yeah.

This is by far the most expensive thing I now own. But that was beside the point. It's beautiful. And knowing Sol, a lot of thought and consideration went into this. He has money, but he doesn't spend it frivolously. He also isn't cheap or stingy. He chose this watch to show me how special I am. That he values me and the life we're building together. This is perfect. Not uber luxurious but I knew it cost a pretty penny, and it gives meaning, which matters most of all.

So we go to dinner, and I couldn't believe the sunset over the lake. The view from the balcony was breathtaking. We dined at a bistro right on the water, and it was perfectly romantic and precisely the way I would have envisioned our very first getaway.

After dinner, we headed to the casino and danced for a bit.

Not quite ready for the night to end, we walked along the lake talking, holding hands, and kissing, of course. A lot of kissing. And talking too. We'd been talking so much, which was perfect. When we got in, we enjoyed the hot tub. And speaking of romantic, it was so romantic under the stars. Yeah. I'd been having such a great time. Just being with Sol was a great time, but here it was… I didn't have the words. Just. All the things. Everything.

I'd called to check on Ma and Daddy once, when we first got in. And they ordered me not to call them back, and that they would be just fine. My Aunt Gloria and Mala were on standby if they needed anything. And I reluctantly agreed.

Today we had plans to take a Gondola before sunset. But. I don't know if we'll make it. Today, we'd literally been wrapped up in each other. That would be cool. But something told me we'd end up wrapped in a blanket together by the fire pit on the balcony, talking for hours and probably sipping wine. Or hot chocolate. That sounded so good, too.

The balcony was my favorite part of this whole cabin. It was grand and expansive. The doors opened to a marble patio floor, and there was a fireplace out there with plenty of furniture. I loved it out there.

This view was my favorite. Lush green trees as far as the eye could see and snowcapped mountains right from the backyard. I took so many pictures. I brought my tote, but I haven't gotten around to sketching anything just yet.

And we've made love out there twice already. I'd never done that before. Made love outside, but I guess it was okay being in a private patio where no one would see us. Actually, we just made love a few minutes ago, and I came out here to the patio shirtless and braless in a pair of Sol sweatpants. Which hung off me, of course. My wild hair flowing down my back.

"You are so beautiful, Indie, my goodness."

"Thank you baby."

I kicked off Sol's pants and my panties before I returned to the bed, lying down right beside him on my back, smiling my ass off. Sol leaned down and planted a wet kiss on my lips, and I pulled him closer, kissing him again a few times.

"You're ready for me already?" He chuckled deep in his chest.

And I laughed too

I was past sore. I needed a massage, and he planned one for me. He had a masseuse on call who would come down and set up when I was ready. Another one of my birthday gifts he told me.

And as lovely as that sounds, I didn't want to leave Sol's arms. Or this room. Get dressed, either. And we hadn't, not since coming back last night. We didn't need to leave. This morning, we showered together, then had pancakes and omelets delivered.

This was the nicest rest I've had. In the nicest place I've ever stayed. Actually, it was the most rest I've gotten in a long time.

And Sol had been spoiling the hell out of me. Waiting on me. Taking care of me. The only thing I had to do for myself was go piss.

I lay beside him naked. Looking into his eyes. He'd began to caress me all over. Up and down my arms. My thighs. My flat stomach. Across my nipples.

My breath caught.

"Mmm."

"You like that, baby?"

"I love that baby."

He spent more time with the tiny gold hoop. He was partial to that one, which was fine with me.

"Ever think of getting the other one done?" He asked me.

"I haven't. Why?"

"Just curious." He kept rubbing his warm hands all over me.

"I could probably get the other one." My lids were fluttering. His warm hands and fingertips felt amazing. He had me pulsating below. I loved it when he played with my nipples. I was extremely sensitive there. He knew that. And I loved that he knew that and that he knew precisely what to do. "Mmm… it wouldn't be a big deal once it stopped hurting." I chuckled light and lazy. "You don't realize how angry nipples can't get until you pierce them and bump them all over everything. Even someone with small tits like mine."

Sol chuckled lightly, too. "I bet."

I felt his gaze as his eyes roamed my naked body. Really felt it. Like a hand touching my bare skin. Warm and gentle.

I wasn't shy, and I let him see me. I lay there. Being vulnerable. Feeling sexy. And free. Desired.

And. I wanted him again.

"India."

"Yeah."

"I like us like this."

"Me too."

When his eyes returned to mine, "I think about kissing you all the time." He told me.

"I think about a lot more than that," I revealed. It was a whisper.

And we didn't wait. His mouth was on mine before the words hardly left me. One sweet, tender kiss, followed by another one. And another one. Deeper than the one before it. I felt his warm hand slip down and settle low on my waist. And I brought both of my arms around his neck. Threaded my fingers into his locs.

He gently pulled me closer as he settled on top of me. And our deep kisses were slowing down. Getting hotter. Wetter. Nastier.

I let him pull me even closer. And I could feel him. There wasn't a question about how much he wanted me. And I wanted him too. Breathless, he gently broke our kiss. Pressing his forehead to mine. "Indie." He chuckled. "I'm not trying to ware you out. If you ask me to stop, I will."

"Who said you're doing the waring out?"

That made Sol laugh. He gave me a deep belly laugh, too. Once he calmed down, he smiled at me. A smile that made me feel like the most desired woman in the world.

More than desired.

Wanted.

Adored.

Loved.

Appreciated.

Yeah.

"Don't want to stop, baby." I whispered. "Just take your time with me… a little sore."

He dipped low, kissing my cheek tenderly. "Always baby."

When he touched me again, his passion and his need for me was glaring. Loud. Like a siren. He pressed into me, and though he moved slowly, gently, my breath would always catch. Sharp. Each time. Every time.

"How are you still this tight, Belle?" he dipped low again, capturing my lips. Then he was under my chin, licking. Sucking. Driving me fucking crazy. "Fuck. I was just here." He chuckled again. "Damn, you're wet, baby. You missed me that much?"

Yeah. I was so wet. Turned the fuck on and still humming from the love we made less than an hour ago. Sol continued his gentle thrusts, and I had a slight… coquettish grin. But said nothing. Moaning. Eye lids fluttering. I looked away for a second, but I swiftly brought my eyes back.

"So you're shy now? That's new." He teased. Flirty.

Yeah. He felt so damn good.

As wet as I was and I was so fucking slippery, I still felt everything. Sol is… *blessed* in this department. And he took such care with me. He held me, talking in my ear and singing my praises. And every move he made felt like tender words softly spoken. We moved together. Slow and intentional. And we laughed. Kissed. Through the heat, the pain, and the pleasure.

The world outside was a blur. It was only us. Only our breath and heartbeats. Sol responded to my body as I pulled him closer. Wrapping my arms around him tighter and anchoring myself the way I love to do. Especially when we're lovemaking.

"Indie… my goodness. You feel so good to me. Fuck baby."

I moaned, then managed to find my voice. "Sol. You feel so good to me too."

It was perfect.

I used to think I understood connection. But what Sol and I had… this was once it a lifetime.

Something steady. Something real.

Something sure.

And our lovemaking.

Making love.

It was already explosive. Delicious. Addicting.

And here in Tahoe, we'd been going at it. Especially today.

It was all I wanted to do.

We didn't move afterward. Not for a while. Neither did we rush to fill the silence. We remained in the stillness and the quiet. I curled up against his chest, a place I loved to be. He held me in his arms, slowly caressing my skin and asking me every so often if I was alright. If I needed anything.

Almost as if to confirm that I was here and that I was real.

Oh sol. I'm here baby.

I'm right here.

I'm here and I'm real.

fifty

INDIA

"This has been one of the best birthdays I've ever had. Thank you Sol. You're really amazing."

"You're so welcome, Belle. I'm glad you could do this." He told me. "You deserve it, you know."

I loved it here in Tahoe. Being unplugged from everything. I had my man, and I had my tote. And that's all I really needed for now. We were curled into each other. Lying up in this impossibly comfortable bed. Chilling. The sun had gone down about an hour ago.

We'd gotten up, taken showers, and changed the linens, too. Then we went outside for a walk and some fresh air.

We grabbed something to-go for dinner from a small restaurant in the plaza.

"Thank you." A beat. "I love it up here. It's just quiet enough. Serene. Gorgeous scenery. I have you here. Got to make love outside." I giggled. "I could get used to this."

"We can come here as often as you like, Belle."

"Really?"

"Really."

I smiled. "I'll hold you to it."

"I hope you do."

Sol looked at me with those reverent eyes he always has.

"Guess what?" He posed.

I smiled again. "What?"

"It's been confirmed. Sam and I are identical twin brothers."

"Sol! That's amazing! Congratulations!" I wrapped my long arms around his neck, pulling him down toward me. Kissing his lips. His jaw. His cheeks. All over. "I love this for you!"

"Thank you." He returned to his comfortable position. He was still lying on his side. His head propped on his hand. A few pillows behind him. Smiling.

"How do you feel?" I'd settled on my back again and cuddled close. Right next to him.

"It's a feeling I can't describe. But. I'm so happy. We're making plans to meet each other. I'll meet his wife. His daughter. My niece… you'll still come with me, right?"

"I wouldn't miss it."

"Having you there will mean so much." He told me. Then he looked off in the distance. Chuckling lightly. "I didn't expect this to ever happen. And I'm so glad about it."

"Me too."

A beat. "Next, I'd love to find out where we're from. Our heritage. Sam knew a few things, but not that part."

"Yeah. Why not. That would be cool. Another piece to the puzzle."

"Yeah."

We were silent. And it was a comfortable silence. The birds chirping outside were the only sounds we heard for a good while. He'd resumed caressing me all over.

"Sol."

"Yeah."

"I'm a twin too."

He stilled his movements.

"A twin? Really?"

I nodded. Saying nothing.

"Wow. Why am I just now learning this about you?"

I shrugged. "It's a sensitive topic."

His hand was moving again.

"Are you estranged?"

"She's no longer here."

He stilled his movements again.

"Oh, Belle. You mean…?"

I nodded. "Yeah. She passed away."

"I'm so sorry."

I smiled weakly. "It's alright. We were premature, and she was here for seventeen days." A few beats. "I wish I'd had a chance to know her. But I'll see her again someday."

"You absolutely will." He leaned down, kissing me sweetly on the temple.

"Want to know something crazy?" I smiled because I loved this story.

"Sure." Sol smiled too.

"When my parents found out they were having twin daughters, they agreed that each of them would name one of the babies. But they wouldn't tell each other or anyone else the names. Just keep it to themselves. When we were born, that's when they finally shared the names with each other."

Sol nodded.

"When the time came to tell each other the names, they couldn't believe the names they'd each picked. Yet, at the same time, they weren't even surprised. My mom named me. She chose my name to honor my father. His pride in his homeland and the stories he'd tell her about his years there as a young lad. You know. Childhood memories. It's why she fell in love with him. His pride and the heart he had for his people. His culture. But he still made room to learn about hers."

"Amazing."

"Yeah. But get this! My dad chose my sister's name: Kenya, in honor of my mom, for the very same reasons."

His eyes were wide. His mouth agape. "What?"

"Yeah."

"So, mom is Kenyan?"

"Yup. My mother's family migrated to the Caribbean and then settled in Guyana by way of Kenya."

"Wow. That's a story."

"Isn't it?"

A few beats.

"What's your middle name?" Sol asked me.

"Ayana."

"India Ayana Rampersaud. Hmm. You're so beautiful with a beautiful name."

"Thank you. What's yours?"

"David."

"Aww. I love it."

"Thank you."

Another beat.

"You know, Belle. Being with you through all of this, I've given a lot of thought to the future. I know we've discussed building a life together." We were eyes on eye again. "When I think about the future and what it looks like, I see you. I want to marry you, and I dream of creating a legacy of our own. A family down the road. Babies. If that's something you want too. I just want you to know where my heart is. It's here with you." After a moment, Sol added, "We're both twins. Wouldn't it be crazy if we had twins?"

I didn't say anything. For a while. Because… honestly. This was always a touchy subject for me. But I knew the day would come when we needed to talk about this.

"It would be." I tried to say it casually, but Sol knows me like the back of his hand. And he picked it up immediately.

"Hey. Belle. You good?"

I sighed, saying nothing.

"India. Look at me, please." His voice tender. Gentle. He rubbed my arm softly.

I did.

"Where'd you go, baby?" he asked in the calmest tone possible.

God, he knew me. This man knew me. And he cares for me. Always fostering a safe space for me to open up. To be vulnerable. But never in a rush about it. Ever. I went somewhere I didn't like to go. A place that hurt. A place that opened old wounds.

But Sol. His eyes were on me. He was still absently caressing me. Validating my courage to open up.

"Sol. Can I please tell you something?"

"Of course you can. Please do baby. And take your time. You know you can tell me anything."

I nodded slow. And it took a while before I spoke again.

Sol kept his gaze on me. His eyes remained fixed on my face, but I looked away. I took a slow breath and revealed something I had never spoken of before. Never. But I wanted to share this with him.

"The topic of kids always kind of messes me up. But it isn't because of you. I love the idea of building a life with you. But a part of me feels scared and undeserving." I took a heavy pause. "When I was younger, I had two abortions. One when I was still a teenager, and another one in my early twenties. The guy I was with at the time… Amir. He pushed me to do it. And I just… I have this mix of guilt and fear. Like, I don't deserve another chance to be a mom. And my parents depend on me so much. I love them and I'd do anything for them. But… I don't want my kids to be burdened with me." I sighed. "I just don't think that I'm worthy."

Neither of us spoke for a moment. I was worried I'd lost him.

"Thank you for trusting me with that." Sol's voice was quiet.

"Do you still love me?" I asked. Before I could stop it. But I wondered.

The emotion was ever-present when he said, "Hey. Come here." He reached for my hand, and we intertwined our fingers. "Belle, I want to assure you, nothing about your past changes how I see you or how much I care about you."

"I worried it would." My eyes went back to his, and they were gentle and steady.

"What happened to you back then doesn't make you unworthy of love, family, or happiness." "You did what you had to do in difficult situations. I couldn't judge you."

"Really?"

"Really. I understand your hesitation about kids. And we don't have to have it all figured out right now. What's important to me is you and me. Let's focus on that for now. Building this solid, beautiful thing while being honest and moving at a pace that feels right. No pressure. No rush. Just us." I smiled at that. I always smiled at that. "All I want is a life with you."

"It means the world to hear you say that, Sol."

"I mean it, Belle. And I don't want you to forget you deserve to be cared for, too."

He leaned down, kissing my cheek, then my lips. I snuggled into him as he wrapped his arm around me. We sat in the settled quiet, and it felt so good to have shared this. Yeah. We were silent for a while. Sol was on his back now. I was still wrapped in his arms.

"Belle."

"Yeah."

"There's something I've been holding off telling you."

I turned toward him immediately. Growing extremely nervous. "What is it?"

"It's exciting. But. I wanted to find the right time to bring it to you. Because this will impact both of us."

Exciting? He didn't seem excited. "Okay." I said slowly. "What is it?"

"I was offered a great job opportunity. Full-time. Tenure track."

"That's great Sol!"

"Yeah. But it's out of state. In Montreal, Canada"

"Oh… wow. That's huge. And you've worked so hard. Congratulations." I tried my damndest to say that sincerely. Because I meant it sincerely. But. My mood shifted. I wanted to laugh. I wanted to cry. I wanted to fucking scream. As happy as I was for Sol… and I am. Genuinely delighted for him. I just… I knew this was too good to be true. Just when I could breathe again… relax again. Settle into this relationship with no worries… then something like this happens.

"India. Baby. You're the first person I thought of when I got the offer. Honest to God. And I know your life is here. I'd never pressure you or want you to leave any of that behind. But I want you to know that I'd love for us to find a way to make this work. Figure it out, whatever it takes. I've told you, you're a part of my future, and that includes wherever my life takes me."

"Sol. *How?*" I begged. A tear rolled down my face, and he gently wiped it away. "That's so far."

"I know baby. I know. But I still chose you. I still want us. Somehow." A few beats. "We can figure this out together. I'm not making any decisions without you. I know your life is here. Your parents. Your work. Your friends. Everything. And I wouldn't ask you to toss any of that aside. At the same time, I couldn't just walk away from you. Or us… Not without fighting for all we've built. We've come too far, baby."

I looked into his eyes. They were tender and emotional. With depth. And I saw… clarity. And confirmation. I knew I could trust Sol's words. And the selfless position he just expressed was all the confirmation I needed. And. Most of all, I was tired of running. I nodded. Tears still in my eyes. "What do we do now, baby? I want us too. And the idea of being so far apart scares me. But I want to try. I know we can find a way somehow. If we both really want this, we can find a way."

He squeezed my hand. Reassuring me. "We will. Whatever it takes. If we're long-distance for a while. Or trying to figure out a move down the line. We can work this out. As long as we keep showing up for each other."

He leaned down, pressing his forehead to mine, and we stayed quiet for a while. The love between us, along with the fear and the certainty that we would face whatever came next together, was almost overwhelming. But I wouldn't worry about it right now. This would affect us both, and it would take more than a few conversations to work through everything. But that was okay. We could do it. We had each other.

"I've never had someone fight for me the way you do," I said softly.

"About time you did. Because I'm not giving up on us, baby. We're going to figure this out."

I managed a smile. "Yes, we will."

After a moment, "You're everything I never thought I'd find. From the beginning, you've seen me. All of me." I laughed. "And you're still here." Sol laughed too. I continued, "I want nothing more than to be with you, baby… can't even imagine doing this with anyone else. Whatever we have to do. I chose you."

I held his gaze again, tears still streaming down my face, and they were happy tears. Sol smiled at me, pulling me into his arms once more. Chest to chest, we lay there. I leaned into him, closed my eyes, feeling peaceful and safe, smiling contentment.

He gently whispered into my hair as he said, "That means the world, Belle. I chose you too. I'll always choose you. Again, and again…" He kissed my forehead. "I'll choose you."

Fifty-one

SOL

"How are you?" India asked me.

"My stomach is in knots." I laughed. "But I'm good. I'm ready." We were settling into our hotel suite. I was hanging a few things in the closet.

My thoughts, my emotions, everything had been haywire all day. The past few days. I hardly slept last night. We flew nonstop from Sacramento to Baltimore/Washington International, and the flight was about 5.5 hours. And thank goodness, I got a little sleep on the flight, so that helped.

Once we got in, we rented a car and drove to our hotel in Columbia. With traffic, the drive was about twenty-five minutes. My nerves were up and down all the while.

We got showered and changed and in just about an hour, I'll be meeting Sam.

I'm grateful he wants to meet me as eagerly as I want to meet him. I couldn't take that for granted. But I'm so very grateful.

After talking for several weeks and texting almost daily and checking in with each other and learning so much about each other. Then, officially confirming what we already knew, we decided it was time.

And now, here we were.

It was tripping me out being here in Columbia, Maryland, knowing that Sam and I are in the same state. The same city. Just a few miles apart.

Aside from meeting each other, Sam and I hadn't made any other concrete plans. I figured at minimum India and I could check out a few things since she'd never been this way.

"You'll do fine, baby." India approached me from across the room, and we embraced. We held each other, and she calmed and centered me. I was so grateful she was here. This was just what I needed to clear my mind.

"Appreciate you being here." I spoke into her mass of curls. Those brought me comfort too.

"I will always be here for you, baby."

After taking a deep inhale, I murmured, "Belle. You smell way too good for my peace of mind."

She tittered, bringing her arms even tighter around me. Sweet and sultry, she said, "Dr. Avery… you can't simply whisper something like that and expect me to function."

She looked up at me. Smiling. It reached her bright eyes.

"You know exactly what you're doing." She beamed but gave me a coy expression. I chuckled then nodded. "Alright. Keep looking at me like that, and we'll have a problem, Indie." I pressed myself closer to her. "If I didn't know any better, I'd think you were trying to distract me."

She threw her head back as she cackled. I took the opportunity to kiss her all over her neck. Licked her there too. I love her long, slender neck. I kiss it almost as much as I kiss her lips. Almost.

"Who's doing the distracting?" She gave me a pointed nod. "You're standing real close. He's not hidden in those jeans, baby." She pressed herself closer to me. "I like it."

"Hmmm."

We stood there, wrapped in a warm embrace, pressed pelvis to pelvis. I loved how tall India is. This afternoon, she wore a pair of black wedge-heeled boots, which made her even taller. These boots nearly reached her knees, making her legs look even longer.

When we stand body to body, we're a perfect fit like two puzzle pieces. I fit right into her sweet spot.

"I like it too baby." I continued to press myself into her. Growing harder by the second.

I felt my phone vibrating in my pocket and I got the feeling it was Sam.

I glanced at my watch. It was.

My Brother Sam: We'll see you all shortly. Dropping off Mina and we'll be headed over.

Me: Bet! We'll see you there can't wait!

My Brother Sam: Can't wait

"Can we pick this up later, baby?" I kissed India's lips tenderly. "We should head out. That way we won't be late if we get lost."

She pressed a few kisses sweetly against my lips. "We absolutely can." A few more kisses. "I'll drive us, baby," India stated around a sweet smile. "Sol, I love you to pieces, but you're a little too jittery for me to trust you navigating this traffic."

We laughed.

"That's fair."

"You know what's funny?" I asked India as I entered the address into the GPS. We were settled in the rental. Seatbelts on.

"What's that?"

"This place we're meeting. It's on Mango Tree Road." I looked over at her into her expectant eyes. "You love mangoes baby. Meeting my brother at a place on a street called Mango Tree Road of all the things it could be. And you're here with me. Taking this step with me. It's all happening the way it's meant to. In the time it's meant to."

India beamed. And it was so beautiful.

"I love that."

She was right about my jitters. As we made our way to the café, my leg bounced nonstop, and I drummed my fingers against my thighs repeatedly.

"Relax, baby," India told me. Gently. "Breathe. You've done plenty of hard things. You can handle meeting Sam." She glanced at me quickly, offering her smile.

That smile.

My. That smile. It was something I could count on. Something I was so sure of. Yeah.

We cruised down I-395 S, enjoying the early-fall East Coast scenery. The trees had changed color, and leaves covered the ground. On this early November afternoon, the sun was shining, but a chill hung in the air. And this East Coast chill wasn't anything like the West Coast one. It was probably in the upper forties. We knew to come prepared and to dress for the occasion.

And. I couldn't name one time in my life I've felt as nervous as I do right now.

"Name one." I playfully challenged.

"That TED talk. You said it was in front of thousands. Thousands more tuned in to watch the live-stream. And millions have viewed it on YouTube."

I nodded. "I was beside myself for sure that day. But this is different."

"Hmm."

Yeah. I've never felt this way.

Not before my TED talk. Not even when I performed on a televised Carnegie Hall stage. I auditioned to be a part of a youth orchestra and beat out tens of thousands of kids from all over the world for a spot. What an honor. I was in high school at the time, but that's an experience I won't forget as long as I live.

And yet. Neither of those compared to how my nerves were moving and flipping, doing somersaults in the pit of my stomach right now.

Our interstate exit led us onto State Highway 32 W toward Columbia, then onto Columbia Pike/US-29 N. I was thankful for the GPS. I could read a map if I needed to, but these highways, freeways, and turnpikes here are quite different. India had this under control, and thank goodness. I'd since taken her hand in mine, and hand in hand, we remained.

And the ride was peaceful, aside from the music filling the air around us. I think she understood I needed it.

India briefly glanced at me.

"Almost there. You okay?"

And I laughed. "Perhaps." By the time I looked to my left, she was looking ahead. But she wore a smile. A smile I'd fallen in love with a long time ago. A smile that anchored me. And brought me comfort. And assurance. "Define okay?" I pressed teasing. Cracking jokes through my jitters was my way of coping.

As nervous as I was, I was just as excited.

"Hmm..." She lightly tittered. Easing my nerves somewhat. "Not backing out. Not asking me to turn this car around. Not fainting or something?" She tossed out in a playful tone.

"Oh. I'm good then!"

We laughed.

"Maybe it is a different kind of nervous. But you can handle meeting your brother." India said.

And the way the word brother landed was heavy. Huge. Significant. And comforting. I smiled at that and inhaled deeply, taking my time with the exhale.

I settled into the resolve that I wouldn't have to wait much longer.

We'd exited the freeway, and when the sign for Busboys and Poets came into view, my stomach really started to act up. I swear I had bubble guts or something.

We parked in a lot across the street, and I went around to the driver's side to open India's door as I got a text.

My Brother Sam: We're seated a little further back. Look for Langston Hughes.

Attached was a painted portrait of Langston Hughes, and that stopped me in my tracks. I showed it to India.

"That is incredible!"

"Right!"

Me: We're headed in now. Just parked.

The chilly air bit at our cheeks, and we were glad to make it inside.

As soon as we crossed the threshold, I felt this shift. It was two-fold. I knew in just a few short moments, my brother and I would be reunited. Finally.

But this space. It was... so rich in culture. The energy. The vibe. It was hard to put into words.

When we planned this meetup, Sam recommended the place.

My Brother Sam: There's a spot called Busboys and Poets, and they have a location near me. Great food. Great vibes.

Me: We'd love to check it out. And that sounds like the start of an artistic expression. 'Two brothers walk into a poetry café..."

My Brother Sam: Man! Doesn't it tho?! Like a song. Or poem. Or the title of a painting.
Me: All three
Yeah.

The ambiance here was artistic and creative. There was vibrant artwork everywhere. And as India and I maneuvered through the dining room, I saw a staircase along the wall lined with pictures of black icons, civil rights activists, musicians, politicians, and educators.

Busboys and Poets reminded me a lot of HomeGrown, almost like they could be fraternal twins. Funny enough.

This place was larger, with seating upstairs and downstairs, both indoors and on the patio. A great spot to gather. The décor was top-notch. I saw a bar. I saw books for sale. Plenty of chairs, couches, and a small stage. It had a casual vibe, and I felt a strong sense of community, creativity, and cultural awareness here. No doubt about that. This place was an experience.

It smelled like fresh roasted coffee. Savory aromas greeted me quickly, and the clinking of plates, the low chatter, and the hum of jazz music were reminiscent of HomeGrown, which gave me comfort and settled my spirit.

India and I were still hand in hand, and I gently squeezed hers when I finally spotted the portrait of Langston hanging over the faces of strangers, laughing, chatting, and breaking bread together.

"I'm here, baby. Right here," she assured.

I halted in my steps and turned toward her.

"I can see the painting. They're somewhere nearby."

No sooner than when I turned around, I saw him.

Sam was waving eagerly. Excitedly.

"Over here! Sol! Right here!"

I looked back at India. Not sure why. Maybe to make sure she was still there despite her hand still being in mine. Or maybe to confirm she'd seen what I saw.

And I was smiling wide, my eyes filled with tears as she gently nudged me.

"There's your brother. Go ahead, baby," she whispered.

I saw a woman next to Sam, speaking in a low voice. They were a few feet away from us. Maybe she was encouraging him just like India had encouraged me.

We both moved toward each other, and when we finally faced one another, eyes locked, we instinctively embraced.

We hugged as if we'd known each other forever. And we basically had. It was as if the years of separation never happened. We held on for so long, neither of us wanting to let go.

I didn't let go until he did.

"This is… damn. This is crazy." Sam said.

And I chuckled. Thinking the very same thing. "I'm saying! It's like looking in the mirror!"

Sam nodded. Smiling as he looked at me.

I did the same. With pride, I studied my brother. We had the same broad smile. Same eyes.

"Well, my locs are shorter," Sam chuckled. Sam had a high fade with short locs on top. Modern with an edge. I like it. Seemed to fit his personality. I kept mine shoulder-length, and I had a low fade. "And you've got a fuller beard," he added.

I have a fuller beard, but I kept it low and neat. Sam had a heavy stubble, but it was trimmed and thick. "Right. Am I taller than you?" I stood beside him with my shoulders back.

"You are. At least an inch."

I stood in front of him again. "This is really happening? Are we really here? Or is this a dream?" Slipped out before I could stop it.

"It's real. It's happening." Sam assured.

We hugged again.

In my peripheral vision, I saw the women embrace. They were standing close together and had been conversing among themselves.

I took the opportunity to meet my sister.

And introduce the woman who had quite literally changed my life. Sam was thinking the same thing.

"Sol. Please meet my wife. Shannon. She's been putting up with me. She knows how much I couldn't wait to meet you."

"Hey Sis."

"Bro!" She returned smiling and bright-eyed.

"Sam. Meet my lady, India." I gently took India's hand in mine. "She's special to me. She's kept me sane from the moment I learned you exist."

Sam gave her a quick side hug.

"Thank you for coming," he told her. "Being here for my brother. Means a lot to me."

"I'm so glad I could be here!" India smiled. "It isn't every day you meet a twin you didn't know you had. I'm so happy for both of you."

The four of us finally sat down. Sam and I sat across from each other, with the women beside us.

India and I sat close. Our shoulders and thighs touching. It was the same for Sam and Shannon.

And my sweet India. My constant emotional support had her soft fingers intertwined with mine under the table.

"I was in suspense for so long!" Sam offered. "I didn't know what to expect. But it's like I already know you. It's strange because the resemblance and mannerisms we share are tripping me out! But doesn't feel like I'm meeting a stranger at all."

"Yeah. Same here. It's a mix of recognition and strangeness." I said. "I feel like I know you like I know myself."

Sam nodded. "Maybe our spirits have been orbiting each other this whole time. It's the physical that needs to be reunited."

"Took thirty-five years to get you two in the same room again. But here you are," Shannon said. "The East Coast version and the West Coast remix."

We all laughed.

Our server came to take our order. We each got a drink and ordered an appetizer to share. The menu looked fantastic, and Sam and Shannon raved about the food.

As our server placed our drinks in front of us, we each thanked her. As she left, Sam chuckled, sitting back, relaxing his shoulders. "You sound just like me."

"You sound like me!" I returned smiling.

We all laughed again.

"I feel like I'm in the Twilight Zone!" India said she was still laughing

"Right?! Even their hands move the same way." That was Shannon.

Sam and I exchanged glances. We both realized at the exact moment that we were still holding our glasses in our left hands, just about to take a sip. Then we locked eyes and shared the same nervous laugh. Soon, the four of us burst out laughing all over again.

"I'm so glad you reached out, Sol," Sam told me.

"I am too. I'm indebted to my student who told me about you after the conference in Atlanta. I'll have to send him a picture and share the rest of the story."

When our food came out, none of us touched it right away. We were wrapped up in our conversation. The women were chatting like old friends. But quietly. So we could have space. India was laughing so much, which didn't surprise me. Shannon was lighthearted, funny, and warm. I saw the love Sam had for his wife. I loved to see that. He kissed her cheek many times.

I wasn't shy about kissing India either.

"Sol. You ever think about what life would've been like if we'd grown up together?"

"All the time. From the moment I found out about you." A few beats. It wasn't awkward. The silence was full and promising. "Honestly, I used to imagine having a brother out there. Somewhere. Strangely enough. But. I kept searching for you, and all leads led nowhere. This is so much more than I could have ever imagined."

"Yeah. It's a blessing. Beyond description." Sam looked off in the distance. "I knew about you. But I couldn't find you. I never thought I would see you. But I thought of you all the time. In my music. In my dreams." A beat. "I'm so glad you're real."

"I'm so glad you're real." I shared. I chuckled. "I wonder if the songs we've written would be different had we grown up together."

Sam laughed easy. "I wonder the same."

We prayed for our food and finally dug into our lunch entrees, and the food lived up to the hype. The presentation was excellent. And the flavors were on point.

I had blackened salmon with wild rice, grilled corn, tomatoes, and asparagus. India ordered shrimp and grits. Sam went with fried catfish, collard greens, and jalapeño grits. Shannon ordered chicken penne pasta.

After our meals and more conversation, we stepped out into the cool late afternoon. There was a calm lake just outside the café, and a gentle breeze moved across the water.

"It is disrespectful out here!" Shannon said, pulling her coat tighter.

India and I were hand in hand, looking at each other, then back at Sam and Shannon.

Reading our confused expressions, Sam offered, "That means it's really cold out here."

As understanding dawned on our faces, Sam and Shannon burst into laughter.

"You've got bicoastal fluency. Right. Fluent in East Coast and West Coast." I nodded. "Makes sense." I laughed again while talking to Sam.

We strolled around the lake, leisurely enjoying our walk. India's gloved hand held securely in mine. Sam's arm rested low, firmly around Shannon's waist. They walked close together.

Sam was still laughing. "Left the West Coast when I was eighteen. But my wife is DMV proud. I had to learn quick!"

"That's right! PG County all day!" Shannon chimed in quite enthusiastically.

We laughed again.

"I can relate. India grew up between Northern California and Berbice, Guyana. I've learned a thing or two from her myself."

"That's really interesting," That was Sam.

"Yeah! That's dope! I thought I heard an accent." That was Shannon.

"I've been telling India she has an accent." I gently teased her while she smiled shyly and looked away.

Shannon continued, "I love Caribbean food. There are some great spots out here, but I'm sure homemade is even better."

"It certainly is! I get all the jerk chicken, peas and rice, and fried plantain I can handle!" I smiled, proud to brag on my woman. "She can cook anything, but she really puts her foot in Caribbean food. Makes it her own with a personal spin."

"Oh Sis! You gotta come by the house and make us something!" Sam said.

We all cackled at that.

We were here for three more days. We talked about visiting the National Museum of African American History and Culture in D.C. before we left. They insisted we see it, saying it was life-changing.

"Indie, would you mind?" I smiled at her, still holding her hand gently. "We can work that out, right, baby?"

Her smile widened into her megawatt smile. "I'd love to. Sure."

"Like tomorrow?" That was Shannon.

"Sure. Tomorrow's fine with me." She looked at Shannon. "I can show you how to make your own jerk sauce, as mild or as spicy as you want. It's not hard at all."

Shannon and India had already exchanged numbers, and they began discussing going shopping tomorrow for some ingredients.

"We can have a jam session at the house tomorrow, too," Sam offered. "We should set up the tripod and film it. This is historic. Maybe we'll even bless the World Wide Web and post it online."

"Oh yeah, man! I'm down. Let's do it!" I replied excitedly.

Today was another one for the books.

Later, back in our suite, India asked me how I was doing and how it all felt. Finally meeting Sam.

And I couldn't quite put it into words, but I tried. I told her it was almost like coming home, as if I had found a missing piece of myself and now everything felt complete. As if he's been part of my life forever. The fact that Sam and I talk all the time prepared me for our meeting. And we talked all the time. About so much.

Another vulnerability I had with India was my fear that Sam might resent me. We had been discussing our lives, and he learned about all the privileges I had. I reluctantly shared those details because he asked and wanted to understand me. I felt guilty and worried there might be resentment since he grew up in the system. He was never adopted and fought for his life literally from birth.

I told him several times how proud I am of him for making a life for himself.

But he didn't resent me. He embraced me as if I were a gift he'd waited years for, and it finally arrived just in time. I shared those same feelings.

And our resemblance is even more striking in person.

Sam proudly mentioned that we would meet his adorable daughter, Mina, tomorrow. I was beyond excited to meet my niece, and I loved that he was such a doting father and a proud husband. He spoke so highly, so lovingly of his wife. My sister. And that was amazing.

Most of all, I loved that not only had I met my brother, but I also gained a sister and a niece.

I'm excited to see them tomorrow.

As we strolled around the lake, talking over the distant noise of cars crossing the nearby bridge, Sam and Shannon had us laughing so hard.

We somehow ran back the confusion we had about the word 'disrespectful' meaning cold outside. So they took the liberty of explaining some more East Coast slang, and I was still trying to understand it.

One thing was about people in Baltimore saying 'Doug' instead of 'dog.' Then Shannon mentioned that some folks in PG County might say 'glizzy,' which means hot dog.

She also tried explaining the battle of the Beltway and the small rivalry between the upper side of the Beltway, where Baltimore is, and the lower side of the Beltway, which is more PG County.

It was hilarious because Shan, as she insisted we call her, got so animated and had us rolling until my sides hurt.

After reflecting on it, I told India that I truly believe the moment I met Sam wouldn't have meant as much if I hadn't shared it with her.

And that was the thing.

Everything good was with my India. My Artist Girl, my Belle, my favorite harmony, my favorite melody, my favorite tune, my favorite song. Everything that made sense, everything that required my full attention and concentration, everything simple, everything complex, everything beautiful, everything captivating, everything extraordinary. Yeah.

epilogue

about six months later
INDIA

As "Celebration" by Kool and the Gang blared through the speakers, we all rose to our feet as the guests of honor made their entrance.

Clapping. Cheering. Whistling.

We were all dressed in our best and packed out at Laguna Town Hall in Elk Grove. It's a modern, state-of-the-art, and fully equipped event space perfect for this momentous occasion.

Tonight, we celebrated Micah's parents' 40th wedding anniversary and their vow renewal.

And everyone was here. They had family from near and far to celebrate this joyful occasion.

Destiney's father was here with his fiancée, Ms. Natalie, and she's so sweet. She's the perfect match for a man like Mr. Evans. He was a widower after Destiney and Daijah's mother passed away from breast cancer nearly twenty years ago. For a long time, he took on the role of a single dad. She seemed to have come along at just the right time, and they had plans to get married early next year. We were thrilled for them.

Mr. Evans and Ms. Natalie were sitting at the same table as Ma and Daddy. And I'm so glad they could come out. In the past, they weren't always so enthusiastic about these things because maybe they weren't feeling up to it. But here they were, and all was well. Daddy has been getting injections in his joints to help manage his arthritis pain. Thankfully, he's been responding well, and it's reduced the inflammation and the pain. He still has bad days, but they are much less frequent. He's been able to work more when he wants to or whenever he feels the itch to build something.

Ma's finally been able to manage her glaucoma better. After trying several options, they found eye drops that work well for her, allowing her to keep her eye pressure under control. She also had a laser treatment. Thankfully, she isn't in much pain, just occasional discomfort. And her vision loss has not significantly worsened. It's been such a blessing that they've been doing so well.

They seemed to be having a great time tonight. I'd gone over to check on Ma and Daddy earlier. They're enjoying themselves.

Also, seated at the same table were Mr. and Mrs. Avery.

Yes. Sol's mother and father.

Our parents met after I met Sol's mom.

A couple of days after the benefit, Sol took me to their house. His childhood home, and his mom apologized.

Profusely.

She apologized for her behavior and asked for a chance to start again and get to know each other.

Sol and I talked about the elite world and all of the fuss with optics and appearance, and I had perspective. I couldn't relate, nor did I agree, but I could see why.

And I was more than willing to start over for a few reasons.

I want to have a good relationship with Sol's family.

I want him to have a good relationship with his own family.

And I want him to have a great relationship with my family.

Mrs. Avery seemed one hundred percent genuine. She was quite emotional. And I believed she meant every word.

And because we all need ease and grace sometimes.

So many people only want grace when they're on the receiving end. We can all do a little better.

But things are well with us. Thank goodness. Mrs. Avery has been wonderful. We talk all the time. We've gone to brunch a few times. And she and Ma have a great relationship, too. The last few times I looked across the room, I saw all three ladies chatting away. Quite engrossed in their conversation.

Mr. and Mrs. Walker, Micah's parents, were finally seated at their table after a dozen pictures, and their standing ovation was over. Their table was beautifully decorated in oranges, yellows, and greens.

The entire event hall was beautifully decorated. My favorite part of all was the backdrop with a sign that said, "40 Years Strong and We Still Do." Everyone went to take pictures under it. I'd be sure to get my photo op before the night was out, too.

Speaking of which, there were two photographers taking pictures of everything, capturing it all. There was also a videographer, along with someone going around interviewing people, asking for their well-wishes for the next forty years, and to share any moments and memories of the couple they had.

Destiney told me, as the family lore goes, Mr. Walker met Mrs. Walker at the skating rink back in the mid-eighties. They were both out with some friends, and he approached her. I love stories like that. And they made such a lovely couple. I've always adored Destiney's mommy in love as Destiney affectionately calls her.

So far, we've all been enjoying the delicious appetizers. A plated dinner will be served soon. There was a dessert table as well for after dinner.

"Des! Look at your in-laws!" I told her once she'd returned to our table. They were out of their seats, dancing together, having a good time. "Still glowing in love. That's amazing."

"Right!" Destiney agreed, taking her seat. She had a plate of roasted artichokes and a couple of eggplant rollups. "To look that good after forty years and still be in love is goals!"

"Girl! Cheers to that!" Ella offered. Destiney and I lifted our glasses of ice water and toasted with the other ladies at our table. The female half of the crew.

Ella sat on the other side of Destiney, and Daijah was on the other side of her. Mala was here too, sitting right next to me. And yeah. Mala was now part of the crew. She'd been hanging out with us a lot more.

I'd just taken a look at the tattoo I did for her right before Sol and I left for Canada. It was a heart-shaped Earth on her forearm, in full color. It healed well, with clean lines and vibrant colors that still popped against Mala's brown skin. It was a good size too, covering a significant part of her forearm. It was perfect for Mala, representing everything she's about. She's so passionate about the world we live in, and she's a lover of people and the environment. I loved her so much for trusting me with that job. It's the largest color piece I've done so far. It took a few sessions, but I couldn't be more proud of it.

I got my license at The Ink Studio, a tattoo shop I discovered that was such a perfect fit and such a great place to be. I wish I had gone sooner. They were new, only a few years in business, with just three women artists working there, including the owner. It was in a modest storefront, but the vibrant artistic energy there made me feel welcome right away.

I met with the owner and showed her my portfolio, which I had started building during my time at King's. I demonstrated what I could do, and I received credit for my other training hours since Kam was willing to sign off on my time at King's.

Yeah. It was such a great fit. They hated that I was moving to Canada. I planned to return to the Ink Studio for the summer. The owner told me I was always welcome there.

"You know something about that, Ella! You and Mal are almost halfway there! "That was Daijah.

"Yeah, you two are the veterans!" Destiney said. She'd already started filling her mouth.

And I felt just like she did. Those appetizers were so good, but I was saving room for dinner.

And I didn't really want to go back to that table.

The various aromas were too much for me right now. I actually needed to get some fresh air. All the smells in here were too much for me right now.

"How long have you and Malachi been married, Ella?" Mala asked, sipping her glass of white wine.

Ella smiled wide. "All our lives."

We laughed.

"No, but it'll be seventeen years this year. Together for twenty years. We're high school sweethearts."

"I love that."

"Me too."

"Yeah, me too."

We all chimed in.

"That does seem like a lifetime only to be thirty-five years old." Daijah offered.

"Exactly. And we're trying to catch up." Destiney smiled.

"Oh, absolutely!" Daijah co-signed. She and Destiney were married just a month apart. That was so sweet. They were nearing year number three soon.

Earth, Wind & Fire's "September" was on now, and people were grooving on the dance floor, and everyone was having such a great time. The space was filled with all the good things. Joy. Love. Warmth. An electric and magnetic energy. There were smiles and laughter everywhere I looked.

And I was so glad to be in the room.

"How are you, Belle?" I smiled when I heard Sol's voice behind me. He leaned down, pressing a soft kiss to my cheek, and I could feel the gentle brush of his hand on my back. "Are you alright?"

"I am. Thank you." I lingered in the space between the chair and him, then stepped into his arms. He held me close, his warmth settling around me like a shield. "I missed you," I murmured, pressing my face against his chest. He didn't even go anywhere, but right now, I felt extra clingy. For some reason.

"I'm right here, baby." Sol's voice was steady. Calm. But there's a hint of something tender that makes my chest tighten. Sol, Micah, Malachi, Julian, and Ray went to a spot near the double doors leading to the courtyard. Ten minutes apart is nothing. But somehow, it's enough to make me crave this.

"And I missed you too. The babies wanted to see the string lights outside. Calmed them down a little."

"Aww." I nuzzled against his neck, inhaling the familiar scent of him, smiling against his warmth.

"Happy to be home?" he asked me. His hand lingered on the small of my back.

"I am. I am. How about you?"

"So glad to be home."

When I returned to my seat, Daijah had her baby, Celine, in her lap.

Celine was about nine months old and as cute as a button. I love her curly hair and her big brown eyes. She's been looking at me. Curious because she knew me, but likely trying to remember from where. It had been a while since I saw them in person, and she'd grown so much. Celine smiled at me every time I smiled at her. Giggling whenever I made faces with her.

"That bartender hooked it up with this margarita. I'm going to get another one." Ella announced.

"Ella! Get me one too, please. I'm pumping and dumping tonight!" Daijah said.

There was an open bar, and a white sangria would hit the spot right about now.

"I'm going with you, Ella," Mala announced. "I need another glass of wine."

"Oh my gosh. I need a glass of wine too. Wish I could have one." Destiney offered.

She was holding her baby boy in her arms. When the men returned, they brought the babies with them. And Destiney's baby, my Godson, is so precious and sweet. And calm. I could just eat him up! I love his chubby cheeks. He was lying quietly on her chest, blinking slow. Seconds away from falling asleep.

"Have some Best," I told her.

Destiney had a look of… hesitation?

"Girl, if you don't have a damn glass! That freezer is full of milk to last Alex the rest of the year!" That was Daijah.

"I can't," Destiney said after saying nothing for a while.

"Girl, you can pump and dump! We won't judge you." Ella said.

"I still can't."

Yeah. I didn't even have to look at Destiney. I already knew.

"Why?" Daijah asked.

When Destiney said nothing, the ladies all leaned in, curious.

"Alexander is going to be a big brother." She finally shared through a smile.

"You're pregnant?"

"Again?"

"Already!?"

The ladies excitedly chimed in all at once.

"Yeah. We are pregnant again. Already. Just found out." Destiney beamed as we all offered our congratulations.

"How pregnant are you?" Ella asked.

"About ten weeks. They'll only be fourteen months apart."

Ella nodded. "Been there." Then she laughed. "I'd do it again too! I loved raising Gabe and Gabby close together."

Mal and Ella's teenagers were close in age and extremely close siblings. And such great kids. Good humans. Well-mannered. Both super studious, super athletic, and super ambitious.

"Yeah, you always wanted two. So, this will take care of that. Maybe it's a good thing you're having them so close together." Daijah offered. "I pray it happens for us soon. We've been trying for another one pretty much as soon as we got the six-week clearance." Her tone was solemn now.

"It will happen, Sibling Bestie. Don't worry. Try not to think about it so much. You know."

Daijah nodded. "I hope so. I'm getting nervous. With Celine, we got pregnant as soon as we started trying. This one's taking a lot longer than I expected it to."

"You guys know what we went through. It was so much work getting him here." Destiney kissed the top of Alex's head softly. He hardly stirred, and I knew he was down for the count. "And then this happened. It was a nice surprise. And a blessing but…I'm a little overwhelmed with the thought of two little ones."

"You'll do just fine. You'll rise to the occasion, and everything will be like second nature in no time." Ella said. "Plus, you've got Micah. He wouldn't let you get overwhelmed. He'll make sure everything's good."

"Oh, you know it! Micah wasn't playing around! I love my husband, but oh my gosh! Last time…" Destiney shook her head, laughing.

And we all laughed.

"Malachi was the same way." Ella was cracking up. "And they got it honest. I mean… their father is the epitome of devoted husband and father. Overprotective and everything else." Ella said pointedly as we all observed Mr. Walker out on the dance floor with Mrs. Walker. He twirled her and they embraced again, continuing to dance close as if no one else was in the room. They laughed at an inside joke and carried on.

Ella and Mala headed to the bar. And Daijah, Destiney, and I watched the couples dancing. Smiling. Relishing. The dance floor was made up of couples of all ages. It was so amazing seeing love across generations represented here. And all the commitments.

Marriages that have lasted a lifetime or two. Love stories just beginning. All of it was astonishing.

"Dance Tonight" by Lucy Pearl was on now, and everyone was still moving and grooving.

My phone vibrated.

It was Sam's wife.

Shan: I love it! I love it! I love it!!!

I'd sent her a picture of Sol and me when we were dressed for the party just before we left the house. She sent a million hearts and heart eyes.

Shan and I have become great friends. I loved meeting her when Sol and I went to the East Coast.

I'm so glad I could be there with Sol when he and Sam were reunited. That was my first time on the East Coast, and I loved it there.

Shan is seriously the dopest person I've met in such a long time.

And she's hilarious. We laughed and laughed like old friends. She kept quoting '90s black comedies, and I laughed until I cried.

Shan is DMV proud, too. I've told her many times how much I love her accent. The way she says daughter, father, and water always makes me laugh.

Also, I had to ask her if she was an East Coast native because her accent had a slight southern twang. She told me she gets that question a lot. It turns out her mother has deep southern roots, and somehow, if you can imagine, her accent has a bit of both.

She's smart as hell and quite accomplished. Academically and professionally.

"India?"

Destiney brought me from my thoughts.

"Yeah?"

"You're quiet. Don't think we haven't noticed you haven't been drinking either. And not that you're an alcoholic, but you'd normally be on your second or third sangria by now!" Daijah said.

We all laughed.

She was right. Sangria's we're my go-to. Or a red wine.

I shrugged. "I'm not feeling my best."

Destiney and Daijah expressed their concerns.

"I'll be alright," I assured. "I'll probably ask Sol to take me outside. I can use some fresh air."

"Yeah. Take a break from all of this if you need to. Best." Destiney knew how I got when I was in sensory overload. I didn't always do well in these settings. "There are a lot of people here. A lot of movement. A lot of noise."

I nodded. "Yeah. I'll get some fresh air soon. I'm sure that will help." I took another drink of my ice water.

"When are you two tying the knot?" Daijah asked after a moment. "I'm only asking. Just curious. I mean, you're there now anyway. You two have such a lovely thing going. I haven't seen anything quite like it. Ever. You're each so passionate, and the level of passion between you. It's palpable. It's fucking hot, actually! So intense! It's like a black romance novel. *Or movie!*

"Yeah!" Destiney chimed in excitedly. "I told you, Indie! Two artists get together and it's explosive! I love the way you two carry on. I bet when you're lovemaking, slow music starts playing." We all laughed. "You're so committed to each other. Living in another country together. What are you guys waiting on?"

I smiled at that. No lies detected.

It really was like an inferno between Sol and me.

Blistering.

Explosive.

I love Sol fiercely.

And his love for me is unrelenting. Unwavering.

Sol is madly in love with me, and he exhibits his love and commitment to me and to us every moment of every day.

His words. His actions.

Sol is amazing.

I smiled at that.

"Nothing, I guess. We've talked about marriage many times. We're just moving at our own pace. Enjoying the journey. But honestly, I'd marry Sol tonight. And I know he'd marry me with the drop of a hat."

"So why haven't you?" Destiney asked.

"I don't know. We just haven't, but I wouldn't mind being Sol's wife. I'd love that, actually."

"Maybe he's waiting on you to bring it back up?" Daijah offered.

"He may be."

"Ask him where he's at with it," Destiney said.

Nodding, I said, "That's a good idea. I think I will."

Montell Jordan's "This is how we do it" came on, and the energy in the place picked up. More of the younger crowd migrated to the dance floor. Daijah, Destiney, and I continued grooving from our seats.

I could see that Ella and Malachi had made their way to the dance floor. So had Mala, and she was dancing with some guy. I'm sure I'd get details on him later. Cousin Ray was out there dancing with his date. We met briefly, and she was cool.

As I sat there thinking about having this conversation with Sol, I started to worry.

I didn't want him to think I'm bringing up marriage for all the wrong reasons.

Like, now that we're here at an anniversary party and vow renewal., I'm pressuring him about it.

We've talked about marriage many times.

Not a big, expensive wedding. Not at all. A marriage.

We've joked about eloping and not telling anyone. And in the meantime, we've been vibing. Cruising and going at our own pace. And everything has been going well. Really well.

But. It had been a little bit since our last discussion. I wanted to see where he was with it. Just to see.

I shared my concern with Destiney and Daijah. And they reassured me immediately.

"I get it, Indie. But Sol knows your heart. You're only asking for the right reasons. He wouldn't misinterpret your motives." Destiney said.

"He won't think that Indie," Daijah told me with care. "Sol is crazy about you. Always has been."

Yeah.

I've been secure in our love for a long time.

The music mellowed. "Lovely Day" by Bill Withers brought that feel-good energy into the space. This DJ had been playing hit after hit. There were no fewer than five generations represented here tonight, and he'd been covering all of them with his song selections.

I glanced across the room again. Sol, Julian, and Micah were hanging out by the bar. Chatting away.

I caught my man's eye and smiled big and bright. His easy smile spread in seconds, and he winked at me. I blew him a kiss, and I beamed as he moved through the gestures of catching it and pressing it to his heart.

Sol went back to his conversation, and I adjusted in my seat, smoothing the fabric of my dress. Then I let my hands rest lightly on my flat belly, almost subconsciously, smiling inwardly.

There was another something I wanted to talk to him about, too. And I will tonight.

As soon as we were home and settled and alone. In our haven of peace, I'll tell him.

And we'll have a conversation about continuing to build our future.

The future we're already building. Something already growing.

I leaned back in my seat as the lively laughter, music, and voices continued around me.

Reveling in love through every decade here.

I'm so freaking grateful to be part of it.

And eagerly anticipating the promises of what's to come.

♪♥♫♥♪

SOL

I couldn't help but smile back when India caught my eye.

She's so beautiful, and tonight she seemed to be glowing.

If I didn't know any better… I swear I'd think…

She looked stunning tonight. All of the ladies did.

I loved that India and I could be here for this occasion. Mr. and Mrs. Walker were like another set of parents, and I wouldn't have missed this for the world.

But the whole crew was here.

Malachi, Ella, and their teenagers, Gabe and Gabby.

Micah, Destiney, and baby Alexander.

Julian, Daijah, and their little princess Celine.

Ray was here with his date.

India's cousin Mala. She came alone, but she seemed to be enjoying herself.

We just got back stateside the day before yesterday, so we were still jet-lagged.

It was a long day of traveling. We flew from Montreal to Chicago and then from Chicago to Sacramento.

There's also a three-hour time difference. Montreal is in the Eastern Time Zone. Three hours ahead of Sacramento.

We'd be home for the summer, and we were so glad to be back.

The University of Montreal wanted me and was willing to negotiate an offer better than anything I could have hoped for. I arranged a 1-1 load. I should mention that it's not typical for a new professor joining a faculty to have such an opportunity, but they were willing to agree to anything reasonable. I also believe my portfolio and CV were so strong that the decision wasn't difficult.

They were glad to decrease classroom hours so I could focus on research and publishing.

I teach one course in the fall. This year, I chose Music of the African Diaspora. The course explores the influence of African music, culture, and philosophy on the development of music in North and South America and the Caribbean.

I taught one course in the spring: Jazz History.

Jazz history documents the cultural, social, and musical development of the genre and its context. It also covers the styles and structures of the music, along with the major creators and innovators who shaped it. Additionally, we explored some surrounding art forms that influenced jazz, as well as others that emerged because of jazz. I enjoy teaching both of these courses, but jazz history is my favorite.

The rest of the time, I'm knee deep in research and grant writing. I attend conferences. Guest lecture. I also mentor and advise graduate students.

I still contribute to music journals. It's nice and very low-key. I was fortunate to basically set my own schedule.

I can still teach, which I believe is one of my callings. And I can still pursue music. It's the best of both worlds.

I've been given room to breathe, and summertime is all mine.

India and I live in an apartment just off campus in Montreal, and it's nice. We have plenty of space and we're comfortable. We got some bicycles, which we've used a lot. But the winters in Montreal are brutal, so we eventually got a car too.

I kept my home here in Sacramento. India and I returned to be with our family and friends. This is our time to reset.

Speaking of which, I knew India would miss her parents and worry about them, so I arranged some support for them so she wouldn't have to stress over anything.

My mother helped us find the best professional household support. We interviewed quite a few until we found the right match. Someone we could trust to handle their needs. They assist with errands, light housekeeping, grocery runs, and meal prep when needed, helping everything run smoothly.

We also have a driver on call to help them get to appointments or handle any other needs. Mr. Rampersaud can still drive, but if his arthritis flares up, they have a driver available if he needs one.

Our parents are good friends. My mother and Mrs. Rampersaud often get together, from what I hear. The same goes for our fathers; they've become great friends.

India FaceTimes her parents almost every day to check in with them. They haven't missed a beat. She and Destiney talk just as much as they always have, and she and Mala haven't missed a beat either. I'm glad she can stay in such close contact with them. She and my mother also have a great relationship. My mother adores India, which didn't surprise me; I knew India is an amazing woman.

Incredible actually.

"Man, look at y'all. Rocking babies like it's second nature." I joked with Micah and Julian earlier when we stepped out into the courtyard.

The women needed a break, and the babies were fussy, so we decided to take them out there.

Mal cracked up at that.

"Hey man, that'll be you soon!"

I nodded. I didn't mind that at all.

Mal continued, "You're gonna figure it out in a minute. It's the best feeling to become a father. Next to becoming a husband." He gave me a pointed nod and knew where this was going.

And I was ready to go there. Been ready. India and I often talk about marriage. We've been chillin', but I felt this unspoken energy. This pull. And this push. To move forward.

I planned to talk to India's father in the next few days, then ask her how she felt about an official commitment. Being my wife. "Right! I wouldn't trade this for the world," Julian said softly, rubbing his hand over Celine's curls.

"I hear you! Same here, man. It's a blessing. And this little boy has me wrapped around his finger. His mom too." Micah chuckled, glancing over at the table where the women sat. "After watching my wife give me my son… after all she went through, there's not a thing she can't ask me for."

"Oh man. Just wait until you have a little girl!" Mal jeered playfully. "Keep that wallet ready!"

Julian cracked up. "I already know. These two women in my life have changed everything for me. I look at both of them and can't believe how fortunate I am."

All of us nodded in agreement. I understood. I felt that way about India.

Right now.

My expression softened. Seeing my boy Micah as a father. And Julian, who's become one of my closest friends.

Yeah. It was all in nuance. The unspoken spaces of fatherhood, they were moving in. Holding their offspring close. Vowing to protect them with their life.

And. I couldn't describe it. I didn't have the words, but it awakened something in me. Almost as if a new chamber of my heart had been cracked open.

It was easy to do. In a space and setting such as this.

Where we all gathered to celebrate a fortieth wedding anniversary. With generations represented. Love represented. New life represented. The security and legacy of something lasting. And the joy of something yet to come.

"I'm glad you guys could make it," Micah said. They had taken the babies back to the women. I checked in with India, gave her a few kisses, and then the guys and I went back to chill by the bar. Well, it was Micah, Julian, and me.

Mal was on the dance floor with Ella. Ray hadn't left the dance floor.

"Me too. This is nice."

By now, the music had mellowed into some old school tunes.

Earth Wind & Fire's "Let's Groove" played, and a moment later, an announcement was made that dinner would be served in the next fifteen minutes.

Laughter was layered in, and conversations kept flowing. I looked back at the table again. India, Destiney, and Daijah were immersed in their chat.

"So. When are you locking that down, bro?"

I burst out laughing at Micah.

"I'd marry her tonight."

Julian and Micah's eyebrows shot up high.

"I'm serious. I've been ready to marry her for a long time, just didn't want to pressure her. She wanted to build things and let things happen naturally at our own pace. But I want a commitment. An official one. I hope she's ready."

"No doubt in my mind she is," Micah said. "She moved to Canada for you. Left her whole life here to be with you. Marry her, man."

I nodded. "She's done so much more than that," I recalled the time we traveled to Columbia to meet Samuel. India was the calmness I needed, and I was so thankful to have her with me.

And meeting Sam.

My twin brother. That's a moment I won't forget for as long as I live. Sam said they plan to come to Sac this summer. I look forward to their visit and am excited to introduce them to everyone.

I'd told my parents about Sam, and they were very support-ive. I understood that my mother needed time to accept it, and I'm so thankful for her support. I needed it more than I realized.

"Mich! Look at them!" I nodded toward Mr. and Mrs. Walker, who were grooving like young people. Well, kind of. Their moves were a few decades old, but this party was all about them. They could do the Cabbage Patch and the robot or what-ever else they wanted to do, and we'd celebrate them all the same. We laughed.

"That's what it's all about, man!" Micah said, shaking his head. He was rolling, probably partly from embarrassment.

"I'm not mad at it!" That was Julian.

"Man! Neither am I!" These people show what love truly looks like. Even after forty years, they still show up for each other. And right here in this room, new love stories and ongoing legacies continue to thrive.

I looked at India again. God willing, we'll be fortunate enough to dance together forty years from now.

Still in love.

Still on beat.

In color and frequency.

the end

♪♥♫♥♪

Thanks for reading, and I hope you enjoyed it!

A quick review on Amazon, Goodreads, or any plat-form of your choice would be a great help to Indie au-thors and help more readers discover these stories.

by way of thanks

India's story began when readers started asking about her. After my first book, so many readers wanted to learn more that a seed was planted. With my editor's encouragement, I started writing, unsure of where it would lead, but I soon realized India had her own story to tell. Pairing her with Solomon made sense, and they fit together so naturally that it seemed they were meant to be from the very first page. It's been both a joy and a privilege to write a love story about these two artists who love so passionately. I'm so very proud of what it has become, and I believe I have done them justice.

I'm incredibly thankful for the people close to me who care deeply about me, this story, and these characters, and who have supported me throughout. It truly made all the difference.

My gratitude goes to:

SB: A big thank you to my amazing Literary Sis! Your insights have really helped shape this story, and I cherish every moment of your support. You've been a fantastic part-time consultant, always honest and kind, and you've patiently answered all my questions about teaching as a college professor and navigating life as a PhD candidate. Your openness and willingness to help, no matter how small the question, mean so much. Plus, during those emotional moments, you were like a therapist and a hype woman rolled into one, always there with encouragement and humor! Your constant support has truly made a difference in this journey. I'm so grateful for your friendship, banter, and all the good times we've shared in these literary streets!

JM: My dearest friend and incredible editor extraordinaire, I truly appreciate you, your time, care, and collaboration. Above all, thank you for your friendship! You believed in this story from the start, even when it was just an idea, and graciously read every word. Your dedication and effort to help make this story the best it could be truly mean the world. You shared wisdom, insight, and patience with such kindness, and your support never wavered, especially when I wanted to set this story aside. You've motivated me every step of the way, and it's such a blessing to have you as part of my team. Here's to

many more adventures together! P.S., I always love hearing about the real-life
Solomons! They always make my day, LOL!

My Father & My Brothers: Thank you! All three of you are incredibly talented musicians, and you have been a great inspiration to me as I developed Sol's character and the band Smoke.

My Sisters: My first and most trusted readers from the very beginning! I love you, and I love our tribe! I'm especially grateful for you as this world, these characters, and this story exist only because you encouraged me to publish my very first novel, *Chasing Destiney*. Just as you cheered me on with my first book, offering support and encouragement, you did the same with this one. Thank you, I'm so grateful for you!

My Babies: Three hearts of mine, this one's for you! Now that I have the privilege of seeing art and music through your eyes, it's a fresh perspective that has greatly inspired me. Keep creating!

My Husband: Thank you so much, sweetheart, for being there. Listening to my frustrations, victories, and all the moments in between, and always knowing the right things to say at just the right time. This story was a challenge for me because it was so different from anything I had ever written. I truly couldn't have finished this without your constant encouragement. Your faith in me helped me get this story across the finish line. You saw light when I couldn't see anything in front of me and kept cheering for me until I found my way again. I love you. I always will. I'm forever grateful for you. ♥♥♥ For me, writing a sweet, sappy love story while in love helps the words flow naturally, and as Sol's character evolved, I often thought of you. I cherish the love songs you've written for me over the years; they are among the sweetest gestures I have ever received. ***My Love, Happy 16th wedding anniversary! 12.12.25*** ♥♥♥ Publishing this love story on our special day was only fitting.

Also by

Vivienne Paul

Chasing Destiney: Sweet Destiney Book 1

Destiney Fulfilled: Sweet Destiney Book 2

Sweet Destiney Series: Collector's Edition

https://www.amazon.com/dp/B0F27F9F5X

Connect with me:
Website: www.vivpaulwrites.com
Instagram: @vivpaulwrites

about the author

Vivienne Paul is a contemporary romance author obsessed with a sweet, sappy black love story, and most days—with a cup of tea or glass of wine in hand—you'll find her reading or writing one.

A Northern California native, she earned her B.A. in Linguistics and Africana Studies from the University of California at Davis. To date, Viv has reached readers in seven countries!

Viv is a wife of close to twenty years and a mom of three, embracing life's tender moments and its beautiful chaos. In the time between, she's an occasional artist and amateur chef.

Viv is currently working on her next book. Sign up for Viv's newsletter to get exclusive updates on upcoming releases! www.vivpaulwrites.com

Viv loves hearing from her readers!!

Follow Viv on IG and drop her a line! @vivpaulwrites

Email Viv at vivpaulwrites@gmail.com